Four brilliant n
Four fabulous

MILLS&

Loves...

Maisey Yates
Barbara Wallace
Aimee Carson
Leah Ashton

Bestselling author Jilly Cooper says…

*"I really am a huge fan of Mills & Boon. Their books have brought a
colossal amount of happiness to their readers. They are always
professionally written with good stories and over the years, when
I have been a bit low, picking up one of these novels has always
cheered me up. The other thing is that they are hugely readable, a
gift always to be applauded. As publishers, Mills & Boon have also
brought joy to a lot of young writers by enabling them to get
published, particularly in these days of recession when it is extremely
hard for a young writer to get started. I cannot thank them enough
and hope they will go on pleasing us for many, many years to come."*

MILLS & BOON
Loves...

Maisey Yates
Barbara Wallace
Aimee Carson
Leah Ashton

Mills & Boon, an imprint of Harlequin (UK) Limited,
Eton House, 18-24 Paradise Road, Richmond, Surrey TW9 1SR

MILLS & BOON LOVES...
© Harlequin Enterprises II B.V./S.à.r.l. 2011

The Petrov Proposal © Maisey Yates 2011
The Cinderella Bride © Barbara Wallace 2010
Secret History of a Good Girl © Aimee Carson 2011
Secrets and Speed Dating © Leah Clapton 2011

ISBN: 978 0 263 88959 8

009-1011

Printed in the UK
by CPI Mackays, Chatham, ME5 8TD

THE PETROV PROPOSAL

Maisey Yates

Maisey Yates was an avid Mills & Boon® Modern™ romance reader before she began to write them. She still can't quite believe she's lucky enough to get to create her very own sexy alpha heroes and feisty heroines. Seeing her name on one of those lovely covers is a dream come true.

Maisey lives with her handsome, wonderful, nappy-changing husband and three small children across the street from her extremely supportive parents and the home she grew up in, in the wilds of Southern Oregon, USA. She enjoys the contrast of living in a place where you might wake up to find a bear on your back porch and then heading into the home office to write stories that take place in exotic urban locales.

Look for Maisey Yates's *The Argentine's Price*, her latest novel from Mills & Boon® Modern™.

Dear Reader,

It doesn't seem like that long ago when I sat down at my computer and wrote the opening line for my very first book. It's been an amazing journey.

To be able to have a job doing what you love is such a tremendous blessing. I find I look forward to Mondays. I don't know very many other people who can say that!

It all started with a contest that Mills & Boon gave through one of their websites. I didn't win the contest, but it made me feel determined to try. I thought if I could survive that "failure", then I might even be able to live through a rejection letter!

So I gathered up my spare bits of courage and submitted a manuscript through the traditional channels. I was fortunate enough to get picked up, and read, by a wonderful editor who saw the potential in what I had written and who was willing to help me bring it out with revisions.

Just three weeks before I gave birth to my third child, I got The Call. My editor telling me they wanted to buy my manuscript! Even at nine months pregnant, that news was enough to make me jump up and down.

I used to dream about what it might be like to see my name on a book cover, which is an incredible thrill, but there's just so much more than that! There's the excitement of cover art, the scary excitement of release day, and the surreal moment of seeing your book on the shelf in your local store. (Yes, I always take pictures.)

Even with all of that, the best part is thinking of new ideas, new characters and places, and sitting down to write them. Because no matter how exciting the rest is, the best part about being a writer is...writing.

The idea for *The Petrov Proposal* was first inspired by the glamour of the jewellery design industry. I loved the idea of putting two people into such a glittery setting who had pasts that were anything but shiny. Two people who desperately needed to heal, and who very much needed to find love.

That's where Madeline and Aleksei came in. I hope you love them as much as I do.

Happy reading!

Maisey Yates

For the Sassy Sisters, Aideen, Barbara, Jackie, Jane, Jilly and Robyn. You've been there for every neurotic moment, and every triumph. You really are my sisters.

CHAPTER ONE

His voice always made goosebumps break out on her arms. Madeline would have thought that after a full year of working for Aleksei Petrov, the startling effect of his rich, slightly accented voice would have faded.

Nope.

"Ms. Forrester," he said, his voice coming in loud and clear through her cellphone, making her stomach tighten, "I trust you have everything prepared for tonight."

Maddy surveyed the ballroom from her place on the entryway steps. "Everything is right on schedule. Tables set, decorations done, guest list confirmed."

"I had to check. Especially after the incident at the White Diamonds exhibition."

Madeline bristled, but kept her voice calm. An advantage, one of many, to having a boss she never saw face to face. As long as she kept her voice steady, he would have no idea of her true feelings. He couldn't read any tension in her face or body. Or see her roll her eyes.

She clenched her fists and allowed her fingernails to dig into her palms. "That was hardly what I would classify as an incident. We had partycrashers, and they took dinners not designated for them. But we solved it. A couple of people went dinnerless for about twenty minutes, but no one was gravely inconvenienced." She hadn't realized he'd heard about that.

This was the first major event she'd coordinated for Petrova, the first event she'd done since her move to Europe. Aleksei had never attended any of the small exhibitions she'd put on in North America. He conducted all of his business from his offices in Moscow and, more rarely, Milan, saving his brilliant presence for the more essential events—which this most certainly was.

And his presence was going to make the event a madhouse. Attempted crashers—both civilian and press alike—were going to be a huge issue. Aleksei was a brilliant businessman, a man who had brought himself, and his company, from obscurity to be the creator and owner of the design house that produced the most coveted designer jewelry in the world.

His success, coupled with the fact that he wasn't the type of man to court media attention, only made him more of a fascination to the public and the press.

This would also be her first time meeting her boss face to face. She didn't know why, but the thought of it made her stomach tight.

"Those who had to wait for their dinner beg to differ," he said dryly.

She looked down at her fingernails and noticed a chip in her polish. That would have to be fixed before the party. "The issue was with the security, not with my planning. And the security does not fall under my jurisdiction."

His deep chuckle reverberated through the phone. Through her. "Your ruthlessness is always inspiring."

Ruthlessness? Yeah, okay, maybe she had become a bit ruthless. Although she'd been kidding. Kind of. But she loved her job, she needed her job, and Aleksei expected perfection. And she always achieved perfection, which meant she wasn't taking the fall for someone else's mistake.

She hadn't recently achieved a promotion within Petrova Gems by taking the fall for other people's errors either.

"Well, I've spoken to Jacob about the measures in place for tonight, and I don't think we'll be having any more issues."

"Good to know."

"You were trying to rile me up, weren't you?" she asked, annoyance and adrenaline spiking in her system.

She was able to hold her cool with everyone, always. But Aleksei Petrov and his sinfully sexy voice rattled her more than anything else in her life. There was just something about him...another reason to be glad they had a remote working relationship.

"Maybe. I would have fired you right away if I thought you were incompetent, Madeline, and I certainly wouldn't have promoted you," he said, the sound of her name on his lips making her arms prickle.

"Then I'll take my current employment status as a compliment," she said, working to put her cool, calm and collected self back together.

It had been so long since she'd allowed a man to become a distraction, so long since she'd allowed anything to be a distraction. When she'd taken control of her own life she'd done it in a big way. She'd moved on, moved up, and had never looked back at the insecure, vulnerable girl she'd been five years ago. She wasn't about to let Aleksei, or his voice, shake any of that.

"But everything is right on track for tonight," she said, her voice still steady. She was anxious to get the conversation back on the topic it should be on. Back in the safe zone.

"That's good to know."

She wasn't just hearing his voice through the phone any-more. It was deeper, richer, filling the empty ballroom and making her feel warm and flushed all over.

The back of her neck prickled.

She turned and found herself at eye-level with a broad, masculine chest. It was covered, quite decently in fact, by a perfectly fitted buttoned-up shirt. But not even that con-cealed the perfect, hard muscles that lay beneath.

She swallowed hard, her throat suddenly dry, tight. Her hands felt shaky. Because it was her sexy-voiced boss, in the flesh. And he was even better looking than she could have possibly anticipated.

She'd hoped that the pictures she'd seen of him had just caught him at good angles, that he wasn't really as hand-some as he seemed like he might be. But pictures didn't do him justice. He was so big, broad and tall, well over six feet. And his face was arresting. Dark, well-shaped brows, an angular jaw. His eyes were deep brown, captivating but completely unreadable. Hard. Everything about him was completely uncompromising.

Except for his lips. His lips looked like they might soften to kiss a woman. She found herself licking her own lips in response to that thought. And then she realized she was standing there, staring like an idiot at her boss. The man who signed her paychecks.

Oh, perfect.

"Mr. Petrov," she said. Then she realized she was still holding her phone to her ear and quickly dropped her hand to her side. "I…"

"Ms. Forrester." Aleksei extended his hand. She was ex-tremely grateful for the reminder of what normal human behavior was in this situation, because all thoughts had been momentarily knocked from her head.

She lifted her hand and clasped his. His handshake was

firm, masculine. His skin hot against hers. She released her hold on him, trying to look calm. Unaffected. She flexed her fingers, trying to make the impression of his touch go away.

She looked over her shoulder, away from him, at the ballroom, which was decorated beautifully, everything in place except for the jewels, which wouldn't be put in their display cases until just before the event started. Until the armed guards arrived.

"I hope everything is to your satisfaction," she said, knowing that it had to be. She didn't do half-measures. If it wasn't perfect, there was simply no point.

"It will do," he said.

She turned to face him. "I hope it will more than do," she said tightly.

"It will do." A slight smile curved his lips and she found herself warring with the desire to keep staring at his fascinating mouth, and the desire to turn and stalk out of the room.

She fought desperately to gain a grip on her control. If he hadn't surprised her, it wouldn't have been an issue. If she had known that he was going to walk in the room when he had, if he hadn't sneaked up on her like that, and if he didn't look like some bronzed Adonis, she would be fine.

Just remember the last time you let your body do the thinking.

That brought her back firmly on solid ground.

"I'm glad you approve," she said, wishing that she had the buffer of the phone again so he couldn't see the annoyance she knew she was clearly telegraphing. And because it was just easier when she couldn't see him.

Aleksei walked down the stairs and into the main area of the ballroom. She waited while he examined the table settings and the glittering white lanterns that were suspended from the ceiling.

"You work hard for me," he said finally.

A rush of gratification flooded her. "Yes. I do."

"I've always wondered why you decided to work for a living. Your family is affluent enough to have supported you."

Of course he knew about her family. They were all so successful in their own right. But her parents hadn't even spoken to her in at least ten years. They hadn't offered her any support as a child. They certainly wouldn't give her any as an adult. And she would never dream of taking one penny from her brother. Gage had already done enough for her. She wasn't going to let him take care of her for the rest of her life, even though he gladly would have.

At least now he had a wife and children to distract him from worrying about her. She would always be grateful for everything he'd done for her, but every time she had a problem Gage dropped everything to make it go away, thanks to his overdeveloped sense of responsibility. She didn't like taking advantage of him in that way.

"I wouldn't get any satisfaction from life enjoying the success of others. I wanted to make my own success. Earn my own reputation."

It had become especially important after her reputation had been destroyed by a youthful indiscretion and the over-zealous media. Although, even now, she wasn't angry at the press. They'd just been reporting her stupidity to a scandal-hungry public. Everything that had happened had been her own fault. She couldn't even pin it solely on her former boss, no matter how much she wanted to.

The only consolation was that the whole thing had died a pretty quick death in the papers. Another day, another scandal. But in the circles she moved in, the damage had been done.

"You've certainly done that. You've had how many people have tried to poach you from me in the past few months?"

"Eight," she said, voice crisp. "And I didn't know you knew about that."

He nodded and made his way back to the stairs. As he got closer, the tension in her stomach wound tighter, that little bit of ease she'd felt proving to be an illusion.

"I make it my business to know what is happening in my company. Especially when someone is trying to steal one of my key players."

"I turned them down," she said. "I enjoy the work that I do for Petrova." Her job enabled her to take part in both practical and creative tasks. She had a huge budget to work with, paid travel, a discount with the hottest jewelry designers in the world and, until today, had never had to deal with her boss. In the physical sense anyway.

Plus, it was high-profile. Every event she coordinated ended up with full-color spreads in some of the most popular magazines in the world. It was a dream job, no question.

But now she was tempted to take the next offer and run.

No. She was stronger than that. She wasn't going to let this...errant...*thing* hamper her success in any way. She was older now, wiser. A handsome face and flattering compliments weren't going to make her lose focus.

Of course, Aleksei wasn't handing out compliments, which helped.

Aleksei stood there for a moment, just looking at her, his dark eyes intent on her. She sucked in a breath.

"I prefer to sit near the displays," he said, gesturing to the empty row of glass cases.

"Of course," she said, making a mental note to shuffle some of the people she'd originally had at the tables near the jewelry display. She'd been planning on seating Aleksei at the front of the room. But he was the boss, and therefore not wrong.

"And that's…for you and a date?" she asked, hoping he was still bringing a date. It put up yet another barrier between them. A barrier she shouldn't even need, but apparently did.

"No, I'm attending alone. My date had to cancel a couple of weeks ago."

Oh, no. She had really, really hoped he was bringing a woman with him.

She took another deep, fortifying breath. "Not a problem."

She could be attracted to the man without acting on it. She could even be attracted to him without being bothered by it. Attraction between men and women was normal. It happened every day. Besides, there wasn't even any reason to believe that he was attracted to her. Even if he were, she wasn't going there. He was her boss.

Been there, done that, made national headlines.

"And the collection will be here?" he asked, indicating the empty display cases.

She nodded. "Yes. Once proper security is in place we'll bring the gems in."

His dark brows snapped together. "I think you should move the cases there." He indicated an expanse of open floor by the windows. She'd considered that spot. The reflection of the gems off the glass when it was dark would make a stunning effect, but for security reasons she'd decided against it.

"It isn't as secure."

"It will look better," he insisted.

She gritted her teeth. So she had to move him and the displays. Lovely. And so not easy only five hours before the big event.

She pasted a smile on her face. "I agree with you about the aesthetics, but the security team has told me it's much easier to keep track of everything if the gems aren't placed by doors or windows."

"What is the point of investing all of this money in an exhibition if the gems do not look their best?"

She fought the urge to roll her eyes. He was standing right in front of her, not talking to her on the phone, so that option was out. That meant the plastic smile had to stay in place. "As I said, for security reasons…"

He shrugged. "Then we'll double security."

"With five hours until the party?" The smile slipped.

"Are you telling me you can't do it?" He raised a dark eyebrow.

The jab hit its mark, right on target. Of course, she was certain he'd known it would. Everything in her responded to the challenge, her blood pumping faster, adrenaline spiking inside of her. Was it an outrageous request? Yes. Could she do it? Of course. And making the impossible possible, and making it seem easy, was a very large part of her job. A part she reveled in. A part that made her feel powerful, in control.

She managed to make the smile reappear. "Of course it's no problem, Mr. Petrov. I'll liaise with Jacob and see that it's done."

He cut her off. "I want this collection displayed to its best effect."

"Naturally, but I was just concerned because they're one of a kind pieces."

He laughed dryly. "I'm aware of that, Madeline, I did create them."

"I think the whole world is aware of that." Tension was making her snippy, and she needed to relax.

But this was the first collection Aleksei had designed in

six years. All of the other collections that had come out of Petrova Gems in the past few years had been by his stable of very highly regarded designers. And every piece designed, or, even better, fashioned by Aleksei, went for millions of dollars at auctions.

That meant media. Lots, and lots of media.

Work was her safety, work was where she was confident, where she excelled. But this was going to be huge beyond anything she'd dealt with before. And she and the press weren't exactly on the best of terms. Well, that wasn't strictly true, she supposed they loved her. She was such a salacious headline. *She* just had a problem with *them.*

"Of course the world knows, Madeline. And that's by design. This is about business, publicity, and that means media attention. That means hype. That means big money. And that is what I'm in business for."

"You actually want the press to swarm the party?"

"Publicity," he said simply. "I would hardly go to all of this expense to put on an exhibition if I didn't plan for it to end up being talked about in any and all media outlets. It isn't as though I'm throwing a party for my own amusement."

She bit the inside of her lip and forced a smile. "Of course not, Mr. Petrov." She doubted Aleksei did anything for his own amusement.

Aleksei allowed himself another visual tour of his event coordinator. She wasn't happy with him at the moment, that much was certain, and he imagined she thought she was hiding it better than she was.

He had always enjoyed her voice when speaking to her on the phone. Low, slightly husky and always, unintentionally, sexy. Even when she was talking about the need to increase the budget for an event. But he had not imagined that the woman would match up to the voice. He hadn't thought it possible.

But she exceeded the sexiness in that smooth, sultry voice. Wavy brown hair that shimmered golden in the light as it cascaded over her shoulders, blue eyes that were enhanced by thick lashes. But it was her body that had his libido fighting to slip its leash. Politically incorrect as it might be, he found her curves captivating. Full breasts, a slender waist, and round hips that drew his attention with their gentle sway when she walked.

She seemed to have a physical effect on him, like strong alcohol. She was intoxicating.

He put his hands in his pocket, felt his cellphone in his right one and gripped it tightly. He suddenly wished he could call Olivia, not because he missed the woman who had been his mistress until a few weeks ago, but because he longed for the distraction of her. But Olivia had been getting clingy. She had started wondering why he only saw her for special events and sex. Had started wanting him to come to Milan just to see her. That was when he'd known it was time to end things. He didn't get any sort of satisfaction out of hurting women. He made his intentions clear from the beginning.

Keeping a casual, long-term mistress was his preference. It was better than going out to bars every weekend to pick women up. After all he'd experienced in his thirty-three years, he felt far too old.

"And what do you intend to do tonight?" he asked.

He could tell she was forcing the smile that was stretched so determinedly across her face. "I intend to do what you pay me to do and coordinate the exhibition."

"I assumed you would have it coordinated at this point."

"The important things, yes. But just in case we end up short a shrimp cocktail or something I like to make sure I'm on hand to ensure there isn't anyone..." she waved a hand in the air "...*sans* shellfish."

"Fine if you need to oversee that, but I don't want you running around the party in jeans and a headset."

"I don't do that," she said.

"Good. I like for everything to blend seamlessly at these events. The only thing the guests should notice is the jewelry."

"I can assure you, Mr. Petrov, that's my aim as well."

"I would prefer if you dressed as an attendee of the party, and not as staff."

He could tell that annoyed her too. The glitter in her blue eyes was in direct contrast with the serene, smooth expression on her face. "I was planning on wearing black pants and a black top, just like the waitstaff."

"But you aren't one of the waitstaff. You work directly for Petrova Gems, and I wish your attire to reflect that."

That was how he ran things. Impeccably. In the design world, looks were truly everything. Nothing else mattered other than the external. So long as the exterior glittered, nothing else counted.

"You should take the time to enjoy the party," he said.

She pursed her pretty lips into a sour pout. "I don't mix business with pleasure."

"I don't either. I prefer my pleasure uninterrupted."

A slow flood of crimson colored her cheeks. It amazed him. He hadn't known there was still anyone in the real world who blushed over casual innuendo.

"And by enjoying the party," he continued, "I mean circulate, listen to conversation, find out what appeals to the guests, and what doesn't. Another reason to dress to blend in."

"So, I'm conducting a covert survey?"

"Not quite. But it pays to learn from critique."

A strange look passed over her face. "Media critique?"

"Sometimes."

"I don't want to say anything out of line, Mr. Petrov, but you've hired me to coordinate the event so..."

"So you want me to trust you rather than dictate?"

She nodded once, brown hair shimmering over her shoulder.

"Sorry," he said, "I did hire you to coordinate, but I'm a perfectionist, and as long as I'm here, I'll see everything done to my standards."

That did make her bristle, that fixed grin seriously faltering. "I can assure you, I do everything to your standards, whether you're here or not."

"That remains to be seen."

"Then, if you'll excuse me, I need to finish some last-minute details. Something to do with shifting seating and doubling security."

The ice in her tone, the fact that she dared to speak to him that way, amused him. He was used to a lot of sycophantic scraping and bowing. That was something he'd always appreciated about Madeline over the phone. She was direct, and she did her job. His ego didn't need another person living to fawn over him. He preferred the fact that Madeline had a mind of her own.

He stuck his hand in his pocket, his cellphone still there. He could call Olivia. Could call a host of women who had given him their numbers recently. Numbers he had kept but never dialed.

Instead he leaned against the railing of the grand marble staircase and watched Madeline clack around the spacious ballroom on her high heels.

Madeline turned and looked over her shoulder, she forced a tight smile when she saw him watching her, but he could see the tension coming off her petite frame in palpable waves.

Something he understood about Madeline: she liked control. And so did he. And he had just come into her domain, as far as she was concerned, and taken her control.

He chuckled softly and took his phone out of his pocket before he walked into the hallway. Maybe he would get a date for the evening. Madeline could add another setting as easily as she'd removed it. He could find himself a woman to keep him company tonight.

And forget about that brief flash of attraction he'd felt when he'd seen Madeline for the first time. An attraction he had no intention of acting on. He didn't date employees, and he had no plan of starting a relationship with a woman who seemed as young as Madeline did.

Because he had no intention of having a relationship at all.

He looked at his phone, then put it back in his pocket.

CHAPTER TWO

HE DIDN'T have a date. Aleksei strode down the long hall-way, his blood pounding heavily in his veins. He had not called anyone. Not Olivia to see if she might want to briefly rekindle their year-long affair. Not any of the jewelry models—beautiful women—who had made passes at him over the past few months.

Because none of them had appealed. The only woman he'd been able envision had been his event coordinator. Beautiful, tightly wound Madeline with the glossy brown hair and curves that seemed to come straight out of every male fantasy.

Beautiful women were easy to come by. He had money, he had influence. If he wanted female company, he could have it.

Yet he was walking to Madeline's room. Compelled to see her again. And he was following the compulsion because, truly, the desire for anything was so foreign to him that he was honestly fascinated by it.

He knocked on the door to Madeline's suite, the one his company, he, in fact, was paying for. He always paid for his employees to stay in the best accommodations when they traveled. Mostly because he never wanted to hear anyone complaining about doing a subpar job because they'd lost sleep on a lumpy mattress.

He heard Maddy's voice coming through the thick door. "Just a second."

He could hear her palms hit the wood as she checked the peephole. When she opened the door, her expression was wary. "Mr. Petrov, is something wrong?"

"Nothing." He walked past her and into the suite.

She moved to the other side of the room, her discomfort with his presence obvious. She was so soft and petite and for a brief moment so lost-looking that he felt a twinge of something...protectiveness, maybe, in his chest.

It was only natural. She was young, maybe in her mid-twenties, and he knew the kinds of things the world had in store for the young and naive. Knew that there was pain out there so intense, that there were rock bottoms so low most people couldn't imagine them. Because he'd been there.

Her eyes clashed with his, her expression guarded for a moment. There was a wariness there, a hardness that didn't match her age. Perhaps she wasn't as naive as he'd imagined. Maybe she knew about the dark side of life already.

She was young, but there was no youthful innocence in her face. Not a trace of naiveté. She was waiting for the angle. Waiting to find out things were about to fall apart around her.

He knew that feeling well.

"I have decided that I would like a companion for the evening," he said.

She gave him a baleful look. "Which means you need me to add the setting that you just had me take away, for the date that you had, but then didn't have and forgot to tell me you no longer had."

A reluctant chuckle got caught in his throat. "Something like that. But I think you'll be able to handle things."

"Well, thanks," she said, her voice flat.

"Madeline, I was wondering if you would like to sit at my table, as a spot has just opened up."

Acid burned in Maddy's stomach. He was just going to have her be his date? Some kind of convenient replacement? It was typical. Most men didn't care who a woman was as long as she was available and willing.

She bit her lip. Hard. She was neither. And she refused to be taken advantage of ever again.

"I'm not actually interested in being your back-up," she ground out.

"That isn't what I was asking. You're an intelligent woman, Madeline. You're ambitious too. I haven't missed that in our conversations together. I thought you might appreciate the chance to sit at my table, to speak to the guests, learn more about the industry. There is room at the table, and I thought you might like the opportunity."

Okay, that was tempting. More than. The fact that she was extremely drawn to the industry of design made her job more enjoyable. She loved everything about the company, and had thoroughly enjoyed the year she'd worked for Aleksei already.

It was tempting because it might give her a chance to learn more so that she could advance into another position at Petrova. It wasn't really part of her five-year plan, but it would be pretty amazing. Something she would readily consider.

"But, as far as the other people at the table are concerned…"

"If you want to be presented as my date so that you aren't treated like the help I have no problem with that at all."

The help. Oh, yes, and people in this circle would treat

her like the help if they knew she was the event coordinator. Working for a living was quite frowned upon in such levels of society.

Not that she cared, but she didn't really want to be the focus of conversation.

She bit her lower lip then released it quickly, realizing what an indecisive, nervous gesture it was. She wasn't an indecisive, nervous girl. This was a chance to further her career a little bit.

But it reminded her too much of working for William, her first boss when she'd graduated from college. Of everything that had happened. Of how incredibly, unforgivably stupid she'd been.

Her stomach knotted fiercely.

This is different.

It was different because she was different. She wasn't some naive girl desperately seeking love and affection. She was a woman. She knew her own mind, she made things happen for herself, and she would never allow herself to be a victim. Never again.

She certainly wasn't going to let past disasters stop her from succeeding.

Besides, she wasn't seducible. She wasn't suddenly going to morph into her past self. Even if Aleksei was the most gorgeous man she could remember seeing, and even if his dark eyes did promise that he might actually know what to do with a woman in bed.

She felt her skin heat and she took a deep breath to try and cool herself down. It wasn't doing her any good to think of him like that. It didn't matter how he was with women, because she would never be among their number.

Didn't want to be. No matter how sexy he was.

"I had some gems set aside for my date to wear tonight, prior to our separation. I would like you to wear them."

The very idea of it made her stomach turn slightly. She didn't like the thought of wearing jewelry meant for another woman, regardless of the fact that this wasn't a date. It was still…well, it reminded her too much of things that had gone on before in her life.

"It probably won't match my handbag. It's a really bright yellow," she said, trying to wiggle out of having to wear the jewels. "And I already have a matching necklace."

He looked at her closely, dark eyes appraising her in a way that had her feeling as though he was looking beneath her skin, into her soul. At all of her secrets.

"I have a piece that would be perfect for you."

The way he said that, *perfect for you,* it was so personal. It made her heart squeeze, and she wasn't really sure why.

"I have a very strict policy on keeping business business, as I said before," she said.

"And this is business," he said, dark eyes impassive again, when before they'd been…hot. "An extension of your job for the evening. Petrova Gems is about romance. It's about making a woman feel as though she's buying not just jewelry but a lifestyle, a fantasy. We need to present a fantasy that goes beyond location, decor and sparkling gems. It's about the woman, how she feels in the jewels, how they make other people feel about her. They are meant to be worn, not simply displayed."

She nodded slowly. "Is that in a print ad or a commercial? Because it should be," she said.

He chuckled, the sound rough, as though he wasn't accustomed to it. "If that's an endorsement, I might have to use it."

"Actually, it might be nice to have something like that written lightly, almost hidden, in script around the display cases for the next exhibition."

"I like that idea," he said, the corners of his mouth curving very slightly.

Why did it made her stomach feel warm when he smiled? It could hardly be called a smile, and she certainly shouldn't be feeling anything. It was just because he liked her idea, because tonight was looking like a serious boon for her career within Petrova Gems. Who wouldn't be happy about that?

"If you would like, I can send over a stylist to help you with your wardrobe."

She bit the inside of her cheek. She wasn't taking gifts. "I have my own dress. Thank you, though."

He moved closer to her, his dark eyes locked on hers. He smelled good. Not like cologne, but just clean. Musky and male. It made her want to draw closer to him, to breathe him in.

She hadn't realized she was verging on pathetically lonely. That was all it was, though. Loneliness. She hadn't seen her brother and his family in too long, and she didn't really have any close friends. She just wanted to be close to someone. She needed to get a cat.

"You are a stubborn woman, Madeline," he said.

"It's been said more than once," she said. "Is that a bad thing?"

"Not at all. I can appreciate the quality since it is one we share."

She felt a smile stretch across her face, without her permission. "Well, I'm glad it doesn't count against me."

He looked like he might move closer. Time stretched on slowly, the air between them thick. "Not at all," he said.

Aleksei turned and walked out of her hotel room, the door clicking shut behind him. Maddy sank onto the couch, suddenly conscious of the fact that her legs were shaking.

She had no idea what had just happened. Well, she was afraid she *did* know. She was attracted to him, to a man who was no different than any other. Discarding women at a moment's notice without any feeling or regret.

It didn't matter how attracted she was. She'd felt attracted to men, from a distance, in the past five years. She simply hadn't acted on it. Of course, she and Aleksei were in close proximity. And it was very likely they would be off and on over the course of the next few months for the different exhibitions for the new line.

She drew her knees up to her chest. Okay, so the attraction was a complication, but it wasn't anything she couldn't handle. She was an adult. She wasn't some naive innocent girl. And she was in control of the situation.

Anyway, other than that brief moment, she had no reason to believe Aleksei saw her as anything more than an efficient little worker bee. And his offer tonight had been strictly business too.

And if he could be strictly business, so could she.

Madeline examined her reflection in the mirror. She was happy with what she'd done. Very happy. Her makeup was natural, making her blue eyes look bright and exotic, and her hair had been tamed into a high, sleek ponytail that cascaded over one shoulder.

She turned slightly, and looked at her bare back, exposed by the low V of her little black dress. She'd seen the dress in a window on her first day in Milan and hadn't been able to pass it up, even though she'd had no clue where she would wear it.

She didn't normally show so much skin, but then, she was usually working when she went to parties.

Always the coordinator, never the guest.

She couldn't actually remember the last time she'd dressed up for something. She liked looking nice, but she always dressed for work, not for going out.

Something that was noticeably absent from her look were the promised jewels. She had a very uneasy feeling that they were due to arrive very soon, with the man himself.

A small shiver wound through her at the thought of Aleksei Petrov. She shook her head. She shouldn't be thinking of him as anything other than her boss. Of course, that had been much easier to do before she'd seen the man in the *über*-gorgeous flesh. Before she'd smelled that faint masculine scent that was so uniquely him.

She made an extremely childish face at her reflection and picked up the canary-yellow clutch bag that had saved her from recycled jewels from the vanity.

When she heard the firm knock on the door, she knew immediately who it was. Aleksei's knock wasn't a request, it was a demand. Like every word he spoke. And that should not, in any way, be a positive quality, and yet she couldn't help admire that in him. The confidence. The absolute surety he seemed to have that he was right.

"Come in," she said, hoping she sounded like the confident businesswoman that she was. At least, she'd been a confident businesswoman a couple of hours ago. It hardly seemed like one meeting with her gorgeous boss should change that.

The door opened and she turned, her breath catching in her throat, making a choking sound. Her face heated. Stupid that he affected her this way. Stupid that she was so obvious. Maybe she should have jumped back into dating, had some flings at least, after The William Fiasco.

Sadly, though, she hadn't. She'd lived like a nun, *sans* habit, and now all of that was starting to catch up with her.

"Does this meet with your approval?" she asked, the question tart because she was frustrated with herself for being so affected by him. And with him for being so appealing.

The slow burn of his gaze made her feel hot all the way to her toes. "It will do."

And why did that—that phrase that was designed to get her hackles up—sound like the most sinful compliment she'd ever received.

"I brought your jewels," he said, holding up a slender velvet box.

She walked to the center of the room. She knew he would follow her, but she had to try and get some distance between them. He was messing with her head, and she couldn't allow that.

"I thought you would have some of the...how did you put it?...*the help* bring my jewels."

She was treated to another slight almost-smile as he walked to where she was standing. "I send others to do my dirty work, not to do pleasant things."

He opened the box and revealed a pair of earrings with yellow pear-cut diamonds at the center and a ring of white diamonds around the outside of the center gem. The cut and clarity of the gems was flawless, the design clean, but arresting.

"These are amazing," she said, touching one of them lightly. "You really are an artist."

She looked up at Aleksei. His expression was hard like granite, dark eyes flat. "They sell well," he said.

"But there's...there's more than that to it," she said.

"No. It's business. There is nothing more to it than the bottom line."

She didn't know why, but the cold, stark sentiment seemed extremely sad, especially when it was said about something so beautiful. She loved Aleksei's pieces. There was something more to them than aesthetics alone. Or maybe there wasn't.

Looking at him now, at his unreadable expression, she

wondered. The man himself was hard, ruthless. Maybe it really was all about the money. It shouldn't bother her. She shouldn't feel anything at all about her boss.

The fact that he made money was good for her. That was all that should matter.

She reached out and took the box from his hand, setting it on the vanity top, and leaned in, putting on the first earring. She raised her eyes and they caught his in the reflection of the mirror. She saw it again, that flicker of heat, and she felt it. Low in her belly, impossible to ignore.

Madeline looked back down at the jewelry box and put more focus than was strictly necessary on putting the second earring in.

"Beautiful," he said, moving nearer to her.

He was behind her, so close she could feel the heat from his body. His masculine scent, the one that had been tormenting her all day, enveloped her.

He reached up and touched one of the earrings. "There is one thing I truly love about working with jewelry," he said. "On its own, a gem is nice to look at. In a well-designed setting, cut to perfection, even more so. But when the jewelry is on a beautiful woman...that's when it truly shines."

Oh, he was good. A far too familiar feeling, an ache, a need, began to grow in her stomach. Beautiful. He'd called her beautiful. It made her want to hear more. She wanted to soak up the attention, the compliments. To feel important and...special.

No.

Madeline had indulged that hollow need before. Had allowed years of neglect to make her vulnerable to a man who talked smooth and offered her things she'd craved most in life. At least William had pretended to offer them to her.

She turned and realized her mistake too late. Her breasts

touched his chest and she gripped the edge of the vanity to keep herself steady.

She forced a smile. "That's nice. I mean, another one for the ad campaign." She slipped past him and moved further from him until she could breathe again. "We should...I should...you can do what you like, of course, but I should head down now. Just some last minute rounds."

He nodded, faint amusement evident on his face. "Of course. Let's go see if this party is as perfect as you've promised me it will be."

CHAPTER THREE

EXTRAVAGANT parties and lavish settings were, almost literally, an everyday occurrence for Maddy. But she worked behind the scenes, coordinating, planning, directing. It was her job to be invisible.

Now, suddenly, she felt quite visible.

People were staring. She knew they weren't really staring at her. It was the jewels she was wearing. It was Aleksei, walking so close to her. The man exuded dark sexuality. Danger and extreme attractiveness in a perfectly tailored tuxedo.

The women in the room were nearly falling out of their chairs to get a closer look. Although, it could have been the jewelry that held their attention so raptly. She doubted it, but it was possible.

She smiled at a passing couple and noticed that Aleksei made no indication that he'd seen them at all. His face stayed rigid, set, unmoving as they walked through the ballroom. He exuded power and charisma, but it certainly wasn't because he was making an effort.

"You might try smiling," she whispered.

He leaned down and she caught another hint of his scent. Her stomach tightened. "Why?"

She took a step to the side, putting some distance between them, as they continued walking. "It's friendly. It's what people do."

"I don't know that I would characterize myself as friendly," he said.

"But you *are* a businessman," she said, the reminder inane and pointless. She continued on anyway. "And selling yourself is a part of selling your product."

He turned to her, eyebrows raised.

"Which you know," she continued.

She didn't really like the fact that she seemed to say stupid, pointless things around the man. She did fine on the phone with him. But then, he wasn't really there when she was talking to him on the phone, and in person he was impossible to ignore.

"Whether or not I smile, the jewelry will still sell," he said blandly.

"Yes, well, I'm sure but…"

"And anyway, if you give people everything they want, they lose interest. Better to leave a little mystery."

Well, mystery he had down. His private life was extremely private. There was never even a hint of scandal, no information on the women he dated. Nothing. Which seemed sort of amazing given the media's ravenous hunger for scandal.

"If the press allows you some mystery, I suppose that's a wise choice," she said, looking away from him.

She looked around the room, and suddenly she felt claustrophobic. She was used to these events, but she was used to being on the outside of them. Being the staff meant she was able to hover around the edges. But actually being a guest, and being with Aleksei, well, that was getting her a lot of attention she'd rather not have.

Maddy had never really known what to do with a lot of attention, having never received a lot of it. And it had only got worse after her time in the unwanted spotlight.

Somehow, it made her feel better that Aleksei seemed to feel the same way she did. She felt him go tense next to her, his hand tightening against her back as he guided her on. She looked at him and noticed a slight line of tension on his brow. His focus wasn't on her, though, but on the table they were heading toward, the table that was already half-filled with guests that were chatting and admiring the display cases filled with jewelry.

He didn't want to sit at the table. And that was when she realized something about her unyielding boss. He was as uncomfortable as she was. He hid it well, his expression almost smooth, but she could feel his discomfort.

She continued on, his hand still resting on her back, and he followed, his movements stiff now.

He did actually smile at the people who were sitting at the table as he pulled her chair out for her and motioned for her to sit down. No one else would know he wasn't completely thrilled to be in their company. He seemed as in control as ever. But she could tell. It was there, his body rigid, his jaw locked tight, even as he smiled.

When he sat next to her and placed his hand flat on the white linen tabletop, instinct took over and she rested her hand lightly over his, the gesture meant to offer comfort. A connection. It ended up being much more than that.

Lightning skittered from her palm up her arm and into her chest, jump-starting her heart and heating her from the inside out. She pulled her hand away slowly and, she hoped, casually.

She looked down at the empty plate in front of her and

hoped that her heartbeat wasn't audible to everyone at the table. She didn't know why she'd done that. She wasn't a touchy-feely sort of person. Most of her life had lacked in physical human contact, and she'd never been overly affectionate as a result. She'd never really had the chance to be.

She had no idea why it had suddenly seemed the most natural thing in the world to touch him.

Aleksei could feel the heat from Madeline's touch, but even more he felt the comfort she offered in the gesture. He swallowed and tightened his fist, turning his focus on the woman that was speaking to him.

"Mr. Petrov, it's lovely to see you here."

"And so exciting to see your new collection," one of the other women purred.

He started to talk about the collection, about the pieces. But his focus was still on Madeline's unconscious touch. He gritted his teeth. It reminded him of things long past. Affectionate touches. Touches that were about more than sex. A connection that went beyond bodies.

He'd shut that part of his brain down. That part of his life was gone. Paulina was gone. Any connection he had imagined between Madeline and himself was simply that. Imagined. He didn't have it in him to give, or receive, any more than that.

Maddy folded her hands in her lap. Her palm still burned.

She watched Aleksei as he spoke. He was confident when he talked about his work, at ease with the subject.

She knew he had passion for his work. She'd seen moments of it, heard it when they'd spoken together on the phone and discussed plans for exhibitions and events. But now, there was nothing. He'd done it earlier in the hotel room. He was a master at creating and maintaining distance, at controlling his interactions with people wholly and absolutely. A skill she wished she could learn.

Sitting next to him, so close his arm kept brushing hers, proved to be disturbing on so many levels. Well, it was really just one level, but it was the one level she was trying to ignore above all others.

Every time he touched her it burned all the way from her shoulder through her body and before long she was wrecked from keeping herself from jumping out of her chair.

"I think I need some air," she said softly, when the plates had been cleared. She also needed to check on a few things and she certainly didn't want to draw attention to the fact that she was staff. It would make it interesting that she was sitting with Aleksei. And she didn't want to be interesting, didn't want to be memorable. Didn't want to be in the headlines in the morning.

Waving politely, a gesture that everyone ignored, she stood from the table and picked her way through the crowd until she'd made her way over to one of the buffet tables. Ah, low on shrimp. She'd expected that to happen.

Rather than finding a waiter to handle it, she skirted the perimeter of the room and made her way out into the long, empty corridor just outside the ballroom.

She nearly sagged with relief when she was away from the loud, frenetic atmosphere. She backed up, heels clicking on the marble floor, and leaned against the tile wall. The chill bit into her bare back. But she needed it, needed anything that could help put out the smoldering flame that Aleksei seemed to have lit inside of her.

"Are you all right?"

Out of the frying pan and right back into the fire.

She turned and saw Aleksei standing there, and suddenly the coolness from the wall wasn't helping at all.

"You don't like crowds?" he asked.

She stiffened. "You don't like parties."

He shrugged and began to walk toward her. "I would

think that was obvious. If I liked them, I would attend more of them."

"But everyone wants to talk to you." The words just slipped out and she wished, she really wished, she could pretend she didn't know what had inspired them. But the lonely girl that still lived somewhere inside her would have loved to go somewhere and have everyone talk to her. Look at her. Think she was special.

She shut the door on those feelings. It was no use feeling sad about things that couldn't be changed. Wallowing in that loneliness...she knew exactly where that led to.

"Yes. Because everyone wants a piece of wealth and power. If I were one of the waiters do you supposed everyone—anyone—would want to talk to me?"

"Having spent the past few years as event staff, I can honestly tell you no. No one would talk to you."

He came to stand in front of her, looking dangerously attractive and like an invitation to every sin she was trying so hard not to commit again. "So then, why should it matter if people want to talk to me when their only concern is for my status, and what it can do for them?"

She looked down at her yellow shoes and admired the way the straps were woven together. Better than admiring her boss in a tux. "I—I suppose it doesn't matter when you put it like that."

He looked over his shoulder, back toward the ballroom door. "I simply don't have the patience for these kinds of events. Not on a regular basis. But it is a part of this business."

She nodded slowly. "I understand that."

"Business comes first for you as well," he said. "I can tell you take work very seriously."

"Having a job is important, necessary. Having a great job is icing on the cake. And having a job I love that garners lots of positive publicity…there isn't anything more satisfying. So, yes, business comes first."

"You enjoy the publicity?"

It was nice to see her name in a magazine without a sleazy innuendo connected to it. Nice to have her name associated with something she was proud of. Although, she always hoped people thought she was a different Madeline Forrester. Really she just hoped they didn't think of the earlier stories about her at all.

"Yes. It's been great for my professional reputation."

"Why work so hard to build a public reputation? Unless you're planning on branching off on your own?"

"Maybe. Eventually. Not now," she said, breathless, knowing she'd just said the wrong thing. "I mean, perhaps in ten years' time…"

His dark brows locked together. "You're planning on leaving Petrova?"

"I'm not planning anything. Not really. Well, maybe. But do you honestly expect that I'm going to work for you for the rest of my life? I have ambition." She looked back down at her shoes.

"What's wrong with working for me?" he asked, his voice soft, smooth, but she could hear the hard note beneath all that civility.

"Nothing. But did you want to be someone's employee for the rest of your life?"

"That's different."

"It's not," she insisted.

"I thought you were the best in the business," he said. "So either you're willing to hand Petrova Gems over to someone who does subpar work, or you lied about your skills."

She narrowed her eyes and pushed off from the wall, not caring, for the moment, that it brought them closer together.

"I am the best. Maybe you can contract my company to do your events and exhibits."

"Your plan is to create your own business co-ordinating events?"

"Yes."

Aleksei felt a surge of annoyance rush through his veins. He had hired Madeline when she'd had very little experience in the way of event planning, and she was intent upon taking that knowledge and applying it somewhere else.

He looked at her, so petite and pretty in her dress. Her eyes full of fear and determination.

"And you feel you could handle the responsibility of running your own company?" he asked.

"I majored in Business."

"A worthless degree in my opinion. You either have what it takes to make it, or you don't."

"Inspirational. You should speak at high school graduations."

A rusty chuckle climbed his throat. Her wit and boldness always impressed him. The fact that she had a viewpoint and her own opinions was one of the reasons he'd hired her.

He'd always enjoyed that in their phone conversations. It was nice having someone ready to engage in a verbal battle when he was in a bad mood, or when he simply needed the challenge. Very few people would dare talk to him like Madeline did. All of that deference got old after a while. Especially when he'd realized what an illusion it was. After he'd realized that none of it meant anything.

"Do you know, I had considered that? But they don't like it when you tell them skip college and get a job."

"Did you?"

College had been nothing more than a fantasy. Finishing high school had been beyond his reach. He'd always had to work. But he didn't resent it. It had made him hard enough to withstand the struggle required to succeed. There had been one bright spot in his life. And then tragedy had extinguished the only light he'd ever known, leaving wounds that had scarred over into granite.

"I had no other option. But I didn't need another option."

She bit into her lush bottom lip, leaving a row of even marks. He fought the urge to extend his hand, to soothe away the impressions with his thumb. "My brother made me go to college."

"Your brother?"

She lowered her eyes, an annoying habit she seemed to be developing. "He's...he's very successful and he wanted to make sure that I was successful too."

She was holding back. He shouldn't care. And yet he found he wanted to know the secret she had nearly let slip. The one she didn't want to tell him.

He did not know why he felt compelled to learn her secrets, only that he did. He shouldn't have even felt the need to follow her out into the hall. And yet when he'd seen her petite figure weaving through the crowd, he had started following.

"So your brother is the one who ensured you got your degree?"

She nodded. "Yes. He has one too, and he owns a massive chain of very successful resorts. So...not so worthless."

He chuckled, surprising himself as much as he surprised her. "I do know who your brother is."

He noticed a flood of red creeping up her neck and into her cheeks. "Of course you do. He's been extremely successful. All my family has been."

"And you needed to keep up?"

"Maybe I just needed to be more famous than the rest of them," she said, a slow smile spreading over her face, while her blush still lingered.

"Somehow, you don't strike me as that type."

She raised perfectly groomed brows. "I don't?"

"No. You practically ran out of the ballroom earlier, so you don't seem as though you're courting fame to me."

"Okay, maybe it's not about fame. I just want to have success on my own."

Her tongue darted out and she slicked it over her bottom lip. He couldn't stop himself from watching the movement, couldn't stop himself from imagining touching his own tongue to that luscious mouth.

She was a very desirable woman. And he hadn't had sex in a long time. He had left Olivia neglected in Milan for a good five months before he had ended the relationship.

"Ambitious," he said.

She looked up at him, blue eyes wide. "What's life without a goal?"

"Boring," he responded.

"Exactly," she said.

He moved nearer to her, so close he could smell the woman beneath the floral perfume. "We are like-minded in some ways then."

She swayed slightly, as though she might be tempted to close the distance between them.

"Strange." She swallowed, and instead of moving closer, he felt her retreat slightly. "Ah…maybe you should circulate some more. And I have to…uh… The shrimp."

"Shrimp?'

"The buffet. It's low on shrimp."

He inclined his head. "Then I'll let you get to that, and I'll circulate."

She walked past him, soft curves brushing against him. His body reacted. Viscerally. Hungrily.

A shame he had chosen to cut ties with his mistress. A shame he hadn't called one of the models, or chatted up one of the women in the ballroom. Now there would be no taking the edge off his need anytime in the near future. His body rebelled at the thought anyway. Olivia wasn't the woman he wanted. Neither were any of women in the ballroom. Not tonight.

"Don't you...? I mean...you were going to go and..." She made a sweeping gesture with her hand.

"Yes, circulate. I'm clear on that. Are you dismissing me?"

She shook her head and her glossy ponytail swung in time with the motion. "No, not at all."

"Because it's bad business to dismiss your boss," he said.

He moved toward her, so close that all he would have to do was wrap an arm around her waist and pull her in to join his lips to hers.

"I'm sure it's bad business to linger alone in empty hallways with your boss too," she said, her eyes fixed on his lips, her expression mesmerized.

"Likely," he said.

Their eyes clashed and held.

"Very bad business," she said softly, before turning away from him.

"I'll talk to you soon, Madeline," he said.

Maddy turned and headed toward the kitchen, her heart hammering in her ears. It was disconcerting to realize that she had so much weakness in her. To realize that men were her weakness. She wasn't tempted as long as she was avoiding them. But it seemed like whenever she was put into close proximity with one...

She braced her hand on the wall and slowed her breathing, trying to clear her head. No, men weren't her weakness. She had just been faced head on with the fact that she was suffering severe sexual deprivation—something she hadn't been conscious of when there wasn't an attractive man around.

Soon things would go back to the way they'd been. They would go back to communicating over the phone and the computer and she would be free of the disturbing effect her boss had on her when they were in the same room together.

She wouldn't have to face the weakness that still lived inside of her.

CHAPTER FOUR

EVERY time Maddy saw a positive headline with her name attached to it, it helped to erase some of the lingering sting left by her experience with the media five years earlier. And this morning, she had a fantastic headline to look at.

The party had been a complete success and the pieces in Aleksei's collection were set to be the must-have items of the year. Of course, most people would only be able to afford the mass-produced pieces, and not the handmade originals. The originals would sell for upwards of a million dollars at auction at the end of the exhibition tour.

Her cellphone rang and she snatched it up from the vanity top. "Madeline Forrester."

"Good work last night, Madeline."

Her stomach dropped to her toes. "Thank you, Mr. Petrov." She sneaked a glance at her own reflection in the mirror and saw that her cheeks were glowing pink.

She tried, valiantly, not to picture what Aleksei might be doing.

"Preparing to head to Switzerland yet?"

"I got a late checkout. My train doesn't leave until two.

The ballroom at the Appenzell is easily twice as big as the one here, so I need to start prep work early."

"Why don't you ride with me, rather than taking the two o'clock?"

"With you?" she asked, parroting.

"I leave at noon and I have a private car reserved. Better than riding in one of the public cars, I would think."

She looked at her reflection head on this time, disgusted by the color in her face and the glitter in her eyes. She was excited. Excited to see him again.

No way was she riding with him. She wasn't spending anymore time with him than was necessary, not until she got a grip on herself again.

"We can talk more about where you plan on being in ten years, professionally, and how we might be able to work your long-term goals into a position at Petrova."

Suddenly, riding with him seemed like a pretty big necessity. Because if she didn't, if she let the attraction she felt for him do potential damage to her career, then she might as well just jump him and ruin her career that way.

She wasn't about to do either. She certainly wasn't going to let fear and insecurity hold her back in her professional life.

"Excellent, what time do you want me to meet you?"

"Meet me in the lobby at eleven and we can share a car to the train station."

"Great, see you then."

When she hung up the phone and set it back down on the vanity top, she realized how tightly she'd been gripping it, how hard she'd had it pressed to her ear. She rubbed at the sore spot near her temple.

A trickle of excitement moved through her, picking up steam as it went. It was because of the possibility of promotion, or eventual promotion. Nothing to do with seeing Aleksei again.

She ground her teeth together as she crossed the room and started flinging her belongings into her suitcase.

Yes, it did have to do with seeing Aleksei again. There. Honesty.

But she didn't want it to have anything to do with him. Didn't want to be curious about what kind of man he was, or what he might look like out of his perfectly tailored suits. The fact that she'd entertained the thought of him undressed at all made her feel…it made her feel dirty.

The fact that she wanted him, that she was attracted to him, made her feel unclean in some way. If she could just ignore her sex drive, she would. And in all honesty, and for the most part, she did ignore it.

And she would just keep ignoring it. Problem solved.

She closed the suitcase lid and pressed hard on it, clicking the locks into place. She didn't have the luxury of hanging around angsting about her own issues. She was moving on, moving forward. That was how she'd been living every day since she was twenty-two and it was how she would keep living.

She wasn't going to allow her mistakes to keep her stuck somewhere. She'd worked hard to get where she was. After her very public fall from grace she'd had to work at horrible catering jobs, awful party-planning companies, doing the worst grunt work, so that she could build up a résumé impressive enough to get hired at the North American branch of Petrova. And she'd worked hard to get promoted and moved to the Milan office a couple of months ago. She wasn't stopping now.

She wasn't going to allow anything, least of all an attraction for her boss, to keep her from reaching her full potential at Petrova Gems.

And if that meant she had to sit across from Aleksei Petrov and talk to him while she tried desperately not to imagine what it would be like to reach out and touch the rough, black stubble of his five o'clock shadow then she would do just that.

Aleksei hadn't been in the lobby to meet her. Which was actually a huge relief. Instead, his driver had been there, sending Aleksei's regrets that he'd had a matter to see to in one of the Milan showrooms.

Her reprieve was temporary, since he was meeting her at the train station, but still, she'd take what she could get.

When they arrived at the train station, Aleksei's driver ushered her from the car and escorted her to Aleksei's private railcar.

Well, without Aleksei, it was a no-brainer how she'd rather travel. The space was large and luxurious, with plush couches and a dining set. The domed ceilings were painted a rich blue and gold trim framed the large windows, designed to give the passengers an unsurpassed view of whatever landscape they were passing through.

It didn't even compare to the cramped seating in a public car. Now, if only she didn't have to share it with Aleksei...

"Good, you made it."

Think of the devil.

She turned and her heart lurched. "Uh...yes, your driver was very accommodating."

Aleksei raised a dark eyebrow. "Good. I apologize that I couldn't meet you."

"You don't have to apologize."

"I know," he said. "But I did."

"Impeccable manners."

"Sometimes."

A small laugh bubbled in her throat and escaped her lips. He made her laugh. He really needed to stop doing that.

"Would you like to have a seat?" He gestured to the long cream couch that stretched across most of the room.

She set her bright pink purse on the floor and sat down on the thick-cushioned couch. Oh, yes, she could get used to this.

"Coffee?" he asked.

"Oh, always," she said.

He pushed an intercom button by the door and spoke quickly in Italian. She lived in Milan now, had for two months, but she was a long way from mastering the language. Aleksei spoke at least three languages. That sort of proficiency was intimidating to be around.

He took a seat across from her in one of the big, dark leather chairs.

"So, what's this about job opportunities?" she asked, trying to disguise the eager note in her voice.

"What are you interested in?"

"What am I...? What do I want to do?"

"Yes. We're just having a discussion, Madeline. You're the one with the ten-year plan. What do you need to feel satisfied with Petrova Gems in ten years?"

He leaned back in the chair, long legs stretched in front of him. She noticed the way his pants pulled tight, revealing muscular thighs. His build was total perfection. He was, hands down, the most gorgeous man she'd ever seen. Black hair, olive skin, sensual lips that she knew could soften for a real smile, even if she'd never seen it.

There was something wrong with her head.

The door to the private compartment opened and a man in a suit wheeled a trolley in with coffee, cream and an assortment of things to sweeten the drink. She thanked him— that much Italian she could manage—and started fixing her coffee, keeping her focus on her cup, and off the man currently melting her brain.

"So this is…anything I want?" she asked when she settled back onto the couch.

"This is hypothetical, but it has the possibility of becoming more."

She felt her face get hot as his words took on an unintended meaning. She took a sip of coffee. "Well, I like the artistic aspect of the event-planning. I like the smaller shows too, dealing with the art galleries and the museums. But, I really like the marketing aspects. I majored in Business—" she ignored the look that he gave her and pressed on "—but I did a minor in Market Research and Advertising. I find that part of the business interesting."

"And if I moved you into Marketing you would stay?"

"Hypothetically," she said, taking another sip of coffee, "I could do that on my own too."

"But not for me. I don't hire out for as many things as possible. I like to work with the same people, within my company, and have as much control of it as possible."

Which she could understand. And it sounded worse when he said it than it actually was. He was a good boss. A great one. Especially when he wasn't three feet away. Yes, most especially then.

"And on your own…you lack job security. Security of any kind, really. It's a competitive field. At least, it is if you're attempting success rather than mediocrity, which I assume you are."

She swallowed a scalding mouthful of coffee. "Naturally."

"In which case staying with Petrova is a better option."

She set her mug down on the trolley and leaned forward. "So…you actually want to keep me on?"

"You're a valuable employee, Madeline."

A rush of pleasure moved through her veins. Being

appreciated was foreign in so many ways. For a moment, she simply enjoyed it. She didn't put a wall up, didn't try to shield herself from her feelings. She'd learned to filter things, good and bad, to protect herself. But she could enjoy this, enjoy that Aleksei Petrov was fighting to keep her on staff.

Could enjoy being wanted. Needed.

"Thank you."

She was actually choked up. Why did affirmation from him mean anything? She should be fine on her own. She shouldn't need a pat on the back from him, or anyone.

But it felt really, really good. And it was tempting to just feel good for a while.

"I have owned my own company long enough to know that, no matter how good I am at what I do, if I'm not surrounded by employees that are as committed and as skilled, true success is not possible," he said.

It was a rare thing, she knew, to have a boss that actually appreciated the work that was done in the trenches and not only that, a boss who didn't see employees as expendable.

At her very first office job, an internship, she'd been so cloistered in her boss's domain she'd got a very good idea that he didn't respect anyone who worked for him. Of course, she hadn't seen it that way; she'd eaten up his explanations of why everyone was incompetent. He'd appreciated her, so he'd said. And she had been...so needy. And so very, very stupid.

She'd allowed that—his proclamation of all other workers at the company as morons—to cut her off from her co-workers. To isolate her. Which had been William's aim, of course. Keep her separate, keep her ignorant. And she had been more than willing to walk right into that trap.

A reminder of why she wasn't going to sit around and indulge in warm fuzzies now.

Although, at least Aleksei acknowledged the hard work of everyone in the company. Not just the designers or the management. And not just an innocent young intern.

"I…well, I really appreciate that you consider me a valuable member of the team. And it isn't like I was planning on leaving Petrova tomorrow."

"When it becomes something you're seriously considering, talk to me."

"I will."

She leaned back, letting the soft cushions take some of the tension out of her shoulders, letting the silence stretch between them.

"You don't want coffee?" she asked.

He shook his head. "I dislike the idea of depending on anything that alters my mood."

Now he did, anyway. Aleksei had come too close, had been too tempted to simply drown himself in a bottle of alcohol when Paulina had died. Had done for a while. It had been easier not to feel. Now, he didn't need a substance to accomplish that. It simply came naturally to him.

But that was why his business was so important. He didn't rely on caffeine, or alcohol. He relied on success. The high of being the best. Of knocking out competition. Becoming the most recognized brand name in jewelry. He had done all of that.

Now he was simply working for more. More success. More wealth. But he had to keep moving. Because when he stopped…well, he just didn't stop. He hadn't, not since that first low. Not since he'd determined he wouldn't let himself sink into oblivion, not matter how much he wanted to.

He very much wasn't in oblivion now, and the arousal coursing through his body when he looked at Madeline was a reminder of that.

He didn't sleep with employees. It was bad for business,

and it was shameless abuse of power. He believed that. He lived by it. But Madeline tested that. Was a temptation beyond anything he had known before.

It was six years since his wife had died. Since he had watched them lower the casket, holding the woman he loved, into the ground. A part of him had been buried then too.

He'd had sex since then, of course. After the physical need had come back, he'd taken care of it. Long-term mistresses being his solution of choice.

But what he felt was basic sexual arousal, a man responding to a woman. Any woman. But it wasn't unique. There was no fire.

When he looked at Madeline, there was fire. Heat and desire on a level he couldn't remember feeling before. The need was for her. The fire burned for her. Not for Olivia. Not for some anonymous woman.

Not even for his wife.

He clenched his hands tight, until the tendons stretched, the mild pain a hope of distraction from the current of need that was washing through him. It didn't work.

Not with her so close, glossy brown hair tumbling over her shoulders in waves, blue eyes bright, the pale, lush curve of her breasts framed by the scoop neck of her deep purple top. She was a call to sin he didn't know if he wanted to resist.

He could. He was certain of that. He'd been to hell and back in his life. Willpower, strength wasn't an issue. But he wasn't sure he wanted to turn away.

The only thing that made him question it wasn't her status at the company—somewhere in the past ten minutes he'd gotten over that—it was the haunted look she got in those beautiful blue eyes. A look he didn't want to take on. A look he didn't want to contribute to.

She sighed and leaned back, berry-stained lips curving

into a soft smile. "I should probably adopt your philosophy. Or maybe start sleeping. But there's always so much to do and…coffee's more readily available than downtime."

"I don't really sleep anyway," he said.

He hadn't slept through the night since Paulina died. But it was good. He used that. He worked. He kept his mind busy.

"I wish I didn't need sleep," she said, misunderstanding.

Good. He didn't wish that sort of nightmarish insomnia on anyone. Living between sleep and being awake, with only ghosts for company.

"There are advantages," he said. "Especially as we have shops in so many time zones, offices in so many time zones. It helps that I'm able to get up and make calls when I need to."

"Mmm," she said absently, sipping her coffee, slender fingers sliding over the ceramic handle of the mug. Which shouldn't be arousing, not in any way. And yet, it was.

It was far too easy to imagine those smooth, delicate hands caressing his body.

When he looked at her eyes again, they were intent on him, the glitter in them hot, longing. Her cheeks flushed with color. Need. Want. Desire. He saw it all there. He saw it because it reflected what he felt.

He met her gaze, dared her to look away. She didn't. But then she blinked and brought down the shutters, her eyes blank of anything other than sheer stubbornness.

Aleksei knew women. He created jewelry for women, to make them feel beautiful, to make them happy. It wasn't often he felt he didn't understand a woman's thoughts.

Madeline continued to look at him, her expression cool now. As if trying to prove to him that he was wrong about the fire he was certain he'd glimpsed.

He was more accustomed to women making invitations,

to them following up a moment of clear physical attraction with an attempt at making it more than simple attraction.

It was clear Madeline was not going to be making any invitations.

"When you're ready, Madeline," he said, "we can discuss what it is you want."

Her eyes widened, her cheeks flushing. "With work?"

He couldn't suppress the rush of pure satisfaction that flooded through him. "Of course."

She nodded. "Yes...that sounds...good."

His heart was pounding faster, adrenaline pumping through his veins. Blood running hotter and faster as he imagined what it would be like to get her to confess her desire for him. Interest. Excitement. Feeling. After six years of experiencing nothing more than basic human needs, this was foreign to him.

He wanted Madeline Forrester. And he intended to have her.

"Oh, please be straight," Maddy muttered under her breath as she finished tacking up part of the large swath of silk fabric.

She was trying to make a swag effect around the ballroom between the wall and the ceiling in an attempt to soften what was a very crisp look. All of the decorations, the table settings, the linens, the lights, would be white, and the idea was to add texture and dimension.

Which was why she was wobbling on the second-from-the-top rung of a ladder, hanging on with one hand and trying to wrangle the fabric with the others.

"What the *hell* are you doing?" Aleksei's deep voice resonated in the empty ballroom.

Maddy wobbled a bit and set the last tack into place, covering it carefully with a fold of fabric, before looking down.

"Working," she said sharply. "And could you not sneak up on me when I'm nine feet off the ground?"

She moved her foot forward, careful not to snag her high heel on the ladder rungs as she climbed down. Her shoe slipped on the last rung and she gripped the sides of the ladder tightly, making a very ungraceful dismount as she plopped both feet on the marble floor.

Her heart was pounding heavily, from the almost fall and from Aleksei's presence. She'd managed to avoid him in the two days since the train ride from Milan. Since the moment she'd nearly given in to the desire coursing through her and touched him. She'd been so tempted. So weak.

She turned and took a step back and nearly ran into Aleksei's broad, muscular body. He reached out and bracketed her in, his hands gripping both sides of the ladder.

"What were you doing?" he asked, voice low and deadly.

"My job," she said stiffly, trying to fight the languor that was spreading through her.

"You were on top of a ladder in high-heeled shoes. Do you have any idea how dangerous that is?"

"No. I mean, maybe it is a little, but I work in heels a lot, and I climb ladders sometimes."

"Don't I pay a very efficient team to help you with the physical aspects of preparing for events?" he practically growled.

"Yes, you do, but I was experimenting with this effect and sometimes it's just easier to execute an idea myself. I'm not always sure how it will come together and…"

"It was a very foolish thing to do."

He was so very close. And he was angry, but he wasn't scary. He was concerned…for her. And that was…that was almost more intoxicating than being close enough to him that with the slightest tilt of her head she could brush her lips against his.

She jerked her head back, because if she didn't do that, she was going to do the opposite. And that would be beyond stupid.

But then he moved his hand, placed it on her back. His large, warm palm spread wide across her shoulderblades, heat seeping through her silk blouse. He moved his thumb slightly, the faint rasp of calluses against the thin fabric audible in the large, empty space.

Everything in her was tangled. Snarled together so tightly that she was immobilized by it. She couldn't do anything but stand there and stare at him. Part of her wanted to move away. To run, as fast as she could. Away from the job, from the man. From the temptation. From the sneaky little hussy that lived inside of her that wanted everything she should never, ever have.

But so much of her wanted to stay. To revel in that touch. The woman in her wanted it, wanted his hands to slide over her body, for the touch to become intimate.

It wasn't normal to be celibate for so long. It just wasn't. And she wanted…she just *wanted*. And really, wasn't that normal? To want a man to want her? To want the man in return? It was hard to have a healthy view on your sexuality when the press had labeled you a home-wrecking slut. It was hard not to see yourself that way. At least, it was hard for her.

And that was why, for five years, there hadn't been anyone. Not a lover, not even a date. No kissing, no caressing. There was no middle ground in her life. There had been work. That was all.

That wasn't right. It wasn't right that she'd let William and his deceit dictate her actions for so long. He never should have had that power. Never should have had any power at all.

But he did. Even with the realization, he still did.

She moved away from Aleksei, and he let her go. "I'm

fine," she said, her voice hard. "And I wouldn't have lost my balance at all if you hadn't come in and yelled at me, so maybe next time wait until my feet are on the ground before you come after me."

He strode toward her, his expression fierce. "Is this a joke to you? Do you know how quickly things end? Do you understand?"

The rawness in his voice shocked her. The depth of emotion. She honestly didn't want to know where it came from. She couldn't handle it. If she knew who he was, beyond being a good boss, if there was any more...she just couldn't.

"I'm sorry," she said, needing to defuse it. "I'll be more careful next time. I'll wear better shoes."

"Have one of the other staff do it."

"Why? They aren't any more smash-proof than I am."

His dark eyes were hard, uncompromising. "Have one of the other staff do it."

He was her boss. Something she needed to remember. "Okay, next time I'll have one of the team do it. Does that satisfy you?"

A muscle in his jaw jumped. "I'm as close to satisfied as I will get," he said stiffly, walking ahead of her and out of the room.

She put her hand over her heart, felt it beating rapidly beneath her palm. She didn't know what had just happened. What had passed between them. What had changed. But something had.

And she knew that there would be no putting things back as they had been.

CHAPTER FIVE

PERFECT. It was all perfect. From the glossy white floors to the white silk draping from the ceiling, Madeline had executed the look of the ballroom with style and grace. It was classic, with a modern edge.

Of course, Madeline had nearly broken her neck for the effect.

It was possible he'd overreacted. When he'd walked into the ballroom and seen her there, nine feet above the marble floor, three inch spiked heels draped over the ladder rungs, the rush of anger and adrenaline that had filled him had been instant.

He would have reacted to any employee, any person, behaving so recklessly. Of course, she hadn't seen her behavior as reckless. Stubborn woman.

"Aleksei." The woman next to him, a woman whose name he hadn't bothered to get, stroked his forearm with long, manicured fingers. "I do so enjoy every piece that you've designed. I have a fabulous idea for your next collection."

He let her drone on. He didn't need ideas, especially not from spoiled heiresses.

Then he caught sight of Madeline. Madeline who was wrapped up tight in a slinky, form-fitting white dress that conjured up fantasies that were hardly pure. Madeline, who had caused him to remain sleepless every night of the week. She was slipping out the side door, making her escape, just as she had done at the Milan exhibition. He was done with sleepless nights. He was done wanting and not having.

He set the champagne glass down on one of the tables and extricated himself from the other woman's hold. She was still talking to anyone who would listen as he made his way across the ballroom and to the door that was nearest him.

It would only take a taste. Something to satisfy the hunger that was eating at him. If he could have that, if he could satisfy his curiosity...that was all he needed.

He looked down the corridor and saw the tail of Madeline's white dress disappear as she exited the hall and went to the indoor gardens.

It had been a long time since he'd pursued a woman, if he ever had. He didn't usually bother. But this woman had burrowed her way under his skin. Until he had her, until he sated his body's desire for her, she would seem like so much more than she was.

She was just a woman. He was a man. They wanted each other. It was that basic. It was nothing more. He just needed to prove that to his body.

She was standing near the door when he walked in, her attention fixed on some of the tropical plants. A striking contrast, the bright pink flowers, Madeline in white, and the deep snow just outside the warm glass sanctuary that shielded all the delicate blooms.

He took a moment to admire her, admire the small dip of her waist, the curve of her hip. Especially that tight round bottom, a feature that made him wonder if she spent time in the gym.

She turned suddenly. "Aleksei," she said, no emotion to her voice.

"You're always running out on your own events. If you don't enjoy them, you might worry about the guests."

Soft pink lips tilted up half-heartedly. "Well, last time I had to get shrimp."

"That's right."

"And this time...I needed...air." She looked away from him and turned her focus to the thick glass walls. "I didn't need it bad enough to go out there and brave the snow so I thought I would compromise."

"You look tired," he said. It was true. There were shadows under her eyes, but it was more than that, it was in the way she held herself. He didn't like to see it. It made him feel... responsible somehow.

She pulled her lips into a hard line. "I don't know that that's an appropriate thing for a boss to say."

He took a step closer to her. "And a friend?"

"You aren't my friend."

No. He wasn't. Anything he said to her, any personal gesture he made, would be made with the aim of getting her into bed. That wasn't the action of a friend. Though, truly he wasn't certain that he had friends. He certainly hadn't gone out of his way to cultivate any friendships. He had never been the social one.

"True." He watched her face, the way she looked at him. The hungry look in her eyes, the one that mirrored his own growing need. "Are you going to pretend there's nothing more between us than a working relationship?"

She pulled her mouth tighter, into a determined pucker. "Yes, I think I should pretend that. Because what's the point of going anywhere else?"

He moved closer to her, half expecting her to back away, but she didn't. She held her ground, arms at her sides.

"Nothing long-term," he said. "But there are benefits to short-term arrangements."

"The woman you were talking to?"

"No one. I didn't even ask her name."

Madeline only looked at him for a moment, clenching and unclenching her fists, shifting her weight from one foot to the other. She stepped forward and put her hands on his cheeks, blue eyes serious as she looked at him. Then she pulled up on her toes and kissed him.

Her kiss was clumsy, a bit inexperienced, but her enthusiasm more than made up for any missing skill. She kissed like a woman who was starving, and he was more than willing to meet her need.

He wrapped his arm around her waist and pulled her to him, groaned when he felt her full breasts press against his chest. Her tongue, soft and wet, slicked against his lips, a timid question in its touch. And he answered, meeting her thrust for thrust, tasting, savoring, enjoying every bit of her sweet mouth.

An enthusiastic sound climbed her throat and vibrated between their lips as she shifted her hands so that she was clinging to his shoulders. He cupped the back of her head with his other hand, sifting his fingers through silky strands.

Just a taste? He wanted a feast. Wanted to move his hands over her curves, without the thin barrier of her dress hindering him. He wanted to feel her skin, smooth and warm. Wanted to taste every inch of her.

As suddenly as she'd started the kiss, she pulled away. And he let her go, watching her. Her eyes were wide, her lips swollen, cheeks flushed, her breasts rising and falling harshly with each breath.

She pushed a hand through her thoroughly mussed hair. "I had to...I had to see," she said, her voice shaky.

"You had to see?" he asked, his own voice roughened by arousal.

"I thought it couldn't possibly be as good as I imagined. It never is, you know."

"And?"

She cursed and turned away from him.

"That good?" he asked.

She turned back to face him. "I can't," she said simply. "It's unprofessional."

"We passed unprofessional a while ago, I think."

"Yes, okay, we did. But continuing would be...more un-professional."

She stood back and looked at him, her eyes hard, as if she was waiting for something. Waiting for him to grab her, or... he didn't know what else. He knew it went with the wariness he saw in her eyes sometimes. Knew he didn't want to take it on. He couldn't be anyone's knight in shining armor. Didn't want to be.

"All right, Madeline, if you don't want to, that's your de-cision. I don't coerce women into bed. I don't have to. But I know you feel the attraction. You've proved it. And as far as professional goes, the line has been crossed with or without actual sex."

She shook her head, dark curls bouncing with the motion. "Office stuff is complicated. I have too much tied up in this job." Her eyes narrowed. "You aren't going to fire me if I say no, are you?"

"I told you, I don't do coercion, and that encompasses asking someone to prostitute herself for a job. I can be ruth-less in matters of business, but I do not abuse people."

Madeline swallowed, but her throat remained dry. She'd just made the second biggest mistake of her life. Okay, pos-sibly third biggest, but it was still big. She never should have kissed him. Ever.

But fantasy never lived up to reality and she'd been so desperate to purge the desire for Aleksei from her system, to do something to get the reckless ache to desert her. She'd been sick with jealousy watching that woman caress his arm and whisper in his ear. It wasn't emotional jealousy, it was basic, physical jealousy. She didn't want another woman to have what she was so set on denying herself.

And with that desire came guilt that was nearly crippling. Guilt because she wanted a man, for the first time in five years. Guilt because she couldn't repress her sexuality anymore. Guilt because she still wanted sex when she'd been so convinced she could let that part of herself go. When she'd been so convinced that she should. Because how could she ever trust herself again?

And then she'd thought, as he was standing there looking so gorgeous it made her body hurt with desire, that she could prove it wouldn't really be electric. She had limited experience with men, only one miserable lover to her credit, and the physical side of things had never been so incredible for her. It had been about emotions, not any kind of true desire.

But Aleksei's kiss had sent a current through her body that had immobilized her with its strength. Had melted her with its heat. She'd meant to close the door on it. Had meant to remind her body that all that physical stuff wasn't everything it was made out to be.

Except it had been more. More than she'd imagined and more than it had ever been for her.

Counterproductive.

"I'm sure you don't." She believed him. Believed that he didn't get his kicks out of abusing his power. He hadn't tried to talk her into it. Hadn't said how beautiful she was. Hadn't said he loved her.

He hadn't lied. And she had kissed him. And lightning

hadn't struck her dead on the spot. There was no scarlet letter out in the snow.

That was all very good to know.

"I just can't…" It was too easy to remember what had happened last time. And it was her boss again, for heaven's sake. Although, if there was a similarity between Aleksei and William she couldn't think of it.

"It's not a good idea," she finished.

"It's not," he agreed.

She folded her arms under her breasts, because she was cold. Because she needed a shield. She put her head down and walked past him, heading to the door.

When he spoke again, his voice was soft, but commanding. "It's not a good idea. But I want you. If you want this to happen, you have to come to me now, Madeline. I'm not playing games, and I don't chase after women."

She didn't turn. "I won't change my mind. I can't."

It crushed part of her to say that. To be such a coward. Because there was common sense involved, yes, but most of it was just fear. And she hated that she was the sort of person who let fear have a hand in her life.

But it was too strong, too real, for her to fight.

He moved so that he was behind her, pushed the door open and held it for her. "And that is your decision. It remains your decision." He didn't believe her. Of course he didn't. She didn't believe herself. "Can I escort you back to the ballroom?"

She nodded stiffly. The best thing to do would be to pretend nothing had happened.

That she'd never felt his tongue slide against hers. Never been held in his strong arms.

She could do it. She could go back to the way things had been. She wasn't weak. At least, she wouldn't be anymore.

* * *

"Hello, Madeline." Aleksei's smooth voice was more torturous now than it had ever been. Now that she'd tasted his lips. Felt his hands, rough and insistent on her. Rough and insistent in a good way. In the way that made a woman feel want at the exclusion of everything else.

"Hello," she responded, her voice coming out short and crisp.

"How is everything shaping up for the exhibition in Luxembourg?"

She leaned back in her chair and arched her back, stretching out her knotted muscles. "Great. Better than great. We have use of the entire castle, which means on the invites I'm going to have guests check whether or not they would like the use of a room in the castle for the night, and to join us for a gourmet breakfast the next morning."

"Extravagant."

"You can afford it," she said.

"Of course."

It was the perfect venue as far as she was concerned. It was turning into the largest event for this collection, and she was very happy with it. The guest list included some of the world's wealthiest and most influential people, and the setting was designed to impress.

"I'd also like to display some pieces from your past collections if there are originals still available."

"Some, although most have been sold at auction."

"Whatever we can get our hands on. Since we have use of the whole space, I want to use the whole space."

She could do this. It was easy to talk work with Aleksei. They meshed there. They connected. On this one plane of existence they connected. And it was really the only way they needed to connect.

Yes, it was. No need to connect in any other way. Not at the lips or…anywhere else.

She grimaced and leaned forward, picking up a pen so she could take notes or something. Anything to keep her mind fully occupied so that it didn't go off on tangents about connecting to Aleksei.

It was better with hundreds of miles between them. Better with the barrier of the phone. She wished, she wished so much, that they had never broken that barrier. It would all be simpler. She wouldn't be having sleepless nights dreaming about his touch, wouldn't get hot every time his name was mentioned in conversation.

"I'm stopping by later today," he said. "We can discuss it further then."

She stood up. "What?" He never came to the Milan office. Well, not in the two months since she'd been there, which didn't really equate to never. But he certainly didn't come often. He'd been in Moscow and she'd been perfectly happy with him there.

"You're looking forward to it, I can tell," he said drily.

"Sorry." She shook her head and cursed herself inwardly. She would kill for a little sexual sophistication right about now. Sadly, she wasn't going to get it in the next hour.

Though she was getting to the point where she was really thinking it was time. She'd allowed herself to be tied up in the horror from five years ago for a long time. Too long. Longer than her former boss, certainly. Likely longer than her former boss's ex-wife. The media didn't even care anymore, hadn't for a long time.

But her name had been synonymous with slut for a good two months. Her brother had done his absolute best to protect her. His misguided best since she'd sworn to him that nothing had happened. A huge weight she carried still.

It was easy to make excuses. For all of it. For lying to Gage—she was embarrassed, humiliated, and, no, of course she hadn't known her boss was married. For any of it happening in the first place—William had said he loved her. But the fact was, there wasn't an excuse. She'd been stupid, she'd been naive and she'd allowed herself to be manipulated.

An affection-starved young woman, barely a woman, who had lapped up every compliment, every ounce of affection her boss had sent her way.

But she was still letting that man manipulate her, and it was a fair bet he couldn't even remember her name. He had likely replaced her, and the wife he'd lost over the affair he'd had with her, ten times over by now.

And she was still stuck. Still wallowing in all the pain and regret of the past. All that moving on and up nonsense was just that. It was a lie. To herself and to everyone else.

Being with Aleksei, sleeping with him, might not be a good idea. But her decision about it shouldn't hinge on things in the past. It should just hinge on the fact that a workplace dalliance wasn't really the brightest move of all time.

"I'll...I'll see you soon then," she said.

She hung the phone up and sat back down. Her heart was pounding hard, her hands shaking. And this time, it wasn't all Aleksei's doing.

She'd had a breakthrough. In ten minutes. She hadn't put her relationship with William behind her. She hadn't moved on. She was letting him control her life, even now.

And it was ending today.

CHAPTER SIX

OF COURSE, Aleksei hadn't simply stopped by. He'd stayed the entire day. And of course, the reason for his visit had been the next exhibition.

Which meant she was involved. In every aspect of his visit. The large staff meeting, the smaller staff meeting, and now she was cloistered in his office after-hours with him, and they were hashing out details between the two of them.

Usually, Aleksei left her job to her. Of course, the exhibitions she'd planned in North America had been less crucial. But this exhibition, this collection was personal to him, for obvious reasons, and he was right in the middle of everything, putting in his own thoughts, changing things around and generally disturbing her.

"So what do we want to do with the necklace?" she asked.

The necklace being the secret piece of Aleksei's new collection. An emerald, diamond and platinum creation that, just in materials, was worth half a million dollars. With Aleksei as the designer, the creator of the piece, it was worth much more. And he had been holding it back for this portion of the tour.

The buzz about the exhibition was already electric.

"I think it should be there when the guests arrive. I want it to be the centerpiece of the show, in the middle of things, but secure."

"Well, we can put alarms around it without obstructing the view of the display case. And of course we'll have security guards. Everywhere." She leaned back in the office chair and stretched her neck. "And then, when the actual event is over, and the guests that are staying in the rooms overnight retire, we'll take the jewels away in the armored cars."

They'd never had a theft attempt, but Aleksei believed in being vigilant. Which was probably why there had never been a theft attempt.

"That all sounds good," he said, standing from his desk and rounding it, coming to stand in front of her.

At five foot three, she wasn't tall, not by any stretch of the imagination, which was why she always gave herself a boost with high heels. But Aleksei was easily a foot taller. And so broad and masculine. He made her feel small, petite. Feminine. The strangest thing was that she sort of liked it.

She blinked, trying to refocus her mind.

She bent down to get her purse before standing. The motion brought her a little closer to him than she'd anticipated. It suddenly felt much hotter in the room.

He was looking at her, dark eyes trained on her face, then dipping to her lips. The tension was thick, physical, like a wire that had been stretched between them had been tightened. Tightened to the point where she felt sure it would break.

Breathing was nearly impossible. "Anything else?" she asked. She needed to escape. Now. Badly.

But she also wanted to stay. Wanted to find out what

would happen if things kept going. She wanted to see what it would take to make the wire snap.

"Only this." He leaned, dipping his head slightly, and brushed her lips with his. She forgot to breathe.

His lips were warm, firm, everything she remembered and so much that she'd forgotten. It was a short kiss, but it made her want more. So much more. Made her want to cry over the frustrating need that was pounding through her. It was as though there was a bottomless pit of need and desire in her, and she'd never known about it until now. Had never known it existed until Aleksei unearthed it.

She wobbled slightly when trying to step away from him, needing distance.

"I thought you were going to wait until I came to you," she said, not summoning up as much accusation in her voice as she'd have liked.

"I was," he said, dark humor lacing his voice, his accent seeming heavier. "But it was only a kiss."

How was something *only* anything when it had the power to tilt your world off its axis?

He was so tempting. But her resolution to let go of the past didn't mean she was going to jump into bed with her boss. Especially when she'd already tried that tired old cliché five years ago.

This had *Bad Idea* written all over it. It had taken her years, professionally and otherwise, to get back to normal after her last disastrous relationship with a man. She hadn't been able to get a job for nearly a year, because the scandal had been related to her work. No one wanted to bring her into the company.

Ultimately, she'd ended up getting a job at a catering company, serving food from a line. No one had cared there. Or maybe they hadn't known. Her boss's wife at the time, the wife she'd been ignorant of, was a semi-famous men's catalog model and B-movie actress. That was one reason her unintended affair had been headline news.

It had been hard to start at the bottom, especially after she'd graduated with such high honors, achieved a coveted, but ill-fated, internship. But at least at the bottom, in a new industry, away from the corporate setting, she'd been free from the ugliness.

But if she started a relationship with Aleksei...too stupid. It would be too stupid.

"Well, don't kiss me again. We're shooting for professional here, and that isn't it."

"Is it because I'm your boss, Madeline? Is that why you don't want this?"

"Partly," she said.

"And the other part?"

"Not your business, because you're my boss and not my lover."

"I'm not opposed to becoming your lover."

She looked at a spot on the wall behind him. She couldn't handle looking at him, not when he was offering her something she was fighting against wanting so desperately. Not when she knew one look in those midnight eyes would undo her completely.

"I know," she said. "But I work for you. That gives you... The power balance isn't fair. There's no way...I would be at a total disadvantage."

"That isn't how I operate. If we were to have an affair—" she cringed at his use of the word "—then I would be your boss during business hours, and your lover when we weren't at the office. As your lover, I wouldn't be your boss."

"And as my boss you wouldn't be my lover?"

"I already told you, I don't mix business with pleasure."

"I think *I* said that. And I also think it might mean something different than colleagues at work, lovers off work."

He shrugged. That he could even make such a casual gesture when she was ready to melt was infuriating. "If it were about a relationship, then, yes, I can see how it would be problematic to separate the two. But I'm not looking for a relationship."

"So, you just want...sex?"

He flexed the fingers on his left hand. "Exactly. I don't do relationships."

Most women would have been upset by that, and she realized that. Even understood why. She'd been one of those women. One who thought sex and love had to go together. Well, she'd been an idiot then.

Now she was relieved. He hadn't lied. He hadn't said he wanted to be with her because she was special. He hadn't said he loved her. He'd said he wanted sex. It was honest, at least.

Those other words...those were lies. Lies men told to make women feel comfortable. To make them feel indebted to them. *Oh, you love me so I owe you my body.*

What a sick joke that was.

"Well, I don't do the relationship thing either," she said, confident in that, if nothing else.

"So we're on the same page."

She laughed, a little hysterical bubble of sound escaping her lips. "I'll bet it's nearly impossible for the two of us to be on the same page."

"You want me," he said. Not a question.

"Yes." There was no point in lying. None at all.

"I want you. Seems like we might be on the same page."

His dark eyes were molten heat, intense, his expression hard and unmoving. He didn't try to coddle her, caress her, seduce her. He didn't add sweet words or a cajoling smile. He didn't try to relax her. Didn't offer her a drink to help calm her nerves.

Her heart was pounding so loud she was certain he could hear it. She knew what was smart. And she knew what she wanted. It was too bad they weren't the same thing.

She took a step toward him, and she knew. Knew that in doing that, she was saying yes.

And then his mouth was on hers, his lips and tongue urgent, his body hot and hard against hers. She moved against him, feeling the hard ridge of his erection against her stomach. She felt an answering wetness between her thighs, her breasts heavy, needing his touch.

Yes.

This was honest. His response couldn't be faked or concealed. He didn't try to make it into more than it was by lighting candles and draping a red scarf over a lamp. This wasn't some carefully plotted seduction. It was need. Beyond anything she'd felt before. It wasn't about emotion, or love, or wanting something, someone, to fill the void inside of her heart.

It wasn't about escape. It wasn't about the future. It was now and it was real. And it was the only thing that mattered.

The masculine growl that escaped his lips as he teased her with his moist tongue was a sound of pure, sexual desire. And that was what she wanted. All she wanted.

Physical, she could do. And she wanted physical with Aleksei. Yes, he was her boss, but there was nothing, nothing about him, that bore any resemblance to William Callahan.

There were no lies between she and Aleksei. No promises either.

Nothing but desire.

She'd thought, been afraid, that being with a man again would put her back in that vulnerable, needy place. Well, she was needy, but not in the way she'd been scared she would be. She was only needy for his touch. For the feeling of his hard body inside of hers.

But she also felt powerful. Felt like she had control. He was so hard against her there was no denying that he was on fire for her too, that he wanted what she did. That she was an equal partner.

She ran her hands over his chest. He was built like a fantasy come to life. Hard, well-defined muscles, broad shoulders. And right now, he was hers to explore. And she wanted to embark on the journey so badly she was shaking with her desire.

Excitement surged through her. She worked the buttons on the front of his shirt and pushed it down his arms, growling in frustration when the buttoned cuffs caught on his wrists. He chuckled and wrenched his mouth from hers, taking a moment to undo the buttons before shrugging his shirt off and letting it fall to the floor.

She swallowed hard when she saw his bare chest. He looked better than he felt. Olive skin, perfectly defined, just the right amount of dark chest hair scattered over his pecs and continuing in a line down his abs until it disappeared beneath the waistband of his dark trousers.

He looked at her, his eyes appraising. He was too calm. She needed him out of control.

She approached him and put her hands on his belt, working the leather through the silver buckle before undoing the button on his pants. She kept her eyes trained on his. His jaw was clenched tight, muscles bunched.

Sucking in a sharp breath, she pressed her hand flat against his shaft, feeling the length of him. He was big. And it had been a long time. Briefly, she worried it might hurt. Her first time had been hellish that way, but then, she hadn't really been all that aroused at the time. She'd simply been eager to please. None of that had been about her.

Well, she was aroused now, beyond aroused. And this *was* about her. About taking something back that belonged to her. Her body. Her desire. Her right to want a man, and to act on that wanting.

Hooking her fingers in the waistband of his pants and underwear, she slid them down his slim hips, revealing his whole body to her. Naked, fully aroused, he was the most incredible sight she'd ever seen.

He was also a little bit intimidating.

"I haven't…been with anyone in a while," she said, looking at his fully aroused body.

"Then I'll make sure you're ready," he said.

And just like that her nerves, what little there had been, were taken care of. He would know what to do with a woman. She trusted that. Because Aleksei was a perfectionist, and he would make this perfect too.

"Now you," he said, putting his hands on the front of her blouse.

She batted them away, replacing them with her own hands. She undid the first button, the second, the third, gratified by the hunger she saw etched into his sculpted face. She let her shirt join his on the floor before shimmying out of her pencil skirt. Then she was standing before him in nothing more than stockings, high heels and a very sheer lace bra and panty set.

And she saw his control snap, the light in his eyes turning feral, just before all of the tension in his body released and he pulled her into his arms.

He moved his hands from her hips, to her waist, up to the catch of her bra. He flicked it open with one deft motion and the lacy garment fell away. She wasn't embarrassed for him to see her, not when it was obvious just how very much he was enjoying the sight.

Those magic hands shifted slightly, his thumbs skimming

her ribcage, brushing against the swell of her breasts. Her nipples tightened, almost painfully. Why didn't he touch her there? She was dying for it. Needed it more than she needed air.

Aleksei didn't look away from her face, his dark eyes trained on hers. He didn't reach straight for her breasts, didn't grope or grab at her. Ironically, she wished he would.

He only continued stroking her skin in maddening circles before encircling her waist with his arms and drawing her up against his hard body.

He kissed her thoroughly, deeply, sensually, his tongue making thorough sweeps of her mouth. Her body shook, and she arched into him, her nipples brushing against his crisp chest hair. A moan of pleasure escaped her lips.

She didn't remember it being like this. She *knew* it hadn't been like this before. This was…everything she was feeling, all of the pleasure, the aching hollow need in her body, it was almost too much. In the very best way.

She moved against him, needing to stimulate the part of her body that was screaming loudest for his touch.

His hand moved from her hip down to her thigh, the sensual slide pure torture in the best sense. Gripping her leg, he drew it up around his, opening her to him, bringing her clitoris up against his hardened shaft.

"Yes," she whispered into his mouth, moving against him, taking everything that she craved.

"Yes," he answered, backing her up until her legs hit the desk.

Lifting her gently, he seated her on the polished surface. When he abandoned her lips, she felt dizzy, dazed. More than a little lightheaded.

Aleksei knelt in front of her and slid his hands beneath her panties, drawing them down her stocking-clad legs, delicately removing them and casting them onto the floor. She was open to him now, exposed. And she still wasn't embarrassed or ashamed.

There was no room for that. Not now.

That filled her with a different kind of exhilaration, one that was quickly overshadowed when he traced a line on her inner thigh with the tip of his tongue. She gritted her teeth. Oh, she had never felt anything like this before. Never experienced a rush of pleasure so divine. Her head fell back and she gripped the edge of the desk, hoping she didn't fall.

Rough, masculine hands moved to grip her thighs, to keep her from scooting away from him as he ran the flat of his tongue over that most sensitive part of her. She arched, tightening her hold on the edge of the desk. This was even better. Even more incredible.

Never, ever had she experienced this before. She'd thought about it, dabbled in the odd fantasy about what it might be like, knew it had to be amazing…but she'd underestimated.

Oh, she'd had no idea.

Aleksei's tongue was expert, and when he slid a finger into her tight passage she nearly flew into a million pieces. The addition of a second digit left her quivering, shaking, close to falling over the precipice she felt like she was on the edge of.

He was merciless, his tongue and fingers moving in time until she was pushed over the edge into oblivion. She let go of the edge of the desk and gripped his shoulders, digging her fingernails into his back. She didn't care. He didn't seem to care.

So that was what all the fuss was about.

She felt weak. Spent. But still somehow unsatisfied. And she knew why. She still hadn't had him inside of her. And it seemed absolutely critical for her to experience that.

"Can you stand up?" he asked, voice husky.

She nodded and stood from the desk. His hands were gentle, but firm, as he turned her so she was facing the desk and pressed slightly on her back. She put her hands flat on the polished surface. She'd never had sex in this position, but she was educated enough on the subject to know what he wanted.

A shiver of excitement ran through her.

She heard the sound of plastic tearing.

"Condom," he said.

A rush of relief flooded her, because she would have forgotten. She'd been too caught up in the moment. She still was. It was hard for her to think clearly, not with the buzz of her first orgasm still lingering, and raging arousal still roaring through her.

The blunt head of his erection probed at her slick entrance and she parted her legs further, trying to make sure she could accommodate him. He thrust into her slowly, painlessly, and she was grateful for that.

Then he gripped her hips and began to move. His rhythm hard, steady, intoxicating. He reached his hand around to the front of her body and cupped her breast, squeezing her nipple lightly. She didn't bother to hold back the moan that climbed her throat, didn't bother to disguise any of her reactions to the pleasure that was rocketing through her.

His hand moved to her clitoris, working in time with his thrusts. She grasped the edge of the desk again, needing something to hold her to earth as another climax started to build.

When it hit her, this time he was with her, his grunt of completion mingling with hers. He placed his hand, palm down, next to hers, resting his head against her shoulder, his breathing ragged, his heart raging.

"I have to move," she said, her knees too weak to support her.

He pulled back, out, and she collapsed into the nearest chair. Her head was spinning, her heart beating on overdrive.

She'd had sex. She'd enjoyed it. The roof hadn't caved in. No one had come in and shouted and called her a whore.

It had even been her boss.

There was no media.

There was no guilt.

For the first time in five years, her body felt like it belonged to her again. Everything, for so long, had been tied up in the man who had stolen what was left of her innocence. Had taken the last shred of her belief in humanity and used it against her.

And because of him she'd locked her desires away, felt guilty for even looking twice at a man, because she felt she couldn't even trust her own body.

Not only had all of that been erased, she'd learned that there really was a lot more to sex than she knew. And she was glad for that. Her few experiences with William had left her disappointed.

She'd wanted so desperately to please him, to be the woman for him. To be worthy of his love.

Tonight, she'd pleased herself. And her lover looked pretty pleased too.

Aleksei turned away from her, discreetly discarding the condom in a wastebasket before picking his pants up from the floor and jerking them on in one fast motion.

She couldn't move yet. She could only look at her clothes, scattered all over the office floor, and wonder what exactly she'd been transformed into in Aleksei's arms.

She looked down and realized she was still wearing her stay-up nylons and high heeled shoes. What a picture she must make. She waited, again, for the guilt. The shame. Nothing. She simply felt…satisfied. Very, very satisfied.

"I…" she said, searching for words.

"It wasn't a good idea?" he asked, buckling his belt.

"No, it really wasn't. But it's too late now."

"It was too late the moment we saw each other," he said, a wry smile on his lips.

"I think you're probably right." She scooted the chair forward and reached down, scooping up her bra and panties. "I don't regret it."

"Good," he said. "Because it's a little late for regrets."

"But it was just sex," she said.

"Yes."

She sighed. "Good sex."

He grunted in agreement as he tugged his shirt on.

"And it shouldn't happen again," she finished.

His movements stilled. "Oh, no?"

"No. We have to work together and now that we've...well, we've got it out of our systems it would be best to go back to work."

One dark eyebrow lifted. "If that's what you want."

"It is." It had to be. It had been amazing and at the moment she felt wonderfully, blessedly detached. She wasn't risking that detachment.

Of course, Aleksei had never promised love. Never promised a ring and a house and a family and everything she'd ever wanted.

She didn't want those things now anyway. They were an illusion. Love was only a mask for control. She didn't believe in it now, didn't want it.

"Yeah, I think...it has to be over now."

He nodded. "I'll let you dress." He turned to walk out of the office, then paused. "I need you to come to the studio tomorrow. I have some things I need to show you so that we can come to a consensus on displays."

"Okay," she said, still feeling unshakeable, unbreakable, in the aftermath of her new experience.

"See you tomorrow." Then he left. And she was alone.

And suddenly she felt very, very alone.

She cursed into the empty room and began to gather her clothes.

CHAPTER SEVEN

IT HAD been twelve hours since he'd been inside of Madeline's body. Twelve hours and his body was still infused with a rush of post-orgasm adrenaline. She had been incredible. Gorgeous, eager, uninhibited.

And she only wanted the one time.

Usually, the promise of one time would settle well with him. He wasn't looking for commitment, not even close. But another taste of the sweet oblivion being lost in Madeline's body afforded? That he would gladly experience again.

He glanced at his watch right when Madeline came bursting through the door of his studio.

"You're late," he said, taking a long moment to admire her beauty.

Her cheeks were flushed from the outside air, and from the run it looked like she'd taken to try and make it on time. Long, slender legs encased in dark, skinny jeans that hugged her hips. A stretchy cotton top with a scoop neckline that molded to her rounded breasts. Breasts he'd had in his hands twelve hours ago.

He hadn't taken the time to taste them, and now he regretted that.

"Sorry...I overslept." She looked down when she said it.

"Didn't sleep well last night?" He certainly hadn't. His body had been hard and aching for round two.

He'd forgotten how good sex was, as strange as it was to admit. Had forgotten the bliss of having nothing on his mind but his own pleasure and the pleasure of his partner. Now he was craving more. More of Madeline.

"Come back this way," he said.

The studio was empty. Most of his designers opted to come in, borrow specific tools, and work from home. It was better that way. Too many artistic egos in one room quickly became chaotic.

He opened the door to his workroom, a room he hadn't been in in maybe two years before these past few weeks, and ushered her inside.

"Do you have the necklace here?"

The note of excitement in her voice was strangely gratifying. "In the safe."

He pressed his thumbprint to a pad in the wall, then keyed in a code that opened his personal safe. There was no such thing as being too careful when jewelry of the quality he worked with was involved.

He took out a velvet box and opened it, watching Madeline's eyes carefully. They widened, obvious approval evident in them. "It's so beautiful, Aleksei."

She reached out, delicate fingers hovering over the gems.

"Touch it if you like," he said, aware his voice sounded rough.

Her eyes met his and she lowered her fingers, caressing the emeralds in a reverent manner. One that made his blood pound hot and fast. He wanted her hands on him again.

Last time had been hot and fast. Incredible. But he wanted more time. Time to savor her body, to thoroughly enjoy every inch of her lovely curves. Desk sex in his office had been amazing, hot, wild, but a soft bed was the preferred venue for good reasons.

"Try it on," he said.

Her blue eyes flew to his. "Why?"

"I want to see it. I have never put it on anyone before. Which means I have never really seen it."

She hesitated, her hand hovering over the box. "I..."

"Let me." He set the box on the desk and lifted the necklace from its satin casing. "Turn around," he said, the echo from the day before sending all of his blood south, making him painfully hard.

It was easy to see her in his mind as she'd been then. Her body stretched over the desk, the elegant line of her back, the indent of her small waist. The curve of her hip, her perfectly round butt. And those long legs, long even though she was petite, with those black stockings still on.

She looked up at him and licked her lips, a glitter of wariness in her eyes. But she obeyed, turning slowly so that she was facing away from him. He lifted the necklace from its case and swept her thick curtain of dark hair aside, his thumb brushing the creamy, smooth skin of her neck.

He'd had sex with her. The mystery should be solved, all questions answered. And yet so many lingered. Her reaction to the first climax he'd given her...it had been explosive, but more than that, she'd seemed shell-shocked. He wanted to know why. Wanted to know why it had been a while since she'd been with anyone.

Mostly, he wanted to know what her pretty pink nipples tasted like.

He looped the necklace around with one hand, fastening it in the back and letting the heavy weight of it rest on her chest.

"Let me see," he said.

He gripped her shoulders and turned her slowly. It wasn't

a line, what he'd said about seeing jewelry on a woman, it was the truth. He never really felt he'd seen a piece until it was being worn.

On Madeline, the necklace was exquisite. Large emeralds and small pear-cut diamonds woven together in a platinum chain. Some of the glittering diamonds dropped to the curve of her breasts, demanding that he look at her ripe, tempting flesh.

"You should wear it," he said.

She touched the lowest hanging diamond, the one that was nearly nestled in the valley of her cleavage. "I *am* wearing it."

"To the exhibition in Luxembourg. It is best displayed on you."

She opened her mouth and he could tell, by the stubborn set of those pretty lips, that she was about to argue.

"Madeline," he said, "don't say anything about professional boundaries. Because those were well and truly breached last night."

Her cheeks turned a deep crimson. "It happened. It isn't happening again, so professional boundaries do matter."

The desire to kiss her, touch her, caress her where those tiny diamonds glittered, was nearly impossible to combat. That by itself gave him the willpower to move away. Anything, any feeling, that was that strong...

It was simply unsatisfied desire. That was all. He'd had his taste, and now he wanted to eat his fill. His reaction was simply that of a hungry man in need of satiation.

Need. It was a word he didn't like. He'd needed someone before, and he had no intention of ever needing anyone again. And that meant he was going to have to deny the arousal that was coursing in his veins.

He could find a blonde. Or a redhead. Variety was always good. And he could go back to the carefully, controlled form of relationships he preferred. The sort of relationships that didn't include spontaneous sex on a desk.

It was better that way.

"I still want you to wear it," he said.

"You could hire a model," she retorted.

"But it looks perfect on you. Why should I pay some skinny woman to walk around in it when it suits you?"

Blue eyes narrowed in his direction. "Did you just imply that I'm fat?"

"No, I implied that professional models are skinny. You have curves. You are a woman." Curves that had fit in his hands perfectly, curves he was longing to touch again.

"Women want to be skinny, Aleksei. Good grief, I thought you were some sort of legendary playboy. Seems like you should know that."

Madeline wasn't really annoyed with Aleksei. Well, not about the skinny comment. She was annoyed at herself. Because the minute she'd walked into the room her sophisticated, blasé self, the one that had got dressed this morning repeating the mantra, "I can have a one-night stand and then face the man the next day, because I'm totally sure in myself," had gone and run for cover, leaving her nervous, and breathless, and a little turned on. Okay, a lot turned on.

And when he'd commanded her to turn around in that same tone as he'd used yesterday... It had melted her. Physically, not emotionally.

It had felt... It had been strange to have him leave after they'd been together. But ultimately, she was glad he had. No point in cuddling up. That was part of *making love.* They had not made love on that desk. That had been nothing but purely physical sex.

And the purely physical part of herself wanted him. A lot. Again. Maybe a couple more agains after that. But she hadn't known that sex could be *so* good.

She'd done the whole crying after, emotional thing before. But she'd never done the pleasure-that-felt-like-it-might-kill-you thing before. And she liked it. Which brought her back to the wanting more thing. Which was really impractical and not going to happen.

But was kind of hard with Aleksei's dark gaze trained on her, his eyes full of heat and, she was sure she saw it, desire.

"I didn't find the statement insulting," he said. "I like your figure."

"Boundaries," she said, not as sharply as she would have liked.

"You like me to cross boundaries."

She thought he might kiss her. But he didn't. He only looked at her. But that look had the power to melt the soles of her shoes. She waited for him to make a move. He didn't.

The disappointment that settled in her stomach irritated her. She shouldn't be disappointed. She was the one who'd said it was one time only. For very good reasons. Aleksei, or rather Aleksei's bedroom skills, were addictive. And whether she was with him one time or ten, they always would be. So there was no point in prolonging it, in making it more important than it needed to be.

More important than it could be.

There was no room in her life for emotional entanglements. And she didn't even believe that love really existed. Her brother and his wife were extremely happy, even after five years. But of course some people were compatible, so it was bound to work.

She'd never seen real love up close in action. Her parents certainly hadn't loved anyone but themselves. Definitely not their unexpected, unwanted daughter. William hadn't loved her. All of his compliments, all of his poetic words, had been designed to manipulate her into bed. Had been to make her docile and happy so she didn't ask why he didn't stay the night, and why they never went to his house. And why it was a secret they were together.

She'd been so stupid.

She never would be again. At least with Aleksei it was just the sex and she knew it.

"I can't deny that I liked it," she said.

Oh, good, and now her cheeks were hot, which meant they were bright pink with embarrassment. She just wasn't a sexually sophisticated person, and one time with Aleksei hadn't changed that.

"But," she continued, "that doesn't change the fact that it was a bad idea, and…and we have to get back to business now."

"I fail to see what any of this has to do with you wearing the necklace. Even if yesterday hadn't happened, now I've seen you in the necklace, you're the one I would want displaying it."

Okay, this was work. It was just work. She was good at this. Besides, the necklace was gorgeous. She admired what Aleksei did so much, saw so much art and beauty in it. She was really almost honored to be asked to wear it.

"As part of my job?" she asked.

"As part of your job."

She nodded slowly. "Okay. I'll wear it."

Because he was her boss, and he was asking her to. But it felt different…and that was because they'd…been together.

All the more reason to just wear the necklace. If she let a few stolen moments of pleasure, the kind of pleasure she'd denied herself for so long, the kind of pleasure she deserved, ruin her job, then she'd have sabotaged her career for sex. And that was even stupider than sleeping with her boss had been in the first place.

"If you need a gown, I will have one purchased for you," he said.

"You sign my paychecks, Aleksei, you know I can afford a gown if I need one," she answered tightly.

"It's for a company event. Shouldn't the company provide it for you?"

She chewed her lip. "Maybe, under normal circumstances."

He shrugged and raised his dark eyebrows. "I thought circumstances were normal."

Maddy made an exasperated sound in the back of her throat. "They are. But they aren't. If you bought me a gown, when you never have before, given what happened, it would make me feel cheap."

"That would not be my intent."

Her stomach tightened. She didn't suppose it was usually a man's intent to make a woman feel cheap. Just like he wasn't lavishing her with attention when all he was really giving her was things.

She'd liked the things William had bought for her. She'd imagined them to be thoughtful. A sign he was thinking of her. Her parents had never bothered to buy her anything, and they didn't care about her at all, so maybe...

Grrrr. She refocused her thoughts. She wasn't going there. She wasn't doing the self-pity thing. The long and the short of it was that taking a gift from Aleksei, at this point, wasn't happening.

"You know why it wouldn't be appropriate," she said, meeting his eyes, feeling the impact down to her toes and at all the interesting points in between.

"You're being ridiculous, Madeline."

"No," she said. "No, I'm not. You're in the position of ultimate power, so you don't get it. I know what it's like to be the one dependent on someone for something. To be the one at a disadvantage. Yesterday happened, and while it isn't happening again, it doesn't change the fact that it did, and that it alters the dynamic between us. I'm not going to let you…buy me, so just let me buy my own dress."

"What's this about, Madeline? Because I'm sure it has nothing to do with me specifically. When have I ever acted like I owned you? Or like I even wanted to?"

"Let's just not talk about it," she said, clipped.

"Fine with me. But I'm buying your dress."

"No, Aleksei…"

"Madeline, last I checked, I was your boss. As you so eloquently reminded me a moment ago, I sign your paychecks. The fact that I had sex with you doesn't mean you can suddenly disagree with everything I say."

"I want to choose it," she said.

"Fine, I trust your judgment as far as fashion is concerned."

Maddy rubbed her forehead, trying to ease the tension there. "Well, that's something."

"I'll have to approve it of course."

"Oh, for heaven's sake, Aleksei!" she hissed. There would be no easing the tension in her head now.

"It's my display, for my jewelry."

"Your *display* is *my* body."

"I will not force you to wear something you're uncomfortable with. I simply want to ensure I'm happy with how it complements the necklace."

She sucked in a sharp breath. Things had got out of hand, and all because of yesterday. She'd been congratulating herself on how emotionless it had been, and now she was feeling extra touchy about everything.

"Okay, fine. I'll buy a few dresses I like and I'll show them to you and return the ones you don't like, fair?" she asked.

"Fair enough," said Aleksei.

He touched her shoulder, his fingers rough from the fine

work he did with his hands, his palm hot. Then he reached around with his other hand and unclasped the necklace, sliding it off of her, the cool metal a sharp contrast to his touch.

How was it possible to be so annoyed at a man and to want him so much at the same time? Maybe that was how it worked when there was no love involved. If desire was divorced from emotion it didn't really matter how she felt about Aleksei. It only mattered that she was still attracted to him.

It made everything inside of her a strange series of compartments. Aleksei her boss, Aleksei the man she'd slept with, Aleksei the man who sometimes drove her crazy.

As long as she was able to keep it all separate, everything would be fine. And she would. Because she had no other choice.

It had been two weeks since Aleksei had been inside Madeline's body. Two weeks since he'd touched her, tasted her. And it was a sad commentary on the power of his attraction to her that he remembered the exact date he'd been with her.

He hadn't found another woman. He'd considered it. Had even considered calling Olivia for a brief and satisfying reconciliation. But he hadn't. Because it wouldn't be satisfying. Not in the way it had been to be with Madeline.

He wanted more of her, and until he had it he could not see wanting anyone else.

He had been working in the Milan office more. It was more convenient at the moment because of the upcoming exhibition in Luxembourg. It was also a form of sexual torture he found almost intriguing. To see Madeline and not have her. To want something he couldn't have. To actually want anything and anyone specifically. It was all fascinating in a way.

He hadn't desired a certain woman in a long time. It had

been more about a need for sex than for anyone in particular. But Madeline...he desired her. Likely because she had ended things before their natural conclusion. Because she had ended things, period. He couldn't remember if a woman had ever ended things with him before. It was always his call to end the relationship.

The intercom on his phone beeped, and his secretary's voice came over the speaker. "Madeline Forrester is here to see you. She says she has the dresses."

A slight chuckle rose in his throat. "Send her in."

Thirty seconds later the door to his office opened and Madeline strode in, three garment bags draped over her arm, her long brown hair loose around her shoulders.

"I come bearing gowns," she said.

He hadn't seen her very often over the course of the past couple weeks. Brief meetings in her office, and he'd passed her a few times walking through the vast lobby of the office building. Every time she was polite, but seemingly unaffected.

Except for the flush of rose that stained her cheeks whenever she met his gaze.

She looked at him and her cheeks darkened. Satisfaction tightened his stomach. She still wanted him. But if she wanted him, it would be her who made the move. He was hardly going to chase after a woman, especially one doing such a good job of feigning disinterest.

She would have to admit it. Would have to acknowledge how much she wanted him.

She stepped forward and draped the bags over his desk. "So, I'll leave them for you to inspect and you can get back to me about which one you like."

He placed his hand over hers, catching it before she could pull it away from the bags. "No, that's not how this is going to work."

"Oh, no?" She lifted one well-shaped brow at him, the curve of her left hip cocked to the side in defiance.

"No. You must try them on for me."

Her mouth dropped open and she pulled that smooth, sexy hand away from him. "That's…objectifying."

"How? You're going to wear one of them in front of me anyway, and I assume all are entirely appropriate for public viewing."

She shut her mouth, her teeth clicking loudly. "True."

"Then what's the problem?"

That bottom lip of hers, so lush and kissable, got a very good chewing on as she decided what to say. He knew she wouldn't have much of anything to say ultimately. Because her issue with it pertained to their having sex with each other and he knew she'd rather chew glass than bring it up.

"Nothing," she said finally, releasing her lower lip.

"You can change in there." He gestured toward the bathroom that was at the far end of his office.

She scooped the garment bags back up in her arms and walked into the bathroom, shutting the door behind her. He had to laugh when he heard the unmistakable click of the lock. Then he had to acknowledge it was probably a good thing she'd locked it, or he might be tempted to go in and help her with zippers or something.

And then he'd end up stripping her bare and having his way with her on the vanity.

His body pulsed in serious approval of that fantasy. He let it play in his mind for a while, much longer than he usually allowed himself, until Madeline came out of the bathroom, perfect curves encased in a long emerald-green gown. It was strapless, but the cut was high and didn't reveal enough of her gorgeous breasts for his taste.

Though, staying on task, the real issue was that he wanted

to see the effect of the necklace on her skin and not on heavy green satin.

"Next," he said.

She shot him a deadly glare. "I like this one."

"Keep it then, but don't wear it with my necklace."

Lifting the skirt and kicking it to one side, she sauntered back into the bathroom. She was sexy, even when she was in a snit. Perhaps especially then. He liked her spirit, liked the fact that she wasn't afraid to have a little verbal battle with him. Women, people in general, usually deferred to him. Even Paulina had looked to him for answers, had waited on his approval.

Not Madeline.

She reappeared a few moments later in a black dress that was fitted all the way until it hit her knees, then billowed out with flowing fabric. The neckline plunged to her sternum, the pale skin on display so tempting it was all he could do to remain at his desk.

The necklace would make the dress more modest, would show hints of those glorious breasts without revealing too much. It would be perfect.

"That's it," he said.

He stood and walked across the room, coming to look more closely. Because he had to.

"I have one more," she said, taking a step back.

"This is it," he repeated.

She quirked her mouth to one side and put a hand on her hip. "Ta-da."

He felt his lips lift into a smile. "Turn for me."

She shot him a glare but turned slowly. The dress hugged that tight rear end of hers that he was so fond of, showed the tiny dip of her waist. Yes, it was the perfect dress. All eyes would be on her with or without the necklace.

She looked up at him and he felt the impact of her

gorgeous blue eyes streak through him. He could remember the last time she'd looked at him like that, her color high in her cheeks, her breasts rising and falling with her rapid breathing.

The last time she'd looked at him like that he'd ended up taking her over his desk.

He could hear the sounds of employees milling around in the next room. Stripping that dress off Madeline's gorgeous body and having his way with her now would be incredibly stupid. Although, even knowing that, it was very tempting.

His teeth ached. He wanted her so badly. He honestly couldn't recall the last time sex had held such power over him. He was thirty-three years old. He'd been in love, been married, had lost his wife. He'd lived a full lifetime by the time he was twenty-seven. With all of that experience behind him, he was a difficult man to captivate.

And yet he felt captivated.

He couldn't understand what it was about this one woman that appealed to him so. Couldn't understand why she brought out desires that had been buried for so long. But he didn't want love from Madeline. He wanted sex. He wanted satisfaction. And that day, she had wanted the same.

She wanted the same now. He could see it written all over her beautiful face. Could see that her entire body was taut with the effort it took for her to hold herself back, to keep from reaching out and touching him.

Her need mirrored his own. And the last time they had given in, it had been explosive. He wanted to give in again. He wasn't a man given to vices. He wasn't a man who gave in to temptation.

But he was considering the benefits of becoming that man.

"You look beautiful, Madeline."

She sucked in a sharp breath, the hollows in her neck deepening. "I don't need to hear that from you, Aleksei."

"Because I'm your boss?"

"Because I dislike it when men use compliments to try and seduce me."

"Happen often?"

She narrowed her eyes. "A couple times that I can think of. I much preferred it when you said you wanted sex, without trying to cushion it with flattery. That was honest, at least."

"So is this. You are beautiful, Madeline, and it has to be said. Even if I never touch you again, I had to say it."

Her breathing increased and she blinked rapidly. He thought he might have seen tears in her eyes. But as quickly as they had appeared, they were gone. No, his prickly Madeline wouldn't cry in front of him.

When had he started thinking of her as his?

"Just...don't, Aleksei, please," she whispered.

Seeing Madeline vulnerable did strange things to him. It made him feel...responsible. It made him *feel*.

"You don't think you're beautiful, Madeline?" he asked.

"It doesn't matter what I think. I just don't trade compliments and lies for sex."

"That wasn't my goal. If I decide to seduce you, you'll know exactly what I'm doing. I would kiss you again, press you back against my desk. I would never lie to get you into bed. I think we've both proven that I don't have to."

She turned red, from the base of her neck to her cheeks. "True," she bit out.

"That's one thing you can count on from me, Madeline. Honesty. As your boss, and as a lover."

She swallowed. "I want to believe that."

"I don't say things I don't mean, and I don't manipulate to get what I want."

"Then…thank you. For saying I'm beautiful." She edged away from him before turning and making her way back to the bathroom and closing the door behind her.

He noticed, after she'd left, that she hadn't promised him honesty in return.

CHAPTER EIGHT

"How is it looking over there, Madeline?"

That voice. That voice that haunted her dreams. Issuing rough, explicit commands, and, more disturbingly, sweet, soft words. That voice that she heard every day on the other end of the phone issuing work-related commands.

Why did his voice have to make her nipples hard and her body ache for him to be inside of her again?

The why didn't really matter. It was that it did, that was the problem. It had been over a month since she'd last touched Aleksei. Two weeks since she'd seen him, since he'd returned to Moscow to take care of some work there.

And she still wanted him.

"Everything looks great, Aleksei," she said, burrowing under the plush covers.

She was at the castle in Luxembourg, preparing everything for the exhibition that was taking place in four days, and she was very fortunate to be staying in one of the castle's many fabulous guestrooms.

It was all very medieval, but with every modern convenience imaginable. It also catered to some latent princess fantasies Maddy hadn't been aware she'd been harboring. But the four-poster bed, complete with gauzy swaths of fabric and lavish bedding, was certainly fit for a princess. And, for now, she was owning it.

Getting the ballroom sorted out had been a big project and she was in bed early in anticipation of working on the smaller displays for the other rooms bright and way too early in the morning.

"And you have the team climbing ladders for you?" he asked, his rich voice sending a little shiver through her.

She squirmed beneath the heavy comforter, wishing that she was still dressed in her work clothes and not in bed in a silky nightgown that barely covered the tops of her thighs.

"I promise my Manolos haven't so much as touched a ladder rung."

"Good."

She shifted and tugged her covers up higher. "What about you, Mr. Petrov? Are you still at the office, burning the midnight oil? Burning the candle at both ends? Burning out?"

"Very nice, Madeline," he said, the humor that laced his voice unexpected, making pleasure curl in her stomach. "And, no, as it happens. I'm at home. In bed."

Her heart lurched and she tightened her grip on the phone. "Really?"

"Yes. Even I have to sleep sometimes."

It was strange to think of Aleksei as a mere mortal. Not when there were so many times he seemed like a lot more than that. "Nice to get…comfy and in your pajamas, I guess."

He chuckled, a sound that made her already tight nipples burn. "I don't wear pajamas."

Her heart hammered hard and her breath was coming short and harsh. And before she could censor herself or think anything through, she asked him the next question that came to her mind.

"So that means you're wearing nothing, I suppose?" Her left hand was curled into a tight fist, gripping a chunk of her thick, down-filled comforter.

"Nothing at all," he responded, his accent thicker, his voice deeper, huskier.

A muffled moan escaped her lips and he chuckled again.

"Madeline, what are you thinking?" he asked.

About pleasure. About the way he had looked, naked and unashamed in his office. About hot, wonderful sex like she'd never known existed before she'd met him.

"About you," she said, her words rushed. "About your body."

There was a slight pause. When Aleksei spoke his voice was rough, strained.

"What about you, Madeline? Do you wear pajamas?"

She bit her lips and brushed a hand over her silky night-gown. Did she continue the game? Or let it end?

Her heart was pounding hard, her body aching. Just a little more.

"I'm wearing a nightgown. It's really silky and short. Pink."

"Perfect. But I think I would like you better without it."

Oh, things were getting out of hand. She shifted beneath the thick comforter, her hand still clinging to it as if it was her lifeline. A link to her sanity. Never mind that it was fail-ing. Never mind that she couldn't think of anything when Aleksei spoke but naked limbs tangled together and the desire for that deep satisfaction only he had ever given her.

It was too easy to imagine him in bed beside her, him without pajamas, his hand exploring the skin beneath her barely-there nightie.

She wanted him to keep talking. Wanted to ask him if he

was hard. If he was as turned on as she was. Her throat was completely dry and her palms were slick with sweat. Her hands were shaking now with desire, nerves and a healthy shot of adrenaline.

She wanted him. She wanted him so much she could barely breathe. It was crazy. Ridiculous. Stupid.

What was she doing? Oh, heaven help her, what was she doing?

"I should go," she choked out.

There was a long pause. The tension nearly killed her. Would he say more? Would he ask her if she was aroused? If she wanted him? And if he did, would she have the strength to hang up?

"Goodnight, Madeline."

Disappointment and relief flooded her in equal measures. Her throat was so tight she couldn't speak. She snapped the phone shut without saying goodbye and buried her face in her pillow. Not even the phone was safe anymore. She couldn't talk to Aleksei, couldn't think about him, and she certainly couldn't share a room with him, without wanting to have a reenactment of those hot, heady moments in his office.

Why not?

They weren't getting back to normal. She'd practically subjected him to a heavy breathing call just now. There was nothing professional about that. She'd had sex with him once already. And nothing dramatic or horrible had happened. She wasn't in love.

Why not do it again? Why not let it run its course?

A jolt shook her body at the thought. Could she do that? A no-strings fling? Well, she wasn't doing one-night stand very well, so why not try a brief fling?

More of Aleksei, his magic hands and lips and tongue.

Her whole body heated at the thought. Then she shivered a little.

She was actually thinking of being a normal woman. Of chasing after what she desired. Of letting go of that horrible mistake she'd made that still controlled so much.

There, she was doing it. She was committed. There was no way to have her relationship with Aleksei be normal, so she might as well have it be what she wanted.

Now all she had to do was re-seduce her boss.

The entire ballroom of the castle had been made to look like a fairytale. The real world was totally absent from the fantasy Madeline and her team had spun from the gorgeous architecture. Glittering gems were displayed on velvet pillows, placed on pedestals.

The only thing that was missing was the gem of the hour. And the woman that was supposed to be wearing it.

Madeline had been noticeably scarce since Aleksei had arrived.

That phone call. Her breathy voice, the moan of desire she'd made when he'd confessed to not wearing anything… it had caused him more sleepless nights than were excusable for a grown man with his level of experience.

He had been so close to embarrassing himself, simply from the sound of her voice.

There were a lot of women at the exhibition. Beautiful women. He hardly saw any of them.

He tightened his hand into a fist and took a slow breath in. Madeline, his experience with her, it was so tied up in fantasy that he must be remembering it as more than it had been. No sex was that good. No woman had that kind of power.

His arms prickled and he looked up. Madeline was descending the wide marble staircase and entering the grand ballroom. Her hair was curled and captured in a ponytail that was fastened low and cascaded over one shoulder. Her eyes, her beautiful blue eyes, were enhanced with the perfect amount of makeup. And those lush lips were painted red.

He wanted to kiss every bit of that red off her lips. See them swollen and pink as they had been that night. He stood from his table and began to walk to her. Her eyes caught his and held. And she didn't turn away.

Heat churned in his stomach. Need. Desire. Lust.

And it was all reflected in her bold stare. Her tempting body was on display, but it was her eyes that held him captive. Her eyes that held the explicit invitation he wanted to accept.

She stopped in front of him and her tongue darted out, slicking over those red lips. "You were right about the dress," she said. "It looks perfect with the necklace." She touched one of the emeralds with her delicate fingers.

"And I was right about you being beautiful."

She looked down. "You don't need to say that."

He took her chin between his thumb and forefinger and tilted her face up so she had to meet his eyes again. "I told you, Madeline. I always tell the truth."

Maddy took a deep breath and extended her hand, touching Aleksei's. "Dance with me?"

His dark gaze was hot and her body responded instantly. Yes, this was the right choice. Otherwise, their one time together would always live in the realm of fantasy. A few heady moments too incredible to be real. There would be no closure.

It needed to be put firmly in reality, rather than being this mythical moment forever frozen in time, and much more important than it needed to be.

It would always be important for one reason. It was the

moment she'd chosen to take control back. But it was about her. Not him. And so was this.

Of course, that didn't mean it couldn't be mutually pleasurable. She fully intended it to be. Part of the rush of power and euphoria from last time had been seeing how she'd affected him.

"Are you asking me to dance as my employee?"

She took a step closer. "Hopefully as your lover." It took every ounce of her courage to meet his eyes as she said that, but she did. She wasn't going to be ashamed of her desire. If he said no, then he said no.

"Come," he said, gripping her hand and leading her to the dance floor.

He placed his hand low and flat on her back and drew her to him. She went willingly, wrapping her arms around his neck, exulting in his touch, his warmth, his scent. She'd missed him.

That realization sent a shock through her system before she shook it off. Of course she'd missed him. Even if the attraction between them wasn't based on love, it was natural for her to miss his touch. That was just the way it was between lovers.

A small smile tugged at the corners of her mouth and she rested her head on his chest.

"Madeline," he said, his voice vibrating against her cheek. "If you keep clinging to me like that I won't make it through the evening."

She lifted her head and drew back slightly. "Well, I worked too hard on all of this for you to miss it. Do you approve?"

He smiled down at her, just a slight curve of his lips. Aleksei didn't do full-blown grins. There was always reserve there. "It's perfect."

Suddenly, her heart felt too big for her chest. She cleared her throat. "Thank you."

She wanted to believe it. Wanted to believe him when he said she was beautiful too. But…it was hard. It was hard to stop looking for the ulterior motive.

He touched her face, brushed his thumb over her bottom lip before leaning in to drop a light kiss on her mouth. It wasn't hot, or hungry, or any of the other things kisses from Aleksei usually were. Of course, kisses from Aleksei tended to result in nudity and they were in a public place, so it was likely for the best.

He rubbed his nose against hers and she nearly melted. Then he pressed a kiss to her cheek, her jaw, the spot just below her ear.

"Oh, Aleksei, please. I won't last through the party if you keep doing that."

"I'm not seeing the downside to that."

"I'm selling the necklace, remember? And I'm supposed to circulate, and overhear conversations, and…"

"Somehow it's slipped my mind." He kissed the curve of her neck and she felt goosebumps break out over her arms.

He pulled his head back and looked at her, his dark eyes unreadable. "What changed your mind, Madeline?"

"I just… Our relationship isn't going back to normal. Why add sexual frustration to the awkwardness?"

He laughed, the most genuine laugh she'd ever heard from him. It made her stomach flip. It was the strangest sensation, as though she could feel his amusement in her. She wasn't sure if she liked the feeling at all.

"That's a good point, I suppose," he said, not missing a beat. Not experiencing the same surreal thing she had just been experiencing.

"It's practical."

"Are you sexually frustrated?" he asked, and this time she could read his eyes. She could feel the heat.

"If I wasn't, I wouldn't have shortcircuited on the phone with you the other day."

"Is that what that was? A glitch in internal wiring?"

"Something like that. Or maybe just…well, it comes back to the sexual frustration."

"And you've decided to relieve that."

"I can't think of a better way." She moved her hands over the broad expanse of his shoulders. "Believe me, I tried."

"That does wonders for my ego."

"Your ego is fine."

"No thanks to you," he said. He nipped the tender skin of her neck and then soothed it with his tongue.

"Aleksei," she said, the warning she'd intended to inject into her tone noticeably absent.

"All right, maybe dancing is a bad idea."

"A very bad idea. But then, since when was any of this a good idea?" She laughed, a nervous, unnatural sound.

Aleksei studied Madeline's face. Her color was high, eyes bright. She looked aroused and nervous and beautiful. And she was right. It wasn't a good idea. Looking at her…it made his heart beat faster. That his heart was affected at all was far too dangerous. She was a flame, and he was captivated, and even though he knew it was a bad idea, he wanted to reach out and touch her.

He couldn't turn her away. He wouldn't. There was no real danger to his heart. That was an illusion. His heart was too hard. The injuries he'd sustained had healed over and left scars too tough for anyone to penetrate. As he liked it. As he intended.

This was simply desire. Strong desire, consuming desire. But it was limited to lust, nothing more.

Aleksei was dimly aware of the fact that there were

photographers near them, and that they were discreetly taking pictures. He was also dimly aware that it was a very good thing. That the photos would evoke romance and show the necklace Madeline was wearing to perfection. But he was only dimly aware of those things. Most of his body was consumed by the need to get across the ballroom and up to his suite as quickly as possible.

"I think the party's over for us," he said.

She met his gaze. He saw her confidence falter. Then she took a breath, tightened her hold on his shoulders. "I think you're right."

He took her hand and led her from the dance floor to the foot of the broad staircase. Madeline looked sideways at the paparazzi. They blended in pretty seamlessly, nothing like the gutter press that charged people in the street, but she still noticed them.

"I was thinking we could find a side entrance and…sneak out," she said.

"Oh, yes, that's kind of your thing, isn't it?"

"No, it's not," she said, "but there's press everywhere."

"All the more reason to make a visible exit. To show the necklace off." He touched the jewels at the base of her throat, his hand hot, sending liquid warmth rushing through her body.

The press. One of her very personal demons. And Aleksei wanted her to walk out, on his arm, her boss's arm, looking very much like they were headed upstairs to do exactly what they were headed upstairs to do.

So does fear still control everything? Or do you?

"I do," she said under her breath.

"Are you ready?"

She met Aleksei's dark gaze and her heart beat strong, steady. She knew what she was doing. She was doing exactly what she wanted, and she wasn't letting her fear win.

"I'm ready."

He put his hand low on her back as they ascended the stairs, and walked out of the ballroom. Aleksei stopped at the double doors and pressed a kiss to her cheek. She saw a camera flash out of the corner of her eye.

She did her best not to flinch.

He put his hand on the back of her neck and soothed the tension there as they walked out of the ballroom and into the expansive corridor. It was packed with people too, eating canapés and drinking champagne, clustered around the small jewelry displays and admiring the different pieces.

"You don't like the press?" he asked, his voice low as they wove through the crowd.

"Not at all," she said tightly.

They were stopped by several people, women who wanted pictures with him, and who wanted to examine the necklace Maddy was wearing. It really was a show-stopping piece. Of course, Aleksei was rather show-stopping himself, in Madeline's opinion.

And he was hers. For a while, he was going to be hers to explore, to pleasure... Her body tightened, ached, with need.

"Let's hurry," she whispered, when they escaped another group of gawkers.

"I knew I hired you for a reason."

The crowd thinned around the curved staircase that led to the guestrooms. Aleksei took her hand and led the way up the narrow passage and Maddy followed, breathless, laughing. Happy.

When was the last time she'd been happy? She worked. She had drive. She had goals and ambition. She was content. But happiness? She wasn't sure if she'd ever been truly happy. But she was now. She felt...free. For the first time in her life, the chains from her past, a past that went well beyond her disastrous affair with William, didn't seem to be holding her down.

"My room is this way." Aleksei gestured to another staircase at the center of a long hallway.

"You have a tower room too?" she asked.

"Of course. The castle penthouse."

She laughed and gripped his hand more tightly, leaned in and pressed her face against his shoulder as they walked quickly up the next flight of stairs.

He reached into his pocket and pulled out an old-fashioned key and put it into the lock. She watched his hands as he turned the key, watched his olive skin stretch over the muscle and tendon. He was so strong. So masculine. Sexier than any person had a right to be.

Internal muscles clenched as she remembered just how masculine he was everywhere. As she remembered what it was like to be filled by him.

He opened the door and she grabbed his hand, pulling him inside. He shut it quickly and wrapped his arms around her waist, twirling her and pressing her back flat against the wooden door.

His kiss was urgent, hungry. There was no restraint. Which was good, because she was fresh out of restraint herself.

She fumbled with his tie, jerked it to the side and loosened it, letting it hang slack while she worked at the buttons on his crisp white shirt. She nearly whimpered out loud when she revealed that toned, muscular chest.

This time she was really going to explore him, take her time and enjoy that gorgeous body. She spread her hands over his chest, felt his heart raging beneath her palms.

"You really do want me," she said, sliding her hands from his chest, down to where his erection was pressing against his black slacks. She cupped his heavy weight and he sucked in a sharp breath.

"I do," he said, teeth clenched.

"Take me."

He didn't waste any time accepting her invitation. He swept her up into his arms and carried her to the bed, depositing her gently on the edge. He worked at discarding his tie, jacket, and shirt, throwing them into a careless heap on the floor. Then he kicked off his shoes and socks.

She reached out and put her hands on his belt, undoing it quickly before she shoved his pants and underwear down to the floor.

She wrapped her hand around his hard length, stroked him, reveled in the grunt of pleasure he made in the back of his throat. The desire to taste him, to do what he'd done to her in his office, overwhelmed her.

She'd never wanted to do this for a man before. Had only ever tolerated doing it for the one man she'd been with before Aleksei. But she wanted Aleksei. Wanted so badly to pleasure him. And she wanted it for herself.

Leaning in, she flicked her tongue over the velvety head of his shaft, her hands still cupping him. He jerked, a raw sound escaping his lips. Emboldened, she continued to explore him with her lips and tongue until he gripped her wrists and pulled her away.

"Not like that. Not this time."

She shook her head. She was on the same page with him, one hundred percent. She needed him inside of her.

He sat beside her on the bed, pulling the zipper on her dress down. She stood and let it fall into a pool of black taffeta at her feet. She was gratified by the heat in his gaze, by the pure, undisguised hunger she saw etched into every line of his gorgeous, naked body.

"You didn't have anything under that dress all night?" he asked, voice rough.

She gave him her best seductive smile. "I had a mission. Underwear wasn't conducive to my end goal."

"Vixen," he grated.

She reached around to grasp the clasp of the necklace.

"Leave it," Aleksei ground out.

She dropped her hands to her sides. For a moment he only stared at her. Her nipples peaked, ached, and she was so hot and ready for him it was amazing. The fact that she didn't want to cover her body was a testament to how bold, how different he made her feel.

"Come here, Maddy," he said from his place on the edge of the bed.

She complied, toeing off her high heels and kneeling on the bed, straddling his body. He put his hands on her hips and tilted his face up so he could kiss her. Slowly, thoroughly. She gripped his shoulders to keep herself from melting at his feet.

He moved his attentions lower, pressing a hot kiss to the curve of her neck, her collarbone just above the necklace.

Then he turned his attention to her breasts. He stroked one nipple with the flat of his tongue before drawing it into his mouth. His teeth scraped the necklace, and her flesh, lightly and she shivered.

He turned his attention to her other breast, where he was just as thorough. He lifted his head for a moment. "I forgot to do this last time, and it has been the staple of my fantasies ever since."

"It was a good one," she said, her voice shaking.

He lay back on the bed and brought her with him. She was astride him, his erection pressing against the part of her that was slick with her desire for him. He scooted them both back and reached into the nightstand that was positioned by the big bed. He grabbed a condom out of the drawer and handed it to her.

She tore it open without wasting any time and rolled it onto his hard length, protecting them both from any consequences. That was the last thing either of them needed.

He put his hands on her hips and helped guide himself into her body. They both made noises of pleasure as he slid into her.

She was almost frantic in her movements at first. She was so desperate for release. Now that she knew what she was after, it was much easier to find the right rhythm. It helped that Aleksei was stroking her clitoris with his thumb as she moved.

"Like that?" he asked, his dark eyes locked with hers.

"Yes, oh, yes," she panted.

He moved his other hand up her back, caressing the dent of her waist before cupping her breast. He teased one hardened bud, moving one of the gems from the necklace over her sensitive skin. The chill from the gold contrasted with the heat of his touch, the stimulation enough to send her over the edge.

As she cried out her release, Aleksei took control, rolling them so that he was in the dominant position and she was on her back. He thrust hard into her and she wrapped her legs tightly around his waist, the aftershocks of her orgasm still pulsing through her as he established his own rhythm, brought himself to the peak of pleasure.

All she could hear was their mingled breathing and the pounding of her heart. Aleksei drew her into his arms and maneuvered them so that she was partially on top of him, their bodies no longer connected.

They stayed that way for a moment before Aleksei sat up. She sat too, intending to collect her gown and get dressed again before heading back to her room.

"No," he said firmly, standing from the bed. "I'm going to take care of things." Meaning the condom, she assumed. "And you're staying."

"You want me to share your bed?" It seemed an intimacy farther than they should take it, and yet part of her wanted to stay with him. Stay near his warmth. Maybe wake up to the kind of pleasure they'd just shared.

She'd never actually slept with a man before. The hazard of having a married lover. Something always came up. Something that meant he had to leave the hotel room. Another clear and obvious sign she'd missed.

She shook her head. She wasn't going there.

"Okay. I'll stay."

CHAPTER NINE

IT WAS still dark when Maddy woke up. Aleksei's arm was curled around her waist and she was fitted snugly against his body. For a moment she just enjoyed the feeling. Being so close to someone else. Skin to skin. Breathing the same air.

It was amazing.

And then, suddenly, the intimacy of it felt like too much to handle.

She wiggled out of his grasp and climbed out of bed, unsure of what she was going to do. The bathroom was the logical first stop. She tiptoed into the room and closed the door behind her.

She took care of the necessities and then washed her hands before pooling cool water in her palms and splashing it on her face. She stood and faced her reflection. She looked thoroughly seduced. Her hair was a disaster, there were remnants of last night's eye makeup on her cheeks and she was still wearing a necklace worth more money than she would ever see in her life.

Reaching around, she unhooked the necklace and decided that figuring out where Aleksei was keeping valuables was next on her to-do list before she made her escape.

When she crept back into the bedroom, gray light was filtering in through the large windows. She swore under breath when she noticed her black gown in a pool of fabric on the floor.

There was nothing else for her to wear. She had come to Aleksei's room in a ball gown, and panty-less, and now she had nothing to return to her room in. There were probably still guests and paparazzi milling around.

The walk of shame indeed.

She looked back at the bed, at the man sleeping there, the covers pushed low on his hips, his upper body bare. What she really wanted to do was crawl back into bed and wake him up in a very creative way.

Instead, she decided to clean up the mess they'd made the night before. She placed the necklace on the nightstand. Aleksei could put it in a safe when he woke up.

She sighed and bent down, picking up her ball gown and shaking out the wrinkles as best as she could before laying it over the back of a chair. She kicked her shoes under the writing desk, then picked up Aleksei's pants, placing them over her dress.

When she went to pick up Aleksei's suit jacket, she noticed a short length of chain lying next to it. She picked it up and moved her hands over it. It wasn't just chain, but in the dim light it was hard to tell what it was.

She turned on the lamp that was on the writing desk and held her find beneath the light. It wasn't a simple chain at all. It was art. Twisting vines, complete with thorns and subtle small flowers sculpted into the leaves, the centers made from varying shades of pink gemstones, the petals fashioned from seed pearls and diamonds. There were hundreds of blossoms, each so delicate and tiny that the little piece of necklace wasn't gaudy at all. It was a study in subtle beauty.

It was only on closer inspection that the labor, the design, was evident.

Aleksei had made it. Had started it. It was obvious. The jewelry he designed was more beautiful than any she'd seen, but this surpassed even what she'd seen of his work. There was something more in it.

"What are you doing with that?" Aleksei's voice, clipped and harsh, startled her and she whirled around to face the bed.

He was sitting, his dark eyes locked onto the small piece of jewelry in her hands.

"It was on the floor," she said.

He looked at her for a long moment and then held out his hand. She crossed to the bed and dropped the length of chain into his upturned palm. He didn't say anything and neither did she. He ran his thumb over the chain, his expression still, eyes distant, mouth tight.

"It is designed to look like *salsola*," he said, his voice rough. "A common weed in Russia. Common in many parts of the world."

"It's too beautiful to be a weed," she said.

A soft laugh escaped his lips. "Yes, some people think that." He let out a heavy breath. "My wife thought so. They grew outside of our home in Russia. She would never let me destroy them."

Her stomach twisted. Wife? He didn't have a wife. He couldn't have a wife. No one, not even she, was that stupid to make the same mistake twice.

"You...you're not married," she said, her voice barely a shaking whisper.

"No, I'm not," his tone was heavy. Final.

Silence settled between them. The question of what had happened hovered on her lips, and yet she couldn't make herself ask. Because she knew, by the way he'd said he wasn't married, that the union had not been dissolved by the court system.

"How long?" They were the only words she could force around the lump in her throat.

"Six years." He set the necklace segment on the nightstand. "I was making this for her. It was meant to be a surprise."

But she'd never got it. And he had never finished it.

It had been in his jacket pocket. Close to his heart.

Maddy put a hand to her chest, to where her own heart felt battered, bruised and bleeding. Not for herself, for Aleksei. Just as she'd felt his humor resonating in her the night before, she felt his grief now. Real. Raw. Deep.

"I...I didn't know."

"It's not a secret. I don't make conversation about it, but it was in the news when it happened. Though, at the time, my success was limited, and my name was only really known in Russia, which means it likely wasn't international news. Although, I honestly couldn't tell you. Media coverage wasn't on my mind at the time."

Six years. It had been six years since he'd designed a collection, until recently. It suddenly made horrible, painful sense. He hadn't designed, but he'd grown his company. Had found worldwide success.

But he'd lost his wife.

"Paulina was killed in a car accident," he said. "I knew you wouldn't ask. It's why this can never be more than this." He gestured to the bed. "I've done commitment. I've done marriage. I won't do it again. I can't."

Her throat was tight, aching. For him. "I don't...I don't want you to. I don't want to marry you. I don't even believe in love."

"I do. But that part of my life is over."

She gritted her teeth, fought against the pressing weight

of pain she felt for him, and against the sense of debt that she felt now. This was why she hadn't wanted to know the reason he didn't do relationships. Because of the emotions churning inside of her.

Because then she would have to tell him why *she* didn't do relationships. Would have to lay bare the most humiliating moment of her life. Would have to reveal her stupidity, her weakness. Would have to admit why she'd been vulnerable to a man like William in the first place.

Her stomach lurched.

"Madeline, come here."

She moved to the bed, her heart hammering so hard she was sure he could hear it. She climbed up and got under the covers. He pulled her to him and kissed her.

"The past doesn't matter. It's over," he said. "What we have is right now. We both understand what this is. We both want the same thing."

She kissed him desperately, passionately. She could handle this. Sex. Need. Lust.

She shoved all of the pain to the side, all of the things she was feeling, for him, for herself, and just embraced her need.

It was all she could handle.

That Madeline had withdrawn after she'd found out about Paulina shouldn't bother Aleksei at all. And yet he found that it did. He didn't talk about his wife. He certainly didn't show anyone the piece of the necklace he'd been designing for her.

He didn't carry it out of grief. Paulina had been gone six years, and while he still regretted her death, the acute pain had faded a few years ago. He carried it as a reminder of what happened when you let yourself love someone.

When someone became your whole world and that world crumbled around you.

Paulina's death had nearly destroyed him at the time. He'd spent a year drinking too much and trying to forget, wallowing in his misery.

And then he'd realized he was going to die along with her if he didn't move forward. Since that moment, he'd moved forward. He'd picked up where he'd left off with his fledgling design company, had finally found the worldwide recognition he'd been trying to achieve before Paulina's death.

He'd succeeded in business. He'd made millions. And while none of it was what he'd dreamed it would be when he was a young man, it was better than falling into the abyss.

Success had been his antidote to depression. He'd simply never stopped, even when it wasn't necessary to his survival to keep climbing the ladder.

He saw elements of that in Madeline. She always seemed to have her armor on. And it bothered him that it mattered at all.

There was a soft knock on his office door.

"Come in."

He looked up and saw Madeline slipping in, looking thoroughly respectable in a tight knee-length skirt and a sweater. So respectable all he could think of was making her look a bit more disreputable.

They hadn't made love since they'd left Luxembourg four days earlier and he was surprised at how much he missed her touch. He'd gone for very long periods of time without sex. Two years after losing Paulina. But for some reason, these four days had seemed like an eternity.

He didn't want to examine why that was. Why he responded to her with such intensity.

"We have a slight problem with the venue for the Paris exhibition."

"Do we?" Aleksei leaned back in his chair and tried to focus his mind on the task at hand, and not on Madeline's gorgeous body. On how much he would like to undo the top button on her prim little sweater...

"Yes. They're double booked. And they want one of us to shuffle the time."

He leaned forward and put his hands on his desk. "The other event can shuffle."

"That's what I said."

"And?"

"And they gave me a very non-committal answer. Said I would have to take it up with Oracle. That would be the company that is also booked for Le Grande ballroom on the same date we have Le Grande ballroom booked."

"I figured as much," he said wryly, pressing his palms firmly on the desk and standing. "What's the number?"

She handed him her cellphone and indicated her last outgoing call. He highlighted the number and pressed Send.

What followed was a flurry of French that Madeline couldn't understand. She spoke a little bit of French, but it was about as good as her Italian. Which wasn't very good, and certainly not proficient enough to engage in serious business negotiations.

When Aleksei hung up he handed her the phone again, his fingers brushing hers, little rivulets of pleasure traveling up her arm and through her body. She could have purred, it felt so good.

And, for the moment, she wasn't going to try and fight the attraction between them. They hadn't had a chance to be together since the exhibition in Luxembourg, but she was still in full *embrace the fling* mode.

"Success?" she asked, putting her phone back in her pocket.

"Of course."

Of course. Spoken like a man who never expected to be

told no. A man who had complete control over every aspect of his life and was completely confident in that.

Except he hadn't always had control. Her heart ached when she thought of his wife, of the pain he'd been through. It disturbed her, just how much it weighed on her.

She smiled. "Of course."

He rounded his desk and took her in his arms. He didn't kiss her, not immediately. He simply rested his head on her hair, his hands stroking her back, warm and comforting. She inhaled his scent, so familiar, so exciting.

When he did kiss her, he put his thumb and forefinger on her chin and tilted her face up, pressing his lips lightly against hers.

"I've missed you," he said.

"Me too." The words were a whisper. An admission that was difficult for her to make, both to him and to herself.

"I need you tonight," he said roughly, kissing her again, this time with very little of the restraint he'd shown the first time.

"Yes," she said, between kisses.

"I have a suite booked at the Hotel Del Sol."

Her heart sank into her stomach. She tried, she tried really hard, to shake off the nausea that gripped her. Aleksei didn't have a wife at home he was hiding from her, and what had she expected? That he would invite her back to his Milan apartment? Like she would invite him to hers? She wouldn't. It would be bringing him into her space, and that just didn't seem like something people involved in a purely sexual relationship would do.

It didn't help. She was afraid she would be sick.

"I... Maybe not tonight," she said, her voice strangled.

She noticed a muscle tick in his jaw and he loosened his hold on her. Pulled away. "A suite doesn't suit you, Madeline? Or is the hotel simply not grand enough?"

"Stop it, Aleksei, I've never behaved that way, and you know it."

Hurt, hurt that had nothing to do with him, an old wound she still carried because of her own stupidity, fueled her anger at him.

He looked away. "If you're busy, you're busy."

"I am," she said stiffly.

"See you tomorrow, Madeline." He went back to the other side of his desk and sat, turning his attention to the computer monitor.

Dismissed. He'd dismissed her. That was loud and clear.

And she was the one who had said no, so what right did she have to be angry and hurt? She gritted her teeth and stalked out of his office.

It didn't matter if she had no right to be angry and hurt. She was.

No matter how much she didn't want to be, she was.

Aleksei didn't beg for women to come to him. They just came to him. That was his experience in life, even before he'd had money. It had only been more frequent since he'd made his first million.

But he was on the verge of begging. His body was unfulfilled and sleep eluded him. He had been cold to Madeline, and then, in the end, he had seen pain in her eyes, pain that went deeper than their simple argument.

And he had turned away. Because he hadn't signed on for her pain. And now it was eating at him from the inside out.

That and the arousal that was coursing through him.

His finger hovered over the speed dial he had programmed in his phone for her.

A picture of her, naked with her black gown pooled at her feet, flashed into his mind, mingled with the image of her standing in his office, devastation in her blue eyes.

He dialed. Pride be damned.

"Hello?" She sounded as though she'd been sleeping. Or crying. His stomach twisted at the thought. Causing Madeline pain was not something he wanted any part in.

"Maddy."

"Aleksei," she said, her voice guarded. "It's past eleven."

"I know. Will you come to my apartment? It's above the studio."

"I...yes."

"Do you need me to send a car?"

He heard rustling, probably covers, in the background. "No. I can drive. I'll be there in ten minutes."

It was a long ten minutes. When he heard the buzzer, he let her in quickly, and when she came to his apartment door he already had it open for her.

He pulled her to him, kissed her. Thoroughly. She wrapped her arms around his neck and pressed her sweet body against his.

"Come in," he said.

She complied and he closed the door behind her. He was short on patience. He'd needed her hours ago, and he needed her even more now.

"The living area isn't very nice," he said, taking her by the hand. "I'll show you my bedroom."

A smile spread across her face, her eyes crinkling in the way they did when she was truly happy. She laughed. "Smooth, Aleksei."

"But it worked, right?"

Her smile broadened. "Of course."

He led her across the vast, open living area and to the double doors that partitioned his bedroom from the rest of the apartment. He didn't usually bring women to any of his personal residences. Hotels were his first choice. And yet he didn't feel as though Madeline was invading. It didn't feel like an imposition to have her.

Of course, for all the time he spent in Milan it might as well be a hotel.

"I like this," she said, looking around his bedroom. "Very manly."

He laughed. "Is it? I paid someone to decorate it."

She smiled and took her jacket off, tossing it on the chair that was positioned near his bed. "Well, they did a good job. The bed is certainly inviting. Though that may be the company, rather than the silky black bedspread. Although, the bedspread helps."

He pulled her into his arms, forked his fingers in that glossy dark hair and kissed her. Kissed her with all of the hunger that was threatening to consume him.

She kissed him back, her hands cupping his face, her soft thumbs caressing his jawline. He lowered her onto the bed and she gave a little shriek when her back hit the mattress. He chuckled and kissed her neck.

"Oh, yes, you're very smooth," she said, wrapping her arms around his neck and drawing her thighs up, parting them so he could settle between them.

He couldn't remember the last time he'd laughed with a woman. The last time sex had felt personal. The last time it had mattered who it was with.

Yes, he could. The last time he'd been with Maddy.

And then thought was impossible to think, because she was pulling his T-shirt over his head and throwing it aside, putting her hands on his chest, exploring him. Torturing him.

"*Milaya moya*, you're lethal," he said, taking her top and tugging it over her head, revealing her hot pink bra and perfect cleavage.

He made quick work of the bra and exposed her gorgeous breasts to his gaze. No dessert had ever been more tempting.

"What does that mean?" she asked, voice breathy as he feathered kisses over the tops of her breasts.

"It means *my sweet*," he said, running his tongue over one of her perky pink nipples. "And you are very, very sweet."

He tugged her jeans off, taking her panties with them and leaving her completely naked. Then he turned his attention back to her breasts. She arched beneath him and her sweet sounds of pleasure gratified him in ways he hadn't imagined were possible. It was always important to him to make sure his partner enjoyed being with him, but it had never felt as essential to his own enjoyment as it did now.

He ran his hands over her body, drew away slightly so he could admire her. Pale skin, full breasts and a flat stomach. She was so beautiful. So perfect.

Desire roared through him. He kissed her stomach, her skin so soft and tender. She wiggled beneath him, forked her fingers through his hair as he began moving his exploration to lower territory.

He loved the taste of her, loved the sounds she made when he caressed her clitoris with the flat of his tongue.

She tugged on his shoulders slightly. "Now," she said. "Please. I need you now."

He stood and took his wallet out of his pocket and set in on the bed before shucking his jeans and underwear and consigning them to the floor with the rest of the clothes.

He opened his wallet and pulled out a condom.

"I've got it," she said, getting up on her knees and taking the packet from his hand.

She opened it and rolled it onto his length. She wasn't overly experienced. He'd realized that the last time they were together. But her confidence along with her obvious desire more than made up for it. And the fact that she tackled the condom application slowly only made it an even sweeter torture.

He lowered himself over her, kissed her and she lay back, parting her thighs for him. He tested her, felt how ready she was before thrusting into her in one motion.

"Oh, yes," she sighed, gripping his shoulders, her nails digging into his skin. The slight pain was just enough to help offset the blinding pleasure, enough to keep him from ending things much too quickly.

She locked her legs around his calves, her head thrown back in obvious pleasure. He kissed her neck, her collarbone, her lips, as he established a rhythm that drove them both to the edge.

She arched beneath him, panting in his ear, her sounds of pleasure the thing that pushed him over, forced him to give up and embrace the hot rush of his orgasm. She followed, her internal muscles clenching tight around him, the pleasure more intense than anything he'd experienced before.

He rolled to the side and pulled her to him. She cuddled against him, her breath hot against his chest.

"I'm sorry about before," she said quietly, her words muffled.

"I hurt you, Maddy. I'm not proud of that, even if I don't know the reason why you were hurt."

She sucked in a sharp breath. "It…it wasn't really your fault. There's no reason you should know why."

He clenched his teeth. Part of him wanted to press for more. The other part wanted to kiss her again, to make it up to her in the best way he could think of. He didn't do pillow talk. Didn't mine his lovers for information.

"Who hurt you?" He tightened his grip on her. And he realized he wanted to know. He wanted to know so he could kill whoever it was that had put that look in Maddy's eyes.

And he wanted to be sure he wasn't the man who had put it there.

She laughed shakily and rolled away from him. "That's a loaded question."

He was caught between the desire to tell her that her secrets were hers to keep, and the need to know more. The need to try and slay her dragons.

He turned so that he was on his side, facing her. "That's okay."

"I guess we can start with my parents," she said, not looking at him. "They just didn't... They weren't really all that into kids, and I was a late-in-life surprise. They had already raised my brother, and they didn't really want... I'm fifteen years younger than Gage. They were done by then."

Aleksei's heart squeezed tight. He shouldn't have asked. What could he do to soothe her pain? Nothing. He had nothing to give. And in Maddy, in this moment, he sensed so much need. So much need he would be unable to meet.

"Anyway, when I was ten they went on a trip...I don't even know what it was for. But they'd let my nanny go and the new one hadn't arrived. I was alone for three days with no food. Not because there was no money. There was lots of money. They just...forgot. I called Gage and he came and got me. I never went back to that house."

There was no pain in her voice, no emotion at all. It was something he knew well. That complete separation from all feelings. Because the other option was to be consumed by misery. And it was obvious neither of them had allowed that. They had moved on. They had chased success and found it rather than embracing destruction.

"Gage made things nice for me," she continued, her voice steady. "He even made sure I went to prom. I don't know if he paid my date to take me, or if it was a dare, but at least I went. I was... I had a hard time with friends and boys because I just didn't...think very much of myself, for obvious reasons. I mean, if your parents don't want you it's hard to believe anyone will. And then I met William."

Adrenaline spiked through Aleksei's system. He knew, just by the way she said the other man's name, that he was going to be fighting the urge to commit a murder by the end of the story.

"He was my boss when I graduated from college. I got an internship. He was really nice to me, always complimenting me and telling me I was beautiful. When he started making advances I was really flattered...and it was so nice to have someone just...want me. No one else had ever...wanted me."

She turned away from him. "I was so stupid, Aleksei. I just wanted to be loved. I was so desperate for it. My parents wouldn't give it to me, and this man was...he was older and powerful and handsome and he said he loved me."

"A lot of young girls make that mistake," Aleksei said, voice rough.

Madeline sat up, letting the covers fall to her waist. "Yes, a lot of girls throw their virginity away on men who profess love but are just using them, I know that. But not a lot of girls break up marriages. I did. And it was in the papers, headline news, because his wife was this semi-famous model and actress. And for a few months I got to be infamous."

"He was married?" Dark rage roiled in his gut. He marveled at the fact that only moments ago he'd considered himself a man with complete dominion over his emotions. That control was gone. If he ever met that man in person...he could not be responsible for what he would do to him.

"I didn't know he was married. I don't think I did anyway. Sometimes I wonder now if I just let myself be ignorant. I didn't talk to the other employees. I didn't tell anyone about William and me. I didn't question him when he took me to hotels and then left right...after. That's my deep dark secret.

Although, if you'd looked me up on Google, you might have found it. Even though it's been five years."

Aleksei looked at her, at her still, tense body. She was still waiting for censure, for him to side with the press.

"It doesn't matter what you knew or didn't know, Maddy." Aleksei sat up and moved toward her. "A man is responsible for keeping his own marriage vows. I never strayed when I was married. I loved my wife, and no one could have enticed me to betray the promises I made to her."

"But I…" Her expression was bleak. "I just should have…I should have made a better choice."

"He took advantage of you. I cannot respect a man who preys on anyone's weaknesses, especially not those of a vulnerable girl. He is not worthy to call himself a man."

She looked down, dark lashes fanning over high cheekbones. "No one else saw it that way. I've never seen it that way. The headlines were right. I'm a home-wrecker."

"The press loves scandal, loves a villain. But don't let them decide how you see yourself. Your boss, he was the home-wrecker."

Maddy drew her knees up to her chest. Her heart was racing, her hands shaking. She'd never told anyone the full story of her life. Not about her parents. Not about William. But it had all come pouring out of her now. Every ugly truth. And Aleksei wasn't looking at her in disgust. His dark gaze was almost tender. She couldn't understand it. Any of it.

As much as it had hurt to see the headlines, it had felt like penance. It had felt necessary. She had embraced the guilt, because it had helped to block out the pain of her broken heart.

"Do you know the worst thing?" she asked, almost desperate for Aleksei to condemn her, to confirm her guilt. "He came to me, after the story broke about the affair. He said he loved me. He said he wanted me to stay with him." She felt a tear slide down her cheek, but she ignored it. "I was tempted. I didn't want to lose him. I didn't want to lose those feelings. He told me how beautiful I was and how special…I think I loved that more than I ever loved him."

"That's why you have so much trouble accepting compliments from me."

Again, Aleksei didn't condemn.

"Yes. They didn't mean anything from William. They were just a means of controlling me. And it worked. The word *love* is more effective at keeping someone prisoner than chains. I was so…desperate. I hate that part of myself. I've done everything I could since then to just not need."

Aleksei just looked at her, his dark eyes unreadable.

"How can you not hate me for everything I've just told you?" she asked.

"Because you don't deserve that, Maddy." He extended his arms, pulled her to him. She crumpled against him, letting a few more tears slip down her cheeks. "You didn't deserve any of it. Not the way your parents treated you, not the way he manipulated you. And you need to see yourself as you are. You *are* beautiful."

Her lungs felt like they might burst and her heart ached. The emotions in her felt too big to be contained. Grief. Anger. Acceptance.

And something else, something that frightened her with its strength.

More tears escaped and, for a while, she simply let them come. She needed the release, needed to wash away the guilt that had lived in her for so long.

She had been a victim then. Young and naive. Both as a neglected child, and then as an emotionally needy adult. But she couldn't let those things control her anymore. She had to let it go. Really let it go.

After the storm inside of her passed, Aleksei still held her, his body warm and comforting against hers.

She inhaled his scent. Deep comfort spread through her, different than she'd ever experienced before. Peace that went deeper than she'd ever known. He simply held her in the silence, and nothing had ever meant more to her.

"You know," she said softly. "You gave me my first orgasm."

A one-note chuckle escaped his lips. "What?"

"I just thought you should know that."

"Now I really want to kill the bastard."

"Why is that?" she asked.

"The least he could have done was made some effort for you."

"At this point, it doesn't matter. I'm happy to have learned all I have from you."

She snuggled into him. At the moment, she was simply happy to be with him. In the morning, maybe she would examine that. And maybe she would even panic. But for now, she was simply going to enjoy.

CHAPTER TEN

"LET'S go out today," Aleksei said from his position on the couch.

Maddy turned to face Aleksei, shocked that he hadn't sent her packing yet. She'd spent the night in his apartment, an apartment he'd been reluctant to invite her to. And then he'd fixed her breakfast, brought it to her in bed.

Now it was nearing noon and he still didn't seem to be champing at the bit to be rid of her. And now he was suggesting they spend the actual day together. Out of bed. Seemed like a violation of 'strictly sexual fling' rules to her. There were rules, she was sure of it. A more experienced woman would know.

"You want to go out?" She walked around the kitchen counter and joined him on the couch in the living room. "We could stay in."

He kissed her lightly on the lips. "Yes, we could. But I want to take you out."

She sucked in a breath. It was noticeably easier to do today than it had been yesterday. As though a weight had been removed from her. In a way, that was exactly what had happened. She'd finally been able to let go of the things that had been holding her back for so many years.

It was only natural she feel lighter. Freer than she'd ever felt before.

"I only have a T-shirt and jeans. Unless you want to stop by my house." She'd rushed over last night, not even bothering with makeup or perfume or any of the things a man of Aleksei's caliber might expect from a mistress.

But he'd wanted her anyway. He'd said she was beautiful. He hadn't judged her.

Her chest felt tight, as though it were too full. It was the strangest feeling. Foreign. Completely new to her. And she had a feeling she didn't want to know the name for it.

Instead of dwelling on it, she took another sharp breath and tried to ease the feeling of fullness.

"I think you're quite sexy in your jeans," he said.

She laughed. She couldn't help it. She just felt happy. She had felt happy since the moment she'd decided to start up her strictly sexual relationship with Aleksei. It was probably part of that feeling of lightness.

"Then as long as you're up for casual we're good to go."

Aleksei took her hand in his and squeezed it, looking right at her, his dark eyes intense, as he lowered his head and pressed a kiss to her palm. "It pleases me to do whatever suits you today."

She pulled her hand away and kissed him on the mouth, trying to ignore the hammering of her heart. Trying to ignore the way she felt when he looked at her like that. When he said things that clearly went beyond the borders of the bedroom.

The antiques market at the Naviglio canal was packed, people walking shoulder to shoulder, the noise of voices, shouting, laughing, talking, making it hard to hear Maddy speak right next to him.

He had never enjoyed things like this. He'd always preferred intimate restaurants, private dining if possible, or small gatherings of people. But the look on Maddy's face made it worth it. Her blue eyes were sparkling as they wandered around looking at different stalls, stopping to admire treasures at all of the booths.

Unless they were in bed, it was rare for him to see her so relaxed. Her dark hair was loose and messy from the breeze and she had pink residue on her lips from the candy floss she'd been eating. And she was smiling.

He was glad to give her a reason to smile. No one else in her life had. He felt the hot burn of anger rising in him again when he thought of all of the people who had wronged Madeline. Fate was cruel. No question.

What had happened to Paulina was proof enough of that. His wife had been so young, with so much yet ahead of her. And it had all been taken away in an instant.

And then there was Maddy. Thank God for her brother or she would have had no one. Would she even have survived her childhood? He knew of her family. They were wealthy, society's elite. And they had left their daughter alone with no food.

He tightened his hands into fists. Then there was her former boss. The man who had taken such perfect, sick advantage of a young girl who had been so neglected that she had been starving for affection. And he had known it.

The bastard.

That was why he was here, at the market. Because she deserved something that made her smile. She deserved to be happy. For someone to treat her with consideration. He couldn't love her, couldn't give her everything she deserved. But he could give her this.

He could make her happy for a few moments in time.

He noticed her blue eyes light up when she saw the large tourist-filled boats moored in the canal. The men in the boats were charging an exorbitant sum for a ten-minute ride, but money was not one of his concerns.

"Would you like a ride?"

She looked at him, her expression so open and sweet it made his stomach clench tight. "It's such a tourist thing."

He shrugged. "Technically, I'm a tourist. I don't spend all that much time in Milan, and you've only been living here for what? Three months? We're both tourists."

She put her hand on her chin as though she was considering it. "True. Okay."

"That didn't take much convincing," he said as he paid one of the men and helped Maddy down into the boat.

She cuddled up against him, looping her arms through his. "I know, but I really wanted to go."

He chuckled, surprised by how easy it was. "I could tell."

It was a silly thing to do, Maddy acknowledged as the boat slid smoothly through the smooth water of the canal. But it was also romantic. A silly smile spread over her face and she pressed her face against Aleksei's shoulder. It didn't even matter that there were ten other people in the boat. She could barely see them. Not when Aleksei was so close.

Dimly, it registered that she shouldn't be looking for romance. She should be running from it. That wasn't part of the bargain at all. Because romance was coupled with love more often than not, and she just…she still didn't trust herself enough.

She'd forgiven herself for what had happened with William, but she should still learn from it. Her desire to be loved had overridden common sense. It had made her behave stupidly, and she had no desire to go there again.

But that wasn't what this was about. This was about the

moment. About being with Aleksei. Their relationship was temporary. It would end when one of them tired of the other one. She knew that now, so there would be no heartbreak later.

She felt a slight ache in her chest and she ignored it. She wasn't going to be heartbroken. Of course, it was hard to imagine tiring of Aleksei. He was just so good in bed. And he was sweet. Considerate. No one had ever taken her to anything like this before. No one had ever indulged her with a boat ride through Milan. Her parents...they never would have taken her to something like this in the first place.

Gage had been so good to her, but he had been so young, he just hadn't thought to provide anything extra. Just having her had been all he could handle, and she had been far too timid to ask. Why would she when, in her mind, no one had time for her?

And with William, everything had been clandestine. So there certainly hadn't been any dates.

So it was natural that she would miss this, would miss him, a little when it came to an end. She suppressed a sigh.

The boat came to a stop where they had started, the short loop completed. Aleksei stood and got out, stepping up on to the stone walkway before reaching down to help her. She gripped his hand and let him pull her up, but her shoe slipped on the edge of the slick stone, she banged her knee on the rock edge of the canal and scraped her other leg down the side of the rough stone before crashing back into the boat, onto the green vinyl covered benches, barely missing another passenger.

"Ow," she said, trying to stand again.

Aleksei was back in the boat in a second, barking angry Italian at the concerned tour guide. He knelt down beside her, his dark eyes fierce. "Are you okay, Maddy?"

"I'm…ouch…I'm fine. I mean, it hurts, but I'm not mortally wounded."

He bent and scooped her into his arms. She squeaked and grabbed onto his shirt as he moved into a standing position and stepped up and back onto solid ground.

"I'm fine," she repeated, when a minute had gone by and he still hadn't put her down.

He narrowed his dark eyes and set her down.

"Ouch!" she said when she put weight on the knee she'd hit hardest.

"You're not fine," he said, his voice harsh.

"Nothing's broken!" she protested.

"You don't know that."

She let out an exasperated breath. "Um, yes, I'm pretty sure I do know that since I'm not incapacitated by pain."

"But it hurts when you put weight on it," he said, wrapping an arm around her waist and helping her walk through the tight knot of people.

"Yes, probably because I have a serious bruise. But nothing more fatal than that."

"Come over here." He led her through the crowd and into a less populated part of the square. "Sit," he said, gesturing to one of the benches.

"Yes, master," she said, but she complied, because her knee really did hurt. And her other leg stung horribly, and she knew she really needed a bandage. Or three.

"Maddy," he growled.

"Sorry, but you're so intense. I fell and scraped my leg."

He knelt in front of her and rolled her jeans up slowly, careful not to scrape the rough material against her injured skin. She'd been right about the bruise. It was already turning a very unflattering color, and it was even getting swollen.

She touched the affected spot lightly. "Ow," she said.

"Well, don't touch it, Maddy," he gritted.

It was strange to see Aleksei concerned for her. He reacted to concern with anger. She realized that now. It was how he'd acted when he'd come in and seen her on the ladder. He'd been angry because he'd been…scared. For her. That was a shocking revelation.

"How is your other leg?" he asked.

She winced. "Likely bleeding."

"Let's go back to my apartment."

The walk back to Aleksei's was short, but it seemed longer thanks to the goose egg on her knee. When they were upstairs and inside, Aleksei sat her on the couch and went searching for the first aid kit. When he returned with it, he regarded her closely.

"You might need to take those off." He gestured to her jeans.

She laughed as she stood and undid the closure on her pants, trying to step out of them as carefully as possible. "Quite the bedside manner you have there."

She kicked her jeans to the side and sat back down on the couch. Aleksei crouched in front of her, propping her leg on one of his thighs as he felt around the swollen part of her knee gingerly.

"Do you feel like you need a brace?" he asked.

She shook her head. "I think I'm fine."

He moved her leg slowly and then took her other one and propped it up. She had a mean scrape down her shin that, while not as painful as the bruise, looked uglier.

He took antiseptic out of the kit and sprayed some onto her wounds. She squirmed when the cold, stinging medicine hit her skin. He looked up at her, concern in his eyes. Her heart felt so full she was afraid it was going to burst.

As Aleksei put a large piece of gauze over her scrape she felt something shift inside of her. When was the last time someone, other than her brother, had cared for her at all? There was nothing in this for Aleksei. Bandaging injuries was hardly seduction material, after all.

She swallowed hard, trying to push the lump in her throat down, trying to ignore the sting of tears she could feel welling up in her eyes. What was wrong with her? She didn't want an emotional attachment, least of all with Aleksei.

He loved his wife. He still carried the necklace.

She didn't even believe in love. She didn't. When had she ever really seen it? Gage had been good to her, but she'd always been afraid that he…that he cared for her out of duty because he was simply too good a man to do anything less.

She took a deep breath, trying to hold back the tears. "I really… Thank you," she said, standing on wobbly legs and picking her jeans up from the floor. She tugged them on slowly, trying not to disturb her new bandages. "I should go."

"Why, Maddy? Neither of us have work tomorrow."

"Because…this is your house and I really shouldn't… impose on you anymore. You've already done more than you bargained for."

"Do you think I resent taking care of you? You're hurt."

"I…I know." That scary feeling was back, taking over, filling her.

He reached a hand out and touched her face. "Who took care of you, Maddy?"

She looked down. "My brother did. He was really good to me."

"Let me take care of you. For now, let me take care of you."

She was powerless to resist his words, powerless to deny the rising tide inside of her. She leaned in and kissed him. Kissing was good. Uncomplicated. It was a lot easier to deal with than him treating her so kindly. Taking her on a boat ride and buying her cotton candy.

It was a lot easier to deal with than the riot of emotions that were pounding through her, making her dizzy with their force.

She couldn't ignore them forever. But she would ignore them for now.

When Maddy woke up, she was naked, in Aleksei's bed, and the sun streaming through the window was fiery orange. She checked the bedside clock. It was seven in the evening. She'd slept for most of the afternoon, after they'd made love.

He'd been so gentle with her, careful because of her very minor injuries. He'd been so concerned about hurting her. She sucked in a breath, trying to ease the tension in her chest.

The bedroom door opened and Aleksei strode in from the *en suite* bathroom, a towel wrapped low around his lean hips. For a moment, all she could do was admire him. How had she got so lucky to have him for a lover? He was so beautiful.

Broad, bronzed chest bare, his muscles shifting as he walked to the bed. He was more than looks, though. He was a good boss, a savvy businessman. He was the kind of man who would get on his knees to clean your wounds.

Her breath caught.

"Feeling better?" he asked, sitting on the edge of the bed.

She pulled the covers tightly around her. "I never felt bad. You were worrying about nothing."

"I don't want to see you get hurt, Maddy."

That sounded more like a warning than anything else. And not a warning against further knee-scrapes.

"Aleksei, I know what this is. I'm the one who instigated it. I don't even believe in love."

"Not at all?"

"No. People make you love them, then they use it against you. Neglect you and remind you that they're your parents, so you love them even if they forgot to pick you up from school again. Or forgot even to send one of the household staff to get you."

"Your parents are unfit to be called human beings."

"No argument," she said.

"I believe in love," he said hoarsely.

Her stomach lurched and her heart pounded, everything in her body on hold as she waited for his next words. There was no reason for that. No reason she should be holding her breath to hear what he would say next. But she was.

"I loved my wife," he said finally. "From the moment I met her. I was eighteen. She was just sixteen. She became my world. For nine years, she was my world. I loved her so much that losing her nearly destroyed me. I know that love is real, because I've tasted the loss of it. I know what it's like for breathing to be physical pain, for it to be harder to live than to give up. That's the power of love, Maddy."

Her stomach hurt. It hurt so much to hear him say that, to know how badly he'd suffered.

"The power of love sounds dangerous," she choked.

"I'm never going through that again," he said, his voice hard, his dark eyes flat.

"Well, maybe love is real," she said softly. "But it seems like it always hurts."

"I don't hurt anymore, Maddy. I don't let myself feel enough to hurt."

Maddy nodded slowly. "I understand that. I've lived most of my life that way. The one time I tried...it didn't end well."

"I won't ever love you. But I won't lie to you either."

The stab of pain in her chest was so sharp, so real, that

it shocked her. She ignored it. "That's all I've ever asked of you, Aleksei. All I've ever wanted was your honesty."

And she had it. Even now, even with her naked and in his bed, he wouldn't even profess the possibility of loving her. It was what she wanted. What she needed.

It was.

"You have that. I promise."

She thought about the necklace Aleksei carried with him. The necklace that he'd never finished. "Your wife must have been a really wonderful woman."

"Paulina knew me before I had anything. She supported me while I worked toward my crazy dreams. When she died...I was getting there, but she never saw me truly succeed. We were poor for most of our time together. We didn't have very much. We had a small house."

"With weeds in the backyard," Maddy whispered.

"Yes," Aleksei said, his voice thick.

She had the feeling that if he could trade his empire for that small house again, he would.

He was right. Love was real. And he'd had it. What could she offer him in the face of that kind of love? She was the girl not even her parents could love.

It didn't matter anyway. He was right. Love was real. And it was pain. A pain she wouldn't put herself through.

"I really should go back home," she said, swinging her legs over the side of the bed, careful of her bruise.

"Do you need a ride?" It hurt that he didn't ask her to stay.

"No. I have my car."

"I'll see you on Monday."

"You'll still be here?" she asked. That was all she said, but it wasn't the only question she had. Were they done? Was this it?

"Until my work here is finished I won't be going back to Russia."

She hated that they were speaking in code. Even though she'd never promised him the same honesty he'd promised her, she had given it. But now she felt she was keeping something from him. She had a feeling it was the same thing she was trying to hide from herself.

"I…" Her words caught. She bent down and scooped her clothes off the floor, conscious that he was watching her and she was naked. She didn't usually feel naked in front of him. But she did now.

She dressed quickly, not about to duck into the bathroom, even though part of her wanted to. But it was silly. Obviously Aleksei didn't feel the shift that had taken place in her. He was still lounging on the bed in his towel. She wasn't about to show him how confused she was. How suddenly everything felt different to her.

"I'll see you Monday," she said softly.

He didn't say anything.

CHAPTER ELEVEN

MADDY wasn't sure what to expect from Aleksei when she came into work on Monday morning. Would he be the cold, brooding stranger he'd been when she'd left his house a couple of days earlier? Or would he be the man who'd bandaged her scraped leg? Would he be the suave lover who had seduced her in his office?

Maybe each of those men were a part of him. Well, they had to be, she supposed. There were moments, small moments, like when she'd told him about her past, when he seemed to care. Then there were moments where he seemed completely cut off from all emotion.

Just like she was. Had been? Forget who Aleksei would be today. Who was she?

She pushed the door to his office open and held out a coffee cup. "I come in peace," she said, setting it on his desk.

"I don't drink coffee," he said.

She pulled a face. "Sorry." She knew that too. He'd told her.

"Thank you," he said.

"For bringing you a drink you don't even like?"

"For the thought," he bit out. "How is everything going with the preparation for the Paris exhibition?"

"Going well now that we have the scheduling thing handled, thank you by the way, and I have the layout planned and all the decorations purchased."

"And how are you?"

"I'm fine. I don't think my leg needs to be amputated or anything." She looked at the lid of her coffee cup.

"I meant how are you? I was...I did not behave well on Saturday night."

"It's okay. We got...very heavy. It's good, I think we know we're on the same page, but maybe we need to keep things in lighter territory."

The corners of his mouth lifted, but there was no smile in his eyes. "Maybe."

"I'm... Do you want to come over tonight? I don't cook, but I have take-out restaurants on my speed dial, and I have a very experienced dialing finger."

She didn't have people over very often. Ever. But she didn't feel strange asking Aleksei to come over. It felt right. It had felt right being at his house, even though she'd been afraid to go at first. Afraid of the intimacy it might add to the relationship.

"I'll meet you there after work," he said.

"Okay."

She still felt a strange distance between them. Like something was missing. And she had no idea what it might be.

"Can you show me your plans design-wise for Paris?"

Maddy blinked and tried to bring herself back to reality, tried to get some focus on the task at hand.

"Sure, I have everything with me." She took her tablet computer out of her bag and flipped open the case. She moved through the screens quickly and brought up the sketches she'd done of the event. "I wanted to go with sort of a retro feel, but still lavish. It's like a very upscale soda shop in all black, white and pink. I think the colored gems will really stand out, and it's a completely different event to what we put on in Luxembourg. Clean lines, very chic, rather than…fairytale chic."

Although she'd been kind of fond of the fairytale.

"And what do you have here?" he asked, pointing to a shaded area of her sketch.

"Oh, this is the stage. I've booked a swing band."

"A swing band, huh?"

"Yes, it's going to be really fun. That's kind of the theme. Fun."

He laughed softly. "What do you and I know about fun, Maddy?"

"I thought we'd done a pretty good job of having it over the past week or so," she said softly, closing the case on her tablet and putting it back in her bag.

"I suppose we have." He looked at her, but his expression was distant, like he wasn't really seeing her.

She sat down in the chair in front of Aleksei's desk as he talked guest numbers, security and all the other incidentals that didn't fall under food, music and decor. She watched Aleksei's mouth as he talked. He really had a wonderful mouth.

She cleared her throat and turned her attention back to her notes. She had to keep the sex thing separate from the work thing. She really did.

"You look tired," Aleksei said.

Maddy looked up and saw him staring at her, a crease between his dark brows.

"Thanks," she said tartly.

"Are you getting enough sleep?"

She thought back to Friday night, the night she'd spent in his bed, and then to the two sleepless nights that had followed. The nights where she'd missed his body. Missed his warmth and his touch.

"I'm willing to bet that I'm not."

He stood from the desk and came to stand behind her, the weight of his hands coming to rest on her shoulders. He swept her ponytail over her shoulder then started kneading her muscles slowly, methodically, sensually.

"You're tense too," he said.

"Yeah." She sucked in a breath. "Really, though, if I gave you a massage are you telling me your muscles would be relaxed?"

"Not at all," he said, his thumbs working the knots that had been tightening in her muscles over the past couple of weeks. "Maybe you should take some vacation time after this event."

Her heart felt like it was going to burst inside of her. The way he spoke to her, so tenderly, so caring. That he noticed she was tired. That her muscles were tight. Of course, he didn't know he was responsible.

No, that wasn't fair. It wasn't Aleksei's fault that their fling was becoming a source of anxiety to her. That she missed him all night when they weren't together. That her emotions were a swirl of confusion.

He'd offered sex, he'd offered honesty, and she'd taken it. Had convinced him, and herself, that that was all she wanted from him.

But it wasn't. It really wasn't. She wanted more.

She could have laughed. She'd fancied herself in love with a man who had never done anything but lie and manipulate her. Had fallen for him, because the words had come so easily to him, and he hadn't hesitated to use them to get exactly what he'd wanted.

But Aleksei would never say the words. He would never feel them either. Not for her. She didn't even have a hope. She didn't even have a lie to cling to.

But that hadn't stopped her. It hadn't kept her from falling in love with him.

She felt dizzy all of a sudden, her pulse pounding hard in her head. She loved him. Had it only been the other day she'd told him she didn't believe in love? Had it only been recently that she'd thought love didn't exist?

She stood from her seat, slipping away from his hold. She looked at him, at his handsome face, so familiar and... essential now. Her heart seized.

How had this happened? How had he become everything?

And what was she going to do when she didn't have him anymore? Because their arrangement was temporary and no alteration in her feelings would change that. Aleksei had been perfectly honest with her from the start. He wasn't looking for permanent. Or commitment or anything resembling it.

She didn't even blame him for it. How long had she clung to all of her superficial hurt and heartbreak? How long had her own mistakes colored her life?

What Aleksei had experienced had been so much more. He had lost his wife. He had lost real love, not the illusion of it. She thought she'd known loss, pain, heartbreak. But it was nothing to what Aleksei had experienced.

She could only stare at him, all words totally frozen in her mind, unable to escape. She just wanted to look at him, memorize every minute detail of his appearance. And at the same time she wanted to turn and run away. To forget about him. To forget that she loved him.

"I...have to go back to work," she said.

He gave her a long look, slight confusion visible in his expression. "I'll see you tonight," he said.

"Actually I can't do tonight, Aleksei. I have...work." She couldn't see him tonight. She couldn't. She had to process all of this. Figure out what it meant.

She needed distance. Needed it more than she needed her next breath.

She left his office and walked through the maze of hallways back into her office. She shut the door behind her and locked it before going to her desk and collapsing into her chair, face in her hands.

It was only then that she realized what it was she was doing.

She was running. She was always running. She'd run from her parents, understandable, since she'd been a child. But it was a demon she'd never faced. She'd run from the headlines when the affair had become public.

She was running from her feelings now.

How much longer could she run until she'd left everyone and everything behind her that meant anything? Until she collapsed with exhaustion?

She wasn't going to find out.

She was done running.

This time he wouldn't call her. No matter how much his body ached, he wouldn't give in this time. He didn't play games. She said she'd wanted a purely sexual relationship, and that meant he wasn't going to fall into any of this female manipulation.

He'd had mistresses attempt it before. Like Olivia. And they were no longer a part of his life.

Even as the thought passed through his mind, he rejected it. Never had he thought of Maddy as his mistress. Strange since it was essentially what she was. They had a physical relationship, one with terms laid out nearly as clear as if it had been a business transaction.

He knew that wasn't strictly true either. Somewhere between sex on his desk and her sharing all of her deepest, darkest secrets that had changed.

His cellphone rang and he picked it up from its position on the coffee table. "Yes?"

"Aleksei." Madeline's breathless voice shocked him, sent a surge of desire, and something infinitely more powerful, through his body.

"What is it? No problems with the planning of the Paris exhibition, are there?"

"No. Everything's fine. Well, the business stuff is fine. Can you buzz me up? I'm standing in front of the building."

He stood from the couch and walked over to the front door, pressing the button to grant her access.

"I thought you were busy," he said.

"Yes, well…" She trailed off and he could picture the faint flush of pink her cheeks would have, the small smile that told him she'd been caught. "I…I decided I had to see you."

There was a small knock at the door and he opened it. And there she was, dressed in sweats and looking more beautiful than any woman had a right to.

She looked down, then back up at him, her eyes bluer, the emotion in them so deep he had to look away.

"I had to see you," she said, her voice strong. "I couldn't stay away."

Her words, so stark and honest, no shame in them, made him feel as though a crack had opened up in the stone wall that was built around his emotions. He gritted his teeth against the sensation, fought against it.

"Aleks." She took a step toward him, touched his face with soft, tender hands. There were tears in her eyes now.

She leaned in to kiss him, her lips so sweet, her touch gentle. She slid her tongue over his lips, then into his mouth, the gentle teasing flicks heating his blood, making it pump faster. Making his heart race.

Those sweet hands slid from his face to his shoulders, over his chest and down his stomach. Her touch just enough to arouse a longing in him that didn't feel familiar at all. He couldn't recall ever feeling such a vast pit of need inside of himself. A need for her body. A need for her. A need that seemed to go beyond words.

He sucked in a sharp breath when her slender fingers brushed over his erection, still covered by layers of clothing.

She looked up at him as she stroked him, her eyes meeting his, the expression there fathomless, intense. She was making love to him. The realization hit hard. Made the dam burst. A tide of sensation flooded through him and he was powerless to do anything to stop it.

"No," he growled, not realizing he'd said it out loud until after he'd spoken.

"What?" she asked.

"Too slow," he said, taking her hands in his, capturing her slender wrists in one of his hands and holding them still while he claimed her mouth.

His kiss wasn't tender. It wasn't exploratory. It was fire, intensity. He poured out every ounce of frustration, every ounce of need that would have to go unmet, into that one kiss.

When he pulled away Maddy's eyes were round, her pink lips swollen, the color in her cheeks dark and prominent. He touched where her lips were puffy from the kiss, running his thumb gently over her reddened skin before leaning in to kiss her again.

She didn't protest. She returned his kiss. The energy coming from her was electric, vibrating through him. Challenging him.

"Bed," he grated against her lips.

"Mmm."

He scooped her up and carried her the short distance into his bedroom before setting her feet gingerly back onto the floor. She pulled her top over her head, dispensing with her bra with equal speed. He worked on his own clothes while she finished undressing.

And then she was back in his arms, soft and gloriously naked.

He cupped her tight butt with one hand, a feeling of possession rolling through him, making his pulse throb, making him ache with a need so fierce it surpassed the sexual.

No. It didn't. This was only sex. Good sex. But only sex.

He wrapped his arm around her waist and gently lowered her onto the bed. He needed to prove it. He needed to wipe every shred of feeling away. Needed the hot rush of satisfaction to remind him that this was only physical.

He drew one of her taut nipples into his mouth and exulted in the purely sexual sound that escaped Maddy's lips. She arched beneath him as he moved his fingers lightly down her belly and in between her thighs, discovering just how wet and ready she was for him.

He stroked her, calling another sound of need from her body, drawn tight as a bowstring beneath his hand. He moved his thumb over the sensitive bundle of nerves and slipped a finger deep inside of her.

Her hands went to his back, fingernails digging into his flesh.

He looked at her face, her skin flushed pink, her eyes closed, her lips parted. Seeing her so caught up in her pleasure, the pleasure he was giving her, felt like a physical kick to the stomach. Never had he seen a more beautiful sight than Maddy in the midst of such abandon.

He'd had her in his bed a few times now, but never had he seen her like this. So lost in the experience, all of her barriers down.

His stomach tightened and he had to labor to draw his next breath.

She opened her eyes, the expression in them so trusting,

so full of caring. He could feel it. Could feel her emotions radiating from her. Radiating in him. His throat felt tight and his body was screaming for release, while his heart was threatening to pound out of his chest.

He moved up to capture her lips, to settle between her thighs, testing her moist entrance with the head of his erection. Heat rushed through him, physical desire strong enough to blot out everything else.

Yes. This was what he needed. It was just sex. Nothing more.

He slid into her body and she let out a little moan of ecstasy that he captured with his lips. He kissed her, sifting her silky hair through his fingers as he thrust into her.

She moved her hands over his back, fingers skimming his buttocks. Her legs locked around his calves as she moved beneath him, perky nipples rubbing against his chest.

She was perfect. Amazing. He couldn't stop himself from telling her. The words fell from his lips as pleasure built inside of him, as he continued to chase down the oblivion that an orgasm would bring.

Anything. Anything to dull the emotion that seemed to be building in his chest. His blood roared in his ears as he neared the peak, drowning out everything except the pleasure that was pounding through him.

A harsh groan escaped his lips as he poured himself into her and he felt her body lock tight beneath him, felt the pulsing of her internal muscles as she gave in to her own orgasm. He was glad she'd found satisfaction, because he'd been too caught up in his own to pay her as much attention as he should have.

She wrapped her arms around his neck and pressed a soft kiss to his cheek. He looked at her, allowed himself to really see the emotion in her eyes. The remnants of the stone wall in his chest crumbled. He was raw, exposed. He was *feeling.*

The intensity of it welled up in him, all of his emotions swirling together, impossible to identify, impossible to pick out one emotion and distinguish it from the rest.

"Aleks," she whispered, stroking his neck, running her fingers through his hair. She kissed him again slowly, sweetly.

He pulled away, rolling to the side and pushing himself into a sitting position.

He turned back to face her. The way she looked at him. With so much trust. He didn't want her to look at him that way. Didn't want to see anything but lust in those beautiful blue eyes.

She sat too, wrapped her arms around her waist, resting her head on his shoulder. He set his jaw, remained motionless. She slid her hand over his chest, her touch arousing him again already.

He moved away from her and swung his legs over the side of the bed. "I need a shower."

Maddy sat still in the center of the bed. She knew that she wasn't invited to Aleksei's shower. The sharp click of the bathroom door confirmed it.

She flopped backward, resting her head on the pillow. She contemplated getting her clothes on and going back home. That was what she would have done…yesterday. She would have run from the tension between them. It was what she had done the other day.

But she wasn't going to do that today. Yesterday, she'd assumed her relationship with Aleksei would be temporary, had counted on it. Today, she was pretty sure it was still going to be temporary, but that didn't mean she wouldn't try to change that.

It scared her, the thought of putting herself out there, laying her feelings bare. The thought of trying for forever. But at the very least, no matter what happened, Aleksei was a man who was worthy of her love. He was worth the risk. They both were.

Even though she wasn't sure if there was any way the risk would work out.

When Aleksei came back from his shower he was still stark naked, droplets of water lingering on his skin. He strode to the bed and slid in beside her. Her heart ached. She loved him. She loved him so much.

He didn't reach for her, as she longed for him to do, didn't draw her against the warmth of his body. But he was there.

Tonight, she wouldn't rock the boat with any declarations. Tonight she would just enjoy being with him. The man she loved. The man who had taught her how to love.

Aleksei woke late, which was unusual. He always got up at six after a night of barely sleeping. But last night he'd slept. With Maddy's deep, even breathing, her scent, the warm weight of her body, he had slept for the first time in six years.

No nightmares. No ghosts.

He pushed aside the realization as he made his way from the bedroom into the kitchen, where he was greeted by a sight of surreal domesticity.

Maddy was moving around the kitchen, taking bread out of the toaster and putting it on a plate next to some scrambled eggs. She was wearing his shirt, the hem riding high on her thighs when she reached up into the cupboard and took out two mugs.

When she turned to face him, that same open, honest look on her face that she'd had last night, his chest seized.

"Good morning," she said.

"You cook?"

"Well, I eat." She walked over to the stove and took a tea kettle off of one the burners—he hadn't even known he owned a tea kettle—and poured some hot water into the mugs. "I will forgive your lack of coffee as you're a caffeine-less Philistine in practice."

She picked up the plates and stood still for a moment. "You don't have a dining room set, do you?"

"No." There was no point. Not here. He wasn't in Milan often, and when he was he didn't have guests. What was the point of owning a dining table? So he could sit at it alone?

Only this morning he could have sat with Maddy. The thought wrenched the tension in his chest even tighter.

"We'll eat in here then," she said, her voice determinedly cheerful as she carried the plates into the living room and set them on the coffee table.

She sat down next to him and pushed her food around instead of eating it. She was upset with him. But he'd never promised her anything beyond what had happened last night in the bedroom and she knew that. If she'd forgotten it now, it wasn't his fault.

"Oh." She set her plate on the coffee table and stood. "I forgot I was making you tea."

"You don't have to make me tea, Maddy."

She started to walk toward the kitchen. "Aleks, it's fine."

And there she was, calling him by a pet name, walking around in his kitchen. Making tea like she was his...

"You're not my wife, Madeline," he said, his voice low and even.

She froze, her body going stiff before she turned to face him. "I know that. I made you breakfast. I'm not trying to be your wife."

"Good. Because I have no intention of ever making you my wife, of ever making any woman my wife."

She turned away again, but not before he saw the bottom-less chasm of hurt behind those blue eyes. His chest felt too full, almost painful, in response to what he witnessed there. For what he had caused.

He gritted his teeth, fought to find his control again. He was a master at controlling his emotions. He had lost his dominion over himself once and he had vowed never to do it again.

There was something about Madeline...last night he hadn't even used a condom. That never happened to him. Protection was an essential part of sex as far as he was concerned. Who could enjoy themselves with the threat of pregnancy or health issues looming?

And yet he'd forgotten last night entirely. Hadn't realized until halfway through his shower. He hadn't said anything to Maddy either. He didn't want to worry her for no reason. The odds of pregnancy were low and he was in good health.

And deep down he acknowledged he didn't want to confess that she'd made him forget. He didn't even want to confess it to himself, but he was forced to.

He heard a spoon clinking against the side of the mug as Maddy stirred the tea too vigorously. She spun around suddenly, her face a study in schooled composure.

"I know I'm not your wife, Aleksei. I'm not even applying for the position because I know you just aren't ready for that. And that's okay. Heaven knows I've held on to plenty in my life. Things that weren't as bad as what you went through. But I do care about you, and if I want to show you that I don't think you should feel threatened by it."

He stood from the couch, his blood pounding fiercely through his body. "I never asked you to care for me. I never asked you to make me breakfast. This was supposed to be a physical affair."

Maddy crossed the kitchen and stepped into the living room. Now that she was closer he noticed how pale she was, what dark circles she had under her eyes. He wanted to touch her. To offer comfort. But he was the source of her pain. It would be too perverse for him to be the one to try and erase what he had caused. What he would continue to cause by not offering her more than a cold, sexual relationship.

"I know what it was supposed to be. I was the one who laid down the terms, wasn't I? But…it's funny, and I didn't expect it, but you…you've healed me, Aleksei," she said, her voice thick with emotion. "I carried so much anger, anger at myself mostly, for what had happened in my past. And I was stuck there, in my mind the little girl that no one loved, the guilty sinner who had an affair with a married man. That was who I was. Maybe not to anyone else, not anymore, but it was who I saw. You changed that."

"No. I didn't change anything, Maddy." He was just another person in her life who had used her. Another person who would hurt her if he didn't end things.

He opened his mouth to speak the words, to tell her to go. An intense burst of pain in his chest immobilized him, stopped him from saying anything.

So Maddy pressed on. "You did. You're the last man on earth it makes sense for me to fall in love with, but I did. I do. I love you. You were the one who showed me that love was real. That it wasn't just something people use against you. Because even now you won't use it against me. I know you won't."

"Your trust is misplaced," he growled. "As is your love."

She looked down, biting her lower lip. "I know you aren't going to get on your knee and confess your undying love, Aleksei. I don't expect that. But that doesn't mean we can't still be together for now."

"I don't think you understand," he said, ignoring the trickle of anguish that was spreading from his chest through his body. "I don't need your love. I don't want it."

"Aleksei…" She moved to him.

"Stop. Maddy, you would take so little from someone? You would take a physical affair and nothing more? Because that's all you'll ever have from me. I will never give you more. I can't. I have my mistresses long term. I find it more convenient. But it doesn't ever really matter who they are so long as they're biddable and available."

He watched the light in her eyes dim, watched her entire being shrink back.

And the trickle inside of him turned into a flood. But if he didn't do it now, if he didn't make her leave now, he would only hurt her worse later. What did one emotionally crippled man have to offer a woman like Madeline? A woman who had her own hurts. A woman who had been so badly abused by those who should have cared for her.

He could give her nothing but his own shortcomings, his own pain. His own failings as a man.

"It's never mattered to me who the woman was, as long as the sex was good."

She jerked back then, as though he had slapped her. And it took everything in him to stay rooted to the spot. To not go to her. To not comfort her. Kiss her.

He had no right to do those things. Had no right to demand love from a woman like Maddy when he could offer nothing of value in return. But he wanted to. More than anything, he wanted to.

She looked up at him, blinking furiously. Maddy wouldn't dissolve, not now. He knew that. She was too strong. Or too stubborn. Maybe both.

"You're right, Aleksei. I...I am selling myself short. I deserve to be loved, not to just give it. I've given it all of my life, and the only person who ever really gave it back was my brother. Everyone else just took what I would offer and used it against me. And I always thought that meant there was something wrong with me. I never thought I deserved more. I do now."

She sucked in a deep breath and put her hand on her stomach, as though it hurt. It probably did. His own pain was certainly real. Physical. Horrible.

"You know, the irony is I learned that from you too. You showed me that I was worth more than I thought. That I was more than my mistakes. More than my parents showed me I was. I'll always be grateful for that. Not for this, though," she said, turning to head back into the bedroom, probably to collect her clothes. "This hurts. And I think you're selling both of us short. I think we could have something, and you're too afraid to take it."

He closed his eyes, ignoring the searing pain in his heart. "No, Maddy. There's nothing. This was nothing."

He'd promised her honesty. Always.

He had broken his promise.

She flinched, her shoulders hunching. But she kept walking, didn't stop. He stood in the middle of the living room, waiting.

When she reemerged she was dressed, her purse slung over her shoulder.

"Will you still be working on the Paris exhibition, or will I need to contract someone else?"

She looked at him, blue eyes hard. "I don't really think it's fair for me to lose my lover and my job on the same day. Plus, I'm good at my job. The best, remember?"

"You'll have your job, any job in my company, as long as you want, Madeline." That he could give her.

She nodded slowly. "Quite the consolation prize. Goodbye, Aleksei."

"Goodbye, Maddy." Her name stuck in his throat, difficult to force it past the lump that had settled there.

She walked past him to the door, where she stopped but didn't turn.

"You know, Aleksei, I finally realized something about myself yesterday. I've been living my life in fear. I let it control what I did, what I didn't do. I let it keep me from so much as going on a date with a man for five years. I don't have room for it anymore. There's no room for fear anymore. Love pushed it away. I hope someday there's a woman who can do the same for you. I know you loved your wife. I know you'll never stop loving her, and I think that's okay. But I hope someday you can let go so that you can move forward."

She opened the door and slipped out into the hallway, shutting the door behind her with a final-sounding click.

Maddy was gone. He'd done what he'd had to.

He waited for the years of hard-won emotionlessness to rescue him from the pain in his body, to rescue him from the dull ache in his head and his heart. From the shattering sensation that was splintering through him.

There was no relief. There was only a sense of bitter loss, a flow of agony that he couldn't stop.

Somehow, over the years, it had come to represent his own.

He had continued on. He had made money, found professional success. But his personal life, who he was, had ended.

He'd thought to protect Maddy by sending her away. The simple fact was he'd been protecting himself. Because he was a coward.

He had loved once. Had loved Paulina as a man should love a wife. Losing her had been devastating. It had stripped him of purpose, and he'd had to claw his way out of the pit it had left him in. Find meaning again.

And yet he suspected he hadn't actually found it. He had found stopgaps, things to fill the void temporarily. Bandages that had concealed wounds instead of healing them. But it had been nothing more than vanity. He had more money than one man could spend, more power than most men could exhaust, more fame than he had ever wanted. And yet it was all worthless. Meaningless. He had nothing of value.

He looked at the necklace again and it was Madeline's face he saw.

Maddy, who called up feelings in him he'd thought long buried, who called up feelings deeper than any he'd ever experienced. Maddy, who had his heart.

And if he was going to be the man for her, he had to let go of fear. He had to move on. He tightened his hold on the necklace and pushed the Scotch away.

Everything was going perfectly at the exhibition. Maddy was standing on the balcony, overlooking the ballroom, watching couples dance to the music.

She smiled wistfully, thinking of the night she'd danced with Aleksei. It seemed like a lifetime ago now. Her memories had a fuzzy edge to them, as though all of it might have been a dream.

If only her pain had the same fuzzy edges as her memories.

CHAPTER TWELVE

ALEKSEI looked at the bottle of Scotch on his coffee table. He hadn't touched the stuff in five years. Not since the very worst of his grief had passed. Not since he'd realized he wasn't accomplishing anything by drinking his pain away.

He was considering it now. Very seriously.

He couldn't lie to himself and pretend he felt nothing for Maddy, not when the agony of losing her was as acute as it might have been if he'd lost her to death. No, not so bad as that. At least she was still here. At least she had a chance at happiness. With a man who could truly make her happy, give her all she deserved unreservedly.

Although the thought of it made him want to strangle the other man, made rage and pain, so severe it felt beyond his control, pour through him.

Maddy was gone. Sleepless nights were back. He had barely slept at all since she'd walked out of his apartment. Out of his bed and his life.

He reached for the short length of the partially completed necklace that was sitting on the coffee table and ran his fingers over the delicate chain. It had always represented his wife's life to him. Beautiful, but far too short. Incomplete.

But it didn't. She missed him so much sometimes she could barely breathe. Over the course of the past week she'd wondered—more than once—if she'd made a mistake.

Being strong and standing on principle, taking all she deserved, was all well and good in theory. It was kind of lonely in reality.

But how could Aleksei—or anyone else—ever respect her if she didn't respect herself? She'd needed to stop letting people who were users dictate the way she saw herself. Dictate the way she saw the entire human race. And she had. She finally had.

It was a hollow victory now, though.

Of course, Aleksei had always respected her. He'd never condemned her for her mistakes. Even in the end he had told her not to accept so little. Not even from him.

It only made her love him more, which just didn't seem fair.

He'd gone back to Moscow the day after. Which was normal. And it was what he'd said he would do. When he was finished in Milan, he wouldn't stay. She'd known then what he'd meant. It was better that he'd done that, really. It made it all feel final. She needed it to feel final so that she could try to accept it and move on.

But, heaven help her, she didn't want to. Loving Aleksei was the most liberating, empowering, terrifying thing she'd ever done. And she didn't want to stop. A good thing, since she wasn't certain she could.

She looked toward the edge of the ballroom and saw Aleksei stride in, looking so amazing in a tailored black suit that she ached with wanting him. He was still so exotic, and yet familiar too. In the very best way. Well, the worst way, really, since she couldn't have him.

He hovered around the edge of the crowd, and she remembered how much he didn't like these kinds of things.

She wished she could go down there. Could go and take his hand, ease his tension.

He looked up to the balcony then, his dark eyes zeroing in on her with unerring accuracy. She couldn't do anything but look back, longing and tension stretching between them, thick and obvious, even with so much distance. The physical distance and the emotional distance.

He stepped into the crowd and crossed the dance floor, his focus still on her. She couldn't breathe. She wanted so much to see him again. Just to talk to him, to be near him, if nothing else. And yet she dreaded it too. Dreaded the kind of pain that would come with something like that.

She watched him walk up the curved marble staircase and make his way across the much less empty balcony. She could only stare as he got closer. She didn't know whether to run from him or run to him. The temptation to do both was as intense as it was impossible.

She noticed the difference in his appearance as he drew nearer. He didn't have a tie on. The collar of his shirt was open at his throat. His cheekbones were more prominent, and slight dark circles under his eyes were showing his weariness.

"Maddy." He said so much in that one word, in her name, that it made her heart swell with emotion.

"Hi," she said, hardly able to speak past the lump in her throat.

"Can I speak with you?"

She offered him a small smile. "You're the boss, Mr. Petrov, since when did you start asking permission?"

"Since I realized how fallible my own decision-making was. Please, give me this time."

"Always," she whispered.

He moved to her, took her hand in between both of his and lifted it to his lips, kissing her fingers lightly. When he lowered his hands, she noticed a shiny patch of lighter colored skin.

"What did you do?" she asked, running her thumb over the mark.

"A burn. I was careless with some metal I was working with."

"Aleksei," she said, "you should be more careful."

"I promise I will be." He didn't release his hold on her hand, but walked her to the open double doors that led to an outdoor balcony that overlooked the gardens.

There were fairylights wound around all of the greenery, casting a bright glow on their surroundings. It was late, and it was cold, so the other guests were inside. But Maddy didn't care about the cold. There was nothing but heat when Aleksei was with her.

Aleksei turned so that he was facing the view, his hands gripping the edge of the railing, his burn turning white as he squeezed the stone. "I went back to Moscow to try and escape you. To try and escape my feelings. I am ashamed to admit this, but you were right. I was afraid. I was living in the past, but not quite in the way you think. I never thought of the rewards that love had given me, only the pain. I was afraid to remember the good things. And then there was you, Maddy. And I wanted you. *You,* not just sex with an anonymous stranger."

She couldn't breathe. Everything in her was wound too tight, her heart pounding too fast.

"And you made me feel," he continued, his voice rough. "I hadn't experienced emotion in so long I hardly recognized it. But I ran from it. I convinced myself I could not be the man for you so I could hide the fact that it was fear that was holding me back."

He reached into the inner pocket of his jacket and pulled out a flat velvet box. "I didn't know if I could be the man for you. But I decided I had to be. Because I can't live without you, Maddy."

He opened the box and Maddy's heart stumbled. "What is this?" she whispered, brushing her fingers over the delicate jewels.

"This." He touched the top of the necklace, by the clasp, the part that was made with intricately woven gold, fashioned into vines with pink gems that resembled small thistle blossoms, the part that looked familiar. "This is my past. I had stopped living, Maddy. I existed, but nothing more. I tricked myself into thinking I had moved on, because I had success, I had money. But it was an illusion."

Maddy felt hot tears burn her eyes, and she let them fall. "What about the rest?" she asked, her voice choked.

The rest of the necklace was made with the same sort of woven gold, but the flowers, fashioned from different-colored gems, grew larger, more open, as they cascaded toward the center. There were emerald leaves, growing, flourishing.

"I had a vision for my life, Maddy, and when that vision changed I simply stopped moving. This…" Aleksei's voice caught and Madeline felt as though her heart might burst. "This isn't how I originally designed this necklace. It's not how I planned my life to be. But it's beautiful, and now…I could not wish it be any other way. My past will always be here." He touched the original part of the necklace. "I will always have love for Paulina. But you have my heart, Maddy. You have reminded me of the beauty of love, have made me open again. You've made me feel. The love I have now…it's endless. Limitless. It's for you. For the family we will have. And it's because of you. I truly understand now what it means to be one with someone. I feel as though you are a part of me. It is unlike anything I've ever known before. I can only hope I have not managed to kill the love you felt for me."

She took a step forward and wrapped her arms around his neck, burying her face in the crook of his neck. She inhaled deeply. Aleksei. Her love.

"No, Aleksei. You haven't killed my love for you. I don't think that's possible."

His chest rose harshly against hers as he sucked in a breath. "Oh, Maddy, you have no idea how happy I am to hear that."

"You are the man that stands before me because of this." She touched the necklace. "I will never ask you to forget."

"I know, Maddy. I can remember now. Remember and feel some happiness for what was, feel hope for what is to come."

She pulled away from him and he set the velvet case on one of the tables that was set up on the balcony. He carefully lifted the necklace from its place in the box. "I love you, Maddy," he said, holding the necklace up and gently looping the ends around her neck, clasping it deftly. "You are my future, my hope. I love you."

She felt a tear spill down her cheek. Aleksei wiped it away. "Aleksei, you know my past, and you love me anyway. You've helped *me* to love me. And I know, with certainty, that you're my future."

He leaned in and kissed her, and Maddy returned it with all of the joy that was fizzing through her body.

When they separated, Aleksei cupped her chin, his dark eyes serious. "I'm so sorry, Maddy. I promised you honesty, always, and I didn't give it to you. I lied to you. I told you I didn't want you or your love, when even then I wanted both so desperately it destroyed me to send you away. But I had to become a man who was worthy of you. I had to let go—" he touched the center gem of the necklace "—to move on."

"Aleks, you idiot. Don't ever try to protect me by breaking my heart again," she said through a watery laugh.

"It broke mine. I didn't realize that was possible." He bent and kissed her again softly, gently. "I love you, Maddy, more than I thought it was possible to love someone. You are essential to me. I feel as though a piece of myself was missing, and now I'm complete."

"Wow, you don't go halfway, do you?"

"Never." He stroked her cheek. "Thank you for making my future more beautiful than I imagined possible."

"I have to thank you for the same thing," she said softly.

"So, you like the necklace?" he asked.

"Of course I do."

"If you want it." He reached into his pocket and produced another velvet box, this one smaller. "I have a matching piece."

"Aleks…"

He opened it and revealed a ring with colorful gemstones encircling an emerald-cut diamond, tiny platinum vines carved into the band. "If you'll marry me, then it was worth the burn that I got making it."

"Yes," she whispered as she held out her shaking hand. He slipped it onto her finger. A perfect fit, in every way.

"When I said future, I meant future. Every day of it. There are no guarantees in life, Maddy, but one thing I can promise is that you have my love."

"Then I don't need any other guarantees."

EPILOGUE

"Do you know how happy it makes me to see you like this? With a smile on your face?"

Maddy looked up at her older brother and squeezed his arm. "Thank you, Gage. It means a lot to me that you came to give me away."

"I wouldn't miss it."

"You really took care of me when no one else would. I don't know if I've ever told you how much that meant to me."

Gage looked at her. "It was never a sacrifice, Maddy. I would do it again in a heartbeat. I love you."

"I love you too."

Maddy smiled and craned her neck to see if she could spot Aleksei down the hill. The wedding was being held outside of the castle in Luxembourg. And tonight they were having their honeymoon in that princess suite Maddy had been so fond of.

The trees had white and red paper lanterns in them, and each chair was draped in white chiffon, the covers tied on with red bows. It was all exquisitely beautiful, and perfect. The wedding of her dreams.

The setting didn't really matter, though. The only thing that really mattered was the groom, and how much she loved him.

The first song ended and Maddy knew the "Wedding March" was about to begin. Butterflies swirled in her belly. Not nerves, just pure, unreserved excitement.

She smoothed the full skirt of her wedding gown and gripped her bouquet of red roses tightly.

"Ready?" Gage asked.

"More than," Maddy said.

As she walked down the green hill and to the aisle, Aleksei came into view. He smiled when he saw her, his dark eyes glittering.

In Aleks's eyes she saw her future. A life stretched before them filled with endless possibilities. A family. Children. Love. So much love that she couldn't contain all of it inside of herself. It was her own fairytale, come to life and more brilliant than anything she could have ever dreamed up on her own.

They had conquered so much darkness, overcome so much to reach this moment. With all of that behind them, there was nothing that could defeat them. Not when they were bound together by so much love.

Aleksei shook Gage's hand when they reached the head of the aisle. Then it was just her and Aleksei.

He took her hand and pressed his lips to her knuckles. "You're beautiful," he said.

And she believed him.

* * * * *

THE CINDERELLA BRIDE

Barbara Wallace

Barbara Wallace has been a life-long romantic and day-dreamer, so it's not surprising she decided to become a writer at age eight. However, it wasn't until a co-worker handed her a romance novel that she knew where her stories belonged. For years she limited her dream to nights, weekends, and commuter train trips, while working as a communications specialist, PR freelancer and full-time mother. At the urging of her family she finally chucked the day job and pursued writing full time—and couldn't be happier.

Barbara lives in Massachusetts with her husband, their teenage son, and two very spoiled, self-centred cats (as if there could be any other kind). Readers can visit her at www.barbarawallace.com, and find her on Facebook. She'd love to hear from you.

Look for a new book from Barbara Wallace in the New Year!

Dear Reader,

I'm married to a sailing enthusiast. On our first date he took me to a maritime museum and while, as a landlubber, I was only mildly entertained by the exhibits, I knew this sea-loving Prince Charming was the man for me. So when I started writing *The Cinderella Bride* it seemed only fitting that Emma O'Rourke's prince sailed into Boston Harbour to sweep her off her feet.

Of course, Emma doesn't recognise her prince. How can she when she doesn't believe in fairytales or happy endings? Then again, neither does Gideon Kent. Both of them are so convinced dreams don't come true they can't see what's standing right in front of them. Fortunately, love has a way of bringing out the dream in all of us. Gideon and Emma are about to find out that, with the right person, fairytales *can* come true.

Emma reminded me of so many women I know— hardworking, dedicated, and practical-minded to a fault. I loved giving her a happy ending. And Gideon—well, I fell in love with him the minute he stepped on the page. I hope you enjoy reading their journey towards each other as much as I enjoyed creating it.

Best wishes,

Barbara Wallace

PS: As I mentioned above, I am a hopeless landlubber, married to a sailor. I tried to get the nautical terms as correct as possible, but if I missed one I hope you'll understand.

To Peter and Andrew, who put up with a lot so I could chase my dream of becoming a published author, and to Mom and Dad, who always believed I could do it.

CHAPTER ONE

NORMAL bosses didn't make their secretaries risk pneumonia hand-delivering financials. They let them stay in nice dry offices, typing on computers and answering the phone.

Unfortunately, Emma O'Rourke mused, she didn't have a normal boss. She worked for Mariah Kent, and when the matriarch of Kent Hotels said "jump," you didn't just jump, you asked how high, how far and if you should pack a parachute.

And so here she was, freezing on the docks of Boston Harbor.

No matter what, do not leave that dock without Gideon's response. Mrs. Kent's orders were beyond explicit. Emma sighed. Days like today she really, really hated her job.

Teeth clacking, she wrapped her blazer a little tighter, the thick manila envelope clutched against her chest crackling. She should have worn a coat. The navy-blue hotel uniform was designed to look crisp and efficient, not to withstand the elements. While downtown the skyscrapers created a sort of insulated bubble, here on the harbor the wind blew off the water, turning an already gray day raw. There was a mist in the air, too, moisture Emma swore hadn't appeared until she'd exited the parking garage.

Off in the distance, a boat zigzagged its way across the water, white sails billowing. Who sailed in New England in October, anyway? Apparently Mariah Kent's prodigal grandson. From the way he kept sailing parallel to the marina, he wasn't in a hurry to come home.

The mist turned to drizzle. Terrific. Now Emma's misery was complete. She freed a strand of copper hair from her damp cheek. By the time she got back to the Fairlane, she was going to look like a drowned rat.

"Hey!"

A brusque voice pulled her attention back to the water. Son of a gun, the boat was actually drifting toward the pier. A lone man knelt at the front, fussing beneath the front sail. He wore a baseball cap and nylon pants. As the boat drifted closer, he lifted his arm, and she saw a large split in the seam of his fisherman's sweater.

This was Gideon Kent, the prized grandson she'd stood freezing for?

Thud! A thick coil of rope landed on the dock. Emma jumped back to avoid it hitting her feet.

"Loop that over the piling."

Apparently he meant her. She looked around for a dry place to leave the envelope. There wasn't one, so she tucked the papers under her arm. The rope was coarse and wet, with a large loop at one end. Grimacing at the sogginess oozing around her fingers, she slipped the loop over a nearby post and stepped back.

"Not like that," he snapped. "Go up through the other eye splice, then over the piling."

It mattered?

"So the other boat can get out," he added, reading her thoughts.

Oh, sure. The owner of the other boat probably couldn't wait to sail on a day like today. She grabbed the rope again.

Naturally, Gideon's boat drifted with the current, dragging the line taut, and forcing her to pull with both hands in order to gain slack. Something that wasn't so easy to do with an envelope under your arm. Eventually, however, after much wrestling, she inched the soggy cable free. She had no clue what an eye splice was, but there was a gap where the other rope was tied to the pole. Water streamed onto her shoes as she folded the rope and threaded it through the space, as if threading a needle. Since no one bellowed a correction at her, she assumed she had guessed correctly.

"When you're done, you can head aft and do the same with the stern line," he said instead.

He was kidding right? He expected her to do this a second time? "Mr. Kent—"

"Boat's not going to secure itself."

"Boat's not going to secure itself," Emma muttered under her breath as she walked down the pier toward the second rope. Like the first, the thick nylon was waterlogged, leaving her hands wet and her legs splattered with seawater.

"The line secure?" he asked a couple seconds later.

If it wasn't, he could secure the darn thing himself. She stepped aside so he could see her handiwork.

"Good job," he stated. Despite her annoyance, the compliment gave her a rush of pride. "Now you can tell me what you're doing here."

Besides freezing to death? Unable to find a place to wipe her hands, Emma stuffed them into her pockets, discreetly drying them on her skirt lining. "I'm Emma O'Rourke, your grandmother's personal assistant," she said.

Gideon didn't respond, choosing instead to look her up and down assessingly. Her brief moment of pride faded, replaced by a familiar self-consciousness that washed over her from head to toe. Suppressing the urge to duck her head, she held out the rain-spotted envelope. "Mrs. Kent wanted me to deliver this."

Still no response. He stared for several more seconds, as if she'd just offered him a drowned rat, then turned away in dismissal.

Emma sniffed in surprise. Maybe he hadn't heard her, what with the wind and all. "Mr. Kent—"

"You can put the financials in the cabin."

Apparently he had heard her. He gave her another one of those assessing looks. "That's what's in the envelope, right? Financials for the last, what, two years?"

"Three."

"Like the extra year would tip the scale." He said the words so softly Emma doubted she was supposed to hear. When Mrs. Kent had first told her of Gideon's visit, she'd said her grandson was somewhat estranged from the family. "Just throw them on the desk," he said, with a resigned sigh that, again, she wondered if she were supposed to hear.

"I'm afraid it's not that simple," she replied.

"Why? Don't tell me you like standing around in the rain."

Oh, sure, didn't everyone? "There's a letter in the packet, and your grandmother expects a response."

"Mariah expects a lot of things." He wiped his hands on his thighs. "Doesn't mean you have to listen."

He was kidding, right? Everyone listened to Mariah Kent. Not listening to her would be like...

Like saying no to your grandmother.

"I only need five minutes," Emma insisted. "Then I'll be out of your hair."

"Appreciate the expediency, but that's five more minutes than I have at the moment. According to the weather forecast, this rain's going to turn into a major storm front. I really do have to fasten down the boat."

Yay, Emma thought to herself. "Exactly how long does fastening down take?"

"As long as it takes." Stepping to the edge of the boat, he ducked his head under the lifeline and leaned close. "So I hope you like rain, Miss..."

Emma blinked. Up close his eyes went from merely scrutinizing to downright penetrating. A shade lighter than a sunny day, they had a blue brilliance that hit you long before you looked into them. Heat, the first warmth she'd felt since arriving at the marina, rippled through her.

He arched a brow, and she realized he was waiting for an acknowledgment. "O'Rourke. Emma O'Rourke. And I'll be fine."

"Fine?" Skepticism laced his voice.

"Don't have much choice, do I? Your grandmother expects me to return with an answer."

"Do you always do what Mariah wants?"

"It's my job."

"It's above and beyond," he replied, returning to the sails. "You must have a masochistic streak."

No, just a healthy distaste for unemployment.

Although at the moment, standing in line at the benefits office did hold a certain appeal. Emma shifted her weight from foot to foot, hoping motion might jump-start the circulation in her legs. What on earth had made her think she didn't need a coat?

"Do you want some help?" she called up to Gideon. "Two hands would make the job go faster."

He glanced at her over his shoulder. "Have you ever been on a boat?"

"Does the Charlestown ferry count?"

"No, it doesn't." He resumed his work. "And you wouldn't

be helping. It would take me twice as long to explain what to do."

Unfortunately, he was probably right. She watched him wrap the sail around the boom with the arrogant grace of a man who'd completed the task hundreds of times. Every so often the wind would gust, causing the canvas to billow, and turning the waves around the pier choppy. But he maintained control, steadying himself on what she realized must be incredibly strong legs. A man in charge of his environment.

In spite of her annoyance, she was impressed.

"You know," he said, jarring her from her thoughts, "playing Little Match Girl won't make me go faster, either."

Emma gave him a confused look. "Playing who?"

"Little Match Girl. You know, the little girl trudging through the snowstorm looking for someone to buy some matches? It's a children's fable."

"I must have missed that one." She wasn't much into fairy tales. Wishing for Prince Charming was more her mother's style.

"She dies."

"What?" Emma looked up in surprise.

"The Little Match Girl. She dies. Freezes to death, actually."

Now that sounded more realistic. "Don't worry," Emma said, pretty sure he wasn't. "I'm not planning on dying."

"Uh-huh."

"Really, I'm fine." Of course, if he actually felt concern, he would give her five minutes. They'd spent almost that long arguing about the match girl.

The drizzle grew heavier, hard enough to qualify as light rain now. Emma wiped the moisture from her face. Maybe she was carrying job dedication too far. Surely Mrs. Kent would understand if she opted against catching pneumonia while her grandson played stubborn little games.

No matter what, do not leave that dock without Gideon's response.

She sighed. Apparently Mrs. Kent knew her grandson all too well.

Oh, for crying out loud... Gideon tied the line off with a yank. Mariah had done this on purpose, sending some willowy, doe-eyed sentry to stand in the rain and make him feel guilty. And it had worked, dammit. Only a heartless ogre could concentrate with those brown eyes watching him.

"Why don't you go wait someplace warm?" he snapped. He wasn't giving her a choice, although she acted as if he was.

"I told you, I'm fine."

Right. That's why she was shivering.

No, not shivering. Bouncing. Rising up and down on her toes and trying desperately to hide her discomfort. Rain beaded on her flimsy hotel uniform as well as on her hair, turning it to burnished copper.

Dammit. Dropping the rope, he channeled all his annoyance into one last sigh and stepped onto the dock. "Come on."

Little Miss Match Girl started; she'd been lost in thought.

"You said you needed five minutes," he said. "I'm giving you five minutes."

As she had with her misery before, she tried disguising her relief, and failed. "I thought you were fastening down the boat."

"I changed my mind. Now come on. And watch your step."

He took her by the elbow and propelled her aboard. The

warmth of her skin surprised him. He would have guessed it would feel as cold as the weather.

"Where are we going?" she asked.

"To the cabin. You might not mind standing in the rain, but I prefer to conduct business inside where it's dry."

Her heels clattered as she dutifully accompanied him, her steps, he noted, matching his stride for stride. For a Little Match Girl, she wasn't all that little. In fact, she was close to his height. That made her, what—five foot ten or so without heels? Funny, when he first saw her, he'd thought she was smaller, more waiflike. He blamed those soft, brown eyes.

Warm air drifted up around them as he removed the hatch boards. He'd fired up the wood stove at sunrise and the trapped heat remained. Feeling it wash over him, Gideon realized exactly how cold he was after hours of exposure in the raw New England air. His body literally ached, he was so stiff and frozen. He could only imagine how Miss O'Rourke felt. Had she really intended to stand in the elements, waiting for him to finish? Because Mariah asked her to?

"Ooomph!"

Distracted by his thoughts, he hadn't noticed his visitor had stopped halfway down the companionway steps. His chest collided with her back, pitching her forward, and he had to grab her around the waist to keep her from falling. He might as well have grabbed a live ember from the stove. Heat rushed from her body to his. No longer cold or numb, he sucked in his breath, catching an intriguing whiff of vanilla as he did so.

He found himself speaking into her hair. "Something wrong, Miss O'Rourke?"

"I—um, no. It's just…this is lovely."

"It's even better once you're fully inside."

"Right. Sorry. For a second, I was… Never mind." She

scampered down the last two steps and into the cabin. "Do you live here? On board?"

"When I can. My main house in Casco Bay."

"In Saint Martin. Your grandmother told me," she explained.

"Oh." What other details about his life had Mariah shared? Certainly not the biggest. That particular skeleton was buried way back in the Kent family closet.

Suddenly he was cold again, particularly his insides. Surprising how quickly the body heat dissipated once Miss O'Rourke moved away. "I need a cup of coffee. You want some?"

She looked at him as if he'd offered her the Holy Grail, but shook her head. "That's all right. I'm fine."

"Fine?"

"Uh-huh, fine."

Fine. It was the fifth time she'd said it, and he hated that word. As far as he was concerned, it the most irritating, dishonest word in the English language. Clearly, she was not fine. She was wet, windblown and hugging that wretched envelope as if it were insulation. And from the flash he'd caught in those brown eyes, she really, really wanted a cup of coffee.

For some reason, her refusal irritated him almost as much as, if not more than, her Little Match Girl act.

Exhaling, he strode toward her, stopping only when the gap between them had closed to a few inches. "Last time I checked," he said, slowly pulling the envelope from her grip, "they didn't give out bonuses for stoicism." He tossed the package on his desk. "So sit down, Miss O'Rourke, and have some coffee."

Emma didn't sit down. She stood frozen in place, listening to the sound of metal clanking against metal coming from the kitchen area. Though she hated to admit it, part of her was glad Gideon was forcing coffee on her. A strange combination of hot and cold, unlike anything she'd ever experienced, gripped her body. Her fingers and toes were number than numb, but her torso, at least the part where Gideon's body had collided with hers, couldn't be warmer.

She hadn't meant to stop short on the stairs, but she'd been caught off guard. From Gideon's scruffy appearance, she'd expected some jumbled sailor's quarters filled with maps and equipment, not a haven of intimate elegance. With its cherry wood and wine-colored upholstery, the cabin was nicer than her own apartment. For a moment she'd been afraid to leave the steps lest she track water on the gleaming wood floor.

Fur brushed her leg, startling her into movement. Squatting, she came face-to-face with a large black cat. He looked at her with yellow eyes that rivaled Gideon's for intensity, and let out a hoarse meow.

"Well, hello there, you." She leaned down and scratched under the cat's chin. A sound resembling a small engine filled the cabin.

"You'll never get rid of him now." Gideon appeared bearing two steaming mugs. He thrust one in her direction. "Here, warm up while you talk. Do you want milk?"

The coffee did smell wonderful. Emma took the mug, pausing a moment to press it against her breastbone. The warmth spreading through her torso wasn't like the heat that had shot through her a few minutes before, but it was comforting nonetheless.

Meanwhile, her furry friend, annoyed that she'd removed her fingers from his fur, meowed and butted his head against her leg.

"Told you that you'd never get rid of him," Gideon said.

"I don't mind. He's very friendly."

"Easy to be friendly when you assume the whole world

exists to do your bidding. Kind of like someone else we know," he added with a smirk. "Do you want milk?"

"No, black is fine."

Gideon gave her a look as he passed toward the galley.

"I thought sailors were superstitious," she called after him. "Aren't black cats supposed to be bad luck?"

"Black cats, maybe," he called back, "but Hinckley doesn't believe he's a cat. More like an old man with fur." Gideon reappeared with a small bowl, which he set on the floor next to the steps. Hinckley raced over and began lapping with abandon, sending splatters of milk across the floor. That's when Emma noticed the space where his left hind leg should have been.

"An old man who's already had some bad luck," she observed.

"You mean the leg. A dog mauled him. By the time we crossed paths, the limb was too damaged to save, so the vet amputated."

"Doesn't seem to hold him back."

"Fortunately, the loss occurred when he was a kitten. It's harder when you're old enough to know what you've lost."

He added the last line in a lower voice, directed more to his coffee than to her. Emma almost thought they were talking about something other than the cat.

Silence filled the cabin as they sipped their coffee. Hinckley, having finished his milk, jumped up next to her and began to bath, using her thigh as a backstop. Smiling, she ran her fingertips through his fur. The cat responded by restarting his internal engine and laying his head on her lap.

"You like that, do you, sweetie?" Emma purred back.

The sound of Gideon clearing his throat brought the moment to an end. "You said you needed five minutes."

"Right." For a second there, she'd felt as at home as the cat, and acted that way. How embarrassing.

She looked around for the envelope, spotting it on Gideon's desk. Retrieving it would mean disturbing the cat. "Your grandmother enclosed a note with the financials, explaining everything."

"Why don't you give me the short version."

There wasn't exactly a long version. The note Mrs. Kent had enclosed was handwritten, and contained, at most, four lines. "She asks that you come to the office this afternoon. For a tea party."

His laugh was rich and throaty. "You're kidding, right? Mariah made you stand in the rain to tell me that?"

No, Mrs. Kent had asked her to hand-deliver the request. He had made her stand in the rain. "She wanted to be certain you received her invitation."

"You mean she wanted to make sure I didn't ignore it."

Was that a possibility? Given his earlier stubbornness, perhaps it was. Mrs. Kent's insistence that Emma stick around was making more and more sense. "She's simply happy you're back in Boston."

"She'd be the only one."

There it was again, the murmured tone that Emma wondered if she was supposed to hear.

"And what time is this little summit with crumpets?" he asked.

"Three o'clock."

"And not a moment before, right?" he said, smiling.

He knew. Emma couldn't help smiling back. Mrs. Kent made a lot of demands and requests, but she had one cardinal rule that trumped everything else: never interrupt her during *All My Loves*. Even her two sons, Jonathan and Andrew, knew the rule. Apparently, so did her grandson.

"Some things never change." For the first time since her arrival, she saw affection light up his eyes. "She still jotting off angry letters to the writers, too?"

"I've typed up five or six."

"She's easing up." Smile still in place, he raised his mug.

He took a long drink. Emma had never paid attention to the way a man drank before, but found herself unable to help watching Gideon. With the tension gone from his jaw, his mouth had a sensual quality to it. Soft and strong at the same time. And deliberate, she thought, noting the way his top lip slowly curled over the rim.

"So—" her own mouth had grown dry and she took a quick drink "—can I tell your grandmother you'll be there?"

Gideon finished his coffee, then set the mug on a nearby table. "I think it's been more than five minutes," he said, standing. "I have a deck to finish."

"What about tea?"

"You're welcome to stay and finish your coffee. Hinckley, I'm sure, would enjoy the company."

"What about—"

"Next time, I suggest you dress for the weather."

"Mr. Kent, please." He had one foot on the stair. Emma stood and caught his arm before he could take another step. She heard his sharp intake of breath as he turned around. Or maybe it was hers, as she reacted to the proximity of his stare. Was it her imagination or had his eyes changed shades, growing darker and more blue? "What should I tell your grandmother?"

That same stare traveled from her face to the hand on his arm. Slowly, he pulled away.

"Tell Mariah," he said, with a look that was enigmatic at best, "that she'll have to wait and see."

CHAPTER TWO

I<small>T TOOK</small> less than a minute for Emma to follow Gideon topside. He felt her before he heard the click of her heels. Funny that, for someone he barely knew, she was quite predictable.

He was tossing fenders over the side to prevent the boat from smashing against the dock. When she passed him, he looked up. Their eyes locked, and he caught the full brunt of her perplexed annoyance. Clearly, she didn't appreciate his parting response. She had expected a concrete answer, and now no doubt thought he was being difficult for no reason.

She didn't realize that where Mariah was concerned, difficult was the name of the game. Especially when she wanted something. And she definitely wanted something. Case in point, sending the intriguing Miss O'Rourke instead of a courier service. Admiration stirred Gideon's blood as he watched the secretary's hips sway in cadence with her long legs. A courier service he could dismiss, but Miss O'Rourke… She was decidedly undismissable. A little too girl-next-door than he normally preferred, but impossible to ignore, nonetheless. He thought of her body pressed against his, and smiled, the memory chasing away the cold.

Definitely impossible to ignore. And dollars to doughnuts, when she dried out, she'd be even more so. He stole another glance, and felt a new rush of heat. He could use a diversion on this visit. Unfortunately, Miss O'Rourke seemed like the kind of sweet young thing who expected long-term, and he didn't do long-term. If such a thing even existed. What number wife was Uncle Andrew on these days? Two? Three?

Then there were Gideon's parents, the poster children for false fronts. If Shakespeare were still alive, they'd inspire one heck of a farce.

No sir, long-term definitely didn't exist.

Why on earth was he thinking about relationships, anyway? Must be Boston, he decided, dropping another fender. Being back churned up thoughts he normally kept buried.

Fifteen minutes later, satisfied that the boat was secure, he returned to the cabin. Mariah's package lay on the desk where he'd left it. Three years of financials. What was his grandmother thinking?

"Does she think I'm going to see the numbers and suddenly return to the fold?" he asked Hinckley.

Well, the joke was on her. He followed the market. Kent Hotels might have stagnated a little over the last couple years, but they were basically healthy. The company didn't need him. Besides, it wasn't as if he belonged there, anyway.

So why'd you come back?

He'd asked himself that question all the way from Saint Martin, and the answer always came back to one thing: for Mariah. Had the request come from anyone else, he would have told them, in no uncertain terms, to leave him alone. But the request hadn't come from anyone else. And Mariah was the one Kent tie Gideon couldn't sever. Mariah, who had touched his cheek and told him his secret didn't matter.

A lie, of course, but one that, at the time, was exactly what his distraught nineteen-year-old mind had needed to hear.

Hinckley yawned and rolled over. Gideon ran a hand across the cat's exposed belly, and the cabin filled with purring. Out of the corner of his eye, he saw the envelope. The stupid thing was mocking him. If he had any common sense at all, he'd ditch the package overboard, turn the boat around and sail back to Casco Bay before Mariah could rope him into whatever she had planned.

Instead, he opened the flap. Rows upon rows of figures greeted his eyes. Along with a single piece of Mariah's personal stationery. "Time to come home, Gideon," read the familiar script. "Tea is at three sharp. Don't be late."

Time to come home. Gideon tossed the package aside with a sigh. "Home" for him was an illusion that had died years ago. Around the same time he'd stopped believing in long-term and true love ever after.

Achoo!

Emma shoved her clipboard in front of her face, hoping to muffle the sneeze. From the look on Mariah Kent's face, it didn't work. The silver-haired woman peered regally over her half-glasses. "You're not getting sick, are you, Emma?"

"No, ma'am." Just cold. This morning's adventure on the waterfront hadn't quite left her bones yet. Fortunately, she'd been able to snag a spare uniform from the employee laundry. The dress was a size too small and rode up her legs every time she walked, but at least it was dry. That was more than she could say for her hair. Her still-damp ponytail hung down her back like the tail of a wet Irish setter.

Mrs. Kent didn't look sold on her answer. "Make sure you order yourself a cup of tea just in case," she said. "We don't want your sniffles turning into anything worse. Is your throat sore, too?"

"No, ma'am." Emma didn't have sniffles, either, but she knew better than to argue. Instead, she gathered her notes and rose to leave. It was almost two o'clock. "Will that be all?"

Mrs. Kent was already on her way to the chaise lounge in the corner of her suite. "I believe so. No, wait!" The older woman smiled. "Tell the kitchen to include extra meringue petit fours. Gideon will like those."

If he shows up, thought Emma as she dutifully jotted down the request. His vague response had rubbed at her the whole way back from the waterfront. Tell Mariah she'll have to wait and see. Emma had stood out in the rain for that?

Mrs. Kent had taken his response in stride, chuckling about her grandson's stubbornness. "He always did hate being told what to do," she'd replied. "He'll be here, though. He's a good boy, and I can always count on him to do the right thing. Eventually."

The sound of voices brought Emma back to reality. She looked to the armoire and saw a beautiful blonde woman sobbing on the television.

"Oh, for crying out loud," Mrs. Kent muttered. "Are you still pining over that ex-husband? Make up your mind already."

Emma smiled as she headed to the door. The change from regal businesswoman to obsessed soap fan never ceased to amuse her. It was a side of the Kent matriarch most people didn't see, the softer, grandmotherly side, and it made it easier to endure some of the more outrageous demands of her job. Like this morning's debacle.

With Mrs. Kent sequestered for the next hour, she had time to catch up on the work she'd missed this morning. Gideon had joked about her diligence, but Emma prided herself on being responsible. After all, someone had to be.

She placed a call to the chef confirming today's tea

service, including the extra petit fours, then boiled a pot of water with the miniature coffeemaker she kept stashed behind her desk. Despite Mrs. Kent's insistence that she order coffee or tea from guest services, she felt more comfortable providing her own.

Fifteen minutes later she was inhaling the soothing aroma of orange pekoe. Mrs. Kent was right; tea did chase away the cold. Closing her eyes, Emma took a deep breath, then another, letting the warmth spread from her lungs to her body. Little by little the chill finally fled. She kicked off her pumps and flexed her nearly thawed toes. How on earth did people like Gideon stand being out in the elements for hours on end? In nothing but a ratty sweater, no less.

Maybe that explained the gruffness, she thought, taking a sip. His insides were frozen.

No, check that. She thought of their collision on the stairs. He was anything but frozen. One brief contact had been enough to melt her insides. The memory made her shiver.

"Told you you'd catch a chill," a voice whispered in her ear.

"What the—" Emma started and dropped her cup. Tea sloshed everywhere. "Didn't your mother ever tell you not to sneak up on people?" she snapped.

The skin on the back of her hand stung where the tea had splashed. Shaking her fingers, she looked up into Gideon's blue eyes.

"On the contrary," he replied. "She preferred I make as little noise as possible." He nodded toward Emma's hand. "Did you burn yourself?"

"Nothing life threatening," she replied, regretting her outburst. "I'll be fine."

He made a sound resembling a strangled cough, and handed her a wad of tissues. "Here, dry yourself off."

"Thank—" The words died in her throat as his fingertips

grazed the back of her hand, causing a flutter in the pit of her stomach. Startled again, she jerked away, letting the tissues float downward.

"Miss O'Rourke?"

"Yes?" His eyes had turned the most mesmerizing shade of sapphire. She couldn't stop staring at them. Not even when he nodded toward her desk.

"Your tea is pooling."

Emma blinked.

Her tea! Shaking off the trance, she saw a brown puddle spreading across her desk. Having ruined the correspondence she'd spent the last hour typing, it was making tracks toward the stack of manila files next to her phone.

"Oh no!" She grabbed another handful of tissues and threw them on the spill, hoping to stem the flow. The file contained original drawings for a renovation project at the Manhattan flagship hotel.

"Allow me." Gideon lifted the file so she could blot underneath. "Looks like your paperwork caught the brunt of the spill."

"Lucky me," she muttered, snatching more tissues. His chuckle would have annoyed her if she wasn't already battling embarrassment. She could feel Gideon watching her, the scrutiny flustering her so much that she nearly knocked over her remaining tea.

"You know," he said, moving the cup out of her reach, "you were pretty lost in thought back there. Mind if I ask what had you so faraway?"

"Nothing important." Just him.

"Must have been somewhat important, because I knocked twice and you didn't hear me."

Emma's cheeks burned. She concentrated on throwing away lumps of wet tissues, hoping he wouldn't notice. "Your grandmother is waiting for you."

"I still have ten minutes. You know how she is about the daily cliff-hanger. Tell me, is anyone else attending this meeting?"

"Only you and Mrs. Kent as far as I know."

"Oh."

His voice had dropped a notch, sounding almost…disappointed? Emma abandoned her futile attempt to save the correspondence, and looked up. "Were you expecting someone else?"

"Not really." His answer had a note of forced nonchalance, then he changed the topic. "What's the damage?"

Substantial. The morning's mail was ruined, as was tomorrow's agenda notes and a half-dozen employee memos. Just thinking about how much time she would need to reprint them made Emma sigh aloud. "Fortunately, you saved the most important paperwork."

"You mean this?"

Opening the file, he started thumbing through the contents, his expression growing thoughtful. "We're renovating the Landmark?"

"So I've been told. Your uncle Andrew dropped off the designs this morning."

"Interesting. What do you think?"

"I only pass along the information," she replied. "I don't evaluate it."

"Is that diplomatic speak for 'I don't like it'?" He leaned forward, his eyes lit with what could only be described as mischief. "Come on, Miss O'Rourke, we both know you looked at the designs, if only to make sure the file was complete. What's your opinion?"

"I told you, I don't have one."

She reached for the folder, but he lifted it away. "Everyone has an opinion," he said. "Give me your-s."

The truth? Gideon had guessed right; she hated the design.

But she would never say so. The designer, Josh Silbermann, was considered the leader in contemporary design, and according to Andrew Kent, they were lucky to snag him. Since Andrew sat on more architectural and museum committees than she could count, she had to assume he knew what he was doing, and that she, in her inexperience, simply missed the point. "Your uncle is very excited about the plans."

Gideon looked unimpressed. "I'm sure he is. Andrew loves this sort of stuff. But you're avoiding my question. What is your opinion?"

"My opinion doesn't matter. I'm not the one making the decision."

He leaned forward. "Humor me."

"Why?"

"Because you're so determined to dodge the question, and that piques my curiosity. For example, what do you think of..." He fished through the file and pulled out a sketch, a stark study of gunmetal and black with splashes of ice blue. "What about this one?

She shook her head. Figures. He'd picked the ugliest sketch in the pile.

"Come on, Miss O'Rourke," Gideon urged, waving the sketch and grinning, "give it up."

Clearly, he wasn't going to stop until she said something. "Fine. It's cold."

"Cold?"

"The room. All that black and blue is far too harsh. I would prefer something warmer." Like the blue of your eyes, she caught herself thinking. "Plus the furniture looks uncomfortable."

"Really? Even these stainless steel padded benches?"

She caught the sarcasm. "I'm not sure even your cat would sleep on those."

"When I left, Hinckley was sleeping in the sink, so I wouldn't use him as a benchmark."

"I'm sure I'm simply missing the point."

"She says, desperately trying to regain her diplomacy," he replied with a chuckle. "Tell me, if you don't like this design, what do you like?"

Emma shrugged. Her experience in hotel rooms, particularly five-star hotel rooms, was limited to the Fairlane. "A comfortable bed."

"That's all? A good bed?"

"Okay, a very comfortable bed. What can I say? I'm practical. After all, that's where I'd be spending the bulk of my time, right?"

He arched a brow. "You don't say."

"Sleeping," she stated hastily. Heat flooded every inch of her, and the mischievous glint in his eye didn't help. "If I'm staying in a hotel room, it's because I need a place to sleep."

"Of course." The glint persisted. Emma fought another rush of heat.

"But," Gideon continued, "if all you want is a bed, you can go to the local motel. You go to a hotel like the Landmark because you want atmosphere."

"The best for the best," she replied, parroting hotel management's catch phrase.

"More than that. You have to exceed their expectations." With the file still in his grip, he perched on the corner of her desk, close enough that Emma noticed his windburned knuckles. Outdoorsman's hands. Raw and weathered from work. The hands of a man who wasn't afraid to use them.

"...fantasies."

She jerked her attention back to Gideon's questioning stare.

"I was saying that for some people, a hotel room is their

way of living out their fantasies," he said. "Which leads me back to my original question. What do you want in a hotel room?" He leaned a little closer. "Surely you have one or two fantasies of your own, Miss O'Rourke."

Beneath her ribs, Emma's heart skipped a beat. She could swear his eyes had grown two shades darker, as if he knew the path her mind had started to travel. It didn't help matters that his ear hovered close to her lips, as if he expected her to confess some little secret.

He's talking about hotel marketing, she reminded herself.

Yet the air between them had grown still. Disturbingly so. She hadn't realized before how Gideon's foot dangled perilously close to her calf. They hadn't made contact, but she could still feel him through her stockings.

She turned to her left, hoping to break the spell. "I doubt I could suggest anything marketing hasn't thought of already."

"Stop dodging the question."

"I'm not dodging." Not much, anyway. She grabbed the first stack of papers available and pretended to sort them. "I'm pretty basic when it comes to fantasies."

To her dismay, that earned her a melodic chuckle. "Anyone ever tell you that you're too serious, Miss O'Rourke?"

Better serious than foolish. "Maybe I'm just easy to satisfy."

"Oh, I hope not. That would be a shame."

Why? Emma glanced over her shoulder at him. He was studying her again, with that probing look that made her skin come alive. "Three o'clock," she said, saved by the chiming of her desk clock. "Your grandmother's free now."

"Time then for my command appearance." He rose and put the sketches back in the file. "This has been a very interesting conversation, Miss O'Rourke. We'll have to do it again sometime."

"Sure," she answered. Whenever you're killing time.

She tried to ignore the way her stomach somersaulted at the suggestion.

Mariah Kent might weigh ninety pounds dripping wet, but it was ninety pounds of reinforced steel. When Gideon entered her suite, he found her seated regally at her desk, the same desk from which she'd run Kent Hotels for close to thirty-five years. How many afternoons had he spent sitting next to that desk, watching her work, listening to her advice?

Treat every guest as if they're special, Gideon. Don't meet their expectations, exceed them.

Yes, Grandmother.

That was a lifetime ago, he thought with a sigh. Back when he'd been a different person and believed Kent Hotels was his destiny.

"This is how you dress to see your grandmother?" Mariah asked, surveying his appearance with disdain. He'd come straight from the boat, and other than exchanging jeans for nylon pants, he still wore his sailing gear. "I distinctly remember telling you when you were growing up to always wear a tie."

"Sorry."

"No, you're not." She raised her cheek for a kiss, then patted his, the sparkle in her pale blue eyes betraying her affection. "You could have at least shaved. Is this how you dress for business in Saint Martin?"

"What can I say? Your summons was rather short notice."

"Not that short. Emma's been back for at least two hours."

"Yes, about that..." He sat in the chair across from Mariah's desk. "Was the personal summons really necessary?"

"I was afraid you might lose your way, after being gone for so long."

"Lose my way or change my mind?"

"With you, both are possibilities." Mariah smoothed the front of her designer suit, a silver that matched her hair. "Fortunately, I knew Emma would see to it you found your way."

As if on cue, his grandmother's assistant appeared, holding open the door for a waiter pushing an overladen tea service. Back in her office, she'd been blocked by her desk, but now he could appreciate how nicely the straight blue dress hugged her silhouette. Too bad she wore the matching blazer. He'd much prefer seeing her arms. Instead, he settled for studying the smooth curve of her calves. The desk had masked them, too.

"Are you ready for them to serve, Mrs. Kent?" she asked.

"Yes, thank you. Did you order yourself a cup of tea like I suggested? You looked a little peaked."

"Yes, ma'am. I have a cup on my desk." Emma's eyes darted briefly in Gideon's direction, sparking the overwhelming urge to wink. If he did, he bet that pale skin would turn a very interesting shade of pink.

"Nice girl," Mariah said after Emma disappeared, leaving the floor butler to serve. "Takes her job seriously."

A little too seriously, thought Gideon. Then again, if their conversation had revealed anything, it was that Miss O'Rourke took a lot of things in life seriously. That didn't feel right, either, her practicality. What kind of woman didn't nurture a few romantic fantasies? The Caribbean was full of women her age champing at the bit for luxury and indulgence, and none of them, he wagered, would stand out in the rain because her job required it. If anyone should want pampering, it should be someone like Emma. But she didn't. She only wanted a comfortable bed.

He frowned. That wasn't right. Emma's lack of expectations were more suited to someone like him, someone with reason to be weary and cynical. Not a fresh-faced girl with freckles dotting her nose.

"Sugar?"

His grandmother's voice jerked him back to the present. From the other side of her desk, she eyed him with curiosity. "Do you still take three sugars?"

"No," he replied.

"Good. Too much sugar is bad for you, anyway," she said. "I'm glad you gave it up."

"I've given up a lot of things over the past ten years," he replied.

"Does that include your family?"

What family? "I've stayed in touch."

"Emails," Mariah said with a frown. "Christmas cards. Phone calls on birthdays. That's not keeping in touch."

"I've been busy."

"No, you've been avoiding us, and it's high time you stopped." She set her teacup on its saucer with a resounding clink. "You need to come home."

As if coming home was even possible. Forcing a lightness in his voice, Gideon replied, "Aren't I already here?"

"I mean for good." Mariah looked him square in the eye, her gaze reflecting every ounce of her mettle. "You're the eldest Kent grandchild. It's time you embraced your birthright."

Once upon a time those words would have meant everything to him. Now they simply lodged in his chest like an undigested meal. "Except for one thing," he replied.

Gideon leaned forward, dropping his voice to a conspiratorial murmur as he said what she seemed so intent on forgetting. "I'm not the eldest Kent grandchild."

Mariah didn't blink. She'd been expecting the comment,

after all. "Your last name is Kent. And I need your help. Those are the only two things that matter."

Surely you have one or two fantasies of your own.

Try as she might, Emma couldn't dislodge Gideon's comment from her head. Two hours after their conversation, his words continued to repeat themselves in cadence with the pages spitting out of the printer. Fantasies, fantasies, fantasies.

Just a comfortable bed.

What was so wrong with her answer? "Excuse me for being practical," she snapped at the printer. Dwelling on things out of her reach was a waste of time. She'd already spent too much of her life dealing with her mother's fantasy fallout. Emma didn't need disappointment of her own.

Which reminded her, she should call her mom and see if she found any leads at the unemployment office.

The printer made a loud clicking sound, drawing Emma's attention. Coming back to the present, she saw a red light blinking on the front panel.

"Don't tell me, I'm out of ink," she muttered. Great. At this rate she'd be forty before she got her desk cleared off.

That's what you get for thinking about fantasies.

Just then the door to Mrs. Kent's suite flew open. Gideon stared at her, his expression a study in tension. "Come on," he said, shutting the door. "I need a drink."

CHAPTER THREE

BEFORE Emma knew what was happening, he caught her elbow and pulled her toward the office door. "Do you know if the King Room serves a decent whiskey?"

"I, uh…" She was still trying to figure out why she was being dragged along.

"Never mind. They serve alcohol. We'll be fine."

"We?"

Gideon gave her a look. "You don't think I plan to drink alone, do you?"

So, what—he planned to drink with her? Nice of him to ask first. "I'm working."

"It's after five, Miss O'Rourke. Workday's over."

"For you, maybe, but I've got a pile of correspondence on my desk that your grandmother expects to go out in today's mail." Correspondence he'd helped delay.

"And the world must do what Mariah Kent expects, right?"

Emma started to say something about entitlement running in the family, but noted the tension in his jaw and thought better. Something had happened while Gideon was sequestered with his grandmother. He was paler, and his eyes, sharp and probing a couple hours earlier, had dulled. In fact, his whole demeanor had a weariness that hadn't existed before.

The transformation jarred her, to say the least. Watching him impatiently pressing the elevator button, she had the overwhelming urge to reach out and squeeze his hand.

Which was why, when the elevator doors opened, she stepped in.

Designed to resemble a gentlemen's club, the King Room was the Fairlane's jewel, a private hideaway where guests could relax in oak-paneled splendor. When she walked through the frosted-glass doors, Emma could have sworn every head in the room turned her way. She could feel the unwelcoming gazes. This was a haven for guests, not hotel employees. Self-consciousness in overdrive, she tugged on her dress, hoping the dim lighting concealed its snugness.

Gideon, on the other hand, crossed the room with the nonchalance of a man who belonged, despite the fact that his sweater and jeans violated the bar's dress code. Emma couldn't help but marvel at his ease. No one rushed forward to politely offer one of the hotel's spare jackets, either, she noticed. Perhaps his last name bought him acceptance, but somehow she suspected the circumstances would be the same anywhere, family-owned establishment or not.

No sooner had they taken their seats than a waitress with a black ponytail and a perfectly fitting uniform approached. She flashed Emma a skeptical look before turning her attention and smile on Gideon. "Good evening. Will you be having cocktails or dinner?"

"Bruichladdich, straight up," Gideon clipped.

Although the name meant nothing to Emma, it must have registered with the waitress, for her eyes lit up with an intrigued gleam. "Certainly, sir." Her voice grew a notch smokier, as well. "It might take a moment, however. Our manager will have to retrieve a bottle from our reserve."

Gideon shrugged. "Fine. Miss O'Rourke, join me?"

"I'll have tea," she replied. "With milk."

The waitress nodded without looking in her direction. Emma wondered if the woman had heard her.

"Tea, Miss O'Rourke?" Gideon shot her a disappointed look. "You're missing out on a seriously good whiskey."

No doubt, judging from the way he'd impressed the waitress. "I'm sure that's true, but I'm also still on the clock."

"Ah, yes, Mariah's correspondence. Tell me," he asked, once the waitress had departed, "do you always do everything Mariah asks?"

That was a silly question. "Of course I do. It's my job."

"That doesn't mean you have to jump when she says jump."

Then he didn't know what working for his grandmother entailed. "What am I supposed to, slack off?"

"Would you even be able to?"

"If you're asking do I take my job seriously, the answer's yes."

"Really? I never would have guessed."

His sarcastic tone rankled Emma. No matter how poorly his reunion with his grandmother had gone, he didn't have to take out his frustration by mocking her. "What can I say?" she snapped. "Not everyone is lucky enough to be born a Kent."

She regretted the comment the second she'd said it. Not only was it beyond impertinent, it caused a shadow to break over Gideon's features, turning them dark and increasing their marked weariness. "Oh yeah." His voice was low and dull. "It's a real stroke of luck."

He lapsed into silence after that, his long fingers drawing

patterns on the inlaid table. Emma stared at his wind-burned knuckles, wishing she'd bitten her tongue.

"I'm sorry," she said. "I had no right." When he didn't answer, she pushed herself away from the table. "Maybe I should just go and let—"

"Don't." Gideon reached out and caught her wrist. Barely a grip, but enough to stop her in her tracks.

"I thought maybe you'd like to be alone with your thoughts," she told him.

"If I wanted to be alone, I wouldn't have dragged you down here."

"But—"

"Sit down, Miss O'Rourke."

Slowly, she met his eyes. The blue had turned smoky, almost indigo in color. A new silence surrounded their table, heavier and more self-conscious than the one before. She looked down to where Gideon's fingers still encircled her wrist.

"Here you go." The waitress's voice broke the spell. She shot Emma an enigmatic look before placing a crystal tumbler in front of Gideon. "Sorry to keep you waiting, Mr. Kent."

Emma noticed that in addition to learning Gideon's identity, the waitress had undone two more buttons on her uniform. And was leaning forward more than usual. "If you need anything else, my name is Maddie. I'll be more than happy to accommodate you."

I'll bet. Emma tried not to roll her eyes. Talk about laying it on thick. Was Gideon impressed? "Do you have any artificial sweetener?" she asked.

Clearly annoyed at having to pull her attention away from him, the waitress shot her a glance. "We keep everything on the table," she replied in a sickeningly sweet voice.

Emma knew that; she was just curious to see what Maddie would do.

The waitress didn't disappoint. "Here, let me get it for you," she said, leaning over far more than necessary to reach across the table. As she did, she angled her body so that Gideon got a good view of her perfectly formed cleavage.

"Thanks," Emma replied, her bravado shrinking. She'd caught a glimpse herself when Maddie had bent over. If there were a real competition, Emma wouldn't stand a chance, and they both knew it.

She waited until Maddie walked—or rather, strutted—to her next table, then pushed the container back into place. "I guess word of your arrival has trickled down the grapevine. Hope you weren't trying to remain incognito."

"Hmm." Gideon was busy studying the contents of his tumbler. He hadn't spoken since asking Emma to stay. She rubbed her wrist, surprised how her skin still tingled. Her reaction to his touch unnerved her, but not nearly as much as his silence did. His withdrawal made her insides ache.

"Mr. Kent?" He looked up from the amber liquid. "Is there anything I can do for you?"

Her question earned her a very strange smile. "Trying to compete with our waitress, Miss O'Rourke?"

"Hardly. You just look…" she shrugged "…out of sorts."

"And you, diligent employee that you are, want to help."

"A simple 'I'm fine' would suffice."

"I hate that word." He smiled again. This time a sparkle appeared with it, one that swept away any annoyance. "How long have you worked for Mariah, Miss O'Rourke?"

Emma added milk to her tea. "A little over a year."

"Most of her assistants don't last that long."

"So I've heard."

"Must be all that diligence."

"I like your grandmother."

"Even when you're standing in the rain?"

Emma laughed. "Even then. As you said, she has a way of making people do what she wants."

"Don't I know it." Just like that, the sparkle dimmed from his eyes. Lifting his glass, he drained the whiskey in one long sip.

"Tell me something, Miss O'Rourke," he continued, studying his empty glass as he spoke. "Did you really dislike the Silbermann designs?"

"I didn't say I disliked them, per se."

"Miss O'Rourke…"

"I think your uncle Andrew is far more qualified to offer an opinion than I am."

"Besides, all you're interested in is a comfortable bed."

"Exactly."

Gideon nodded, and went back to studying his tumbler. Emma sipped her tea and tried not to squirm. Why did she feel like she'd given a wrong answer?

Surely you have one or two fantasies….

"Maybe we should put that theory to the test," she heard a voice say.

She lifted her eyes in time to see Gideon's mouth curve into a devastating smile. Awareness washed through her, pooling in one deep, very inappropriate spot. "Wh-what?"

Those eyes were bluer than blue as he leaned forward. The pool got a little deeper. "How would you like to go to Manhattan?"

Emma almost spat out her tea. "You mean, New York City?"

"Unless they move the buildings someplace else, yes, New York City."

"Oh, sure," she replied, realizing the question was rhetorical. Had to be rhetorical. "Right after I get back from Paris."

"I'm serious."

He was? She studied his expression. He was. "Why?"

"Why what?"

"Why are you asking me to go to New York?" There had to be a catch. The request was too spectacular, too out of the blue. People didn't just hand out trips to the Big Apple.

"Because I have to go, and I could use an assistant," he replied with a shrug.

And there it was. He needed a secretary. Emma should have realized that. Why else would he ask her?

"Does your grandmother know you're poaching her employees?" she asked.

"No, but I don't think she'll mind. The trip was her idea."

Emma sat back. "Really?"

"Unfortunately, yes. She wants me to meet with Ross Chamberlain."

Emma recognized the name from various memos and correspondence. He was Kent Hotels' largest nonfamily shareholder. "Why you—?" Her hand flew to her lips as she realized how insulting the question must sound. "Sorry. I only meant why isn't she sending one of the other Mr. Kents?" Why summon Gideon back to Boston, then send him to New York? That seemed a trifle eccentric, even for Mariah Kent.

"That, Miss O'Rourke, is the sixty-four-thousand-dollar question. Let's just say Mariah expects me to go."

And the world always did what she expected. Suddenly his earlier mood made sense.

But still, why take Emma along? Kent Hotels had a host of secretaries at his disposal. Both here and in New York.

"I don't want one of the secretaries in New York," he replied when she asked. "I want you."

She tried not to feel flattered by his answer. "What about your grandmother?"

"Believe me, Mariah will survive." He grinned. "I mean, it's not like I'm taking away *All My Loves*."

"Now that would be a real loss," Emma replied with a laugh.

"Then it's agreed. We'll leave tomorrow afternoon."

Emma's chuckle faded. "Tomorrow afternoon?"

"Is that a problem?"

"No, I suppose not. I just didn't realize you wanted to go so soon."

"The sooner I run this little 'errand,' the sooner I can get back to my own life. Can you arrange for the jet?"

"Certainly." Her head was swimming. She was flying to Manhattan. Tomorrow. That sort of thing didn't happen. Not in her world. A thrill tripped down her spine. "I'll go make the arrangements right now."

With that, she pushed herself away from the table. "Good night, Mr. Kent. Thank you for the tea."

"You're welcome. Don't work too hard. Oh, and Miss O'Rourke?" She was almost clear of the table when he called out to her.

"Yes, Mr. Kent?"

"We'll be staying at the Landmark." The corner of his mouth slowly quirked in a teasing smile that curled Emma's toes. "I'm looking forward to hearing how you like the bed."

"Manhattan?" Leaning against the counter, Janet O'Rourke tapped her cigarette against the ashtray she held in her freshly manicured hand. "Don't they have secretaries in New York? Why'd he ask you?"

Emma shrugged. "He said he didn't want a secretary from New York. He's going on a business trip for his grandmother. Maybe he feels more comfortable taking someone from her office. And since I'm the only one he knows..." She shrugged again. Since Gideon issued his invitation, she'd asked herself the same question multiple times, and that was the best answer she could come up with.

"Or maybe—" her mother's eyes widened "—he's interested in more than business."

"You've been watching too many movies, Mom."

Leave it to her mother to raise that theory. Janet O'Rourke saw romance everywhere. That was one of her biggest problems.

"You never know. Is he good-looking?"

"Attractive," Emma admitted. And yes, she did know. She knew because of all the times she spent alone, fending for herself because Janet found true love—again—only to have to nurse her through a broken heart days later.

Emma's shoulders suddenly felt heavy. "How'd job hunting go?" she asked, changing the subject. "Any good leads?"

"Nothing that piqued my interest."

Not a surprise. Most work failed to interest her mother. "Well, maybe tomorrow."

"Actually…"

Emma stiffened. Whenever her mother started a sentence with the word *actually*, what followed wasn't good.

"Mary O'Leary and I were thinking of heading to the casino tomorrow. With luck, I'll hit big on the slots and won't have to worry about work."

"Wouldn't that be nice." Another one of Janet's pipe dreams. Her mother had dozens of them, every one leading to disappointment.

And Gideon Kent wondered why Emma didn't want more than a comfortable bed. As far as she could tell, wanting more only cost you in the long run. You were better off not wanting at all.

Life was safer that way.

CHAPTER FOUR

"YOU expect me to what?"

Gideon couldn't decide which entertained him more: Hinckley making himself at home on the chaise lounge or the look on Mariah's face when he told her she would be cat-sitting. "I can't very well leave him locked on the boat while I'm gone. Someone has to feed him."

"That's what staff are for."

He didn't have the heart to tell her that in Hinckley's book, she was staff. Out of the corner of his eye he caught Emma's discreet smile, and resisted the urge to flash a conspiratorial wink.

Mariah's secretary was looking particularly blue today. Blue skirt, blue blazer, light blue turtleneck. Too bad this outfit wasn't as form-fitting as yesterday's dress. He liked seeing the curves.

"It's only for a couple days," he told his grandmother. "You won't even know he's here." Not much, anyway, he added silently as he watched Hinckley flop on his side. His length took up more than half the seat. "You're the one who asked me to go to New York."

"I didn't realize my request would result in wild animals being left on my doorstep. Bad enough you've stolen my secretary. By the way, Emma, do you have the latest earnings per share projections?"

"Yes, ma'am. Jonathan Kent dropped them off this morning."

Hearing his father's name, Gideon felt a dullness akin to an ache form in his chest. Since his return to Boston, he'd noticed the man who'd raised him had been conspicuously absent. Gideon couldn't really blame him. No one liked being reminded of his mistakes. Or his wife's. If he were in Jonathan's shoes, Gideon would stay away, too.

He swallowed back his emotions. "I'd like a copy of that report."

"Already done, Mr. Kent."

"I should have known. Now you know why I stole her," he said to Mariah. "Who could resist such efficiency?"

"Hmm. And making me suffer for sending you on this trip had nothing to do with it," his grandmother replied.

"Don't be silly. That's Hinckley's job. Miss O'Rourke sealed her own fate."

She stared at him, her eyes impossibly large and dark. "Excuse me, I what?"

"With your efficiency," he replied. "How could I possibly take another assistant? Especially on such an important trip."

Actually, he didn't really know why he had asked her along. He didn't need a secretary for this meeting. Hell, he didn't have to stay overnight. He could wrap up his business with Chamberlain in a few hours. Maybe he did want to punish Mariah.

It was that conversation they'd had about the Landmark, that's what it was. The whole exchange had started as harmless flirting, a diversion while waiting for Mariah's show to end. But then Emma refused to offer her opinion. For crying out loud, his secretary in Saint Martin shared her opinions on everything, from the state of office supplies to Hinckley's habit of leaving 'dead mice' on the office doorstep. Ninety-nine percent of the time, Gideon didn't even have to ask.

But he practically had to drag the answer out of Emma. Why? Especially when her opinion made sense. The design was cold.

And who on earth wanted nothing but a comfortable bed? That particular comment had gnawed at him all night long. Emma's pragmatism bothered him. A woman like her, fresh and sweet…shouldn't she be full of silly romantic notions like sunken tubs built for two and balconies looking out at the stars?

She definitely should want more than a good night's sleep, he thought, eyeing her blue-clad figure.

"As long as you keep Gerard Ambiteau in his place, you can take every secretary we have in the building," Mariah was saying. She pressed her fingers to the bridge of her nose. "That man has no scruples whatsoever. I can feel him out there. He's waited years to find our weak spot, and now he's just waiting till the timing is right to make his move."

You couldn't miss the stress in her voice. Though he'd grown up listening to rants about Gerard Ambiteau, this was the most worked up Gideon had ever seen his grandmother. She was worried—genuinely worried. She also had a point. Right now, Ross Chamberlain was a weak spot that Ambiteau could easily take advantage of.

"I'll talk sense into Ross, don't you worry," he assured her.

She smiled. "I know you will, darling. It's one of the reasons I asked you back home."

One of. He knew the other. The plan wasn't going to work.

Emma cleared her throat. "If you want to avoid rush hour

traffic, we should consider leaving soon. I've already called
the front desk. The car's ready whenever you are."

"See?" he said to Mariah. "Irresistibly efficient."

"I know. That's why I hired her."

"And why I poached her." He leaned over to kiss his
grandmother's cheek, then stepped over to scratch the top
of Hinckley's head. The cat was already sound asleep.
"Behave," he said.

"Are you talking to me or the creature?"

"I'll let you two fight it out. Be careful, though. Hinckley
fights dirty."

"So do I," Mariah replied.

Emma had retrieved her overnight bag and was already
at the elevator when he finished his goodbyes. He caught up
with her just as the doors slid open. "Are you ready to take
a bite out of the Big Apple, Miss O'Rourke?"

"Ready as I'll ever be," she replied with a nervous smile.

She looked uneasy. Had done so, he realized, since he'd
walked into Mariah's office. What was shyness yesterday
was now far more pronounced, almost anxiety. He could
see the tension in her ramrod posture as she stood beside
him, watching the numbers count down. Guilt pricked his
conscience.

"Everything all right?"

He watched her shoulders stiffen. "I'm fine," she replied
shortly.

"Are you sure?" There were smudges under her eyes, dark
hollows a shade lighter than her uniform. "You look tired."

"Really, I'm fine."

Then why was she chewing the inside of her cheek? It
was the Little Match Girl act all over again, he thought with
irritation. Why didn't she just say what was wrong instead
of playing martyr?

Unless… A thought struck him. "Miss O'Rourke," he

stated, "you're not anxious about being in New York with me, are you?"

She whipped her head around, her eyes a little wider than usual. "Of course not."

"Because I realize this trip is a little unorthodox."

"And I realize you wouldn't be anything but professional, no matter what— Never mind." She shook her head, leaving him to guess what she'd been about to say. "I'm fine, I promise."

He hated that word. There was no way on earth he was going to listen to her say it every five minutes on this trip.

The elevator doors parted and Emma started toward the lobby. "One minute, Miss O'Rourke." He stepped in front of her, blocking her progress. "Before we leave, we need to set a few ground rules."

"Ground rules?" Her features furrowed in confusion. "Like what?"

"First of all, I don't believe in mindless autonomy. I prefer my associates speak their minds. I expect you to speak your mind. Understand?"

She nodded.

"Good. Which leads me to ground rule number two. The next time you say the word *fine*, I'm going to hang you by that copper-colored ponytail of yours."

"What?" Her eyes grew dark and large, giving him a firsthand view of how expressive they could be. Expressive and innocent. Like the rest of her face. His own eyes fell to her lips, parted ever so slightly in surprise, and for a second he forgot what they were talking about.

She reminded him, however. "You don't want me saying the word *fine*?"

"No, I don't. Like I said, I prefer honest answers."

"'Fine' isn't honest?"

"My dear Miss O'Rourke." He caught her chin, forcing

her gaze to meet his, so there would be no misunderstanding what he was about to say. "Fine is the most dishonest answer there is."

He released her, surprised at how reluctant his fingers were to break contact. "Now," he continued, stuffing his hand in his pocket, "let's start over. You look a little off this afternoon, Miss O'Rourke. Is everything all right?"

"Everything's fi—" She caught herself. "I was up late working. This trip came on short notice, so I had to put in extra hours to make sure my desk was cleared." Her concluding scowl was worthy of the most sulky of teenagers.

"Now, that's more like it." Gideon felt a chuckle rising in his throat. Her eyes were sparkling now, like two big, annoyed diamonds. He liked the look. Slipping the overnight bag from her grasp, he swung it over his shoulder, cutting off her impending protest. "Come along. We have a plane to catch."

What kind of person banned another person from using a word? Especially a perfectly useful word like *fine*? Emma wondered, annoyed. She chewed the inside of her cheek as she allowed Gideon to guide her through the private terminal at Logan Airport. Bad enough her racing thoughts had kept her up half the night. Now she had to make her tired brain think of synonyms? She was having enough trouble acting as if she knew how to navigate her way through an airport.

The terrible truth was that she wasn't fine. She was uptight, exhausted and nervous as could be. Though not, as Gideon suggested, about going to New York with him. No, she was nervous about getting there. Although she'd arranged dozens of flights on the Kent corporate jet, she'd never actually seen the plane up close—she'd never seen a plane up close, period—and she was desperately trying to fake a practiced air.

Then there was Gideon, who overnight had morphed into a completely different person. Yesterday's sailor, while rugged and compelling, still had an element of accessibility to him. Blame the ratty sweater and faded jeans, or the day-old growth of beard, but she'd felt as if she could talk to him. That man was gone, replaced by a businessman in a charcoal-gray suit and a crisp shirt the color of his eyes. He dripped with wealth and power. Skycaps, attendants, security guards—they all straightened respectfully upon his approach. He moved through the terminal with entitled nonchalance, raincoat draped over his arm, wordlessly communicating to everyone that he was a man not just at one with his environment, but in command of it. A sexy prince, to the manor born.

When she boarded the jet, Emma could barely suppress her gasp of surprise. She wasn't sure what she'd expected, but it definitely wasn't this. The spacious cabin more resembled a living room than a plane. A nicer living room than her own, she noted, realizing it was the second time this week Kent family transportation outclassed her living space. In this case, she stood in an airborne version of a Kent hotel, complete with Oriental carpet and crystal light fixtures. Instead of seats, leather divans lined both sides, with a small table set in the back for conferencing. A heavy gray curtain blocked her view of the front, but through a gap in the material she glimpsed the stainless steel gleam of kitchen appliances.

"First time?"

"Excuse me?" Gideon's question broke the spell.

"Flying the Kent friendly skies. Is this your first time on the corporate jet?"

"It's very impressive."

"Beats domestic travel, that's for sure." He tossed his coat over the back of a divan and gestured for her to take a seat. "Make yourself comfortable, Miss O'Rourke. Or do you plan to stand the entire flight?"

Emma settled in across the aisle. The leather was so supple the seat molded to her instantly, like a glove. She tried to lean back and enjoy the sensation. A seat belt latch nudged her hip. She looked around for its companion. Was it too early to buckle up? Did she even have to?

Meanwhile, across the aisle, Gideon remained unrestrained and looking more at home amid the opulence than a man had a right to. He must have noticed her squirming, for he glanced at her curiously.

"Are you sure everything is all right?" he asked.

"Everything's fi—" She caught herself and sighed. This was going to be a long trip. Maybe she should ban his asking if she was all right. "Why wouldn't it be?"

He shrugged. "No reason. Except your spine is stiffer than a steel rod. You are allowed to relax, you know. This is a business trip, not a kidnapping."

"Thanks for clarifying."

"Just making sure you knew."

Before Emma could answer, a disembodied voice filled the cabin. "We'll be taxiing into position shortly, Mr. Kent. The weather's a bit choppy over Connecticut, so we might encounter a little turbulence."

Emma buckled her seat belt. From across the aisle, she could feel Gideon watching. She tried to avoid the sensation by rummaging through her briefcase for reading material. Her insides were jittery enough without the added voltage that seemed to flare whenever she looked in his direction. It was as if her body had some kind of electrical switch when he was around. He only need move into her vicinity and her nerve endings got all twittery, disrupting her equilibrium.

The plane lurched forward, having begun its taxiing in earnest, and pitching Emma off balance in the process. She righted herself, using the shift in position to camouflage another tug on her seat belt.

"Did you bring the Silbermann file?" Gideon asked.

She looked up. Leaning back on the divan, legs stretched across the aisle, Gideon was the picture of comfort and ease. An incredibly handsome picture. She caught her breath as the inevitable charge passed through her. "Yes," she replied. He'd asked her to pack the design sketches when he'd arrived with Hinckley. "I've got them right here."

"Good. Let's take a look."

To her surprise, he crossed the aisle and buckled himself into the seat next to hers. "You need to look at them, too."

"I do?"

"Didn't I say I expected you to give your opinion?"

"Yes, but—"

"So you might as well start now. What is it about these designs, exactly, that makes you think they're cold?"

Oh Lord, they were back to that, were they? "A tad moot, don't you think? Your grandmother already approved the project."

"Humor me." He took the file from her hands and leafed through until he found a sketch of the suggested lobby refurb. "What don't you like about this one, for example?"

Emma stared at the drawing, trying her best to focus on design and not the thigh pressing against hers, or the seductive hint of limes and spice emanating from his skin. Talk about futile. Worse, she knew next to nothing about interior design. How on earth was she going to make an intelligent comment?

"Well?"

He wouldn't give up until she said something. For whatever reason, he seemed hell-bent on getting her commentary.

"The color," she said finally. "I don't like the color."

"You don't like blue?"

Actually, no. She hated blue, navy especially. More so now that the color dominated her wardrobe. She didn't tell him, though. "It's the wrong shade," she said instead. "This blue is too harsh, too icy. It should be more…"

She looked up into Gideon's eyes, causing the rest of her sentence to die on her tongue. Maybe she didn't hate all blue….

"More what?" he asked.

"Brilliant."

Realizing what she'd just breathed, she jerked her gaze to her lap. "Not a very helpful suggestion, was it?"

"On the contrary, I understand perfectly."

"You do?" She couldn't help herself; she looked back up.

"Sure," Gideon replied. "Color evokes emotion. When speaking viscerally, you can't always name a shade."

"And here I thought I was simply verbally inept."

"I seriously doubt you're ever inept, Miss O'Rourke."

The compliment sparked more satisfaction than it should. "Oh, you'd be surprised, Mr. Kent," she replied, deflecting the sensation. "I can be plenty inept when I put my mind to it."

"Further proving your efficiency. True ineptitude doesn't require effort. By the way," he added softly in her ear, his conspiratorial tone setting off a new batch of shivers, "we're in the air."

"What?" She looked out the window. Sure enough, Boston, along with the rest of New England, was rapidly receding from view. She'd been so distracted by Gideon, she hadn't noticed their liftoff.

Which had been the point, she realized. "How did you…?"

Gideon shrugged. "Lucky guess. Plus you had that seat

belt of yours locked in a death grip." Emma blushed. "You don't like flying?"

"Actually, I don't know if I like flying or not. This is my first time. In fact..." if she was going to confess, she might as well admit everything "...I've never been farther than Providence."

"Huh."

Something about the way Gideon said that one syllable unnerved her. Especially since he fell silent for the minute or so that followed. Was he regretting dragging her along? Worrying she might not know how to act in front of Ross Chamberlain? Normally she'd find such concerns insulting, but he looked so regal and elegant in comparison to her that suddenly she was worried about her ability to perform, as well.

She fiddled with the buckle on her seat belt, lifting the metal latch up and down. "See?" she said, breaking the awkward silence. "I told you I had areas of deficiency."

"Inexperience is hardly a deficiency. In fact—" he shrugged "—maybe it's a benefit. Really," he added when Emma scoffed. "You see things with a fresh perspective."

"Like cold interior design," she remarked self-deprecatingly.

"Don't forget comfortable beds."

The smile accompanying his reply shorted out her internal electrical switch. Her nerve endings flared. Covering the reaction, she peered into her briefcase. Thank goodness for business talk. "I printed out last year's correspondence with Mr. Chamberlain, along with some of the most recent news articles from the trades. I thought you might want them for background. Would you like to review them?"

"Later." Gideon was actually fishing through his own attaché. "Much as Mariah thinks otherwise, I do have a business of my own to run."

"Fishing charters."

He chuckled. "You've been listening to Mariah too much. Castaway Charters is a little more extensive than a fishing business. We do sailing vacations, island getaways, world-wide tours. Mariah makes it sound like I'm standing on the beach flagging down tourists."

"I'm surprised."

"What, that I'm not flagging down tourists?"

"That you didn't go into the hotel business. I would have assumed, what with growing up in the industry…"

A shadow crossed his face. "Yeah, well you know what they say about assuming."

She did, indeed, and she should have known better than to fall into the trap. Assumptions were as bad as fantasies. No good came out of either.

They spent the next half hour or so in silence, Gideon engrossed by work, Emma trying not to think about the firmness of his shoulder pressed against hers. Now that they were in the air, she thought he might move back across the aisle, but he didn't. He remained buckled next to her, a large, silent, impossible to ignore presence. She cursed herself for not bringing work of her own along. She'd been so intent on gathering everything Gideon needed, not to mention stress-ing out about her first flight, that she forgot. Now, without the distraction, she was hyperfocusing on the unhealthy images she'd buried earlier.

Desperate to stop her train of thought before it got going, she pulled out her organizer and began writing unnecessary reminders on her to-do list. Silly things like "pick up trash bags" and "laundry" just so she'd have something to do.

Unfortunately, she ran out of items within a few minutes. It didn't take long before she traded staring at her calendar for stealing glances at the man next to her. Gideon was lost in his own thoughts and didn't notice. He stared off in the distance, absently tracing the tip of his gold pen along his lower lip. Emma felt a surge of envy, watching the pen go back and forth. He had a remarkably beautiful mouth.

What thoughts distracted him? she wondered. Something pleasurable, no doubt, for his features had relaxed, the tension erased from his jaw. Daydreaming looked good on him.

Everything looked good on him, she realized. The suit, the plane. Even that ratty sweater. A prince to the manor born, she repeated to herself. Which made her what?

The poor Little Match Girl. On a corporate jet, heading for Manhattan. She turned and checked the view from her window. The plane appeared to be descending; they were no longer above the clouds. Far off in the distance, she saw a cluster of buildings that had to be New York City.

She would never admit it out loud, but looking at those buildings, she felt a thrill passed down her spine.

She was heading to New York.

They had to be kidding. Andrew Kent wanted to renovate this place? As Gideon guided her through the Landmark lobby, Emma couldn't help swiveling her head like a tourist. Everywhere she looked she saw something—a vase, a painting, a carving—that took her breath away. She'd always thought the Fairlane to be the height of luxury, but this place... With its gold embossed ceiling and dark red marble, she felt as if she'd walked into a palace.

Complete with a handsome prince.

"The ceiling is supposed to remind you of Cortez's lost city," Gideon said when she glanced upward. "In fact, this whole design has an Aztec motif. Very popular during the Art Deco period." He pointed behind her, to the large mosaic hanging above the main entrance, a swirling mass of color and motion. "That's Quetzalcoatl, the Aztec sky god."

"It's breathtaking," Emma replied.

"Yes, it is." His eyes were on her as he answered, making her stomach flutter. "Don't tell Mariah..." he leaned into her

space, the upturned collar of his overcoat tickling her cheek
"...but I think this place could rival the Fairlane."

"Careful, that's heresy," Emma replied, though she understood his point. "The Fairlane is more mainstream, more modern. This place has an...I don't know...an energy, maybe? I feel like I'm stepping back in time."

"Andrew would call that feeling dated."

"Maybe, but I like the look. It's—"

"Let me guess. Warm." He shot her a grin that, had he been anyone else, would have earned him a smack on the arm.

Emma blushed. "Are you teasing me?"

"Not at all. I'm agreeing with you. You have an eye for design, Miss O'Rourke. You should share your opinion with Mariah."

Hoping the color flooding her cheeks again wasn't too evident, Emma looked away. Gideon's words flattered her more than she wanted to admit. She'd never been told she had a flair for anything. Other than hard work, that is. To cover, she laughed them off. "I'm sure your uncle Andrew would love that."

"Andrew spends too much time listening to Suzanne."

"Who?"

"The latest wife. No doubt she's the one who pushed for Josh Silbermann in the first place."

"Oh." Emma knew who he meant. A statuesque blonde several years Andrew Kent's junior, she always dressed stunningly and never acknowledged Emma's existence. "Well, she is very stylish."

"Pretentious, Miss O'Rourke. The word you're looking for is pretentious. As well as superficial, hard to please and short-term. Andrew tends to like them that way.

"Sort of a Kent family tradition," he added with a wry smile.

Including him? Emma kicked herself for letting the

thought cross her mind. Gideon's preference in women was none of her business. It wasn't as if she would make the list, anyway. In fact, she couldn't believe she was even entertaining the idea.

"I better go check on our rooms," she said, determinedly returning to business matters.

"No need. We've been spotted." He nodded toward a short, ruddy-faced man marching in their direction.

"Mr. Kent!" the man exclaimed in a clipped, semi-British accent. He clasped Gideon's hand in both of his. "Welcome back."

"Sebastian. You haven't changed a bit."

"Well, not so much that a little hair color won't hide, eh?"

"You have gray hair?"

"You should know. You caused most of it." He turned and smiled at Emma. "You must be Miss O'Rourke. I see this rascal hasn't talked you into taking your shoes off yet."

"Why would I take my shoes off?" She looked at Gideon who, to her surprise, actually had color in his cheeks.

"One time, Sebastian," he replied. "That was one time. And the floors were freshly waxed. I couldn't help myself."

"He couldn't help himself with a lot of things. Gave his grandmother fits, he did. He and those cousins of his." Sebastian's smile grew serious. "It's good to have you home again, sir."

"Just a short visit, Sebastian. Nothing permanent."

"Of course." There was no mistaking the disappointment in the manager's voice. It was so evident that Emma felt disappointed herself. Everyone, it seemed, wanted Gideon to stay.

Breaking the silence, she turned to Sebastian. "I was just about to check on our rooms."

Like any good employee, he quickly righted himself. "Of course. Two suites, just as you requested."

No, not as she requested. She'd reserved one suite for

Gideon and a standard room for herself. "Actually..." She paused, trying to think of a way to correct the situation without calling attention to the manager's mistake.

"Thank you, Sebastian. I knew I could count on you."

Emma frowned at Gideon. "You changed the reservations?"

"Last night, and before you ask why, I like having you close by.

"Don't worry," he added with a chuckle. He spoke just behind her ear, his breath tickling the hair on the nape of her neck. "The beds in the VIP suites are just as comfortable as the ones in the standard rooms. I promise."

Ten minutes later Emma stood in the middle of a parlor opulent enough to rival Mrs. Kent's. A VIP suite. What was Gideon thinking?

She looked around the living space, an elegant study in jewel tones and gold. There were three distinct areas. At one end, framed by a pair of floor-to-ceiling windows, a decorative fireplace flickered merrily, its flames complementing the darkening Manhattan skyline outside. Nearby sat a small dining table, perfect for a candlelit dinner.

At the other end was a large—no, make that a huge— conference table, wet bar and desk. Everything an executive would need for business.

Both orbited a third space, a cozy sitting area with a velvet sofa and matching Queen Anne chairs. For those in-between moments, she supposed, when the rich just wanted to relax and read the financials.

And all of this was contained in one of the three rooms. What was she doing here? What did Gideon expect her to do with so much space?

A soft cough drew her attention. A waspish man in a crisp red blazer hovered in the doorway. Her personal concierge, he explained when he arrived with the bellman. "Excuse me, madam. I had your luggage placed in the boudoir. Would you like me to call a maid to help you unpack?"

A maid? Emma blinked in surprise. What would the woman do, hang up Emma's one suit? "Thank you, but I can unpack myself," she replied.

"Very well, madam. My name is Robert. If there's anything else you need, just ring the desk."

"I doubt I'll need anything. I'm only staying one night."

"Of course, madam."

The formality and courtesy unnerved her. Especially since it was unnecessary. Surely he recognized her hotel uniform?

"Excuse me, Robert," she called out as he was leaving.

He turned, his expression expectant. "Yes, madam?"

"Emma," she corrected. "There's no need to be formal. After all, we are both hotel employees, right?"

"Except you're staying in a VIP suite. And we've been given specific instructions to afford you every service and amenity."

"Instructed?" Emma wasn't quite sure she understood.

"By Mr. Kent. He made it quite clear when he called last night that you were to be treated as his special guest."

"He did?" Robert's answer unnerved her more than the solicitousness. Gideon had called her "special"? Why would he do that?

"Yes, ma'am. He said you were to be exposed to every amenity the Landmark had to offer." The mask of indifference slipped slightly, and the concierge smiled kindly. "So I guess that makes you a little more than another hotel employee."

"No, I'm not," she said to herself after Robert left, more to quell the butterflies in her stomach than anything. She didn't know what Gideon was up to, but she wasn't sitting in a VIP suite because she was special. That was an idea her mother would fall for.

Emma wouldn't think about how enticing the idea sounded.

On her way back toward the corridor that divided the parlor from the rest of the suite, she stopped and studied her reflection in one of the mirrored doors. A pale, tired woman stared back. Not a woman who enchanted billionaire businessmen, but a woman who needed a nap.

Satisfied that she'd put Robert's comment well out of her head, she kicked off her heels and carried them through the boudoir into the bedroom. One thing was certain, she conceded as she entered the room. The bed did look comfortable. More than comfortable, it looked downright decadent. There had to be a dozen pillows, a literal sea of them, and the mattress seemed so high and thick she wondered if she wouldn't float away when she lay down.

She did so, and sure enough, a down topper enfolded her with softness.

"Wow, a girl could get used to this." She ran her hand across the damask duvet. The sapphire silk reminded her of the ocean.

Or Gideon's eyes.

Suddenly, the image of those eyes boring into her from above flashed through her brain, accompanied by a hot, needy quiver.

Surely you have one or two fantasies….

Her eyes flew open and she scrambled off the bed as if it were on fire.

This was her mother's fault. If she hadn't raised that ridiculous theory in the first place, Emma wouldn't be entertaining any of these thoughts. Foolish, inappropriate, completely unrealistic, waste-of-time thoughts. Gideon had booked her into this room because he wanted her nearby. For business reasons, nothing more. This suite, this trip—they were a onetime deal.

She was overtired. That was it. Strung out from nerves

and new experiences. A hot shower—that's what she needed. Something to unwind her tense muscles.

Like everything else in the suite, the bathroom was spacious and luxuriously designed. The marble tub had to be the largest she'd ever seen. She'd never really been much of a bath person, mainly because she could never lounge comfortably. Her legs would stick out if she submerged her shoulders, and vice versa. Either way, she got cold. Plus baths were time-consuming; she usually had too much to do to indulge in them.

She had time now, though, didn't she? Their meeting wasn't until tomorrow afternoon, and Gideon…well, she imagined Gideon had friends in the city he wanted to spend time with.

And the tub was big. The size of a small swimming pool, really. She could lie down flat on the bottom and her toes still wouldn't touch the edge.

Why not? When was the next time she'd get an opportunity to swim in a tub? With bubbles, no less, she thought, grabbing a bottle from the vanity. Feeling silly and rebellious at the same time, she turned on the water and dumped the contents under the stream. Seconds later the room filled with the sweet aroma of citrus and ylang-ylang.

She was just about to submerge her toes in the bubbles when a knock sounded on the door.

Concierge Robert, she thought with a sigh. He'd ignored her protest and sent a maid to unpack her things, anyway.

A large white robe hung on the back of the bathroom door. Throwing it on, Emma went to answer the door.

Only to wish she'd thought to use the peephole first.

CHAPTER FIVE

"Is this a bad time, Miss O'Rourke?"

It was Gideon, not the concierge, standing in her doorway. "I wanted to review the Chamberlain correspondence." His blue gaze raked her length, lingering, or so it seemed, on her belt. "Guess I should have called first."

When she didn't respond, he frowned. "Is everything all right?"

"Yes, I…" Emma shook coherent thought back into her head. "I wasn't expecting you."

"Obviously." His grin grew wider.

"I mean, I assumed you would have plans…."

"Ah, didn't your mother teach you about making assumptions?"

In more ways than one, thought Emma.

"Besides," he said, "why go out when I can spend a stimulating evening reviewing financials with you? May I?"

He nodded toward her hallway. It took a moment for Emma to realize what he was asking; her head was stuck on his last comment. But eventually she stepped aside to let him pass. "Are you sure I'm not interrupting you?" he asked.

Emma thought of the lavender-filled bath growing cold. "No. Nothing important. My briefcase is in the bedroom. I'll go get it and meet you in the living room."

"Sounds good." He took two steps down the corridor, then turned. "Oh, and Miss O'Rourke?"

"Yes?"

"While you're in there, you might want to put something on under your robe. That belt doesn't tie very securely."

Emma gasped and clutched her collar. She didn't need a mirror to know her entire body had just turned crimson; the heat washing over her said as much. Holding the neckline tight, she dashed toward the bedroom, stopping halfway there when she realized her clothes were in the boudoir.

Check that; tomorrow's suit and her pajamas were in the boudoir. The rest of her clothes lay on the bathroom floor. She turned back, grateful that the parlor was out of view. It was bad enough that she heard Gideon laughing to himself as she rushed off.

When she emerged a few moments later, still bare-legged but dressed, Gideon had already made himself at home. So at home that Emma had to catch her breath. He looked amazing. It was as if yesterday's sailor and today's prince had decided to merge, creating the perfect combination of casual sophistication. He'd shed his jacket and tie in favor of rolled-up shirtsleeves. Though the cotton garment had gone through a day's travel, on him it looked sharp as a tack. Even the five o'clock shadow on his cheeks was appealing. She glanced down at her uniform, wrinkled and not nearly as attractive looking, and self-consciously ran a palm across the front of her skirt.

He'd turned on the television and was clicking through stations with the remote. "I hope you don't mind, but I wanted to catch the market wrap-up." He looked up, saw her and frowned. "You didn't have to put your suit back on."

Instantly, her self-consciousness doubled. "Either that or my pajamas," she replied.

"You didn't pack anything else?"

Why would she? "I wasn't planning to stay more than tonight."

He made a clucking noise with his tongue. "We're going to have to do work on that practical streak of yours. Pajamas, by the way, aren't a problem if you'll be more comfortable."

"I wouldn't be."

"We'll have to work on that, too."

She wished he'd stop saying "we," as if they were a team. Every time he did, her stomach fluttered, and the sensation disturbed her. Especially after the thoughts she'd had earlier.

Curse her mother for putting those thoughts in her head.

There was a matching chair across from the sofa. Emma tucked herself in the corner and propped her briefcase on her lap like a shield. "Which would you like first, the correspondence or the figures."

"The fig— Damn, the Dow took another late-day tumble."

"A big one?"

"Big enough for me to appreciate being a privately held company. Wonder how Kent Hotels did."

"I should think, being mostly privately held, the company did well enough. Unless someone impulsively decided to sell…" All the pieces suddenly slid into place. "That's why you're in New York, isn't it? Your grandmother is afraid Mr. Chamberlain will sell his stock, isn't she?"

"Ross has taken some big hits. Not to mention last year's very expensive divorce. Buzz on the streets says he's looking to shore up his liquid assets."

"And Mrs. Kent thinks he'll sell his Kent Hotel stock to do so."

"Exactly."

Emma paused, recalling what little she knew of the Kent-Chamberlain friendship. From the tone of Mrs. Kent's correspondence, the families had been friends for years. "Surely he wouldn't just sell, not without letting your grandmother know."

"Never underestimate the power of a greedy ex-wife breathing down a man's neck. Did you hear how worried Mariah was by a man called Gerard Ambiteau?"

Of course she had. "Your grandmother makes me run news searches on the name every week."

"Glad to see the internet's making Mariah's obsession easier. Ambiteau, or more specifically, Gerard Ambiteau, is Mariah's archenemy. Ever since he tried to buy Kent Hotels following Edward's death. He made the mistake of implying the hotel business was too much for a young widow with three children to handle."

"Ouch. Bet that went over well."

The smile Gideon flashed made Emma's toes curl. "About as well as a hydrogen bomb. Needless to say, Mariah took the offer as a personal affront. I swear she expanded the Kent empire as much to spite Gerard Ambiteau as anything."

"The ultimate revenge. Your grandmother's a formidable woman."

"Mariah's a survivor, that's for sure. Then again, married to Edward Kent, she'd have to be, right?"

Emma had heard the stories; Edward Kent's womanizing and debauchery were almost as legendary as his business acumen. "Surely it wasn't all bad," she said. "They did have three children."

"Ah yes, children, the ultimate indicator of true love." The bitterness in Gideon's voice made her shudder.

"Sorry," he quickly added. "I should learn to keep my cynical views to myself."

"That's all right. I understand what you're saying."

"You do?"

Was that surprise in his voice? "I was raised by a single mom, remember?" Emma of all people knew children weren't a guarantee of marital bliss.

Heck, few things were. She certainly knew of far more failures than successes. "Makes you wonder sometimes why people ever bother getting married in the first place."

"Exactly."

It was the succinct, definitive answer of a man whose mind was made up. Emma didn't know why, but her insides twisted at his decisiveness. Maybe it was the sudden change in atmosphere that followed. Gideon's cynical comments had caused him to fold into himself, taking the warmth from the room.

It was as if he were a human thermostat, Emma realized. When he was "present" the room pulsed. But as soon as he withdrew, the air grew cold, the coziness sucked away. It made her want to burrow next to him on the sofa and prod him teasingly until he returned.

However, since those actions were far too intimate and familiar for her to carry out, she settled for switching to a lighter subject. "How do you think your grandmother and Hinckley are getting along?"

Gideon didn't return completely, but his half laugh erased some of the fatigue from his face and brought back some of the warmth. "Right now I'm guessing they're arguing over who gets the bulk of the sofa."

"Wonder who will win."

"Hinckley, without question. When it comes to his comfort he's extremely stubborn. Mariah has met her match."

"Is that why she's cat-sitting?"

"Why, Miss O'Rourke, are you suggesting I foisted my spoiled, entitled, stubborn cat on Mariah as payback?"

"In a word, yes."

He pressed a hand to his chest. "I'm crushed that you could think such a thing. I was merely acting as any loving pet owner would, making sure my beloved cat was as comfortable as possible."

"My mistake. I apologize."

"She says while laughing."

Emma couldn't help it. His feigned indignation was so over the top, she had to. "Sorry," she repeated, trying to rein in her smile. She failed.

Earning herself a grin to beat all grins from the man across from her. A grin that not only brought back the warmth and coziness, but was bright enough to light Manhattan. Seeing it, Emma felt her insides tumble.

"I guess I can forgive you," he said. "But—" he pointed at her with the remote "—this means I get to choose the room service order."

"Wait a second. Your father sent an email about that subject a few months ago...."

She was smart, that's for sure. Watching Emma search her laptop for a memo about Kent's overseas projects, Gideon couldn't help but be impressed. One mention of a figure and she could recall a document or memo, sometimes months old, referencing the conversation. Moreover, she had an intuitive ability to link content from one document to another seemingly unrelated one. No wonder Mariah was so keen on her secretary. Like with the hotel decor, the woman had a real feel for the business.

She was adorable, too. The way she stuck her nose in the computer, the tip of her tongue protruding in concentration... She'd relaxed enough to move from the chair to the floor, where she sat with her long legs curled like a cat's.

Her shoes were off, and he could see her bare toes digging absentmindedly in the carpeting.

Again, adorable. He felt bad for letting his cynicism color the mood earlier. This atmosphere was far more pleasant.

"Here it is." Emma beamed with victory. "I knew I read those figures before. See?" She pivoted the computer screen so he could look. Sure enough, there was the memo outlining in great detail their upcoming Dubai project, including its impact on revenue.

"Management's very high on this new property," she said. Based on projected earnings, he could see why. "Of course, the numbers are still a few years out."

"True, but unlike a lot of investments, this one promises to turn a profit fairly quickly." He gave a quick nod of approval and turned the screen back toward her. "Good call, Miss O'Rourke. This might be exactly the carrot we need."

"Just doing my job." She was trying to sound nonchalant, but he caught a hint of pink washing her cheeks.

"Is it your job to remember every detail of every memo Kent Hotels has ever issued?"

"No, but with your grandmother, a good memory helps."

"I suppose it does. Lord knows hers is long enough. Mariah's lucky to have you, you know."

"In this economy, I'm the lucky one. Good jobs don't grow on trees."

"Don't sell yourself short. Mariah doesn't sing praises easily, and she definitely sings yours."

Another blush. Gideon leaned back against the sofa, taking in the woman across from him. For someone so competent, she sure wasn't use to compliments. Hard to believe. You'd think she'd be swimming in them.

"Have you ever thought of applying for a management position? You have a nose for business."

She laughed, clearly deflecting the suggestion. "Down in the lobby you said it was an eye for design."

"So I did. Maybe you've got both, a nose and an eye."

"Goodness. I can't wait to find out if I have a mouth."

Oh, she did...a gorgeous one. It was Gideon's turn to look away as a half-dozen images, all of them inappropriate, popped into his head. That she seemed clueless to the innuendo made the remark all the more arousing. How on earth could a woman be so oblivious to her charms?

He pushed himself to his feet and moved to the window. Nighttime had claimed the sky, transforming the view into a study of shadows, shapes and light. After years of endless tropical horizons, he wasn't used to seeing buildings clustered so close together. It looked strange to him.

"What an amazing view."

Emma approached, her eyes wide as she gazed out at the skyline. "It's breathtaking."

"Absolutely." Though he wasn't thinking about the view. Like this afternoon in the lobby, he found her expression far more captivating than his surroundings. Watching her made the male part of him flood with awareness. Forget sweet. She was beyond sweet. Why weren't there men lined up to spoil her?

Then again, maybe there were. Maybe there was a guy back in Boston spoiling her to death. For some reason Gideon found that idea unsettling. Probably because if there was a guy, he was doing a pretty poor job. A spoiled woman wouldn't blush at every compliment. Or lack expectations.

There were elements to Miss O'Rourke that just didn't line up.

"What building is that?"

Her question drew his attention. Emma had moved closer and was pointing to an angular structure a couple blocks away. She looked at Gideon expectantly.

"I'm not sure. The skyline's changed since my last visit. I think maybe a bank."

"Oh."

Dammit if he didn't feel he'd let her down. Determined to make up for it, he steered her by the shoulders until she stood in front of him. "Here," he said, "look to the left. That's the Chrysler Building."

He watched as she craned her neck to get a better view. Though he hadn't meant to, his maneuvering left her cradled against his chest. He could feel her body heat through his shirt. When he turned his own head to follow her gaze, his nose caught a hint of her vanilla-scented skin.

"You can't get views like this from the second floor," he said. It was taking all his self-restraint not to bury his nose in the curve of her neck and inhale.

"No, I don't suppose you can."

She smiled at him over her shoulder. A shy, half-lidded smile. Bedroom eyes, thought Gideon, his blood heating, with bedroom lips to match. So pink and luscious. He bet they tasted as sweet as everything else about her. All it would take was a little dip of his head...

"Would you like me to type up in one document what we discussed this evening?" Emma's voice suddenly dissolved the spell. "That way you can have all the figures in one place when you review them in the morning."

Breaking free of his orbit, she moved back to the center of the room, back to where their paperwork lay strewn across the coffee table.

Back to business.

Just as well, thought Gideon. He swallowed his sigh and straightened his shoulders. "Thank you, Miss O'Rourke. That would be very helpful."

* * *

Talk about making a fool of herself. After Gideon left, Emma slipped the dead bolt in place, then rested her forehead against the door. What had she been thinking? She'd come this close—this close—to kissing Gideon Kent! One second she was looking at the Chrysler Building, the next she was gazing into those beautiful blue eyes and drifting slowly toward them. Thank God rational thought had kicked in at the last minute. Before she'd completely embarrassed herself.

It was the suite, she decided. The opulence made her act like an idiot. Well, that and Gideon. He had this way of making her feel unnerved and relaxed at the same time. Not to mention he was gorgeous, funny, smart, sexy...

Listen to her; she was going on like her mother summing up a potential boyfriend. The man was her boss, for goodness sake! And after tomorrow he wouldn't even be that. He'd be wrapping up his visit and she'd be back to typing Mrs. Kent's correspondence.

Leaving the doorway, Emma padded into the bathroom. The robe lay on the floor where she'd discarded it, along with her stockings. She picked up the garment and returned it to the hook on the door. Then she sat down on the tub's edge. The water had long ago grown cold, the bubbles and lavender aroma dissolved. So much for indulging. Then again, maybe she'd indulged enough for one night.

She unplugged the drain and headed back to the parlor.

She wore an evening dress. The kind princesses wore. Her shoulders were bare. A muscled torso pressed against her back; hot breath sounded in her ear. She sighed as strong hands caressed her shoulders. "Show me your fantasies, Miss O'Rourke...."

The sound of ascending chimes cut through Emma's dream and her eyes flew open. What the—?

Her phone. It was ringing. Blinking in the darkness, she groped along her nightstand, telling herself her rapid breathing was from being startled awake, not from the dream she'd been having.

"Hey, sweetie, how's New York?" Her mother's high-pitched voice bellowed from the other end. "Mary and I are on our way home so we thought we'd see how you were doing. We're not interrupting anything, are we?"

"Huh? No. I'm in bed."

"And?"

It took her a moment to realize what her mother meant. "No!" Emma repeated vehemently. "I told you, Mom, this is a business trip."

"What, you don't think men like to combine business with pleasure?"

Flashes of her dream popped into Emma's mind. She shook them off, replacing them with Gideon's gentlemanly departure last night. "Not Gideon."

"Ooh, Gideon, is it?"

"Mom, he's my boss. Quit trying to imply something else." Quit putting stupid thoughts in my head, was what she really meant.

Out of the corner of her eye she noticed the clock on the nightstand, and something her mother had said clicked. "Did you say you were on your way home? It's five-thirty in the morning. Were you at the casino all night?"

"What can I say? We met some new friends and time got away from us."

There was the sound of giggling on the other end and Emma winced. Not again. "What's his name?" she asked, settling in for the usual download of information.

"Tony, and he's absolutely amazing. He's got a house on the Cape. And a boat. We're going to have the best time this summer. Maybe you can join us."

"Sure, sounds fun," Emma replied flatly. Inwardly, she sighed.

Her mother was talking rapidly now, clearly on a high from last night's "friendship." She'd be living on enthusiasm and coffee for the next couple of days. Until she either drove this Tony person away or he got bored and stopped calling. Then it would be days of bitterness and depression.

"And not one of those little fishing boats, either. This one sleeps five people, and you can water-ski behind it." Prattling on, mostly about Tony and how wonderful he was, Janet didn't even notice her daughter's silence. "We're meeting him and his friend Jimmy at the Prudential for drinks later today. As soon as we've had a chance to go home and change, that is."

Guess looking for work was out this week. Her mother would be far too busy hitching her wagon to Tony from the Cape. Life would be so much easier if her mom would just see it a little more realistically.

Like you were doing last night? a voice in Emma's head asked.

"Yes," she answered back. Because unlike her mother, she caught herself before the foolish ideas took hold.

And besides, even if she did do something stupid, which was highly unlikely, she was smart enough not to pretend there was a fairy tale ending on her horizon.

CHAPTER SIX

"Wow, Ross Chamberlain sure knows how to talk. Too bad he doesn't say anything interesting. No wonder his wife wanted out. She probably feared being bored to death."

Speaking as he went, Gideon strode into Emma's suite ahead of her, not waiting for an invitation. They were back from their meeting, and rehashing what had transpired. It turned out Mrs. Kent's worries were well founded. Gerard Ambiteau had put out a few feelers, hinting that with her getting on in years, Kent Hotels might not be such a solid investment for a man with financial constraints.

Fortunately, Gideon had managed to persuade Chamberlain, through numbers and more than a little personal charm, to honor their families' long history. Emma was still a little breathless from the display. He'd been a sight to behold, a heat-seeking missile exuding charisma and business acumen. Ross Chamberlain never stood a chance.

"Should we call your grandmother and tell her the good news?" she asked.

"Later. First I say we toast our success." He made a beeline for the bar by the windows.

Emma watched in puzzlement as he uncorked a cut glass carafe and poured himself a drink. With his business concluded, she was surprised Gideon wasn't in more of a hurry to get his things and leave. By her calculations they could be back in Boston within a few hours. She certainly didn't understand why he was making himself at home in her suite.

"Join me?" he asked.

She shook her head. "I'm not much of a whiskey drinker."

"The bar's fully stocked."

"Then maybe a bottled water."

He rolled his eyes and tossed her one of the plastic bottles lined up by the ice chest. "Really, Miss O'Rourke, we have to work on your relaxation skills."

"Sue me, I like to stay hydrated."

"Is that what you call it," he teased, with a smile that curled her toes. Then he raised his glass. "To us."

"To keeping the wolf at bay," Emma retorted.

"For now, at least."

"What do you mean? I thought Mr. Chamberlain was fully on board." That sure seemed to be the case when they'd left him.

"Oh, he is, but I'm afraid we've only plugged a small leak. There's still the bigger question of when Mariah steps down. Andrew's reputation as a manager is shaky. He's made more than a few questionable decisions. Especially lately." Although Gideon didn't say so, the words *since he married Suzanne* came through loud and clear.

"What about your father?" From the way the brothers met with Mrs. Kent in tandem, she assumed they ran Kent Hotels the same way. "Surely his reputation is solid."

"Oh, definitely. Jonathan has an impeccable reputation. He's very good at presenting what people want to see." Gideon didn't even try to hide the edge in his voice. It was so sharp, Emma could feel it on the other side of the room.

"Unfortunately, he's not very good 'when the rubber hits the road,' as the saying goes."

Watching Gideon toss back his drink, she thought, not for the first time, that his comments must refer to more than the family business. "What do you think they'll do?"

"Short of Mariah living forever, which—" he jabbed the air with his index finger "—isn't out of the realm of possibility, I don't know. Her grand plan certainly didn't work."

"Grand plan?"

"Nothing. Just something between her and me. It doesn't matter."

He was folding into himself again, and the air chilled as a result. Without waiting for him to ask, Emma approached the love seat, slipped the glass from his fingers and refilled it. Blue eyes met hers as he accepted the drink. With a whoosh, the chill disappeared and the air began to crackle with a kind of tense heat. She wondered if Gideon noticed the change, as well, for he cleared his throat before taking a sip.

Needing to break up the atmosphere, she reached for the hotel phone and a safe topic. "What time would you like me to have the driver bring the car around?"

"Why? In a hurry to leave?" Gideon asked.

"No. I mean, I'm fine." He arched a brow and she stopped. Apparently the word ban was still in place. "It's just that we've done our business in the city, and I didn't think you wanted to spend more time here than necessary."

"I appreciate the consideration," he replied. "But what about you?"

"What about me?"

"You didn't get to see many sights during your first trip to New York."

"I'll live. Besides, what I did see was great. The view from the window..." A flash from her dream popped into her head. She took a quick drink from her water to cover her flush.

Fortunately, Gideon didn't notice, as he was too intent on arguing his point. "A hotel view and a couple of car rides hardly count as 'seeing the city.'"

"Oh, well. Maybe next time."

"Hmmm, next time." He frowned and disappeared into his thoughts for several seconds before abruptly draining his drink and slapping the empty glass on the coffee table. "I've got it," he said. "Go change."

"Change?" She wasn't sure what he meant.

"Into your evening clothes. I'm taking you out for the quintessential New York experience."

"Excuse me?" Emma took another drink to drown the butterflies Gideon's suggestion released in her stomach. Surely she misunderstood. "Did you say go out?"

"Yes, for dinner. To celebrate today's success, and to show you more of the New York than a window view. What do you say?"

What did she say? Emma didn't know what to say. Dinner with Gideon? The idea was…well, it was…

"It's not necessary," she replied.

"Why not? You've earned it. I wouldn't have been able to pull off today without your input. Your background knowledge was invaluable. And that report was fantastic."

She blushed. "All I did was merge a few files."

"You did a lot more than that." When she blushed again, he chuckled under his breath. "What's the matter, Miss O'Rourke, afraid you might enjoy seeing the city with me?"

"No!" The protest came out far quicker than she intended. "I mean, yes, I would love to see New York." Especially with him. Which was why she hesitated. His proposal sounded too good to be true. "I don't want you to delay your return to Boston to take me sightseeing, though."

"Even if I want to?"

He wanted to? The butterflies took flight again. "But your grandmother..."

"Mariah can wait twenty-four hours. Now go change."

Emma looked down at her gray wool skirt with its coordinating black turtleneck, the only nonuniform outfit she had, and winced. "I can't."

"What do you mean you— Oh that's right, you didn't pack other clothes." He let out a long breath. "I swear, you must be the only woman on the planet who packs light."

"I didn't plan on taking a sightseeing tour," she said with a sheepish shrug. "But no worries. I don't have to change."

"I wouldn't want you to," he said, in a voice so low its timbre hummed through her. "Not one bit."

He meant her outfit, right? The way he looked at her, with his eyes heavy-lidded and unreadable, it would be easy to assume something else.

Ah, but didn't he warn you about assuming...?

"Besides—" she covered her thoughts with a laugh "—isn't the quintessential New York experience a hot dog in Central Park? Hardly necessary to dress up for that, right?"

"I had a slightly different experience planned."

Like what? she wondered, fighting the urge to speculate. "Sorry I ruined your plans."

"Who says they're ruined? Just go downstairs to the boutique and find something to wear."

His matter-of-fact answer made Emma laugh. She'd seen this "boutique." A tiny designer enclave off the lobby with accessories that cost more than her weekly paycheck. "How about I stick to my suit and we get the hot dog," she replied.

"Miss O'Rourke..." Gideon's eyes narrowed; she was about to get reprimanded.

"Really, Mr. Kent. A hot dog in the park sounds terrific." And cheaper. She wasn't about to max out her credit card on some designer dress no matter how tempting the idea of dinner sounded. Her mother splurged enough for both of them. Emma couldn't afford to fall down the same slippery slope.

"In fact," she continued, "I'm so hungry I might eat two hot dogs. With cheese and chili. Just let me get my bag."

"Miss O'Rourke." As she started past, he gently grabbed her arm. "You know that I meant for you to charge the dress to the room, right?"

No, she did not. Emma looked to the ground, embarrassed that she hadn't understood what he was saying. Now that she did, her head was spinning. He'd offered to buy her a dress? "I can't do that."

"Why not?"

"Because." Because it was too surreal. He'd already booked her into a luxury suite, flown her in a private jet. Things like this just didn't happen to her.

"Consider it a bonus for a job well done," he said, cutting her off. "I meant what I said before. I wouldn't have pulled off today's meeting without you. And don't say you were just doing your job."

"I don't need a bonus." Really, it was bad enough that his compliments were making her head spin.

"No one needs a bonus, Miss O'Rourke. But you do deserve one."

She shook her head. "Really, I—"

"Hey, Emma." He caught her chin, stopping the protest. "Let someone do something nice for you."

When had he closed the space between them? With him standing near her this way, his body teasing the boundaries of her personal space, she couldn't think sensibly. She got too lost in the combination of his body warmth and unique scent.

"Go to the boutique," he said in a low voice. "Indulge

yourself. I insist." His set expression told her he wasn't about to stop insisting, either.

Looking into his eyes, now the color of a stormy sky, Emma felt her resolve fade away. Well, now she knew how Ross Chamberlain felt. A person didn't stand a chance when Gideon locked you into his sights.

The boutique, called Christine's, was empty and about to close when Emma got to the lobby. Even so, a stunning blonde with perfect posture greeted her at the door as if she was the first customer of the day. "Miss O'Rourke," she said with a smile, "I'm Christine. Mr. Kent said you were on the way down. You're looking for a cocktail dress?"

"Nothing too fancy," Emma replied. Once out of Gideon's mind-altering presence, she'd regained her senses, making up her mind that while she was going to buy a new dress, she'd pay for it herself. Her credit card didn't need the charge, but she would feel more in control. Something that seemed to be rapidly disappearing during this trip. "I'd like to wear it more than once."

"One little black dress coming right up," Christine replied. She led Emma toward the rear of the store. As they passed a rack of brightly colored party dresses, Emma felt a stir of longing. They all looked so vibrant and alive.

Be practical, she told herself. If she was going to spend a lot of money, she should buy an investment piece, not a trendy swath of silk.

Meanwhile, Christine was pulling back the curtain in a large dressing area. "I took the liberty of selecting a few outfits you might like," she said. "If none of these suit your taste, we can keep looking."

A dozen dresses of various styles, lengths and colors lined the wall. Emma fingered a beaded jacket sleeve. "How did you know my size?"

The look she received in response was simultaneously knowing and discreet. Gideon. A thrill buzzed through her at the idea that he'd studied her figure. And studied quite accurately, she realized, looking at the size.

"As I said," Christine continued, "these are only a few suggestions. We have others, as well."

"I'm sure one of these will be fine." Emma couldn't help noticing that none of the dresses had price tags. Not a good sign.

Investment, she repeated. Investment. She held up a black crepe sheath. The little black dress of little black dresses.

"That's the perfect investment dress," Christine said, reading her mind. "You could wear it for years and never be out of style."

Couldn't get more practical than that, could you? Or duller, she thought, turning the garment from front to back. Plain, simple, shapeless but not too shapeless. Switch the black to navy blue and you'd have her uniform.

"You can always dress it up with accessories," Christine offered.

Sure, she could. Scarves, jewelry. Emma knew all the tricks, thanks to the other women at work. They never really worked, though. In the end, you still wore a plain, simple dress. On the other hand, she was already wearing matching shoes, which would cut down on expenses, and she knew she could wear the style. If the dress fit, it was the right choice.

Maybe once she tried it on, she'd feel more positive.

She was halfway out of her turtleneck when a flash of color caught her eye, stopping her in her tracks. There, hanging on the discard rack, was the most brilliantly blue dress she'd ever seen. Sleek and sexy, the satin material shone under the track lighting, reminding her of Gideon's eyes. Maybe that's why she lifted it from the rack.

"Oh, that dress is one of my favorites," Christine said. "Isn't the color magnificent?"

Still thinking of Gideon's eyes, Emma replied, "Gorgeous." Hypnotic even, the way the garment called to her.

"I know you wanted a little black dress, but your hair and coloring would be perfect with this shade. You really should try it on."

"I don't think so." She couldn't. The gown was way too impractical. She would never wear the thing after tonight. In fact, it was probably too fancy for tonight. "I should stick to basic black." Dull, serviceable basic black.

"Are you sure? The dress is your size. Maybe fate's trying to send you a message."

"Yeah, right."

"Why don't you try it on for fun," Christine prodded. "You don't have to buy it."

Emma knew what the saleswoman was trying to do. She'd noticed Emma's hesitancy and was now trying to sway her to what was obviously a more expensive item.

Still, the dress was extraordinary. She fingered a cap sleeve. The material glided beneath her fingers, smooth as ice. She bet it would feel amazing on a person's skin. A longing, fierce and sudden, welled up inside her.

Go on, a voice whispered in her head. You know you want to.

What the heck. She already knew she was buying the black crepe. When was the next time she'd get to try on an unspeakably expensive designer dress? Why not have a little fun? The color would probably look awful on her, anyway. Saleswomen always told you what you wanted to hear.

A soft rustle filled the room as she stepped into the dress. She'd been right; the satin did feel amazing. After slipping on one sleeve, then the other, Emma zipped the side and looked in the mirror, expecting to discover the dress was too tight or too misshapen or woefully garish against her skin. Instead, she gasped. Behind her, Christine gasped as well.

The dress fitted perfectly. The modest neckline showed a hint of cleavage, while the back draped nearly to her waist, revealing a sexy expanse of creamy skin. The skirt skimmed her hips perfectly, almost too perfectly, revealing lines and curves she didn't know she had. Surely this body wasn't hers.

"Don't move," Christine said. She drew closer. "Do you mind if I do something?"

Before Emma could reply—not that she could speak at the moment, since her reflection had her too stunned—the woman pulled the hairclip from Emma's hair. Her copper-colored locks spilled around her shoulders, but only briefly before Christine swept it back in a kind of semi chignon.

"This dress calls for a more sophisticated updo," she said. A small change, but a stunning one nonetheless. Emma blinked, transfixed by the transformation.

"And shoes," she heard Christine saying. She disappeared into the main store and returned with a pair of silver sandals. "Here, put these on."

Still stuck in her trance, Emma obeyed. The heels were higher and strappier than she'd normally wear, but they suited the dress perfectly. For the first time in her life, Emma didn't mind the endless stretch of leg.

"Still think you should stick to basic black? That dress was made for you," Christine said. "I told you, fate was giving you a message."

"You think?" She still couldn't believe her reflection. Who knew one dress could make such a difference? With the hair and the shoes, she felt like a celebrity.

Or a princess.

She looked at the crepe dress waiting on its hanger. This dress probably cost more than she made in a month. The black was the best choice. The practical choice. The responsible choice. Her gaze flickered back to her reflection.

"I'll take this one." The words shot from her mouth unbidden. The moment she said them, her nerves began to tingle. What was she doing?

Christine didn't give her a chance to change her mind. "Great," she gushed. If Emma didn't know better, she'd swear the woman was genuinely excited about her choice. "Now, let's touch up your makeup."

Fifteen whirlwind minutes later, Emma had become a different person. Christine didn't so much "touch up" her makeup as make her over. Her eyes were turned sultry and exotic. Crystal earrings dangled from her lobes, catching the light. Throughout it all, Emma felt lost, as if she were watching herself in a dream. A wild, unimaginable dream.

"Perfect," Christine said when Emma finally stepped from the dressing room. She looked over her shoulder for affirmation. "Don't you agree?"

"More than perfect." Gideon stood leaning against the counter, raw appreciation lighting his eyes. "Breathtaking."

The bottom fell out of Emma's stomach.

He handed her a heavy knit shawl that wasn't hers, but complimented the dress. Emma was too focused on his seductive gaze to protest. "Shall we?" he asked.

Feeling as if she were floating on air, she took his arm and let him lead her away.

The floating sensation stayed with her through the lobby and onto the street. While they'd been inside, the city had been shifting gears from business to social. Even though the sun was disappearing, its heat continued radiating from the pavement and buildings, keeping the air warm. Emma took in a deep breath, reveling in the encroaching summer night. After days of cold and gloom in Boston, the reprise felt wonderful.

"Is the restaurant very far?" she asked.

Gideon shook his head. "No. Why?"

"I was wondering if we could walk a little. The warm air feels good."

Smiling, he guided her past the doorman. "We can do whatever you want." His palm skimmed the small of her back, and the spark running up her spine made her feel so alive she could have run a marathon in her high heels. "Tonight's your night."

Her night. Her insides did a foolish little dance. Slipping her arm free from his, she pointed at the buildings lining the horizon. "Nice to finally see the top of the skyscrapers, isn't it?"

"Yeah, goodness knows you don't get to see that every day in downtown Boston."

She responded to his sarcasm with a smirk and a slight push to his shoulder. "Seriously, it's nice to see the sky change colors behind the buildings. All the different shades of pink and gray. Looks like a painting."

"Why, Miss O'Rourke, that sounds almost whimsical. Careful, whimsy's one step away from fantasy, you know."

"A momentary slip, I assure you," she replied with a laugh.

"Oh, I hope not. I'd like to think we've awaken a sleeping giant. Emma O'Rourke, dreamer."

"Afraid not." She fiddled with her wrap. There'd been a honeyed note in his voice that made her nerves hum with an uncomfortable awareness. "I suppose these sunsets pale compared to what you're used to seeing," she said, changing the subject.

"A little. In Cabo San Lucas, there's this place called Land's End where the sun literally drops off the edge of the world. You'd swear you were watching a big red ball sink into the water."

"Why, Mr. Kent, that sounds almost whimsical." She earned herself a smile and a salute.

They paused at an intersection to let a taxi pass. "There are days when I wouldn't mind sailing off into the sunset," she told him.

"Why don't you?"

"What, and leave all Kent Hotels has to offer?"

Her attempt at offhandedness failed. The look Gideon gave her was unsettling at best. "Seriously, why not?"

"Not everyone can take off. Someone has to stay and work."

"Who decided that someone had to be you?"

Life did, thought Emma. "Because that's the way it's always been," she said softly.

Somberness followed her answer. "Not tonight," Gideon replied in an equally low voice. "Not tonight."

They walked on in silence. Emma welcomed the respite. Following his words, she felt more aware of Gideon than ever. Every look, every movement registered in high definition on her brain. Like the way his sleeve brushed against her arm as they walked. Or how his fingers hovered oh so near hers, touching but not touching. A miniscule shift to the left would break contact, but she couldn't bring herself to move.

Instead, she stole a glance at his profile. If Gideon noticed, his expression didn't indicate. He stared ahead, his eyes focused on a point somewhere in the distance, as if scanning the horizon. Recalling those tropical sunsets, perhaps?

"You must be looking forward to going back."

He glanced at her, his muzzy expression that of a man yanked from his thoughts. "To Saint Martin," she added. Or Cabo, or whatever locale had dragged his thoughts away.

"With your 'errand' complete, you'll be able to go home soon."

"Mmmm," he replied. "I suppose so."

She was surprised how much his answer disappointed her. What did she expect him to say?

Quickly, she changed the subject before the emotion could take hold. "I have to admit I'm getting hungry. I don't suppose I can get a hint as to where we're going for dinner? Since you're not buying me a hot dog, that is."

"Nope. You'll have to wait and be surprised. We're only a few blocks away now. And I promise, you'll like it just as much as a hot dog."

"Promise? Because I happen to really like chili-cheese dogs."

Immediately, she regretted her teasing tone, because the smile Gideon flashed back was beyond sexy. As was his voice. "I promise, Miss O'Rourke. This will be a dinner you'll never forget."

Gideon didn't know why he'd picked this particular restaurant. He'd never eaten here himself, having always considered the place a five-star tourist trap. But as soon as the elevator doors opened and he heard Emma's gasp, he knew he'd made the right decision. Thirty-five stories above Manhattan, the entire penthouse dining room was a glassed-in paradise. Outside, the skyline beckoned from all four sides. Inside, crystal chandeliers bathed the room in light softer than candles, while real flames adorned glass-topped tables. "Like dining in midair," the restaurant ads touted.

Manufactured romance, Gideon had always thought, but seeing the wonder on Emma's face, worth the effort. Her eyes danced, they sparkled so brightly. Pleasure shot from his head to his toes. Not sexual pleasure, but the thrill of having pleased her. Her lack of pretense fed his desire to treat her like a princess. The more she refused to indulge herself, the more he wanted to shower indulgence on her. He thought back to her earlier comment, about being the one to stay back and work. He wished he knew who or what had convinced her she couldn't have more.

"What do you think?" he asked, slipping the wrap from her shoulders. "Better than a hot dog?" Her speechless nod only made his satisfaction swell more, and compelled him to lean in closer. "Wait till you see the view up close."

Just then the maître d' approached them, a crisp, slim man in a silk suit. "May I help you?" he asked in a clipped voice.

Gideon introduced himself, and the man instantly snapped to attention. "Yes, of course. Mr. Kent. Right this way. Your table's waiting."

He led them through the crowded dining room to a table in the back with an unobstructed view of the Chrysler Building, just as Gideon had requested. A bottle of champagne was chilling in a nearby stand, also as he'd requested. Gideon waited until Emma had been seated, then slipped a generous tip in the man's palm. Normally he detested men who threw money and entitlement around, but tonight he made an exception. He wanted Emma to have an experience she wouldn't forget.

"Okay, I admit, this is better than a hot dog," she said once the maître d' had left them. "This view is beautiful."

Emma's eyes sparkled in the candlelight. He hadn't noticed before, but the brown had flecks of green. It made them glitter even more than usual. A man could get lost studying those eyes.

And that dress... Christine had outdone herself. He'd sent her a Little Match Girl and got a copper-haired siren. When Emma stepped from the dressing room, every ounce of air had rushed from Gideon's lungs and he was still having trouble getting it back. The woman sitting across from him wasn't his adorable Miss O'Rourke; she was a woman who swept coherent thought straight from a man's head.

"Not as beautiful as you."

He probably shouldn't have said the words aloud, but when her blush seeped past her collarbone, regret faded in favor of his growing arousal.

Arousal that kicked up a notch when she looked away and began fiddling with her silverware. He watched her set and reset the angle of her salad fork a half-dozen times. The woman honestly didn't know her own appeal, he realized. The stirring in his blood grew stronger.

Their waiter arrived and poured the champagne. When he departed, Gideon raised his glass. "To a memorable trip," he said.

"To keeping the wolf at bay," she replied, repeating her toast from earlier. He noticed her hand shook as she raised the glass to her lips.

"You're not nervous, are you, Miss O'Rourke?"

Another blush colored her cheeks. "A little, maybe. This is all so different for me. I feel like everyone in the room's staring at me."

With that dress, they probably were, thought Gideon.

She swiveled the stem of her flute between her fingers. "It's like I have a gigantic *O* on my forehead for Out Of Place."

"Everyone feels out of place a little when they visit somewhere for the first time."

"Right. Even you?"

"Even me."

He reached across the table and squeezed her hand. A mistake, because Emma's eyes immediately darkened with awareness, sending his arousal into overload. It was all he could do not to raise her wrist to his lips and trail kisses up the inside of her arm until those eyes darkened to black.

Abruptly, perhaps because she could read his intention, she pulled her hand away. The motion was so quick Gideon nearly knocked over his champagne. By the time he recovered, she'd tucked both hands onto her lap. Out of his reach.

Dammit.

"Have you traveled to a lot of places?" From the way she chewed her lip, he guessed she was trying to change the atmosphere.

"Depends upon what you consider a lot," he replied, obliging her. "Not nearly as much as you think. The larger my company gets, the more I seem to stay in one place. The irony of the hospitality industry."

"How large is your company?"

"We opened an Australian office last year, and next spring I'm setting up shop in the Pacific Northwest. That'll make..." he tallied the number in his head "...thirteen locations worldwide."

"Wow," she replied, "definitely not a fishing charter business."

He felt himself smile like an idiot at her impressed tone. "No, definitely not. Though it did start out as one."

"Really?"

He nodded and sipped his drink. Thanks to the champagne, and the whiskey he'd had earlier, he was feeling quite mellow. The personal history tripped off his tongue easily. "When I first arrived in the Caribbean, I didn't have a dime, so I had to work the boats to make a living. Eventually, I saved up enough to buy a boat of my own. One boat became two. The rest naturally followed."

"You're being modest. If it were that easy, every fisherman would be a millionaire." She leaned forward, chin cupped in her hand, face rapt with interest. "No wonder your grandmother wants you to take over Kent Hotels."

She bit her lip and quickly looked down at her place setting. "Sorry. I probably shouldn't have said that."

Embarrassment looked so cute on her. "You figured out Mariah's grand plan, did you?"

"Wasn't hard. Mrs. Kent said a couple things. Then there was the summons home, the visit to Mr. Chamberlain. Doesn't take a rocket scientist to connect the dots."

"I suppose not. Then again, Mariah never believed in subtlety, either."

"She doesn't have to. People do what she asks regardless."

"Gee, and what makes you say that?" Gideon teased.

"Oh, I don't know, this trip to New York maybe?" she teased back.

They grinned at each other, enjoying the shared joke for a couple seconds in silence. There were times, thought Gideon, when he felt he and Miss O'Rourke were reading the same page. Like two peas in a pod. Though her pea was by far the more delectable of the two. He studied the way she raised her glass to her mouth, appreciating how the liquid made her lips glisten. "You're curious," he said, guessing at her thoughts. "About why I don't want the job."

"Family politics is none of my business," she replied. "Besides, I would think you have your hands full running your own company."

"Nice to see someone at Kent Hotels recognizes that fact."

Curiosity continued to lurk in her eyes, but she said nothing. Nor would she, he realized gratefully. She would never push. The knowledge made him feel closer to her than he'd felt toward another person in a long, long time, and for a wild second he considered sharing his true reason for walking away from Kent Hotels. What would she say then? he wondered. To learn he wasn't really a Kent?

A voice in the back of his brain said she wouldn't care nearly as much as he did.

"Mariah will have to find someone else." While he spoke, he reached for the champagne and refilled their glasses. "Last time I looked, there were more than enough Kents to choose from. Andrew's son, Alexander, for example."

A slight frown crossed her pretty face.

"You have a problem with Alexander?" Gideon asked.

"I don't know Alexander."

"Then what?" He didn't like that her smile disappeared. He wanted it back.

"Nothing."

Not nothing. Something. Her dismissal made him all the more curious. Unlike her, he would press. "Miss O'Rourke, I thought when we left Boston, we decided you would share your opinions."

"About hotel business," she reminded him. "Not Kent family business."

"When it comes to the Kents, family business and hotel business are one and the same. Besides, call me quirky, but I like it when you speak your mind. Now, what bothers you about Alexander?"

"Nothing. I told you, I don't even know Alexander Kent."

"Yet you frowned when I mentioned his name. Why?"

"Well…" She went back to playing with her flatware, obviously searching for a diplomatic response. "I couldn't help noticing you refer to your family in the third person. It's always 'Mariah' or 'Andrew.' You never say 'Grandmother' or 'Uncle.'"

"Would you own up to Andrew as your uncle?"

To his relief, she laughed. "If only we could choose our relations," she said. "Life would be so much easier, wouldn't it." It was a statement, not a question.

Tightness gripped Gideon's chest. She understood. He could see the understanding reflected in those luminous brown eyes. How she knew, he couldn't say, but she did, and the realization was more intoxicating than all her beauty and sweetness combined.

He wanted to grab her and pull her into his arms then and there. Instead, he raised his glass, silently toasting her as he drank. "Wouldn't it, though," he said. "Wouldn't it."

Emma had fallen down the rabbit's hole. Sitting in this glass tower, surrounded by the night, she'd been dropped in a different world. A beautiful, magical world of sparkling light.

She smiled at the man across the table. He smiled back, and her insides danced. There was magic in the way Gideon looked at her tonight, as well. It was as if every glance set off a flume of bubbles that started at her toes and floated to her brain, making her feel lighter than air. It certainly wasn't how a secretary should feel when eating with her boss; in the morning she would be kicking herself for getting carried away. But at the moment, with Gideon's eyes beckoning invitingly, she couldn't resist.

He was as perfect a dinner companion as she could imagine. While the waiter brought one gourmet treat after another, Gideon entertained her with stories of life in the Caribbean and the eccentric travelers that crossed his path. With each tale, her enchantment grew stronger. The rest of the dining room faded away until she wasn't aware of anything but Gideon. She studied the graceful way his fingers held the handle of his knife, watched the curve of his mouth as he laughed, with new, acute awareness, enjoying what seemed to be their own candlelit world.

Unfortunately, like all fantasies, dinner ended. While the elevator brought them back to earth, Emma closed her eyes, savoring the last few moments. When she opened them, she saw Gideon watching her with a curious smile.

"What?" she asked, shyness sweeping over her.

"Nothing," he replied, still smiling.

They walked outside to discover the city's second life in full swing. Neon lights threw colored patterns on the sidewalk, and high-heeled pedestrians replaced the commuter traffic. In silent agreement, Emma and Gideon began walking back to the hotel. Remnants of dinner's magic followed.

After a few feet, she turned to him. "Thank you. That was..." Words failed her.

No matter. Gideon seemed to understand, for he smiled. "I couldn't take you to New York and fail to show you anything but the inside of a hotel room, now could I?"

The innuendo in his words did nothing to quell the pull she was feeling toward him. "Still," she replied, "there's dinner and there's...this. All of it. The restaurant, the dress— Oh my God, the dress!" She clapped a hand to her mouth. "I forgot to pay!" She'd been so enchanted by her transformation she'd forgotten.

"Relax. When I called the boutique, I told Christine to charge everything to the room. I had a feeling you'd ignore my request."

Emma blushed. "Am I that predictable?"

"Afraid so."

"You didn't have to pick up the bill."

"I know. I wanted to. You deserved it. You deserved this whole night."

There was such tenderness in his voice, Emma felt herself falling. Perspective was getting harder and harder to keep. "For a job well done," she said.

"Because I wanted to," he replied again, reaching for her.

A gasp escaped her lips as the back of his fingers brushed her cheek. She looked up, saw the earnestness of his expression and tumbled a little further.

"So let me, okay?"

Lost in his indigo gaze, Emma could only nod. They were standing impossibly close. Yet again, he'd merged their space without her realizing it. Barely a breath separated them; she could feel his body almost touching hers. "You know what else I want?" he asked.

"What?"

The glint behind his smile made her heart race. "Come on. I'll show you."

"I can't believe I let you talk me into a moonlight cruise."

"You can't go to New York and not look at the Statue of Liberty. She is a symbol of freedom, you know."

"At least she's made of stone. I don't think I'm going to feel my toes for days."

"A couple hours soaking in the tub and you'll be fine."

They were in the corridor, in front of Emma's suite. Emma had replaced her shawl with Gideon's jacket, which she'd wrapped tightly around her. Cold feet aside, she'd actually loved the boat ride. There was something incredibly serene about floating on the water, away from the hustle and bustle. Without street noise, the city looked like a picture postcard. She and Gideon had stood at the railing and watched the buildings float silently by. Later, when they turned and Lady Liberty greeted them from the outer harbor, Gideon had moved behind her, to shield her from the wind. Emma had viewed Staten Island from the shelter of his arms, barely feeling the cold. She was sorry to see the trip end. She was sorry to see the whole night end. Who knew when she'd ever experience another night like this one?

"Thank you," she said, for what had to be the millionth time. "I can't tell you how incredible tonight has been."

"Even with the cold toes?"

She laughed. "Yes, even with the cold toes."

"Good." He reached out and flipped a lock of hair from her shoulder. "And you don't need to keep thanking me. Tonight was my pleasure."

They stood smiling at one another. Emma twisted her key card in her fingers, unsure what to say next. If this had been a date, she could invite him in for a drink.

But this wasn't a date, right? Drinks wouldn't be appropriate.

To play it safe, she returned to her comfort zone. Work. "What time would you like to leave tomorrow?"

Gideon gave her an odd look, one almost of disappointment. "Back to business, are we, Miss O'Rourke?"

No sense dragging out tonight's fantasy longer than necessary, right? "I don't want to delay you any more than I already have. I know you're eager to head back to Saint Martin. Plus your grandmother's no doubt annoyed you've kept her waiting." As far as Emma knew, he had yet to call with the news about Ross Chamberlain.

"Ah, so you're protecting me from the wrath of Mariah," he teased. "Don't worry, I'll be fine. If not, I can always unleash Hinckley on her again."

"Oooh, that'll teach her," Emma exclaimed. Joking with him was so easy. There were moments, like this one, when she felt like they were on the exact same page.

Perhaps it was a good thing he planned on returning to Saint Martin soon. A woman could easily mistake familiarity for something more. Especially when he smiled the way he was smiling at her.

She cleared her throat. "Well, I should let you go. I know you said to stop, but thank you again for tonight."

"Told you I'd give you a New York experience."

"Yes, you did. For the record, though, I would have settled for the hot dog in the park."

"I know."

While he spoke, she'd started to shrug his jacket off, but he stopped her, reaching out to take the garment by the lapels. She could feel his thumb caress the material. His expression had turned strangely serious. "You're an original, Miss O'Rourke, that's for sure. No fantasies, no need for extravagances, no expectations. Why don't you want more?"

She couldn't. "More" led to disappointment. "I have enough." The thickness in her voice made the words sound hollow.

Fingers brushed her skin as he slipped the jacket from her shoulders. Her breath hitched. When had his hands gotten so warm? They were like fire against her skin.

"Do you?" he asked, his voice low and gravelly. "Because I think you deserve more."

More? "Like what?"

She felt her body leaning toward him, closing the distance between them. She saw his head dip, his eyes grow heavy-lidded.

"Like everything," he whispered.

Everything. He made the word sound so possible. Except she didn't need everything. Right now, right here, she didn't need anything.

Then she felt his lips touch her cheek. A gentle lingering kiss that made her knees buckle and her heart stop. Instinctively, she turned toward him, seeking the taste of his mouth. To her disappointment and surprise, he pulled away.

Leaving her wanting more.

"Good night, Miss O'Rourke," he said with a parting caress.

She watched in stunned silence as Gideon disappeared around the corner, while she pressed a shaky hand to where his lips had touched her skin.

CHAPTER SEVEN

THE next morning was business as usual. Neither mentioned the night before. They made small talk during the ride to the airport, and the moment they boarded the plane, Gideon barricaded himself with work. "Jamilla, my assistant in Saint Martin, is almost as efficient as you," he teased. "She's managed to fill my in-box in less than twenty-four hours."

Emma smiled, but said nothing. She sat across the aisle, updating her day planner. While part of her appreciated the silence, another part hated that her thoughts had free rein to wander. She knew exactly where they would head, too.

Don't get carried away. How often had she thought those words when her mother met a new potential beau? And yet she'd done the exact same thing last night. Too much champagne and candlelight had made her forget reality. Emma pressed her fingertips to her cheek, recalling the feel of Gideon's mouth, hating the stirring the memory caused in her chest. At least now she understood her mother a little better. She could see how easily a woman could get sucked in by romantic fantasy. Last night she'd felt so indescribably special it had been like flying. If that was how her mother felt, then Emma understood why she continued to chase the dream. The high was incredibly addictive.

Except, as with any addiction, when the high ended, you came crashing down. Like she had this morning when she woke up and became plain old Miss O'Rourke again.

She stole a glance across the aisle. Saddest thing was, even knowing about this morning's crash and burn, she would trade her soul for another night like last night.

"Wouldn't you rather go home?" Gideon asked. "I'm sure Mariah doesn't expect you to come in today."

"I want to check my in-box," Emma replied.

They stood watching the parking garage elevator count down the floors. Gideon had hoped Emma would drop him off at the Fairlane and head home, instead of insisting on coming upstairs. He should have known better.

Hopefully, Mariah wouldn't insist on meeting too long. He needed some space to clear his head. Maybe a sail. The brisk air might help. Last night played like a video loop in his head, with every taste, every scent, every touch captured in Technicolor detail. What was he thinking, spouting all that nonsense about her deserving everything? She did, but that wasn't the point. The point was that somewhere between wanting to indulge her and Ellis Island, he forgot his own rules. He actually started buying all that manufactured romance.

That's what happens when you spend time with sweet young things, he told himself. He was beginning to get why all the Kent men continued to make fools of themselves.

Fortunately, his non-Kent genes had kicked in just in time, saving him from doing something he'd really regret. Like kissing her senseless and making love to her all night long.

Now if only his body would forget how amazing her skin

tasted. He'd had to take a cold shower last night to cool his blood. If a simple peck on the cheek stirred him that much, then her mouth would probably be the death of him. Being stuck in close proximity to her body was bad enough. Every turn, she assaulted him with her doe eyes and vanilla-scented skin. He'd been fighting his body's reaction since LaGuardia.

Maybe he should have gone with the hot dog in the park, after all.

"Should we stop at the front desk and pick up Hinckley's carrier?" Emma asked, all business as usual. She acted as if last night had never happened.

"Hinckley hates the carrier," he replied. "One look and he'll hide. Best I wait till he lets his guard down."

The elevator doors opened and he moved back to let her board. As she passed, vanilla drifted with her. The urge to lean close and inhale gripped him, and he had to struggle not to give in.

By the time he joined her, Emma had already inserted the keycard and stood studying the control panel as if it contained the secrets of the universe. Briefcase in one hand, the other gripping her purse strap, she was an expressionless, efficient, trench-coated statue. Another urge gripped him, this time the desire to grab her shoulders and shake her until she showed some kind of reaction.

Instead he took a position on the other side of the elevator—best he put as much space between them as possible—and checked his watch. "Almost two o'clock. If the elevator doesn't move quickly, I'll have to sit through her soap."

Emma's lips curved slightly, not enough to qualify as a full smile, but enough to make his blood heat. "Maybe she'll make an exception for you."

"Only if hell froze over while we were in the air."

The smile grew a little wider. Gideon wanted more. He wanted a full-blown grin like the ones he'd seen last night.

Let it go, Gideon. Be grateful she's not calling you out on your behavior. Last time he checked, kissing your secretary, even if only on the cheek, wasn't exactly proper business behavior.

There was a soft ding, and the elevator doors parted. The small waiting area that served as entrance to Mariah's quarters was empty.

"Odd," Emma said, twisting the door handle. "Your grandmother usually keeps her door unlocked during business hours."

The hair on the back of Gideon's neck prickled. He looked at his watch again. One fifty-nine. "Have you spoken to her today?"

"Earlier, before we took off. We didn't discuss any last-minute appointments." Emma frowned. "Mrs. Kent wouldn't schedule anything for two o'clock, anyway."

"No, she wouldn't," he replied.

He waited impatiently for Emma to unlock the door. Before they could even enter her office, Hinckley was upon them, meowing hoarsely and twisting around their legs. He was the only sign of life.

Emma looked up at Gideon, her face reflecting his worry. "Any reason your grandmother would lock him out?"

"No." His insides turned cold.

The door to Mariah's suite was sealed tight. Their eyes met. Neither of them had to say a word.

The television set wasn't on.

"Mariah!" Gideon hollered, banging on his grandmother's door. "Mariah, are you in there?"

Without waiting for a response, he kicked the door open, knocking the wood panel from its hinges. Emma followed, less than a step behind.

Mariah's sitting room was empty. The television was off. "Mariah!" he called again.

"Gideon?" The faint cry came from the bedroom. In tandem, they ran to the doorway, only to stop short. Gideon's heart sank to the pit of his stomach.

Mariah lay on the floor by the bed, legs tucked awkwardly beneath her. When she saw them, she attempted to sit up, only to wince and fall back again.

He recovered from his shock and rushed to her side. "What happened?"

"I felt dizzy. I went to lie down and I fell. I must have hit—ooh!" She winced again. "My chest. It hurts."

"Shhh, lie still. I'll take care of everything." He stroked her silver hair, hoping he sounded calm, because he sure as hell didn't feel that way.

Emma knelt beside him. "An ambulance is on the way," she said. "And I asked the front desk to track down your father and uncle."

"Thank you."

"This couldn't have happened too long ago. The bed's made." Meaning the maid had already come and gone. If they hadn't arrived when they did, Mariah might have lain on the floor for God knows how long.

Gideon felt Emma's hand touch his shoulder. It was exactly the reassurance he needed. He gave her a brief, grateful nod and turned his attention back to Mariah. Her pale blue eyes glistened with moisture. Gideon's own vision blurred for a second. All of sudden he was nineteen years old again, his bags packed, listening to Mariah tell him that blood or no blood, he'd always be her grandson. That she would never give up on him.

He stroked the hair from her pale cheek. "Don't worry

about anything, Grandmother." Emotion tightened his voice. "I'm here now. I'll take care of everything."

"What's taking so long?" Andrew Kent jammed his fingers through his silver hair before pushing himself from his seat. "We should have heard something by now. Where on earth is Dr. Crenshaw?"

"She said she'd find us as soon as she had some news to share," Gideon replied, in the same firm yet gentle voice he'd been using all afternoon. Jennifer Crenshaw was Mrs. Kent's personal physician. She'd arrived earlier and taken charge of her patient's tests.

Andrew shook his head. "I don't like how long it's taking."

"You can't rush these things. When they do talk to us, I want them to have facts, not speculation, don't you?"

"Gideon's right," Jonathan Kent said softly. "Mother's in good hands. Let Dr. Crenshaw do her job."

Andrew let out a frustrated breath, but didn't argue any further. Like she had in New York, Emma marveled at Gideon's command. He seemed to recognize Andrew's bluster ran in direct proportion to his nerves, and managed his uncle accordingly.

The past couple of hours had been a blur of activity and confusion. Gideon had accompanied his grandmother in the ambulance, while Emma followed behind in the SUV. His father and uncle had arrived at the hospital a short time later. Jonathan Kent looked shell-shocked, while Andrew almost immediately began demanding information, growing frustrated and belligerent when none was forthcoming. That's when Gideon took charge. Watching him calm Andrew down and communicate with the staff, Emma understood immediately why Mrs. Kent wanted him to run Kent Hotels. Calm and collected, even though she knew inside he was as distraught as the others, he was a natural born leader. Her heart swelled with admiration.

Stuck in the middle of the melee, Emma did what she could, getting coffee and retrieving doctor's numbers. But mostly she sat in the corner observing, superfluous to the action around her.

Gideon's father surprised her. Usually charming and loquacious, he sat wordlessly apart from his son, watchful yet distant. Emma might have attributed his aloofness to worry—maybe he was someone who withdrew into himself when faced with adversity—had he not managed to charm the hospital staff, even going so far as to apologize for Andrew's outbursts.

Gideon, she noticed, barely spoke to him, either. There appeared to be a line drawn between the two that neither wanted to cross.

And yet, as separated from one another as the three men were, they were still an entity unto themselves. A united Kent front, separate and superior.

After what seemed forever, Dr. Crenshaw appeared. She went directly to Gideon. "Your grandmother had a mild heart attack," she told him. "Nothing too severe. More of a wake-up call than anything. She'll need to make some lifestyle changes. The chest pain she complained about was actually from a cracked rib. Apparently she struck the corner of the nightstand when she fell forward."

"So she'll be all right?" Jonathan asked.

Dr. Crenshaw nodded, and all three men's shoulders relaxed with relief. "She'll be up and bossing people around in no time. She's already lecturing the nurses about patient hospitality."

"Heaven help the hospital," Gideon murmured.

"Can we see her now?" Andrew asked.

"Keep it short. I want her to get some rest." Dr. Crenshaw addressed Gideon. "She's asking to see you. When you go in, do me a favor and tell her no hotel business for at least twenty-four hours."

"Like she'll listen to me."

The doctor smiled. "You have as good a chance as anybody."

Gideon disappeared behind Mrs. Kent's hospital door. Emma immediately shivered. With him gone, the corridor felt cold and empty. Andrew and Jonathan turned their backs to her and talked to each other in low tones. They seemed unaware that Emma was even there.

Why was she still here? she wondered. For Gideon? He didn't need her. He had his family. She was merely the secretary.

Tossing her empty cup in the trash, she left.

"You gave us quite a scare, missy," Gideon admonished, upon entering his grandmother's room.

"I scared myself," Mariah replied. She looked tiny buried under the covers of her hospital bed. "I hate being helpless."

"Really? I never would have guessed!"

There was a small stool in the corner. He pulled it to the side of the bed and sat down. The sudden change of height reminded him of younger days and made him smile. "You're going to have to start taking better care of yourself, Mariah."

"I like it better when you use 'Grandmother.'"

So did he. Gideon looked down at the hand resting on his arm. The long tapered fingers were crooked from age, but the touch was as firm as ever. Tightness gripped his chest as he covered those fingers with his own.

"Thank you," she said.

"Shouldn't you be thanking your soap? If you weren't such a creature of habit, we might not have realized something was wrong."

"I'll write the producer a note. I meant thank you for coming home. I've missed you, Gideon."

"I missed you, too." The tightness got a little stronger. This uncharacteristically emotional side of Mariah threatened to dislodge all the feelings he usually kept under control.

He rose to leave. "I better go. Dr. Crenshaw told us not to tire you out, and your sons are pretty eager to check on you."

She squeezed his arm. "Come back tomorrow."

"Of course."

His father and Andrew passed by him on his way out the door. Jonathan looked in his direction for a second, but said nothing. No different than it had been all day, really.

Though there had been one moment. A fleeting instance when, while pacing back and forth, his father had looked in his direction and nodded. As if he was glad Gideon was there with them. And damn if the feeling didn't shake him to the core.

Because he liked it.

A sudden gulf of loneliness opened inside him. Now that the crisis was past, his control slipped and he felt unsteady and adrift. He needed a mooring, an anchorage to steady him.

Emma. He needed Emma. From the moment they'd found Mariah, Emma had been there, steady and reassuring. At the peak of the confusion, when Dr. Crenshaw was nowhere to be found and Andrew was bellowing at the nursing staff, Gideon had just had to look at her, sitting quietly next to a rack of linens, to regain his bearings.

He needed some of her steadiness now. Instinctively, he turned to the chair next to the linen rack.

The chair was empty.

"Emma, open up. It's me."

Emma frowned at her front door, trying to figure out who "me" was. The voice sounded like Gideon Kent's, but that was impossible. He was at the hospital with his family. What's more, he didn't know where she lived.

But it was Gideon. Peering through the peephole, she saw his steely eyes looking back, and a thrill passed through her. Quickly, she quashed her excitement. If Gideon sought her out, it had to be because something was wrong.

She unlatched the door, apparently yanking it open with more force than necessary, for Gideon started. Either that or he was taken aback by her blue plaid flannel pants and pink sweatshirt. Upon coming home from the hospital, she'd been too tired and unsettled to care about matching pajamas. "I woke you up," he said apologetically.

"I was watching television," she assured him. "Is something wrong with Mrs. Kent?"

"Other than being cranky about being laid up, and taking it out on the entire hospital, she's doing all right."

She breathed out in relief. "Good. I'm glad."

On the other hand, something was clearly wrong with Gideon. His cheeks were ruddy, red and windblown, and tension lined his face. He still wore his suit from this morning, though he'd shed the tie and undone the top two buttons of his shirt. The gap revealed a patch of tan, smooth skin.

Amazing, thought Emma. Tired and burdened as he looked, he was still devastatingly handsome. She tugged the hem of her sweatshirt in a vain attempt to look fresher. "Would you like some coffee? Tea?"

He shook his head. "I'm caffeined out. Though if you have anything stronger…"

"I don't have whiskey. Will beer do?"

"Beer would be perfect."

"Domestic okay?"

"As long as it contains alcohol, I don't care if you brewed it in your sink."

She headed to the kitchen. Gideon followed, opting to lean against the counter and watch while she fished around in her utensil drawer for a bottle opener. The scrutiny made her suddenly, incredibly sensitive of her surroundings and how far removed they were from the suite at the Landmark, or even his boat. Emma's landlord had spared every expense decorating her side of the duplex. The white laminate cabinets were chipped, and the beige countertops looked as cheap as they probably were. Gideon seemed like a piece of fine art at a flea market in comparison. So why was he here?

"You left the hospital without saying anything," he said.

She was surprised he'd noticed. No one else had. "I didn't want to disturb your visit with your grandmother. Why, did you need something?"

He gave her a long look. "Yes, I did."

"Oh." The hiss of air rushing from the beer bottle filled the kitchen. "I'm sorry. But you said Mrs. Kent was all right, yes?"

"Yes." She handed him his drink, and he took a long sip. "Dr. Crenshaw wants her to stay in the hospital for a night or two."

"I bet she's thrilled about that."

"About as much as you'd expect, but she's resigned to her fate. I think today frightened her more than she wants to admit."

He took another long drink. Two sips and the bottle was nearly empty. Something was off. Gone was the commanding presence from the hospital, replaced by weariness and shadows. "Her accident frightened you, too, didn't it?" Emma murmured.

His response was to drain the last of his bottle. "Got another?"

Yes, this afternoon had definitely shaken him.

"Funny," she said, popping the cap from a second bottle and handing it to him, "but I always think of your grandmother as indestructible."

"She certainly gives that impression. But then, the Kents are very good at false impressions."

What an odd response. He'd said something similar about his father yesterday.

"Nice place you have here," he said, abruptly changing the subject. "Do you live alone?"

She tried hard to pretend his question didn't make her skin tingle. "Yes, why?"

"No reason. Just wondering if I should expect your mother to pop in and join us."

"Good Lord, no. She lives a couple blocks away. We would kill each other if we lived together.

"Besides," Emma added, thinking of the text message she'd received earlier, "she's off on a 'romantic adventure.'" She framed the last two words with her fingers.

"Your mother's got a boyfriend."

"This week, anyway."

That earned her a crooked smile. "Sounds like she took a page from Andrew's book."

"Only without the marriages."

"That could be a good thing. Saves on attorney's fees."

"About all it saves."

"True. They always forget about the collateral damage, don't they?"

A lump stuck in Emma's throat. Talking about her mother only reminded her of last night, and with Gideon standing as close as he was, it was the last thing she wanted to think about. Especially when his voice had that tired, melancholy tone that made her want to comfort him.

Then again, if he had that tone of voice, maybe talking about her mother was a good thing. A verbal cold shower stopping Emma from doing something stupid.

Needing to distract herself from the thickness growing in the room, she grabbed the kitchen sponge and began wiping invisible spills off the Formica. "You said you needed something. What was it?"

"You."

The sponge slipped from her fingers. She gripped the edge of the counter to keep from buckling. "Me?"

"I wanted to thank you. For your help this afternoon."

"Oh." She should have realized. "I only made a few phone calls." He'd been the real unifier.

"You did more than you think."

"Right, I got coffee, too." She gave the counter another unnecessary swipe.

"You were there when we needed you, which means a lot."

How she wished his soft reply didn't make her feel all fuzzy inside. "You could have told me this by phone. I'm sure your family—"

At the word *family*, he gave an irritated snort. "My 'family' will do just fine without me. They have so far."

Not from what Emma had seen at the hospital.

"Funny thing, family," he continued, his voice distant. "What's that old saying, you can pick your friends but—"

"Family's forever."

"I had a different phrase in mind," he said, "but that'll do."

The loneliness behind his words made her heart ache. Was he, she wondered, regretting his estrangement? Or his return?

Meanwhile, Gideon had become intently interested in peeling the label off the bottle neck. The tearing of paper sounded like a foghorn in the silent kitchen.

"Did you know I was raised to run Kent Hotels?" he asked, without looking up.

Emma wasn't surprised, though she was surprised he chose to share the fact with her. "But you don't want to."

"I did once." He raised the bottle to his lips. "But things change, right? Life doesn't always turn out how we plan."

"Seldom does," Emma replied.

"And yet people like Mariah keep fighting to the bitter end. You'd think she'd realize that some things even an iron maiden can't fix." With one final swig, he emptied the bottle and slapped it on the counter.

"I'm tired," he said abruptly.

"I'm not surprised. Days like today are draining. Especially when the person hurt is someone you care about."

Gideon's eyes met hers. Despite the bright overhead lights, the blue was so dark she couldn't tell where pupil ended and iris began. They were eyes full of despair. "I wish I didn't," he replied, his voice tight.

"Didn't what? Care?" She couldn't imagine that was what he meant.

But it was, because he nodded, and in that one simple gesture, Emma saw all the vulnerability and loneliness he kept tamped down. Her heart swelled, not with pity, but with an emotion far deeper. One she didn't want to contemplate. She simply wanted to offer comfort. To somehow let him know he needn't feel alone.

With a boldness she didn't realize she had, she raised her palm to his face. She didn't say a word. She let her touch do the talking.

The air around them ignited. Suddenly the loneliness in Gideon's eyes disappeared, replaced by something far hotter and primal. Seeing it, Emma's own desire sprang to life. She traced her fingers down his cheek, letting the stubble burn the tips. Gideon's gaze dropped to her mouth. Anticipation ripped through her body. Her breathing grew ragged. Her lungs couldn't get enough air.

"Emma," he whispered hoarsely.

It was all he said before sweeping her into his arms.

CHAPTER EIGHT

THERE was no tentativeness, no slow build. Gideon held her tight, his mouth slanting across hers with a passion that, if Emma could breathe, would have taken her breath away.

Her body responded without hesitation. Clinging to the lapels of his coat, she pressed her length to his. Common sense fell away. He needed her. And she wanted him. Wanted this more than she'd ever wanted anything in her life.

"Emma, sweet, sweet Emma." Gideon chanted her name between kisses. Hearing him say her first name sounded strange, but incredibly right. His hands slipped under the hem of her sweatshirt and skimmed the hollow above the waistband of her pajama bottoms. Emma let out a sigh. She knew this touch. It was the touch from her dream.

With a soft whimper, she arched closer, while her hands wrestled Gideon's coat from his shoulders. Who cared if tonight had no future, or that in the morning she'd have to deal with reality? Tonight nothing mattered but this.

Propping himself on one elbow, Gideon stared down at the woman sleeping beside him. She lay curled on her side, lips parted. A strand of hair curled across the bridge of her nose. He smoothed his hand across her forehead, brushing the strand away, and she sighed a sweet sigh.

When he'd left the hospital, he'd only thought to find Emma to talk. He'd called the hotel and cajoled the night manager into looking up her home address, and then he walked here, hoping the combination of brisk night air and Emma's calming presence would rid his head of thoughts he couldn't put words to. Making love had been the last thing on his mind.

Hadn't it?

Stop kidding yourself. He knew when Emma answered the door in all her disheveled innocence that this visit couldn't end at simply talking. Being with her was...

He couldn't match words to his thoughts. Only that when she looked at him with those luminous brown eyes, he felt... Why couldn't he think of the right words? Understood? No longer alone?

All he knew was the sensation filled his body. He'd reached for her because he couldn't not reach for her. He'd needed to feel her, to have her sweet warm presence surround him. She touched something deep inside him in a way that was thrilling and disturbing at the same time.

Emma stirred and pressed closer, her legs entwined with his in unconscious possession. A satisfied smile played on her lips. He'd caused that smile. Male pride swelled even as guilt assailed him.

What happens next? Mind-blowing night together or not, he was venturing into dangerous territory by sleeping with Emma. She wasn't the kind of woman a man tossed aside after one time, and while he was pretty sure she understood his views on commitment, he didn't want to see her hurt.

Next to him, there was more stirring, and he heard a soft voice say, "Penny for your thoughts?"

Emma's doe eyes were shy and uncertain. Instantly, Gideon's chest constricted. "I was thinking how beautiful you look when you sleep," he answered truthfully. "Like an angel."

Color flushed her skin, reminding him how, only a short time before, she'd flushed with passion. He brushed an imaginary strand of hair from her face, pleased when she shuddered. He wanted her again with a fierceness that shocked him.

"You were smiling," he said. "Good dream?"

"Mmmm." Eyes closing, she burrowed her head in the curve of his neck. "The best."

He wanted her again, more urgently than the first time, if that was even possible. Emma nestled closer, her breath warm on his skin. It was like someone flicked a switch in his body, into the On position. Even the caress of her breathing aroused him.

This was more than dangerous. If he was smart, he'd get up and get out before he dug himself in any deeper.

Only being smart wasn't what he wanted right now.

He gave his sleeping beauty a little nudge. "Hey, don't slip too far into dreamland."

To his surprise, she stiffened and inched off his body. "Sorry, I didn't mean to…."

Was that disappointment in her eyes? The emotion disappeared too quickly for him to tell. That and the fact that Emma had rolled over, putting her back to him. "Have you seen my sweatshirt?" she asked.

"In the kitchen," he replied, snaking his arm around her waist. Surely she wasn't getting dressed? "You don't need to cover up on my account," he teased.

"I'm not. I'm cold, that's all."

Well, he knew how to remedy that situation. Only to his

dismay, Emma was slipping from beneath the covers and covering her gloriously naked body with a chenille throw.

"Where are you going?" he asked, pushing himself into a sitting position.

"To get my robe. It's on the hook in the bathroom." She had the throw pulled so tight he wondered how she could breathe.

"Why?"

"I told you, I'm cold."

"I meant why are you getting up at all?" He was beginning to sound like her, asking why, but he couldn't help himself. Since rolling over, she'd yet to look directly at him, which made him a little bit nervous.

"It would be rude to lie in bed while you let yourself out, wouldn't it?"

"Let myself…?"

"Of course. I didn't expect you to stay."

Why not? "I wasn't planning on—"

"It's okay. You don't owe me any explanations."

He didn't?

"It's been a stressful day. You needed a port in a storm and I—I wanted to give you one."

Finally, she looked at him, though in the dimly lit room he couldn't tell if her expression matched her casual tone. If only he'd thought to turn on more lights when they'd stumbled in here.

"You were more than a port in a storm, Emma" he said.

"Figure of speech." She flashed him what looked like a tremulous smile. "I only mean I know how these things work."

His stomach tensed. What should have given him reassurance for some reason made him more uneasy. "You do?"

"I'm a big girl, Gideon. I knew exactly what I was doing, and the repercussions. So don't worry, I don't expect anything. Now, will you give me a minute? I don't want to walk you to the door naked."

She closed the bathroom door. A few seconds later, Gideon heard the sound of water running.

He sank back, his skull whacking the headboard. What just happened?

Congratulations, Emma, you handled that pretty darn well.

Eyes burning, she blinked at her reflection in the bathroom mirror, barely recognizing the face blinking back. Tousled hair, swollen lips. She was looking at the face of a sexually satisfied woman. When it came to lovemaking, Gideon was, as always, a man in command of his environment.

It had been glorious.

Don't get carried away, she quickly reminded herself. Gideon had been looking for comfort after a stressful day, nothing more. She'd known that when she'd returned his overtures. She wasn't going to compound the situation by expecting more. Nor would she embarrass herself by clinging. She would handle this with sophistication and maturity. She wouldn't think about Gideon's touch or how it made her feel like the most desirable woman in the world. She wouldn't let her lover's prowess cloud reality.

Why, then, did her heart feel as if it was ripping in two?

Drying her face, she slipped on her robe, cringing when she saw the coffee stain on the front, then kicked herself for cringing. A little late to worry about impressions now, wasn't it? She twisted her mussed hair into an even more mussed topknot and opened the door.

Gideon was buttoning his shirt when she walked out. Avoiding his eyes, she crossed the room to her bureau, saying in as casual voice as she could muster, "If you give me a moment, I'll drive you to the marina."

"No need."

"I don't mind. It's late. You'll never catch a cab at this hour." And there was no way he would spend the night. Making small talk over breakfast would be unbearable.

What did one wear when driving home a one-night stand, anyway? She rummaged through the drawer, angry that it mattered to her. She'd finally settled on a beige sweater when a hand came down on her forearm, halting her search.

Apology lined Gideon's face. "Don't."

Her knees faltered, along with her veil of sophistication. She floundered for footing, desperately thinking of something neutral to say in response. "Feels like it's getting colder. I wouldn't be surprised if we have snow flurries. But then that's New England for you, right? Snow in October."

He opened his mouth to reply. She cut him off.

"It's all right, Gideon. I already told you I understood." And she wasn't up to rehashing. "You don't owe me any explanations." Or apologies. Please, no apologies. "Now let me get dressed so I can take you to your boat."

"Don't get dressed," he said. "I'll walk. It's not that far."

"Oh. Sure." He wasn't apologizing, after all; he was just eager to escape her company. How embarrassing. She furiously blinked back the tears springing to her eyes.

Wordlessly, they headed to where the night had begun—her kitchen. His coat lay in a heap on the floor, the sleeve draped over her discarded sweatshirt, an intimate reminder of what had transpired. Emma looked away. The awkwardness in the room was growing exponentially. No wonder Gideon wanted out quickly.

"Can I get you some coffee? For the road," she added, in case he thought her offer a ploy for him to stay. "I've got travel mugs."

"I think I've had enough to drink, coffee and otherwise."

Yes, she thought, casting a glance at the empty beer bottles, maybe he had.

Too bad she didn't have the same excuse.

She waited while he shrugged into his jacket, then led him to the front door. To her relief Gideon didn't try to draw her into conversation. That is, until she touched the door handle. Then he reached out and covered her hand. "I don't want—"

"Gideon, I'm fine," she said, determinedly bright. Other than wanting to melt back against him as soon as he touched her, that is. "Tell your grandmother I'll be by first thing tomorrow morning. If you'd like, I can call first. To make sure I don't interrupt any tests." Along with giving them a chance to avoid each other.

An unreadable emotion flickered across Gideon's face as he brushed a strand of hair from her temple. The tenderness nearly killed her, and she had to brace herself against the door to withstand the impact.

His fingers trailed downward, along her cheekbone, until they curled around her jaw, drawing her forward. Her traitorous body began to hum. It took every ounce of her resolve to turn her head at the last second.

Didn't matter. He found her lips, anyway. "Good night, Emma," he whispered.

She mustered a smile. "Goodbye, Gideon."

"Another arrangement? Good grief, don't these people have something better to do with their money?"

Emma wondered the same thing. Mrs. Kent's hospital room resembled a florist's shop. Three deliveries arrived during her visit alone. Large, expansive arrangements from Boston's top florists. They dwarfed the small get-well bouquet she'd purchased at the hospital gift shop, and filled the air with thick fragrance.

She'd so had enough of flowers today.

Before visiting the hospital, she'd stopped by the hotel, where the concierge told her a dozen red roses were waiting. At first she'd thought they were for Mrs. Kent, until she noticed the card addressed to her. Gideon had sent them. Roses, apparently, were the obligatory custom following a one-night stand. She'd left them in the box, hoping out of sight would equal out of mind. But all these flowers were quickly proving that theory wrong. Maybe she should bring Gideon's bouquet here. Let them blend in with the others.

"They're from the governor." She read the card stuck amid the blooms. "He wishes you a speedy recovery." Gideon's card had only his name. Could've been worse, she realized. He could have added some lame closing, such as "Fondly."

She looked around the room. "Where would you like me to put it? Space is at a premium."

"Send the foolish thing to the nurse's station. As a matter of fact, send all the plants there," Mrs. Kent replied. "I can't take the smell."

Emma couldn't blame her. All the flowery scents were giving her a headache. "Unfortunately, I doubt this is the last. If you'd like, I can arrange for the flowers to go to other patients. Maybe the geriatric ward?"

"What a wonderful idea. Let them brighten up someone else's room. Take an arrangement for your desk, too," Mariah added. "You look like you could use some brightening."

So much for the concealing powers of makeup. After Gideon left last night, Emma had spent an hour or two curled on the sofa, mentally kicking herself. Then, because she couldn't bear the idea of sleeping on sheets that bore his scent, she'd spent the rest of the night doing laundry. As a result, she looked like the walking dead, pinched and drawn in her jeans and dark sweater.

"I'm fine," she lied. "Just tired after yesterday. You gave everyone quite a scare."

"So my sons keep reminding me. They're making a far bigger fuss than necessary, if you ask me."

Her protest might have carried more weight if she hadn't attempted to sit straighter while speaking, and gasped in pain.

"They're concerned about you," Emma replied. "Do you want the bed raised?"

"What I want is to go home to my own bed," Mrs. Kent grumbled. At that moment she resembled a petulant child rather than the matriarch of a billion-dollar empire.

To hide her smile, Emma grabbed the plastic water jug next to the bed and topped off her employer's ice water. "Dr. Crenshaw's also concerned."

"Dr. Crenshaw is a middle-aged worrywart."

"Dear God, this place looks like the inside of a florist's."

Gideon's voice sounded from the doorway, causing Emma to jerk her hand back and send water sloshing over the nightstand. For once she was grateful for her clumsiness, because she could avoid looking up. She grabbed a handful of tissues and tried not to think about the man whose footsteps were entering the room.

To her chagrin, the footsteps rounded the bed and stopped behind her.

"Sorry I startled you," he murmured. His breath was warm against the back of her neck, reminding her of last night, when that same breath had been hot and steady on her skin. Just like last night, Emma's insides began to tremble.

"Good morning," she heard him say to Mariah, followed by a soft noise that sounded like a kiss on the cheek.

"I see you decided to look your best for this visit," Mrs. Kent said in greeting.

"And I see you're feeling better. How did this morning's tests go?"

"Humph, tests. Dr. Crenshaw's a little too fond of tests.

If you ask me, she's using them as an excuse to run up my bill."

"Really? I thought you said she was a middle-aged worrywart." Emma could hear the smile in Gideon's voice. "Wasn't that the phrase she used, Miss O'Rourke?"

Emma kept her eyes on the table in front of her. "I believe so, Mr. Kent."

"Nice to know you two are keeping records of everything I say. I thought you were coming by earlier."

"I stopped by the hotel to pick up Hinckley before he took over your bedroom."

"Too late. That three-legged monster made himself quite at home on the first night. On my cashmere throw, no less."

"That's Hinckley. Nothing but the best. Right, Miss O'Rourke?"

Why couldn't he ignore her presence and talk to his grandmother? Reluctantly, she looked up. Please don't let there be indifference in his eyes, she prayed. That would be worse than the flowers.

She should have prayed for something else. Like her legs not turning to jelly, or for Gideon not to look quite so perfect.

No wonder Mrs. Kent had made a comment about his clothes. He'd reverted back to sailor mode—faded jeans and that ratty Irish-knit sweater—and looked as beautiful and awe-inspiring as ever. Emma's heart gave a sad little lurch.

"I'll send the throw out to be dry-cleaned," she said.

"Never mind." Mrs. Kent waved away the comment. "Gideon might as well take it with him, since that creature is so fond of the thing."

"Ah, but then he won't want to sleep on it anymore," Gideon told her. "Where's the fun in sleeping on something you're allowed to sleep on?"

Or with, thought Emma bitterly.

"Sorry to interrupt," a nurse said, knocking on the door,

"but it's time to check Mrs. Kent's vital signs." Her eyes swept over Gideon with obvious attraction as she approached the bed. Gideon smiled back, causing Emma's stomach to knot with jealousy.

Knock it off, she told herself sternly. You don't have any claim on him.

Meanwhile, the nurse practically beamed, she smiled so brightly. "If you'd like to wait, I promise I won't take long."

Seeing her chance to escape, Emma scooped the flowers from Mrs. Kent's bedside table. "I'm going to take this to the nurse's station and make those arrangements we talked about." After which she'd slip into the elevator, and finish visiting later, after Gideon left.

Or not.

Ten steps from the room, she heard Gideon call out, "Emma, wait!"

Her heart urged her to pretend she didn't hear. Unfortunately, her brain told her that wouldn't work, so she stopped.

"Apparently the nurse watches *All My Loves*," he said, catching up. "At least I hope so. They're in there discussing who fathered some woman's baby."

"The ex-husband," Emma replied automatically.

"How do you know?"

"It's always the ex-husband."

"You'd think I'd know that by now." Without asking, he took the floral arrangement from her. "So Mariah's giving flowers to the nurses?"

"Among others." She told him the plan to deliver flowers to other patients.

"Nice idea. Yours?"

Hating how his compliment made her insides turn mushy, she focused on the flecks embedded in the gray linoleum. "Your grandmother wanted to spread the wealth."

"Just don't give away all the flowers that get delivered."

She paused, then realized what he meant. "The roses."

"Good, you got them. I was going to send them to your place, but didn't want them sitting on your doorstep all day." His mouth quirked. "For some reason I figured I'd have better luck sending them to you at work."

"They're lovely," she replied quietly.

"Not nearly as lovely as the recipient, I assure you."

Again, her insides melted. "You don't have to do that, you know."

"What, send flowers? I wanted to."

"I mean the compliments. There's no need to let me down easy. I told you last night I didn't expect anything."

He regarded her for a long moment. "Most women would."

"Guess I'm more realistic than most."

They reached the nurse's station, where the head nurse was on the phone, updating someone on a patient's condition. When she saw them approach, she signaled that she'd be another minute.

Gideon set the flowers on the counter. "Do you really think I'm trying to let you down easy?"

"Aren't you?"

"Funny, I thought I was showing my admiration."

The nurse on the phone signaled that she'd be a few more moments. Emma busied herself with the arrangement, repositioning chrysanthemums.

Gideon's voice came from behind her shoulder. "What are you doing tonight?"

"Tonight?"

"Yes, it follows this afternoon."

"Why?"

"Because I thought we could have dinner on my boat," he replied.

"That's not necessary."

"Why don't you let me be the judge of that?"

She adjusted another stem. From the corner of her eye, she saw the nurse wrapping up her phone conversation.

Or so Emma hoped. She needed the interruption. Gideon's question gave birth to an optimism she didn't want to feel. He was only inviting her out of guilt, trying to make amends for last night. Like with the roses.

"I have to make arrangements for the flowers," she said.

"You haven't accepted my invitation yet." He lowered his head towards her. To the nurses at the station, it would look as if he was merely speaking confidentially. Except that he used the same maddening lover's voice he'd used in her bed. The one that coaxed her to do whatever he wanted. "You know you want to."

Heaven help her, but she did. She wanted another night with his hands on her skin and his voice murmuring lover's words in her ear. What good would it do, though, except to pull her back into the orbit of a man she was better off forgetting?

Gideon's fingers curled around her shoulders. "I'm waiting."

The fissure dividing common sense and want widened. This whatever-they-were-doing had no future, no point. Only a glutton for punishment would say yes.

She sighed. "What time?"

Was she making a mistake? Probably, but making a mistake apparently didn't stop her from finding her way to the marina at sundown.

Gideon's hatchway was open. Light and the aroma of Italian food spilled out into the cockpit. He'd told her to dress warmly and she had, in jeans and a wine-colored sweater she knew set off her hair. Even so, a shiver ran through her as she stepped aboard. What are you doing? she asked herself yet again. Another night would only make the inevitable that much harder.

Suddenly changing her mind, she turned to leave, but before she could run, Gideon's head appeared in the hatchway opening. "I thought I heard footsteps," he called. "Come on down."

Emma found she couldn't say no. With tentative steps, she headed toward him.

The cabin looked different than the last time she'd seen it. For one thing, the brass lamps were dimmed to their lowest setting. As their gimbals swayed with the current, they flickered like candles. The table was set for two with fine china and silver. With slight amusement she recognized the pattern as the same one from the Fairlane dining room. A vase with a single rose graced the middle. An open bottle of wine waited next to two crystal goblets.

It reminded her of New York.

Gideon never looked better. He'd shaved, and ditched the sweater in favor of a white shirt that pulled tight across his chest. Dark curls teased the open neck. He was gazing at her like he'd never seen a woman before. The unabashed desire stirred hers.

"You wore your hair down," he drawled. "I like it."

"Thank you."

He moved forward, eyes locked on her. Emma's mouth went dry. She regretted wearing such a heavy sweater, because she was suddenly quite hot. Another couple steps and there'd be no space between them.

"I'm looking forward to dinner," she said.

"Me, too."

He came closer. Emma started to tremble with need. "I'm hungry," she managed to say.

"Me, too."

He reached the stairs, then reached for her. Emma's vision glazed as she melted into his embrace. Immediately his fingers tangled in her hair, urging her mouth to his. "Let's start with dessert."

CHAPTER NINE

"I'M rearranging deck furniture, aren't I?"

Hinckley blinked at her. At the moment he lay sprawled across the seat cushion, far more interested in having his fur stroked than listening to her ramble.

It had been three days since Mrs. Kent's heart attack. Three nights with Gideon. Here, on morning four, Emma found herself repeating the same argument as days one through three—that being with Gideon was a bad idea with a capital *B*.

"Our ship's going nowhere but down," she told Hinckley. "I should get off before I drown, right?"

Except she wasn't entirely sure she wasn't over her head already.

She stared at the red streaks painting the horizon. Gideon was below, sleeping. Or so she presumed, from the soft snoring she'd heard as she slipped from the sheets about an hour before. As had become her habit these last couple of days, she'd gone on deck to watch the sunrise. This morning the October wind blew wet with the remnants of last night's fog. Shivering, she pulled the sweatshirt hood over her head, only to shiver again because the thick cotton smelled like Gideon. She inhaled deeply, savoring the aroma like a woman in a fabric softener commercial. Maybe he'd let her keep the shirt when he left.

When he left. Her heart sank a little. As much as she tried to live in the moment, thoughts of his inevitable departure dogged her, anyway.

Bringing her back to the deck chairs.

Hinckley nudged her thigh, demanding attention. "Yeah, I know, stop talking and put my fingers to better use," she replied, finding the sweet spot between his two shoulder blades. The action flipped a switch, and the feline immediately rolled onto his back, his three limbs stretching straight in the air so she could scratch his belly. The purr in his throat rivaled the fishing boats' engines.

"If only we could all be more like you," she told him.

"Please, the world couldn't handle that much self-centeredness."

Gideon emerged from the hatchway, two cups of coffee in his hands. His smile flipped Emma's switch, and her heart sped up. Lord, but he was handsome in the morning. He was handsome any hour of the day, but mornings, when his eyes were the bluest part of the world, were especially good to him. Today he'd showered before coming up. His damp hair had a little bit of curl in the back.

"I thought I'd find you up here," he said, handing her a cup. "You're turning into quite the sea dog, you know that?"

She breathed in the steam wafting from her mug. "I never knew how pretty the harbor could be this time of the morning. The solitude's very peaceful."

"That it is." Settling on the other side of Hinckley, he gave the cat's jaw a scratch. Which of course Hinckley responded to by stretching and making room for more hands on his body.

Gideon chucked. "Reminds me of someone else I know," he teased. "Must be my magic hands."

Emma stuck out her tongue. He didn't need the encouragement, even if he was right. "More likely it's having two sets of hands on him at once."

"True. Heaven help him when he has to go back to one-person attention."

Meaning when Gideon left Boston. They hadn't talked about his leaving, but with Mrs. Kent out of the hospital, the time was coming. A lump rose in Emma's throat. To ignore it, she studied the trails their fingers made in Hinckley's fur. "I'm sure he'll adjust. Cats always do." Same as she would.

"I don't know. He's pretty spoiled."

"I think he's proved he can roll with life's punches, don't you?"

"Maybe, but you can roll only so many times."

It didn't feel like they were discussing Hinckley anymore.

The sun had breached the horizon and was painting the gray with pink streaks. She pointed toward the light. "Red sun at dawn, sailor's forewarned, right?"

"Listen to you quoting seamen's myths. Next thing you know you'll be singing sea shanties and munching hardtack."

"Don't forget the parrot on my shoulder."

"A parrot, huh?"

"A girl's got to assimilate."

"And you assimilate so adorably, too." He leaned over and kissed the tip of her nose.

This was how they worked. Deliberately steering the conversation to lighter fare, sharing but not sharing. As if they both knew delving too deeply would be a mistake.

Indignant that their teasing interrupted his massage, Hinckley stretched and got off the bench. Gideon used the opportunity to scoot closer to Emma. She leaned back against his chest, and together they watched the sun rise higher.

"Tell me," he said after a few moments, his chin coming to rest on her shoulder, "does this new assimilation of yours mean you're planning to accept my offer?"

Sailing lessons. Last night he'd offered to teach her.

Emma shook her head. "I think I'll draw the line at forecasting. I told you last night, the ocean's a bit too cold for me at the moment."

"And I told you, you could come to Saint Martin. *Mi casa es su casa.*"

"I thought they spoke French on your part of the island."

"Okay, *ma maison est votre maison.* Or should I say *mon bateau est votre bateau?*"

My boat is your boat. She couldn't think of anything more enticing than being with Gideon on a tropical island, but they both knew the invitation wasn't serious. "Thanks, but I think we're all better off if I stay on dry land."

"You navigated the water all right last night."

Color crept into her cheeks as she remembered how they'd made love to the rhythm of the waves. "That was different. The boat wasn't actually moving."

"Says you."

He caught her chin, reeling her in for a quick kiss. His touch was so warm and gentle, and felt so good that Emma was surprised she didn't start purring like Hinckley. "You'd make a helluva first mate," he said against her lips.

When he dropped his voice like that it was hard to remember this was only banter. Emma bit back a sigh. Her index finger traced his lower lip before trailing to his collar. He wore a white button-down shirt. "You're dressed for business," she mused.

"Breakfast summit," he explained. "Mariah issued an edict for first thing this morning."

"That's right. I forgot." Arranging the breakfast had been one of Emma's first tasks when Mrs. Kent came home.

She took a long, fortifying sip of coffee. "I better head to the shower."

She moved to get up, but he caught her wrist. "Whoa, no need for you to rush."

"Are you kidding? When your grandmother says first thing, she means first thing."

"For her sons and me. For you, on the other hand, there's absolutely no reason to rush. She'll have you doing her bidding all day. Take your time, have a second cup of coffee, pleasure Hinckley. Better yet, think about ways I can pleasure you later."

With that, he leaned forward and kissed her. She expected he meant the kiss to be a quick peck, but as usual, what started innocently enough quickly ignited into something more, erasing all coherent thought. Emma sighed into Gideon's mouth as he pulled her tight. He tasted of coffee and spearmint and something more. Something unmistakably Gideon. It was incredible, and totally, completely addictive. She was putty in his hands.

"Emma," he whispered, when they finally broke apart. He pressed his forehead to hers, his ragged breathing matching hers. "I so don't want to go to breakfast."

She so didn't want him to go. "But your grandmother..."

"I know." He broke away, but not before emitting a guttural groan. "We'll continue this tonight, okay?"

Emma nodded. She couldn't have refused if she wanted to.

When did his uncle become such a pompous ass?

Gideon sat back in his seat, listening as the man described, of all things, coffee grind and eggshell facial wraps. Had to be Suzanne's influence. The man was working overtime to make this marriage stick. Good luck with that.

Gideon tried to picture Emma having a coffee grind facial, and failed. No matter. He'd much rather picture her as she'd been this morning, anyway. Hands and head tucked in his sweatshirt, with only her face visible to the morning. Well, her face and her legs. Those long, long legs. He shifted uncomfortably and wished for the umpteenth time he had stayed with Emma on the boat. From the disappointment he'd caught in her eyes when he'd disembarked, she did, too.

Funny, he'd thought he would have gotten her out of his system by now, but the opposite held true. If anything, the past three days had whetted his appetite for more. And given Emma's uninhibited response to his lovemaking, he had to assume she was as hungry for more as he was.

Why didn't she want to go to Saint Martin, then? They were having a good time together. Why not extend the fun a little longer under the hot tropical sun? He could show her all the sights he'd described to her. Those places that made her eyes light up with fascination. Maybe they could jet over to Cabo. He could picture her face now as she watched the sunset. Eyes growing wide, lips parting in a small O, the way they did just before she—

"Gideon?"

"Hmm?" He jerked his attention back to Mariah.

"I asked if Ross had anything else to say when you met with him," she stated.

"Nothing I haven't already told you. He seemed satisfied that Kent Hotels had a solid future. Why?"

"Because I got a message yesterday from Gerard Ambiteau. He was inquiring about my health."

"You did have a heart attack, Mother," Andrew said. "He's simply showing professional courtesy."

"Nonsense. Gerard Ambiteau doesn't believe in courtesy.

He smells blood in the water. That's why we need to make sure we have Ross Chamberlain's loyalty. Thank goodness I didn't have my heart attack twenty-four hours earlier."

"Mother!"

"I'm simply pointing out a fact." Mariah set down her tea. "We dodged a big bullet the other day. There's no guarantee that next time we'll be so lucky."

Gideon sipped his orange juice, which had suddenly lost its flavor. He didn't want to talk about a next time, with regards to business or Mariah's health. Both topics churned his stomach and made his heart burn. It didn't help that Jonathan sat through the entire meeting like some kind of stone statue, barely saying a word. If not for the occasional sidelong glance, one would think Jonathan didn't know his supposed firstborn was even in the room.

Using his glass as a screen, Gideon stole a look to his left. Jonathan was intent on his egg-white omelet and didn't look up. Gideon's heartburn kicked up a notch. From the hollow sensation beneath his rib cage, he was pretty sure the acid had burned a hole in his chest.

As soon as this breakfast ended, he was taking Emma for a long solitary walk and some fresh air.

"And then there's our other shareholders," Mariah continued. "What about them?"

"Most of them are family," Andrew noted.

"Being family doesn't equate loyalty. The way this family's gone to hell in a handbasket the past few years, I wouldn't be surprised if they lined up to sell us out. Unless they feel Kent Hotels is in good hands."

"And how do we convince them of that?" Andrew asked.

Mariah looked unwaveringly at Gideon and raised her teacup to her lips. "Simple," she stated. "We name a successor."

* * *

"Gideon, wait!"

Emma was returning from the business center when she heard Jonathan call his son's name. His tone, unsure and soft, stopped her in her tracks. She hovered outside her office door, uncertain what to do.

"Yes?" she heard Gideon say.

"I—we—never thanked you for everything you did the other day. With your grandmother. Keeping Andrew under control."

"You don't need to thank me. I was simply doing what needed to be done." He sounded like her, Emma thought with a smile. She'd have to tease him later.

"Yes, we do," the elder Kent insisted. "If you hadn't arrived when you did..." Silence filled the air. Unable to help herself, Emma peered through the door crack. Gideon and his father stood face-to-face, much closer together than she would have guessed from their stilted voices. Jonathan Kent was looking down, toeing the carpet with his Italian loafer. "Your grandmother didn't tell me you were coming to Boston." He looked up with a nervous smile. "I think she feared I would bolt."

"I'm surprised you didn't," Emma heard Gideon say under his breath.

"Guess I deserved that. It's been a long time."

"Ten years."

"You've done well for yourself."

"You paid attention?"

"Of course." Jonathan's expression was one of forlorn surprise. A mirror, Emma suspected, of Gideon's face seconds before. "Why wouldn't I?"

"Because it's been ten years."

Emma knew she should back away. This was an intimate moment between father and son, one she had no business watching. But she couldn't move. Gideon stood with posture so erect and proud it broke her heart.

Again, Jonathan toed the carpet. "I suppose you'll be heading back soon, to Saint Martin."

"Well, there isn't any real reason for me to stay, is there?" Emma's heart crumbled when she heard Gideon's answer.

"There's your grandmother's offer. I thought perhaps you might reconsider. The family..." Jonathan cleared his throat. "Your family needs you."

"My family?" Gideon responded with cynicism.

"Yes, your family. We need you." Jonathan touched Gideon's shoulder. "I know what you're thinking, but no matter what, your last name is and always will be Kent. That makes this your family. It makes you my family."

There was no response. Emma saw Gideon bow his head. Jonathan kept his hand on his son's shoulder. "I should have told you that a long time ago. But then you left, and I kept waiting for the right time, and..." He gave a halfhearted shrug. "The more time that passed, the less sure I was you'd listen."

"Why?" Gideon's voice cracked, as if he was choking on the words. Emma's heart cracked with it. "Why now?"

"In a word? Mother. Her heart attack made me realize that if I kept dragging my feet, I might run out of time altogether. Then I'd never get to tell you at all."

More silence. Gideon was weighing his father's words. "Are you sure this has nothing to do with Mariah's offer?" he asked after a moment.

"Perhaps a little. You should be where your heart is, Gideon."

"And you think my heart's in Boston?" His disdain was palpable. Emma felt the stab.

"I think only you can answer that question. But why else would you come back?"

"Because Mariah asked me to."

"And you've stayed…"

Again, no response.

Jonathan started toward the elevator. Emma ducked around the corner so Gideon wouldn't catch her eavesdropping. She'd just made it when his voice called out.

"Jon—Dad, wait." He caught up with his father. "I'm going to be here a couple more days. Would you like to have a cup of coffee…or something?"

Gratitude lit Jonathan's expression in a way Emma had never seen before. "I'd like that. Are you free now?"

"Yeah," Gideon replied in a hoarse whisper. "I'm free now."

The elevator came and went, leaving Emma alone. She stayed hidden around the corner, not yet ready to leave her coward's hideout.

Nothing to keep me here. You think my heart's in Boston?

Talk about a wake-up call. More like an air siren blasting in her ear.

It wasn't as if she hadn't expected that. Hadn't she been saying pretty much the same thing to Hinckley this morning? At least now she knew when her ship would sail: in a couple days.

A couple more days, then back to reality.

Reality came sooner than she thought. It arrived about eight hours later, when her mother turned up at her apartment in tears over her latest heartbreak.

"Tony and I had a connection, you know?" she said between sniffles. "We had a bond."

"I know, Mom." There was always a connection.

Janet had wedged herself into the corner of Emma's couch. Her knees were pulled tight to her chest, and she was taking shaky drags on a cigarette. An ashtray filled with cigarette remains rested by the sofa arm. Mascara streaked her cheeks. It was the only makeup she still had on, the rest having been cried or worn off.

"He was so nice," she continued, before pausing for another puff. "Did I mention he had a boat? And a house on the Vineyard? We talked about me visiting, for cripe's sake."

She ground the butt in the ashtray, grabbed her pack and lit another. "What did I do wrong?"

"Nothing, Mom." *You just read too much into the conversation. As usual.* "He's a jerk, that's all."

"But I really, really liked him."

She always did. And as she got older, she fell faster and harder, the endings more bitter and dramatic.

"It's not fair," Janet said. "Why do they always dump me?"

Emma's stomach churned as she handed her mother a fresh tissue. They'd been through the breakup regime dozens of times. No sense suggesting her mother caused her own misery, since she wouldn't listen. Besides, this time Emma actually had a little sympathy for Janet's woe-is-me sobs.

After all, she was heading for same scenario.

Nothing to keep me here. She shook off Gideon's words. Now wasn't the time. Her mother would cry her eyes out for at least another couple hours, before falling asleep on the sofa. There would be plenty of time for a pity party then.

As she listened to Janet ramble on about heartache and the inequities of life, Emma wondered how many times the universe would have to crush her mother's romantic dreams before she got the message. Janet's meltdown was just one more reminder that her own affair with Gideon was a one-way cruise to nowhere. She refused to be like the woman in front of her, crying over a love affair that existed only in her mind.

Time to abandon ship.

* * *

It was two hours later when she arrived at the marina. When she'd called to cancel their date earlier, Gideon had told her he would welcome her no matter what time she arrived, but now she wondered if she should have waited until morning. The boat looked dark.

Drawing closer, however, she saw a light in the front berth. Gideon was in bed. She pictured him propped against the cushions, his chest bare and muscular in the dim light.

Maybe one more night...

No, no more nights. That's how she'd gotten into this mess in the first place. One night would stretch to two and then three, and before she knew it, Gideon would set sail along with whatever chance she had of keeping her dignity intact. No waiting until morning, either. Because come morning, she'd only find another reason to stall. Either she ended things now or she ended them never.

Squaring her shoulders, she stepped aboard and knocked on the hatchway door. Gideon answered within moments. "Emma!" he said in surprise, before his expression softened in what seemed to be genuine pleasure.

He looked exactly as she'd pictured, shirtless and sexy as could be. Emma's heart immediately lodged in her throat. This would be harder than she'd thought.

"Can I come aboard?" she asked.

"Of course. Why didn't you call? I would have picked you up. You shouldn't be wandering around alone this time of night."

"I didn't want to be a bother."

He rolled his eyes. "What will I do with you? Come on," he said, extending a hand, "get inside before you let the cold air out. Is everything all right? You sounded off when you called."

"My mother had a temporary crisis. Nothing I haven't dealt with before."

"You sure? You look tired."

Gentle concern marked his expression. Emma tried desperately not to fall under its spell. Too much tenderness would make her task impossible. "Dealing with my mother can be draining."

"Obviously. Let me get you something to drink."

"You don't have to."

"Will you stop being a martyr?" He gave her shoulders a gentle kneading. "I know I don't have to anything," he whispered. The huskiness in his voice went straight to her insides.

Please stop being so wonderful, she begged silently.

He disappeared into the galley, leaving her alone. The respite helped her regain her bearings, and she took a long last look at her surroundings. Of all the wonderfully luxurious locations she'd seen since meeting Gideon, the boat would always be her favorite. The jet was incredible, the Landmark was luxurious, the restaurant beyond words, but this space felt...real. Her eyes began to burn.

"Penny for your thoughts."

Why did his voice always manage to send tingles down her spine? "I was thinking about the first time I came on board," she said, blinking her eyes quickly.

"A rain-soaked Little Match Girl." His chest was a breath away from her spine. He slipped an arm around her waist and pulled her close. "I'm glad you didn't freeze to death that day."

"Me, too." She looked down at the mug Gideon had placed in her hands. "Tea?" she noted with surprise.

"I grabbed a box while stocking supplies. Figured you might appreciate having some on board. That is your blend, no?"

"Yes." Her eyes began blurring again. Why was he making this so hard? "Thank you."

If Gideon noticed her strangled tone of voice, he didn't comment. He was too busy nuzzling her neck. "I told you, *mon bateau est votre bateau*. Besides, it's all part of my master plan."

"Master plan?" She was trying not to arch her neck in response to his kisses, and failing miserably.

"I figure if I stock the boat with your favorite foods, your practical nature will force you to visit me in Saint Martin. Because I know you don't like to waste food."

He trailed kisses up her neck, his tongue flicking the skin under her jaw. Emma squeezed her eyes tight, willing herself not to melt. "I'm not visiting you in Saint Martin." She managed to grind out the words.

"So you say now. I haven't finished implementing the plan yet. Food is only part of the strategy. Care to guess the other part?" he asked as he nipped her earlobe.

"Not really."

Somehow she summoned the strength she needed to break their embrace and move to the other side of the cabin. As distance went, it wasn't much, but it was enough to clear her head. A little.

She could feel Gideon frowning at her back. "What's wrong? I thought you said everything went okay with your mother."

"It did."

"Then why are you so tense? Did something else happen?"

A whole lot had happened, beginning with her waking up. "I'm not going to Saint Martin," she repeated.

"Why not? We both know you'd have a terrific time. You, me, the tropical breezes…"

He closed the distance between them in three short steps, causing Emma to curse the narrowness of sea vessels. If she'd been smart, she'd have insisted on staying outside to talk.

"There's so many things I want to show you," he continued in that lover's voice she'd come to adore. "Places you wouldn't believe exist."

As he spoke, he traced a path with his index finger down the side of her neck and along the curve of her shoulder. Her sweater did nothing to stop the heat of his touch from reaching her skin. "Beautiful, tropical hideaways where no one can find us. What do you say, Emma. Will you let me show you?"

It sounded heavenly. Beyond her wildest dreams. She sighed. Then, just as she felt her defenses begin to crumble, an image of her mother sobbing popped into her head, renewing her resolve.

"Like you showed me New York?" she asked, breaking away. "Another treat for the poor travel-deprived secretary?"

Gideon's evasive expression told her she'd hit upon some truth. Sensing her opportunity, she continued. "That's what this has been all about, hasn't it? Expanding the poor Little Match Girl's world? Giving her some fantastical memories?"

"Since when is it a crime to treat a woman like a princess?" he asked.

Except she wasn't a princes, she was a secretary. "It's not a crime," she replied. "Just very seductive."

"And that's a bad thing?"

He reached for her, but she sidestepped in time. "Yes, it is. Because eventually the experiences have to end, and the pretend princess has to go back to her life. Don't worry, though, I knew exactly what I was getting into when we started this little fling."

A shadow crossed his features, making his expression impossible to read. "Is that what you think we're doing? Having a fling?"

"What else would you call it? You don't do relationships, remember?"

Saying the words out loud hurt more than she expected. Needing a moment to collect herself, she gulped down her tea. The hot liquid burned her throat, but she didn't care. It made her temporarily forget the pain in her chest.

Gideon, of course, said nothing, which spoke volumes.

"Like I said, don't worry," she repeated, as much to reassure herself as to reassure him. "I'm a big girl. I never harbored expectations that what we were doing would lead to anything more."

"You didn't." He sounded as if he didn't believe her. She supposed because he was used to the opposite.

"I learned a long time ago that life isn't a fairy tale, Gideon. Happy endings are few and far between. And I've seen more times than I can count what happens when you base your future on false hope." She forced a tremulous smile. "Better to live in reality then nurse a fantasy. Wouldn't you agree?"

He didn't answer. Trying to think of an appropriate response, no doubt. What, she wondered, did someone say in a situation such as this, other than goodbye? Surely nothing that would make the ending any easier.

And so when Gideon finally did open his mouth to speak, she pressed her fingers to his lips. "Don't. Let's not belabor what we both know is the truth. Why don't we both walk away while we're still friends, happy with the fun we had together?"

He didn't answer. She didn't let him. That didn't stop disappointment from hitting her hard. In spite of everything, part of her wanted him to argue the point, even though they both knew there was no point in doing so. Proof she was right to end things between them.

It was time to go. Her teacup was empty. Setting the mug down, she gave Gideon one last smile, backing away when he reached for her. She wanted nothing more than to taste one last kiss, but she knew doing so would hurt far too much. "I want you to know that this...us—" she waved her hand between them "—was amazing. I don't think I've ever felt... Never mind." She had been about to say *special*, but the word sounded trite. "Goodbye, Gideon."

He stared, shocked. "You're leaving?"

"We'd both be better off if I did, don't you think?" She grabbed the railing. "Have a safe journey home, Gideon."

Before he could utter another word, she bolted up the stairs.

CHAPTER TEN

Too stunned to say a word, Gideon watched as Emma raced away. It wasn't until he heard the footsteps above him that he realized what had happened, and sprang into action.

"Emma, wait!"

He bounded up on deck. "Emma!" he bellowed. Nearby a cormorant grunted in protest, the only noise besides Emma's rapid footfalls.

Ignoring the cold on his bare feet and torso, he started after her, calling her name yet again. She didn't stop. In fact, when he hollered, she picked up her pace, going from a brisk walk to a jog to finally an all-out run. He followed her as far as the sidewalk, in time to see her jump into her car and peel off.

What the hell? Confusion swirled in his muzzy brain. It didn't make sense. They had a good time together. Check that, they had an amazing time together. Making love was a near religious experience, at least for him. No, for both of them. She was enjoying their time together as much as he was. So why cut and run when they still had several days left to enjoy each others' company?

"Hey, be grateful," he said to himself. "She's right, you don't do relationships." He'd been dreading saying good-bye, anyway. That was half the reason he'd invited her to Saint Martin, right? To postpone the unpleasantness. Now he didn't have to feel bad. Emma had done him a favor. He should be relieved. He could move on with a clean conscience.

Slowly, he walked back to the boat, waiting for the relief to wash over him.

It didn't come.

A week later, Gideon stomped into his cabin, feeling cold and miserable. Hinckley opened an irritated eye as he barged past on his way to the galley and the coffeepot. Which, he soon discovered, had about an inch of coffee left in it.

"Damn!" He slammed the pot on the burner, sending a metallic rattle reverberating through the boat. He was going to have to make a fresh pot, and the blasted canister was empty. What idiot had decided living on the water was a good idea, anyway? His hands were so numb he could barely feel them. How hadn't he noticed how cold Boston Harbor was before?

Blowing on his fingers, trying to jump-start some kind of circulation, he scanned the supplies, looking for a spare can of coffee. If he had to make instant, he would not be responsible for the damage. As he reviewed the various cans, his eyes fell on a bright red box. A sinking sensation hit him in the gut. Tea. Emma's tea.

He leaned a shoulder against the wall. It had been seven days since she'd pronounced them over and had taken off. Seven long days. He'd tried to reach her. She conveniently managed to be absent whenever he arrived at the Fairlane, and she wouldn't take his calls. He'd left messages at work,

on her cell phone. In fact, he'd left so many messages he was starting to feel like a stalker.

This desperation wasn't like him. He didn't chase women. But Emma... He couldn't get her out of his head. No woman had ever gotten under his skin the way she had. He thought about her when he ate, when he showered, when he worked on the boat. The worst was at night, when he lay alone in his bed with nothing but thoughts of Emma to lie with him.

The simple truth was he missed her. Missed making her smile. Missed hearing her gentle breathing as she slept. Missed the fullness that swelled in his chest when she looked in his direction.

Conversely, the past week had brought him closer to his family than he'd been in years. Since their awkward conversation the other day, he and his father had forged some new bonds. Tentative ones, but he had hope they would grow strong. For the first time in his life, both of them were talking—really talking—and more importantly, listening. They discovered they shared a lot of traits, such as pride and stubbornness, and Gideon was starting to wonder if maybe DNA didn't matter, after all. He was even reconsidering Mariah's offer to take over Kent Hotels.

A decision he'd love to discuss with Emma.

His back pocket buzzed, telling him he had a call. The Fairlane, according to the call screen. When he saw the number, his pulse quickened. Maybe his stalking had finally paid off.

It hadn't. Mariah's voice greeted him from the other end. "Good morning to you, too," she said.

"Sorry, Grandmother." He tried to push the disappointment from his voice. "I was hop— I thought you were someone else."

"I'll forgive you, since you called me Grandmother."

He smiled to himself. "What can I do for you, Grand-mother?"

"You can come to tea," she replied. "I want you to look at some concepts the advertising agency sent over."

"Isn't that Andrew's concern?"

"I want you to see them."

Gideon shook his head. He wondered if, in his grand-mother's mind, he'd ever turned down her offer. "All right," he replied, "I'll be there. What time?"

"One o'clock."

"Sounds good. I'll see you then." Emma, too, he realized with a thrill. That is, if she didn't hide again.

Suddenly, an idea hit him. "Grandmother," he said, "will you do me a favor?"

"Make sure those letters go out in today's mail," Mrs. Kent said. "Tell Marketing and Legal I don't want them bickering about the words, either."

"Yes, ma'am," Emma answered, not entirely certain what she was answering "yes" to. Since breaking things off with Gideon, she'd been on autopilot. Her perpetual fog showed, too. She made stupid mistakes. Yesterday, she'd even sent a phone call through to Mrs. Kent during *All My Loves.*

Speaking of Mrs. Kent, her boss's pale blue eyes were impossibly intent as they studied Emma. "Is your headache any better today?" she asked in concern.

"A little," Emma replied. A migraine was the excuse she'd given for yesterday's mistake. It wasn't too much of a lie. She did have a headache.

"Hmmm, maybe you should see someone." Mrs. Kent was frowning now.

"I'll be fine." There was only one person she wanted to see, and he was off-limits. "I should be feeling better soon."

After all, it had been seven days, for crying out loud. Her

mother bounced back in two. Emma should be over Gideon by now. Instead, he dominated her every thought. Every time she heard him on her voice mail, it was like a knife in her midsection. She was beginning to wonder if she'd ever stop thinking of him.

Mrs. Kent had a few more housekeeping items for review, so Emma forced herself back to the present as best she could. Still, she only half listened. Hopefully, her automatic notes would fill in the blanks. When her meeting was over she walked robotically back to her desk. If she was lucky, work would distract her for a few hours at least.

"Hello, Emma."

She stumbled, she stopped so quickly. Gideon stood in the doorway. Every emotion she'd been struggling to forget rushed at her simultaneously, forcing her to grab hold of the printer table for balance.

"I didn't know you were stopping by." He looked more handsome than a week ago. Obviously, he hadn't spent the past week tossing and turning the night away.

She didn't want to think how he did spend the night, either.

"I asked Mariah not to say anything. So you wouldn't have a chance to hide," he added when she frowned.

"I haven't been hiding," Emma snapped. She hated that he'd read her thoughts. "I've been very busy. Your grandmother is making up for the work she missed while in the hospital."

"Then why haven't you returned my calls?"

"I just told you. I've been very busy."

"Liar." Challenge sparkled in his eyes. Emma looked away. She didn't have the energy to fake an argument, so she surrendered. "I didn't see the need," she said, fiddling with the table edge. "We said everything that needed to be said the other night."

"Really? As I recall, you did all the talking."

"You didn't argue."

"You didn't give me a chance. You blindsided me, then took off before I could recover."

"I didn't think we had anything more to say."

His voice dropped a notch. "I've missed you, Emma. You're a hard woman to let go."

He spoke plainly, without a shred of seduction. The simplicity was far more devastating, anyway. "If I'd reacted faster the other night, I never would have let you walk off the boat. I would have taken you out to sea and refused to let you go."

In spite of herself, Emma had to smile at the image. "Pretty big gesture for a guy who doesn't believe in relationships," she said.

"Guess I'm not ready for this relationship to end yet."

"*Yet.* That's the magic word, isn't it?"

"What are you talking about?"

"You said *yet.*" She leaned against the table. "You miss me now and you don't want our affair to end *yet.*" Meaning eventually it would still end.

"What should I have said?"

How about, Don't go. I love you.

Suddenly, in one fell swoop, it hit her. She'd become her mother. Despite all her safeguards, all her vows of maintaining perspective, she'd fallen, anyway. Emma was in love with Gideon. She didn't want yet. She wanted more. She wanted him to love her back.

An impossible desire, to say the least. "That's what happens when you look beyond a comfortable bed," she muttered.

"What?" Gideon seemed completely baffled.

"Nothing. You wouldn't understand."

"Try me."

She didn't want to. Now that her feelings had made their way to the surface, she needed to leave. To put some distance between them before she made a fool of herself.

Check that, a bigger fool. She pushed herself toward her desk. "I have to go meet with Marketing. Your grandmother wants this letter to go out today and Legal has a problem with some of the language. I need to—"

"Don't dodge my questions. You said something about a comfortable bed. What was it?" He paused, and she saw understanding crest in his eyes. "Does this have something to do with what you said the other night? About nursing fantasies?"

Trust him to listen too well. "Let it go, Gideon. What I said or didn't say doesn't matter."

"It does to me." His fingers wrapped around her forearm. "I'm not letting you go until you tell me what you meant."

"Your grandmother—"

"When will you learn that my grandmother can wait?"

Emma looked down at the hand on her arm, gentle but immovable. "Fine," she snapped. Maybe if she explained, he'd understand and finally leave her alone. "I said this is what happens when you look for more than a comfortable bed. You end up wanting too much."

"Too much?"

"As in things you can't have."

His eyes were two probing blue beams. "What is it you want, Emma?"

"What do you think I want?" she retorted, furiously yanking free of his grasp. A week's worth of fatigue and misery finally got the best of her, and all her frustration and pain just bubbled over. "The happy ending, the fairy tale. I want you not to say 'yet.' I want you!"

She slapped her hand to her mouth. Oh Lord, she hadn't meant to say that.

Gideon stepped back, stunned. Her cheeks felt on fire. Maybe they were. Could she be a bigger idiot? Why not scream "I love you" too, and make her humiliation complete? Hot angry tears sprang to her eyes as she groped desperately on her desk for something, anything, she could use as an excuse to escape this hideous embarrassment. She settled for a random stack of papers. "I have to go to talk to Marketing...."

"Wait."

"No. I've already said too much. Let me go." She tore herself away from his restraining hand and practically ran out of the office.

She wanted him, thought Gideon, dazed. His chest was so full he swore it would burst. It was as if a missing piece of him slid into place. Emma wanted him....

"Are you going to stand there daydreaming, or are you going to chase her down?"

He turned around to see Mariah in the doorway. How long had she been listening? She admonished him with a sharp stare. "Well?" she asked imperiously.

Her question kickstarted him into action. "Excuse me, Grandmother." He left the room at a run. This time Emma wasn't going to make a proclamation and then walk away. Not without hearing him out.

She wanted him. And she was standing by the elevator, trying to escape.

"Don't you dare leave this floor, Emma O'Rourke!" He bellowed so loudly a nearby housekeeper dropped her towels. Emma, though, true to form, didn't pause a beat. In fact, she pushed the elevator button.

"Son of a—" He jogged down the hallway toward her. "You are not running away from me before I can say my piece, do you hear me?"

She jabbed at the button again. "What else is there to say,

Gideon? I wanted something you can't give. You said so yourself."

"So you simply walk away?"

"It's called cutting my losses," she said shortly.

Cutting her... For crying out loud. Frustration ripped through him. "Dammit, Emma, how am I supposed to get through to you?"

The elevator doors opened. Emma stepped on, but he threw his arm between the doors, preventing them from closing.

"I thought you were kidding about that bed. I can't believe you actually think that way."

"Well, where I come from, there's no sense wanting more than you can have," she retorted hotly.

"Instead you decide to want nothing at all?"

Emma glared at him indignantly. "What's that suppose to mean?"

"It means you're afraid."

"I am not afraid," she almost snarled, stepping off the elevator.

"Aren't you? You said it yourself. You're afraid you'll like life so much you'll want more. So you abstain altogether. No harm, no foul, right?"

Emma's temper finally snapped, because he was so utterly right. "Can you blame me? Do you have any idea what it's like watching your mother fall for man after man on some fruitless search for the one of her dreams? Do you know how many times I had my life tossed upside down because she was certain this week's Prince Charming was 'the one'? I promised myself I would never be disappointed the way she was. That I wasn't going to spend the rest of my life regretting or mourning something I could never have."

Gideon looked at the ground. Emma's furious confession had knocked him square in the gut. "I don't know what to say."

"There's nothing to say," she stated coldly, reining in her anger. "I said all along I knew what I was getting into. You don't have to feel guilty."

Guilty? Her words sent a fresh round of frustration rolling through him, and he groaned aloud. "Will you stop?"

"What? All I said was that I knew what I was—"

"I know what you were saying. Would you stop assuming I don't want a commitment?" God, he wanted to throttle her then and there.

She was looking up at him, wide-eyed with disbelief, waiting for his next comment. A thousand tangled emotions stormed in her beautiful brown eyes. Amazing, Gideon thought suddenly. He could look at those eyes forever and never figure out every different emotion.

Forever.

The word hit him like a stone. His whole life, he'd mocked the idea, but when it came to Emma, the word forever flowed effortlessly. The fight went out of him, and when he spoke again, his voice was calm.

"How would you know what I want, Emma?" he asked. "You've never let me participate in the conversation."

"Of course I did. You never answered."

"Because you always ran away. The other night. This afternoon. Even the first night we made love you had me out the door before I could catch my breath. You've never given me a chance to say anything."

Emma blinked in shock. She'd given him plenty of chances.

Hadn't she?

But that didn't matter. The fact remained he wasn't going to hang around. "I heard you tell your father you didn't plan to stay."

"My father? When did I say…?" He paused as comprehension dawned. "Now I remember. Last week, after breakfast. You were eavesdropping."

"I was coming around the corner when I heard you," she said defensively. "You told your father you had no reason to stay in Boston."

"I was talking family. Not about you."

"Great," she said with a bitter laugh, "I didn't even make the equation. I feel so much better now."

She turned to summon the elevator again, only to have Gideon lift her arm away before she could push the button. "What I meant," he said, "was that I was planning to take you with me. Remember? That's why there was nothing keeping me here.

"Look," he continued, "I know what it's like to have your parents' love lives turn your own life upside down. Believe me, I know that chaos better than you think. And until recently—very recently—I followed the low-expectations road, too. Stay away from relationships, stay out of trouble. But I'm realizing that road might not be the safest one, after all."

"Why not?"

Cupping her cheek, he forced her eyes to meet his. "Because I met a Little Match Girl, and I didn't realize how cold and lonely my boat would be without her on board."

Emma stared into his blue eyes, looking for some sign, any sign, that she shouldn't believe him. Of course, it was hard to tell with her own eyes tearing the way they were. "Your boat's cold?"

"Freezing. Quiet, too. Don't tell him I said so, but Hinckley's a lousy berth mate. He just doesn't spoon into my body the way you do."

Emma looked away. "So you're looking for a bed warmer."

"I'm looking for a first mate," Gideon replied, drawing her attention back. "I told you before, you'd make a terrific one. The job's yours if you're interested."

"First mate, huh?"

Gideon nodded and she smiled shyly. She'd never heard such a wonderful offer.

But... She caught herself before she could accept. What if she was reading too much into the invitation? What if she was making the same mistake again?

Protect yourself, a voice urged. All the old familiar voices chimed in. Be realistic. Don't get your hopes up. You'll only get your heart broken. She saw her mother crying pitifully over yet another failed relationship. Did Emma want to end up like that?

But wasn't she already miserable? Wasn't being with Gideon even for a short while better than the heartache she was enduring now? Longing rose up inside her, urging her to take a chance.

"I'm scared."

She didn't realize she'd spoken aloud until Gideon smiled and brushed his thumb across her cheek. "Me, too. Thinking long-term is uncharted water for me."

"Same here," Emma replied.

"Then I guess we'll have to navigate those waters together."

Together. The word held such hope and promise. With tears of happiness filling her eyes, Emma smiled and buried her face in the crook of his neck. Gideon wrapped his arms around her tightly. "I've missed you so much," he whispered as he kissed her temple.

"I've missed you," she told him in a choked voice.

They stood quietly, letting the warmth and safety of being in each other's arms wash over them. After a few moments— or an hour, Emma wasn't sure—Gideon pulled back, revealing eyes that were bluer and brighter than anything she'd ever seen. The emotion shining in their depths was unmistakable, and her heart swelled with love. "So," he said with a smile, "are you up for the voyage, Miss O'Rourke?"

She caressed his jaw. "For as long as it takes, Mr. Kent."

"Good. Because I have a feeling it's going to be a very long journey."

"How long?"

He moved closer, bringing his breath to her lips. "How do you feel about forever?"

Emma didn't think it was possible, but her heart filled even more. "Forever sounds perfect, Captain." She leaned forward to complete the kiss.

Suddenly a thought came to her, and she pulled back. "Your grandmother," she gasped. "She's probably wondering what happened. We should go explain."

"Oh, we've got time," Gideon replied. With a triumphant smile, he showed her the time on his wristwatch. "It's two o'clock."

Three months later, Emma stood on deck, watching the sun fall off the edge of the earth in all its breathtaking glory.

"Beautiful," she murmured.

A pair of strong arms wrapped her waist from behind. "So, is it everything I promised?" Gideon asked, pulling her to him. She leaned into his chest, marveling for the millionth time how safe and happy his embrace made her.

"More than everything," she said.

"Good. After all, we aim to please." He nipped the curve of her neck. "And please, and please, and please…"

Nipping became nuzzling, and Emma giggled. She'd had no idea life could be this magical.

Gideon had made peace once and for all with his family. He told her about his parentage; how his mother didn't know who had fathered her son. Emma agreed with Mariah and the others. His DNA didn't matter. He was a Kent at heart. It took a while, but Gideon was slowly realizing that same fact.

At the moment, however, he appeared more interested in peppering her shoulders with kisses. The man was insatiable.

Not that Emma minded. Making love to Gideon never grew old. They discovered something new about each other every time.

"Mmm," she said, letting her head fall back to allow him better access. "I'm going to hate going back to work, after all this sunshine."

"Well, we can always extend the honeymoon another few weeks." He teased her ear with his tongue. "Or years."

"Don't you have a hotel chain to run?" Last night, he'd called his grandmother to officially agree to be her successor. They were scheduled to meet with the board of directors next week.

"I suppose," he replied with a sigh. He didn't bother disguising his disappointment. "Though running a hotel chain isn't nearly as fun as teaching you how to sail."

"Oh, is that what we're calling it now," she teased. "If it helps, I'll be right by your side." She planted a kiss on his nose. "Just like a good first mate should."

"You, sweetheart, are hardly a first mate. More like a co-captain."

"How about admiral?"

"As long as we've got Hinckley, I'm afraid that position is filled." With that, Gideon adjusted their positions so his mouth hovered just above hers. "Have I told you today how much I love you, Mrs. Kent?"

Emma smiled. "Yes, but I'll never get tired of hearing it. Or telling you I love you back."

And as the sun disappeared, she kissed him with all the happiness she felt in her heart. "Thank you," she whispered, "for giving me everything."

Everything, she thought to herself, and more.

* * * * *

SECRET HISTORY OF
A GOOD GIRL

Aimee Carson

The summer she turned eleven, **Aimee Carson** left the children's section of the library and entered an aisle full of Mills & Boon® novels. She promptly pulled out a book, sat on the floor, and read the entire story. It has been a love affair that has lasted for over thirty years.

Despite a fantastic job working part-time as a physician in the Alaskan bush (think *Northern Exposure* and *ER*, minus the beautiful mountains and George Clooney), she also enjoys being at home in the gorgeous Black Hills of South Dakota, riding her dirt bike with her three wonderful kids and beyond-patient husband. But, whether at home or at work, every morning is spent creating the stories she loves so much.

Her motto? Life is too short to do anything less than what you absolutely love. She counts herself lucky to have two jobs she adores and incredibly blessed to be a part of the Mills & Boon® family of talented authors.

Look for Aimee Carson's new novel, *How To Win the Dating War*, in December 2011.

Dear Reader,

Reading a book by a new author is a bit like going on a blind date—awkward in the beginning, but ripe with possibility and the anticipation of the unknown. So, dear reader, in celebration of my debut novel I'd like to ease this first-meeting awkwardness by sharing my favourite recipe for the perfect romance:

Aimee's Favourite, Melt-In-Your-Heart Romance Recipe

- 1 heroine – handpicked for her sassy attitude, quirky imperfections, and the ability to laugh at herself; virginity is optional

- 1 hero – selected for his hotness, audacious charm, and sprinkling of faults; sense of humour a must…see sassiness of heroine above

- dash of personal growth and gut-wrenching emotional truthiness

- pinch of conflict

- toss in a few surprises and a generous helping of FUN

Stir until ingredients are combined, the fun is evenly distributed, and lumps of faults and imperfections are of a tolerable size. Bake, let cool, and frost with your favourite setting. My choice was easy—although the various hotels, clubs, and restaurants mentioned in my book are fictitious, South Miami Beach's Ocean Drive and the sparkling Atlantic are very much real.

Aimee

To my kids

CHAPTER ONE

WELL, this was it. She'd come full circle. Back to where her dream of organizing glamorous events had been born and was now about to be realized. If she could get the job, that was.

But first she had to conquer her lame phobia of gilded front doors.

Alyssa Hunt stared across South Miami Beach's Ocean Avenue at the Samba Hotel. As part of the renovations, workmen in overalls applied touch-up paint around the arched windows, the afternoon sun glinting off the glass. A salty Atlantic breeze rustled the fuchsia-tipped hibiscus lining the path to the staff entrance in back.

Years ago, she'd donned her waitress uniform to work at least a dozen catering jobs at the luxury hotel. And always, *always* entered via the rear.

She tugged on the jacket of her off-the-rack gray suit, shifting her gaze from the ornate front entry to the walkway that led to the service entrance. No mocking doorways back there.

With a frown, she let out a soft sigh of exasperation and gripped the handle of her tote.

Come on, Alyssa. Quit being such a wuss. It's time to take your business to the next level. And hovering in a quasi-purgatory state of indecision won't get you what you want.

She took a deep breath and waited for a break between cars. When it came, she crossed the road, boldly striding for the front door.

Fifteen minutes later Alyssa exited the elevator into the bright sunshine of the Samba's rooftop deck, heading toward a row of chaise longues. She was too stunned to take in the scenery. And as the realization she was one step closer to success finally sank in, she stopped to set her tote down and clutch the back of a chair, pressing a hand over her eyes.

"Are you all right?"

The deep baritone voice echoed across the water of the pool, but Alyssa ignored the interloper.

Of course she was all right. She'd shown up. She'd conquered her ludicrous fear of fancy entryways. Best of all, she'd scored an appointment for an interview. For a gig she wasn't quite qualified for. Oh, she could do the job. She knew she could. It was exactly the kind of contract she'd been preparing for since she started Elite Events. Unfortunately, now she had to convince the owner. Not the manager, the *owner.*

Her stomach rolled, and she dropped her palm to her belly, as if she could soothe the jittery butterflies engaged in a feeding frenzy over her nerves.

"Lady, maybe you should take a seat before you keel over."

The voice was followed by a rhythmic splash of water. Whoever it was, he was swimming in her direction. And though she wasn't about to keel over, thank you very much, maybe his advice was sound.

Besides, she'd hate to find out she was wrong and ruin her skirt.

She rounded the chair, dropping into the cushioned seat. Elbows on her thighs, forehead against her fingers, she stared down at her feet and blew out a breath.

So what if none of the events on her résumé were as grand as those at a five-star hotel? So what if she'd chosen safer— albeit less exciting—small corporate events? She'd learned a lot since she started her business. And she was good. She *knew* she was good.

Arrange a kickass employee appreciation party on a budget? No problem. Keep her cool at a retirement luncheon as the intoxicated retiree barfed on her shoes? Bring it on.

But *jeez...*

Ten years after her royal screw-up, and five years after starting her business, she was finally applying for a job that catered to the moneyed set. A class of society responsible for countless humiliating memories. It had taken her all night to psyche herself up to ask for a meeting with the manager. And now she had to face the billionaire owner, Paulo Domingues.

Billionaire. With a boldfaced capital *B*.

Her stomach flipped again, and she closed her eyes, using deep breathing exercises to regain control. Which went well until sparkles of light began to shimmer behind her eyelids. It took a moment for her to realize she was teetering on the edge of hyperventilation.

Clearly her relaxation technique sucked.

"Here," the man said from beyond the twinkling darkness. "Take this."

She forced herself to inhale slowly, lifted her lids, and caught sight of her high-heeled sandals—the token designer accessory she'd added for a hint of style. Oh, good, no more annoying sparklies in her peripheral vision. With her breathing finally in line, she shifted her attention forward and spied bare masculine feet, water pooling on the deck around them.

Her gaze slid up past a pair of muscular thighs. With a growing sense of unease, she moved on to lean hips enveloped in a Speedo and then a flat abdomen. This was followed by an underwear model chest, complete with the obligatory ripples. Sunshine glinted off rivulets coursing down the sculpted torso as the man held out a bottle of water in her direction.

Alyssa was handling the disturbing image just fine until he gave a shake of his black hair—and flying water droplets landed close to her pricey high heels.

With a faint disgusted sound she leaned over to check the leather. She'd paid a mint for those shoes. She lifted her head, preparing to give the man hell...

Until her gaze met his. Dark eyes. With a hint of heat. Eyes housed in the handsome face of Paulo Domingues. Her mouth froze, and her blood drained lower, her head growing light.

Great. What sick, twisted turn of karmic fate was this?

He continued to hold out the bottle, his forehead creased with concern. "You look pale."

Uh...yeah. Because all her blood had reconvened south of her belly button.

Like many in this city, his muted Latino heritage was tinctured with an American flavor that matched his accent. But just because she'd been presented with a vista of downtown Miami to the west, cerulean sky over the Atlantic to the east, and a shimmering pool garnished with a fantasy-worthy, ridiculously wealthy male specimen, she was not going to swoon.

She *never* swooned. Damnit, she was better than that.

He nodded at the bottle in his hand. "Drink this." A sexy half-smile flickered across his face. "And then I'll get you something stronger."

There wasn't enough alcohol in the world to get her through the next few minutes.

Her heart thrummed beneath her ribs, and she accepted the offer with a nod of thanks.

As she sipped the icy water, her gaze followed him anxiously as he crossed to a table piled with clothes and swiped a towel down his legs. He pulled on jeans over his bathing suit, and she relaxed in relief. But then he returned to stand in front of her, folding his bicep-laden arms across his beautifully naked chest, scanning her face as if to assess if she was okay.

The concern was nice, but for crying out loud, what was with the shirtless Taylor Lautner impression? And why couldn't she finish her panic attack in peace?

Hoping he'd take the hint, she checked her watch and then looked up at him, searching for a gracious way to tell him to take a hike. And, please God, don't let her hick accent surface. "I believe we have an appointment in fifteen minutes."

His eyes lit with a twinkle. "Nice to know you can speak." He headed for a nearby corner bar, bypassing the table with his remaining clothes. "Otherwise it would have been a very short interview, Ms....?"

Shoot, he was *still* bare-chested. "Alyssa Hunt."

"So, Ms. Hunt," he said as he pulled out a soda and raised it in offering. "Would you like some caffeinated sugar?"

Really? That was his idea of something stronger? Alyssa simply declined with a shake of her head.

"It might help you prepare for the interview," he went on.

Prepare. Well, there was an idea. Last evening, when she'd heard about the sudden opening at the Samba, she'd learned as much as she could about his property. A shining star regarded as the industry's hippest new hotel. But there was no time to read about the owner. Other than his rebel image, aided by his shocking departure from his family's mega resort chain, she didn't know much. And she never went in so blind about a client.

"I'll admit the short notice left little time for research," she said.

"My event planner's departure yesterday took me by surprise, too." His half-grin turned into a full, complete with dimples. "So, just to be fair, I'll give you ten minutes to pump me for information."

With a little grimace, she wrinkled her nose delicately. At least she hoped it was delicate. "That sounds so harsh. I prefer the phrase..." She searched for a more acceptable term. "Tactical reconnaissance."

His brows rose. "Are you preparing for an interview or a combat mission?"

Confident her professional air had finally returned, she stood, smoothing a hand down her jacket. The concrete and steel forest of downtown Miami gleamed in the distance beyond him. "You can always hope for the former," she said coolly. "But it's best to prepare for the latter."

A glint of awareness appeared in his eyes. "Should I be afraid?"

His suggestive tone set her on guard, but she held his gaze, refusing to play. The bad boy image was all well and good, but she had no time for games. "I doubt you scare so easily, Mr. Domingues."

As his lips twitched, she braced for his reply. But when it came, it was without his previous undertones. "What would you like to know about me?"

She hesitated. Anything she said was likely to reveal

more about her than him, and the male expanse of chest was most troubling. But the opportunity was too good to pass.

Alyssa picked up her bag and crossed the teak deck, sitting on the barstool across from him. "What do you think I should ask?" she said with a polite smile.

Obviously tickled by her reply, he braced a hand against the counter. "You're going to make me do all the work?" She lifted a noncommittal shoulder, and he pursed his lips. "Okay. I would want to know if I'm dealing with a straight-shooter or someone who beats around the bush." Alyssa tipped her head in question, and he answered, "Straight-shooter."

The roguish look returned to his face. "On the other hand..." His eyes boldly swept down to her waist and back, triggering a barrage of disconcerting sensations in her body. "You should ask if you'll have my undivided attention or if my gaze will repeatedly drift to your legs."

Ignoring the hammering in her chest, she resisted the urge to roll her eyes and folded her hands on the counter. Her tone was careful. "Fascinating. That isn't a question I would have considered."

"You would have considered it." A grin flashed. "You just wouldn't have asked it."

True. And she always appreciated blunt honesty. "And the answer is...?"

His dimples grew deeper. "Yes to both."

Cocky little charmer. While most people were working hard for their pay, here he was swimming in the middle of the day, but his easygoing nature was hard to resist. "I appreciate the warning." She hiked a brow drolly. "Should I be aware of any other chauvinistic character traits?"

"Oh, I'm much more subtle than that."

Ha. There was nothing subtle about him. Neither his confidence nor his to-die-for looks nor his bazillion-dollar smile. Feeling the need for a shield, she folded her arms across her chest. "So exactly how hard a sell are you during a job interview?"

He parked his elbows on the counter, bringing his face level with hers, his eyes flickering with an unmistakable light. "Depends on the bait."

Bait? She blinked. Whatever allure she held, it was nothing compared to his thick eyelashes. The chin-length black hair brushed back from flawless skin. Or the dark slash of eyebrows that added a rugged touch and contrasted nicely against full lips.

She leaned back to gain some distance and crossed her legs. And while she sensed his teasing was all in fun, it was best he learned Alyssa Hunt didn't take crap from anybody anymore. She sent him her well-perfected I-won't-be-tempted smile. "I don't dangle myself in front of anyone, Mr. Domingues."

The man tipped back his head and laughed. Deep. Rich. Radiating humor to its very core. The kind that wrapped around you, encouraging you to join in no matter what your troubles. And he was clearly trouble.

When his chuckle finally died out, he said, "Sure we can't continue this over a drink?" His gaze turned positively wicked. "A mojito, perhaps?"

Alyssa's body froze. During her luncheon for the Hot Bods Agency, with every hunky Miami model in attendance, she'd been hit on repeatedly. And she'd had no problem dealing with the six-pack of tall, dark and handsomes at her table. Surely she could handle just one?

Her lips twisted dryly. "I think I've learned enough." And then some. "Perhaps, since you were so kind, I should return the favor?"

"Lady." His face filled with skeptical humor. "I don't need to pump you for information."

Pow. He really knew how to hit where it hurt. He was the rich hotelier and she was the peon with a rinky-dink business.

Alyssa bit her tongue, holding back the snarky retort. Wealthy charmer or not, he stood between her and her dream account, so she forced the pleasant expression to remain on her face.

"But I suppose a few questions wouldn't hurt," he went on. "Where did you work last?"

"Actually—" pride crept into her voice "—I have my own event planning business."

"Freelance?"

Heck yeah, because she'd worked her tail off since she was fifteen, occasionally getting treated like a lowly servant by the guests. But that was okay. She appreciated the valuable lesson. The only orders she'd ever take again were from her clients.

She lifted her chin. "I prefer to be the boss."

"Me, too." The glimmer in his eyes returned. "Doesn't bode well for us, now does it?" What did he mean by that? While she dealt with the confusion at his words, he continued. "And I'm looking for an in-house planner."

Maintaining his gaze, she ignored the deficiencies in her résumé and focused on the accomplishments. "I think if you listen to my pitch you'll change your mind."

The amusement returned full force. "You think so, huh?" His mesmerizing eyes held hers as he rounded the bar to lean his wonderfully muscled swimmer's frame against the counter.

Suddenly, she *did* regret refusing a drink. And forget the fruity mojito. She needed a shot of whiskey. Because the man looked very comfortable in his skin…all that wonderfully exposed tan skin drying in the sun. The urge to drop her eyes to his chest was strong, but she steadfastly held his gaze. Looking down would be sensual suicide.

After a pause, he finally went on. "Don't you have an interview soon?" He raised his eyebrows meaningfully. "Wouldn't want to be late." He cocked his head, eyes sparkling with humor. "First impressions are important."

She pressed her lips together, holding back the laugh. Oh, he was smooth. Very smooth. But she had the sale of the century to pull off, so she sent him her best self-assured smile. "That's right," she said, and inwardly cringed at her twangy words. After years of practice, the country accent still couldn't be totally contained. "So, if you'll excuse me." She slid off her seat and picked up her tote, lifting what she hoped was a dignified brow. "I have a job to land." And with a confidence she didn't feel, she turned and walked toward the exit. Other than the clap of her heels, silence followed until she was five feet from the elevator doors.

"Good luck with your pitch," he said, his voice sounding amused again.

Paulo watched the lady walk away with a regal air, hips swaying gracefully.

Outrageous. Abso-freakin'-lutely outrageous.

The combination of professional businesswoman and spunky attitude was riveting. The fitted skirt hugged a shapely backside and extended to her knees, her spectacular shoes the only style in a painfully bland outfit. With a push of a button, the swish of the elevator door, she disappeared behind a curtain of stainless steel, and his body slowly began to unwind from the knot it was cinched into.

After spending a hot morning outside, conferring with the landscaper, he'd needed a dip in the pool before checking the contractor's work in the penthouse. And now his instincts—instincts that never failed—hadn't been able to determine if Ms. Alyssa Hunt shared in the attraction or not. But *he* needed a shower. Maybe two. And most definitely cold.

He also needed to get his head out of the gutter.

But ten minutes later Paulo decided frigid showers were overrated in their ability to quash an attack of lust. His certainly hadn't helped. After pulling on clean clothes, he left the room he'd kept for his personal use during the renovations still preoccupied with thoughts of Alyssa Hunt. His mind was filled to the brim with a delicious picture of her, and Paulo's slow simmer kept returning to a rolling boil.

Smoky eyes. Delicate features. Her look had screamed professional. But the sharp tongue—tinged with an intermittent drawl—hinted at the possibility for passion beneath. And the killer body couldn't be disguised by the uptight business suit.

As he turned down the hallway leading to his office, anticipation coiled around his libido and his body tightened in response.

Paulo paused in his doorway, taking a moment to enjoy the sight of the woman in the chair across from his mahogany desk. Honey-colored hair fell in a sleek line to her shoulders, and she sat with a dainty precision. Back straight. Legs crossed. Hands folded on her lap.

When their eyes met, he felt a current of awareness, and he held her gaze as he crossed the floor. He'd give anything to see her sassy side return. "Before we get started, would you like to ask me any more questions?"

The cool gray eyes didn't flicker. But the luscious strawberry-colored lips sent him a genteel smile. "I'd prefer to explain why I'm the answer to your event planner problem."

He leaned back against the front of his desk. He had a problem, all right. Several of them.

After the smooth purchase and renovation of the Samba, now everything was falling apart. The event planner had deserted him. His general manager had left to deal with an emergency at another one of Paulo's hotels. And, to top it off, the band scheduled for the grand opening had reneged on their contract.

Typical. It *would* happen when the most important opening of his career was just eighteen days away. He'd waited years to prove Marcos wrong about the Samba.

With a small frown, he pushed the thoughts of his brother aside. "I hope you can help me too," he said. "But I need to learn a lot more about you first."

Desperation flit across her heart-shaped face before it went blank. What was the flash of panic for?

As soon as the thought formed, he squashed it. Her vulnerabilities had nothing to do with him. Whether or not he hired her would be based on her abilities.

After half a decade of killing himself at Domingues International, Paulo had finally wised up and broken free to carve out his own business vision, in his own way. No more sacrificing his life on the altar of success for a family who never noticed. No more following the Domingues creed of eating, sleeping and breathing the job, while reaping none of the rewards. Work hard and play hard, with his own needs as the goal. That was the motto he'd learned, and he wasn't about to let anything—*anyone*—distract him from it.

He realized Alyssa Hunt was still staring at him and he broke the train of disturbing thoughts. "Let's start with your résumé."

With a firm set to her delectable mouth, she reached into her tote on the floor, pulling out a folder. She handed it to him and silently sat back.

He allowed himself a brief scan of shapely calves and then, with a harsh internal reminder of what this interview was *supposed* to be about, he scanned her résumé instead. And the more he read, the more discouraged he got. When he reached the end, brows pinched with doubt, he met her gaze again.

"Your experience consists of minor corporate functions. Our social events will be on a much larger scale. And certainly more..." He paused, searching for a tactful approach. Wouldn't want to expose her vulnerabilities again, and his unwanted twinge of sympathy. "Sophisticated."

He failed at his task, because her posture and the polite expression went brittle enough to break. But the sexy drawl returned, stronger than before. "I'm perfectly capable of handlin' the work, Mr. Domingues."

He crossed his arms, amused. "I'm sorry to disappoint you." And he meant it. Because the woman fascinated him. But he couldn't let the most important business acquisition of his life hinge on an unqualified event planner, not without supervision. And he'd decided the woman would definitely be a distraction. The thought strengthened his resolve, and he set her résumé on the desk behind him. "Besides, I told you," he went on, "I'm looking for an in-house planner."

Her delicate chin climbed higher, and this time her words were as crisp as her posture. "And I believe as your strategic *partner*, I would make a better choice."

Paulo's lips twitched at her carefully worded description. "I don't do partners." Neither professionally, nor personally. He'd learned both in one neat and tidy bout with betrayal.

So thoughtfully provided to him via his family and his ex-wife.

The memory kicked up a dust cloud of bitterness, choking off his good humor. Seeking a zen-like calm, he picked up the autographed baseball displayed on his desk and rolled it between his hands. Because calm was okay. Actually, calm was good. But forgetting...?

Absolutely not.

So now he limited his relationships to those that went as

deep as easy listening Muzak. He liked his women soothing, occasionally diverting, but relegated to the background of his life.

After a few seconds, Paulo realized Alyssa wasn't gathering her tote to leave. If anything, she looked even more rooted in her chair. Interesting.

But, as enjoyable as this interview was, he was late for his meeting with the contractor. With a touch of regret, he pushed up from the desk and set the ball aside. "You have my answer, Ms. Hunt," Paulo said. "My secretary will see you out."

As he headed for the door, he heard her heels hit the wood floor and follow. A surprised grin shot to his lips. Determination appeared to be the lady's first, last and middle name.

"If you would just give me a chance." Alyssa Hunt laid a gentle hand on his arm.

The soft Southern accent and skin-on-skin touch stopped him mid-step, cranking up the achy need with a visceral response that left him smoking. His grin died as he turned to stare at her. Damn. Torture was definitely the order of the day. And while she was busy twisting him in painful knots, her face remained cool and collected.

And how moronic would it be to pass on a planner that could solve his problem? It wouldn't be the first time he'd had to resist the allure of a beautiful woman. She was clearly tenacious, and he could use someone with that much fire on his side.

At the very least he could give her a chance to change his mind. Because his secretary was too overwhelmed to help, and he needed somebody now. Someone who at least had a *clue*. Rubbing his jaw, he considered his next move, and realized he had only one choice.

He would just have to continually beat it into his head not to flirt with the woman.

"Okay, Ms. Hunt." Paulo crossed his arms, breaking their contact and the resulting sizzle, his tone all business. "I have to check the contractor's work in the penthouse." He nodded toward the elevator down the hall, his lips smiling in rebellious anticipation. "You have until we reach the top floor to convince me to hire you."

After two blinks and three pounding heartbeats, the words penetrated Alyssa's brain. Gaping open-mouthed would hardly be polite, but her eyelids managed to do a decent imitation. Because there wouldn't be time to give an address and phone number, much less pull off the impossible.

But at least he'd agreed to hear her pitch. She discreetly bit her lip and looked at Paulo, now dressed in jeans and a black T-shirt. She guessed the wealthy son of a powerful family and owner of a successful line of hotels didn't need a suit. She wished she had that option. With a tiny sigh, she wiggled her toes, cramped in her designer heels.

Perhaps if she pried that silver spoon from his smart-alecky mouth, it would wipe the sexy smile from his face?

Well, she wanted this account and she wasn't giving up. She forced herself to focus. "Okay, Mr. Domingues." He set off down the hallway, and she followed along beside him. "I'm familiar with the boutique concept of your hotel line." They entered the lobby, her heels clicking on the wood, and she went on. "And I admire its emphasis on personal service."

As they crossed the floor, she snuck a peek at Paulo. His face looked almost bored.

Her heart slunk lower as they reached their destination. "I have excellent people skills. I'm committed to customer satisfaction." With the push of a button, the elevator doors opened and they entered. When the doors slid shut behind her, she said, "And I work well under pressure."

This seemed to prick his interest. "Do you really?" he said as he stepped closer.

His proximity, and the smolder in his eyes, pushed her closer to the edge, and every cell in her body ceased what it was doing to take notes. She inhaled, only to catch a whiff of masculine soap.

Easy, Alyssa. Remember what's important.

She forced herself to maintain a neutral expression. "Would you like me to cite specific examples?"

A dimple appeared as he leaned closer, pushing a button on the panel beside her. "I'd rather see for myself."

Was that what this torture session was all about? Palms damp, she felt her stomach lurch as the elevator lifted. A pinging sound began as they passed each floor, coming way too quickly for comfort, but she pressed on. "I'm a stickler for detail. I'm organized and efficient." She made the mistake of lifting her gaze. His face was now two feet away.

And suddenly she was drowning. Drowning in those better-than-mocha-cappuccino eyes. More golden-brown than dark. Beautiful. With tiny little specks of green.

He had to know exactly what he was doing to her as he patiently waited for her to go on. Ignoring the pesky rate of her heart, she searched for a safe focal point, but couldn't find one. "And I'm particularly good at creative solutions to last minute problems," she said.

"A thinking-outside-the-box kinda girl?"

"Definitely."

Ping... His brow lifted expectantly. "Go on."

His mischievous expression morphed gorgeous into irresistible. And although he wasn't even close to touching her, he didn't need to.

He slayed her with a look from those bedroom eyes.

She glanced at the elevator panel, her mind scrambling for something brilliant to say.

Ping... One floor left. A thin line of sweat broke out along her upper lip.

Come on, girl. What's wrong with you? Your goal, remember? To produce the high-end events that lured you into the business in the first place, and to heck *with the past.*

The last ding sounded in the small compartment.

Alyssa swore under her breath and reached out to push the emergency stop button. The elevator halted with a jolt that had them bracing against the mirrored walls for support.

Paulo's expression shot to one of total surprise. "What are you doing?"

After dedicating every waking moment to her business, indulging in a daydream that included her and a potential client was certainly understandable. It just wasn't acceptable. No matter how tempting. She forced her shoulders back. "I told you. I'm good at creative solutions."

His forehead bunched in suppressed amusement.

But this was her *dream* she was fighting for. Nothing funny about it. "Look, Mr. Domingues. I know every vendor in town for putting on a reception." His amused expression didn't budge. And, really, he was standing entirely too close. "You want exotic flowers? Use Lynn's Boutique. They aren't as fast as Beth's Florals, but worth the wait if you have the time." She sucked in a breath, dizzy from her efforts and the handsome man in front of her. "Catering a seafood buffet? Use Dominic's. Their stuffed scallops are fantastic but they don't do prime rib so well."

A lock of hair fell forward across her face.

Alyssa reached up to brush the strand back into place, Paulo's eyes following her every move. And by the end of the maneuver his gaze was dark. Even as she fought the rising tide of awareness, she knew it was hopeless. The surge of desire had swelled to new heights. Enveloping her. Fogging her brain.

"But whatever you do..." The tight sound of her voice was foreign, but the familiar twang was thick. "Don't order your ice carvin' from Jenny's Designs." Alyssa waited for him to ask why, but Paulo just stared at her. Was he even listening anymore? Nerves stretched to the max, she pressed on, answering the unasked question. "Their sculptures suck."

Paulo let out a low chuckle. "That wasn't a very professional critique."

"I tried professional." She frowned. "But you weren't paying attention."

"Oh, trust me." He took half a step closer, sending heat slithering along her veins. "I'm definitely paying attention."

Hypnotized, she tried to become one with the elevator, pressing her back against the door. Wicked messages skittered like skipping stones along her every nerve. Because that mouth would entice the strongest of women.

And, sadly, she was learning she wasn't as strong as she thought. She longed to run a finger along his lower lip and then drop her hand to the awe-inspiring plane of muscle on his chest. The mirrored elevator would certainly provide an atmosphere for incredible sex. A person could see everything. And making love with this man would rate a category five on the hurricane rating scale.

"Time's up," he said.

His gaze radiated a heat hotter than the sands of South Miami Beach at high noon, and Alyssa watched in utter amazement as Paulo slowly leaned forward.

Did he think he could just *kiss* her?

Those hazel eyes, those wonderful, heavy, sexy eyes, lingered on her mouth. Molten lava pooled, shortcircuiting her brain. His lips were full, sensual, and slightly parted.

Closer...

His left arm lifted. Where was that hand going?

Closer...

"You'd better brace yourself," he said huskily.

Her body's reaction to his words prevented any hope of a coherent thought, and his meaning didn't become clear until she heard the pop of the emergency button beside her. But by then it was too late, and when the doors slid open she began to fall.

CHAPTER TWO

PAULO stepped forward to catch Alyssa just as her fingers clutched his shirt, and, like a Jackie Chan swivel kick to the chest, the contact blasted his intentions to smithereens.

His body cataloged every glorious sensation. The intoxicating feel of her gentle hips beneath his hands. The knuckles flat against him. But her thighs pressed to his were the most disrupting. Everything about him was hard, while she was soft, supple, bringing sultry visions of hot Southern nights. Entwined limbs. And sated bodies.

He'd wanted to know if the attraction was mutual, but the expression that flashed on her face when her gaze dropped to his mouth...

Man, some things a guy just couldn't be held responsible for.

So he'd opened the door to escape her and get his reaction under control, triggering a nuclear explosion.

He seized hold of his response and cleared his throat. "Next time someone tells you to brace yourself, you should listen," Paulo said as he slowly set her back, ignoring the protests from his body. She released his shirt, but her frozen expression gave him no inkling what she'd do next. At this point, all he knew was to expect the unexpected from this woman. He lifted a brow. "Are you planning on following me into the penthouse?"

Something flickered across her face he couldn't interpret. Maybe awareness tinged with annoyance? "There's nothing I need to see in the penthouse," she said with a slight frown.

His lips twitched at the tone that implied he'd meant something lurid. Or maybe that was his libido providing the translation. Hell, he shouldn't tease her either, but he couldn't help himself. "Oh, I definitely have something you want to see." He suppressed the grin and headed for the door at the end of the hall.

Watching her deliver her presentation, the cool demeanor slowly slipping away and the occasional—and increasingly stronger—hint of attraction, had been the highlight of his month. Maybe the last three months. At least until the pull became so magnetic the need to push her up against the wall and kiss the reserved professional right out of her had all but overwhelmed him.

As he neared the suite, he heard her scurry down the hall behind him just before she joined him at the door.

With a lift of her chin, the poise was back. "We've reached the top, Mr. Domingues. My pitch is over. Do I have the job or not?"

Paulo propped a shoulder against the wall, struck with the need to keep her as off balance as he felt. And if she tipped that chin at him one more time, pretending she didn't return the attraction, he'd forget his good intentions and take the kiss he'd been dying for during their riveting ride up. "Too busy to take in the view from the penthouse, huh?"

A myriad of emotions crossed her face, as if she was baffled how to handle their interaction.

Welcome to the club, lady.

Finally, she sent him an overly patient look. "Not everyone is born with money to burn."

He bit back the grin at her indirect slur. "And I'm not convinced you have the necessary skills to handle this job."

"I can do this job better than anyone else you can find."

His eyebrows shot higher. She had zero experience in social events. And her confidence amused him. "Can you?"

"Definitely."

He continued to hold back the smile. He was enjoying the exchange way too much. And he'd made the decision to hire her the second she'd hit the stop button in the elevator.

But after the desertion of his old event planner and the band for the grand opening, he felt the need to make a point. It was imperative she follow through. He had no tolerance for false promises, employees who talked big but failed to deliver.

He tipped his head and went on. "I have a little task that needs attention. In six months the mayor is having her fiftieth birthday party at the Samba. Nothing has been done on it yet." He maintained a straight face, despite the lie. "Do you think you could prepare a complete event proposal?"

"Naturally."

The corner of his mouth twitched in amusement. "Can you have it ready by tomorrow?"

Her eyelids flared briefly, and she hesitated. He could almost see the smoke from the wheels turning in her brain. No doubt trying to come up with a tactful way to tell him to go to hell. He waited, itching to hear her carefully worded no.

"Of course," she finally said.

His amusement came to an abrupt end. It was an impossible task, and she should know that. As he stared at Alyssa, for a moment he considered changing his mind about hiring her, wondering if she suffered from delusions of grandeur.

But he'd laid out his plan, and until she signed a contract he wasn't stuck with a crazy employee.

And he absolutely *had* to see what she would come up with next.

"Good," he said with a sharp nod. "Until I'm confident in your skills, you'll be under the supervision of my manager. But, assuming your references hold up, you're hired." He finally pushed away from the wall. "On your way out, stop by and see my secretary to sign the permission form for a reference and background check."

Alyssa Hunt went so still she could have doubled as a photograph.

What now? Had she had a fight with a former client? He bit back the grin, imagining the incident. "Shall I escort you back to the reception desk?"

With a small frown, Alyssa hiked her tote higher and looked at him coolly. "I'm perfectly capable of finding my way."

His grin finally reappeared. "I have no doubt you are."

Clever little bastard. Who the heck did he think she was? A naive country bumpkin who didn't know the score? As if the accent she couldn't completely suppress somehow made her gullible. She hated being stereotyped.

Happy to finally have exchanged the restricting suit for her well-worn jeans, Alyssa leaned back on the leather couch in her apartment. She propped her bare feet on the glass coffee table, wiggling her still hurting toes, glad to be free of the designer high heels.

Why couldn't they design a little comfort into their hideously expensive shoes? If people weren't so fixated on external image, she wouldn't bother with the dreaded torture traps. Of course, the casual style Paulo sported suited him. He looked like a bazillion bucks with no effort at all.

She blew out a breath and sank deeper into the couch.

And his "little" task, as he so casually labeled it, couldn't be done in one night. And certainly not without interviewing the mayor. She'd smelled the trap the moment he asked for the proposal by tomorrow. But why? To get her to admit it was impossible? To see how much she knew?

Peeved, she'd blurted out her response, preparing to go home and do the best she could by gleaning a little info about the mayor off the internet. It wouldn't be her finest work, just a rough idea to get things started.

And then she'd discovered it was completely unnecessary.

Irritation surged again as she remembered her conversation with his secretary. Figuring her meeting with the woman should be put to good use, Alyssa had asked her about the upcoming party. And learned that, sitting in a file in Paulo's office, was the previous event planner's completed proposal.

And a pretty good one, too. Alyssa knew that for a fact. Because she'd seen it.

Fuming at what Paulo probably thought was cute little ploy to test her, she'd sent the secretary up to the penthouse to ask him a question and then snuck into his office, found the file, and made a copy.

Alyssa looked at the document splayed across her coffee table. Now that she had all the notes about the mayor's preferences, and the event planner's ideas, Alyssa couldn't decide what to do with the information.

Chewing on the tip of a nail, she eyed the papers, pondering her next move.

It was a decent proposal. With a few tweaks of the less inspiring elements, and some computer-generated graphics, it had the makings of a humdinger of a report. And if she didn't change it too much, Paulo would recognize his former employee's work.

A small smile slipped up her face as she pictured him stumped, trying to figure out how she'd gotten hold of the file. He wouldn't, of course. Avoiding the discreet security camera in the lobby had been the perfect test of her expertise.

Not that she was particularly proud of her childhood skills. But, with the background check, Paulo was going to find out about her criminal record anyway.

With a sigh of resignation, she dropped her head back to rest on the couch.

When she'd started her business, with the first three jobs she'd gone after she'd been completely honest, telling the prospective clients about her history. It was in the past. She wasn't that person anymore. And she refused to hide in shame.

But the information had lost her every one of those accounts.

After that, she hadn't volunteered a thing. And not one of her clients had asked for a formal background check since. Until today.

A familiar feeling of defeat threatened to swamp her, but she pushed it aside. One thing she knew for sure: the secret to dealing with Paulo Domingues was to never let him get the upper hand. Always leave him guessing. Keep the cocky man just a little unsure of himself. So she'd show him exactly who Alyssa Hunt was.

Someone who wasn't afraid to take him on, tit for tat. *Mano a womano.*

And if he was going to change his mind about hiring her because of her history anyway, well…then she'd go out in a blaze of glory.

With a renewed determination, Alyssa sat up and reached for the copy of the proposal.

* * *

At seven forty-five the next morning, Alyssa sat in a cab on the way to the Samba, cradling her latte with its potent double shot of caffeine. Sleep had been in short supply last night, but there had been plenty of room for work.

And now that she knew she found Paulo attractive, that he bound her insides up so tight blood could barely find its way to her toes, she'd skipped the designer shoes for less torturous heels. There was only so much constriction a girl could take. Unfortunately, her taupe pantsuit wasn't comfortable either. But today, to provide her ensemble with a little flair, she'd added a Prada tote. At least it didn't inflict pain.

A squeak of tires sounded as the taxi slowed and stopped at the curb. Alyssa grabbed her things and climbed out onto the sidewalk, giving the door a solid push. The decisive smack was a jolting boost to her courage. She had her proposal, her laptop, and enough caffeine on board to keep her charged for weeks.

After marching up the steps, she pulled open the heavy door and entered the spacious lobby. Stainless steel and stone accents lent a modern touch. Gleaming hardwood floors added warmth. And in the center of it all a huge bar was set against a slate backdrop, water sheeting down the rock wall. The soothing murmur provided a cool place to escape the scorching tropical sun with frosty drink in hand.

And she could use a little soothing because, when she spied Paulo approaching, her body reacted with a mixture of heat, dread, and mutinous anticipation.

Alyssa brushed her hair from her cheek, composing herself.

"Good morning." He stopped in front of her and studied her closely. He wore black jeans and a white dress shirt, sleeves rolled to the elbows, his well-muscled forearms displayed in all their glory. "You're much too young to have dark shadows under your eyes, Ms. Hunt."

"At twenty-eight, I'm much too old to be called young," she said. "And anyway, youth does not preclude a person from hard work." Lord knows she was living proof.

"Work? That's the cause of the circles?" He shook his head, and a wave of gorgeous, devil-may-care hair fell across his forehead. "I thought maybe you'd thrown your proposal together and then stayed up late having fun with friends." With a smile, he went on. "Or maybe with a date."

She forced her brow to relax. He really did think he was cute. And after their elevator ride, rife with sexual tension, clarifying her position on *that* particular topic would be smart. Like the fact she refused to be tempted by his charms. "I'm too focused on my company to date."

His eyes narrowed. "You don't date," he repeated slowly, as if unable to digest her statement. "So you either sustain yourself on a string of one-night stands or you're celibate."

Damn. How had the conversation taken such a radical turn? Alyssa raised a single brow as delicately as she could. "You have a rather limited take on the concept of dating."

He looked amused. "It doesn't begin and end with sex, true. But it should at least include it." His eyes crinkled in question. "Are you seriously forgoing a social life for work?"

Gone were the teasing undertones, and the genuine curiosity in his expression made her feel like an oddball. Her nonexistent sex life hadn't been a conscious decision, only one of necessity. Once she began her business, she hadn't had time for the kind of relationship that went deep enough for that kind of intimacy.

Not to mention there was always the sticky issue of her past.

But unfortunately it appeared declaring her lifestyle upfront had only piqued his interest instead of squashing it. Really, the man should come with an instruction manual.

Buck up, Alyssa. You can be cool. You can be elegant.

After securing her hair behind her ear, she smiled politely and turned the topic back to safer waters. "Don't we have business to discuss?"

"Straight to the job at hand." The killer grin returned with a flash. "I like that."

He placed a hand under her elbow, the assault on her senses cutting off her response. Smooth skin caressed her arm as he steered Alyssa toward the staff area. She tried to ignore his touch, the heat, and the memories of yesterday. It didn't go so well.

Paulo guided her down a hall with offices on either side—the largest of which was his—to a doorway at the end. He stopped and held out an arm. "This space was reserved for the event planner's use."

She entered the room, and her jaw went slack in surprise. The office wasn't huge, but the exquisitely crafted cherry desk, dark wood filing cabinets and Persian rug that lay between were lovely. No, *beautiful*. And it sure beat the dining room in her apartment. She set her bag down and touched the desk longingly, aware of Paulo's eyes on her.

"But as an in-house planner," Paulo added, "she worked exclusively for the Samba."

The words spurred her to face him, and Alyssa frowned. Was he suggesting she would take advantage of the space? "You don't need to worry I'll abuse my privileges, Mr. Domingues. I'm a professional."

His gaze didn't waver. "Being a professional doesn't make up for your lack of experience." As the seconds ticked by, they stared at each other—a silent battle of wills—before Paulo went on. "So why don't you show me your ideas for the mayor's birthday party."

A ghost of a smile formed as Alyssa reached into her bag and withdrew the work she had spent yesterday afternoon and a good part of the night putting together. The new and improved proposal, reprinted on *her* business letterhead.

"Of course." Alyssa held out the document, complete with the added glossy photos and sketches.

Paulo's expression was worth every minute of lost sleep.

She boldly held his gaze and continued. "My ideas, as requested."

With a stunned look, he accepted the folder, and she went on in a brisk, businesslike tone. "I also have a detailed cost analysis. In case the client chooses to go with the proposal." It took all she had not to giggle as she passed him the second document.

Paulo took the report, disbelief radiating from his face. "How did you manage all this?"

"I told you." Game. Set. And end of the match. *Ha!* "I can do this job better than anyone else you can find."

Long moments ticked by as he flipped through the documents, his movements growing slower and slower. She knew the second he recognized the information, because an unmistakable look of understanding flashed in his eyes. After another pause, he carefully set the reports on the desk before turning back to her. "Impressive," he said.

That would teach him not to underestimate her, hick accent or not.

She sent him her best "aww, shucks" smile and fluttered her eyelashes, just a touch, for effect. "Thank you."

In response, a glint of amusement flared in his eyes. "You did all this without help?"

She could fess up. Give it to him straight. But something held her back. Maybe it was the way he kept challenging her. Let him figure it out all by his little ol' self.

"I told you," she said, eyeing him levelly, "I'm good at creative solutions."

Take that, Mr. Smooth-Talking Charmer.

His lips twisted, and he tipped his head up. For a moment, he looked as if he would burst out laughing. Instead, he wiped a hand down his mouth and stepped closer—*too* close—and Alyssa's awareness shot from coffee shop grande to extra-venti.

There was no denying he was good at the counterpoint move.

Frozen in place, she gripped the desk behind her and resisted the urge to shrink away, holding her breath. Unfortunately she didn't think to stop breathing until after she'd caught a whiff of his scent...sandalwood, mixed with desire, and a generous dose of danger.

"*Very* creative, I see," he said. "Are you sure you produced the reports single-handedly?" His right eyebrow climbed a tiny degree higher, as if waiting for her to respond. "No help from any..." He paused, as if allowing her time to fill in the blank. Heart thumping madly, she forced herself to maintain his gaze, a cool smile plastered on her face. "Friends?" he finished.

Due to his scent and his nearness, it took several seconds for her muddled brain to send a message to the muscles in charge of her mouth. "None whatsoever."

Paulo slowly leaned forward, reaching for something on the desk behind her, his six-foot-plus frame dwarfing hers. Her nerves scrambled for cover as he came close enough to almost touch her. Thick eyelashes and sensual lips brought memories of yesterday's elevator ride. And then he straightened up, holding out a file. "Our contract."

When she managed to take it, he folded his arms across his chest and turned to sit on the desk, creating enough space for her to breathe again. And the look that crossed his face told her she was in trouble.

He cleared his throat. "In light of your..." pausing, he pursed his lips for a moment before going on "...*superior* performance, I've decided your work won't be supervised by my manager."

"Excuse me?" Shoot—the drawl again.

There was no smile, only an expression bordering on a smirk. "You'll be reporting to me."

A bolt of electrical energy deep-fried her nerve-endings. Alyssa chewed on her lip and willed her heart back to a reasonable rate. Her little deed had earned her the eagle eye of the boss instead of an immediate firing. But didn't he have better things to do than torment his new event planner?

Paulo cocked his head. She couldn't tell what he was thinking, but at least his tone was businesslike. "Do we have a deal?"

Alyssa rounded the desk, not stopping until it was between her and Paulo. It was much easier to handle him from a distance. And her voice was clearer, too. "Of course."

"Good," he said, and then headed for the door. "I have a few things to discuss with my secretary." He stopped at the threshold and turned to face her. His eyes communicated exactly what he wanted to see the woman about. The file. The twinkle appeared in his eyes again. "Anything you want to tell me before I go?"

"No," she said coolly. "Not a thing."

The light in his eyes grew brighter as he acknowledged the stalemate with a sharp nod. "Okay. I'll be back to see how you're doing at the end of the day." And then he turned and headed out the exit.

Alyssa flopped into her chair and dropped her head back, staring at the door he'd closed behind him. Oh, joy. He was coming back to check on her. More nerve-racking moments to look forward to. This game of cat and mouse was doable until he stepped closer and she could *feel* the attraction, an almost physical presence. It was like being caught in a tractor beam.

Sucking her in.

And on the off chance her background check didn't get her fired, now her job would involve daily direct contact with Paulo Domingues. *Daily direct contact.*

How in the world was she going to handle the constant scrutiny of the bedeviling man? Even more crucial, how was she going to survive the undeniable way he made her feel?

"Look," Nick Tatum said. His sandy brown hair stuck out beneath the baseball cap perched backward on his head. "Right there." Paulo's friend hit the pause button on the security video, and an image of Alyssa from yesterday froze on the TV. She was standing at the reception desk of the Samba, in her boring gray suit. "Do you see that?" Nick pointed at Alyssa's right hand where it rested on the counter. "Her fingers are angled in a different position."

Paulo frowned and leaned in for a closer look at the screen.

Right after he'd spoken with his secretary, he called Nick. Friends since junior high, there was no one Paulo trusted more. For the last twenty minutes they'd been reviewing the tape in the security guard's tiny office, and Paulo's frustration was mounting. "That doesn't prove anything."

After calling a few of her former clients yesterday, every one of them singing her praises, Paulo had decided Alyssa might be able to cut the mustard. When she'd handed over the mountain of work she achieved overnight, his fascination had reached for the roof.

And the thought of leaving her supervision to Charles had left him feeling cheated.

At first he'd assumed she'd asked the secretary for the report, but that had turned up false. Then he'd thought she'd helped herself to the file from his office. But when he'd found the document in his filing cabinet, he'd run into a dead end. The security tape was supposed to give him the answer. And still he had nothing.

"It doesn't make any sense," Paulo said.

"I'm telling you." In cutoffs and a T-shirt, Nick leaned back, pulling his bowl of popcorn from the table and balancing it on his lap. "She took the file."

"But the file is still in the cabinet."

"Dude." Nick popped a piece of popcorn in his mouth. "She copied it."

"There wasn't time." Aggravated he couldn't solve the perplexing mystery, Paulo raked a hand through his hair. "She had to pull the document from my filing cabinet, use the copier in the staff hallway, return the papers to the office, and then get back to the counter. But every passing sweep of the security camera clearly shows she never left the reception desk."

Crunching on his snack, Nick frowned, as if disappointed by the huge hole in his theory.

"Unless…" Paulo said, a slow realization dawning as he glanced at the watch on her wrist. Why hadn't he thought of it before? "She knew exactly when the camera would be making its sweep, timing her movements to return to stand at the counter at precisely the same spot between each task." He lifted a brow in triumph and glanced at his friend.

Nick's eyes went wide as he let out a low whistle. "Now, *that's* cool." He gazed at the TV screen. "Who'd she organize parties for in the past? The *Mission: Impossible* team?" After a moment's pause, he sent Paulo a grin, his green eyes lit with humor. "If I'd known your workday was this entertaining, I would have hung out here more often."

Entertaining. His new event planner had pulled off a heist in broad daylight, and, short of dusting for fingerprints, Paulo couldn't prove a thing. Granted, she hadn't actually stolen anything, and it would have been information she would have had access to anyway, but that wasn't the point. The point was…

Paulo's thoughts trailed off as he stared at the beautiful woman on the monitor. He couldn't remember his point anymore.

Nick tossed a kernel into the air, caught it in his mouth, and then wagged his finger in the direction of the video recorder. "Let's rewind the tape and watch it again."

Paulo shot Nick a wry look. "Glad you're enjoying the midday movie."

"You're just ticked she bested you at your game."

No, he wasn't. And that was the problem. He wasn't angry; he was massively, massively intrigued by his new event planner's cunning and finesse.

Intrigued and attracted. Not a reassuring combination.

Paulo was saved from dwelling on the growing concern when his cellular phone beeped, and he pulled it from his pocket. Scanning the text message, he felt his snowballing curiosity reach gargantuan proportions. "The results of her background check," he said, waving his phone in the air. "Ten years ago she was convicted of stealing."

They both turned to view the woman on the screen.

After a moment's pause, Nick said, "Why would she risk a stunt that could trigger a look at her record?"

It was the first question Paulo had a ready response to. Eyes fixated on his new event planner, Paulo answered, "She's sending me a message. She doesn't care if I know."

The ticking of the clock on the wall was loud, until Nick finally broke the shocked silence. "Wow. I think I'm in love." His tone proved just how impressed he was. "If you fire her, I'm hiring her at my club."

And miss out on the most exciting woman he'd ever met? Not a chance in hell. Paulo continued to stare at Alyssa's image. "She doesn't want to be one of your many girlfriends." He shot Nick a quick look from the corner of his eye. "And I financed that club, remember?"

"And to return the favor I found you the perfect replacement band for the opening of the Samba." Nick stood and set his popcorn aside. "Seven o'clock. Old Beachside Park. Be there tonight and you can hear their stuff."

Right now Paulo was too distracted to think of much outside his new employee. He stood, arms crossed, absorbed by her demeanor on the screen. Her posture was dignified as she waited at the counter, her tote hanging from her shoulder. Very professional. How had she retained such a calm expression during her caper?

"Ahem." Nick waved his hand in front of Paulo's eyes. "Beachside Park? Seven o'clock?" Paulo turned to face Nick. His friend looked amused as he continued. "Maybe I should just leave the two of you alone."

Paulo ignored the comment. "I'll go see the band tonight," he said. He was more wound up than he'd realized. "Thanks for finding them. I owe you big time."

Nick shot him a grin. "Always good to keep my obnoxiously rich friend indebted to me. Could come in handy again someday."

Paulo let out a soft snort. "You're such a moron."

"Coming from you, that means nothing," Nick said, and then his grin grew bigger. "Now I'll let you get back to your new girlfriend." After a salute, he headed out the door, chuckling all the way down the hall as he left.

Paulo returned his gaze to the monitor, taking in the curve of Alyssa's backside, the slim calves and the delicate ankles above the spectacular shoes.

Who was this unflappable lady that had descended like Wonder Woman upon his hotel, promising to solve his problem? A woman with enough poise to greet the Queen of

England, enough spunk to take on Hell's Angels, and the ability to fight dirty when pushed into a corner.

But she hadn't hidden what she'd done. Instead she'd flaunted it. Gleefully waved it under his nose. Daring him to say something.

While most aggressive go-getters learned to think outside the box, she upped the ante and thought outside of the whole shipping container. And he was developing a deep admiration for his wily new employee.

Admiration, intrigue *and* attraction.

Man, he really was in trouble.

At six-thirty that evening Paulo sat on his motorcycle in front of the Samba, waiting for Alyssa to show. Traffic zipped by on Ocean Drive. Pedestrians meandered along the terracotta walkway, passing hotels and trendy shops, enjoying the cooler evening breeze.

Alyssa appeared and headed down the front steps of the hotel, turning north on the sidewalk. Her respectable pantsuit was paired with a purse that added a bit of chic. Yesterday it was the shoes; today it was her bag. And, though she handled herself with decorum, he was beginning to get a better taste of the woman beneath.

A delicious concoction he'd never encountered before.

As he watched her walk, his eyes dropped to her feet. Before she'd left the building, she had exchanged her heels for a pair of athletic shoes. Interesting.

He started his bike and pulled up beside her, flipping up the visor on his helmet. "I like the new shoes," Paulo said as he balanced the slow-moving motorcycle with his feet. "If you're going home on foot, I can give you a lift."

She kept walking and sent him a tight thanks-but-no-thanks smile. "I'm fine."

"You must be tired after producing such a detailed report."

She ignored his dig and continued her sexy saunter on the sidewalk.

He tried again. "Do you always work this late?"

"The more I get done now, the more time to solicit new events later." She turned to look at him as she continued on her way.

His eyes dropped to take in the translucent pink of her lipstick. The fierce need those full lips created was enough to require a "caution—contents hot" label.

"More events, more income," she said. "I'm sure you understand the benefits of more income."

The words triggered a cascade of memories, every one of them leaving an acrid taste in his mouth. Profit had been the singular concern at Domingues International. But no matter how much he'd added to the bottom line, busting a gut, sacrificing everything to match his brother at work, he'd never obtained that elusive Holy Grail: his father's recognition.

He pushed the bitter thoughts aside, turning his focus back to the feminine challenge before him. "Your long hours are none of my business. All the better for me, I suppose. But personally, I don't think work is worth ruining your health over."

Alyssa stopped mid-step. "Poverty doesn't increase your lifespan either," she said dryly.

Paulo halted beside her, taking a quick glance at her bag, amused. "Is Prada the latest trend among the destitute?"

Her lips quirked, as if holding back a smile. "I bought it secondhand."

"Chic, yet frugal." He stared at her, more intrigued than ever. But what did he expect? A confession that she'd swiped it? "That's a rare female combination of traits." Everything about this woman was exceptional.

"As the daughter of a teenage mother working for minimum wage, I didn't have much of a choice," Alyssa said, and started up the sidewalk again.

Hmm, now he was getting somewhere. Because he was burning with curiosity about her past. With his twist of the throttle, the motorcycle revved in response, and he pulled forward on the road to follow along beside her again. "I imagine that was a tough way to grow up."

A small smile graced her lips, but she didn't turn to look at him. "No offense, Mr. Domingues," she said as she continued her stroll, her silky hair swinging against her shoulders. "But I really don't think *you* can."

Paulo grinned. He got a kick out of her refreshingly sassy mouth that kept lobbing subtle barbs in his direction. There was no resentment in her tone. Nor any sign of anger. Only a slight impatience, as if she was in possession of super-secret knowledge he wasn't privy to.

With the roaring pop of a wheelie, he pulled up on the sidewalk in front of her, and had the pleasure of seeing a startled look fly to her face as she came to a halt. "I have to check out a potential band for the grand opening," he said. Pleased by her expression, he struggled to keep a straight face. "As my new event planner, you should be there." While she stared at him, he sent her a measured look as he tipped his head toward the back of his bike. "Hop on."

CHAPTER THREE

ALYSSA looked down at the candy-apple-red, ultra-modern motorcycle, more suited for a racetrack than a city street, and her body reacted. Heart stomping. Stomach swirling. Nerves churning. She hoped her eyes didn't resemble those of a tree frog. "You want me to ride there on *that*?"

His look was deceptively bland beneath the matching red helmet. "It's just a Ducati. It doesn't bite."

As she continued to eye it dubiously, he straightened up, balancing the idling motorcycle between his legs. "Are you afraid?"

The hint of an I-dare-you tone and the suggestive question pricked a nerve. "Of you—no," she said firmly, hoping to convince herself. She wrestled with the alarming and distressingly heady idea of touching him again. "Of splattering my brains on the pavement—yes." It seemed a logical enough excuse.

With a look of suppressed humor, Paulo took off his helmet and held it out in offering, waiting patiently.

"What about you?" she said.

The angular, masculine features, combined with the

waves of hair and Latino coloring, made him hot enough to star on the silver screen. "I'll risk it."

Her lids dropped to half-mast. "I just bet you will."

Unfortunately, he'd addressed her safety concerns. Any more excuses would look too obvious. And he was right; she needed to be there to hear the band. Blowing out a breath, she wordlessly accepted the helmet and clamped it on her head. After securing her bag on her shoulder, she threw her leg over the back of the bike. She leaned forward, struggling to hold on to Paulo with dignity and still keep her distance.

"Hang on tight." Paulo pulled her arms firmly around him, spooning her body against his.

The surefire kick to the solar plexus restricted air entry into her lungs. Every solid inch of him was hard, from the back plastered against her breast, to the chest beneath her arms and the thighs between her legs. Alyssa fought for breath as Paulo twisted the throttle, and with a rumbling whine they were off.

For the next few minutes she concentrated on the view of the Atlantic and the sun on her shoulders while trying to rein in her response. The decadent agony ended when Paulo stopped at a park bustling with people and dismounted.

He nodded toward an ice cream vendor. "Vanilla or chocolate?"

Alyssa paused in the midst of pulling off the helmet, a smile of surprise threatening to hijack her mouth. The handsome man wearing a rakish expression looked more inclined to buy her a beer or a whiskey or a Blue 32 shooter. Ice cream sounded so innocent.

"Vanilla," she said.

While he made their purchases, Alyssa headed toward one of the few empty benches and sat down. When Paulo joined her, he handed her a vanilla cone and kept a chocolate for himself, taking a seat beside her. Desperate to ignore his proximity, she studied the scene.

Sun sparkling off its surface, the Atlantic Ocean spread out before them in shifting shades of blue moving from aquamarine to dark indigo as the ocean floor dropped away. People in shorts and bathing suits milled about on grass dotted with palm trees, while the band set up their equipment on the outdoor stage.

One by one her muscles relaxed, her posture easing against the seat. And the vanilla treat tasted like heaven.

After a few minutes, Paulo interrupted the silence. "Where did you grow up?"

Alyssa tensed. *Here we go. Time for the third degree.* She turned to look at him as calmly as she could. "I thought you didn't need to pump me for information?"

A dimple popped into view. "Maybe I spoke too soon."

The nonchalant words were harmless enough, but she wasn't fooled. And she wouldn't volunteer anything more than he asked directly. "I was born in Okeechobee County and moved to Miami when I was five."

"A country girl at heart, huh?"

"Country. City." She shrugged and sent him a pointed look. "I prefer not to be characterized in such a shallow way."

A second dimple popped into view. "How would you characterize yourself?"

She met his gaze, refusing to give anything away. "As an excellent businesswoman."

"Any other traits I should be aware of?"

Alyssa's brow pulled tight as her words from their first meeting were being thrown back in her face. And as she studied him—the expression, the knowledge in his eyes— she knew. He'd run the check and heard about her record. Asking her to come see the band was an excuse.

She was about to get canned. Again.

With the bellowing dive alarm of a submarine, her stomach descended to her toes. Her dream job was coming to an end before it began. And she was so tired of being labeled by her past. So very, very tired.

But she wasn't going to cower like a coward. She crossed her legs, summoning every ounce of poise she possessed. "For a self-described straight shooter, you beat around the bush a lot, Mr. Domingues," she said. "Why don't you just tell me what's on your mind."

"I read about your conviction."

Though her heart pounded, her gaze didn't flinch. She hated excuses, and she wasn't about to offer him one. But she hated being defined by that moment even more. And what was she supposed to say? She hiked an eyebrow. "So…?"

Paulo loosely shrugged a shoulder, as if it were no big deal. "So, I want to learn more."

His casual attitude toward the issue grated, and irritation flared, reflected in her tone. "The rest is none of your damn business."

He leaned back in surprise, whether from her cuss word or her response, she wasn't sure. "You're my employee," he said.

As if that entitled him to dig into her most private moments.

"I'm your *partner*," she said.

"I told you," he said easily. "I don't do partners. Especially ones I can't trust."

Irritation made way for anger, skewering her insides further. Ten years later and the whole world refused to let her move on. Tethered her to the past like she was a mangy dog. No matter how hard she worked, it meant nothing. Emotion had the words tumble unchecked from her lips, her accent strong.

"I made some mistakes. I paid for my crimes." She sat up higher in her seat. "But I can produce the kind of events that will knock the socks off your guests. If you're going to fire me, Mr. Domingues, then do it. Otherwise—" she sent him a frown "—quit jerkin' me around."

He lifted his lips into another crooked smile. "I don't want to fire you."

The words knocked her off kilter, defusing her anger with a single sentence. Her brow shot upward of its own accord. "You don't?"

"Do you still steal?"

Confused, she frowned harder. "No."

His smile grew bigger. "Then we don't have a problem."

He wasn't going to fire her like the others.

Dumbfounded by the unexpected turn of events, she slowly settled back against the bench and turned her face toward the crowd, feeling overwhelmed. No matter how much she hadn't wanted to care, a part of her had always been hurt by the clients who changed their minds about her when they learned the truth. Sad they couldn't see beyond her mistakes to the hardworking woman she was now. She had poured everything she had into her business.

Impatient with herself, she blinked back the sting of tears, refusing to let him see her cry. She didn't want his pity. Concentrating on the scene, she watched the band began to warm up, listening to the chords as the lead singer strummed his guitar.

Paulo was her first client not to boot her to the door after the news. Of the three others, two had given her a false smile and excuses about why she wasn't right for the job, while the third had been more up-front. She preferred the honest approach. After two years of suffering at the hands of her snooty, rich college classmates, she had no patience left for false airs and pretense. But, rich as he was, Paulo Domingues didn't fall into that category.

Honestly, she had no idea what category he belonged to anymore.

She finally composed herself and found her voice. "If you aren't going to fire me, why are you pushing me so hard for information?"

He leaned forward, his face lit with curiosity. "I want to know how you got hold of that file."

So it wasn't her record that bothered him. It was not knowing how she'd pulled off her cheat. Despite the lingering emotion, delight spread through her body. At this point she'd work for him for free, just for the fun of keeping him on his toes. She widened her eyes innocently. "What file?"

His lips quirked as he stared at her a moment more. "Never mind. The details aren't important. I've learned enough for today." He shifted on the bench, his knee pressing against hers, and a nervous thrill skittered along her limbs. "Like the way your drawl gets heavy and that cool exterior slips when you're angry." His gaze traveled across her face, and the transformation to lazy charm was instantaneous. "It also happens when you're fighting the attraction between us."

Her heart tripped before picking up speed.

With a hard swallow, she refused to look away. Because that would be admitting he was right. And as she met his gaze, she could feel the old awareness rise from the ashes like a phoenix. She clutched her cone, back rigid, as a breeze blew her hair across her face, partially veiling her vision. But Alyssa couldn't move. And, no matter how much he knew, acknowledging it out loud had to be a bad idea.

"I think you're confusing irritation with attraction," she said, shooting for a lofty, confident air, but knowing she fell horribly short.

His eyes went dark. "Am I?" he said as he swept the hair from her face, his fingers lingering on her cheek.

A shower of shivers coursed down her spine, and the resulting blaze melted the tension in her back and muddled her brain. She was vaguely aware ice cream dripped onto her fingers. But the cold droplets did little to extinguish the heat in her body. She sat, paralyzed, as his eyes dropped to her lips, increasing her internal Fahrenheit reading to the boiling point.

"A challenge like that is impossible to resist," he murmured.

Alyssa's breath paused in her throat while he slowly lowered his head, as if he was reconsidering his actions along the way. But when his mouth touched hers, he came alive and opened her lips wide. Boldly invading the soft recesses. Taking what he wanted. And the demand for submission kicked her reaction into overdrive.

She leaned into the kiss. The taste of sweet vanilla mixed with rich chocolate as his tongue mated with hers, an act that left her achy with need. Fire swirled like a tornado in her stomach, creating a force that pulled the warmth down, concentrating the heat between her legs. Lordy, her *body* was melting...

Wanting more, needing more, with a groan she gripped his shirt, her response taking on a quality too sinful for a public place.

And then Paulo pulled back, his breathing heavy, his eyes darkly curious. "Exactly how long has your ban on dating been going on?"

Every nerve working overtime, she released his shirt and tucked her hair behind her ear, fingers trembling from the shock and awe to her senses. She swiped a napkin down the hand holding the cone, pretending to be concerned about the drips of ice cream before recovering enough to meet his gaze. "That's none of your business either."

"I disagree," he said. "It's very much my business." He lifted a meaningful brow. "Because your sweet-as-molasses drawl is thick when you're turned on."

It was just a silly little kiss.

Fingers wrapped around the handle, Alyssa stared into her open refrigerator, the cool air seeping in her direction. But her body was still hot. She wasn't hungry for breakfast, and gazing blankly at the shelves, continuing to pretend she wasn't affected by yesterday's events, wasn't helping. With a frown, she finally closed the door.

Time to admit the kiss hadn't been little and was far, far from silly. But it was only a temporary lapse. A one-time slip-up. Obviously abstinence was affecting her reactions.

Fortunately, after listening to the first couple of songs, Paulo had decided the band was perfect, and Alyssa had been more than eager to leave. Sitting next to him, trying to concentrate on the music, had left her antsy. When he had offered her a ride home, she'd politely declined and taken a taxi.

Unfortunately, the scorching encounter had left her coiled tighter than the box springs beneath her mattress. Sleep had been impossible.

If she wasn't careful, her business would start to suffer.

Her cell phone buzzed on the dining room table, and she crossed the kitchen to pick it up. "Elite Events."

"Lyssa."

At the familiar sound of her mother's syrupy voice, Alyssa knew the conversation wouldn't be quick. She clamped her phone between her ear and her shoulder, gathering her things for work.

"I popped by the Samba yesterday to see you," her mother

went on. "But the manager said you'd already left. A darlin' man, though a tad too serious. And I told him he'd better treat my baby right."

Alyssa scrunched her eyelids closed. Her mother's mouth had always been set on "shoot to kill and ignore the questions later." Through the years, working in a country and western bar as a waitress had honed her manners to a sharp point, while Alyssa's business had necessitated softening the edges. And now Charles, Paulo's Chief of Operations, a man Alyssa hadn't even met yet, had been reprimanded by her mom.

Perfect.

With a quiet sigh, Alyssa reached for her keys. "Mom, please tell me you didn't."

"Oh, relax, Lyssa. He probably thought I was joking," her mother said. The whoosh of a melodramatic exhale came from the phone. "It's just this new job of yours makes me nervous."

Alyssa ignored her own doubts and tossed her keys into her purse. "Paulo Domingues already knows about my record."

"It ain't your record I'm worried about."

Of course not. Alyssa slowly shook her head, a baffled grin creeping up her mouth. Her mother's attitude never ceased to amaze her. "Mom, I was convicted of shoplifting." She set her purse on the table. *"Twice."*

"Oh, who cares about that?" her mother said with a dismissive tone, as if the arrests were irrelevant.

Alyssa gaped mutely at the cellular. Did she really think no one did? Then again, in the world according to Cherise Hunt reality was optional. As a matter of fact, it was often actively discouraged. Only fourteen years older than Alyssa, her brash personality was an eclectic combination of both soul sister and quirky parent, and Alyssa was never sure which role her mom would assume.

Her mother went on. "Between Paulo Domingues with his money and a hotel full of hoity-toity guests, well..." Her voice trailed off.

Alyssa gripped her phone with her hand. Was she worried her daughter would screw up again?

"I just don't want to see you get hurt, baby," her mom said.

The concern in her voice melted Alyssa's heart. As frustrating as her mother sometimes was, as many mistakes as she'd made, it had always been the two of them against the world. She'd taught Alyssa how to skirt a security camera, and she'd fought tooth and nail to keep their two-person family going during some desperate, destitute years. Alyssa owed her everything. And, while her mom sometimes made things more difficult, she always meant well.

Alyssa's tone grew soft. "I won't get hurt."

"Good. Because watching those highfalutin' college classmates of yours treat you like dirt near broke my heart."

Alyssa's fingers clamped harder around her cellular as a self-directed slap of anger surged. "Things are different now."

She was different now.

No longer was she the delinquent eighteen-year-old who'd believed people would give her a second chance after her first conviction. And although the narrow-minded behavior was always disappointing, it never surprised her anymore. Which was why she still couldn't wrap her brain around the fact Paulo hadn't fired her. Did he really not mind, or was he just stringing her along, waiting for a more opportune moment to lower the boom?

Confused, Alyssa dropped into a chair at her dining room table. "I've got to get ready for work, Mom."

"Good luck, baby. I'll bring you dinner tonight to celebrate your fancy new account."

Alyssa signed off and set her cellular aside, staring at her computer on the dining room table. Maybe it was a bit premature to be celebrating.

Because, no matter how hard Alyssa tried, she couldn't shake the thought Paulo still might use her past against her. It didn't seem the sort of thing he would do, but she'd learned long ago to never take anything for granted. It was one of many luxuries she couldn't afford. And arming herself with knowledge via a friendly bout of internet searching couldn't hurt.

After powering up her laptop, Alyssa tapped Paulo's name into the keyboard and hit Enter, dismayed by the list that popped onto the screen. The number of entries was so large she could read for a month and never reach the end. Apparently it wasn't just his star factor as the industry's cutting edge, unorthodox entrepreneur that made him hugely newsworthy.

Frowning, she typed in Paulo's name and "Domingues International Resorts," and another long list of articles was displayed. She scrolled through several screens until one from a local tabloid instantly caught her eye.

Paulo Domingues Ditched by Wife for Brother.

The headline punched with a powerful force.

Damn. Alyssa sat back and stared at the screen. She wanted a little dirt on the man, a tidbit to throw back in his face should he decide to investigate her further. But this kind of news was too low for her to use. No one should have something so despicable and painful wielded as ammunition against them. Her eyes dropped to the next headline.

Local Hotel Magnate Removed from Country Club by Police.

Now she was getting somewhere.

This one was on the same date as the caption above, and she doubted it was a coincidence. Unable to stop the snooping about his breakup now, she clicked on the article and began to read.

At lunchtime, Paulo made his way into the empty hotel parking garage. The sun was scorching, and the sidewalk along Ocean Drive was full of female tourists in short shorts and midriff-baring tops. But his mind was stuck on a bland suit filled with the luscious body of Alyssa Hunt.

He hadn't stopped by to see her yet today, wanting to delay their meeting until he felt more in control. The make-out session yesterday had left an indelible heat that couldn't be washed away with a hundred cold showers. Paulo was still steaming from that one, chock-full-of-trouble kiss. He'd spent a good part of his morning being interrupted by fantasies starring Alyssa. Most of them involved him entering her office, hoisting her onto the desk, and taking her, right then and there.

Man, he was slipping.

With a grunt of disgust, he threw his leg over the back of his motorcycle. His frown grew deeper when he heard Alyssa's voice.

"I learned a few things about you today," she said.

Paulo looked up and watched her approach, her heels tapping on the concrete, the sound echoing off the walls. But it was the sight of her prim navy pantsuit that wiped the frown from his face, because he'd learned something, too.

Alyssa was all passion, kept tightly contained within a package of sassy Southern priss.

But that didn't mean he should linger in her company. He reached for the helmet hanging from the handle of the Ducati. "What did you learn?"

"Apparently you've had a run-in with the law yourself."

He froze in the midst of lifting his headgear, and slowly lowered his hands back down. "Decided to do a little research to get even?"

"Not to get even. That would be petty." She came to a halt beside the bike. "I figured it was only fair I knew more about you."

She would. And it amused him. "And did you succeed?"

"I guess I was busier the first year of my business than I thought. I missed out on quite a few stories about you in the local newspapers five years ago. Several in the *Miami Insider*."

The amusement instantly died. Leaning back, he schooled his face into an easy expression. "Don't believe everything you read. Journalists like to embellish. Especially ones at that tabloid." He shrugged easily, as if the topic didn't disturb him. "Conflict sells. That's why I don't answer reporters' questions."

"Never?"

With a growing need to escape, he pushed the start button, and the Ducati came to life with a purr. "Never."

She raised her voice over the idling bike, the purring sound reverberating in the deserted parking garage. "I just have one thing I want to ask."

Staring at her, he considered driving off. He'd spent a whole year of his life fielding questions about that day. Being chased by the paparazzi. Journalists camped out, waiting for him to walk by. Pouncing as soon as he appeared. The only safe havens had been home and Nick's club, but that was only because Security there had been trained to recognize every reporter in town and toss them out the door.

And hell if he'd start answering questions now.

Hoping to knock her off course, he sent her a scorching look, his gaze sweeping down her pristine suit to her designer shoes and back up, lingering along the way. By the end, he was wound tight again. And he wondered if the look got her as worked up as it did him. "I'll answer your question right after you drive this motorcycle."

Her hesitation was incredibly brief. "Deal."

Paulo slowly raised his brows. There seemed no end to the ways this woman would surprise him. She'd called his bluff again. And, as usual, he was too captivated to resist. He shut off the motorcycle, the silence vibrating around them.

His statement came out as more of a question. "You're going to drive the Ducati."

"After you show me how."

He bit back the smile. "I didn't realize that was part of the conditions."

"It is now." A fleeting look of concern crossed her face. "And I have one more. No kiss."

He allowed a small grin to lift the corner of his lips. On that subject they were in perfect agreement. "Absolutely no kiss." He crossed his arms, eager to see how she'd pull off driving his motorcycle. No doubt with her pinky lifted, as if holding a delicate cup of tea, all the while cussing under her breath. "So what's the question?"

"Is it true the police were called to kick you out of the country club?" she said. "For fighting with your brother?"

The mention of Marcos skidded helter-skelter down his spine, leaving skidmarks of anger along the way. He sent her an indifferent look. "It wasn't like I was arrested."

She colored slightly and scowled at him. "You caught a break because of your wealth."

"Maybe. But it wasn't my fight that got me thrown out."

"So why did they boot you out the door?"

His answer came out smooth, but only because he'd had a year of practice giving it. "I got kicked out because I refused to put on a coat and tie." He shrugged. "Too bad, too. Missed out on a good meal of lobster and prime rib."

She stared at him, her gaze scanning his face, as if looking for more beneath his expression. "That's what you told the *Miami Insider* reporter." She placed a hand on her hip and looked unconvinced. "So it had nothing to do with the fact you'd just learned your wife left you for your brother?"

He hadn't been left. He'd been *played*.

The bitterness went deep, leaving a wide gash. And the festering wound refused to heal.

Strung out from his years on the fast track at Domingues International, he'd thought a little easy company at the end of a long day would be nice. A union with a childhood friend, his father's goddaughter, a woman who understood the family and its dedication to the business, had seemed smart.

In retrospect, it had been anything but.

Three months after exchanging vows with Bianca in a simple ceremony, Paulo had known it had been a mistake. And even though they'd started out caring for each other, he'd been miserable. She'd been miserable. And the affection had started to wane. But he'd stuck it out because he'd made a promise. And if Bianca had simply asked for a divorce because it wasn't working, because he refused to conform to her tastes in clothes or behavior, he'd have chalked it up as a learning experience and moved on. Instead, she'd walked out when he had threatened to leave Domingues International and hooked up with the man who inherited the company. His *brother*. It was then that Paulo had finally realized the truth.

Bianca had wanted the Domingues name, the money and all the status that came with it.

Resentment burned his gut, leaving another black mark on his soul.

He forced an easy expression on his face. "Nope, the country club incident had nothing to do with her leaving.

Marcos and Bianca are welcome to each other." Made for each other, more like it. Paulo hadn't talked to either of them since. No point.

Alyssa's face softened. "I don't think you really mean that."

"You're free to believe whatever you want."

For the first time, she looked unsure of herself. "For what it's worth...I'm sorry."

Her expression was so honest he almost believed she was concerned he'd been betrayed. That the only family he'd ever had that cared—his wife—had walked out on him. Turned out her affection was all an act.

His gut burned from the memory. "Nothing to be sorry about."

"Is that why you left Domingues International when your father died?" she asked.

Another flicker of emotion came and went inside—this one just as strong, just as intense—but he locked it up tight before it could fully escape. "You used up your one question." He kept his hands on the handlebars as he dismounted, holding the bike upright. "Time for the lesson."

She glanced at the Ducati, a worried look creeping up her face. "Before we get started, can you explain why people who live in a state known for its tropical storms choose transportation without doors and roofs, seatbelts for safety..." Her voice died out as she looked down at her dress pants and then back at the motorcycle. "Not to mention regular seats to maintain your dignity?"

After glancing around the deserted garage, Paulo sent her a wry look. "I know it will be difficult for you, but there's no one here you need to impress." The frown on her face grew bigger as she eyed the motorcycle, and he had to suppress the grin. "Are you going to back out?"

Her shoulders snapped back. "Of course not."

This woman seemed incapable of backing down from a challenge. And he was starting to enjoy himself now. The look on her face was almost worth the miserable trip down memory lane. "Why don't you take a sec to get a feel for her?"

"Her?" Alyssa blew out a breath and stared at the motor-cycle, feeling foolish. What about this monstrosity made it female? And why in God's name had she agreed to this plan?

She knew why. Paulo and his exasperating mix of male magnetism and good looks. The more she learned, the more she wanted to know about the man. And his blithe treatment of his family's actions was astonishing. Not once had she seen a sign the conversation disturbed him. The laid-back, carefree attitude was firmly intact.

And, dangerous as it was, she had to admit she enjoyed his company.

But the amused look in his eyes couldn't be ignored. She wiped a damp palm down her pants. Finally giving in, she gingerly threw a leg over the bike and gripped the handles.

With a little more of a wiggle, she sat back on the seat. *"She* feels fine." Alyssa glanced down at the hard concrete, and her stomach twisted with fear. "I'm not so sure I do, though."

"Trust me. You're going to love it."

"I'll admit I enjoyed the ride yesterday." What little she remembered beyond touching him included the wind whipping by, the salty ocean air, and the bright sunshine on her skin. There was a sense of freedom that she hadn't antici-pated. "But driving one...?"

One hand on the handlebar, Paulo leaned closer. "Afraid?"

Her heart began to misbehave at his proximity and the *café con leche* eyes. This time she told the truth. "Yes." She kept her voice even, resisting the urge to look at his mouth.

"Especially of exotic-looking ones that are worth a bazillion dollars."

He tipped his head quizzically, his eyes crinkling with a curious humor. "Are we still talking about my motorcycle?"

A warm flush filled her stomach. "Of course." She cleared her throat. "I wouldn't want to ruin her."

A wry smile twisted on his lips. "Excellent point." Paulo threw his leg over the seat behind her and, like a slice of green tomato dropped in boiling oil, her nerves came to life with a sizzle.

Well...*hello*. This wouldn't help her concentration any.

Her back was pressed against his chest, her hips sandwiched between his thighs. She gripped the handles of the Ducati, her knuckles turning white. And maybe her dignity wasn't the most important thing she had to lose right now. Maybe it was her mind.

Neither of them moved for a moment. Being wrapped in Paulo's lean form was an odd combo of security and danger, and Alyssa's confused senses couldn't decide which she liked better.

"I never fully appreciated the motorcycle as a sexual symbol before," he murmured, his mouth at her ear. Paulo turned his head, nose at her neck, and inhaled. Her breath caught as goosebumps pricked her skin, and the fiery heat left her feeling oddly damp all over. "Now I do."

"Paulo..." The protest died when he placed his hands on her thighs and her mouth lost the ability to articulate.

"Don't worry." The rumble of his voice was at her ear. "I'm only here to keep the bike from falling over on you while you learn. I'll keep my promise. No kiss."

Shoot, who needed a mouth when hard muscle enveloped you like a second skin? In hindsight, it seemed a worthless condition. And how the heck was she supposed to follow his instructions now?

But the longer she sat frozen in place, the longer she'd be subjected to this torture.

Ignoring her body's chaotic response, she followed Paulo's directions and started the engine, easing the lever out. The bike crept forward. The minor accomplishment fueled her courage, and she grew more daring, gingerly twisting the throttle to pick up speed.

Over the next thirty minutes Alyssa managed to survive the distraction of Paulo's hands on her thighs *and* several trips around the first level of the garage. With each pass, the triumphant feeling grew stronger until, finally, she ventured to the top of the building and back. By the time she came to a stop on the ground floor, she didn't bother to contain her excitement.

Alyssa turned in the seat to flash Paulo a smile, her words a heavy drawl. "That was fantastic."

The smile died the moment she met his gaze, inches from hers. Thick lashes framed hazel eyes that glowed with an intensity hot enough to burn a hole in the ozone layer. There was no grin. No shared amusement. His hands scalded her through her pants. And the sight of his sensual lips, so close to hers, had the blood howling in her veins.

And suddenly Alyssa was sorry she'd made him promise not to kiss her. Because she longed to taste him again. To feel those large hands touch her between the legs. She shifted her hips, hoping to end the agony, only to wind up pressing her backside against his hard erection. Streaks of white-hot desire blazed, and she nearly groaned out loud.

His hand slid higher on her thighs, holding her hips in place, his voice husky. "If you don't want me to kiss you, you shouldn't look at me like that."

Heart pounding like a bass drum, Alyssa stared at him. Long denied, pent up desire demanded to be satisfied, and need finally overruled her good sense. "Maybe I've reconsidered my condition."

Several beats passed before he narrowed his eyes a fraction, gaze lingering on her mouth, as if considering her blatant offer. "No," he said softly, and her heart dropped at the word. "I made a promise, and I intend to keep it." And with that, he dismounted.

Dazed, every cell punch-drunk with the buzz of desire, she stared at him.

Paulo looked down at her. "I think you should go to lunch." He leaned forward to unhook his helmet from the back of the bike, his face achingly close to hers. "Before I change my mind."

She gripped the handles hard, fighting the urge to close the distance between their lips. But pride drove her chin higher. "Who's to say I won't change *my* mind?"

He flashed her a deliberate look, as if he knew all her secrets. "We both know you won't."

CHAPTER FOUR

THAT was it. No more trying to get the upper hand, or any other part of her anatomy, on Paulo Domingues.

Alyssa sat at an outdoor café, ignoring the patrons droning on around her and shredding her napkin, alarmed on so many levels her mind spun from the turmoil. Down the street, the gorgeous gold marquee of the Samba glistened in the sunshine. She'd needed to get away, because eating lunch at her desk wasn't conducive to recovery.

The kiss at the park obviously hadn't been an aberration, and she didn't trust herself around the man anymore. It wasn't that she had—in a roundabout way, anyway—just asked her client for a kiss. It was worse than that.

The horribly, terribly, awful part was she'd practically *begged* him for it.

And not only with her words, she knew. She had begged in every possible manner. With her tone. Her gaze. In the way her body had leaned, *screaming* in its intent, closer to his.

She planted her elbows on the glass tabletop and groaned, dropping her face to her hands. No one could miss that blatant a come-on. And then, with desire etched in her every attitude...

He'd turned her down.

The turbulent chaos in her body intensified as she relived the sharp stab of longing followed by the crash of disappointment.

After the vow she'd insisted he take, she had shamelessly encouraged him.

How could she be so dumb?

In college, when rumors about her arrest in high school began to circulate, the effect had been swift and immediate. Labels had been attached to her faster than a game of pin the tail on the donkey.

Because if she was a thief, she must be easy too, right?

And, though the rumors weren't true, that hadn't stopped her classmates from indulging in a bit of fun, the stories growing more elaborate as they were passed along.

Alyssa rubbed her overheated cheeks. So what must Paulo think of her?

She'd set out to secure the account at the Samba, and then let the world's hottest hottie muck up her priorities. Outmaneuvering him might have been fun. It might have felt good. But letting down her guard and burning it up with him between the sheets wasn't going to impress Paulo.

Work. That was how she needed to impress the man. She was good at her job. *Excelled* at it. She needed to show him what she could do.

Feeling better now that she had rescrewed her head on right, she checked her phone. An email from the caterer doing the grand opening blinked on screen, reminding her about their meeting tomorrow morning to discuss the layout for the buffet. Alyssa picked up her fork and dug into her pasta salad, gazing at the message.

But, no matter how hard she worked on the last minute

details of the opening, it was still someone else's creation. She needed to solicit a new client for the Samba. And not just any event. It had to be something amazingly spectacular. Something that allowed her the creative freedom to produce a dazzling party that showcased her talent.

And she didn't have much time.

She had to get Paulo to give up this need for a supervisory role. Because if she spent many more days in "daily direct contact" with him, who knew what she'd do next?

The following afternoon Paulo entered the lobby of the Samba and grabbed a bottle of water from the refrigerator behind the bar. The sound of the rock waterfall backdrop failed to calm the pulsating memory of yesterday's ride with Alyssa.

The lilac scent of her neck.

Her hips, firmly pressed between his thighs.

After twisting the cap off the plastic, he slugged back an icy sip to ease the churn of desire, his gaze drifting across the lobby to the staff hallway. Alyssa's first no-holds-barred smile from the day before was forever branded in his brain. And her look of unleashed desire? That particular expression had kept him up last night. Refusing to kiss her had been tough, but he wanted to prove to himself that he could.

The only thing walking away had proved was that he was deep in denial.

Their relationship was past the point of no return. She wanted him as much as he wanted her. And the more he fought it, the more securely he was caught in the web of attraction. Now the only way out he could see was to take it to its predictable conclusion. In bed with Alyssa. A few nights spent with her in his arms would free him to move beyond this frustrating fixation.

The familiar tap of heels on hardwood caught his attention,

and he turned to see Alyssa crossing in his direction. Fresh, lovely, and bound up tight in a silk blouse and skirt. All he wanted was to strip the fabric away and discover the body beneath.

He rounded the bar. "Ready for another lesson?"

She came to a halt beside him, looking uneasy. "I don't think I'll ever be ready."

He was beyond ready.

Paulo propped his foot on the rung of a stainless steel barstool. At least she wasn't freezing him out with her professional face. Definitely progress. "It's not unusual to be a little apprehensive at first."

"I'm not apprehensive."

"Seemed that way yesterday." His tone shifted lower. "Until the end, anyway."

She ignored the innuendo and climbed onto a seat, primly crossing her legs.

Was she sending him a message?

"I have a more important matter to discuss," she said. "The caterer for the grand opening told me the pipes burst in the Twin Palms' ballroom today."

He shrugged. "That's the price one pays for working with historic hotels."

"Yes, well, it's left Rachel Meyer without a venue for her wedding reception."

She waited, as if this were something that affected his life. Other than feeling sorry for the engaged woman, who clearly lacked good sense, it was nothing to him.

Alyssa went on. "She's a best actress nominee for that indie film she did last year."

"I know who she is."

"She's a hot commodity in Hollywood right now, so her wedding is sure to generate terrific coverage."

Looking nervous, she touched the tip of her pink tongue

to her lower lip, and the sight tackled his libido and pinned it to the ground. Maybe yesterday's fantasy should be adjusted. Her desk would be good, but if he pushed up her skirt even a barstool—

"The reception is two nights before our official opening, but I want to go after the account," she said.

His eyes still fixated on her mouth, the racy vision of the two of them dispersed with a pop.

She wanted to *what*?

Staring at her, he slowly lowered his foot to the floor. Long ago, when he'd still worked for Domingues International, he'd fought with his brother over the viability of the Samba. Marcos had wanted to sell it. Paulo had wanted to reinvent it.

His brother had eventually won.

And when Paulo had finally set out on his own business venture, every hotel he'd bought and turned into a prosperous enterprise, every dollar he'd earned, had been to guarantee that—if the Samba came up for sale again—he was ready to prove Marcos wrong. Now he was close to unveiling his vision, and she wanted to risk a catastrophe before they even opened?

"I realize the situation is a little unusual," she said, smoothing a silky strand of hair behind her ear. "But it's an opportunity to really market the Samba."

He couldn't decide whether to strip off her clothes and make love to her or send her to have her head examined. Instead, he gripped his bottle. "Or splash a very public nightmare across the papers if it's a disaster."

She didn't look discouraged. "It wouldn't be a disaster."

"And you know this *how*?"

Alyssa drew herself up to her full height. "Because I'll be in charge of it."

"It's only fourteen days away."

She opened her mouth, most likely to argue, when his Chief of Operations greeted them as he approached, saving her from herself.

When the man stopped beside him, Paulo kept his eyes on his overzealous, perplexing event planner and made the introductions. "Charles, this is Ms. Hunt. Alyssa, this is Charles Belvidere, my right-hand man."

The manager turned to Alyssa, and instantly she felt like a bug under a magnifying glass. Middle-aged, slim, with streaks of silver in his dark hair, he was tall. Distinguished. Between his black suit and his staid nature, he exuded the aura of a funeral director.

"Ah, yes," he said, his face was solemn. "I met your mother."

Her mouth went dry. It was obvious he had something more to say.

"She's quite…" Charles paused, as if searching for just the right word.

Alyssa didn't have an English degree, but she was pretty sure such a word didn't exist. With a small sigh, she rested her elbow on the counter, knowing this could take a while.

"Distinctive," Charles finally finished.

She added "politically correct" to her list describing the manager.

"Alyssa wants to go after the Myer reception," Paulo said.

Irked by his tone, she shot Paulo a frown. Both men were looking at her as if she'd declared she wanted to organize the inaugural ball for the President.

Charles adjusted the wire-frame glasses on his nose, looking uncomfortable. "I'll leave you two to your discussion."

She watched Charles walk away and then turned back to Paulo, prepared to resume the debate. "I'm quite capable of handling this job."

"You have no experience with an event of this size, and there's not enough time."

"Everything for the reception is in place. There's plenty of staff to help." She held his gaze, feeling less then steady despite her tone. He hadn't been this worked up during the conversation about his wife. His red T-shirt hugged the muscles beneath and, combined with the well-worn jeans, fostered a James Dean look. But this rebel most definitely had a cause. And its name was the Samba. "They just need a new venue," she added.

A few beats passed as his eyes slowly narrowed to questioning slits. "Did you have anything to do with the pipe incident at the Twin Palms?"

She rolled her eyes. "Oh, for goodness' sake."

"No strategic sabotage?" Her cheeks flamed as he went on. "Or convenient accident?"

Alyssa forced her chin to remain level. "I'm not going to dignify that with a response."

He waited a moment before going on. "Well, unless your days consist of more than the usual twenty-four hours, how are you going to pull this off in two weeks? *And* deal with the last-minute details of the grand opening?"

"I'll manage." Of course it wasn't quite as easy as she'd made it out to be, but she wasn't afraid of hard work. He simply stared at her, and she exhaled with a force that matched her frustration. "I'm *tryin'* to do the job you hired me for."

"Yes." He set his water bottle on the bar and sent her a grim look overflowing with doubt. "A job I'm not entirely convinced you're ready to do," he finished softly.

Alyssa's heart slowed to a dull thud. He didn't think she could do it.

That was what this was all about. He simply believed she wasn't capable.

As the depressing thought settled deeper, her chest grew tight. When he'd kept her on, despite her record, she'd thought it signaled he had some respect for her abilities. That all those events listed on her résumé—the ones she'd sacrificed so much to organize—counted for something. *Meant* something. But, when push came to shove, they didn't matter enough. And his doubt hurt, because the one thing she was absolutely sure of in her life was her skill as an event planner.

And to think she'd almost begged this man for a kiss.

"You don't trust me," she said.

He paused before replying. "This is business. It isn't personal."

The words cut off her breath in her throat. It was personal when your work was all you had. "It would be foolish to pass on this opportunity," she insisted.

His face shifted through a sequence of emotions until it landed on resigned agreement. "You're right." He stepped closer, and her heart responded to his proximity, though his reluctant tone did little to repair her wounded pride. "But let me make myself clear." His frown grew deeper. "You're not to make a single decision without checking with me first. I want to know what you're doing every step of the way. And I expect detailed daily reports on your progress."

Breathing hard, she met his gaze. He wanted reports? She'd give him reports. Squaring her shoulders, she said, "Not a problem."

Feeling the need to flee, she turned and headed for her office. Hand in a fist, her palm was damp. And not just from nerves.

He pushed her sensual buttons just by entering a room, torching her blood and leaving her in flames. When she'd come out of her office and seen him across the lobby it hadn't mattered how many lectures she'd given herself, every cell in her body had done a happy dance. How could she have the hots for a man who didn't respect her work?

Her whole life was wrapped up in her business.

Her nails bit into her palm. Okay, so she would show him just how good she was. He'd never doubt her again. And she would enjoy watching him eat the crow she served him.

Once Alyssa had sold the bride-to-be on relocating her displaced event to the Samba, the two weeks passed in a flurry of activity. On the surface, Paulo had managed to keep his interactions with Alyssa strictly businesslike. Their daily meetings, complete with printed reports rivaling the size of the Dade County phonebook, had been brief.

Because Alyssa never stood still for long, working nonstop.

This morning the hotel had been crawling with temporary hires hustling to produce today's miracle. And directing the chaos, calm and in control, had been Alyssa with her phone…displaying the to-do list that consumed her life.

A to-do list that had served its purpose well, because tonight the reception had gone down without a hitch. And now his concern wasn't that she couldn't do her job, it was that perhaps she did it *too* well.

At first he'd been pleased with how hard she worked, but as the days wore on watching her slowly kill herself organizing this event had had him rethinking his opinion. So did the exhaustion in her face. No one should work that hard. Ever. Especially when someone else reaped the majority of the awards.

Namely…him.

Disturbed, Paulo frowned as he rode the elevator to the top of the Samba. Not satisfied with merely shifting the arranged event to his empty hotel, Alyssa had set out to exceed the bride's previous expectations. Guests had lingered in the lobby, enjoying cocktails from the waterfall bar, before moving on to dinner in the reception hall. But by far her greatest coup had been the dance area she had created from scratch on the rooftop deck.

Paulo exited the elevator and took in her efforts. Hurricane candelabrums lined the railing, while floating candles adorned with white orchids drifted in the pool, casting a gentle light into the nighttime sky. Low sectional couches of dark mahogany and white cushions were arranged in cozy groups, emulating a trendy nightclub. An ethereal gazebo of draping swaths of white fabric made up the temporary dance floor.

And now that the last guest had finally left the building he needed to find the woman who was driven to perfection at her business.

He spied Alyssa standing at the far rail and, like a cell phone set on vibrate, his body hummed with awareness.

In the days since their disagreement, every night had been filled with dreams of her. And every morning he opened his eyes to find his body tangled in the sheets, soaked with sweat and burning for Alyssa.

The multitude of tasks she'd had to accomplish for tonight, every one of which he'd overseen, had thrown them into constant contact. Alyssa had gone back to pretending the attraction didn't exist. But with every activity the underlying sexual tension between the two of them had climbed higher and higher. Until he'd thought he'd spontaneously combust.

Paulo studied her. In her standard suit and pumps, she radiated confident professionalism, but she was so much more than that. Now his need for her was about more than putting out the fire and ending his preoccupation. He wanted Alyssa to learn to release her passionate side. To immerse her in the kind of pleasure that would remind her she was a beautiful, sensual woman.

With mounting expectation, he approached her. Alyssa's

face glowed from the flickering candlelight and the neon lights of South Beach beyond. Her black jacket was tailored, but a slip of silk peeked from beneath.

"Are you ready to kiss and make up?" he asked.

"That would turn this personal," she said coolly.

He resisted the urge to smile. "You're still mad at me."

"More like disappointed."

He leaned an elbow on the rail. Dishes clinked in the distance as the staff gathered dirty cocktail glasses, bustling to clean up the aftermath. "I'll admit I had serious reservations about your abilities. But never let it be said I can't admit to being wrong. And as for the kiss during your motorcycle lesson..." A fleeting look of desire crossed her face, only to be replaced by one of embarrassment, and he leaned close, hoping to bring the first expression back. "On that issue, I concede to your wisdom, too."

Staring at him, she tipped her head. "Have you considered you might be overestimating your charms?"

His smile finally won. "It's high time we give in to the inevitable." To bring his point home, he brushed a strand of hair from her cheek, savoring the smoothness. "I already have." Her eyes went from silver to slate, and fierce need slammed into him with the force of a head-on collision, killing his grin.

Hell. He was right back where they'd left off the day of their ride.

Hard. Wanting her.

By now her poise was back in place. "Nothing is inevitable," she said. But despite the words her protest sounded thin, and there was a husky quality to her tone. "And don't you have better things to do than monitor every move your event planner makes?"

"Monitoring my event planner's moves has become a favorite pastime of mine."

"Yes," Alyssa said dryly. "And I can't figure out how you've managed to build a thriving enterprise with priorities like that."

Paulo's lips quirked at her tone. As if success could only be achieved by those who bartered their soul to the devil along the way. Like the years he'd spent consumed by his job. He'd almost given up racing his motorcycle, and though Nick had always stopped by the office to see him Paulo had never once enjoyed the club he'd helped his friend finance. Not until he left Domingues International.

"I'm living proof you don't have to kill yourself to build a prosperous business," he said. And that was just one of many lessons he wanted to share. Starting tonight. "I worked hard for the last ten months, restoring the Samba, but I still found time for the things I enjoy." Doubt radiated from her face, and he lifted an eyebrow. Fun shouldn't be this hard to sell. "With the pace you keep, eventually you'll burn out. Something I learned firsthand."

"I've never seen you in a suit and tie. So I can't picture you as a burnt-out executive."

"Life's too short to spend it with a noose around your neck." He let out a small scoff. "A concept my family never understood." Paulo gripped the metal rail with both hands, staring at the city lights and fighting the threatening return of bitter memories. "I don't do suits and ties. Ever. But burnt-out executive I know well. Now…" He sent Alyssa a mock stern look. "Have a seat while I go find us a drink," he said, and then headed for the bar.

Alyssa stared after him, wondering how a man could look so dashing in simple dark pants and a navy dress shirt. Despite the hellish work schedule, she'd missed their earlier easy camaraderie. With a flutter of nervous anticipation, Alyssa settled onto a couch. One of the staff wandered by, snuffing out the candelabrums that lined the railing, slowly lengthening the shadows on the deck.

When Paulo returned with two champagne flutes, he handed one to Alyssa and sat down beside her, throwing her instantly on guard.

Hoping to keep a lighthearted atmosphere, Alyssa sent Paulo an assessing look. "I always pictured you more as a beer connoisseur. I'm surprised to see you drink champagne."

"I do, but only when forced."

His words made her smile. "Who's forcing you?"

"The situation," he said as he threw his arm along the back of the couch. And though he didn't touch her, the potential was hard to ignore. He raised his drink between them. "To South Miami Beach's event of the year, and Elite Events for making it possible." Paulo tipped his flute against hers, and the delicate ting of crystal on crystal rang in the air. "Seriously," he said, his face reflecting his words, "you did an amazing job."

The sincerity in his tone floored her—one of those moments of candor that knocked her off her feet, affecting her as powerfully as his touch. Her smile melted away as warmth seeped into her heart. And it had nothing to do with the kind of heat Paulo usually excelled at creating. This kind seeped all the way to her soul. How could one man's words so effortlessly swing her from abject misery to unadulterated high? She was *supposed* to be gloating.

"Thank you," she said, surprised by the pressure of tears behind her lids.

Jeez, Alyssa. Blubber like an idiot, why don't you?

Feeling silly and overemotional, she sipped her bubbly champagne before continuing. "You worked hard, too."

And he had. Paulo had been there every step of the way, working alongside her. Wherever an extra set of hands had been needed, he'd rolled up his sleeves and pitched in. She'd learned that, despite his charm and piles of money, he was no slacker. Because when the linen vendor arrived late, and Alyssa had briefly panicked, it was Paulo who'd helped her spread the tablecloths on the dinner tables.

And the sexy billionaire hotelier surrounded by swaths of hot pink had been a sight to behold.

She shifted her gaze away from his, taking in the ambience. Dinner in the reception hall had been lovely, but the deck was her creation. Her baby. And throughout the evening she'd hovered behind the scenes, ensuring everything went smoothly, proudly watching from afar as the affluent crowd enjoyed her efforts.

To date, the most satisfying moment of her life.

Paulo set down his glass. "But I didn't come just to sing your praises." The only light now came from the candle on their coffee table. "I came to convince you to lift your embargo on men."

Her heart relocated to her throat and picked up its pace. Alyssa gripped her champagne glass, but didn't reply. Respect as colleagues was one thing, but a relationship was a more difficult can of worms. One she wasn't sure she wanted to open.

As her silence lingered, the side of Paulo's mouth twitched. "Last I checked, a vow of celibacy wasn't a requirement for an event planner. Wouldn't be much competition if it was. And the time to break that vow has come." Paulo shifted closer, his hard thigh pressing against hers. And the look he sent her lit her more effectively than if he'd doused her in brandy and set her ablaze. An Alyssa *flambé*.

Time for the close-to-the-bone truth.

She'd never wanted another man the way she wanted Paulo. Which was probably why it had been easy to give men a pass for a while…until now.

"I was hoping to start our new affiliation with a dance." Paulo glanced at the band members who were packing up their equipment. "I'm sorry I didn't get to salsa with you."

"I don't know how."

"Too bad. Because one of my prerequisites for involvement with a woman is the ability to salsa." The left corner of his mouth tipped up. "But in your case I'll make an exception."

Alyssa ignored the thrill of desire coursing through her veins. Obviously he had picked up on her weakening resistance and was feeling cocky. Too cocky. She worked hard for a deadpan face. "Am I supposed to be flattered?"

His dimple grew deeper. "Very."

Holding back the smile, Alyssa pursed her lips. "That's an interesting assortment of rules." She lifted her hand and ticked them off on her fingers. "No suits. No ties. No women who can't salsa." She arched an eyebrow, letting him know the last one was rip-roaringly ridiculous. "Any other additions to the list I should be aware of?"

"Only one more."

"And what's that?"

"No more engagement rings."

There was no mistaking the warning.

Paulo leaned closer, his eyes searching hers. "Is that a problem?"

His dark hair hung seductively to the side of his forehead, and his proximity sent her temperature spiraling, bringing memories of him wrapped around her on the Ducati. The rest of her body was busy remembering as well.

She stared back, breathing in his sandalwood cologne, knowing she'd regret it if she pushed him away. By the end of her motorcycle lesson, deep down she'd known the war within was over.

And she'd spent the last two weeks in Paulo's constant

presence, thinking about the possibilities the entire time she'd been planning this event. Tormented by every accidental brush of his arm. Every brief touch of his hand. The occasional searing look. Until his simple presence robbed her of the ability to breathe. And finally she'd concluded she wanted to know, *had* to know, how it would be between them. The fact he'd stated up front it would be limited to a brief affair made it seem almost attainable.

Because did her past really matter if a permanent relationship wasn't part of the equation?

Rubbing the condensation on her glass, she finally replied, her words soft. "No. That's not a problem."

Eyes dark, he ran a finger down her neck, trailing flames as he went. "You're lucky I'm a patient man."

"Lucky?"

"Yes."

"You think highly of yourself, don't you?"

"I suppose." He laid his hand at the base of her throat, and the warmth it generated rivaled the effect of an entire bottle of champagne. "This morning, I almost dragged you out of the reception hall and back to the office."

Goosebumps pricked. She knew the exact moment he was referring to, but she sent him a false innocent look. "To discuss work?"

He leaned close, his mouth almost touching hers. "Nope." A light brush of his lips across hers evoked electrifying messages. "You see, I have this ongoing fantasy involving you, me…" he took her lips again, this time drinking deeply before pulling back a fraction "…and the top of that desk of yours."

Lips aching for more, the pulse in her neck throbbing beneath his hand, she swallowed hard. "And do I get any say in these fantasies?"

"Absolutely." The fire in his eyes set her belly blazing,

and his hand slid lower, dipping under her jacket. "I'll let you tell me all about them in my room." Their gazes locked, and his fingers brushed the curve of her breast.

She slowly shook her head, quaking with need. "You'll *let* me?" Obviously the man required a little more humbling. With a deep breath, Alyssa stood, bringing a startled look to Paulo's face, and she bit back a grin. "I should check on the staff." Fingers trembling, she drained the last of her champagne, trying to appear nonchalant. "Besides, I think it would do you some good to wait a little longer." She sent him a small smile. "You know, heighten the anticipation a little."

He stared at her blankly, as if she was speaking Greek. "You gotta be kidding me."

His expression was priceless. Working hard to keep her composure, she enjoyed the sensation of power, and her smile got bigger. "Why, Mr. Domingues, where is that infamous patience of yours?"

His eyes narrowed with growing suspicion. "Is this some sort of payback?"

Chuckling, she leaned forward, bringing her lips within inches of his. "Of course." She raised a brow, dropping her gaze to his mouth and enjoying her effect on him way too much. "Afraid I'll change my mind?"

"Hell, yeah," Paulo growled back, his eyes black with desire.

"You should be." Alyssa straightened up and sent Paulo a coy look. "I'll come find you when I'm done."

CHAPTER FIVE

As the last of the staff left the building, Alyssa glanced at her watch.

Almost 1:00 a.m.

Fatigue settled in her chest like dead weight. The moving crew had hauled away the rental furniture, and she had just finished her survey of the reception room and was on her way to the pool for its final inspection. As she crossed the lobby, she wondered where Paulo had wandered off to.

Maybe he had given up on her and gone home. Disappointment rose at the thought. But as she entered the elevator footsteps sounded behind her. Alyssa looked up and caught Paulo's reflection in the mirrored wall.

Her fatigue vanished as the doors slid shut behind him, and the elevator waited patiently for someone to push a button. But patience was the furthest thing from her mind. Still keyed up from their earlier encounter, she was a conflicted mass of nerves and need. "Where are you taking me?"

"The first time?" Paulo's eyes held hers in the mirror as he stepped closer. "Here."

Her mind balked at the answer, but her body didn't care as it began a chant of encouragement. She stared at Paulo's reflection, and then at her suit, unsure what to do next. The coy feeling of control from before was long gone.

It had been fun.

It had also been an act.

He must have seen her concern. "No more thinking about your work." He lowered his mouth to nuzzle her neck. "Now it's just you and me." Nipping a path toward her jaw, each rake of his teeth made her sizzle. But the starkly vivid vision of them in the mirror was too much, so she tried to turn in his arms for a kiss.

He stopped her by pulling her flat against his muscular frame, his erection hard against her backside. Moisture flooded her panties, and her heart thudded harder, as if pumping blood to all those suddenly engorged parts of her body took extra work.

"I know what you want," he said at her ear. "And we'll get to that, I promise." His arms encircled her, his cheek level with hers, his dark hair tickling her face. "But first..." Holding her gaze in the mirror, he began to undo her jacket, winding her tighter with every release of a button. "I want you to see yourself as I do."

Though awash in a sea of longing, she blinked twice, suddenly petrified. She knew how the guys in college had seen her. As trashy. Cheap.

A guaranteed lay.

Shame churned her stomach. She'd been hit on repeatedly, and with as much delicacy as a freight train, while they'd tried to prove the rumors true.

"How do you see me?" she said hoarsely. She was almost afraid to hear.

With a grasp of her lapels, Paulo peeled her coat down her

arms, the fabric falling to the floor. "I see a lady who wears a crisp business suit," he said.

Her nerve slipped lower as he released the catch on her skirt. With a push, it landed at her feet, leaving her in just her camisole and panties.

A wolfish grin appeared. "With a daring red thong beneath."

Daring. The frantic beat of her heart made the term kind of ridiculous.

"Not so daring if no one sees it," she said quietly.

"*I* see it." Hooking her panties with his thumbs, he dragged the scrap of lace past her hips. Once her thong joined her skirt, with her help, he lifted her camisole and tossed it aside. Eyes devouring her, the grin on his face died. And so did the last of her frayed nerves.

Paralyzed, Alyssa stared at her reflection. A woman about to engage in a sexual exploit in an *elevator.*

She felt bared. Stripped of her constricting clothes. But without them she wasn't the cool business owner. The competent careerwoman. Her suit, her identity—her armor—lay in a pile at her feet.

And the moment was so blatantly sensual, so highly charged, it was overwhelming. Sure she'd make a fool of herself, she turned her face away from her image, trying for a light tone. "I just see a naked lady."

Holding her chin, he gently turned her face toward the mirror again. "A very *sexy* lady," Paulo said.

Her nipples tightened, and she knew Paulo noticed by his voice.

"One capable of great passion," he murmured huskily.

Was she? Her usual insistence on darkened bedrooms sometimes left her satisfied. Kind of. Then again, it always afforded her some measure of cover. And protection. But this...?

He slid his hands down and around to the front of her thighs, her eyes growing wider as he went. Fingers threading through her curls, he brushed his thumb across her clitoris. As the pleasure pierced her, she gripped her cheek between her teeth, staring at the risqué vision of the two of them.

No man had ever watched her reaction, and the scrutiny heightened the anticipation. Made it more acute. Left her edgy. But it was almost too erotic. And when he brushed her again, shooting sparks down her limbs, her thigh muscles clinched reflexively. She *couldn't...*

"It's okay," Paulo said. "Relax and enjoy the moment."

The pounding in her chest hurt. "It's not so easy for me," she whispered.

"I'll take care of you," he said. "Just open your legs."

Her breath hitched at his words, and she instinctively parted her thighs. Eyes on her face, he slid two fingers between her wet folds, and her jaw went slack at the sweet pressure. His free hand cupped her breast, caressing the tip.

Her senses were keyed up. Wired. And those magical hands were strong, sure, and so adept she wanted to weep from the pleasure.

"More," he demanded.

Mesmerized by his touch, she did as told and spread her legs wider, finally letting him in. Allowing him complete access. Placing herself in his care. Never had she had a moment where the attention was so purely on *her* needs. Just the freedom to be. To feel.

And, dear God, did she feel.

Thumb stroking her nub, he took the ecstasy higher, until it was sweet torture. Every nerve-ending was eager. Every touch, smell, even the sound of their breathing was amplified. And he played her body until it hummed. As the delicious rhythm bombarded her with volley after volley of need, she clutched his wrist, mouth open, frozen, afraid if she moved she'd break the spell. But Paulo would have none of that.

"Stop holding back," he said roughly against her ear. "Take what you want."

"I can't."

"Yes." Paulo's gaze bored into hers as he increased the pressure of his thumb. "You can."

She choked back a cry of pleasure, and tentatively began to rock her hips in time with his hand.

It was too much and not enough, all at once. A flame of desire shot straight between her legs, where his thumb captured it and stroked it even higher. Every sensation built on the one before, magnifying it.

Until her need teetered so high, so precariously, it was frightening.

The bone-melting heat in his eyes and the building tension left her trembling, her knees shaky. Driving her into sensual oblivion while he watched. She couldn't look away, trapped by his gaze and their reflection in the mirror, Paulo's one hand between her thighs, the other on her breast. Lips parted, a gasp escaped her throat with every in-and-out slide of his fingers.

"Make some noise, Alyssa." His hazel eyes looked black. "Just let go."

And suddenly she was tired of holding back.

Tired of denying herself.

Releasing the last of her doubt, Alyssa groaned and lifted her arms to thread her fingers through his hair. Cheeks hot, hair damp at the nape of her neck, she arched her hips.

Her movements grew stronger. Desperate. Wanting more. Demanding more. Her consciousness slipped to a higher level, a new state where she existed outside herself. A state of bliss. Euphoria.

And the mirror contributed to the out of body experience.

Paulo, eyes on hers, whispered shockingly explicit words of encouragement in her ear as her body, in sync with his, moved with complete abandon. Uninhibited. Wanton.

Until, with a burst of light, the orgasm finally hit. The pressure of pleasure exploded outward, shocking in its ferocity. Her muscles convulsed around him, driving her hips to a frantic pace, riding the waves as she repeatedly cried out his name, the loud words echoing in the small space.

The silence that followed was marred only by her labored breaths. She closed her eyes and let go of his head. Every cell throbbed with each erratic thump of her heart.

"That was beautiful," Paulo said, kissing her damp temple. "*You* are beautiful."

She opened her eyes, still wrapped in Paulo's arms, her legs limp. If he let go, she would surely slump to the floor in a heap.

"Was it worth waiting for?" Paulo asked.

All she could manage was a whisper. "Yes." And then some.

Paulo looked at her with intense scrutiny. "Hmm. No snappy comeback. No sharp retort to keep my ego in line." A slight lift of his lips. "Little Alyssa must have been moved."

Moved? Good Lord, she'd been rocked to the core. Her muscles still ached from the force of her climax, as if she'd just spent the day running through deep sand. How was she going to make it to the hotel room now? "I don't think I *can* move."

Paulo chuckled as he released her. "No problem." He began to undo the buttons on his shirt. "You don't have to."

Doubt overcame her weakness, and she whipped around to face him. What was he planning now? "Aren't we going to a bed?" With a lift of an eyebrow, Paulo reached for the bottom button. Her voice sounded strangled. "But—"

The word died when he peeled off his shirt. His chest

was lean. The abdomen taut. She stared up at him, the wave of need returning. Because she wanted him again. With a fierceness that was alarming. As if the most amazing orgasm she'd ever experienced wasn't enough. Paulo pulled a condom from his pocket and then pushed his pants and briefs to the floor, kicking them aside. Now he was gloriously naked, his erection in full view, and desire sent her heart rate soaring again. But *how…?*

When Alyssa glanced at the marble floor, the uncertainty in her face was adorable, and Paulo felt compelled to reassure her. His little event manager had so much to learn. "No hard floors, I promise." Staring at her, he rolled on the condom, fascinated by the pink tint to her cheeks. "We'll do this standing up."

Her color rose higher. "That's impossible."

Paulo stepped forward to cradle her breasts. "It absolutely is possible," he said softly.

He brushed his thumbs across her nipples, and her mouth opened with a groan, wiping away her doubtful look. Satisfied, Paulo took her lips, slaking his across hers. And hers were warm. Sweet. Passionate, and yet surprisingly submissive. The aggressive, take-charge attitude was replaced with an eagerness to follow his lead. And the sense of power was exhilarating.

The mating tongues filled his mind with the image of what he wanted. Paulo lifted one of her thighs, wrapping her leg around his waist. The tip of his erection nudged her, a very frustrating touch too high. Grasping her buttocks, he shifted her up.

She pulled her mouth from his, her chest heaving. "Paulo, I don't think this will work—"

Her words ended when he thrust inside, and they both went still, staring at each other.

She was hot. Wet.

And so, so tight.

Struggling for breath, senses reeling, he pressed his forehead to hers as he fought the urge to pound into her, the feeling violent. The self-induced, masochistic plan to concentrate purely on her pleasure, to immerse her in sensation, had backfired. Now his own need was so great he was afraid he would hurt her. Jaw clenched, hands on her buttocks, he pinned her against the mirror and began to gently rock his hips.

But with every dig deeper Paulo felt his greed grow.

With every thrust inside his tempo increased.

Until the buck of his hips was strong. Hard. He'd never get enough of her. He burned with the fire she lit in him. Cheeks flushed, her mouth slack in a silent cry, careening sounds of pleasure began to slip from her throat. He recognized the call. The sharp bite of her fingernails on his shoulders. She was close.

Unfortunately he was closer. He wanted her with him when he peaked, to feel her shatter around him again. For some inexplicable reason, if she wasn't experiencing that same powerful force his release wouldn't be as satisfying.

One hand supporting her, he reached between her legs to caress her slick center. The tip of his index finger landed where his shaft stroked her body, and the sense of possession was so fierce he almost came.

Gritting his teeth, embedded deep inside her, he paused again, his heart pounding. And as he stared at her it hit him. This was about more than simple satisfaction. More than just moving beyond a frustrating obsession. He had advanced, and she had retreated. He had thrust, and she had parried.

But right now, in this moment and time, she was *his*.

He reached up to pull her hand from his shoulder and press it between them, his fingers on top of hers, so she could feel where they were joined. Alyssa inched her leg

higher on his hip, offering him more. At her silent acknowledgment he began to move again. High on the double pleasure of knowing she was experiencing the taking of her body
in two ways, not just one. Thrusting harder and harder between her legs. Demanding. Rough. Ruthless in his pursuit
of their pleasure, pushing it higher.

And when Alyssa let out a cry that bounced off the walls,
her body clenching, the sound of her letting go drove him
wild.

The feel of her orgasm made him crazy.

And with a flash of blinding light he followed her into
oblivion.

Two days later Alyssa stood at the end of the staff hallway,
watching the sunshine stream through the arched floor-to-
ceiling windows of the Samba lobby. The tinkle of stemware
and murmur of conversation filled the room. In the corner,
the band played soft Latin music. The grand opening was
well underway. And Paulo, in khakis and a dress shirt, mingled with the guests, looking relaxed and at ease.

Alyssa was anything but.

Because she couldn't delay the inevitable any longer.

When Paulo had finished with her in the elevator, he'd
carried her to the penthouse. And what had come next was
stupefyingly unbelievable. Alyssa had eagerly followed
along wherever he led her, over and over again, leaving her
limp from the pleasure. It had been more than she could
have imagined. Better than what she'd heard. But when she'd
opened her eyes in the morning she'd been handed a major
reality check.

She'd slept with a client. A man who had never asked her
for a date. Heck, she didn't even know where he *lived*.

And as her gaze had roamed the dim hotel room, the
heavy brocade curtains blocking the light, an uneasy feeling

had welled inside. The penthouse bedroom was beautiful. Opulent. But coldly formal. Completely lacking in any reflection of Paulo's personality.

But the worst part had been, even after a long night in his arms, she was hungry for more.

She'd turned her gaze to his beautiful face as he slept peacefully, his long, muscular legs tangled in the sheets. And the craving to wake him by sliding her tongue up his thigh and taking him in her mouth had been strong. Shocking in its intensity. She'd stared at him, struck dumb and utterly, utterly aroused, lost in the daydream.

And tortured by what it would say about her.

She was *supposed* to be a professional. And her sleek, polished air was hard to maintain when holed up in a dark, impersonal hotel room, preparing to throw herself at a man like a naughty nymphomaniac.

With fumbling fingers she'd dressed and quietly slipped from the room. After changing into the spare outfit she kept at her office, she had found the hired crew and thrown herself into the middle of the cleaning frenzy to prepare for today. Frantic for some space to regain her equilibrium.

But there was no avoiding him now. Of course their first meeting would be easier if she knew whether they'd just had a one-night stand or if Paulo intended for it to happen again.

And what would she say if he did? Or if he didn't? And why couldn't she decide which was worse?

She bit the tip of her fingernail, hating the feeling of uncertainty her life was filled with of late. Normally she set her sights on a goal and pursued it with the determined focus of a pitbull on Ritalin. Sometimes to her own downfall, as her mother loved to remind her.

And then, as if conjured by her thoughts, she heard her mom call her name.

Alyssa turned to watch her mother approach. With her

voluptuous figure brazenly accentuated in a suede skirt, fringed Western shirt, fancy boots and her best cowboy hat, Cherise Hunt looked like a middle-aged rodeo queen.

All she needed now was a sash emblazoned with the words "Alyssa's Mother."

After all these years Alyssa was used to her dramatic entrances, but this one was particularly spectacular. She held back a dry smile as her mom drew closer. "Nice outfit."

Cherise touched the bleached-blond bob beneath her hat. "Just keeping in touch with my roots."

Alyssa's brow rose in amusement. "You've never been on a horse in your life."

Her mother fluttered a hand. "Details, Lyssa." Her eyes swept around the room. "Fancy-shmancy little shindig you cooked up here." She looked Alyssa up and down, and her gaze lost a little of its luster. "But Lordy, hon, must you dress like a repressed virgin?"

The amusement choked and died as heat flooded Alyssa's face. She took her mother's arm and steered her toward the staff hallway, away from the crowd. "Mom, please."

"Oh, for Pete's sake, Lyssa. No one is listening." She eyed Alyssa's black pantsuit critically. Granted, it was more conservative than usual. But after her night with Paulo it felt appropriate. Her mother, however, looked concerned. "You're not, are you?"

With a sigh of confusion, Alyssa felt obligated to ask, "Not what?"

"A virgin?"

"Mom." Alyssa stopped inside the doorway to the back hall, sweeping her hand toward the crowd. "Does this look like the appropriate place to discuss this?"

"You never want to discuss anything important with me."

"That's not true. I just prefer private discussions take place in *private*." Alyssa lowered her voice to a whisper.

"And, just for the record, for some people celibacy is a legitimate lifestyle choice."

Her mother sniffed delicately. "Ridiculous. What's the point of a lifestyle without the life?"

Three days ago Alyssa would have had several ready responses. After her adventures with Paulo she had none.

"Ms. Hunt."

Alyssa chimed "yes" in unison with her mother, turning to face the crowd as Charles approached them. But he wasn't addressing her.

The manager, looking refined in a pinstripe suit, held out his elbow to her mom. "Would you like a tour of our facilities?"

Beaming up at him with all the subtlety of a spotlight, Cherise Hunt slipped her hand through his arm. "Well now, sugar, aren't you the sweetest thing?"

Alyssa winced at her mother's endearment.

"Ms. Hunt," Charles said, this time looking at Alyssa. "Mr. Domingues would like you to join him in greeting the guests."

Greeting the guests? Alyssa clutched the hallway doorjamb, staring after Charles as he led her mother away, and then switched her gaze to the growing crowd—a host of South Miami Beach's richest and most influential people. Nausea formed a rock in her stomach.

A little awkward post-sex meeting paled in comparison. So far Alyssa had been working the event in the background, making sure everything went according to plan. Truthfully, there wasn't much to do, but all that wealth accumulated in one room was too much to face.

This is what you wanted, Alyssa. This is what you've been working for.

Good God, what had she been thinking?

She pressed the heel of her palm to her forehead and

gulped for air. After a few seconds she dropped her arm to her side, shaking her hands to release the tension.

Do it, girlfriend. Just go.

With a smile plastered on her face, she stepped across the threshold, scanning the crowd for an approachable-looking group. Then she spied Tessa Harrison, mother of an old college classmate and a wealthy woman with a majestic air, a bazillion dollars' worth of jewelry gracing her designer pantsuit. Alyssa's steps faltered as fragmented visions flashed in quick succession.

Being treated like a servant at a catering job in the woman's home. Her condescending attitude during a charity banquet Alyssa had worked. The mocking tone of her daughter at college. And then the procession of shame landed on the granddaddy memory of them all: the parent-student luncheon her sophomore year at Osten College...the party that had ended with Alyssa being hauled out in the hands of the police.

The second time in her life her outfit had ended up accessorized with a pair of handcuffs.

Her ears filled with a threatening buzz as her head grew light. Her lips tingled. Sweat beaded at her temples. Jeez, maybe she should take a moment to collect herself.

Heart thumping in her chest, Alyssa spun on her heel and crossed back into the staff section, sliding her hand along the wall to steady her steps as she headed away from the crowd. When she reached the far end of the hallway, though tempted to keep going, she leaned against the exit door for support. She closed her eyes and dropped her head back, concentrating on the music drifting up from the lobby.

You knew this day would come. You knew it.

Footsteps padded up the hall and came to a stop in front of her. She recognized the cologne. Paulo's spicy scent was forever entrenched in her memory after a night in his arms.

Oh, good grief. Could this moment get any more complicated?

"Are you all right?" he asked.

She kept her lids closed. "I'll be fine," she said. "Just feeling a little..." Terrified? Horrified? As if she was the shining star in the *World's Lamest Losers* reality show? And she sure wasn't referring to weight loss. "Intimidated."

"Why?"

She drew in a deep breath. "I don't function well around the wealthy."

"They're just people like you," he said. There was no irritation in his tone, only a pragmatic reassurance. "No better. No worse."

Alyssa opened her eyes and Paulo stood before her, a plate of chocolate-covered strawberries in his hand, a line of concern between his brows.

She blinked several times, and after a moment her heart recovered a bit. "Next you'll be telling me to picture the guests in their underwear."

A smile tugged the corner of his mouth. "I'd prefer you picture *me* in my underwear. Or, better yet, while you're making the rounds around the room..." He leaned closer. "Picture me naked."

The sound of music faded as she looked into thickly fringed smoky eyes, the slanted cheeks framed by dark hair. Her heart threatened to make a comeback. "Not exactly the vision I need right now."

With a puckered brow, he searched hers eyes for a moment, and then he leaned back, holding out his dish. "Do you want to talk about it?"

Her laugh was harsh. "Not particularly."

His voice went quiet. "Is this about your arrest?"

As she stared at his troubled face, she realized she had to

say something. By now he must think his event planner was a total basket case.

She lowered her gaze to the fruit on his plate, nausea rolling again, and gathered her courage. "In high school I got caught shoplifting and was referred to a youth diversion program. I was assigned a job with a caterer." A weak smile lifted her lips. "An excellent teacher and a great boss. She paid me way more than I was worth." She let out a small scoff. "Which was a godsend."

His frown grew deeper. "You needed the money?"

She briefly lifted her eyes to his. "We needed the money."

A space of several seconds ticked past, as if he was waiting for her to elaborate. But she wasn't about to.

After returning her gaze to his plate, she concentrated on selecting a strawberry, as if the fate of the not-so-free world depended on it. It made telling the story easier. "But the first catering event I worked after starting college was at the home of a student from my freshman English class. Her parents' anniversary, I think," she said with a frown, trying to remember. Not that it mattered. "In my initial pass around the room with a tray of appetizers, my classmate spilled her drink on my shoes." Alyssa remembered that part well. She finally picked a berry. "Before the night was over two of the girl's friends had tipped their drinks onto my tray."

"Not a coincidence, I gather?"

"No. And unfortunately that night was just the beginning." Alyssa cautiously nibbled on the end of her strawberry before continuing. When her stomach didn't complain, she swallowed. "Most of my classmates ignored me. Some were superficially polite, but others…" Her attention drifted back toward the lobby. "Some of the others were offended that I'd sullied the hallowed ground of their precious school. And Tessa Harrison was just one of several parents at Osten College who felt that way."

The grimace on his face spoke volumes. "Osten College?"

She lifted a helpless shoulder. "My boss was chairman of their board of admissions and pulled several strings to get me in on a scholarship. I figured a prestigious school would look good on my résumé." She cleared her throat before going on. "Better than a criminal record, anyway."

With a thoughtful expression on his face, Paulo set his plate on a hall table and then turned back to her. "Tessa Harrison is a shrew with three ex-husbands, every one of whom left her for a younger woman. Just remember that if you bump into her out in my lobby."

She shot him a grateful smile. His attempt to reassure her was sweet. Not exactly a word she would have associated with the man. But the thought of bumping into the woman had her stomach considering issuing a rejection slip to its contents. Alyssa pitched the rest of the strawberry into a nearby trash can and rubbed her temple, hoping he wouldn't notice the tremble in her fingers. "I'm not sure I can go out there."

He placed a hand on the door beside her head. Alyssa's heart rate skyrocketed as he ran a finger down her cheek, staring at her lips. Desire battled fear for her attention, and as the moment lingered desire began to win out.

She swallowed hard. "Aren't you tired of your event manag—?"

His mouth landed on hers.

Her body trained from their night together, Alyssa reacted immediately. The last vestige of her panic gave way to a monsoon of need. Opening her mouth for his tongue, she let his lips take hers as a hard thigh pressed against her intimately, and she arched against him, a sigh escaping her throat.

She was back in his arms again, and for one shining moment she forgot everything. The people in the lobby. Her past. All that was important was this man and the all-consuming power he had over her body. The kiss lingered until bells of warning rang in her head, signaling the need for air, and Paulo finally lifted his head.

"Yes, you *can* go out there." His breathing was ragged, and a twinkle appeared in his eyes. "And, no, I *won't* be tiring of the delicious challenge you present anytime soon."

Looking up at him, her heart battering away, Alyssa arched an eyebrow, trying her best to appear calm as the blood throbbed in her veins. She hadn't exactly fought his kiss. "Not much of a challenge anymore."

"I disagree. After an amazing night, I woke up alone."

Amazing night, indeed. And the noises that had come from her mouth…

Flushing at the memory, she fought to regain her composure. "I needed to supervise the cleaning crew."

"No," Paulo said, shaking his head. "I'm not buying it. You're just not used to the morning-after scene." He cocked his head. "You know how I knew?"

"I think we both know how. But I'm sure you're dying to tell me anyway."

"With every orgasm you had such a look of surprise."

She turned her face away, gnawing on her cheek. She'd wanted to know what sex with Paulo would be like, and now she did. Unfortunately she hadn't counted on getting such a delicious taste of what she'd been missing all these years. "I never knew they came in so many…flavors." Feeling ridiculous, she let out an embarrassed laugh.

He looked at her curiously. "Do you regret sleeping with me?"

She stared at him. Ever since she'd made him an exception to her rule, she had been putting herself through an emotional wringer. Unable to decide how she felt. Waffling between dismay and total delight. But, whatever happened next, he deserved an honest answer. She might question the future, left to muddle her way through unfamiliar territory, but there was no question about their past. "I'm not sorry I slept with you."

"Good. I hope to make it a regular occurrence for the next few weeks or so."

Her heart did a perfect backflip in her chest. Okay, that answered the one-night stand question. And, as crazy as this relationship was, as crazy as it was making her feel, she wasn't ready to give it up. But she'd worked too hard to build her business to let it slide. She'd just have to figure out how to manage extra time for Paulo. And that meant setting some ground rules.

"I want to make one thing clear," she said, tucking her hair behind her ear. "My work comes first. Everything else, including us, comes second. No exceptions."

He lifted a cynical brow. "I appreciate your dedication, especially since it benefits me as well. But I can't say I look forward to constantly competing with your never ending to-do list."

"My business is my only priority, Paulo."

"I'll accept the condition as long *you* understand one thing."

"What's that?"

A glint of mischief appeared in his eyes. "I'm going to focus all my free time on changing your mind," he said as he reached up to rub her bottom lip.

Her body basked in the electric sensation he created. She lifted her chin, fighting for what she hoped was an artless smile. "I hope you're not afraid of hard work."

Humor lit his gaze. "And you said the challenge was over."

"A girl should always keep a man guessing."

A grin crooked the side of his mouth. "With you, I never

know what to expect next. Now," he said, taking her elbow, "let's go show these people what you're made of."

Looking down the hall at the lobby, she took a deep breath and squared her shoulders. She was as ready as she'd ever be. Certainly better than she'd been a few minutes ago. And it was time to clear this final hurdle. Ignoring the tension in her body, she let Paulo lead her down the hallway and into the crowd.

CHAPTER SIX

PAULO leaned back in the leather chair in his office. Twenty-four hours after the grand opening and he was still wondering what the hell had just happened. Finding his sassy event planner cowering in the staff hallway had been a surprise. For a brief moment he'd considered leaving her alone. Marriage had taught him he was no good with overly emotional women. He didn't do wedding rings anymore, and he most definitely didn't do drama.

But the look on Alyssa's face—the *panic*—had cut him in ways he hadn't imagined.

So he'd distracted her the only way he knew how. And the kiss had proved a success, and highly stimulating.

Now he was the one in need of a distraction, because he couldn't set aside the disturbing knowledge that she'd spent her teen years working. He'd assumed her childhood must have been rough, but something in the way she'd said "we needed the money" told him she was downplaying the ugly truth. And coming face to face with her hardship rankled.

An unwelcome tug snagged him somewhere deep.

Alyssa never asked for sympathy. Or pity. And if he

hadn't known her so well she would have looked every bit the polite businesswoman as they'd made their way around the lobby. But her nervous habits had grown familiar: a tuck of silky hair behind her ear, the swipe of a palm down her pantsuit, the tight smile and the thicker accent.

So what had happened to his spunky event manager? Where had her gumption gone? She didn't seem the type to let mistreatment by a bunch of hypocrites bother her.

His eyebrows pulled together in deliberation.

She worked hard to maintain the stoic mask. The cool professional fixated on her work. But over time, with him, that mask had cracked wide open, and when he'd finally watched her shatter in the elevator mirror she had made him ache. And the single night they'd shared had changed everything. Making love to her. Listening to her cry out. His body coiled tight at the memory.

He'd never felt so satisfied. But after an incredible night together he'd woken up alone. Ditched without a goodbye. A scowl infiltrated his face.

Watching her come apart in his arms was addictive, but he had the impression if he left her alone she wouldn't complain. She would continue on, business as usual. Fixated on her job. And the thought left him intensely *un*satisfied.

So the challenge was far from over. Not until Alyssa learned to apply as much passion to her life as she did to her job.

His thoughts were interrupted by a knock at the door and the arrival of his Chief of Operations. Charles had a newspaper in his hand, and his navy suit looked stifling for the sweltering temperature outside. Sometimes Paulo really pitied the man.

"I have some news," Charles said as he adjusted his wire-frame glasses. "First, the Ocean Inn in Boca Raton was just placed on the market. It could be a profitable enterprise." He paused and shifted on his feet, looking uncomfortable and infinitely more grave than usual. "And your brother called today, requesting your cell phone number."

The flare of anger was instantaneous. What could Marcos possibly have to say? *I'm really enjoying your wife? Thanks for warming her up for me?*

Paulo's frown grew deeper. "I hope you told him no."

"Naturally."

"Good man, Charles."

"He left a message for you to call." There was a minor pause before Charles continued. "And one more thing before I go. I wanted to show you this. The phone has been ringing nonstop since this morning." He held out the newspaper.

At the sight, Paulo tensed, preparing for bad news. To this day he still couldn't read a headline without flinching. The mention of his brother made his response that much worse. But when one of his manager's rarely dispensed smiles appeared, Paulo relaxed.

Charles said, "It appears we're the new popular South Beach venue for an event."

Paulo reached for the society section of the local newspaper. There was a spectacular array of photos of the Samba on the front page. Wedding guests at the lobby bar. A happy bride and groom dancing. And a stunning night time picture of the rooftop decked out in all its glory. He scanned the article quickly, a grin of satisfaction crossing his face at the glowing report. "I'll have to thank our strategic partner for her outstanding work."

"Yes, sir," Charles said. "But before you do you should know that you already sent Ms. Hunt flowers, thanking her for her efforts on behalf of the Samba."

Surprised at the news, Paulo set the paper down. "How thoughtful of me," he said dryly. "What kind of flowers did I choose?"

"A delicate blend of orchids and gardenias." Charles frowned, suddenly looking concerned. "I hope you don't mind my doing so, sir."

"No, not at all, Charles. It's your job to make me look good. And you do it well."

"Thank you," he said, his somber air returning. "Have a good evening."

As Charles left, Paulo raked the hair from his forehead.

Man…he'd spent an incredible night with a stunning, sexy woman and it was his manager who had thought to send her flowers. Not for the sex, of course, but because of the bang-up job she'd done promoting his hotel. So he'd had two good reasons to send Alyssa flowers and he hadn't. Paulo frowned.

If he wasn't careful he'd wind up as self-absorbed as his brother.

With a sigh, he looked at his watch. He was supposed to meet Nick at the racetrack in two hours. His frown faded to a grin. But first there was a luscious lady down the hall he needed to see.

The sweet smell of gardenias filled her office, bringing a smile to Alyssa's face as she ticked off her day's accomplishments, happy with her progress. She'd updated her priority list, compiled the catering bids for the Mayor's birthday party, and reviewed her notes on the new audiovisual company.

Transfer of her revised to-do list complete, she disconnected her phone from her laptop just as a knock sounded in the room. Paulo poked his head through the door, a devilish look on his handsome face. And faster than a high-speed internet connection she wanted him again. Her nipples tightened in response. *Whoa*. What had this man turned her into?

"You busy?" Paulo asked.

Alyssa crossed her arms across her breasts to hide the reaction. "Depends on what you have in mind."

Paulo stepped inside, closed the door, and leaned against the wall, hands behind his back. The look he gave her made her skin tingle. "Oh, I definitely think you're going to like what I have in mind." He tipped his head, his eyes lit with mischief. "Are you done with work for the evening?"

She couldn't control her body's response to the words. Anticipation hummed, the heated blood in her veins warming her to her toes. Since their night together not ten minutes had passed without a picture of Paulo popping into her head. And in every one of them he was naked.

She really was a degenerate.

"Paulo," Alyssa said, growing serious as she glanced at the door, "I'm not sure the office is a good idea."

"Why not?" His voice took on a hint of danger, leaving no doubt what he had in mind. "It's six o'clock. Everyone in this hall is gone." Hands still behind his back, he approached her. "I locked the door." His eyes dropped to her chest and his voice turned to a throaty rumble. "And the walls are thick enough to block all that noise you'll make."

Alyssa ignored the blazing heat that flared higher. "And you won't be making any noise?"

His eyes went dark. "It turns me on just listening to you…" His voice died away, leaving Alyssa breathless, too. "Get ready to make some noise, Ms. Hunt." Paulo sent her a cocky grin and pulled his hands from behind his back, dropping a newspaper on her desk. "A little light reading for your evening enjoyment."

Confused, Alyssa reached for the paper. Across the front page was a gorgeous spread of photos of the hotel. Recovery from the abrupt turn of events was slow, but she finally managed to skim through the article, her smile growing as she registered the praise. When she reached the end she read it again, just for fun. Feeling positively giddy, she looked up at Paulo and let out a laugh.

Eyes sparkling with humor, Paulo perched on the edge of her desk. "Charles says people are clamoring to schedule the hotel for their receptions. Things are about to get even busier around here." His voice wicked with amusement, he went on, "And you thought I came in here for something else."

Alyssa shot him a scolding look, but it was half-hearted at best. "That's what you wanted me to think." Even worse, she was disappointed he'd only been teasing. She had an overwhelming urge to make him squirm in return. Her eyes landed on the gardenias. "Paulo, I meant to thank you…" She didn't have to work hard for the dreamy quality in her voice. "Sending me these beautiful flowers." She watched his grin fade, holding back her smile. "I can't tell you how much they mean to me."

For a brief moment Paulo looked positively speechless. Alyssa reached for her phone, snapping a photo of him.

"What was the picture for?" He asked, clearly stumped by the sequence of events.

Alyssa let out a small laugh. "To capture the struggle on your face as you worked out how to explain the flowers weren't from you."

"How did you know?"

Alyssa pulled the card from the arrangement, releasing the scent of gardenias, and read, *"'Dear Ms. Hunt. Thank you so much for your efforts. Your diligence, efficiency and attention to detail made for a delightful evening. Sincerely, Mr. Domingues.'"*

Alyssa arched an eyebrow. "Either Charles sent it…" she lobbed him a look as she tossed the card on her desk "…or you need to work on your moves, Mr. Domingues."

"There's nothing wrong with my moves." He grinned

down at her, and his voice dropped. "You want me to show you one of them now?"

Stunned, she bit the tip of her tongue. Yes. She wanted to tell him *yes*! It was what a modern woman would do. Take charge of her sexuality. Embrace the temptation that was consuming her. Her temperature spiraled higher, and she opened her mouth to answer.

But a randy rendezvous on her desk would be way out of line.

At the last second she chickened out, glancing at the cell phone in her hand. "I still need an hour or so to answer my messages."

The moment the wimpy words left her lips she wanted them back. A look of challenge flashed in Paulo's eyes, as if she'd thrown down a gauntlet. And then his gaze turned from milk chocolate to dark.

He took her phone, set it aside, and lifted her chin with his finger. "Maybe I should remind you of what you're missing."

Heat infused her limbs, leaving them weightless, and she waited in anticipation as Paulo leaned forward and touched his mouth to hers. Small whisper-kisses. Subtle, feathery kisses. A gentle exploration that was more of a tease than a touch—until he finally opened her mouth with his. Her lips went soft, and her body followed close behind. With a sigh, she leaned into him.

She'd missed this. It had only been three days, but she missed how he made her feel. The delicious slide of tongue on tongue left her craving more.

And more was what she got when Paulo hoisted her onto the edge of the desk. With his mouth still on hers, he pushed her skirt high, and she wiggled her hips to aid his efforts. She didn't mount a peep of a protest when his hands slid under her blouse to release the front clasp of her bra. He cupped her bare breasts, and his thumbs began to circle her nipples. The tips tingled, grew hard, and her groan was loud against his lips.

He leaned back to watch her face, his breathing heavy. As his hands drove her temperature to critical, he whispered, "Shall I go and come back in an hour?"

Eyelids stretched wide, she stared at him. Not fair. He was teasing her. And how did he manage to get her so hot and bothered while he still had the power to pull back? She frowned. "Listen, mister," she said with a decided twang. She grabbed his shirt and hauled him closer, pulling him firmly between her legs. "Don't you *dare*."

The brash demand and bawdy action brought a warm flush to her cheeks. Maybe she'd been too aggressive? One night together and she thought she'd learned all she needed to know. Had experienced everything. It was frightening to discover she hadn't plumbed the full extent of her passion, her sexuality. Just how deep did it go?

And how lewd could she get?

But the grin on Paulo's face was huge. "That was hot."

And then he kissed her again, hard, as if inspired, chasing away the doubts. His tongue stroked hers in time with the drag of his thumbs across her nipples. Swallowing her moans, Paulo thrust his hips, his hardness rubbing against her center until Alyssa was so ready for him she let out a cry and dug her nails into the tight muscles of his backside. A wordless plea to end her agony. To be filled. By Paulo. No other man would do. Her response to him was singularly unique. Special.

Paulo pulled back again, his eyes dark with desire. "I don't have a condom."

Shocked by the cruel news, she choked back a sob of protest.

Hands on her breasts, his tone was firm, insistent. "What else do you want?"

Her blood turned to sludge in her veins, her heart so loud in her ears it was hard to hear. "I don't know."

"Yes, you do." The frank honesty in his face didn't budge. "So say it."

Seconds ticked by. "I can't." Oh, dear God, why did she always sound so juvenile? At twenty-eight, too. How lame was that?

His hands dropped to her hips, his gaze refusing to give. "Try anyway."

She opened her mouth, but couldn't speak. Every time she thought of a response memories choked it, the long-ago words whispering in her head: Trashy. Easy. *Slut.*

But she wanted him so much. And as she stared at his dazzling face the alluring promise in his eyes sent a frisson of excitement up her spine. She was torn with this desire that effortlessly destroyed her cool faster than the old fear could rebuild it. Until she couldn't take it anymore.

Alyssa slowly leaned back on the desk, lifted her hips, and slid her panties down. If the words were too hard, she would show him. She tossed her underwear aside and spread her legs, begging him with her eyes.

His gaze burned into hers, and he laid a scorching hand on her bare thigh. "That's a good start." He didn't move, and the waiting expectation on his face slayed her all over again.

"Just a start?" she said.

"I want you to trust me enough to tell me what you want."

Her chest clenched tighter around her heart. "I'm happy with whatever you give."

"No." His hand gripped her thigh and he leaned forward, looking down at her with an intensity that was compelling. "That's not enough."

Tears of frustration stung her lids. He demanded too much. The impossible.

"I'm afraid I'll sound vulgar," she whispered, closing her eyes, terrified at the thought. "Or crude."

He laid a hand on her cheek and she lifted her lids. "Alyssa." His voice was soft, his gaze tender. "You couldn't sound crude if you tried."

And then Paulo shifted down her body, casting gentle kisses on her skin as he went, murmuring reassurances. When he got to her inner thigh, her legs trembled. Anticipation surged as his lips drew close to where she wanted them, where she *needed* them to kiss her. But he hovered at the edge, not giving her what she wanted. Her body burned. Ached.

She was one giant nerve-ending, waiting on Paulo.

He opened her with his fingers, his words whispering across her swollen, sensitized skin. "Say it, Alyssa," he demanded.

"Please." Her voice broke. "Take me in your mouth."

His lips closed around her nub and suckled. The wicked touch seared her nerves and Alyssa let out a cry, arching her back. Cradling her buttocks, he brought her closer, and she almost wept with relief.

She was lost in a sea of sensation. Riding high and growing ever higher. Waves of pleasure swelled, and then receded. Each time cresting to new heights, sweeping her along in a treacherous current until she was too raw with need, too exposed to care anymore.

Breathless, she threaded her fingers through his hair and told him what she wanted. More pressure. Or less. Faster, or slower.

The pleasure was eating her alive. Spreading her legs wider, she strained up toward the unrelenting sensation. And her words grew bold, explicit. Until she was demanding the rake of his teeth, or the slick slide of his tongue.

And he obliged. Feeding her fantasy.

Until a final rasp of his tongue drew a loud groan from her lips, sparks bursting behind her lids. She clutched his head, the orgasm washing through her with shimmering waves of fire and light…and the delicious feel of her sex clenching beneath his mouth.

Forty-five minutes later Paulo steered the Ducati into the circular drive at the Samba. Tense didn't begin to describe how he felt. The word failed to capture the tumultuous battle for supremacy raging in his body.

And just who was in control here? Him or his hormones?

After their tryst in her office—and the hint of a sexually assertive side to Alyssa—he'd muttered a weak excuse and bolted to take a cold shower in one of the hotel rooms, hoping to extinguish the blazing fire. Massive fail. Thinking a ride would help, he'd gone for a spin around the block.

Unfortunately, getting caught doing a hundred in a thirty-mile-an-hour zone wasn't an option, and the painfully slow putter behind a pack of sightseers had only exacerbated the agony. What he needed was a full-throttle, high-speed race around the track. Because not a tiny dent was made in his need for her.

With a frown, he parked his bike by the front curb of the Samba. What was wrong with him? He'd never had this kind of trouble with a woman before. Letting an affair run roughshod through his life. Clearly, with the emergence of the racier Alyssa, he'd have to try a little harder.

As a stretch BMW pulled up behind him, Paulo dismounted the Ducati. He stepped on the kickstand, ignoring the limo until a familiar figure emerged from inside. The sight shot his mood from agitated to outright antagonistic. His body went rigid. Stunned, he flipped up the visor on his helmet and watched his brother approach. In an Italian suit and leather shoes worn with the intent to impress, he strode toward Paulo like he owned the Samba. Which he didn't.

Not anymore.

Marcos stopped a few feet away. He'd aged since their last apocalyptic meeting; his short dark hair now had a hint of gray at the temples. The hard face and set of his mouth were just like their dad's, all the way down to the disapproval in his eyes. But Paulo had never cared what Marcos thought of him, only his father.

The sheer nerve of his brother to show up at this hotel had Paulo seething, teeth grating as he pulled off his helmet. Reining in the familiar fury, he turned his back on Marcos and hung his helmet on a handle. "What are you doing here?"

"If you had returned my message, you would know."

The curt response drove Paulo's anger higher, but he'd be drawn and quartered before he'd let Marcos see how much his presence affected him. "I have nothing to say to you." He headed for the entrance to the hotel. Nearing the doorman, he jerked a thumb in the direction of his motorcycle. "Keep an eye on her, will you, Jerry?"

The elderly man tipped his uniformed cap. "Sure thing, Mr. Domingues."

Paulo was a few feet up the granite staircase when Marcos's voice called out.

"Believe it or not, Paulo, this isn't all about you. This is about Dad's will."

The sharp, indignant stab of resentment brought Paulo to a halt. "Dad's will?" He turned to look down on his brother, annoyed to see he was following him. "That was years ago. He gave you the company. And, sorry, I sold the shares of Domingues International he left me to buy my first hotel." He shot Marcos a piercing look. "You can't have those, too."

Apparently being sole heir had left Marcos feeling a touch

guilty—or maybe it was the fact he'd pilfered Paulo's wife—because his eye twitched at one corner. "Quit being so difficult."

The irony sent Paulo's eyebrows skyward. "*I'm* being difficult?" He knew from a lifetime of experience that, if he didn't get Marcos to leave they would end up goading one another until it disintegrated into an ugly debate. Paulo sent him an empty smile. "If you don't like my attitude, feel free to go, big brother."

Paulo pivoted on his heel and nodded as Jerry held open the front door. He crossed the busy lobby and moved down the hallway leading to his office, managing to resist the urge to slam the door behind him as he headed for his desk. The forest-green walls of his office were soothing. But, even better, they didn't contain his brother.

The sound of the door opening behind him made his insides twist. Damn, the man wasn't going away. Hoping to keep his hands busy—and maybe control his anger—Paulo picked up his autographed baseball as he rounded his desk. He flopped into his leather chair and leaned back, propping his feet next to his computer and waiting for Marcos to speak.

Frowning, his brother strode into the room. "Don't walk away from me."

The arrogance was familiar, but no less infuriating. "My hotel. My rules." Paulo began tossing the ball lightly in his hand. "I'll do whatever I want."

"I see you still dress like a slob."

"You got something against jeans and a motocross T-shirt?"

Marcos pushed his Armani jacket back, hands on his hips, gold Rolex gleaming in the light. "Never mind your appalling lack of couth, we need to discuss Dad's will."

The old resentment flared again, and he was getting tired

of its return. Paulo gripped the baseball tight, fighting the need to hurl it at the wall. "There's nothing to discuss."

"Dad left me with a job that I intend to complete. I was put in charge of a trust that comes into effect on the fifth anniversary of his death," Marcos said, his mouth white, pinched with anger. "Did you even realize how long it's been?"

"Yeah," Paulo replied slowly. "I'm well aware of the date." Even though it was hard to miss a father who barely noticed you were alive, his passing had still hit Paulo hard. Because it had been the end of any hope for a little praise from the man.

And those dark days had been about more than just the loss of his dad.

"Which means yours and Bianca's wedding anniversary is coming up, too." Paulo hiked a scornful brow. "Shall I send you two a card? I could draw little red hearts on the envelope if you like."

Marcos ignored the remarks and plowed on, lines of aggravation engraved around his mouth. "You were named a beneficiary of Dad's trust. It leaves you an additional fifty-million-dollar inheritance."

Paulo tossed the ball onto his desk. It landed with a thunk and rolled off to hit the floor.

Money. Always about the damn money. It was the only kind of success his dad had understood. And after investing years of hard work, with barely a word of acknowledgment from his old man, the final insult had come at his father's death. Marcos's role as the favorite child had payed off big-time when he was handed the throne.

And now Paulo had been beaten out by his brother for his dad's attention one final time.

His gut buckled under the weight of the memory. "I'm not interested."

"Don't be childish."

Paulo couldn't believe the words. After the stunt Marcos had pulled, he was calling *him* childish?

"Dad wanted you to have it," his brother went on.

"Your wife is addicted to the finer things in life. She couldn't stand the thought she might have to live on less." Paulo speared his fingers through his hair. "So why don't you give the money to her?"

Marcos didn't move, and something unrecognizable flickered in his eyes. "Money isn't the reason Bianca left you."

The verbal smack hit Paulo hard, and his hand landed on the desk with a thump. "She left me when I threatened to leave the company, hooked up with you, and then took another vow of forever right after you inherited it all." He cocked his head in disbelief. "That's a helluva coincidence."

Marcos's titanium steel gaze bored into Paulo's. "You never did understand her."

Undaunted, Paulo stood up from his chair, staring back. "I understand her better than you think." He would not waste his time debating his ex-wife with his brother. "It's time for you to go."

Face red, Marcos looked ready to blow. "We'll discuss this again later."

Paulo nodded toward the door. "This discussion is over."

CHAPTER SEVEN

ALYSSA sat in the empty bleachers, bathed in the light of the setting sun. The rumbling roar grew louder as the pack of motorcycles zoomed by, leaving the acrid smell of hot rubber in its wake. Alyssa held her breath as Paulo leaned deep to take the curve, his knee almost dragging the pavement. When he was safely around Alyssa relaxed, remembering to inhale.

Everything about the man left her breathless. And when Paulo had stopped back at her office to invite her along for his practice run she should have said no. But she'd said yes. Partly because she was still dazed from the moment on her desk an hour earlier. And partly because…well, because she wanted to.

It had been so easy for Paulo to sidetrack her today. What started as a simple kiss had turned her into someone she hadn't recognized. And she still couldn't believe some of the things she'd said to him.

Worrying the button on her cuff, she watched Paulo pull off to the side and dismount, the first one to finish. His lean form was encased in a protective racing suit. The uniform only increased the man's sex appeal, and her body started that crazy internal cha-cha again. She let out a self-directed, chastising snort.

Paulo Domingues, able to take a woman from borderline frigid to knocking on nympho in ten seconds flat.

When Paulo headed into the concession stand, her tension eased a touch. And then the second place finisher parked next to Paulo's Ducati, flipped up the visor on his helmet, and scanned the bleachers. Surprised, Alyssa watched him lope up the stairs in her direction.

"You must be Alyssa." He came to a stop in front of her bench, propping a foot on the seat beside her. "Nick Tatum," he said as he pulled off his headgear. "Owner of the hottest nightclub in South Beach and Paulo's oldest friend." He stuck out a hand, his green eyes twinkling. "In duration, that is, not in age."

Alyssa returned the shake, laughing at his disclaimer. "Nice to meet you."

He was good looking in an all-American way, his brown hair sun kissed with glints of gold. "Anything you want to know about Paulo, just ask."

Alyssa studied him closely. A very noteworthy statement. And one that left her wondering if it was a warning. But she kept her tone light. "Is there anything in particular you think I should know?"

A rakish grin appeared. "A very perceptive woman, I see." He paused before going on. "But on second thought..." He tipped his head. "I wouldn't want to kill the mystery."

"Is mystery a good thing or a bad thing?"

He leaned closer, as if sharing a secret, his grin so big Alyssa had to smile. "Depends on who you ask," he said.

Paulo appeared behind his friend, a tray laden with two hot dogs in his hand. "Are you done flirting?" The tone was easy.

Too easy. Because Paulo's expression was hard, his eyes sharp. The moment froze, tension snapping in the air like heat lightning on a summer evening.

Nick's forehead furrowed in amusement. "Ease up, bro." Removing his foot from beside Alyssa, he straightened up. "I'm not moving in on your territory."

Paulo switched his gaze to Alyssa. "I didn't say you were." He held a hot dog in her direction and took a seat in the exact spot where Nick's foot had been.

The position was intentional, and Alyssa bit back the laugh, strangely tickled at Paulo's discomfort. It was such an unexpected turn of events. But she should at least pretend to be offended. As she reached for the hot dog, she shot them both a grow-up look. "Territory?" she said dryly. "Is that really a term you two use?"

"Hell, no," Paulo said.

"At least not in mixed company," Nick added. "My Neanderthal-looking friend here is exuding more testosterone than usual, so it seemed appropriate." Paulo was now scowling outright, but a grin lit Nick's face. "But don't worry," he said as he clapped Paulo's shoulder. "I just wanted to meet Alyssa and find out what's responsible for your win tonight." The man rubbed his chin with a finger. "Whatever it is that has you bugged, you sure seemed willing to put your life in peril."

As he looked at Alyssa, Nick jerked his head in Paulo's direction and continued. "Watching him bang his head against the wall in frustration might be more fun than Lady Gaga in concert, but it's also a guarantee he'll risk life and limb to beat me on the track."

Alyssa looked curiously at Paulo.

But by now Paulo's face was bland, and he lifted a brow at his friend. "Are you going to stand there and be helpful all night?"

"Easy on the sarcasm, my friend. You might hurt your-self." Nick shot Paulo another grin, obviously undaunted by his friend's hint to leave. "I'm just keepin' it real." He looked down at the hot dog Alyssa was holding. "By the way, in case you didn't know, Paulo's loaded." Eyes sparkling, he nodded at her food. "You should hold out for a better dinner. And now," Nick said, sending his friend a salute, "she's all yours." He shot Alyssa a wink and then turned to lope back down the bleachers.

Nick's comments were interesting, because she had sensed Paulo's strained, almost dark mood when he'd picked her up. Gazing out over the track, she ate her hot dog, pon-dering the source.

Finally, she had to ask. "Why do you take the risk?" When he sent her a questioning look, she nodded toward the track. "The dangerous speeds. The death-defying corners." She shook her head. "It's crazy."

He gave a careless shrug. "The key to speed is keeping tight control over your bike."

Remembering their blistering encounters, her voice went low. "You like to keep everything under your control, don't you?"

Paulo lifted a brow, his eyes now glowing with amuse-ment. "Let's not turn this into an attempt to psychoanalyze my personality." He looked at her half-eaten hot dog and then at her, his voice rumbling sensually. "Now, finish up so I can take you home."

The promise in his statement had her heart rate doing double time, creating a hum of desire as she stared at him, her insides twirling. Clever little maneuver he had there, wielding his charm to redirect the conversation.

After finishing her hot dog, she leaned back on her hands and watched him polish off his food. "It's not going to work, you know." His eyebrows lifted in question, and she tipped her head. "Trying to seduce me with the adrenaline-junkie attitude."

"It won't?"

"I'm afraid not."

"Hmm." His voice low, he leaned in, bringing those better-than-chocolate eyes closer. "What will it take?"

Desire skipped along her nerves. Shoot. She really needed to work on being harder to get. "Sorry," she said softly. "But I have to make you suffer a little first."

His gaze moved to her mouth. "As if you hadn't already," Paulo said. "The Alyssa that finally came out to play today was inspiring." His voice dropped to a rough whisper. "I've never been so turned on in my life."

She bit her lip, her heart thumping. "I was a bit…graphic."

"Oh, yeah. And I want more from where that came from," he growled. He narrowed his eyes. "But maybe you should wait until I have the equipment to follow through."

"Consider it revenge for shamelessly seducing a woman who was trying to work."

His lips twitched. "I look forward to letting you seduce me instead." He stood and took Alyssa's hand, pulling her to her feet. "We can start the celebration of my win with a drink at your place," he said, and turned to lead her down the steps.

The words and his tone, combined with the feel of her fingers entwined with his, sent her desire heavenward. Suddenly, exerting a bit of control of her own seemed vital. "Are you inviting yourself over to my apartment?" she scolded, her tone teasing. She gently shook her head. "Your invitation. Your idea." They reached the ground and headed in the direction of the Ducati. She sent him a deliberate look. "I think it should be at your place."

Every fiber in Paulo's being immediately balked at the idea, and he fought the need to frown. Listening to the gravel crunch beneath their feet, he was careful to keep his expression shuttered as he wrestled with the thought of her at his house.

Because it went against his rules. He kept his affairs separate from his private life. Out of his home. Out of his space. It made it easier to get them out of his life. And the thought of *Alyssa* in his bed was like moving too fast into a curve, flirting with disaster. Knowing one false move and their relationship would spin out from under him, hurtling them both toward a painful crash.

He didn't want to give her the wrong impression. And he sure as hell didn't want to think about all the reasons this woman was a risk to his hard-earned peace of mind. All he wanted was to get lost in the rare chemistry they shared. To watch Alyssa enjoy it, too. Especially after the day he'd had...

Wound tight from his seduction efforts. Enduring his brother's visit. And now his ridiculous reaction when he saw his friend standing so close to Alyssa.

And why had seeing them together bugged him so much? Nick was an accomplished flirt. He hit on every female he found easy on the eye. But just because Nick managed to make Alyssa laugh, it didn't mean anything. And even if it *did* mean something, it shouldn't bother him. The jealousy was new, sophomoric, and damn irrational.

All the more reason to stick to the *Paulo's Plans for Dating Handbook.*

"It would be easier if we went to your apartment," he said.

She stopped, forcing him to halt beside her. "Who said anything about making this easy?" With a light tone, she continued. "Those are my terms. Take it or leave it."

Clutching her hand, Paulo looked out over the mostly vacant parking lot. Every time he tried to teach Alyssa a lesson, he was the one who paid the price. He blew out a frustrated breath and took in her exquisite face, leaning in close. "Like I have a choice."

Her eyes sparkled with humor. "You always have a choice, Mr. Domingues."

Paulo stared at her, enjoying her look of amusement. Her sweet scent grew stronger as he swept the hair from her cheek. Her gaze turned dark at his touch, and his body grew tight. "No," he murmured. "I don't think I do."

After providing a tour of the Samba facilities, Alyssa said goodbye to the couple searching for a reception site and took a seat at the rooftop bar to jot down her notes. The bartender set an iced tea in front of her, and Alyssa nodded her thanks.

The Atlantic sparkled in the distance. Soaking up the warm midday rays, guests relaxed in lounge chairs or took a dip in the cool water of the pool.

Normally she would consider the relaxing view a distraction. But her desk, where memories of Paulo were vivid, was worse. And, after the fabulously successful wedding reception, work was getting busy. Every day her to-do list grew longer. But she was having trouble focusing, thanks to her disturbingly handsome, insanely seductive client.

Last evening, after leaving the track, Paulo had taken her to his house and straight to his bed. Another jaw-dropping, amazing night. Sometimes she'd led and sometimes she'd followed, but she had never hesitated to tell him what she wanted. And the sense of empowerment had been liberating. Paulo had enjoyed it, too.

She'd thought she'd won a victory when he agreed to take her to his home. But when she'd opened her eyes at dawn, a gentle light had lit the bedroom walls filled with racing photographs, baseball memorabilia, and pictures of historic hotels in South Beach. A smile had crept up her face when she'd spied a pair of jeans draped over a chair. It was all so much more personal than a cold, sterile hotel room.

But he hadn't wanted to bring her there, insisting from the beginning this was a short-term affair. And her smile had died as she was struck by the thought that, suddenly, she wasn't satisfied.

Their temporary arrangement had allowed her to ignore her doubts and indulge in a little free time with a funny, sexy, drop-dead gorgeous man who made her feel things she hadn't thought possible. A temporary arrangement which had seemed perfect...until now.

Unnerved, she had crept downstairs, called a taxi, and gone home. After a quick shower and change of clothes she'd arrived at the office early, desperately burying her worries in the familiar routine of work.

Ice shifted in her glass with a clink, and she realized most of it had melted. Frowning, she glanced at her watch. She'd been sitting there for fifteen minutes. Doing nothing.

Okay, girl. You have *so* got to get your head together.

Pen poised in her hand, she stared at her blank notepad. But every five minutes her mind drifted back to the fact that she was now unhappy with the limits on their relationship. Apprehension whittled away a little more of her courage, and she set her pen aside, giving up on the task.

She picked up her cold glass and pressed it to her cheek, heart tapping loudly. Her mind churned with questions. How was she going to handle this growing desire to have more of him in her life? And would he even be interested in an ex-con as a steady girlfriend?

"I woke up alone again."

Alyssa jerked and set down her glass, turning in her seat. Paulo was in a T-shirt and cut-offs, every muscle in her arms and legs exposed. Her mouth went as dry as hot sand baking on a beach.

Heart hammering harder, she carefully controlled her expression. "I have a lot I want to accomplish today," she said evenly.

He leaned against the counter, bringing a deluge of images from their night together. She wrapped her hand around her chilled glass, fighting the warmth he generated, vainly trying to steady her heart. Obviously overexposure to Paulo's touch was *not* desensitizing her to his presence.

"You could give a guy a complex," Paulo said dryly.

Alyssa bit the inside of her cheek, repressing the threat of a nervous giggle. The thought of Paulo with confidence issues was laughable. "Just trying to please my new client," she said.

His eyes lingered on her face. "You already have," he murmured.

"Then why the complaint?"

"Did you enjoy last night?" he asked.

"You know I did."

"So why is your work so important you'd choose to spend a Saturday morning here rather than in my bed?"

As he scrutinized her face, he seemed to be waiting for her to respond. But her budding doubts about their relationship and his disturbing proximity momentarily left her speechless. And then a glimmer of determination finally appeared in his eyes.

"I was hoping to convince you to share the reason by upgrading my dinner plans from the racetrack to the top of the Ritz." He paused and cocked his head inquisitively, as if waiting for an answer. "Best restaurant in town... Excellent mojitos..."

A jumble of confused feelings ensued. Their discussion at the grand opening had probably left him believing she was a downtrodden former juvenile delinquent who'd never been given a fair shot. But what would he think if she told him the whole story? The reason why her work was so important?

Blowing out a breath, she eyed him warily. "You're asking me out on a date?"

Humor lit Paulo's face. "I'm asking you out on a date."

Nibbling on a nail, she considered the offer. Essentially, she had two choices. End this affair, or push it forward. At least dinner at a nice restaurant would signal a step toward a more conventional relationship. And if it just so happened she worked up the nerve for a full disclosure—a swell of nausea tumbled in her stomach—well, at least the public location would keep his response tolerable. She let out a small sigh. "Okay."

"Good. I already had one of the staff make dinner reservations for eight," Paulo said. "I'll pick you up at seven-thirty." His expression was one of a man with a target in sight.

And Alyssa could almost see the bright bull's-eye glowing on her past.

The limousine was an unexpected surprise, but not Paulo's lack of a coat and tie. His dark pants and navy dress shirt were nice, complementing Alyssa's royal blue blouse and skirt. As they exited the elevator onto the top floor of the posh high-rise, the snobby hostess started to protest Paulo's lack of proper attire. But when they stepped closer, recognition abruptly changed the woman's attitude.

So did the smile Paulo flashed her.

Alyssa watched the exchange with awe. Paulo lived in a world where people were happy to give him what he wanted. Where a respected name and oodles of money opened doors closed to others. The complete inverse of her world.

Her history slammed doors firmly in her face. Did she have the nerve to share the complete unvarnished truth?

Tension filled her body as the hostess led them to a table with a spectacular view of skyscrapers, the lights of Miami blazing against the night sky. Nestled in the corner, their secluded location detracted from the safety of a restaurant full of people. Paulo held out her chair, his fingers brushing her shoulder as she took her seat.

The scorching feel of Paulo's skin stung her nerves, and her concentration faltered. After lacing her fingers in her lap, she drew in a breath to psych herself up while he sat down and placed their drink order.

When the hostess left, Paulo settled back. One corner of his lips lifted. "I recognize that expression on your face."

Unless he'd seen her being led before a firing squad, she was pretty sure he didn't.

She'd spent a long time preparing for—and dreading—this conversation. Wondering how honest she should be. But they could sit here until kingdom come, and she still wouldn't be ready.

And then his half-smile turned into a full one, tripping up her focus. Dark hair framed the square-cut features and slash of eyebrows. But, as usual, it was the speckled milk-chocolate eyes that held her attention. Or maybe it was the sexy curve of his mouth?

"You have that determined look on your face again." He crossed his arms, and his shirt stretched across broad shoulders, blitzing her last coherent thought. "All I want from you is the truth."

The truth. Well, there was a mood killer. And he had no idea what he was asking.

She dropped her gaze to the table, her voice soft. "Sometimes it's uglier than you think."

"It can't be that bad."

The outright confidence in his voice brought her gaze back to his. "That just proves how much you don't know."

"I'm a big boy." He looked so relaxed. So at ease with his request. Totally clueless as to what he was letting himself in for. "I'm sure I can deal with whatever you have to tell me."

"Can you?" She laid her hands flat on the table and leaned forward, looking at Paulo with total concentration. "What if the reality of my life is more truth than you can handle?"

"Alyssa," he said dryly, a faint look of amusement on his face. "Your life isn't a remake of *A Few Good Men*. There's nothing you can tell me that I can't handle."

"I was six years old the first time I helped my mother steal a box of cereal."

The humorous glint was doused from his eyes and his body went still.

Little did he know she was just getting started. Alyssa met his gaze, realizing if she looked away her courage would falter. She supposed she could have eased into that statement, but his absolute faith in his capacity to understand had finally pushed her over the edge.

And there was nothing like jumping in with both feet. Because then there was no changing your mind.

But, boy, the cold shock to the system was more effective than five iced lattes.

As they stared at each other the waiter appeared, placing their drinks on the table. Without sparing him a glance, Paulo ordered the special for them both, and the man retreated again, leaving them alone. Alyssa held his gaze as she took a sip of her mojito. The fresh mint, lime and rum were refreshing, and the alcohol warmed her stomach, relaxing her a touch.

Which could only help—because this went beyond the professional. Beyond his belief in her ability to do her job. And when had his *personal* opinion come to mean so much?

Her stomach did a sickening slow roll, but she forged ahead. There was no backing out now. "It was ridiculously easy, you know," she said. "I snuck out with the box under my sweater while my mother distracted the clerk. And who would ever suspect a kindergartner as an accomplice?" Her lips twisted wryly. "Of course, considering it was eighty degrees outside, the sweater should have been a red flag."

After a long pause, his face stunned, he said quietly, "You were so young."

"Yes. I was."

He picked up his drink with a frown. "How often did you have to do that?"

Alyssa scrunched up her face at the impossible question. She was digging herself deeper and deeper into a gaping pit. "Whenever the money ran out before our month did. Which was frequent when I was little, but dwindled to a rarity by the time I started high school."

Paulo seemed to recover from the initial shock, and with a muttered curse he plopped his glass down. "I can't believe your *mother* taught you how."

His defense of her wasn't a surprise. But it also wasn't fair.

"My mom is..." Alyssa shifted her gaze to the window, looking beyond the lights to the black sky above "...frequently frustrating, often intentionally obtuse, and occasionally incomprehensible." She let out a little huff of surrender. The description really didn't do her mother justice. "When I was in second grade I found this pretty little notebook with a beagle on it. I loved it, and I needed one for school. But of course we had no money. So I took it." She gave an apologetic shrug at the words. Good grief, no wonder he had that expression on his face. "My mom made me take it back."

Paulo looked dumbfounded. "So stealing cereal was okay but a notebook wasn't?"

"Welcome to the world of my mother." With a sigh, Alyssa leaned back. All of his judgment seemed directed at her mom. How could she explain the unexplainable? "She had a very definite idea of what was allowed and what wasn't. Cereal or a jar of peanut butter was fine. Potato chips and soda were out. Which would lead one to assume it was based on nutritional content, except an occasional candy bar was okay—but only if it was chocolate." Knowing it didn't make sense, she sent him a weak smile. "I never could figure out her logic. Then again—" she slowly shook her head "—I often still can't."

"Faulty logic." Brows furrowed, as if struggling to comprehend, he went on. "She taught a kindergartner it was okay to steal."

"When I was born, my mother was fourteen..." Alyssa leaned forward again, scanning his eyes. "*Fourteen.* A runaway foster kid who had absolutely no trust in the social welfare system. She did what she had to do to survive."

"Refusing to accept government help wasn't fair to you."

"At first she was afraid they'd take me away. After a while, the way of life became a trap."

Paulo shook his head, his hair falling across his forehead. He pushed it back, looking unconvinced. "I appreciate your loyalty to your mother. And I also realize that I have no comparable experience to draw from, but—"

"That's right," she interjected in a low voice. "Unless you've gone to bed hungry, you don't." She refused to soften her gaze. Or reduce the strength in her tone. "Judgment is easy from a comfortable, cushy distance."

They stared at each other, and the galaxy of differences between them expanded to include a new solar system. He couldn't understand. It was too much to ask of anyone. Which was why she never had. Until now. She rubbed her forehead, trying to remember why.

"So what changed?" Paulo said.

She pushed aside the doubt. "Ironically enough, it was my

arrest in high school." She propped her elbows on the table. "With the money from my catering job, suddenly we didn't have to choose between eating and paying the electric bill anymore. And that was it. My mother declared stealing was no longer allowed and—boom." She spread out her hands. "We were done. And from then on, as far as she was concerned, we have always been law-abiding citizens." And her mother had avoided all conversations on the matter since.

Even when Alyssa had slipped up again.

Damn.

With trembling fingers, she reached for her drink, the guilt eating at her. "We were both ready to put it all behind us, and my catering job was the way out."

"Was that what college was? A way out?"

The queasy feeling returned, and she abandoned her glass. "Yes. I thought after two years of clean living, good grades in high school and working hard at my job I was ready to take on Osten College." Her lips twisted wryly as she laid her cheek against her palm. "Even now, I'm still amazed at my own stupidity."

Frustration carved on his face, he leaned forward, his eyes boring into hers. A prickle of shock and awareness skittered down her spine, dispersing her thoughts. She fought to control the rate of her heart and her breathing as he spoke.

"I don't get it. You have so many choices as an event planner." His face full of doubt, he said, "Why would you choose to work with the class of society you fear?"

Jeez, what a hopelessly loaded question.

Struggling to cover the emotion, she dropped her gaze to her hand, trailing a trembling finger on the tablecloth. "I'm not afraid of them, really. I just..." Her voice died. She opened her mouth to try again, but nothing came out. She knew she needed to go on, but was unsure how to finish the story. After deliberating for hours, she still didn't know.

How could she explain she wasn't worried about being exposed to their ridicule again? The ultra-wealthy of the world only served as a reminder that her ultimate humiliation was due to her own failure. Her *weakness*.

Up until now, his skepticism had been directed at her mother. Alyssa gripped the napkin in her lap. All in defense of *her*. But what about when he learned what she'd done in college? Would he lose all respect for her? There would be no more outrage on her behalf, for sure. And any illusion he had of her innocence would be killed cold. Tears pricked the back of her lids, and she turned her face to the window.

God, was she destined to be stuck in this spiral of shame forever?

"Paulo," a feminine voice called out.

With a colossal sense of relief at the interruption, Alyssa turned to see an elegant redhead approach. In a strapless black dress, she had her arm wrapped around the elbow of a man who seemed vaguely familiar, a massive diamond ring on her finger. "I stopped by the Samba this afternoon to invite you over for dinner, but your reception clerk told me you were out." Her smile was so bright Alyssa thought she would go blind from the flash of white. "Fortunately she was kind enough to tell me about your plans to dine here with Ms. Hunt."

When Alyssa pivoted her gaze to Paulo, the look on his face put an end to her relief at the interruption. If his expression and the white-knuckled grip on his glass were any indication, this would be no pleasant interlude.

Paulo's voice was soft, but his face was hard. "What are you up to, Bianca?"

The name came from the blue and blindsided Alyssa, knocking the breath from her lungs.

Bianca. Paulo's ex-wife.

Which meant the man looked familiar because he was

Paulo's brother. Though he was sporting a gorgeous black suit, and his dark hair was cropped short, he was as tall as Paulo, with a matching bitter expression to boot.

Either she didn't notice, or didn't care, but Bianca's face didn't register Paulo's terse manner as she glibly pressed on. "I thought Marcos and I could join you for a drink." The redhead turned to Alyssa. "I was hoping to get these stubborn men together to discuss the money Paulo's father left him. You don't mind if we join you for a moment, do you?"

Alyssa's mind scrambled for a diplomatic response, but Bianca didn't wait, reaching to pull out a chair.

Paulo didn't bother with diplomacy. "I mind." His words stopped the woman cold. And, though he was talking to his ex-wife, his gaze was fixed on his brother. "I will not pretend we're a happy family sharing a pre-dinner drink."

A flicker of annoyance came and went in Bianca's eyes. The tension upgraded from uncomfortable to stifling, triggering a pause that ground out the seconds into a sci-fi-worthy time warp that lasted forever. Alyssa shifted uncomfortably in her seat, her gaze moving from Bianca, to Paulo, and then to his brother.

Marcos's expression was one step away from pure stone. "This is a waste of time, Bianca." The man said nothing to his brother. "He won't discuss the trust."

The woman turned to her husband, still oddly upbeat. "I'm sure Paulo will be reasonable."

"No, I won't." And without further explanation Paulo stood. "So, if you'll excuse us, Alyssa and I will be leaving."

Bianca's shiny veneer cracked, her desperation oozing to the surface, while Marcos's face took the final step, taking on a look of granite. But at least he was finally acknowledging his brother's presence, even if it was with a glare.

Paulo tossed a thick wad of money on the table and shot

Marcos a smile laced with sarcasm. "Enjoy the meal. And give our regards to the waiter."

Desperate to escape the unhappy atmosphere, Alyssa began to stand, but stopped when Bianca touched her arm. "I believe we have an acquaintance in common, Alyssa." Her rediscovered smile would have done Malibu Barbie proud.

What a piece of work. How could she stand there and pretend everything was fine?

Bianca went on. "At the South Beach Historic Society's luncheon yesterday I ran into Tessa Harrison. We were discussing the wonderful newspaper article about the Meyer reception when your name came up."

The blood in Alyssa's face made a beeline for her toes; it was a good thing she was still sitting or she might have collapsed. No doubt Tessa Harrison had gleefully described Alyssa's arrest. And as her heart rate slowed, each beat growing more forceful than the last, she was sure the thudding vibration would shake the table.

"I have a party I'm planning at the country club." Bianca pulled a business card from her clutch purse and held it out to Alyssa. "I could use some expert advice. Perhaps you could call me sometime to discuss it?"

Acting purely on protocol, Alyssa accepted the card and discreetly removed her arm from the woman's hand. She rose from the table. "Perhaps," she said vaguely. Right about the time she sprouted wings and learned to fly. With a tight smile, she gave a polite nod. "Enjoy your dinner."

Paulo took her arm and steered her toward the elevator. Alyssa trudged along, grateful to escape but still mortified and unable to focus.

"You've lost every ounce of color in your face," he said. After coming to a stop at the door, Paulo pushed the down button, staring at her with a frown. "I'm the first to admit my family is hellaciously unpleasant, but why would the mere mention of Tessa Harrison upset you so much?" With a muted ding, the doors slid open and Paulo led her inside.

Alyssa leaned weakly against the glass wall, ignoring the lights of Miami as the elevator began its descent down the side of the building. Maybe the bottom would swallow her up and ferry her directly to hell. That would be fitting.

"It's nothing," she said, avoiding his gaze.

"You're a lousy liar. You look like you've run into a ghost." He gently turned her face to meet his gaze, his eyes troubled. "What are you not telling me, Alyssa?"

She pulled her chin away and dropped her head back against the wall, exhausted from the encounter. She guessed the decision of how to finish the story had just been made for her. "Osten, the college that was supposed to save my reputation, kicked me out."

"You were expelled?" When she nodded, there was a pause before he asked the inescapable question. "Why?"

She slowly rolled her head along the wall to meet his gaze. "Because I got arrested again."

CHAPTER EIGHT

"DRINK this," Paulo said, breaking the silence.

He held out one of the two tumblers of bourbon in his hands and waited. As Alyssa sat on his living room couch, head resting against the back, eyes closed, he grew concerned by the lack of response. She hadn't said a word since the elevator. After her stunning declaration, he'd silently hustled her to the limousine, because Alyssa looked too strung out for questions.

Her face was white. Lips devoid of color. The circles under her eyes so well defined his gut clenched reflexively at the sight, a twinge pinching his chest.

It was damn disturbing.

But one glance at her and there had been no question he would bring her to his home. He didn't care about the run-in with his duplicitous brother and his ex-wife. Could even put aside hearing about the trust again. Everything was overpowered by the need to ease Alyssa's pain.

Finally, she sent him a weary expression and accepted the drink. "Aren't you tired of watching me fall apart and then shoving refreshments in my hand?"

Though relieved she'd recovered enough to speak, he watched to make sure she took a sip. He should have fed her first, but he suspected they both needed a bit of false courage.

"Aren't you going to say anything?" she said.

"I'm waiting for you to tell me what happened."

"I thought I already did."

He hated how she looked. Vulnerable. Defeated. As if someone had pulled the plug on her sassiness, sucking her spirit down the drain. The need to see the spunk return was fierce. Some color in her face wouldn't hurt either.

As he took a seat his hip brushed hers, sending a firestorm of signals that lit the deep, dark depths of his body. It wasn't a planned move, but Alyssa's cheeks turned pink. While that was a good thing, he pushed his need for her aside.

Now was not the time for a sensual road trip.

He fortified his resolve with a sip of bourbon. "You told me the beginning and the end. I want to hear the middle."

Staring at the drink in her hand, she rubbed her fingers along the glass, as if gathering her thoughts. It was a full minute before she spoke.

"For two years I attended Osten College. Every day I left my rundown neighborhood, taking several buses to reach the beautiful campus filled with beautiful people." Her gaze was unfocused, her voice distant, as if lost in the memories. "I tried to upgrade my wardrobe, just enough so I wouldn't stick out so much. It was hopeless, of course. But all I really wanted was to pretend my past didn't matter."

"That's understandable."

"Perhaps. But my mom kept telling me Osten was a mistake." With a rueful twist of her mouth, she went on. "That most people didn't believe in second chances. But I didn't want to listen." Threading her fingers through her hair, she dropped her voice a notch. "I was so sure she was wrong."

With a forced exhalation, Alyssa leaned forward and rested her elbows on her knees, her drink clutched in her hands. "Except while I was desperately trying to get my degree, to forget about my record and move on, when my classmates found out they made sure I never forgot."

Paulo would have endured a thousand meetings with his brother just to wipe away her unhappy memories. "Life is rarely fair."

"And I *knew* that. But I was too pigheaded to accept it." She frowned, massaging her temple. "I had to push."

"How?" Paulo asked softly.

Her hand dropped to her knee. "Every year Osten arranges a parent-student luncheon. A horribly pompous affair, where the main topic of conversation is who has more money." With a pause, she stared down at her bourbon. "My sophomore year I volunteered to organize it."

"Why am I not surprised?" he said.

"My first official event." She let out an endearingly unladylike snort, but kept her attention on her drink, as if avoiding his gaze. "I spent hours putting it together because I wanted…" Her drawl died out as her fingertips went white against her glass. "I wanted to show them what I could do. To prove that I was more than a hick accent and a criminal past. That I had what it took to produce a glamorous social affair." And then she lifted her gaze to his, the gray eyes haunted, and his chest hitched again. "Ridiculous, right?"

Hit with the need to kiss those eyes closed, to heal her, Paulo gripped his glass instead. Touching her would be dangerous. "Not ridiculous. I busted my ass working for my dad for a similar reason." He laid his arm on the back of the couch. "Everyone wants their work appreciated."

"True," she said with a thoughtful nod. And then, after a sheepish glance, she looked back at her bourbon. "But I was tired of always wearing a waitress uniform to parties. And this was *my* event. So I wanted once, just this once, to wear something special." Her voice turned brittle. "And that's where my motivation runs amok."

She swiped a palm across her eyes, as if to collect herself, and then dropped her hand back to her drink. "I saved for months to buy a designer outfit. And I finally found the perfect one." This time the wan smile was filled with guilt. "Pretty, but not too pretentious. I know it's stupid…" She dropped her gaze to her drink, swirling the amber liquid in her glass. "But when I tried it on in the dressing room it made me feel like one of those guests I was always serving. You know—" she lifted her glass "—classy. Chic. But still me." She tossed back the rest of her bourbon with a grimace. "Of course reality is always the kicker."

"I can see where this is going."

Her mouth turned grim. "Not so hard to figure it out."

"You didn't have enough."

"I was fifty dollars short."

She plunked her tumbler on the coffee table, her words escaping in a defeated rush. "God," she said. "I can't begin to describe how disappointed I was. The party was one day away, and while I sat in the dressing room, trying to figure out what to do…" Pressing her fingers to her mouth, she dropped her voice, the drawl growing thick. "I kept thinkin', 'What's one more time? If I never do it again after today, what difference will it make?' And so I—"

Her voice broke, and she closed her eyes as if unable to go on. Another piece of Paulo's heart melted, and he ignored the alarms clanging in his head as he reached out, lacing his fingers with hers. He could feel the years of remorse in her grip on his hand.

When she turned to look at him, she'd recovered a bit. "I would have succeeded except the owner of the shop was at the party and recognized me." She let out a humorless laugh. "How's that for being served your just deserts?" Pausing, she fixed her gaze on Paulo, the smudge of purple beneath her eyes stark against her pale face. "And two years at Osten was nothing compared to the disgrace of being arrested at an event I'd organized."

The question in her eyes pulled him in as silent seconds passed into a full minute.

Paulo stared at her. He knew she was waiting for him to speak. Waiting for his reaction to her news. But he couldn't put it all together. Her soft skin, her delicate scent, and—far worse—the emotion in the squeeze of her fingers distracted him. The words wouldn't come.

And while he groped for a response Alyssa shot from the couch and crossed the room. "Don't you dare feel sorry for me," she said as turned to face him, folding her arms across her stomach. "Don't you get it? The real tragedy of this story?"

There were so many tragic parts he didn't know where to begin. But he knew what came next was important, and, as painful as it was to watch her suffer, he remained silent. Because he needed to know the answer. *Her* answer.

"It's not the poverty, or the way I was treated, or any of that." She tapped her chest with her fist, enunciating every word. "I wasn't strong enough to rise above it."

She began to pace with a frenetic energy. "I let a few superficial phonies matter. And I forgot the employer who took a risk on me. Forgot the pact I made with my mom. I let

them both down. Let myself down." She clapped her hand
to her forehead and came to a stop. "All over somethin' as
dumb as an *outfit*," she said, as if after all these years she
still couldn't quite believe what she'd done. She closed her
eyes and leaned against the wall, her voice sounding weary.
"Some epitaph that would make. 'Brought down by vanity
and the lust for a designer dress.'"

Gutted by the look on her face, he felt the truth hit him
like a lightning strike, blinding in its clarity. Slowly, he
set down his drink. "I've been racking my brain trying to
figure out why you work so hard," he said, watching her
from across the room. "Why you push yourself." He stood
and went to stand in front of her. He reached out to squeeze
her fingers again. "It isn't going to be enough."

Confusion filled her face. "What?"

"Take it from someone who knows. Whatever you think
you're trying to prove with your business, it won't be
enough."

She drew in a wobbly breath, her hand clamped around
his. "Without my business, I'm nothing more than a—"

With a press of his lips to hers, he cut off the sentence
before she could complete it.

He had no idea what words she would have used to finish
the statement. But, whatever was about to spill from her
mouth, it wasn't true. Whatever she believed about herself,
she was wrong. And, though he'd only meant to stop her, he
allowed himself a moment to gather her lips deeper, to linger
in the softness and the woodsy-sweet taste of bourbon.

After releasing her lips, he lifted his hand and gently
cupped her jaw, but his tone was firm. "Everything you've
been through has made you strong. Your business wouldn't
be the success it is today without that trait."

He could see the rebuttal forming on her lips, and he cut
her off, trying again. "The most respected people on this

planet are those who can admit where they went wrong and go on to be better people. Just like you." The uncertainly in her face triggered a powerful protective urge, and his voice went low, insistent. "Everyone makes mistakes. No one is perfect. And while you're hell-bent on this life sentence you've appointed yourself—" hating the doubt in her eyes, he pulled her into his arms "—you're missing out on a future."

With a sigh, she leaned her forehead against his chest. "I'm not missing out. I'm just..." Her hands clutched his shirt, as if holding on for dear life. And with a sniff she went on, her voice fragile. "Just puttin' it on hold."

His heart slipped as he gathered her closer, like tires spinning out from beneath him. The momentum was frightening. And if he wasn't careful he'd crash for sure.

"Concentrate on who you are now, Alyssa," he said softly. "Let the past go."

As the minutes passed, he struggled to regain his equilibrium. But then he felt her fingers fumbling at his shirt, opening his buttons, and her lips landed on his skin. A kick of desire shot from his chest and landed with precision in his groin. Adding more weight to the unbalanced feeling.

His body demanded satisfaction, but he eased his hips away. "Alyssa," he said in warning. He couldn't do this now. No matter how much he wanted her. But she just popped the last button and looked up at him, her lids rimmed red. With a look of trust in her eyes that flattened him.

What had he done?

"No." He reached for her elbows. But she ignored him, pulling his shirt from his pants. Her hands slid down his chest as she brushed kisses along the open path. When her mouth landed on his abdomen, his muscles clenched in pleasure. "Alyssa, wait."

And then she dropped to her knees and nipped his erection through his pants.

Flames flared, and Paulo hissed, pulling her chin up. *"Don't,"* he said, staring down at her face. "You're tired. Feeling vulnerable." The frank passion in her luminous gray eyes was almost his undoing, but he felt wrung out. Too close to her. All the carefully constructed barriers he'd been fighting to keep in place had just received a potentially lethal hit. And being caught between the need to regain some distance and the maddening desire to consume her was pure hell. Ignoring the disappointment, he went on. "Now isn't the time."

"Yes…." Alyssa pushed his hips firmly against the wall and tugged open his zipper. "It is." After tugging down his pants, she palmed his shaft and ran her tongue from the base to the tip. The visceral hit was brutal, and a second hiss escaped his lips. He should push her away. But all he managed was to feel the sweat beading at his temples.

"I want you like this." Her words drawled against his skin. "And—" she licked his head "—don't stop before you're through." She lowered her mouth.

With a groan, Paulo arched his hips, delving deep. Alyssa moaned her approval, the sound vibrating around his erection. And, with her mouth boldly pleasuring him, she reached up to rake her nails down his chest, catching a flat nipple on the way.

Paulo shuddered and snapped.

Alyssa heard Paulo swear. He grabbed her wrists and pulled her up, whirling to pin her hands high on the wall above her head. Stunned, she stared at him. His shirt open, their bodies were pressed together from his bared chest down to his hips. His tone was low, harsh. "Why are you doing this?"

The words burst from her mouth. "Because I want you to stop holding back." She pressed her lips together, hating that she sounded so desperate.

Because now, after sharing her story, this man who knew all she'd done still looked at her the same way. *Still* had faith in her. A faith that scrubbed away the last traces of shame that clung to her like a tenacious stain.

And left her with a need that went beyond anything she'd felt before.

Yet every time he'd made love to her she'd known he was steering the event. Keeping his passion in check while she was reduced to a whimpering mess. And she wanted to drive him so crazy that he let out a shout. Like he did to her.

As she watched the internal battle in his eyes, tears pricked her lids. He'd had such a profound impact on her life. Touched her on so many levels. She was afraid that every time they'd made love it had been all about *her*.

And hadn't left a dent in his memory.

"I need you to lose control," she said.

Fury flared in his eyes as he thrust his erection against her belly, and the thrill had her body softening in response. His voice was rough, ragged. "You think I can control this?" He arched again, his shaft a band of steel. His eyes dropped to her breasts, mashed against him, and the tips puckered in response. "Your nipples beg when I walk in the room and it drives me insane."

They stared at each other, chests heaving. The demand for release intensified. With every brush against hard muscle, her body grew tighter.

Paulo lowered his mouth to her ear, and the growl in his voice dropped an octave. "Do you know how much I crave the feel of you coming against my lips?" Her breath caught, drowning in fire. He lifted his head, his mouth hovering over hers as he held her against the wall, his face angry. "Hearing your spicy Southern words egging me on?"

Alyssa cried out and crushed her lips to his, and their mouths melded in desperation, frantic. She wanted to touch him. To stroke his skin. Anywhere. *Everywhere.* To fuse them together. To hold on to this moment so it would last forever.

Frustrated by the impossibility, she pulled her hands free and clutched his face, nipping hard at his lower lip. Paulo shoved the hem of her skirt to her waist and lifted her, pinning her with his hips. With her legs wrapped around him, their mouths still locked, he dragged his thumbs across her nipples. The stab of pleasure was followed by a desperate thrust of his hips, and she savored his power, his passion. It was heaven. Nirvana. Supreme bliss.

This savage need they shared.

Then he shifted her higher, and Alyssa dragged his face to her breasts. She dropped her head back with a moan as Paulo feasted on her body through fabric, driving Alyssa to rock her hips. "Take me. *Now,*" she gasped.

His hands cupped her buttocks, and Paulo's mouth hungrily sought out her lips as he carried her down the hall to his bedroom.

"You know I can't resist you." He deposited her on the bed, yanking off his shirt and her panties, not bothering with his pants or her clothes. Fingers gripping her thighs, he spread her legs. She was overcome with the need to give him everything. All that she had.

This man who wanted her so badly, who saw her for who she was.

And liked it.

With no time for her to catch her breath, or for her body to gently adjust to his, he drove his shaft deep.

Paulo heard Alyssa's gasp and began a demanding rhythm, a mating that was pure possession. It was wild, unruly, bordering on too much, too soon. He knew he should slow down, let her body acclimatize to his, but he couldn't. Because she hitched her knees higher, hot, wet, begging him for more, her skin damp. And with every reach of his hips he went a little deeper. Surged higher.

Straightening his arms, he arched his back to better angle his hips between her legs. "Alyssa," he groaned.

The muscles in his chest and biceps tensed as he plunged deep, again and again. The feel of his body joined with hers drove him forward. This terrible, destructive desire to imprint himself on her. To leave a mark and brand her his forever.

The room filled with the slick sound of skin on skin, the smell of sweat. The erotic sensations worked their magic, softening her, until Paulo buried himself to the base of his erection. "Oh, God," he breathed. But still...it wasn't enough.

Damn it. Why wasn't it enough?

Agitated, he clasped her shoulders to hold her in place as his movements grew rough, reckless. He felt feverish. Burning with the fire that was consuming him. Tearing him down and building him back up. Hating the loss of control.

And loving it.

He stared down at her, and their gazes locked. "Is this what you wanted?" he said hoarsely.

"Yes." She should look frightened, as disturbed as he felt. Instead, there was only ecstasy. *"Yes."*

With a guttural groan the last of his reserve splintered, and his hips bucked madly. Eager, throaty gasps escaped her with every thrust. Arching her neck in pleasure, Alyssa braced her hands on the headboard, inflaming him with her provocative words. The bed thumped against the wall. He was desperate to end the agony. To satisfy this need that was devouring him bit by bit. Bite by bite. Taking pieces of him he knew he'd never get back.

And then she came undone.

With a final violent thrust, Paulo threw back his head with a shout. Alyssa clutched his body, holding him deep inside her as the powerful orgasm released its hold on him, the magnitude crushing in its painful pleasure.

Alyssa woke at midnight to the sound of distant thunder and the feel of Paulo's body spooned against her back, his arms around her waist. A storm was approaching. She could hear the gusts of wind, the rustling of tree branches, and their occasional scrape against his bedroom window.

Between the grueling discussion about her past and their explosive lovemaking, she had been mentally and physically whipped. Paulo had fixed a simple meal and brought it to her in bed. Once they'd eaten, she'd been incapable of anything beyond the need for sleep. He had pulled her close, the tenderness in his touch like a healing salve, and she'd drifted off, at peace. And full of something she hadn't felt in years…

Optimism. Hope for the future.

Ten years of being petrified she'd let her image slip— saying the wrong thing, *doing* the wrong thing—was a grinding wear and tear to her psyche that had slowly eroded her strength. She was exhausted from the sheer effort of keeping up her guard. But with Paulo she didn't have to measure her every word, her every response.

In bed or out.

And the happiness was so new, so unexpected, she wanted to cling to it for as long as she could. She didn't want to waste precious time with Paulo engaged in an internal debate about the choices she'd made since her arrest. That could come later.

Much, much later.

A streak of lightning lit the room, and Paulo shifted. "You're still here." His words hummed against her ear. "I thought I'd wake up alone again."

Raindrops began to splatter against the window, and she snuggled closer to Paulo, his king-size bed warm and inviting. "I'm too comfortable."

"Good," he said as he tightened his arms around her waist. "Because the whole point of the morning after is to indulge in more of what went on the night before."

"I don't know if I want to repeat all of tonight."

"Mmm," he murmured. "How about just the best parts?" he said with a sexy rumble.

A second smile touched her lips. But despite the incredible memories his words had resurrected, the awkward moment with his brother and ex-wife flashed in her mind. Obviously that was one part of the evening *he* didn't wish to repeat. He hadn't broached the subject of their encounter with his family, and she was positive he wouldn't bring it up. Watching his tight face during the encounter had been difficult.

Alyssa absently rubbed her fingers against his arm, the rough hair coarse. "I'm sorry about the run-in with Marcos and Bianca."

A few moments passed before he replied, "It doesn't matter."

Her fingers stalled on his arm. He'd been nonchalant about the subject before, and this discussion was never going to be easy, but surely, after everything they had just been through he would feel more at ease talking to her now?

"It had to have hurt when she left you for Marcos." When

he didn't respond, she went on. "And your brother's actions must have hurt your relationship with him, too."

His harsh scoff came out close to her ear. "The only thing Marcos and I ever shared was an unfriendly competition at work."

Alyssa twisted in his arms to look up at him. "You two were never close?"

Another jagged flash of lightning lit his face, complete with a Rochester-esque scowl that would've had Jane Eyre swooning in her shoes. When the accompanying grumble of thunder finally arrived, Alyssa waited for the sound to pass, and then his reply. But the silence was only broken by the increasing force and frequency of pattering rain.

Paulo rolled onto his back, his left arm still beneath her waist, and finally spoke. "Six months before I left the business, I approached my father about creating a boutique line within the company." It wasn't an answer to her question, but Alyssa waited, knowing the story was important. "I wanted to take our older, smaller hotels and renovate them. Restore them to their original designs." The light was dim, but as he stared up at the ceiling she could just make out the frown on his mouth. "And I wanted the Samba to be the first. But, as usual, Marcos and I..." He hesitated before going on. "We disagreed about the idea."

She sensed those disagreements had been heated. "So what happened?"

"My father had a stroke, throwing the company into chaos. And then, four months later, while Marcos and I were still arguing about my proposal, Dad died from complications."

The story was recounted with as much emotion as it took to read a grocery list. But the loss of his father must have been tough. "I'm sorry."

His reply was wooden. "Don't be."

She couldn't tell if he was glad his dad was dead, or missed him terribly, or any of the countless variations in between. And his refusal to talk was daunting. Ignoring the pang of disappointment, she boldly pressed on. Persistence was her only ally. "If Marcos and Bianca's relationship doesn't bother you, why are you refusing to talk to your brother about the trust?"

The frown grew deeper. "Because there's nothing to talk about."

Her forehead crinkled with concern. "You don't expect me to believe that, do you?"

"I don't want the money."

Alyssa propped her head on her hand. "Why not?"

The fingers beneath her hip growing tight. "Because I don't need it."

"But don't you feel an obligation to honor your father's last wishes?"

With his free hand, Paulo raked his hair from his forehead. And as she waited the frustration grew. One night of feeling unbelievably close to him had rocked the very foundation of her world. She was different. Irrevocably altered. Hadn't it changed anything for him? Hadn't he felt the slightest shift in their relationship?

Feeling an overwhelming need to press the issue, she went on. "Why won't you answer the question?"

Paulo pulled his hand from her waist. "It's been a long day. And we're both tired." His voice was low, laced with fatigue. He rolled over to face the wall. "Get some sleep, Alyssa."

She stared at his back, listening to the sound of the rain pummel the window, confused. And hurt. After letting every ounce of her soul pour out for him to see, he still didn't feel comfortable talking to her.

With an ominous feeling, a massive caution light was

blinking in her brain. Flashing brighter than the lightning that streaked across the night sky. And if she were smart she'd start paying attention. Problem was, when it came to Paulo nothing about her was smart. And she realized she'd gone and made another mistake. Another *horrible* mistake.

She'd fallen in love with Paulo Domingues.

CHAPTER NINE

AT 2:00 a.m., Paulo leaned against the wall of the patio outside his bedroom, staring at the shifting lights in his pool. The storm had passed, leaving the smell of damp earth and a heavy humidity, and it pressed in on him. Despite the rain, it was still hot. And the temperature, the black night, along with the moisture in the air, all combined until it became a wet, oppressive box. Inside the house, it was air-conditioned and cool, but Alyssa still slept in his bed, and he didn't want to wake her.

He felt bruised. Battered. And beat up.

When he'd brought her to his home he hadn't counted on being completely gutted by her story. The unbearable need to put her world right. Much less the alarming look of absolute trust she'd given him. And when she'd finally unleashed her wild side, a hellcat in bed, it had knocked his control out of the park.

Once that wall had been breached, he was powerless to stop it.

Restless, he crossed the small porch and leaned his elbows on the rail, frowning as he watched the pool light shimmy, flickering blue ghosts against the trees. He should have ended their affair when she'd continued to question him about his family. But he couldn't seem to bring himself to do it. Instead, like an idiot, he'd told her about the argument with Marcos. Granted, it was a diluted version of the story—like watered-down Scotch, it didn't sting as much going down—but he'd thought it would satisfy her. But it hadn't been enough.

Would probably never be enough.

And the more he gave, the more Alyssa would want. She was tough. Tenacious. With her childhood, she'd had to be. But as she'd continued to push and push, the warier he'd become…and the more she'd sounded like Bianca.

Stifling him. Cutting off his air just as surely as a constraining wedding ring around his finger. Over the course of his year of marriage Bianca had grown pushier, needier, and that circle of gold had grown tighter, until it had felt like he was choking.

And he was choking now.

He sank into the patio chair and scrubbed his face in frustration.

From the moment he'd met Alyssa he'd been in over his head. What he needed now was space. Room to catch his breath. Things had gotten out of hand and way too intense. It was time to back off for a bit. With any luck, by putting a little distance between them and this evening, he could ease them back into the simple affair this was meant to be.

And if that wasn't enough for Alyssa, then it would be time to move on.

Three days later Alyssa sat on her couch, a shot of whiskey in her hand. The publicity from the wedding reception had taken on a life of its own, and her cellular had been ringing non-stop. And thank goodness, too, because she was left with nothing but work to keep her busy.

After the life-altering evening with Paulo, he'd told her to see Charles with any problems and then left for Boca Raton to check out a hotel for sale. This afternoon he'd called to ask her to meet him at Nick's club tomorrow. The conversation had been short, with Paulo avoiding every question she'd asked.

With a sigh, she tucked her bare feet beneath her. Things were going so well at work there was little doubt Paulo now had complete faith in her abilities as an event planner. She'd reached her goal. Secured her dream job. And she'd ruined it all by falling in love with a man who didn't do wedding rings anymore.

Love.

Damn, girl. Don't pretend you didn't see this parade of pain coming.

Her breath whooshed out in a hiss, and she traced the furrow between her brows. He'd offered a few weeks of fun and sex, and now she wanted more. And there was a vast void that spanned the space between a casual fling and forever.

A sharp knock was followed by a jingle of metal. There was only one person who had a key to her apartment.

Her mother entered and spotted her on the couch. "Oh, here you are." She closed the door and tossed the keys on a chair. "I dropped by the Samba to find out your plans for dinner…" Her gaze fell to Alyssa's glass, and her movements grew slow, as if sensing the negative vibes. "I think I'll join you." She headed into the kitchen and grabbed a glass from the cupboard, returning to plop down next to Alyssa. "So, what's wrong?"

Alyssa rubbed her glass with her fingers. "Work has been busy, and I wanted to relax." As she summoned the energy to tell the truth, she watched her mother pick up the almost full bottle of whiskey from the coffee table and pour herself a shot.

"It's six o'clock and you're already home." Her mom narrowed her eyes, her gaze dropping back to Alyssa's hand. "You're not turning into an alchy, are you?" Without waiting for an answer, she plunked the bottle on the table. "I think you need to slow down. Lord knows, the pace you keep would drive me to drink." She brushed at her bright blond feathery bangs, frowning at her own glass. "Though I'd prefer a beer to this stuff. Anyway, my friend told me about this new rehab clinic down on—"

"Mom," she said, unable to take it anymore, "I'm not an alcoholic."

Her mother settled deeper into the sofa, as if preparing for a long story. "So what's the problem?"

"I slept with Paulo Domingues."

"Lyssa." Her mother sat up, twisting to face her on the couch. Alyssa braced for her reaction, and after a moment of shocked silence her mom reached out to touch her hand. "I'm so proud of you."

Flabbergasted, Alyssa rested her glass on her jean clad knee. "After five years of working hard to build my business, you're *proud* of me for sleeping with a client?"

"You took a risk. You put yourself out there." She gave Alyssa's hand a final pat. "Good for you."

Alyssa briefly closed her eyes. Not so good for her. She'd taken a risk and fallen hard. Her voice went low, and she asked the question that had been swirling in her mind since Paulo had left town. "How am I supposed to work with him now?"

"Well, if you quit, would it be horrible of me if I dated his manager?" As Alyssa absorbed the news, her mother tried to look innocent while sipping her whiskey. "Charles asked me out to dinner." For the first time ever, Alyssa saw her mother blush. "He's really very sweet."

Sweet. Charles. *Sweet?* Alyssa blinked, trying to picture it, and then finally gave up. Some things were just beyond her comprehension. And, since her mother was one of them, perhaps the two were meant to be.

Unlike her and Paulo. A piercing fear robbed her of her breath.

"I reckon that's enough about me. What do *you* want?" her mother said.

The impossible, apparently. "I want Paulo," Alyssa said. "I love him."

"Then go after him, honey."

"He doesn't want commitment."

"Fiddle-faddle. Men don't know what they want. It's up to us to show them."

Alyssa sent her a wan smile. She'd inherited her mother's stubbornness, and her accent, but she didn't come close to touching her confidence. As time ticked by, Alyssa couldn't think of a response, and a sober look slowly washed over her mother's face.

"I was too young to be a parent," her mom said. "And I know I made mistakes."

Alyssa went still, stunned by the expression and the words. Her mother rarely admitted to anything. She preferred to pretend all was well even when things were falling apart, which had been constant when Alyssa was little. "It's okay, Mom."

"No, it's not."

"You did the best you could."

"Maybe. I'm real sorry my choices made your life so difficult." She shook her head, her massive hoop earrings swinging. "But I never regretted having you." The fine lines around her eyes eased as her expression softened. "That's all I want for you, baby. A life without regrets."

A lump formed in Alyssa's throat, and she swallowed hard, trying to clear it.

"So," her mom said, the easy-breezy smile returning to her face. "How 'bout I swing by the Samba tomorrow and take you to lunch?"

Amused by the lightning change, Alyssa sent her a tiny smile. "I'd like that."

"Good." Her mother pushed up off the couch. "Now, while you think of a way to straighten out your boyfriend, your momma is gonna make us some dinner."

Watching her go, Alyssa slumped against the couch and twirled a lock of hair in her finger.

A life without regrets.

It sounded good, but where did she go from here? Just thinking about her feelings for Paulo left her lungs tight and a sick feeling in her stomach. And after tossing and turning all night the only thing she knew for sure was that she couldn't give up. But how did you reach a man who refused to talk about his feelings?

With the sound of pots clinking in the kitchen, Alyssa listened to her mother singing a country song. Despite their problems, she could always count on her mom. Her love. And her loyalty. And, although Alyssa's childhood had been difficult, there was one thing she was beginning to truly understand: being wealthy didn't necessarily make it any easier.

She knew Paulo's time at his father's business had been tough. And if his family's only concern was money and success, maybe communication wasn't a priority at his home? Perhaps he didn't talk about the painful parts because he'd never been shown how?

Despite his horrendous treatment by Marcos and Bianca,

it was his father that he refused to discuss. And maybe, just maybe, if she learned the secret to their relationship, convinced him to accept the money and get past whatever was eating at him, it might allow him to let her in, too. Outside of Nick, who was probably too loyal to share the truth, the only other person who might be willing to discuss the matter with her was Bianca.

Alyssa dropped her gaze to her cellular, resting on the coffee table. When she'd opened the email from Paulo's ex-wife, requesting her help again, Alyssa had planned on deleting it, but never got the chance. There was no telling what Tessa Harrison had said to Bianca, and Alyssa dreaded the thought of dealing with her plastic smile again, but it was one way to learn about Paulo's father. A long shot, maybe. And, considering how Paulo might feel about it, definitely risky. But she was used to both.

Alyssa twisted her whiskey glass on her knee, eyeing her phone with apprehension. When he'd called today, Paulo wouldn't even elaborate on why he wanted to meet her at the club. Somehow she didn't think it was to profess an undying love for her.

With a sigh, she reached for her cellular and began her search for Bianca's number.

Bianca Domingues was the only woman Alyssa knew who made a white tennis skirt and a ponytail look chic.

"I can't thank you enough for helping me, Alyssa," Bianca said.

Her kindness was surprising, but so was Bianca's request for help with her *wedding anniversary.*

Alyssa's apprehension had climbed higher at the news, and she'd hesitated. But after a few seconds of intense deliberation she'd proceeded anyway. Because, although she planned on trying to learn a little about Paulo's dad, her arrangement with Bianca wasn't personal. It was purely a business deal.

And if anyone would understand that, it was Paulo.

After questioning Bianca for half an hour on the phone, Alyssa had landed on the perfect theme. When she'd arrived at her home today to present it, Bianca had graciously served up refreshments in her manicured backyard, the view overlooking the tennis courts and the Atlantic beyond.

"The country club has been marvelously accommodating on such short notice," Bianca said. "But their ideas were a little—" she wrinkled her nose, shifting the sprinkle of freckles on her sun dappled face, red hair gleaming in the light "—ordinary," she finished. Her eyes lit with excitement as she leaned forward. "I absolutely adore your idea for a theme."

It was impossible to hold back a smile at her infectious enthusiasm. "I'm glad you're pleased." Alyssa took a sip of her iced tea before going on. "We were lucky the vendor's casino tables were available. Passing out chips to your guests and indulging in a Monte Carlo fantasy will certainly be different."

Bianca's smile grew bigger. "Marcos loved the gaming clubs during our honeymoon there."

Which hardly matched Alyssa's impression of the man. Then again, nothing was turning out as expected. After all the time she'd spent fretting about meeting the woman again, it had turned out to be a wasted expenditure of angst.

"Up until now, we always left town for our anniversary." Bianca's smile slowly faded. "After all the vile things the newspapers printed after we married…" She blushed, and with a delicate shrug abandoned the sentence. "But this year Marcos has been working so hard, has been gone so much, I decided at the last minute it was time to celebrate at home." Bianca squarely met Alyssa's gaze, as if daring her to question the decision.

But Alyssa understood the need to stop running from the past. "I'll finalize the plans with the vendor today."

Bianca reached out to touch Alyssa's hand, her eyes full of gratitude. "Thank you," she said. "I know I'm paying you for your time, but if there is anything I can do for you—anything at all—please let me know."

Suspicion snaked along Alyssa's stomach. The same sensation she'd had when she talked to Nick at the track. She couldn't shake the feeling Paulo's ex-wife was trying to tell her something. Twisting her glass on the table, Alyssa gathered her courage. "I was hoping you could tell me a little about Paulo's father."

Bianca looked surprised at the question. After a moment, she picked up her drink and paused, studying her glass with great care. "Ricardo was my godfather. He was a wonderful man and very generous to me." She took a sip before going on. "But he wasn't overly affectionate toward his sons. And he was particularly hard on them after they joined the company." She set her glass carefully on the table and went on. "Most would probably say he was too hard. But I believe he had the best of intentions. Running Domingues International is not for the faint of heart." Pride crept across her face. "Marcos is very good at what he does."

After another pause, Bianca reached for a canapé. "Which brings me to a second favor I'd like to ask of you. You seem to have captured Paulo's attention," Bianca said. Alyssa's eyes widened a fraction, and Bianca sent her a deliberate look. "I was hoping you could convince him to come to my party."

Blinking back her surprise, Alyssa sat back in her chair. Despite Paulo's insistence that his brother and ex-wife were welcome to each other, she doubted that extended to Paulo attending their anniversary party. "I don't think he would listen to me," she said truthfully.

Hors d'oeuvres in her hand, Bianca's face hardened with determination. "I really want to see Paulo put an end to this ridiculous vendetta. Marcos has suffered enough."

Marcos has suffered? She watched Bianca daintily nibble on a cracker topped with crab salad. How could the woman say that with a straight face? Because from where Alyssa was sitting—admittedly a position that was starting to feel like complete ignorance—Marcos wasn't the one who had suffered.

"Did Paulo leave the family business because of you and your husband's marriage?" Alyssa said.

Bianca coughed and wiped her mouth with a napkin. With a frown, she finally lowered her hand to the table. "Paulo didn't tell you?" Heat crept up Alyssa's cheeks, which must have been answer enough. "Of course he didn't." Bianca leaned back and crossed her arms. "He hasn't changed a bit. Even after a year of marriage, I never could get him to share anything with me, either."

The news was hard to hear, and Alyssa felt like a lead weight was growing in her chest.

The redhead continued. "It was never made public knowledge, but when my godfather died he left the business to Marcos. That was when Paulo left."

Alyssa stared at Bianca, shocked by the news. Dissed by his own father. What kind of man favored one son over another? And why should she have to learn everything about him off the internet and from his ex-wife?

Bianca seemed oblivious to Alyssa's shock. "Paulo was so driven to outdo Marcos and prove himself to his dad," she went on. "I could have been happy, despite his grungy clothes and workaholic ways, if he had simply opened up." Bianca's face turned pensive, and profoundly...sad. "But finally I accepted the fact that he could never learn to love me the way I loved him."

The lead weight in Alyssa's chest grew heavier. This was not the story she'd come to hear. Nor was it the story the newspapers had told. Fashion snob, maybe, but the cold, calculating woman was nowhere to be found.

"And then my godfather had a stroke—" Bianca's voice broke a little, and she cleared her throat before she continued. "I was so unhappy, and Paulo was no help." Her gaze drifted to the turquoise waters, hurt evident in her expression. "Every time I tried to discuss it with him, he'd turn his back on me."

The words struck with the force of a twenty-foot tidal wave, and the blood slowly seeped from Alyssa's face, robbing her of the power of speech. She remembered the sight of his back and the feeling it produced. Heart pounding, Alyssa desperately reached for her iced tea. She took a tasteless sip, struggling to get it down, only half listening as Bianca went on.

"But Marcos was wonderfully supportive. And as we dealt with Ricardo's illness, we grew closer." Bianca looked at Alyssa again. "Over time, I realized I'd married the wrong brother."

Alyssa felt ill, the nausea growing with every passing second, and she *so* didn't want to throw up here.

"I'm sorry," Bianca said softly. "I know how frustrating it is to love Paulo and not be able to reach him."

Alyssa didn't want to hear anymore. Didn't want to discuss Paulo with Bianca. She needed to escape. Her hands fumbled as she reached for her purse. "I should be going now. I have an evening appointment," she said as she stood.

In truth, she had to meet Paulo at Nick's club.

How ironic.

"I'll call you after I've made the final arrangements with

the vendor," Alyssa said with a tight smile, and then took off across the closely cropped lawn.

She managed to get about five feet before the woman spoke again. "Alyssa?" Bianca said.

Alyssa's heart dropped. There would be no escape yet. She stopped and slowly turned to face the lady.

"Tessa Harrison told me she contacted a *Miami Insider* reporter about you," Bianca said. Alyssa's heart sank further, settling to her toes like a stone as Bianca continued. "Your past is none of my business, so I haven't discussed it with anyone." Compassion filled her face. "But I thought you deserved to know."

Staring at her blankly, Alyssa managed to mutter her thanks, and then headed off again, her mind reeling from the double dose of bad news.

But the truth about Paulo's marriage was more disturbing than a vague threat of possible exposure in a tabloid magazine. Dazed, she made her way toward Bianca's driveway, and then she heard the distant sound of the surf. On impulse, she slipped off her pumps and carried them, cutting through the sea oats on a well-used path.

Feet sinking in the sand, she aimlessly wandered along the beach, lost in thought. The marriage itself hadn't bothered her. Plenty of people made the commitment, only to have it fall apart. Divorce didn't ruin a person for relationships forever.

When he'd insisted he didn't make promises, Alyssa had assumed it was because he was wary of being hurt again. But ratcheting up her torture meter to intolerable levels was the news he'd hurt Bianca first. Repeatedly. Treating his wife the same way he was treating Alyssa now.

With a heavy heart, Alyssa climbed the steps of a boardwalk running along a public beach, her legs tired from trudging through sand. An empty bench nestled under the cool cover of a palm tree was too tempting to pass, and she collapsed onto the seat, gaze fixed on the sunlight glistening off the water. She smelled salt. She felt the warm breeze.

But would she ever feel normal again?

A couple wandered by and settled onto a towel to soak up the sun, making goo-goo eyes at each other. The sight of people in love, enjoying their life, had never bothered her before.

She let out a heavy sigh. Life had been so simple before Paulo coaxed her into an affair. She'd been satisfied with days full of nothing but her business. But now...

A Pandora's box of discontent had been thrown wide open, and there was no going back.

And it wasn't as if the thought of strolling along the beach *alone* was appealing. She wanted Paulo with her. Forever. Alyssa gripped the edge of the wooden seat.

He'd turned his back on Bianca, just as he had her.

She pressed her lids closed. But she couldn't simply take Bianca's word about their less than ideal marriage. It wouldn't be fair. There were two sides to every relationship story, and she needed to know Paulo's.

And, no matter how much he didn't want to discuss it, when she met up with him tonight she had every intention of finding out.

"Do you always park the Ducati on the sidewalk entryway?"

At the sound of Alyssa's voice, Paulo turned from the rail lining the dance floor of the cavernous club fashioned after an old warehouse. Neon lights pulsed in time with the music. People filled every nook and cranny. But in jeans and a pink blouse, hair pulled back in a matching scarf, Alyssa was more beautiful than every woman in the room. His body went incredibly hard and inexplicably soft, all at the same time.

"The security guys at the door watch her for me," he finally said.

She lifted a brow dryly. "I hope you at least pay them for babysitting."

His lips twitched, and she sent him a tiny smile as they stared at each other.

He had done what he'd set out to do, spending the last two days buried in his review of the numbers at the Ocean Inn. Taking a breather. Clearing his head. Now he was just glad to be back, struck with the urgent need to hold her again.

Not wanting to break the spell, he silently took her hand and led her onto the now dimly lit dance floor, pulling her close as a slow song started up. "It's good to have you back in my arms," he said. He leaned in to inhale her floral scent.

"I've been waiting to talk to you."

"Talk?" Fingers flexing against her hips, he brought her flush against him, and a dark look flickered in Alyssa's eyes. Pleased with her reaction, he leaned in for a kiss.

Alyssa stopped him with a hand to his chest. "Look, Romeo," she said dryly. "You can't just waltz back into my life and start putting the moves on me."

He shifted his gaze to her hair and rubbed a silky lock between his fingers, forcing the conversation back to a light tone. "I don't think I should be compared to Romeo. His plan was flawed. Worse, he fell for a lady who made poor choices, too." He hiked a brow. "What kind of woman stabs herself through the heart?"

"A woman devastated by the loss of love." She stared at him, and the pause stretched as the blood grew heavy in his veins. "Because, unlike us, Romeo and Juliet were *really* involved."

Paulo frowned at her serious expression. He might not want anything permanent, but he wouldn't pretend their time together wasn't special. His movements slowed until their feet were barely shifting on the floor. The sensual slide of thigh on thigh left a smoldering ache in its wake, and his grip on her hip grew tight. "We've spent an extraordinary amount of time together for two people who aren't involved."

Alyssa's chin rose stubbornly. "Time together at work doesn't count," she said. The pink tinge to her cheeks brought out her gray eyes, and the way she hitched her breath had her lovely chest heaving erotically against him.

Damn if he didn't want her again.

And he wouldn't let her dismiss their sizzling chemistry so easily. He lowered his mouth close to hers and arched his body against hers, nearly groaning out loud at the instant agonizing pleasure. "How about when you pushed me against the wall of my living room?" His voice was husky from the memory. "Does that count?"

Shifting from pink to red, her face lost a little of its confidence. "No, the sex doesn't count either."

Frustration surged. "The hell it doesn't," he growled, and took her lips with his.

One hand securing her neck, he slaked his mouth across hers, while the other hand clutched her buttock, pressing his erection firmly against her. He wanted her to *feel* his powerful reaction. Because, despite her words, it was a reaction they shared. Her lips went soft, compliant, and the desire expanded until it devoured him.

Alyssa ripped her mouth away. "Stop." She pushed against him. He stared at her as he fought for breath, his chest heaving, his heart thundering beneath her hand. "You can't seduce your way out of this conversation," she said.

Paulo stepped back, raking an aggravated hand through his hair. He wanted to have this talk about as much as he wanted to contract a deadly disease. And certainly not with an audience.

He took her hand. "Let's take this to the VIP room."

CHAPTER TEN

As they threaded through the crowd, Alyssa's body still vibrated from the scorching kiss. It was hopeless. Being in love made her reaction to the man unbearable. But, as painful as it had been to pull away, she couldn't let him distract her.

Blinded by nerves, she followed along as he led her up a metal staircase along the far wall, across a landing, and into a small room with leather furniture. A massive picture window overlooked the dance floor below.

Paulo rounded the corner bar. "Would you like a cocktail?"

"Club soda, please."

"Sure you don't need a splash of something in it?"

Alyssa took a seat and crossed her legs, bracing for the discussion. "Quite sure."

He poured her a drink. "So what do you want to talk about, Alyssa?"

"Us." He cocked his head, waiting, and she went on. "You know every gory detail about me, yet I know very little about you." She'd *thought* she did. But today had proved just how mistaken she'd been. And it cut to the quick. "I'm not happy with how one-sided our relationship has become."

He carefully set the bottle of club soda down, a line between his eyebrows as he studied her. "You were on board with my conditions from the start."

"The conditions that our relationship would be based on work and sex?" She'd been stupid enough to think that would make it *easier*. Heaven help her, how wrong could she get? "Your plan also allowed for a couple of weeks, at best."

Frowning, he dropped his hand to his side. "Maybe I've changed my mind about the time limit."

Hope swelled, but she ignored it. She linked her fingers at the end of her knee. "An affair that lasts an eternity can't replace a relationship that's deep enough to have an honest discussion."

As he crossed the floor with her club soda, his tone went firm. "There's nothing to discuss." With a guarded expression, he handed her the drink. Heat flashed in his eyes as their fingers brushed.

Skin tingling, her stomach took a free fall in desperate need of a parachute. Good Lord, the man could befuddle her brain with a simple touch. Clutching the glass, she held his gaze. But it was time to get to the meat of the matter. "I picked up a new event today." Confusion swept across his face, and Alyssa took a sip before going on, regretting it wasn't stronger. "Bianca hired me." As his expression slowly fell, her heart rate rose.

Courage, Alyssa. Courage.

"I'm helping with her anniversary plans," she finished.

With a stunned face, he stared at her, his voice gruff with disbelief. "You're organizing my brother's anniversary party?"

She worried her lower lip, alarm sending her heart rate

soaring higher. "Not organizing it, no." She adjusted her scarf with shaky fingers. "I'm helping her with the theme."

Gaze fixed on hers, he looked at her as if he'd never seen her before. "Is this your way of manipulating me into discussing my family?"

Her heart stumbled and fell, getting bruised in the process. "Manipulating you?" Though shocked, hurt by his words, Alyssa managed to tip her chin in defiance. "No honor among thieves, you mean?" When he kept silent, she went on, despite the painful wound. "This is my way of learning more about you. Because *you* refuse to be honest enough to tell me."

A dark look flitted through his eyes before they went cold, glittering. His voice dripped with accusation. "My ex-wife is none of your business."

Alyssa froze, staggered by the callous words and frigid delivery. She had hoped for an opening for a frank conversation. But there was none. Only an insult and a harsh reminder she had overstepped the boundaries he'd placed on their relationship.

She bit back the bubble of a hysterical laugh, the absurdity of the moment not lost on her. "I guess she's my business now."

White lines of anger etched firmly around his mouth, he said, "And I'm sure my brother appreciates the use of your skills on his behalf." And then, almost as an afterthought, he went on with a scoff, "No doubt Bianca will be pleased with your work, too."

Marcos. Just like at the restaurant, his anger was directed mainly at Marcos. So who was he mad at most? Bianca, for walking out on him, or his brother for replacing him? Hearing about Paulo's behavior during his marriage, watching his reaction now, she knew it was the latter. Heart growing heavy, she finally touched on the worst discovery of all. The thought she'd been avoiding all day. She'd hoped he'd simply buried the pain, because the memory of being hurt by an old love she could fight.

But if Paulo was simply incapable of love...?

And, as much as she hated to, she had to admit all the evidence was pointing in that direction. Which meant the outlook for a future with Paulo was growing dimmer and dimmer. She closed her eyes against the mounting pile of anguish, trying to focus on her original goal.

After swallowing hard, she met his gaze. "I think Bianca would be more pleased if you accepted your father's money. And ended the feud with your brother," she added.

The look he shot her was sharp. "Then perhaps she shouldn't have dumped me for him."

Her palms grew damp, but she forced herself to remain calm. Because she had to speak her mind. She'd seen the pain on Bianca's face. It was real. Alyssa knew leaving hadn't been easy for her. "Bianca isn't perfect. No one is, as you so prophetically told me yourself. But at least she tried to make the marriage work. Truthfully." She lifted her chin at his budding expression of disbelief. "I think you drove her away."

Paulo stepped closer to the couch. The skeptical fury in his eyes as he stared down at her was a force to behold, and his voice was harsh. "And just what the hell would you know about it?"

She blinked back the hurt, because she knew plenty now. The expression on his face as he froze her out had been chilling. And his thunderous look right now was shattering. "Actually, I know quite a lot," she said unsteadily. And what she'd learned matched Bianca's account, not his. "We had a very illuminating conversation about you."

"She used me."

"I don't believe that."

"You're going to take my ex-wife's version of the truth over mine?"

"When it corresponds with my own version of the truth?" she said. "Yes."

"And what *is* your version of the truth?"

He wouldn't like what she had to say this time either, but she said it anyway. If any hope remained for the two of them, no matter how tiny, it had to come through a ruthless look at his past. An *honest* look. "That you hold back from the people in your life. From me. From your brother. And at one time from your wife. You may have married Bianca, but you never tried to make it work."

He returned to the wall and propped a shoulder against the glass, sarcasm oozing from his voice. "Is that what you think?"

"That's what I think."

"At least I have a life. *Friends.*"

Alyssa ignored the jab. "Friends that don't require much from you."

His eyebrows reached for the roof. "Now you're attacking my loyalty to Nick?"

She shook her head in frustration. "I didn't say you weren't loyal. You are. But Nick doesn't make any demands on you. An aren't-we-good-buddies friendship allows you the freedom to give what you want, when you want, and nothing more." The conclusions she'd reached as he'd treated her so callously came tumbling out, her fingers crushing her glass. "You want a lover for your bed, an easygoing friend, but you don't want anything that resembles a deep relation-ship because—"

"I tried commitment once," he said with a scowl. "And I hated it."

"You didn't try. It was just a ring on your finger and a legal paper filed in your office. And you don't want commitment because it's all about *Paulo*. You want to choose when, what, and how much, if any, you'll share, and—"

"You know what?" he said, cutting her off again as he pushed away from the glass wall. "I didn't sign on for this." He thrust an agitated hand through his hair. "And I have no intention of competing with your idea of the perfect boyfriend. I didn't want to compete with my wife's idea of a perfect husband, and I sure as *hell* got tired of competing for the role of perfect son."

"Don't you get it?" She shot off the couch and crossed the floor to stand in front of him, her tumbler clutched in her hand. "That's what the Samba is all about. You're *still* competing with Marcos." Why was he so blind to the truth? Why couldn't he see it? "But now it's just a pitiful competition for the attentions of a ghost." Surely somewhere, buried beneath all that anger, there must be pain. Dying to get him to let her in—just a little crevice that might lead to more— she reached out to touch his arm as she tried to steady her drawling voice. "Sooner or later you're going to have to let that go, Paulo." Her voice dropped low. "Because you can't win the approval of a dead man."

He pulled his arm from her hand and turned to face the glass. She was left looking at a familiar image. His back. Devastated, she stood still, feeling empty, drained and defeated.

He'd made her laugh, teased her and flirted shamelessly. But he'd also treated her with great tenderness. That proved he was capable of caring, didn't it? Or maybe she was just hoping that was true. Her heart, already bleeding, bled a little more. "Is this really who you want to be?" she croaked hoarsely. "Someone so cold?"

His voice was devoid of emotion. "Are you done?"

She closed her eyes against the pressure of hot tears.

My God, I'm being dismissed.

Paulo stared down at the dance floor for a full minute, filled with the distant thump of music. From her silence behind him, Paulo knew Alyssa was shocked, but she finally replied.

"Not quite done," she said, her voice shaking and thick. "Take your own advice. Let it go, already. Go see your brother. Accept the money from your father. Because the only one you're makin' suffer is yourself."

Paulo felt it all caving in on him again.

Then he heard the sound of the door opening, music spilling loudly into the room and then growing muffled with a click of the latch as it closed.

Alyssa was gone.

Anger bowled into him, returning with such a ferocious impact he had to move. He speared his fingers through his hair and turned to pace the floor. He'd been made the fool again.

Played.

He'd taken off for a few days to get his head on straight, and Alyssa had snuck off behind his back and gotten chummy with his ex-wife.

The turbulent emotion grew exponentially with every step. And he was glad he had stuck to his guns about the commitment. Because as he had stood at the bar, listening to her sabotage any hope of continuing their casual relationship, he'd been tempted to reconsider. And then came her announcement that she'd gone to see Bianca, was planning their *wedding* anniversary, and it had felt like a shotgun blast to the chest, knocking him back with a furious hit.

Footsteps ringing against the wood floor, he reached the wall and turned to keep going. He had been systematically stabbed in the back by every member of his family. His father. His brother. Even his wife. No way was he lining up for more.

He stopped pacing and braced an arm against the window, his mouth working, tightening his grip on the raging emotion.

There was no changing what had happened between them: Alyssa seeking out Bianca and choosing her version over his. Him striking back with his words.

Paulo balled his hand into a fist against the glass and stared, unseeing, down at the dance floor. He still couldn't believe what she'd done. Then again, it had taken him months to recover from Bianca's actions, too. His only solace this time was that the press wasn't involved.

Somehow the consolation didn't help one bit.

Paulo cut through the water, stretching his arms further, pumping his legs harder. His muscles screamed to take a rest. But each time he reached the end of his pool he flipped and kept going, his mind furiously at work.

Over a week had passed since the disaster at the club. And in that time Alyssa had been working from her apartment, while he spent every night at home, punishing himself in the water, both with hard exercise and by replaying their finale in his head.

He had yet to find a safe haven.

They had shared too much at the office. The track offered no relief. And his place was full of memories he'd be struggling to forget until the dawn of the next millennium. Everywhere he went he swore he smelled her perfume. In his living room. In his bedroom. Even on his bike.

There was no escape.

And every time the elusive lilac scent hit him, her absence made him ache, and he got angry all over again. But eventually that began to fade, and he couldn't even decide who he was mad at anymore. Alyssa, for hurting him? Or himself, for letting it happen? Finally he was left with nothing but this huge gaping hole. A void. And the silence no longer allowed him to ignore the word she'd used to describe him. The word that echoed relentlessly in his mind, even as he tried to push it away.

Cold.

If he hadn't known better, he would have thought she was talking about his father. The word described Ricardo Domingues to a T. Distant. Aloof. Paulo had never been able to figure out what made the man tick. Growing up, the only approved topic of conversation had been Domingues International. And while Marcos and his dad discussed business, Paulo had always felt left out. So he'd done what most kids would have done—sought the affections of his old man any way he could. But nothing had worked. When Paulo finished college, he joined him at the office, hoping he would finally be able to live up to the standard set by Marcos and earn his father's approval.

Pathetic. Pathetic and stupid.

Paulo reached the edge of the pool, executed a forward roll and pushed off, the hard kick of his legs propelled by his anger.

When he'd walked away from his father's business, he'd thought he was done. Was free of his family. He'd been proud of rising above the Domingues family trait of being defined by success. He scowled, water sleeking past his body, Alyssa's words ringing in his ears.

It had never occurred to him he was making the same mistake. That he was still letting his father influence him.

And this time it was his own damn fault.

Pain seared his thighs, enveloped his shoulders, but still he kept going. The repetitive slap of his arms and legs against the water was satisfying. And if Alyssa was right about his sorry excuse for a life, what else was she right about?

Something slapped the top of Paulo's head, and he stopped swimming. His T-shirt floated in the water, and he looked up to see Nick holding two beers in his left hand.

"Dude, as official best friend," Nick said as he approached, lit by pool lights, "I have to inform you that there *is* such a thing as too much exercise."

Paulo swam for the side and placed his elbows on the ledge, his chest heaving from exertion. "If you really cared about my health you'd be handing me a bottle of water, not a beer."

Nick shot him a mock shocked look. "They sell water in bottles?"

Despite his foul mood, Paulo let out a scoff of reluctant amusement.

Nick took a seat, dangling his legs in the pool, and handed Paulo his beer. They sat in silence as the water bucked and swayed from the aftermath of Paulo's strokes, pool lights flickering off the tile.

"I got an invitation to your brother's anniversary party." His friend paused, and the sound of lapping water filled the air. "It's this weekend."

Paulo set his bottle down with a clink. "I know when their anniversary is. I got an invitation, too." Raking a hand through his wet hair, he looked at Nick. "What is it you're really trying to say?"

It was the first time Paulo had seen his friend struck mute. But it didn't take long for Nick to recover.

"Okay...since you asked." Nick waved his hand to encompass the pool. "Is this your big plan? To hide out like a little girl because Alyssa said something you didn't want to hear?" He looked at him seriously. "Avoid her like you avoid your brother? Cuz I gotta tell you, bro. If it is—" he shook his head skeptically "—your plan reeks."

Paulo exhaled slowly through pursed lips. Nothing like

the brutal honesty of an old friend. He picked up his beer and took a sip, the dark brew cooling his throat as he watched the pool light shimmy in the palm trees beyond the deck.

"What did Alyssa say to you, anyway?" Nick said.

"The abridged version?" Paulo gripped the hard glass in his hand and turned to look out into the dark beyond the trees. "That I'm an ass."

Nick chuckled. "Always knew she was a perceptive woman."

"Yeah," he said slowly. "That she is."

"So what's your next step?"

Paulo hesitated. He had spent hours pondering that question, and one thought refused to quit tailing him. No matter how hard he tried to shake it.

He wanted Alyssa. He wanted her in his life. But he couldn't make that happen without letting go of the last stronghold he'd been defending. Because the thought of taking a risk again always made his chest squeeze tight, constricting his lungs.

Scaring the hell out of him.

He shoved a hand through his hair and considered his choices. The tasks before him seemed insurmountable.

Alyssa's final words came back to him, and it seemed as good a place to start as any. "First, I'm going to go see my brother about the trust."

Located in downtown Miami, Domingues International headquarters dwarfed the surrounding buildings in both luxury and height, blocking the fierce noontime sun. Paulo parked in the circular drive and passed through the revolving glass door lined with gold paint.

Every muscle in Paulo's body grew heavy with memories as he rode the elevator to the suite that encompassed the top floor. His dad's old office.

Now it was his brother's.

Paulo exited the elevator and paused in a small alcove to look out the window, jamming his hands in his pockets. The view was one he would remember until the day he died. After every frustrating meeting with his father, Paulo would come to this spot, wondering if it was time to leave the company. Struggling between the need to stay and the desire to strike out on his own.

"What are you doing here?"

He turned and saw Marcos standing five feet away, wearing an impeccable suit and nothing short of a scowl on his face.

Hands planted on his hips, his brother said, "Did you come to give me more grief?"

Paulo supposed he deserved the terse greeting and unhappy expression. For a long time his own behavior had been fueled by anger. Anger was easier to handle, more familiar. Had become an old friend. And old friends were hard to say goodbye to.

"No, Marcos," Paulo finally said with resolve. "I'm done giving you grief. I only came to sign the trust papers." Another eternity passed as they stared at each other, and then, with no more than a curt nod, Marcos turned toward his office.

Paulo followed him into the spacious suite with its modern look that consisted of chrome, glass, sparse furniture and a bird's eye view of downtown. Marcos pulled a document from his desk and handed it to him. The thick legal file was heavy, and Paulo stared at it blankly.

The last legacy of his father.

He hadn't expected to do more than give a cursory signature to the papers and then leave the bloody building. There was nothing for him here. Certainly nothing worth reminiscing with his brother about. But when he saw his dad's familiar signature Paulo was hit with the irrepressible need to make sense of his father's actions—although he expected it was probably too late. The only man with the answers had been buried long ago.

Paulo tossed the file onto the glass top of Marcos's desk. "What did Dad expect to accomplish with this?" With a heavy sigh, he took a seat opposite his brother and flipped through the document, searching for the first line needing his signature. "That five years after his death he could make up for snubbing me in his will?"

"I never knew why Dad did anything that he did." Marcos sat in his leather chair across from Paulo. "And I was as surprised as you were when he left the entire company to me."

A harsh laugh rose from Paulo's throat as he wrestled with chronic, debilitating memories. "I don't know why. No matter how hard I worked, I could never compare to you." Not in school. Or later in college. And certainly not in the business—though he'd near killed himself trying. Jaw clenched, he reached for one of the pens perched in a silver cup, avoiding his brother's gaze. "Every time I accomplished something Dad would call me into his office—not to compliment me, but to compare my work to yours." Eyes fixed on the papers, he flipped through the document, not bothering to read as he scrawled his name in the marked spots. "And he made it plain that mine was never up to par."

"He did the same thing to me about you."

Shock reverberated through his body, and Paulo froze in the middle of his last signature, staggered by the news. Words failed him as he slowly looked up at his brother.

Marcos settled back in his seat, his stern face growing reflective. "Remember when I purchased the Hawthorne line of hotels? Dad had talked about the deal for two years, and I worked night and day to push the acquisition through. When I finally did..." He let out a forced breath, rubbing his chin.

"The only thing he said to me was how the new boutique line *you* were proposing had more potential for growth."

Pen clutched in his hand, the world as Paulo knew it took a decided tilt in a different direction, and then began to rotate in reverse. "You're kidding me."

"I wish I was," his brother said, his expression harsh.

Struggling to reconcile the news with his memories, Paulo finished signing and closed the file, wishing that closing this chapter of his life could be accomplished as easily. As he tapped his pen on the desk, he gazed out over downtown Miami. "Why would he pit us against each other? It doesn't make sense."

Marcos said dryly, "Probably because he was a complete bastard." The lines bracketing his mouth grew deeper. "But that could be my resentment talking." He met Paulo's gaze with a level one of his own. "Bianca would say it was to push us to achieve more. To train us for the cutthroat world of business."

"You've discussed this with Bianca?"

"Of course I have. She's my wife."

The moment stretched tight, the tension so taut he could have bounced a quarter to the moon off the surface. All the things he'd wanted to say when his brother ran off with Bianca ran through his mind. The muscles in his jaw worked as he grappled for an appropriate response.

But he couldn't find one.

After a long pause, his brother spared him the effort. "She didn't leave you because of the money, Paulo," Marcos said, his voice low. And, though Paulo's first instinct was to reject the words, there was no lack of sincerity in his brother's tone. "The reason she left was because she was afraid."

Paulo cocked a disbelieving brow. "Afraid?"

"Yes," Marcos went on, his face set. "When her parents

died she was barely out of high school, and she turned to Dad for support. She relied on him for everything."

Paulo shifted in his seat, uncomfortable with the direction of the conversation. "I know. Dad adored her."

"She adored him in return," Marcos said. "And when he had his stroke she was frightened. That was when she turned to me." With his pause, his eyes turned dark. "She had no one else to lean on. Because, even though she was married to you when Dad got sick—" he shot Paulo a hard look "—she was still very much alone."

Paulo slowly leaned back in his chair. Try as he might, other than a few cursory comments, Paulo couldn't remember discussing his father's illness with Bianca.

Not once.

But he remembered growing uncomfortable as she'd grown weepy during her attempts.

A wave of guilt slowly washed through him, and he tossed the pen to the desk with a grunt of self-disgust. He was the one to start asking the questions, but apparently there was no guarantee he would like the answers. It was time to own up to his role in the sordid mess that had been his marriage.

After wiping a weary hand down his face, Paulo finally responded. "Yeah." He dropped his hand to his lap. "I was a lousy excuse for a husband. Especially after Dad's stroke." His lips set, he shot his brother a rueful look. "I was too busy arguing with you about the business."

Marcos slowly nodded his head.

After a hard swallow, Paulo asked one final question. "So why did you two marry?"

Marcos hiked an eyebrow, as if the answer should be obvious. "We got married because we fell in love."

Paulo absorbed the blow, the blunt truth ricocheting, tearing holes in his long held beliefs.

Marcos went on. "Look, the months following Dad's

stroke were chaotic. We were all under enormous stress." His shoulder rose and fell. "I can't say I handled it any better." He leaned his elbows on his desk, his fingers steepled together, studying Paulo over his hands. "But one thing I should have known was that your idea was never in danger of failing. Just like Dad, you've always been a shrewd businessman." Marcos stood and crossed to the plate glass overlooking downtown. "I should have listened to you about starting the new line," he said, staring out the window. "Maybe Dad knew you were better off running your own show." Finally, he turned and fixed a steady gaze on Paulo. "It could be he left the company to me as a way of forcing you to take that step."

Pursing his lips, Paulo considered the scenario. The concept was difficult to buy, but certainly within the realm of possibility. And, after all he'd just learned, someone could accuse his dad of being a foreign spy and Paulo would believe them.

"Maybe he did." Paulo sent his brother a dry smile. "Or maybe he *was* just a bastard, through and through." Marcos let out an amused scoff, and Paulo shrugged in resignation. "Either way, we'll never know."

And, while the overdue conversation with his brother had come with several surprising revelations, Paulo was only sure about one thing…he didn't care anymore.

Marcos crossed back to his desk and leaned his hands on the surface, looking at him intently. "We could merge the two companies."

Paulo watched his brother, the offer hanging between them. But as far as his business was concerned he had everything he needed. And he was right where he wanted to be.

In the driver's seat.

"Thanks for the offer," Paulo said as he stood. With a wry

grin, he stuck out his hand. "Why don't we just figure out how to be brothers?"

Marcos let out a small laugh, his face relaxing as he returned his handshake.

Paulo's grin grew bigger. "I don't do partners so well."

As soon as the words left his lips, his thoughts turned to the one person he *did* team well with. Alyssa had felt like a partner in every sense of the word. At work. At play. And in bed. The longing to see her again was fierce, and brought a sucker punch to his stomach.

As Paulo headed for the exit, he was keenly aware of the huge, yawning space left by the one woman who had taken a piece of him when she'd left. Now that he'd completed the first task he'd formulated after his swim, he was at a loss over how to approach the second—and much more important—of the two.

How the hell was he going to make things right with Alyssa?

CHAPTER ELEVEN

It was late when Alyssa entered her apartment with her shopping bags, disappointed her mom's retail intervention had failed. When her mother had stopped by and seen the state Alyssa was in, she'd given her a hug and dragged her out of the house. But after two weeks of crying, moping, working, and working some more, nothing could wipe away, even briefly, the vision of Paulo's back as he had dismissed her at the club.

As she placed her bags on the sofa she heard the sound of Paulo's voice on her answering machine, asking her to pick up the phone, and her footsteps faltered. A wave of longing hit—so strong she pressed a hand to her chest.

She missed Paulo. Her heart ached for him. His sense of humor. The way he made her feel. Real. Free. And alive.

Gloriously, gloriously alive.

Entering the dining room, she listened, slowly sinking into a chair as he gave up asking her to pick up and went on. His voice was serious, the volume low as he spoke. "There's something we have to discuss." Her throat closed over and her heart expanded until it felt too big for her chest. She'd been waiting two miserably endless weeks for some sign of a breakthrough, and she prayed this was it.

Paulo went on. "I'm afraid the success at the hotel has made you worthy of gossiping newspapers. I don't know if you've seen today's *Miami Insider*, but I wanted to warn you. There's a small blip detailing your criminal record." Numb, Alyssa listened to him let out a sigh, sounding frustrated as he continued, "We can discuss it at my brother's anniversary party tomorrow."

The click of the phone disconnecting was loud, and pain flashed bright, hot. And—just like a laser beam—it cleanly separated her heart into two. Neatly cauterizing the edges. No hope for healing remained. After treating her so coldly, there still had been no apology. Worse, Paulo hadn't even called to talk about the two of them.

He'd only called to warn her the past had caught up with her.

Motionless, she stared at the answering machine. Right now, countless Miamians were reading about her shady history. She should feel...something. Humiliation? Defeat? Yet nothing.

All she felt was a crushing sadness. After days of hoping Paulo would finally come through, it was time to admit their relationship was circling the dead-end cul-de-sac of his heart. There was nowhere to go. No matter how stubborn she was, she had to face the fact that the man she loved couldn't love her back.

Sagging against the table, she covered her face with her hands. He'd warned her from the start he was unavailable, but she hadn't listened. And now he was going to pay the price for her mistake. Because who would want to schedule their precious functions at the Samba with a known criminal as its event planner?

The lonely silence grew as she dropped her hands and

looked around her dining room. Her phone sat on the table next to the invitation to Bianca's anniversary party. In lieu of a cupboard, several filing cabinets lined the wall, containing all the information she'd gathered over the years. Vendors, contacts, events she'd organized. Her gaze landed on the newspaper article about the reception at the Samba, now hanging on her wall. Everything that used to be important.

But what she wanted had changed.

Paulo was right: she'd paid her debt to society. She deserved to be happy. To pursue her dreams. She exhaled slowly, combing shaky fingers through her hair. But she had to quit her job at the Samba. Because, no matter how much he'd hurt her with his words at the club, the consequences of the article should be hers and hers alone.

She sat up and reached for the anniversary invitation on her dining room table. She hadn't planned on going. And after the tabloid article about her it would be best if she stayed far, far away. But she refused to cower like a mangy dog anymore. Plus, she had to put things right for Paulo.

The Samba was important to him, and she couldn't let the man she loved suffer because of her.

Alyssa concentrated on keeping her breathing easy as she stood in the doorway to the country club ballroom. Casino tables and roulette wheels circled the dance floor. While dealers shuffled cards and took bets, a small jazz band played in the corner. The sound of poker chips and laughter rang in the room as guests in cocktail dresses and suits milled about. She'd passed the Ducati on the way in, which meant Paulo was here.

Perspiration dotted her lip, and Alyssa ran a hand down the crepe jacket of her designer pantsuit, focusing on the texture. It was airy. Pretty, yet casual. And blessedly comfortable.

You look great, Alyssa. Now go in there and get this done.

After squaring her shoulders, she made her way through the crowd and, with no idea where Paulo was, randomly headed for the roulette wheel. As she passed the blackjack table she spied Tessa Harrison. For a moment their gazes locked, and the stunned expression above the lady's hand of cards was almost funny.

But Alyssa just ignored her and kept walking, too distracted by queasiness to give the woman much thought. The bumbling butterflies dancing in her belly were getting pretty rowdy. Because giving Paulo up, even if all they had left was a work relationship, was going to be tough. She'd never see him again.

Her heart crumpled at the thought, and she stumbled slightly in her casual high-heeled sandals.

"I was hoping to see you here," Paulo said from behind.

She cringed and came to a halt, bracing for the hurdle she had to clear. The one she wasn't ready for. The one she would never be ready for. Slowly, she turned to face him.

He was wearing a tuxedo, black hair trimmed but still long enough to keep the roguish look. And the mocha cappuccino gaze was the same. He looked too gorgeous for words. A tinge of unwanted desire slipped out before she could contain it.

His level gaze was guarded. "After the article, I wasn't sure you would come."

She fingered the edge of her jacket, hoping to soothe her frayed nerves. But she had a job to do. And, come hell or high tide, no matter how difficult, she was going to do it. "I've never run away from anything in my life," she said. "And I certainly don't intend to start now."

"You ran from my bed that first morning."

She blinked, searching for a response. "I was just postponing the inevitable."

"And the second morning?"

Frowning, she tensed her forehead. "I had work to do."

"Convenient, all these excuses," he said as he stepped closer.

The deep voice and his proximity had the butterflies in her belly shifting from the Texas Two-step to thumping hip-hop. She turned to look out the window overlooking the bay, collecting herself before meeting his gaze again.

"We have a few things to discuss," he said with a determined tone. "But why don't we start with a dance?"

Heart beating furiously, she gripped the strap of her purse. She couldn't get sidetracked by how good he looked, or how wonderful it would feel to be in his arms. And putting this off wasn't going to make it any easier. "The time for dancing has ended, Paulo." She swallowed against the lump in her throat. "I'm moving out of the Samba. I'm going to rent office space for Elite Events."

His brows pinched together in doubt.

"I'm going to tell Charles to hire an assistant," she continued. "Someone who can help coordinate things while he looks for another event planner." Alyssa cleared her throat, trying to loosen the tight muscles, but it was hard to keep her voice even. "I'm not renewing our contract."

A dark look flickered in Paulo's eyes. "Why?"

She stared up at him, torn by the answer to his question.

Shifting even closer, Paulo looked down on her. "You keep saying you don't run. So what does this qualify as?" His stare was intense. "A fast walk in the opposite direction?"

Was he really trying to convince her to stay? Her work wasn't that important. She could be replaced. And hadn't he thought about what the newspaper article would mean? "It qualifies as me trying to do the right thing," she said. "My past is now widely known in Miami."

A furrow of disgust appeared on his brow. "That sleazy newspaper is a worthless piece of scum."

Dear God, was he *trying* to make this more difficult for her? With her fist clenched, she tried again. "It could affect business at the Samba."

"I doubt that. And it doesn't matter if it does."

She pressed her hand to her temple, forcing herself to go on. And this time she included a part of the truth. "I can't have you paying the price for my sins."

"To hell with the article. You've paid the price already. You shouldn't have to keep on paying."

She closed her lids, cutting off the vision of Paulo. The sound of the roulette wheel clicked in the background as conversation lagged. She hated how weak he made her feel. Hated how a few little words could sap her resolve to let him go.

But just because he'd come to Bianca and Marcos's party, just because he was a man of principle who believed she'd paid her dues, was willing to brave the effects of bad publicity, it didn't mean anything had changed. The rest was nice, but there were bigger issues at hand. Like the fact she loved him. And he couldn't love her back.

She opened her eyes. "I can't work with you anymore," she said, and turned to walk away.

He grabbed her hand. "Don't go." His fingers firmly held her in place while his eyes searched hers, and then he shoved both hands in his pockets, staring at her as he shuffled his feet. An odd anticipation settled in her gut. She'd never seen Paulo nervous.

"I have something to give you," he said.

Her gaze dropped to his tuxedo pocket. His fist was bunched, as if curled around an object. And, despite all the fresh air circling around them, Alyssa couldn't find enough oxygen. Because with absolute certainty she knew Paulo had a ring in his pocket. Her heart lost speed, its rate barely able to supply blood to her brain, and time lapsed into slow motion.

Without saying a word, without so much as a peep of explanation, he began to kneel down, and Alyssa's heart stalled completely.

Her lids stretched wide. That was it? She blinked. No discussion needed? The rushing rise of emotion blasted through her body, her thoughts swirling. Because popping the question and giving her a ring didn't necessarily signify he was ready for an honest relationship.

He had put a ring on a woman's finger before and it had meant nothing.

The pain she'd felt each time he froze her out came roaring back, and she dragged in a breath, her chest hurting. She needed him so much, and the thought of being married to Paulo, waiting for him to participate, was too painful to contemplate. Waiting…like Bianca had.

She couldn't live like that. Which meant she had to refuse his offer.

His knee landed on the floor, and her thoughts raced. He'd chased her so hard. Dragged her out into the sunshine to breathe the fresh air of a life beyond work. To feel. To want. To *love*. And along the way he'd annihilated every ounce of her reserve.

As he began to pull his hand from his pocket, her legs turned to jelly.

She couldn't do it. She wouldn't be strong enough to say no.

When he flipped open the box without a single word panic seized her, and she pivoted on her heel, blindly pushing her way into the crowd.

Paulo stared, dumbfounded, at the sight of Alyssa disappearing into the small mob that had gathered around them curiously.

She was leaving.

The granite floor was hard against his knee. The collective held breath of the crowd around him was strained. But every cell in his body was too stupefied to move.

Alyssa was walking away. With his intentions so clearly stamped in his posture, she was leaving him. But it wasn't as if he hadn't been through this before. This feeling of desertion. Some of it was deserved, like Bianca. Some of it wasn't, such as his father. His brother was a bit of both. But every single incident—every one of them—had hurt.

But *nothing* compared to the excruciating pain of watching Alyssa walk away.

He closed his eyes, clamping the jewelry box shut. The crowd began to murmur and shift, flowing around him, resuming their activities. But Paulo couldn't move.

When he'd read that blasted article in the paper, his first instinct—right after squashing the need to tear the journalist apart—had been to fix the problem. Make it go away for her. But it was a done deal. There was no undoing the damage.

And then all he'd wanted was to find her and pull her into his arms. To protect her. But, because of his dumb actions, he didn't have that right. And he *wanted* the privilege of being the one to take on the world for her. He'd thought he could make this easier by skipping past all the awkward parts and going straight to what he wanted...a life with Alyssa.

Truly, he was the King of Stupid.

He opened his eyes and stared in the direction of the exit. He should chase her down. Talk to her. Try to convince her to change her mind.

Frowning, he lowered his hand to his knee. Or maybe he'd hurt her so much that she couldn't forgive his asinine behavior. And what if he let go, cracked his chest open and let it all spill out, only to have her refuse his proposal again?

How would he recover?

With a scowl, Paulo slammed the door on the cowardly thought and stood up. Alyssa had faced down her fears so many times, in so many ways, it defied comprehension. Yet he didn't have the guts to do it once.

Not *once*.

And if he didn't have the courage to go after her, he didn't deserve her. If he didn't go after her *now*, she'd be lost to him forever. Her smile, her spunk, her cool wit and their combustible passion relegated to a distant memory—until he grew so old and bitter he wouldn't be able to stand being on the same continent with himself.

Paulo shoved the ring in his pocket and took off toward the exit.

She didn't have time to call for a taxi. Hoping to hail one from the street, Alyssa hurried up the country club driveway, her steps faltering when she heard a shout from behind. Her heart constricted, stealing her breath.

Paulo.

Moving quickly, she rounded the gate and dashed across the northbound lane, the cars held back by a red light. When she landed on the palm-tree-lined median, her heels sank into the grass. She glanced back and saw Paulo approaching. With her teeth clamped on her lip, she turned to stare at the cars whipping by between her and the sidewalk on the other side. Maybe she should take her chances. Just dart across and hope her timing worked out.

Good grief. She was desperate, but she wasn't crazy. Her chest heaved as she blew out a sigh. And if Paulo was ready to talk, ready to have a *real* heart-to-heart, this was as good a place as any.

Mentally preparing for battle, she turned to watch him wait for a break in the streaming line of vehicles freed by the traffic signal. She'd had a moment to collect herself. To push aside her hurt. And that made way for the other growing emotion.

Anger was now riding shotgun with her pain.

When the line of cars stretched far enough apart, he jogged across the lane and came to a stop in front of her. "That absolutely qualified as running away."

The words smashed the last of her restraint. "No." She tried to stomp her foot, but her heel caught in the ground. Frustrated, she went on. "That was me refusing a proposal that was nothing more than an empty romantic gesture. And I'm not the one who's running." She finally wrenched her shoe free. "You are!"

"Alyssa—"

"You think you can just show up and offer me a ring in front of a crowd?" she said, her drawling words loud. "As if whippin' out a piece of jewelry suddenly makes everything okay?" Her nails dug into her palms, and she forced herself to slow her words. "I don't want you down on your knee. I don't want a public proposal." She stepped closer, looking up at him. "I want *honesty.*"

He crossed his arms, his tuxedo jacket drawing tight on his broad shoulders. "You want honesty? How about this? It's hell watching your wife walk away, even if it's mostly your fault." Shocked by his admission, she was struck mute. The pause stretched, traffic now whizzing by on both sides. "And up until now there was no way I was going to put myself through that possibility again."

She couldn't belittle his fears, but she also couldn't ignore her own. "She left because of the way you treated her."

He didn't bother to deny it. "Yes."

"So how do I know this time will be different?"

He sighed and raked his hair from his forehead. "To start with, for once I'm actually in love."

Her heart soared, but her head pounded, keeping her focused. "That's wonderful. But let me tell you something. If you don't have the actions to back it up, it won't be enough." Feeling surer of her argument, she tipped her chin, her voice stronger. "And you know what? You were right. I *do* deserve a life. And I'm not going to settle for less anymore. So if you want me, than you have to put yourself out there. *Really* take a risk. Because if you can't—" She blinked back the stinging threat of tears. "If you can't, we don't stand a chance."

"I don't know where to start."

"Start with telling me what you want."

After a pause, Paulo held out his hand, the velvet box in his palm. "I want you," he said as he flipped open the lid. "Marry me."

A large diamond solitaire sparkled in the sun, and the pounding in her temples spread to her chest as she stared at it. Everything she wanted was right there in front of her. Unfortunately she hadn't heard all she needed to hear.

A semi-truck swooshed by, kicking up a diesel-scented gust of air that blew her hair across her eyes. Blinking, she swiped away the strands, her hand shaking. But she remained silent.

With an apprehensive expression, he glanced around and then turned his gaze back to scan hers. "Is this not unromantic enough for you?"

"It's not about the location. It's about your words."

After a brief hesitation, ring still displayed in his hand, he said quietly, "You're not going to make this easy, are you?"

"Life isn't easy. Marriage won't always be easy." She glanced down at the ring and back to his beautiful face, gathering her strength to press on. There was no other choice. "You have to convince me this time around will be different."

His chest rose and fell on a huge breath. "Okay." With a determined look, he stepped closer, his voice burning with the same intensity reflected in his eyes. "From the first moment you showed up at my hotel, sassing me by the pool, I've wanted you. I kept telling myself it was a temporary fling." He frowned, looking down on her. "But I couldn't let you go."

"Maybe that was just the sex."

"It was more than just sex." He paused and shook his head. "But I was too dense to recognize it. And then you faced me down and sided with Bianca, and it was too painful to deal with."

"I sided with the *truth*."

He placed his fingers on her mouth, and her body instantly began to purr. She fought the urge to lean closer.

"I know that." His eyes grew gentle, followed by his tone. "At least I do now." His lips tipped up into that killer half-smile. "And a heartfelt confession strong enough to make up for some serious sins is hard to pull off when I keep getting interrupted." He dropped his hand, and instantly her lips felt lonely.

She swallowed, her throat burning with emotion. "I'll shut up."

"Just until I finish." He cupped her jaw with his free hand and shifted closer, until they were toe to toe, the offered ring still between them. "I've never been in love before, Alyssa." His face was tight, a hint of fear beneath the sincerity. Her vision blurred, and she blinked hard at the tears as he continued. "Didn't *want* to be in love. After my experience with family, all the rejection, I figured life was easier that way. Because after a while…" A flicker of raw pain crossed his face, cutting her deep. "A guy starts to wonder if there isn't something inherently wrong with *him*."

The sheen of tears finally breached her lashes, and her vision cleared as they slipped down her cheeks. The cocky charmer, full of self-doubt? Who would have guessed?

"Can I say something now?" she asked.

He rubbed the wet track on her face with his thumb. "Only if it's something I want to hear."

She laid a loving palm on his cheek, her voice full of conviction. "There is nothing wrong with you." With a small sniff and a wobbly smile, she amended her statement. "At least nothing that a swift kick in the ass won't fix."

He chuckled softly. But as the amusement died away he grew serious again, his eyes searching hers. "I want to believe that. But I'm still scared senseless that you'll discover you were wrong about me and take off. It's a scary thought." He sent her a look that was breathtakingly frank. "But nowhere near as scary as living the rest of my life without you." Paulo glanced down at the ring he still held between them. "My arm is getting tired," he said, and a flicker of panic crossed his face. "Please tell me you'll marry me."

She laid her palm on the box. "I'll marry you."

His fingers closed around her hand and he let out a sigh of relief, leaning his forehead against hers. His voice was rough, his hazel gaze glowing. "Now tell me you love me."

Alyssa looked up at him, letting it all shine in her eyes. "I love you."

His mouth closed over hers. With a tiny squeak of relief, she reached up with her free hand and gripped his lapel, pulling him closer. Paulo's lips grew more insistent, and she savored the taste of him. The hard chest beneath her fingers.

A few discordant honks peppered the air, and a wolf whistle from a passing motorist had Alyssa pulling away.

With shaking fingers, she smoothed the wrinkles she'd left on his jacket.

Paulo smiled as he stepped back, holding out his arms. "You never told me what you thought of my tuxedo."

An unfamiliar feeling of joy bubbled up in her heart. "It will be perfect for our wedding."

He shot her a suspiciously winning grin. "Hmm," he said as he dropped his hands to her hips. "Now that we're engaged, are you going to tell me how you got that file?"

Raising her eyebrows, she struggled to maintain a deadpan face. "It will be my gift to you on our fiftieth wedding anniversary."

The mischievous spark in his eyes grew brighter, and he pulled her against him. It was like coming home. His voice went low, seductive. "Make it the twenty-fifth, and I guarantee it'll be worth your efforts."

Alyssa finally let out a laugh, giddy with happiness. "It's a deal."

"Do I still get to keep you as my strategic partner?"

"Of course," Alyssa said, sending him a smile that must rival the blazing sun above. "But you, Mr. Domingues, now hold the permanent number one position on my to-do list."

* * * * *

SECRETS AND SPEED DATING

Leah Ashton

An unashamed fan of all things happily ever after, **Leah Ashton** has been a lifelong reader of romance. Writing came a little bit later, although in hindsight she'd been dreaming up stories for as long as she can remember. Sadly, the most popular boy in school never did suddenly fall head over heels in love with her...

Now she lives in Perth, Western Australia with her own real-life hero, two gorgeous dogs and the world's smartest cat. By day she works in IT and by night she considers herself incredibly lucky to be writing the type of books she loves to read, and to have the opportunity to share her own characters' happy-ever-afters with readers. You can visit Leah at www.leah-ashton.com.

Dear Reader,

I started writing this book while visiting Vela Luka, a picturesque town on the island of Korcula, Croatia. I'd become engaged just weeks earlier and was still at the stage where I'd stare at the ring on my finger and smile. Actually, I still do that!

I couldn't have asked for more romantic inspiration, could I? But back then all I had was the opening line (I'll let you turn the page to see what that is!). Who was the woman who'd said that? And why? Well, once I knew why Sophie said what she did, I just had to write her happy-ever-after, even though I knew it was going to be a little bit different.

Secrets and Speed Dating was the winner of the 2010 Mills & Boon® New Voices competition. Winning the competition was one of the most unexpected and thrilling experiences of my life. If you read my entry, you'll see that Dan and Sophie's story has evolved, but I'll think you'll like the changes. To see how far *Secrets and Speed Dating* has come, you can visit www.romanceisnotdead. com.

I'd like to thank everyone who was brave enough to enter New Voices and every single person who voted for my entry. You've made my dream of publication come true.

And if you're meeting Sophie and Dan for the first time, I hope you enjoy their story. As the stars of my first published novel, they will always be special to me.

Leah

For Linley—who started it all.
I'd like to thank Nikki for—everything.
I couldn't have done it without you.

I'd also like to thank my editor, Meg Lewis, for giving
me every chance to get this book right. You had faith
in me when I didn't.

To the Monday and Tuesday Night Dinner crowds, thank
you for the food and for the laughter. I love you all.

And thank you, Regan, for proving to me
that heroes really do exist.

CHAPTER ONE

The Sophie Project (Project Manager: S. Morgan)
Task One: Find a boyfriend

'Just so you know, I can't have children.'

Sophie Morgan watched her date's expression morph from a twinkly-eyed grin to slack-jawed surprise at her calmly delivered statement. She took a sip of her vanilla martini and met his wide eyes as she continued. 'I *really* can't. It wouldn't matter if I "stopped trying" or "went on a holiday" or "just relaxed".' She shrugged. 'It just won't happen.'

Her date had barely blinked, so she gestured vaguely at her flat stomach. 'Things down there just don't function properly...*reproductively* speaking, of course. I mean, I *can* have sex. That's all normal.'

The poor guy spluttered into his beer. 'Ah, isn't this conversation a bit...premature? We've known each other five minutes.'

He was being literal. A moment later the high-pitched chime of a small silver bell silenced the room.

The hostess of the speed dating evening—a depressingly

stunning model-type who Sophie was sure would never need to attend such an event herself—waited until all eyes were on her. Unlike Sophie, her hostess looked completely at ease in the *über*-modern bar, with its black granite floor, chrome and glass furniture and leather couches. Back in Sydney, this type of place had been Sophie's domain. But now, in Perth, with her old life three thousand kilometres away, she felt like an impostor.

'Okay, gentlemen, time to say goodbye and move on to your next date.'

Her date still look dazed, so she tried to explain quickly, hopeful that she didn't sound like a completely unbalanced lunatic. She *did* know blurting out her infertility wasn't exactly normal behaviour. 'Look, everyone here wants a relationship, right?'

He nodded. In fact, this speed dating event was specifically for people seeking long-term relationships.

'So, when most people picture a relationship, they want the whole package deal—wife and kids. With me, that's not possible. I just thought it was only fair you should know.'

He shook his head. 'Not everyone wants that. I don't know if I want kids.'

Sophie smiled, but shrugged. 'I still think it's better to be up-front, get it out in the open. What you want now can change a heck of a lot in the future.'

People changed their minds. She knew that far too well.

Her date smiled at her. Reassuringly, he now looked more bemused than ready to run screaming away from her—that twinkle was even back in his eyes. 'Who knows about the future?' he asked as he stood. 'Why not let a new relationship just flow? Why worry about it now?'

She watched him sit down at the neighbouring table, his attention already on his next date. She envied his naivety. The ability to live a relationship in the moment, to pretend that all you needed was each other. But Sophie wouldn't do that again. She couldn't.

Not that she didn't want the fairytale happy ending. She did. She'd love to grow old with her perfect man—whatever that meant. Definitely someone who didn't want kids. And *really* didn't—although she really had no clue how she could unequivocally determine that. Maybe someone who'd already had his children? Or was older? Not that she really went for much older men.

She took another sip of her cocktail, a humourless smile quirking her lips. Clearly she didn't know what she wanted. She just knew that she wasn't about to waste her time—or risk her heart—on some guy who would dump her once he knew what she couldn't give him. Getting it all out up-front was definitely a good idea. An *excellent* idea, even.

Still, when she'd flipped over her date card she quickly circled 'No' beside her last date's name. As she had for the four dates before him, and probably would for the remaining five.

Wait.

No. She needed to—*had to*—think positive.

She wasn't ready to admit that speed dating was a mistake. After all, it was the first task on her list. If she couldn't do this, what chance did the rest of her project have?

And if she knew that dropping her bombshell was abnormal behaviour, she *certainly* knew that the very existence of her project tipped her over the edge into…well…a little bit nutty. Knew it—but was determined to carry on regardless.

After the amorphous, directionless mess of the past six months she needed a goal—needed a *plan*.

Reaching into the handbag hanging on the back of her chair, she ran her finger along the sharply folded edges of the piece of paper that had led her here this evening.

A single piece of paper. Flimsy—it could so easily be crumpled and thrown away. But she wouldn't be doing that.

Instead, it gave her focus. Just as when she'd sat down at her laptop and methodically put the document together. Soothing lists of tasks and deliverable dates—familiar in their structure and yet so different in their type and intent from the project plans she was used to. For this time Sophie Morgan, Project Manager, was *not* implementing a major software upgrade, or rolling out new hardware, or co-ordinating a change management program.

No, this time the project was her life. Her *new* life.

Sophie took a deep breath. Straightened her shoulders.

It didn't matter that she didn't know who or what would make her circle 'Yes'. She just owed herself—and her remaining dates—her full attention, and at least the tiniest smidgen of hope. No premature circling of 'No'.

And definitely—*definitely*—still disclosing her...uh... situation.

So far the reaction to her announcement had been almost comically consistent, except for the beer-spluttering of her last date. That had been new—but then so had her rather graphic description. She grinned at the memory. She probably shouldn't have done that, even if her more than slightly sick sense of humour had always helped her deal with her problems, infertility or otherwise. She figured that was healthier than the total denial of her mid-teens to early twenties: *I never wanted kids, anyway. They're just snotty alien spew-makers. Yuk!*

Her next date settled into his seat. Middling height, with bright red hair, he beamed at her, and she couldn't help her grin becoming a smile.

'Hi,' he said, obviously about to launch into a well-practised line. 'Why on earth would a stunningly beautiful woman like yourself need to go speed dating?'

But she laughed anyway, determined to enjoy the next four and a half minutes.

And then she'd let him know.

* * *

After his third or fourth surreptitious glance, Dan Halliday decided to just give in and look. Something about the woman who'd stayed long after the other speed daters had left kept drawing his attention. Unsurprisingly, the appeal of polishing wine glasses or counting the night's takings really couldn't compete with the beautiful woman propping up his bar.

She was twisted slightly on her seat, so she could stare out of the window that ran the length of the Subiaco Wine Bar. He had the feeling she wasn't people-watching, though, as the one time he'd asked if she wanted another drink he'd felt as if he was interrupting, that she'd been lost in her own little world. He'd left her alone since then—surreptitious glances excluded.

If she *had* been watching she would have seen the constant stream of cars and the packed café tables of a few hours earlier transition into a rowdier, typical Friday night club crowd. The cafés and restaurants that spilled onto the busy city street were now mostly closed, and only the late-night pubs and clubs remained open. His bar needed to close too, and she was the last customer.

Her hair was long, dark blonde, and swept back off her face in a ponytail—which he liked. He'd never understood women who hid behind curtains of hair. This way he had an unrestricted view of her profile: pale, creamy skin with a touch of colour at her cheeks, a long, slightly pointed nose and a chin that hinted at a stubborn streak.

He couldn't tell her height, seated as she was, but he'd guess she was tall. She wore a deep red silky blouse that skimmed the swell of her breasts, and he could just see her crumpled, obviously forgotten speed dating name-tag stuck beside the V of pale skin her top revealed. But he was too far away to read it.

And then she turned her head and locked her gaze with his. 'Are you closed? Do you want me to go?'

Even from where he stood, a few metres away, he was caught momentarily by the intense colour of her eyes. They were blue—but unlike his own boring plain blue, hers were darker. Richer. More expressive.

He gave himself a mental shake. *Dan Halliday philosophising over the colour of a woman's eyes? Really?*

Dan cleared his throat. 'Yes to the first question, but no to the second. You're welcome to stay and finish your drink.'

'You sure? I must have been here for...' she glanced at her watch '...almost *three* hours, and I've only had half of my cocktail. You could be waiting a while.'

He put down the glass he'd been not polishing while he'd stared—*leered, maybe, Dan?*—and walked to her end of the bar. 'Really, I don't mind. I'll tell you what—how about I give you a fresh cocktail on the house and you can get back to that serious contemplation you looked to be doing while I finish up?'

She shook her head. 'Thank you, but no. I'm sure you don't want me staring out of the window like a zombie any longer. I'll go.'

'So it's all figured out, then?'

Her brow furrowed. 'What is?'

'Whatever it was you were contemplating—it's all sorted? Done and dusted?'

She laughed, but it was a brittle sound. 'No. Not sorted.' She sighed. 'But, trust me, one more cocktail is not going to sort out the total mess of my life.'

Dan knew he should just let her leave. That right about now all his instinctive confirmed bachelor alarm bells should be ringing. This was a woman who had just attended a speed dating evening and had a self-confessed messy life. That was one alarm bell for 'wants a relationship' and another for 'has baggage'. The noise should be deafening.

Instead, he reached for a fresh martini glass, and didn't bother analysing why he didn't want her to go. 'Stay. Stare like a zombie all you like.'

A moment passed. Then another. But eventually she smiled, and nodded. 'Thank you.'

His gaze flicked to her name tag.

Sophie.

A deep aversion to her mother's inevitable requirement for a blow-by-blow account of her speed dating 'adventure', as her mum insisted on calling it, was the reason Sophie had lingered at the bar. At least that was the original reason. But hours had passed since she'd sent a 'Don't wait up' text message, fully aware she was only delaying the inquisition, and still she didn't go home.

At some point she'd stopped making up stories about the diners she could see through the bar's window. She'd stopped imagining which couples were on a first date, who was out for dinner for their birthday, or who was a tourist. The stories were a habit she'd fallen into over the past few months—an effective distraction from actually thinking. It was far easier to analyse and deconstruct a stranger's life than her own. Even her ill-fated plan had been all about striding forward. She hadn't been brave enough to look back.

But tonight she'd let her eyes unfocus, her vision blur, and for the first time in what felt like for ever had let the jumble of memories in.

Sydney.

Rick.

Rick's new girlfriend.

Rick's new *pregnant* girlfriend.

Lost in thought—in contemplation, she supposed, like the bartender had said—she hadn't noticed the other customers leaving. And somehow—remarkably, really—she hadn't noticed the fact her bartender was drop dead gorgeous.

She'd felt him watching her, but had expected a 'finish your drink and leave' type of glare when she'd looked up.

He'd surprised her. He hadn't been glaring—not even close. There'd been undeniable interest in his hooded gaze.

She lifted the fresh martini to her lips and studied him over the rim of the cocktail glass as he methodically counted money from the till. He stood with his hip resting casually against the stainless steel counter, his long legs clad in darkest grey jeans and the breadth of his shoulders emphasised by his fitted black shirt. The sleeves were rolled up, revealing rich olive skin and arms that looked strong—as if he did a lot more than just pour drinks with them.

With his short cropped black hair and sky-blue eyes he was far more handsome than any of her speed dates that evening. Of course it hadn't been her dates' looks, intelligence, charm or even their reaction to her unsolicited medical announcement that had been the problem.

She twisted in her chair so she faced the window again, her back to the bartender. She watched a gaggle of young women spill, laughing, out of a restaurant across the road. Hmm— Maybe they were on a hen's night? Or maybe they worked together and were having particularly enthusiastic Friday night drinks?

No. Focus. Her free drink was for contemplation, not daydreaming.

Okay. The problem was that she'd been wrong. She just wasn't ready for a relationship.

Her bruised heart didn't care that she had a perfectly scheduled five-week plan practically burning a hole in her handbag. It turned out that, no matter how hard she tried, she wasn't able to self-impose a 'get over it' or 'move on' deadline.

So, sexy bartender or not, she'd take his offer at face value: continue her zombie-like staring out of the window, finish her drink, then leave.

'How's that contemplation going?'

Sophie jumped, surprised to hear him so close. She looked over her shoulder to see him wiping down the bar.

'Fine, thanks! Plus I've nearly finished my drink, so I'm

almost out of your hair.' She held up her near-empty glass in demonstration, then turned back to her window.

'Anything you want to talk about?'

She spun around in her seat at that, ignoring the concerned look in his eyes. 'Nope!'

She gulped the rest of her martini and plonked the empty glass down a little too hard on the bar's polished surface.

The bartender raised his eyebrows. 'I've owned this bar for ten years. Trust me, I know when someone needs to talk.'

Sophie slid off the barstool, slung her handbag over her shoulder and headed for the exit. The click of her heels echoed in the near-empty room. A cleaner swept near the door, but he paused to open it for her.

She wasn't sure what she'd expected. That he'd follow her? Tell her to stop?

The fact that he did neither, and that of course he wouldn't—she was a total stranger!—made her pause.

She couldn't unload to her mother and sister. They were too quick to interject, to judge. Too desperate to give her a solution when all she wanted was someone to listen.

The temptation to talk to the bartender—a man who didn't know her, whom she was unlikely to see again—was too strong to ignore.

She turned and walked back to the bar.

He was calmly polishing a wine glass.

Sophie took a deep breath. 'My fiancé dumped me two months before my wedding.'

He didn't say anything for a moment. He just looked at her, as if he was thinking something over.

'Ouch,' he finally replied. 'Let me get you another drink.'

CHAPTER TWO

The Sophie Project (Project Manager: S. Morgan)
Task One: Find a ~~boyfriend~~ date?

THE words hadn't come tentatively. Not at all. Instead they'd leapt, tripped and tumbled in a big, rambling rush from her mouth, desperate to be heard.

Sophie wasn't sure how long she'd been talking, but she'd talked *a lot*. More than she had in six months—probably way more than the bartender had expected. Poor guy. He sat beside her on a barstool, still drinking his first bourbon and coke, his jean-clad knee only a few inches from her own. Earlier he'd switched off most of the lights, so the room was lit only by the soft, multicoloured glow of the backlit rows of spirits and liqueurs lining the wall behind the bar.

Now the bartender knew Rick had ditched her for another woman—a work colleague of theirs, no less. He knew she'd had to leave her job, as working with her ex and his new girlfriend each day was—obviously—not an option. He knew she'd sold her share of the house to Rick and promptly spent all her money backpacking through Asia. And he knew that, with barely a cent to her name, and no job or home to return to, here she was back in Western Australia. Living with her well-meaning, wonderful, but suffocating, mother.

But she hadn't told him it all. Of all the things she'd told him, she'd withheld what she'd told every other man that evening. Why?

That was easy. She'd well and truly had her fill of shocked looks that evening. Somehow the combination of the disaster with Rick *and* her infertility was just too much. Too pathetic. She didn't want the bartender's pity.

And she also hadn't told him the absolute worst bit—about what Rick had said to make her feel simultaneously all hollowed out inside and full to the brim with lead. An impossible emotion—one that surfaced far too often and one she wasn't even close to willing to share. Even with her stranger the bartender.

Wait. *Her* stranger?

It didn't matter—the important part was that with him she had opened the floodgates. Given a voice to all those swirling memories and shards of anger that she'd barely let herself think, let alone speak to anyone about. And she'd been able to because she'd never see him again.

Now she'd finished, and her sad little story was all blurted out, it was as if the bartender was coming back into focus. As she'd talked she'd paid no attention to anything except the fact that he was listening to her, and that had been all that mattered. But now she was finding it difficult to ignore the reality of him—the sharp angles of his face, his towering frame and the obvious muscled strength of his thighs so very close beside hers.

'Why did you come speed dating tonight?' he asked, his velvety voice almost a shock after what had been—if she were honest—pretty much two-hour tipsy Sophie mono-logue. He'd asked a few questions earlier, while she'd still felt a bit awkward, but once she'd got going—and, boy, had she—he'd just let her talk. She took a long drink of her cocktail in an attempt to keep an unwelcome surge of embarrassment at bay. She'd have plenty of time to be mortified at all that she'd told him tomorrow. And probably for quite some time after that.

'For the usual reason, I guess—I wanted to meet someone.'

He raised his eyebrows. 'Are you sure? After all you've just told me, you don't sound like a woman who's ready to jump straight into a relationship.'

'I know,' she said, her shoulders slumping. 'It was a stupid idea. But it seemed like a good idea at the time and all that.' Her gaze fell away. 'And I really wanted to kick off my proj—'

As her brain belatedly caught up with her traitorous mouth she slammed her lips shut. Her bartender had already heard more than enough from her tonight—no need to add *totally unhinged* to her list of flaws.

'Project?' he asked.

Too late.

'It's nothing,' she said, with a brisk shake of her head. And a desperately unwanted heating of her cheeks.

Busted.

'Really?' he said, leaning forward, curiosity shining in his gaze. 'You said you're a project manager—what type of projects do you normally manage?'

'IT,' she said quickly, hoping to distract him. 'I pick up contracts for big companies. For example, my last project was for a bank in Sydney, rolling out new software. And before that I worked at a university for about six months. And...uh...'

Her words tapered off under the weight of his steady gaze.

'Did either of those projects require speed dating?' His grin was wicked.

She glared at him. Fine—so he really wanted to know?

Sophie put her glass back down on the bar with calm deliberation, then reached down for the large handbag at her feet. Without meeting his eyes, she slid out the folded A3 piece of paper and spread it out on the bar's surface.

'I got the idea from planning my wedding,' she said. 'If I had a plan for that, why not have one for life in general?' She kept her gaze on the neat list of tasks and the horizontal bars indicating her timelines and deadlines, bracing herself for the laughter she was sure would come. 'I've always liked keeping lists and being organised, so this just seemed a natural next step.'

When he remained silent, she lifted her head to find him watching her. The absence of his teasing grin surprised her. Instead, his lovely blue eyes seemed to look right inside her.

Great. He felt sorry for her.

What had she been thinking? She hadn't even shown her mother the plan, knowing that she wouldn't understand. *No one* would understand.

Especially not a handsome bartender who didn't even know her name.

She reached out, untidily refolding the project plan. 'Forget it. It's just a stupid idea I had...'

His hand covered hers, instantly stilling her movements.

'It's not a stupid idea,' he said.

His hand was warm, much bigger than hers, his olive complexion a stark contrast to her pale skin. Milky-white her mother called it. Totally impractical for the Australian climate and irritatingly fast to burn—that had always been Sophie's opinion. But right now she liked how her skin looked against the bartender's. Delicate—something that at five feet ten she rarely felt.

She met his eyes. 'It does make sense,' he continued. 'You're a project manager who wants to get her life back on track, so you're using what you know. If it works for you, why not?'

It shocked her when her lower lip started to wobble. She'd managed not to cry throughout the telling of her whole sad story—she was *not* going to start crying now over what was basically a glorified spreadsheet!

She swallowed, sliding her hand away from under his and immediately missing his touch. 'You haven't looked at the plan properly,' she said, pleased at her wobble-free tone. 'You may change your opinion.'

Across the top of the page the next five weeks were clearly marked, each week crammed with deliverables— many unthreateningly achievable: *Update CV. Move out of home.* Others, after tonight's speed dating failure, seemed laughably optimistic: *Find a boyfriend.* That was the worst of the lot, and of course it was a dependent task for much of the rest of the plan. Including the big one—the task that had started it all, its beribboned and embossed invitation landing in her mother's letter box like a ticking time bomb only a week earlier.

It lurked at the bottom of the task list, where she'd highlighted it in bold bloodred letters. Appropriate, she'd thought.

Attend Karen's wedding.

Three words. And such a joyous event—a close friend's marriage. And yet the prospect filled her with dread. In fact, now that she realised she'd be attending alone, she could upgrade 'dread' to 'sense of impending doom'.

'Speed dating was part of Task One?' he asked.

She nodded.

He met her eyes. '*Did* you have any luck, then? With the speed daters?'

She shook her head vehemently. 'No, not at all. I'm so far from ready for a relationship it's laughable. They were all nice guys. They deserved better than for me to waste their time.'

Sophie was almost certain she saw a subtle relaxation of the bartender's posture. Surely he couldn't be relieved? Because she didn't think talking about her ex for hours on end and then introducing her obsessive organisational skills were particularly effective flirtation techniques.

But you're not interested, remember?

'So, now do you move onto the other sub-tasks?' he asked, refocusing her on the plan and away from her misguided train of thought. *Online dating. Sign up for a new class...* His head popped up. 'Dare I ask what type of class?'

'Salsa dancing. Life drawing. Something like that.'

Now he grinned. 'Is that how you think you'll find your new boyfriend?'

She narrowed her eyes. 'Yes—and it would have worked,' she said, with total conviction. 'My projects are always a success.'

'I don't think it's possible to plot out your love life,' he said.

'I disagree,' she said simply. She'd always lived a structured life—even her adventure through South East Asia had included a carefully scheduled itinerary. And—excluding the rather massive hiccup with Rick—that life had worked for her. 'Just because you wouldn't do it that way doesn't mean it won't work.'

'How do you know I'm not a speed dating and life drawing classes kind of guy?'

It was her turn to grin. Life drawing classes for this bartender? Only if he were the model.

She ran her gaze over him. She hoped subtly. Tall, dark, handsome. Tick, tick, tick.

If he were the model at a life drawing class she certainly wouldn't be looking at any other men.

I shouldn't be looking at any men.

That was the point—she'd just decided she wasn't ready for a relationship. Imagining her bartender naked was not conducive to that goal. All that lovely, muscled skin...

She gave herself a mental shake.

It went without saying that he wasn't the speed dating type, either. He probably had women throwing themselves over his bar each evening—not that she was about to tell him that. And she was pretty sure he wasn't looking for a 'wife and white picket fence' future, like the men she'd met speed dating.

She snuck another glance at the bartender. He was undeniably sexy—from his short-cropped hair to his leather-clad toes.

Yeah, he was definitely the 'love 'em and leave 'em' type. Guaranteed to break a woman's heart.

'You aren't that kind of guy,' she said firmly.

'So sure?' he said, crossing his arms. 'Even though you know nothing about me?'

The reality of the past few hours of self-absorbed conversation washed over her like a bucket of ice-cold water. First the sad and sorry Rick story. Then her stupid plan.

Rapidly her icy skin was replaced with the burning heat of what felt like an all-over blush. 'I'm sorry. You must be bored out of your mind.'

He shrugged, completely unperturbed. 'You needed to talk. So I listened.'

But she realised now she wanted *him* to talk. She wanted to know more. Find out who he was, what he did outside of work—besides not going speed dating and not drawing naked people.

And wanting that was even more stupid than imagining him in the nude.

She'd talked, he'd listened, and she *did* feel better. Now she should go.

But she wanted to stay. The way he looked at her—not all the time, but sometimes—was addictive. When his gaze morphed from calm understanding to something tinged with heat and intensity, it felt…fantastic.

And it had been so incredibly long since she'd felt anything good. Anything untainted by sadness, humiliation or rejection.

It was on the tip of her tongue to offer to leave. Thank him, pay him for her many cocktails, then walk out never to see him again. Let her bartender remain just a generous and ridiculously attractive stranger.

Instead, she put down her glass and reached out her hand.

'Hi, my name's Sophie.'

'I know.' He smiled, and his gaze dropped to her chest.

She looked down, and there it was—her name in big black felt-tip capitals. 'So much for thinking I was being all mysterious.'

She ripped the forgotten name tag off and crumpled it into a ball that she dropped on the bar. Then she reached out again, determined to do this belated introduction properly.

'I'm Dan,' he said, and gripped her hand firmly.

An electric jolt flew up her arm before settling down low inside her.

A dangerous, but delicious sensation.

'Hi, Dan,' she said softly, and their eyes met. His big hand held hers just a few moments longer than absolutely necessary. 'So, if you don't think project planning is the way to meet someone, what do you suggest instead?'

* * *

Buying a woman a drink and asking if she wants to talk.

Actually saying the words had been a very near thing. Followed closely by an invitation to dinner.

But he'd stopped himself. His initial instincts had been right—very right. Sophie epitomised the type of woman he went out of his way *not* to date. She was unequivocally the long-term relationship type—with the added bonuses of recent significant emotional baggage and a project plan that was both eccentric and surprisingly endearing.

She was about as far from the type of woman he usually dated as it was possible to get.

So Dan didn't answer her question. 'I don't do relationships.'

It was a reminder to himself. No matter how lovely she was, with her mane of silky blonde hair, porcelain skin and deep pink lips, she was a woman he needed to avoid. Because the commitment that women like Sophie wanted was just not something he was capable of giving.

'Why not?'

He shot her an incredulous look. 'After your experience, you have to ask?'

'You don't want to get hurt?'

For a moment the innocent question staggered him, the words slicing through his insides like a knife.

A decade of determinedly ignored emotions simmered up inside him—but hurt certainly wasn't the most dominant. In fact it paled in comparison to the others.

Betrayal.

Loss.

Guilt.

'No,' he said. 'I just don't believe in settling down with one person.'

His tone did not invite further questioning.

But she ignored that. 'Do you want to talk about it?' she said softly. 'It's the least I can do.'

'No,' he said, more harshly than he'd intended. She'd been leaning towards him and now she straightened up abruptly, her eyes wide. 'There's nothing to talk about,' he said, more gently.

But she tilted her head, looking at him sceptically.

He ignored her assessing gaze. He'd been happy to listen to her. After a week of stupidly long hours—the result of a bartender resigning and half his staff being struck down with the flu—it had almost been a relief to just sit still for a while and let her words flow over him.

But he wasn't about to trade stories with her.

Besides, he hadn't lied. As far as he was concerned there was *nothing* to talk about.

'I thought you said you weren't ready for a relationship?' he asked, unashamedly changing the subject.

She blinked, but nodded. 'I'm not,' she said, then gestured at the project plan, still lying on the bar in its colour-coded glory. 'And it totally stuffs up my plan.'

'What do you mean?' he said, returning his attention to the task list. He hadn't got much further than the first few lines.

Sophie didn't strike him as the kind of woman who thought she needed a man. All the tasks he'd read she could do perfectly well herself: *Find new job. Buy a car. Buy sexy underwear...*

His head popped up at that one. 'Underwear?' he asked, raising an eyebrow.

Her cheeks turned pink. 'That isn't important,' she said quickly, then tugged the plan closer to herself and stabbed her finger at the final task on the list. '*That's* the problem,' she said. 'I have to go to a *wedding.*'

She infused the word with the kind of loathing he usually associated with dental appointments and bad breakfast radio.

'Can't you just not go?' he asked.

'No!' she said. 'It's a schoolfriend's wedding. I want to go.'

He looked at her blankly.

She smiled, taking pity on him. 'It's the first wedding I've been invited to since I cancelled mine.'

He nodded as realisation dawned. 'And you don't want to go alone?'

'Exactly,' she said, the grin falling from her face. 'I was hoping I'd meet someone new. Both as company at the wedding—someone to just hold my hand, really—and as proof I've finally gotten over Rick.'

She sighed, looking utterly defeated.

'You could still do the first one,' he said. 'The hand-holding bit. You know—ask a friend to go with you or something.'

'Yeah, I did think of that,' she said. 'Earlier, when I was doing all that contemplating at the bar.' He nodded. 'But it just seems a bit sad to take a friend. Like I can't handle it myself—even though I guess that's the whole point of all of this. A boyfriend just *looks* better.' She looked up to watch a taxi swoosh by outside—the first movement on the street in hours. 'And, trust me,' she added, 'I know how many types of wrong it is for me to be thinking like that.'

'Can you ask someone to pretend to be your boyfriend?'

He didn't know why, but finding a solution to Sophie's problem suddenly seemed vitally important. Maybe because he could picture just what she'd be like at the wedding if she went by herself—quietly strong and probably a bit distant. As she'd been when he first saw her at the bar.

She shook her head. 'Five years in Sydney means my

social circle back here in Perth is minuscule—and sadly bereft of single men prepared to fake date me.'

He knew it was very wrong to be a little relieved. But he couldn't help it. He didn't like the idea of Sophie dating anyone—real or otherwise. All very irrational and caveman of him. But the truth.

'It's a pity,' she continued, leaning over and propping her chin on her hand as she studied her plan. 'It would be a great project. I could schedule in fake dates to get to know each other and figure out a back story, and there's even a barbecue being held in a few weeks for another schoolfriend's birthday that we could attend...'

He watched her, fascinated, as she ran her finger down the list, her brow furrowed in concentration. A minute later she sat up rapidly, twisting in her chair to face him directly. 'I'm going to do it,' she said, a broad smile lighting up her face. 'Thank you—it's a brilliant idea.'

Slightly stunned, it took him a moment to reply. 'I thought you just said you had no one to ask?'

'Minor problem. I've decided I'll just hire someone.'

'What?'

But her attention was back on her plan. 'Do you have a pen? I wouldn't mind updating the plan now, if you don't mind.'

'What do you mean, *hire* someone?'

'Actually, I've got a pen in my bag I think,' she said, picking it up from near her feet and plopping it onto the bar to search through. Pen in hand, she finally answered his question. 'Just like I said—I'll advertise. Or maybe try to find an actor.'

'You said you had no money?'

She scribbled out *'Find a boyfriend'* as he watched. 'I put a little aside for rental bond and a car deposit. I can use that,' she said, totally matter-of-fact.

He slid off his chair, unable to sit still. She didn't notice, her head down as she wrote furiously.

'Sophie?' he asked.

'Mmm-hmm?' she said, her attention squarely on her plan.

He reached out, meaning to still her hand as he had before, but instead he found himself rubbing his knuckles lightly— and very briefly—down her cheek, hooking a finger beneath her chin to gently tilt it upwards.

Immediately he was caught in the indigo depths of her eyes—even more compelling now he understood the sadness behind them. For a few moments they just stared at each other in silence.

Dan cleared his throat. 'Are you sure this is a good idea?' he asked.

The pen dropped with a clatter onto the bar as Sophie pulled away from him. 'What else am I meant to do?' she asked, her gaze focussed everywhere but on him. 'I don't want to go alone and I've got no one to ask.' She laughed— that terrible brittle laugh again. 'The only single man I know in Perth is *you*. And you won't do it.'

'Why are you so sure?' he said, the words out before he could capture them.

She shook her head. 'Why would you? I bet you go out with only the intimidatingly beautiful. Women who have their lives together and don't blubber all over total strangers. Women who aren't so desperate they resort to asking total strangers to be their bogus boyfriends.'

'I'll do it,' he said.

Finally she met his gaze, her eyes wide. 'I don't think that's a good idea,' she said.

If he thought he'd been stunned before, now he was totally floored. 'Pardon me?'

'You and I,' she said, pointing at Dan, then at herself, then back at him, 'would never, *ever* work.'

Even though he agreed, her rebuff was a shock to his system. Women rarely—actually, *never*—rejected him. It took him a moment to recover.

'I'd agree,' he said, 'if this were genuine. But it's not. And we're adults. We can separate the fake from the real.'

Very slowly, she nodded. 'Okay. But it's not just the wedding, you understand? If I'm going to do this, I want to do this right.'

He couldn't imagine Sophie doing anything halfway.

'But I'll make it worth your while,' she continued. 'I'll need to check my accounts, but I should be able to get the money transferred early next week—'

'I don't want your money,' he said.

Now she looked as shocked as he assumed *he* had a few minutes earlier.

'Then why would you do it?'

He had no idea.

No, that was a lie. He knew exactly why. He was being an irrational, protective caveman.

It was a mistake, and he knew it. The chemistry between them was too palpable, and the last thing Sophie needed was a guy like him—in and out of her life in a flash. A guy whose longest relationship in the last ten years had lasted just over a month.

He was not the one to give Sophie back her faith in men.

But of course that wasn't what he'd offered to do.

Now he just had to come up with an explanation for Sophie.

'It's simply business,' he said, suddenly struck by inspiration. 'I'm understaffed at the moment. If you work every Saturday night until the wedding I'll be your date.'

The bar *did* need extra help, and he always had trouble

finding staff to work Saturdays. It was a legitimate business transaction.

Right.

She worried her bottom lip as she considered his words. 'That seems fair,' she said, 'as I'll need you a few hours each week for boyfriend practice.'

He liked the sound of practising.

Dan had a pretty good idea what expression he wore to warrant Sophie's cutting look, and he held up his hands in mock surrender.

But she didn't need to worry. He'd be on his very best behaviour over the next five weeks.

'Thank you,' she said with a smile. 'This is really nice of you.'

Nice was not something he associated with the idea of attending a wedding with Sophie. The opportunity to pretend to be her boyfriend—to touch her, pull her close and feel her body pressed against his...to kiss her...

Okay, maybe his *best* behaviour was pushing it. But he'd try.

'So, when are you free?' she asked. 'I'll just need to update my project plan and then we should catch up—maybe start talking about our back story?'

Already she was in project manager mode.

'How about we discuss that tomorrow...?' He glanced at his watch, not unsurprised to see it was nearly three in the morning. 'Or rather tonight?'

Her brow furrowed. 'What do you mean?'

'I mean that we'll have plenty of time to discuss our first project meeting, or whatever you want to call it, tomorrow.'

He started to collect the empty glasses, and Sophie slid off her barstool and hovered awkwardly beside him.

'Your shift starts at 5:00 p.m.,' he clarified finally. 'Wear black.'

CHAPTER THREE

The Sophie Project 2 (Project Manager: S. Morgan)
Task One: Establish ground rules

SHE was early. She always was—for everything from super-important oversize-tables-with-Sydney-Harbour-view boardroom meetings to Saturday afternoon coffee with friends.

Or, as it turned out, unexpected second careers as a bartender. Or as a waitress—or as whatever job she was actually supposed to be doing that evening.

She'd been far too busy processing Dan's offer the night before to think to ask what exactly he'd just bartered himself for. She suspected she'd still been a little slack-jawed with shock when he'd bundled her into a taxi at the end of the night.

No. Not night. At stupid o'clock *that morning.*

Now she sat at a white-clothed table in Dan's bar, downing a much needed cappuccino, as she waited for Dan to arrive. If the other staff members considered her sudden recruitment strange they said nothing as they carried on their business around her with barely a curious glance.

The bite of the double-shot coffee sharpened her cocktail-fuzzed synapses, allowing more lucid consideration of Dan's offer. Which mainly focussed on the whole *Why on earth would he do this?* issue.

It sure as hell wasn't because he was desperate for a new waitress…or something.

A fancy place like the Subiaco Wine Bar didn't just hire anyone—she was sure of it. The intimidatingly efficient staff buzzing around her made that patently clear.

Another alternative job occurred to her: kitchen hand.

Oh, she hoped so. She *knew* how to wash dishes. Waiting tables? Mixing drinks? Not so much.

And she really wanted to do a good job. Desperately, even. Because she was pretty sure that Dan had offered to be her fake date for no other reason than because, under all that sexy playboy exterior, he was a bonafide knight in shining armour. Obligated to rescue all damsels in distress—even tipsy ones with project plans in their handbags.

The noble thing to do would be to let him out of it. He'd gone far above and beyond his knightly duties—listening to her babble about Rick surely met any chivalry quota.

But then she'd have to go back to her original plan and hire someone, and that prospect held zero appeal.

Plus, it would be bad for the project. If this *were* an IT project she wouldn't be knocking back the star analyst who wanted to join the team, would she?

So, to be fair, if Dan was going to sacrifice himself honourably—so to speak—for *her*, then the very least she could do was be useful. No, *better* than useful—she wanted to be the best damn temporary employee he had ever seen.

Punctuality was a valuable employee asset—so she could

give herself a big tick for that. And she wore head-to-toe black clothing, as requested. Another tick.

Beyond that she was a bit lost.

At home, she'd watched online videos on waitressing skills, and beside her coffee cup she had her hastily purchased and encouragingly titled *Cocktail Bible.*

She had a feeling that her questionable memorising of cocktail recipes and a few instructional movies wouldn't get her very far. But still she'd try:

Margarita: tequila, triple sec, lime juice, salt. Martini. Ah, yes. Lubricant of choice for sad gibberers to total strangers and, on a more positive note, unexpected purveyors of handsome wedding dates.

Gin, vermouth… But how much of each? Um…

Between The Sheets… Honestly—who thought up *that* name? White rum, brandy and…uh…

But any chance of remembering the other ingredients evaporated as Dan walked into the room. He emerged through a door at the back of the bar marked 'Staff Only', looking tall, and fit, and every bit as handsome as she remembered.

Dressed in loose, long shorts that hung low on his hips, a fitted T-shirt with some surf company's logo splashed across it and flip flops, he looked younger than the mid-thirties she'd guessed him to be. As he walked closer she took in the dark stubble that shadowed his jaw and implied he hadn't yet shaved that day—and then she watched him watching her.

The sweep of his eyes set her skin to tingle.

She shivered.

Damn. Ignoring her attraction to Dan was going to be more difficult than she'd expected. Unfortunately she couldn't just tick *'Forget how hot Dan is'* or *'Erase all memory of the way he looks at me'* off some imaginary emotional checklist.

She reached for the project plan as if it was a safety blanket, extracting it from amongst the pages of the *Cocktail Bible. That* was what she needed to remember: the plan. That was far more important than any five-minute fling with Dan. He'd lose interest in her in seconds, and where would that leave her?

Dateless at Karen's wedding and back to square one.

And also, she suspected, with fresh bruises all over the heart she was working so desperately to heal.

With that in mind, she stood to greet him, hand extended, fully in business mode.

'Good afternoon,' she said, making herself look him square in the eyes and training her expression—she hoped—to 'slightly remote professional'.

He raised an eyebrow. 'I think we're a bit past shaking hands,' he said.

'I don't,' she said. 'This is a business deal, so I'm treating it like one.' She straightened her shoulders and reached towards him again. 'Hi, I'm Sophie Morgan,' she said.

He wrapped his hand around hers and instantly she knew she'd made a mistake. 'A *pleasure* to meet you, Sophie,' he said, the words a rich caress down her spine. 'I'm Dan Halliday.'

This was not the brisk handshake she'd intended. It was slow and deliberate, and when Dan brushed his thumb over her knuckles and the delicate bones of the back of hand it became *tingly*. Sensation emanated from that point and grew, spreading throughout her body.

She should let go, but she couldn't. Not because he wouldn't let her, but because she seemed to have lost the ability to try.

Still holding her hand, he leant close, his breath a hot whisper beside her ear.

She froze, waiting.

'How are you today?' he said, without any sexy inflection, just quiet, genuine concern. 'Did it help last night—the talking?'

It was so unexpected. She'd anticipated—no, *braced* herself for—some flirtatious comment. But he'd surprised her.

She nodded, her throat muscles suddenly tight.

He dropped her hand, and now it was as if he was channelling a more professional version of himself. It was disconcerting, this shift from sexy to seductive to concerned to businesslike.

Who was she kidding? He'd maintained *sexy* all the way through.

She cleared her throat. 'So—uh—what will I be doing tonight?'

'Have you waitressed before?' he asked.

She shook her head. 'I worked at a fish and chip shop when I was at uni, if that helps?'

He coughed—suspiciously as if he was covering a laugh. 'Working here will be a little different.'

'I know,' she said, very aware that in this environment her Masters degree was less than useless. 'I've been doing some research,' she continued, gesturing at the book propped open on the table. 'Making cocktails, how to wait tables—that sort of thing.'

He smiled. 'You *are* always organised, aren't you?'

'I try,' she said. 'Although it was hard to prepare when I didn't know what I'd be doing. Guess I should have focussed on waitressing, then?'

Dan nodded. 'Yeah. We need an extra person on the floor tonight.'

'I'll do my best.'

They stood in awkward silence for a moment, before Dan said gruffly, 'I'll ask Kate to come show you the ropes. Any questions—ask her. I'll be behind the bar.'

With a nod, he walked over to a small, dark-haired woman whom she assumed to be Kate—the lucky lady with the task of transforming Sophie Morgan, Project Manager, into Sophie Morgan, Waitress.

Waitressing. Not as reassuringly straightforward as washing dishes—although it was a relief to stop worrying about martinis, Caprioskas and Fuzzy Navels, or the final ingredient of Between The Sheets.

She couldn't stop herself running her eyes over the impressive width of Dan's shoulders as he spoke to Kate, his back to Sophie. Or letting her gaze dip lower, admiring *all* of his rear view. *Geez.* She even found the dark hair sprinkling his calves attractive.

But at least she'd solved the mystery of that cocktail's name.

Yep, she'd bet a woman had named it.

Right after meeting a man like Dan Halliday.

Much earlier that day—like at four in the morning—Dan had walked the short distance from the bar to his townhouse, reassuring himself that he *hadn't* just made a huge mistake.

With the whisper of a breeze ruffling the leaves along his tree-lined street the only accompaniment to the dull echo of his boots on the bitumen, he'd done his best to justify his actions.

Sophie was hurting. He felt sorry for her. He was helping her out.

End of story.

For a while he'd believed that, too. He'd been comfortable in that knowledge all day.

As he'd swum his regular laps along Cottesloe Beach he'd

even smugly considered the brilliance of the business side of the arrangement. A few hours of his time for a free employee—excellent!

Of course seeing Sophie again, her black clothes highlighting the paleness of her skin and her deep golden hair, had reminded him of his less altruistic reasons.

Touching her had only underlined them.

He could spin it any way he wanted, but the truth was he *liked* Sophie. He liked that she was smart, he liked that she was beautiful—he even liked her project plan.

What he *didn't* like was that some moron had damaged her. He didn't like that at all.

So he could tell himself he was just being a nice guy, but it was more than that. He'd wanted to see her again.

Actually, he wanted more than that. Quite simply, he wanted *her*.

And not in the happy-ever-after way that Sophie needed. In a much more primal, 'twisted sheets and tangled naked limbs' kind of way.

But that would be a very bad idea.

If he stuck to the plan they'd be fine. Sophie would get her wedding date, he'd get an extra employee—and surely it wouldn't take long for the heat between them to cool? Then the arrangement would be purely business. Just as he'd told her it was.

Yes. That was it. He'd just wait it out. Sophie would be out of his life in five weeks, and he could go back to dating more suitable women.

All he had to do was keep his hands off Sophie and it would work out fine.

With that in mind, he remained resolutely professional whenever she came to the bar to collect drinks, treating her exactly the same as he did his other employees.

If—very occasionally—he watched her take an order, or

walk away from the bar, while admiring the dramatic curve of her waist and hips in a very non-employer/employee appropriate kind of way—well, it couldn't be helped.

It was while he talked to a regular customer, rattling a cocktail shaker as they spoke, that he heard the unmistakeable crash and smash of many plates hitting the ground.

He looked over to see Sophie, standing smack bang in the centre of the restaurant part of the bar, the remnants of some unfortunate customer's dinner dumped at her feet. For a second it was silent as diners and staff turned to look at her as one.

Her face was totally white as she stared at the mess. Then she lifted her gaze—straight to him. As she did, the murmur of conversation and the clink of cutlery clicked back into place and the noise that had disturbed them was forgotten.

'I'm really sorry,' she said—or maybe just mouthed. She was too far away for him to hear. He smiled—he hoped reassuringly—but she still looked totally stricken.

He quickly poured the cocktail, then headed over to Sophie, who had knelt down to collect the pieces of broken crockery.

He squatted beside her, dropping the tray he'd carried from the bar onto the floor and started piling pieces of shiny white porcelain onto it.

'I'm sorry,' she said quietly. 'I know I'm sucking at this.'

'Don't stress,' he said. 'Everyone makes mistakes when they're new. You look to be doing fine to me.'

He reached across her to grab the last section of broken plate, causing their shoulders to bump gently together.

She twisted to look at him. 'You really think that? I keep forgetting the specials, and I have a bad feeling I've served at least one person the wrong meal. Or the wrong drink.'

'I'm sure you haven't,' he said. Miss Organisation wasn't

about to make that type of mistake. 'And besides, I didn't expect perfection.'

She gave a little huff of frustration. 'But I *want* to be really good at this, you know? To make this whole wedding date thing a fair deal. And all I've managed to do is break your plates and ruin someone's dinner.'

'Hey,' he said, and their shoulders touched again as he shifted his weight. 'I'm happy with the deal.'

She narrowed her eyes. 'Why? What are you getting out of it other than a dodgy waitress?'

It was terrible timing, but his gaze dropped—completely without his permission—to her lips.

She went completely still.

And then her eyes widened, before travelling south, too.

Really? Was he thinking about kissing Sophie surrounded by splattered risotto and chilli mussels and in a room full of people?

And it had been less than an hour since his decision to keep his distance. Pathetic.

He needed to do better than this.

Without a word he stood and forced himself back into professional bar-owner/manager mode—mollifying the intended recipients of the ruined dinner with a free meal, organising a kitchen hand and a mop to fix the rest of the mess, and then going back behind the safety of the bar, pouring wine and mixing cocktails with one hundred percent concentration.

He'd treat Sophie just as the employee she was. Nothing more.

It was a pity he couldn't quite make himself believe that.

Sophie stood patiently as the chef made his finishing touches to the three desserts she was awaiting for Table Two. The desserts were in the same style as the rest of the menu—

simple, unpretentious and delicious. Or at least she assumed delicious, given the very little food left on the plates she'd been clearing all night. She hadn't had a chance to eat yet. Or stand still. Or talk. Or think.

She couldn't remember the last time she'd felt so completely exhausted or so completely incompetent.

Or so completely flustered?

She'd felt Dan's eyes on her—a constant tingling awareness that had scrambled her brain at the most inopportune moments. Like when customers were ordering their meals. Or when she was—possibly a bit too optimistically—carrying too many plates at once.

She'd just about convinced herself that his attention was that of a concerned bar-owner—to the point of cultivating a little righteous frustration that it was *his* fault she kept flubbing the specials and had discovered her previously dormant clumsiness.

But then there'd been those few minutes when they'd knelt side by side on the floor, and any logical explanation for why he'd been looking at her had gone right out of the window. She'd seen the heat in his eyes—and known what it meant.

He'd been thinking about kissing her.

And just for a moment—maybe even less than that—a *millisecond*—she'd been thinking the same thing.

Not good.

Finally the chef finished adding chocolate sauce flourishes to the individual baked cheesecakes. She rocked side to side on her aching feet, trying to figure out how to handle this.

Was that why Dan had agreed to be part of her project? Did he think she was up for a no-strings-attached fling? Maybe he wasn't quite the magnanimous knight in shining armour she'd cast him as.

She would almost not blame him, if that *was* what he planned. She was sure he knew that she was attracted to him. She had, after all, basically turned into a puddle of lust when he'd simply shaken her hand.

But she'd already decided that starting something with Dan was a bad idea, and she wasn't about to be convinced otherwise. Despite the actions of her traitorous hormones.

The chef pushed the finished desserts plates forward for her, and she carefully arranged them—two plates on one arm, one on the other—just as Kate had shown her. Another waitress watched with obvious trepidation.

'You sure you've got those?' she asked, but Sophie wasn't worried.

This time she was determined to deliver the food un-scathed—through pure willpower alone if necessary.

With a reassuring smile she headed for the single remain-ing occupied table and managed to serve all three cheese-cakes with barely a wobbly moment.

Triumphant, she walked back to the bar rather than the kitchen. She knew she should be wiping down tables, or some other end-of-the-night, wannabe-best-employee-ever task, but instead she went to Dan. They needed to sort this out.

He was wiping down the counter top, but he glanced up as she approached. He'd shaved earlier, after his shower, but she didn't even get to miss his sexy stubble as he easily looked just as good clean-shaven.

But of course his perpetual state of gorgeousness would *not* cause her to waver in her decision. If he'd really only agreed to be her wedding date to get her into bed then she needed to end this now.

'I bet you didn't think you'd be working here this time yesterday,' he said.

Sophie's eyes darted to the clock above the bar. It had

been twenty-four hours since she'd accepted Dan's offer to talk. It felt a million years ago.

'No, definitely not.' Without her asking, Dan poured a glass of water and put it on a coaster in front of her. 'Thank you,' she said.

She watched him over the rim of her glass as she drank and he polished yet more stemware. She needed to just come out and say it.

'How long ago did you open the bar?' She figured she'd work her way up to the 'if you're just in this for sex you're out of luck' thing.

'Ten years ago,' he said. 'I bought the other bar five years later.'

'Other bar?'

Dan nodded, putting the last glass away and then hanging the cloth on a bar beneath the sink. 'Yeah, in Fremantle. It's almost twice as big as this place.'

She was impressed. This bar wasn't exactly small. 'You must have been pretty young when you bought this place, then?'

'Twenty-five,' he said, then grinned. 'What is this? Twenty questions?'

She felt her cheeks heat. 'I'm just curious,' she said. 'You know so much about me, and I know nothing about you.'

Also, every minute she spent in his company further convinced her that she'd gone way off track with her theory. Even as they spoke two young women perched at the opposite end of the bar were watching Dan with undisguised interest. And how could she have forgotten his easy banter with customers all evening? Women hung off his every word. And she had thought Dan was having her work in his bar, pretending to be dating her, just to get *her* into bed? *Sophie Morgan?* When he could have his pick of anyone?

Now it seemed ludicrous. Dan didn't need to jump

through hoops to get sex. He probably just needed to shoot a smouldering look in some unsuspecting girl's direction.

'What do you want to know?' he asked.

Who are you? Ruthless player or gallant knight?

'Have you always wanted to own bars?' she asked instead.

'No,' he said. 'I used to be a lawyer.'

'Really?' she said, surprised. She couldn't imagine Dan cooped up behind a desk all day.

He laughed, obviously able to see what she was thinking. 'I know. But it's true—and for a while I loved it.'

'What changed?'

His gaze slid away from hers, but she didn't miss his fleeting grimace. 'Nothing,' he said, 'It was just time for a change.'

She didn't believe him. His expression was reminiscent of one from the previous night—when she'd made the mistake of asking if he was scared of being hurt.

Her every instinct was to push—to ask him again and find out what—or rather *who*—had made Dan turn his life upside down.

But before she had a chance the girls at the end of the bar gestured to get his attention and he walked over.

The final table had finished their desserts, and so she'd lost her chance to ask more questions—although she was certain he wouldn't have been forthcoming. His shuttered expression was as good as a 'Keep Out' sign.

By the time she'd cleared the table, and the customers had paid their bill and left, the other staff had started to filter out of the kitchen, heading for the door and throwing goodbyes over their shoulders. The same cleaner from last evening swept the dining area, and she smiled at him as she headed back to the now empty bar. If he was surprised she'd been transformed from customer to employee he didn't show it.

Sophie picked up the coasters and empty glasses the

young women who'd been eyeing Dan had left behind. The scrawled name and phone number on one of the coasters didn't surprise her one little bit.

See! He can have anyone.

Dan was counting the money from the till when she walked behind the bar and dropped the coaster on the counter beside him.

'I think this is for you,' she said, in what was supposed to be a casual tone but instead ended up stiff and awkward. She swallowed, hoping he hadn't noticed.

No such luck.

He grinned and raised an eyebrow. 'You disapprove?'

She shook her head. 'Of course not!' Again, not the relaxed, breezy tone she'd hoped for. 'Why would I? It's none of my business.'

None at all.

She stacked the empty wine glasses into the dishwasher tray with a little more force than necessary.

What was wrong with her?

Out of the corner of the eye she saw him slip the coaster into his pocket. She clenched her teeth. Then realised what she was doing and relaxed her jaw. Took a deep breath.

'I'd like to organise our first project meeting,' she said.

There. That was better.

'Sure,' he said. 'Just tell me when and where.'

'Tuesday—at whatever time suits you,' she said. She was the unemployed one, after all. Then she named a nearby café she thought would be suitable.

'How about you meet me down at Cottesloe Beach?' he said. 'I swim laps most afternoons, and it's supposed to be hot this week. You could come for a swim, too.'

'No!' she said. Dan with his shirt off and all those rippling muscles—she was sure he had them—and her in a three-year-old faded bikini and deathly white skin? *No way.*

He shrugged. 'Just a suggestion.'

'I just want to keep things professional,' she said.

'I suggested a swim on a hot day,' he said. 'Not rolling around together on the sand.'

Not an image she needed.

He laughed at her shocked expression.

'Calm down, Sophie,' he said. 'I get it. You want to stick to the plan.'

She swallowed. 'Yes, I do. This is no different to one of my work projects. It's a professional arrangement—each of us trading our services. No funny business involved.'

'Funny business?' he said with a laugh. 'What are you? One hundred years old?'

She glared at him. 'You know what I mean.'

He held his hand to his heart. 'I solemnly swear that I, Dan Halliday, will not ravish Sophie Morgan.'

When he put it that way, she felt completely ridiculous.

'I'm sure you'll be able to restrain yourself,' she said dryly.

'I will,' he said, than added mournfully, 'somehow...'

'Stop it!' she said, reaching out without thinking to shove him gently. 'I just think it's easier if we know where we stand. Before—when I dropped the plates...' The words trailed off and she blushed as Dan caught her gaze. He knew exactly what she was talking about.

'It's okay. I agree with you. You and I would never work.'

They were the same words she'd used, but somehow when Dan said them they made her feel a little empty inside.

She *really* needed to pull herself together.

'That's good,' she said simply. And it was. She just needed to keep reminding herself of that.

'But more seriously,' he said, looking at her without humour in his gaze, 'if we're going to pull this off we'll need to put on a show for people. Touch, hold hands, kiss—that sort of stuff.'

She nodded slowly. 'I guess. But maybe we should have some ground rules. Just so neither of us gets the wrong idea.'

He reached out, and she froze as he tucked a loose lock of hair behind her ear. He leant close. 'So this would be okay, then?' he said, his voice deep and seductive. 'Touching you like this?'

She took a step back. 'There was no need for the demonstration, but yes,' she said, a little unevenly. 'And definitely no kissing,' she said firmly.

She had a terrible feeling that if Dan kissed her she'd find it impossible to stop at one.

'I don't think that'll work,' he said. 'We're supposed to be a couple in love.'

'Fine,' she conceded. 'But only on the cheek.'

He shrugged. 'Cheeks only it is. Whatever you want, Sophie.'

Ah, but this wasn't about what she *wanted* from Dan. Every traitorous bone in her body *wanted* Dan.

But what she *needed* was a 'no fuss' date to Karen's wedding. That was all.

In keeping with their reaffirmed arrangement, Dan was brisk and businesslike as he finished closing the bar for the evening. Lights finally switched off, and everything locked up, he walked her across the tiny, crunchy-gravelled car park to her mum's faded red hatchback.

She unlocked the door, but stopped before she opened it, turning to look up at Dan.

'Thank you for doing this,' she said softly.

He shrugged. 'I just need some extra help at the bar.'

Yes. That was all it was. Time to stop over-analysing and searching for ulterior motives. He wasn't some dastardly playboy hell-bent on seduction, and neither was he her own personal knight in shining armour.

He was just a guy helping her out. And she was helping *him* out. That was it. The end.

She opened the door and slid into the car, then reached out to pull the door closed—only to have the movement blocked by Dan's broad shoulders as he leant towards her.

'You did great tonight,' he said, his voice a smooth whisper against her ear.

And then his lips touched her cheek, instantaneously soft and firm.

Perfect. But in a split second his touch was gone, and he was unfolding himself back to his full height.

She couldn't stop her hand creeping up to touch her face where he'd kissed her.

'Thought I'd better try out this cheek-kissing thing,' he said, his tone only a little louder than before. 'Get some practice in. I don't know about you, but I think that one was pretty good.'

She nodded, her ability to form coherent words deserting her.

'Good,' he said again.

A minute or two later, just when she thought he was about to lean down and kiss her again, he turned and walked away.

CHAPTER FOUR

The Sophie Project 2.0 (Project Manager: S. Morgan)
Task Two: ~~Planning Meeting No. 1~~ *Rewrite Plan*

'SERIOUSLY, Sophie, a suit?'

Dan stopped a few metres away from the café table, running his eyes appreciatively along the fitted lines of Sophie's light grey skirt and baby pink blouse. At least she'd hung her jacket on the back of her chair as a small concession to the warm November afternoon.

She looked up from her laptop. 'I've been meeting with some contacts in the city, as unfortunately I need to get a job at some point. This,' she said, casually pointing down at her clothes, 'is not for you.'

Maybe not, but he could still enjoy the view.

'So we're not going all formal and hand-shaking again, then?' he asked, raising his eyebrows.

'No,' she said, her lovely blue eyes sparkling but direct. 'But we're still keeping this one hundred percent professional, right?'

'I don't think we could've been any clearer than in our last conversation,' he said wryly.

That was, of course, if you ignored his total lapse of judgement in the car park. That kiss had come from no-where, minutes after he'd silently berated himself for teasing her when she'd so awkwardly attempted to establish her 'ground rules'. Why, when he agreed with her, had he teased her?

And why, when he knew it was wrong, had he kissed her?

He took the seat across from her, dropping his backpack at his feet—he'd come straight from the beach—and his sunglasses onto the table. They were at the back of the café, surrounded by empty tables—a stark contrast to the busy alfresco area outside. All those sensible people were basking in the sea breeze, icy cold drinks in hand.

Instead he'd got a table full of project plans, checklists and...his own file.

He reached for the black folder with some trepidation. His name was printed clearly on the spine. 'Uh, Sophie—what's this?'

'That's your project file. I thought it would be easier if I put everything together for you.' She grinned. 'It's pretty cool, huh?'

He opened it and flicked through the section dividers: *Our History, About Sophie, About Dan, Task Schedule* and, of course, *Project Plan*.

The *About Sophie* section documented her basic information: date of birth, the schools she'd attended, her parents' names—that sort of thing—while all the others remained blank.

'You don't think this is a little excessive?' he asked.

'Probably,' she said, shrugging unapologetically. 'But hey, if you're going to do something, might as well do it right.'

He didn't even know why he was surprised—the file was

pure Sophie. He flipped back to her section, reading the first page with interest.

'I thought a lady never revealed her age,' he said. She was twenty-nine—six years younger than him.

'In this instance it's essential,' she said, in what he assumed was her sensible project manager voice. 'You never know what we're going to get asked at the wedding, or at the barbecue. Given we're—apparently—madly in love, we'll be expected to know that type of stuff.'

'Is that the barbecue you mentioned the other night?' he asked.

'Yeah,' she said. 'It's in the project plan.' She pushed his file aside and spread the plan in front of him. It was large enough that she'd needed to tape several sheets of paper together for it to fit. She ran her finger three quarters down the page. 'See? There. A good friend from school is having it for her birthday. It's perfect, as Karen and her fiancé will be there too, plus a lot of the guests.'

'Right.' He nodded, scanning the page. He saw that each task was marked with pink for Sophie, or blue for him. There were a *lot* of blue tasks. Actually, nearly all of them.

He checked all the pink tasks. 'What happened to underwear shopping?' he asked.

She narrowed her eyes. 'I've got two versions of the plan. Yours is a condensed version, just with the parts from *The Boyfriend Plan*.'

For a moment he just stared at her.

'The whole thing I'm calling *The Sophie Project*,' she clarified, 'because that's what it is. But I'm calling your bit *The Boyfriend Plan* to keep it all straight in my head.' She smiled at him. 'I know what you're thinking, but I promise I'm not totally insane,' she said. 'Just organised.'

'I'll take your word for it.'

'Anyway,' she hurried on, 'it'll make more sense when I walk you through it. But first—here.' She passed him a pen.

He half expected it to be emblazoned with his name, but thankfully it wasn't. 'Can you fill out this questionnaire?'

She passed him a few typewritten sheets of paper that matched the pages he'd seen in her file. But all the details were blank. There was space for him to answer each question—everything from where he'd been born through to the name of his last girlfriend.

As Sophie returned to typing away on her laptop, he began to answer the questions.

Siblings? None.

Cultural background? Australian/Croatian.

Parents/Grandparents? One set of each. His father's parents long dead; his mother's Croatian parents still going strong.

Ever married? His hand stilled.

He read the next question. *Any children?*

He put the pen aside and slid the questionnaire into the folder. 'I'll finish this later,' he said.

She looked up, surprised. 'Are you sure you can't do it now? We need to start studying each other's backgrounds right away.' She paused, then added, 'Actually, I just like seeing "100% Complete" beside as many items as possible. It's compulsive—what can I say?'

She grinned, but he didn't smile back.

'I have an appointment after this. I don't have much time.'

Her eyebrows drew together. 'I thought you said this was your day off?'

'Something came up,' he said firmly. He didn't like lying to her, but he wasn't about to fill out the questionnaire, either.

'Oh,' she said, frowning. 'Well…uh…let's go through the project plan instead.'

She stood, dragging her chair beside his so they could both look at the plan the right way up.

She reached across him to grab her pen, close enough that

he could smell the coconut scent of her hair. It was distracting, having her so close. Annoyingly so.

Having her close heated his skin, disrupted his thoughts, messed with his head. It reminded him of why he'd kissed her in the car park. It reminded him of why he wished that sanity hadn't prevailed and he'd kissed her on the mouth instead of walking away.

It reminded him of why, when he'd pulled that coaster out of his pocket, he'd thrown it away rather than calling the woman as he'd intended.

Her knee knocked against his. 'Sorry,' she said, turning her head as she spoke.

She gasped as she realised how close they now were— their foreheads, noses, *lips* mere centimetres apart.

Within seconds she'd shoved her chair backwards and retreated to the other side of the table. 'It'll be easier if I show you from here,' she said. 'More room.'

'Good idea,' he said, and it was. An excellent idea. Space helped neutralise the sparks between them enough that Dan could actually pay attention to what she was saying, rather than imagining how good she'd look in that sexy underwear she was planning on buying.

And paying attention was clearly a *very* important thing to do, once he began to register what some of the tasks assigned to him actually were.

'Wait,' he said, interrupting her. 'Did you just say *clothes shopping*?'

'Yes,' she said patiently. 'For the wedding. I'll buy you a suit.'

'I have plenty of suits,' he said, appalled. 'I don't take women out for dinner or go to industry functions in board shorts and flip flops.' As he was currently wearing. 'Don't worry, I won't embarrass you.'

'Oh, I didn't mean that!' she said, blushing a deep red. 'Not at all. You always look great.'

He raised his eyebrows. 'You think so?'

She tilted her head, widening her eyes innocently. 'What? You didn't notice all the women swooning in your wake today?'

He grinned. 'Sadly, no.'

'I'd imagine it must get tiresome, wading through the resulting piles of besotted women.'

He laughed out loud. 'Sweetheart, you have no idea.'

Her gaze shifted as she scanned his face. He could as good as see little cogs turning as her brain ticked over. 'It must be unusual for you, having a woman uninterested in you.'

Uninterested in how little he could offer her, definitely. She was lying to herself if she pretended there was no chemistry between them.

You deserve better than a guy like me.

He said nothing.

Sophie gave a little shake of her head as she refocussed on her project. 'Anyway. The clothes shopping was just about getting the look I want. The wedding date is like the final project deliverable. I want it to be perfect.'

'You do know I'm not a doll you get to play dress-up with? Just tell me what colour your dress is and I'll wear something that won't clash. Easy.'

'But—'

'No clothes shopping,' he said.

She explored his face for a few moments, as if she was gauging whether to argue further. 'Fine,' she said finally, reluctantly. 'I'll update the plan.'

Over the next half an hour Sophie walked him through the task lists—which mostly seemed to consist of planning meetings to map out their back story and quiz each other on pertinent facts about their life histories. Not exactly thrilling stuff.

'So that's it?' he asked, when Sophie finally reached the

end. 'Coffee meetings and quizzes for the next five weeks, one barbecue and one wedding?'

'Yes,' she said.

'It's a good plan...'

'But...?' Sophie asked.

'I think you're going about it the wrong way.'

She crossed her arms defensively. 'How do you mean? I spent hours working on this. I can't think of any better way to prepare.'

'I think that's the problem,' he said. 'You've got a meeting to plan how we met, and then another meeting for our first date, plus all those quizzes so we can get to know each other. All that effort and time spent *preparing*, when it would be a heck of a lot easier to just *do* it.'

'Do what?'

'Date,' he said. 'And before you start over-reacting, not for real. Fake date. Just like a real date—where you have dinner, find out about each other—with the added bonus that we're actually *experiencing* the date we're supposed to have had.'

'I guess then it wouldn't feel like such a lie,' she said quietly. 'That's good. That's really the only flaw in the plan...the having to lie bit.' She chewed on her bottom lip. 'But it would still be all make-believe, yeah?'

'Yes,' he said. 'But about a hundred times more enjoyable than learning each other's life history by rote.'

'Hmm,' she said, a blond-ponytailed picture of scepticism. 'But what if we don't cover everything in the file?'

'Why do we have to? Can't we just say we met speed dating last weekend, then started dating—and get to know each other like normal people?'

'I guess...' she said, her attention on the pen she twirled around and around with her fingers. 'But wouldn't you rather spend your evenings with women you're *actually* dating?'

'I'll squeeze you in,' he said.

'You really don't have to. I'm happy just to keep meeting during the day—'

'Sophie, I was *joking*. Despite your flattering assessment of my appeal to women, I'm not seeing anyone at the moment. I'm all yours…so to speak. Until the wedding.'

She nodded slowly. Then rotated the project plan so it faced her again. He watched as she scanned the tasks, her brow knitted in concentration.

'This could work,' she said after a few minutes. She crossed out one of the planning meetings. Then another. 'Actually,' she said, her voice warming with enthusiasm, 'it's actually a really efficient way of doing this. Streamlines the whole project. I like it.'

'Good,' he said as he stood, hefting his backpack over his shoulder. 'I'll pick you up on Friday at eight, then.'

'Where are we going?'

'It's our first date—it's a surprise.'

She shook her head. 'No, I really don't like surprises. I like to be—'

'Prepared?' he said.

'Exactly!' She gave him a relieved smile.

But then, for no other reason than he liked seeing perfectly coiffed, perfectly organised Sophie Morgan rattled, he said, 'I know. But bad luck. I'll see you Friday.'

CHAPTER FIVE

The Sophie Project 2.1 (Project Manager: S. Morgan)
Task Three: The First Date

SOPHIE paced from one end of her mother's living room to the other, her heels loud on the half-century-old jarrah floorboards.

'That won't make him get here faster, you know,' her mother said, curled up in the corner of the beige leather sofa with the paperback she was pretending to read on her lap.

'I don't *want* him to get here faster,' Sophie replied, making herself turn away from the window and the view of the street it offered.

'Whatever you say, darling,' her mother said, with an irritatingly wise nod.

Sophie put her hands on her hips. Her fingers slid against the snug-fitting silky fabric of her dress—a dress that might or might not be suitable for her mystery date destination.

'*Mum*, you know what I'm like. I'm fidgety because I don't know where I'm going—and I *hate* that. It's got nothing to do with Dan.' When her mother replied by raising one of her perfectly manicured eyebrows, Sophie huffed in frustration. 'You're not being at all subtle, you know—doing the whole *I'll just happen to be reading on the couch next to the front door when he arrives* thing. I see right through you.'

Her mother sniffed. 'As if I'd miss *this*! It isn't every day you get to meet your daughter's fake boyfriend.'

Unfortunately telling her mother about the plan had been unavoidable. Partly because she could come up with no valid explanation for her sudden transformation from virtual recluse to arriving home in the silly hours of the morning, but mainly because she hated lying to her mum. Her mother might be equal parts nosy and opinionated, but she was also an unquestionably awesome parent. Bringing Sophie and her sister up by herself could never have been easy—and then when years of hospital stays were thrown into the mix...

'You need to remember that,' Sophie said, making herself sit beside her mother and ignore the hum of tension resonating through her body—or at least try to. 'The fake bit. It's not real. It's totally platonic.' Up went her mother's eyebrow again, so she added, 'Look, we're not even *attracted* to each other.'

That outright lie managed to drop her unflappable mother's jaw.

'Well, maybe a little bit,' she conceded. Sometimes she was sure her cheek still burned from his kiss. 'But nothing's going to happen. We both agree.'

With a sigh, her mum scooted closer and wrapped an arm around Sophie's shoulder. 'Are you sure you're ready for this, hon?'

Her attention steadfast on the fastest of the super-kitsch porcelain ducks that flew across the pale yellow wall, she said, tone firm, 'I just said—it's *fake*.'

'Let's for argument's sake imagine it isn't.'

The urge to leap up from the cocooning softness of the

leather couch and restart her pacing was near impossible to suppress. But instead she made herself turn to face her mother.

'I'm not ready to jump into something new,' she said. 'That's why I'm doing this rather than speed dating, or online dating, or however else I'd been planning to find a *real* boyfriend. Getting a real boyfriend for Karen's wedding was the dumb idea. *This* is the sensible one.'

A rather liberal definition of 'sensible', for sure. More sensible than expecting to let go of all her hurt and anger and sorrow and fall in love conveniently in time for the wedding anyway.

'You don't *need* a date for the wedding, you know.'

It wasn't the first time her mum had pointed out this unarguable truth.

Of course she didn't need a date for the wedding. Every strong, independent bone in her body knew that—in fact *rebelled* against the idea that she should even consider a wedding date a necessity.

So she didn't *need* a wedding date.

But—and she hated this reality—she *wanted* one. Badly. Desperately, even.

A short seven months earlier she'd attended a wedding with Rick. Of course she'd had not even the tiniest inkling that anything was up, or that her perfectly constructed life was about to dissolve before her eyes. No, *instead* she'd had a wonderful evening, loving both the utter romance of the wedding and the opportunity for her brain to observe, analyse and file away snippets and ideas for her own wedding. She'd even taken a few notes in a tiny notepad hastily stuffed inside her clutch, for goodness' sake!

And it *had* been beautiful, that wedding. More than once, with an excited squeeze of his arm or a touch on his thigh at dinner, she'd whispered to Rick, 'The next wedding we go to will be ours!'

The next wedding she was going to would be Karen's.

That wasn't how it was supposed to be.

The unmistakable slap of leather shoes on her mother's authentic 1960s cement front porch, followed shortly thereafter by a deliberate knock on the door, saved Sophie from attempting to explain.

With yet another raised eyebrow and a long look that Sophie could only interpret to mean *Be careful* or possibly *Don't do anything stupid*, her mother curled back into the corner of the sofa. Sophie smoothed her hands down the midnight-blue fabric that covered her thighs and with a deep breath channelled her best impersonation of a calm, totally-has-her-stuff-together woman.

Half believing it herself, she walked to the door and twisted the handle.

You're nervous because you don't know where you're going. You're anxious because of the upcoming wedding.

The butterflies are not because Dan is standing behind the door.

She swung the door open.

Dan stood there, tall and dark, his face a kaleidoscope of shadows thrown by the sensor light that had flickered on behind him.

'Hey,' he said.

He wore dark grey trousers and a crisp white shirt, no tie—a whole other type of handsome from bartender Dan or board shorts Dan. She liked those too, but this version was a particular favourite. Maybe because she liked the contrast of his stark white shirt against the olive skin the two unfastened buttons at his collar revealed. Or the unbidden question it raised—was he that colour all over?

Or maybe it was because she knew he was about to whisk her away on a date—just the two of them, alone together.

No. Wait. *What?*

Unbelievable. One glance at Dan and she'd forgotten this

was a facsimile of a date. Fluttering tummy butterflies and romantic notions had no place here.

Flustered, and realising she'd been standing dumbstruck and silent for far too long, she said the first thing that occurred to her.

'You look great.'

Not ideal, but at least she'd managed to form words. Unfortunately now she had to scramble to provide adequate justification. 'I mean, I appreciate that you made an effort—like this is a *real* date. Which it *isn't*, of course. I know that. But I guess it's possible we could bump into someone I know, or maybe someone would—'

'Sophie?' he said, cutting her off. 'I get it. And just for the record...?'

She nodded, waiting as his gaze swept over her, leaving a wave of tingling sensation in its wake.

He cleared his throat. 'You look way better than great.'

Five minutes later Sophie was settling into the leather passenger seat of Dan's jet-black, low-slung, two-door sports sedan. The car suited him—darkly attractive and effortlessly sexy.

But totally impractical and completely unsuitable in the long-term.

She couldn't forget that.

'Your mum's nice,' he said, pulling away from the kerb. 'No probing questions or veiled threats against your honour. Always a plus when meeting the parents.'

Sophie gave an inelegant snort of laughter. 'And how often do you bother to meet a girl's parents, exactly?'

He nodded. 'Fair point. But believe it or not, when I was much younger and sillier, I may have been known to do so—once or twice.'

There it was again, a flash of something—anger? Regret?—

across his face. 'Who were these lucky ladies who persuaded you to do such a thing?'

He lips quirked up in a grin as he saw right through her. 'Nice try. But past girlfriends aren't a standard first date topic of conversation, are they?'

Sophie sighed. 'But this *isn't* a real date.'

'It isn't one of your project planning meetings in disguise, either. Let's just go with the flow. See where the night takes us.'

She didn't like the sound of that. Or rather, she did—which was the problem.

'Where are we going?'

She was rewarded for that question with a deliberately raised eyebrow. 'The flow, remember?'

She crossed her arms, jiggling her legs in frustration. The action slid her dress further apart from her knees. Why had it never seemed too short until she slid into Dan's car?

With a subtle smoothing of the fabric, she attempted to hide a gentle tug to pull it lower before Dan noticed.

No such luck. She felt his eyes on her the moment his attention flicked momentarily from the road. She shouldn't be surprised—men always seemed to have a special radar for displays of naked flesh.

She also shouldn't have been surprised when her skin goosepimpled beneath his gaze. Annoyed at herself, definitely, but not surprised. She should be used to the way her body responded to Dan. And by now she should be a heck of a lot better at ignoring it.

'Are you close to your parents?' she asked, both to say something and because she wanted to know.

Dan glanced at her across the centre console. 'Are you asking for your questionnaire?'

'No,' she said, shaking her head. That hadn't even occurred to her. 'You met my mum, and I'm curious about yours. And your dad too, of course.'

Her own father had walked out long before she was old enough to remember him.

'Well,' he said, 'I have one of each. Mum is tall, Croatian, bossy and a fantastic cook, while Dad is taller, a fourth generation Aussie, and loves to eat her food. That's about it.'

'What do they do?'

'Enjoy the leisurely life of the retired and lament my early exit from the family profession and my rejection of anything resembling settling down.'

That sentence was easily the most candid Dan had uttered since she'd met him.

'They were lawyers too?' she asked.

He nodded. 'But I think that's enough sharing of family history for a first date, don't you?'

She didn't miss the infinitesimal tightness of his voice, and it was enough to silence the many questions teetering at the tip of her tongue. She knew Dan well enough now to see she needed to quit when she was ahead.

'Fine, then—what should we talk about instead?'

'Normal first date stuff. Like what are your hobbies?'

'Other than spreadsheets?'

He grinned. 'Yes, other than spreadsheets.'

'Well, in my spare time,' she said, deadpan, 'I like to make lists…'

Dan laughed. 'I just bet you do.'

They ended up at one of Perth's best fine dining restaurants—a tiny, exclusive venue nestled behind the dunes of Cottesloe Beach.

So, yes, she was appropriately dressed—which was a huge relief.

Actually, no. Not really.

As they pulled into the restaurant's car park and their destination became clear, that tight coil of tension in her belly should have instantly loosened. Dan hadn't planned an evening skydiving, or any other ridiculous date possibility that she'd considered.

But it didn't. She felt just as wound up, and not one of those darn tummy butterflies had reduced its fluttering.

They continued their flapping as Dan asked the sommelier for wine recommendations. 'Sophie doesn't like red,' he said.

Wines ordered, and sommelier on his way, Sophie looked at him with surprise. 'How did you know that?' she asked.

'I've been reading your file.'

She narrowed her eyes. 'I didn't think you believed in the file. Aren't we supposed to be getting to know each other "like normal people"?'

'Normal people don't dot point their life stories into two pages or less.' He shrugged. 'Of course I read it. Just don't expect me to answer any spot quizzes, okay?'

She laughed, knowing arguing her relative normalcy was a pointless battle. Fake dates and colour-coded life plans didn't exactly paint a flattering picture. 'So what else did you learn?'

'Apart from about your fascinating teenage career as a newspaper delivery girl?' he said. 'Well, in addition to your dislike of red wine, you also don't like coriander.'

She grimaced. 'I really went all out with the mesmerising content, huh?'

Dan grinned. 'I wasn't bored,' he said, 'and I learnt all sorts of random stuff. Like that you went to school with my cousin—Melinda Halliday.'

Sophie nodded. 'Yes, I did. She was in the year above me at high school.'

She spoke without thinking, but immediately realised her mistake. She held her breath, waiting.

His brow wrinkled. 'I thought the file said you were twenty-nine?' he said. 'The same age as Mel?'

She breathed out slowly. Of *course* he was going to ask questions.

'I am,' she said, then paused, considering. How to explain? 'I…uh…had to skip a year.'

'Why?'

It was the obvious question, but the answer—not so much. There was a reason she'd left this little detail from her file, after much typing and deleting and typing and deleting.

Could she use Dan's line? *It's probably not first date conversation.*

She could, and it would have the added bonus of being the absolute truth. Stories of childhood illness didn't really set the scene for a hot and heavy first date, did they?

But this, of course, *wasn't* a real first date.

'Cancer,' she said simply. 'Mine. I was ten and in and out of hospital for months. I got so far behind at school I took the rest of the year off to recover and had to repeat.'

For a long moment Dan just stared at her, his face stiff with shock. When he spoke, his voice was rich with genuine concern. 'Oh, Soph, that's terrible.'

It was the first time he'd shortened her name. As if he was a friend, and not just part of her project plan.

'Uh-huh,' she said, with a weak attempt at a smile. 'That's one word for it.'

His expression quickly morphed from shock to concern. 'But are you okay now?'

She nodded. 'Yes, perfectly.'

The words slipped out effortlessly, as easily as if they'd been true. Oh, she'd beaten the cancer, but it hadn't left without a struggle—or without leaving its mark. At one time, in her teens, she'd imagined she'd done a deal with the devil: her life in exchange for her unborn children.

She was no longer that angsty, overly dramatic seventeen-year-old, but the reality remained. Chemotherapy had made her infertile. In an immovably permanent, no-chance-of-a-miracle-baby-*ever* kind of way.

'I don't normally tell people about it—being sick,' she said. 'I only tell people really close to me.'

'I'm sorry. I shouldn't have asked.'

She shook her head. 'Don't worry about it. I didn't have to tell you.'

It was true. She could have come up with something else. Her illness was an unlikely topic of conversation for the barbecue or the wedding, so a white lie wouldn't have done any harm to her project.

But she hadn't liked the idea of lying to him. For a relationship that had been formed solely to perpetuate a lie, it was an unexpected realisation.

Dan was just looking at her, his gaze exploring her face as if he was waiting for her to speak again. And she *should* speak, she knew. She kept almost doing it—almost opening her mouth to start saying the words where she'd tell him the *whole* truth.

Just so you know, I can't have children.

But she remained silent. Why?

Her decision always to announce to men her infertility like a newspaper headline—bold and harsh and up-front—meant she needed to get over this. This might not be a real date, and he had no prospect of becoming a real boyfriend, but why not practise with Dan?

Just so you know, I can't have children.

Just eight words. When she'd told him everything else. Why not this? She'd told total strangers that she was barren. Why not Dan?

He doesn't need to know.

A valid justification because—well, he *didn't*. Her ability or otherwise to carry a child was about as irrelevant and unrelated to their deal as it was possible to get.

But that wasn't the reason she wasn't telling him. She wasn't telling him because she didn't *want* him to know.

And she didn't want to even begin to analyse why that was.

It was a lovely meal, but Dan barely tasted a mouthful despite wiping his plate clean. It was Sophie rather than his tastebuds getting his full concentration.

She'd changed the subject, awkwardly and rapidly, from her illness to safer, more generic first date topics of conversation. Travel. Reality TV. Movies.

As she spoke he studied her. Not the upswept shimmer of her hair or the perfect paleness of her shoulders, nor the hint of cleavage the heart shaped neckline of her dress revealed—although he wasn't exactly ignoring any of those things. Instead, he studied her with fresh eyes.

His heart ached for the ten-year-old Sophie. He hated—*hated*—the idea of her being so sick and stuck for months in a hospital bed. Irrationally it made him angry—angry that it had happened to her and angry he hadn't been there to help her.

Although what good a sixteen-year-old boy who'd spent his every waking moment studying would have been to her he had no idea.

Maybe he could have held her hand.

'My birthday's October 20.'

She stilled, her fork and its piece of salmon hovering midway between her plate and mouth. 'Pardon me?'

'And I'm an only child.'

Her gaze sharpened, and then she smiled. 'The questionnaire?' she said.

'Yeah. Figured it couldn't hurt to answer a few of your questions.'

Especially when the past *she'd* just revealed left him humbled. Suddenly it seemed petty—juvenile, even—to hold his past so close to his chest. What she'd said in the café was true. He knew all about her, while she knew nothing about him.

'Thank you,' she said. 'Can I take notes?'

He laughed, even though he knew she was completely serious. Sophie didn't joke when it came to her project. 'I think you should quit while you're ahead.'

'Okay,' she conceded. 'Go on, then.'

She placed her fork on her plate and settled back in her chair, waiting.

'This feels like a job interview,' he said.

She took pity on him. 'Maybe we should combine what we both want. You want this to be like a normal date, and I want to tick an item off my project plan. So—' she reached forward, picking up her wine glass and taking a sip '—how about I pretend to be a particularly nosy first date...' he raised his eyebrows at that '...and you pretend to be the kind of guy who would *not* totally freak out if you were asked these questions on said first date.'

He nodded. 'Fine.'

'Good,' she said, then leant towards him, her voice low and unexpectedly sultry. 'So, Dan, what high school did you go to?'

He blinked at the incongruity of her tone and the question.

She grinned. 'I was trying to cancel out the job interview vibe.'

He leant closer himself, running his finger down her cheek before she had a chance to pull away. 'Goal achieved,' he said roughly.

'Oh, good,' she said, in a slightly uneven version of her project manager voice, straightening up in her chair. But her prim and proper act was far too late—heat radiated between them and warmed her cheeks to a deep pink.

He cleared his throat. 'Guildford Grammar,' he said.

'Ah, private school boy—I should have guessed,' she said with a teasing grin, and the tension eased—a little.

While they waited for dessert she peppered him with questions—where he went to university, how he liked his coffee, that sort of thing. Nothing too scary, even if he did feel the need to question the necessity of them every now and then. And Sophie always answered the same way: 'I like to be prepared.'

Finally she got to the question he'd been dreading.

'I think I already know the answer to this one,' she said with a smile across the two complicated looking desserts between them, 'but have you ever been married?'

He took a moment to respond, still questioning his decision to tell her the truth. He *never* spoke about his past. To anyone. As far as the women he dated were concerned he'd been allergic to commitment from birth.

Sophie filled the silence as she poked at her crème caramel with a spoon. 'I know—silly question. But I thought I should ask—'

'Yes, I have.'

The spoon clattered onto the fine china serving plate, smudging the chocolate sauce flourishes around the rim.

'What?' she said. 'I mean—sorry—uh—*when?*'

He counted back the years. It was a lifetime ago—a whole different version of Dan ago. 'I got married thirteen years ago. Divorced three years later.'

She still stared at him, agog. *'Wow.'* She tilted her head and chewed at her bottom lip. 'I thought maybe a woman was why you quit law, but I never thought you'd been the marrying type.'

'You thought a *woman* was why I bought my bar?' he asked, surprised she'd spent any time thinking about it at all. Maybe he shouldn't be—she probably considered it research for her project.

She nodded. 'Yeah, a few times you've gotten all tall, dark and distant—I put two and two together.'

'It wasn't a woman.' He paused. 'I just realised my life was on totally the wrong track.'

'The marrying-super-young track?' she asked. 'You must have only been—what?—twenty-two? Twenty-three?'

'Maybe,' he said. 'Although more likely the marrying-for-the-totally-wrong-reasons track.'

Her eyes widened with interest. 'And what were they?'

He met her gaze for a long moment. 'That wasn't on the questionnaire.'

Dan half expected her to push, but to his relief she just nodded with only slightly disappointed understanding.

'But can I ask just one more question?'

'How about we eat dessert and go back to pretending this is a normal date? Without the nosy question-asker?'

No such luck.

'It's an important one, and given I got the marriage one so wrong I really have to ask.' Her gaze flicked downwards, and she absently moved her spoon around her plate. 'Do you have any children?'

'No,' he said immcdiately. Too quickly, probably.

But Sophie didn't seem to notice. She laughed—maybe a little unnaturally—and said, 'I'm relieved I didn't read you completely wrong, then.' She scooped up a piece of dessert with her spoon, but didn't make a move to eat it. 'Would you do it again? I mean marriage?'

And repeat his past mistakes? Regress to the person he'd once been but now barely recognised?

'No,' he said. 'Never.'

CHAPTER SIX

The Sophie Project 2.1 (Project Manager: S. Morgan)
Note to self: Maintain professional distance from Dan
(Important!)

AFTER dinner they walked across the car park to a soundtrack of barely muffled music and loud conversation from the pub across the street. Sophie walked in silence beside him, glancing occasionally at the crowd almost spilling from the open ground-floor windows.

'Do you want to go in for a drink?' Dan asked.

'Oh, no,' she replied. 'I used to go there when I was at uni. We're not the target demographic. And besides, what I'm wearing is all wrong.'

He needed no excuse to run his gaze down the tailored lines of her dress. It was just like her, that dress—elegant, subtle, classic. And sexy. Very, very sexy.

'Who cares what you're wearing?'

The patrons he could see wore everything from collared shirts and sparkling tops through to dresses and shorts that had obviously come straight from the beach.

'I care,' she said. 'Besides, the agreement was dinner only. You don't have to do this.'

What if he wanted to? Not go to that pub, particularly, just spend more time with Sophie?

'Do you only ever do things you've planned?' he asked, coming to a stop in the middle of the car park, directly across from the entrance to the pub. 'Never try anything that isn't perfectly scheduled into one of your project plans?'

'Of course not,' she said. 'I can be spontaneous.'

'Great,' he said. 'Let's go grab a drink, then.'

He could see her battle with what to say. Argue—and prove his point—or acquiesce and walk into the pub— *shock! Horror!*—over dressed.

'Fine,' she said. 'One drink.'

'Watch out,' he said. 'Don't go all wild and crazy on me.'

She shot him a cutting look. 'I know how to have a good time.'

'Really?' he asked, remembering something she'd said that first night at his bar. 'Dinner parties and long walks on the beach with Rick, right?'

She went silent, staring down at her sparkling silver heels, and for a moment he was sure he'd gone too far. But then she surprised him by reaching out to grab his hand. Her eyes were bright. Determined.

With a tug, she pulled him towards the road. 'Come on,' she said. 'Let's go.'

She led him past the pair of burly bouncers and into the dimly lit and heaving pub. People were crammed into every inch of space in front of a window-framed backdrop of star-scattered sky and the thick black ocean beneath it.

Sophie had been right. He was easily ten years older than the majority of... No, make that *everyone* else there. Sophie's comparatively ancient status appeared to be doing her no harm, though—more than one young male head swiv-

elled in her direction as she strode into the room. Make that
a hell of a lot *more* than one young male head.

He used the hand she still held to slow her rapid pace
and to draw her closer towards him. Close enough that their
shoulders bumped as they walked.

She shot him a questioning look but made no move to
drop his hand. Good.

The crowd at the central bar was easily four deep, but
Sophie guided them through to the front with absolutely no
effort at all. At her destination, rather than ordering, she
turned and leant against the polished chrome bar as if she
owned the place.

'What can I get you?' she said. No. *Purred* was a more
appropriate description.

Where was the woman who'd subconsciously plucked at
the fabric of her dress when she'd answered the door—who
had just two minutes ago anguished over the suitability
of her clothing? He dropped her hand, searching her face
for signs that this was all an act. For cracks in this sudden
veneer of ultra-sophistication.

There were none.

A shove from amongst the crowd suddenly pushed him
towards her, and for long, long seconds they were pressed
together, chest to chest, hip to hip, thigh to thigh. Her softness against his hardness.

His hands had landed at her waist and she'd turned her
face up to his, her eyes rapidly changing from shocked to...
Well, he guessed he was looking at her in exactly the same
way.

He swallowed a groan. They were as good as embracing
already—it would be so easy to close the gap between their
mouths and make it real.

Her tongue darted out, moistening her lips.

It was all the invitation he needed...

But as he shifted his weight forward, moments from the kiss he was beginning to think had always been inevitable, she sucked her full bottom lip between her teeth in a movement he'd seen her perform many times before. When thinking. Worrying.

It was the crack in the veneer—an unwanted reminder that stopped him in his tracks.

He stepped back. 'I'll have a bourbon,' he said.

She closed her eyes, her black mascaraed lashes a harsh contrast to her porcelain skin.

When she opened them again Miss Sophistication was back, and she smiled brightly, not meeting his gaze, before turning to order their drinks.

Minutes later, drinks in hand, they managed to fight their way through the masses to a coveted space near a window. The evening ocean breeze tugged long strands of Sophie's hair free of whatever women called the complicated roll she'd fashioned her blond mane into.

She took a long drink of her cocktail, meeting his gaze over the rim. 'I'm not as boring as you think I am.'

'I never said you were boring.'

'Lacking spontaneity, then,' she said.

He shrugged. 'That's kind of unavoidable when you live your life to an immovable, predetermined schedule.'

'I don't,' she said. 'I know how strange my project plan is. But it's a one-off thing—a guide to getting my life back on track.'

'But it isn't the project plan that had you stressing about where we were going tonight, and umming and ahhing out in the car park before.'

'I came for a drink, didn't I?' she said, nodding at the martini glass in her hand. 'And, for your information, I *did* have fun when I lived in Sydney. Rick preferred to stay at home, but I'd go out with my girlfriends, or hit King Street Wharf on a Friday after work.'

Now he could add *dull* to Rick's list of sins.

'But you *did* plan that fun, didn't you? Organise it a few days in advance? Take clothes to change into after work? That sort of thing?'

Sophie opened her mouth to disagree, than snapped it shut before nodding with much reluctance.

'So you might not have had a project plan stuck on your fridge, but it was there nonetheless.'

She narrowed her eyes, shifting from *deny* to *defend*. 'Fine. If, like you say, I *am* marginally over-organised, what's wrong with that? Why is it wrong to want some control over my life?'

'Is that what it is?' he asked. 'You need to be in control?'

She slowly shook her head. 'No, that's the wrong word. It's, uh...' Her forehead creased in concentration. 'I guess I like how when I put something on a list it happens. And then you cross it off and it's gone.' A shadow passed across her face. 'Even the bad stuff.'

He stepped towards her automatically—to do what, he didn't know. Touch her arm? Hold her?

He forced himself to do neither. Accidental top-to-toe contact might have been okay at the bar, but touching her now would certainly cross whatever line they were both dancing so close to.

'What bad stuff?' he asked.

For what felt like minutes she stared at him, deep into his eyes. Assessing him. Chewing her bottom lip again.

She placed her glass down gently on the windowsill. 'When I was sick, my mum had a calendar of all of my treatments. On the fridge, actually. We'd talk about what was going to happen, and how it was going to make me better— so even though it was scary I always knew what was going on.' She paused as the crowd around them cheered the opening bars of an iconic Australian rock anthem, then raised her voice to be heard over the resultant joyful, drunken singalong. 'And then we'd come home from the hospital and I'd put a big red cross over that treatment because it was done. Gone.'

She shrugged. She had spoken in the matter-of-fact tone of someone who had figured something out long ago.

But had she really?

He realised that the woman who'd dragged him into the bar was the same woman he'd seen glimpses of before—a sparkle in her gaze here, a teasing comment there. It was as if she was wearing her super-organisation like armour, only occasionally letting people see the real Sophie through the chinks.

He wanted to see more of that Sophie.

But how to encourage her to take detours off the path she'd mapped out for herself?

He might not have had a project plan, but he knew all about travelling full steam ahead with blinkers on down the wrong path. Not that his solution—quitting his job, buying a pub and swearing off serious relationships—would be of much use to her.

Sophie was watching him, waiting for him to say something. Her brows were drawn together as she over-thought whatever she imagined he was about to say, making him want to reach out and rub those worried lines away.

Beside her a couple barely out of their teens began to kiss enthusiastically, and then a board-shorts-wearing man with bleached blond hair came within millimetres of sloshing beer down Sophie's dress as he barrelled obliviously past.

They couldn't have this conversation here. They shouldn't even *be* here. His interest in walking in had been driven purely by Sophie's reluctance to do so.

'This place is awful,' he said. 'Do you want to go?'

Sophie nodded eagerly. 'I'm sure I've reached my spontaneity quota for the night.'

A few minutes later they were outside, and the breeze had cooled enough for Sophie to hug her arms as she walked. He had no jacket to offer her, so he did what felt natural—he wrapped his arm around her shoulders, pulling her close.

At his touch she paused mid-stride, turned to look at him. Her height and her heels raised her to near his eye-level, resulting in a negligible gap between her lips and his. Convenient.

'Very chivalrous—but a little touchy-feely for a first date, don't you think?' she said, but made absolutely no effort to move away.

He responded by tugging her closer, turning slightly towards her to block suddenly stronger gusts of wind. 'No,' he said. 'Do you?'

She was shaking her head almost before he'd asked the question. 'I guess not.'

They started walking again, the distance to his car annoyingly short. He liked how she fitted against him—how they almost instantly figured out a perfect rhythm to their walk.

Part of him questioned what the *hell* he was doing. Touching her. Considering the practicalities of kissing her. Wondering if maybe it wouldn't be *that* bad an idea to make this date one hundred percent real.

But it was only a small part of him doing the questioning. The vast majority—capitulating pathetically to the will of his baser self—thought that wrapping his arm around her was the *best idea ever* and had all sorts of plans. Starting with taking advantage of how little distance there was between their mouths.

They reached the car, and rather than unlocking the doors

he found himself turning Sophie so her hips and lower back brushed against the passenger side window.

More strands of her hair had pulled loose and whipped about in the breeze. A dull cheer originated from the pub as yet another mid-eighties classic blasted out onto the street.

He'd dropped his arm from her shoulders, and while he still stood close they didn't touch at all.

Sophie was thinking. He could as good as see the pros and cons list he was sure she was rapidly constructing in her mind, and knew he should probably be doing the same.

Kissing Sophie:
Pro: I get to kiss Sophie.
Con: …

Ah. No prizes for guessing which part of him was writing that list.

'You think it's stupid, don't you—all my planning and crossing off of things?'

'No,' he said, imagining a tiny version of Sophie standing in the same kitchen he'd been in earlier that night, a red pen gripped tightly in her hand. 'Not stupid. Brave.'

'Maybe when I was ten.'

'No,' he said. 'Not just then.'

'I needed something after what happened with Rick—to focus on, you know?' She dropped her chin, focusing on the small stitched logo on the left side of his chest. 'But I guess I sometimes take it a little too far.' She laughed—a hollow sound. 'And start to verge into obsessive/crazy territory.'

He reached out, tucking a finger beneath her chin and dragging her gaze back to his. 'You aren't crazy. And I can relate to being a little obsessive about a goal.'

'With your bar, do you mean?'

He nodded. 'Yeah.'

And his previous career. And university. And his marriage.

She shook her head, and his hand fell away from her face. 'You're nothing like me. You *are* spontaneous. You have fun with women, you totally change your career and can even agree to be a total stranger's fake wedding date.' She sighed noisily. 'Geez, if some guy had asked *me* to do something like this I probably would have whipped out a damn SWOT analysis.'

'A what?'

'Strengths, weaknesses, opportunities, threats…' Another long sigh. 'My God. I *am* boring, aren't I?'

He smiled. 'Wrong again.'

'You're just being nice.'

He leant forward, close enough so his shirt just brushed against her chest and he could whisper into her ear. 'You know what, Soph? I'm really not that nice a guy.'

To prove his point, his hands stole out, sliding up to rest at her waist. Not lightly. *Firm.*

'I've had an idea about how you can shake things up. A small diversion from your project plan.'

Despite all that she'd just said, she stiffened. 'I can't drop anything from the plan. I *do* need to find a job, and go to the wedding, and—'

He ran his thumbs gently up and down her sides in an attempt to distract the cogs working overtime in her brain. 'Don't panic—the plan stays. I just think it will do you good to have a little fun along the way. Be more spontaneous.'

'And does this fun by any chance involve you?'

His breath was hot against the delicate skin beneath her ear. 'If you're interested.'

Okay, so it wasn't an entirely selfless suggestion.

She pulled back just a little—enough to give her room to twist slightly in his arms and meet his gaze. A streetlamp illuminated her satiny skin and reflected off her cobalt-blue eyes.

'What exactly are you suggesting?'

'Doing what I'm pretty sure we both want to do.'

It was too dim to see the blush that flushed her cheeks, but he knew it was there.

'I thought you said that you and I would never work.'

'I've changed my mind,' he said. And he had. He'd been so sure that starting anything with Sophie could only end badly—that he'd only add to the hurt she was already experiencing. But maybe he'd had it all wrong. As long as they both knew the score, why *not* explore this unarguable attraction between them? Maybe a distraction—an activity that was certainly *not* on her project plan—was exactly what she needed?

'But you don't do relationships.'

Now it was his turn to go tense in her arms. Here it was—proof positive as to why this was terrible, horrible—the *worst* idea. He was thinking of a hot kiss up against the car and how badly he wanted to see Sophie in the new underwear she was going to buy—and then remove it as quickly as possible—while she jumped straight to talking about *relationships*.

'I don't,' he said, the words triggering the slightest tightening of Sophie's jaw. 'But I do flings. Why don't we have one? A no-strings-attached, *spontaneous* fling from now until the wedding? With the added bonus of avoiding the need to lie to your friends. At the wedding we would really be together.'

'But not in a relationship?'

'No.'

The corner of her mouth kicked up, but there was no sparkle in her eyes. 'And this is going to be *good* for me? Is this your version of helping me out—a bit of charity for

the sad, recently dumped and compulsive maker of lists?'
She pressed her palms to his chest and gave a light shove.
'Thanks, but no thanks.'

He stepped back, but let his hands fall from her slowly.
Reluctantly. He shrugged. 'Sophie, I like you. I *want* you.
And I think we could have fun together. Charitable is the last
thing I'm feeling right now.'

Instead he was itching with the need to touch her again, to
drag her into his arms and kiss her the way he badly wanted
to. To convince her with his body after totally failing with
his words.

He made himself take a further step away from her, and
reached into his pocket for his keys. Sophie had leant back
against the car, her head turned as she gazed out across the
deserted beach and beyond to the inky black sea.

With a press on his key the car was unlocked, and Dan
strode around the car to the driver's side door. Sophie pushed
away from the window and turned to open her door just as
he opened his. Across the patent black roof of the car their
eyes met.

'If you change your mind, Soph, all you have to do is say
the word.'

CHAPTER SEVEN

The Sophie Project 2.1 (Project Manager: S. Morgan)
New Task: Visit to Fremantle (<u>not</u> a date)

WHEN Sophie pulled into the wine bar's car park fifteen minutes prior to the start of her Saturday night shift Dan was leaning against the hood of his car, watching her.

Waiting for her?

She pretended not to notice as she climbed out of the car and swung her handbag over her shoulder. Ignoring him was hard work—because it would be so much easier to let the heat of his undivided attention incinerate all the sensible, logical, *necessary* decisions she'd made.

Like not agreeing to a no-strings-attached fling with Dan.

That was the big one. But that decision was the culmination of a whole heap of smaller but equally important ones. Because as they'd stood beside his car after their date, her skin goosepimpling and her body shivering for reasons unrelated to the buffeting breeze, she'd had many tough choices to make.

For example, when his hand had curled around her waist

she could have a) Brushed him off. Stepped aside. Something! Or b) Done nothing.

And then, later, when he'd made the boundaries of his suggestion crystal clear—that anything between them could only ever be temporary—she'd warred with herself. *Could* she shove aside her logical self and seize the moment? *Could* she, a woman who had only a series of committed relationships behind her, really let go and leap into the madness that would be a fling with Dan?

She'd been so close—*so* close—to answering yes. But then her logical self had piped up, loud and obnoxious: *He feels sorry for you. He thinks ruffling the feathers of crazy project plan lady would practically be a community service.* And, even worse: *You like him. He'll hurt you.*

That realisation had made her last decision easy.

Slide her hands up his chest to: a) Creep higher to loop behind his neck and pull him closer. Or b) Push him away.

And so she had—although it hadn't felt as right as she'd hoped. That little throwaway comment across the roof of the car hadn't helped either, but she'd managed to restrain herself from doing or saying something unwise throughout the whole drive home. Dan's apparent ability to instantly forget that he'd just propositioned her had made that a heck of a lot easier too. He'd been clearly far from cut up over her rejection.

Humph.

So now she walked across the car park, all senses in overdrive as her brain over-analysed the situation and her body over-reacted to the force of his gaze. Avoiding him was impossible as he'd parked right beside the rear entrance to the wine bar. And there wasn't even a reason *to* avoid him—apart from the certain knowledge that the amount of time she spent with Dan was inversely proportional to the strength of her self control. Not that she thought she'd jump him in the middle of a public car park, of course...

'Right on time,' he said as she slowed to a stop in front of him. He didn't move from his position propped against the car, his legs crossed at the ankles.

She nodded. 'I always am.'

He grinned, reaching with a strong tanned hand to slide his sunglasses off. He wasn't in any of the uniforms she was familiar with—not the beach uniform or the bartender one. Instead he wore jeans and a slim-fitting charcoal T-shirt that clung to the width of his biceps.

'Always?' he said, raising his eyebrows. 'You never lose track of time? Sleep in? Get distracted?'

'No. That's what alarm clocks are for.'

He looked a little stunned. 'So you've never been late for work—ever?'

She laughed. 'Of course I have. Ferry strikes, that sort of thing.'

'But only when it was outside of your control?'

She nodded, again. 'Yes.'

'Never taken a sick day when you weren't sick? Never wagged a day off school, right?'

'Of course not!' she said. 'I would *never* do that.'

Again that cheeky grin. 'Calm down. I'm not impugning your character, here. Just setting the scene.'

She eyed him warily. 'For what, exactly?'

He pushed away from the car and opened the passenger side door with a flourish. 'Climb in,' he said. 'We're blowing off work today.'

It took her a moment to grasp what he was saying. 'Pardon me?'

'We're taking the night off. I thought we could go into Fremantle. Watch the sunset or something. I could show you the other bar.'

'Take the night off?'

'Uh-huh. It's a pretty simple concept.'

She shook her head. 'Why would we do that?'

'Because we can. I'm the boss, and choosing when I take time off is a big perk.' He shrugged. 'It's really not that big a deal. Come on—it'll be fun.'

'But the whole reason I'm working here is because you're understaffed. This doesn't make any sense.'

Finally Dan seemed to realise that she wasn't going to obediently leap into his car, and he swung the door shut with a heavy, muffled, this-is-an-expensive-car-sounding thud. A bit different from the creaking slam that was all her mum's little red hatchback could manage.

'That was last week. I've hired a new bartender and one of my waitresses is back from sick leave. The bar will survive without us for one night.'

'Does that mean the bar doesn't need me at all any more?'

'No, just not tonight.'

'Hmm.' She looked at him sceptically. 'Look, maybe we should go back to my original plan to pay you to be my wedding date. You don't need an extraneous, only mildly competent waitress. Our deal has to be fair.'

Plus, if she paid him, it pushed the agreement back into pure-business-deal territory. After last night they certainly needed a good shove back onto the straight and narrow. She really didn't want Dan having any ideas that she might change her mind.

And *she* definitely didn't want to be having those kinds of ideas, either...

'The deal stands,' he said, his tone firm. 'University exams start in a week, and some of my staff are taking time off. I still need you—just not tonight.'

'Then why didn't you just call to cancel my shift?'

She knew she was being difficult, but she was stalling.

Was he just planning to pick things up from where they'd left off last night?

Dan took a long, deep breath. 'Because this isn't in the plan. We're low on reservations so I decided to take the night off and go have some fun. With you. That's it. And I didn't call because you never would have agreed over the phone.'

True. Distance from Dan always had a positive impact on her ability to think straight.

'I'm not going to change my mind,' she said, unable to look at him as she spoke. There was no need to clarify what she meant.

'I know.'

Her eyes flicked back up to his. If she ignored the charged atmosphere between them—and she had to, because her only other option was to abandon the project and put as much space between herself and Dan as possible—she could tell herself this wasn't about their fling. Or rather, the fling they weren't going to have. So why? Why take her to Fremantle? He'd already made it clear he didn't want a relationship, so he couldn't be asking her out on a real date.

'Oh, is this to replace the fake date we've got planned for next week? Doesn't Wednesday work for you any more?'

Yes, remember: it's all about the project.

She started mentally shifting her plan around. Moving next week's task up a few days wouldn't hurt. In fact, it...

Dan took a step forward, and now they were centimetres apart. His nearness scrambled her thoughts and heated her skin.

'This has nothing to do with your project,' he said. Low and quiet. 'Let's go to Fremantle for absolutely no reason at all. Not because of your project, but just because we can.'

He gaze locked on hers—and then, for the first time in as long as she remembered, she ignored all the sensible, sane lists of reasons in her head and did something totally unexpected. And definitely unwise.

Sophie nodded. 'Okay,' she said. 'Let's go.'

Rather than climbing into Dan's car, Sophie had made him follow her home—both to return her mother's car and so she could change.

He really shouldn't have been surprised.

But then, when she'd walked down the driveway in a floaty green dress that nipped in at her waist and showed off her fabulous legs, well, any niggling frustration at her obsession with appropriate clothing was swiftly forgotten. That dress was well worth waiting a few minutes for.

And those legs...

He was doubly pleased that she'd agreed to come out with him. Although for a while there it had seemed far from certain. In the car park she'd studied him with calculating eyes, weighing up every word he'd spoken as she searched and searched for the *why*.

But the thing was, there wasn't one. Not really. It was as simple as realising that it was going to be an unusually quiet night at the bar and suddenly having the—*he'd* thought—brilliant idea of spending the evening in Fremantle instead. With Sophie.

He hadn't bothered figuring out *why*. He'd just decided that was what he wanted to do. And he had the vague sense that it wouldn't do Sophie any harm to do something so out of the blue. It was becoming a habit, this compulsion to push her a little off-balance—to see that fire in her eyes as she threw everything into sticking to her plan.

They drove to Fremantle engaged in easy conversation, avoiding their wedding date agreement entirely. They discussed Sophie's job hunting so far—good, with a few interviews lined up the following week—and his opinion on the best beaches in Perth—Cottesloe and Scarborough. By the time they drove into the port city Sophie was smiling at him like a woman living in the moment—one without spreadsheets and to-do lists and project plans.

They parked in the centre of town, detouring through the century-old Fremantle Markets on their way to the beach. They walked past stall after stall of fresh fruit and vegetables before entering 'the hall'—a maze of handicrafts and souvenirs and food and—well—everything else you could think of. It was packed with locals and tourists, and the scent of incense battled with spices, fragrant candles and buttered popcorn. Here they took their time—Sophie looking at handmade jewellery, Dan buying a paper cone filled with candy-covered hazelnuts.

He paused outside a shop he hadn't been to in years. So long ago he'd forgotten it had even existed.

'Oh, how cool!' Sophie said, stepping past him and walking inside. He followed her to the far wall, where she perused such fine wares as rubber vomit, whoopee cushions and fake dog poop.

'My dad used to bring me here when I was a kid,' he said. 'As a reward for getting good grades, I could choose whatever I wanted.'

Picking up a bag of hot chilli lollies, Sophie grinned at him. 'Your mum must have loved that.'

'She was a pretty good sport, really. Although the fake cockroaches in her bed didn't go down quite as well as I'd expected.'

Sophie laughed. 'I can imagine.'

She put the lollies back and then examined the intriguingly labelled 'Pot of Snot'. 'So you did well at school?' she asked.

'With fake mucus on offer? Of course.'

She nodded. 'Yeah, me too—just without the bodily fluids. I was kind of obsessed with studying.'

He slapped a hand to his chest in mock surprise. 'No!'

She raised an eyebrow. 'Very funny,' she said dryly.

'I was the same,' he said. 'Nose in a textbook every night and all weekend.'

She turned to face him, rubber chicken in hand. 'You are the *last* guy I would have guessed to be such a good student. I would have picked you to be the guy making out with the most popular girl at school behind the sports shed—not the one studying away in the library.'

He met her eyes. 'Who says I didn't do both?'

She blushed, swinging the forgotten chicken absently from its feet. 'I should have known.'

The chicken smacked against the side of the display table, squeaking in distress. This earned them both a stern look from the shopkeeper, so they made a hasty retreat, grinning at each other. Back in the crammed maze of aisles, they followed the swell of bodies out onto South Terrace. Lined with cafés and restaurants, the busiest street in Fremantle was packed with everyone from retirees to families to the terribly trendy. Plus, of course, the definitive bohemian Fremantle residents—musicians and artists adorned with dreadlocks, piercings and colourful clothing.

'Where to now?' Sophie asked, holding up a hand to shield against the glare of the rapidly setting sun.

'The beach, I think—for the sunset.'

'We'll miss it,' she said. 'We're too late.'

Dan shook his head. 'Too far to *walk*, maybe. Follow me.'

He braced himself for a barrage of questions, but they never came. Instead she let him lead her down a side street, and he began to hope that this was all going to be *way* easier than he'd imagined. Until she saw where they were headed.

'No way,' she said, and stopped dead on the foot path.

Ahead sat a neat row of scooters behind a red-and-white 'For Hire' sign. 'I don't do motorbikes.'

'They aren't exactly motorbikes.'

'Close enough,' she said, crossing her arms. 'They're dangerous.'

'Not if we keep to the back streets and go slow. It'll be fine.'

She shook her head firmly. 'No. Look, I know tonight is all about me being spontaneous and everything—but there is no way I'm getting on one of those things. They freak me out. One little nudge and it's all over.'

'It's safe, Sophie—really. Not that you need one for these things, but I've got a motorcycle licence. I'll look after you.'

'You and your licence are welcome to go for a spin. I'll just wait here.'

Dan shoved his hands roughly into his pockets. 'Would it help if I went and asked the owner about his safety record? Surely statistical analysis would reassure you?'

'Nice try, but no. I have no interest in wavering from my four-wheel motorised vehicle policy.'

He'd known Sophie would resist his brainwave of hiring scooters, but this was getting ridiculous.

'Fine,' he said. 'We don't have time to go back to the car, so how about we get a ta—?'

'Oh, look!' she exclaimed, walking to the end of the second row of scooters. 'Why don't we hire *this*?'

She pointed at a two-person, four-wheeled—importantly—golf buggy/scooter amalgamation. Painted on its side, in childish lettering was its name: 'Scoot Car.'

'No,' he said. It was tiny, bright yellow and had more than a passing resemblance to a circus vehicle. The type usually overflowing with men wearing wigs and with white-painted faces. *He* would look like a clown if he folded his six-foot-one body inside it.

'But it's safer than a scooter. It's perfect!'

'There is no way I'm getting in that thing, Sophie.'

Understanding seemed to dawn, and she grinned a wicked grin. 'What, Dan? Are *you* worried about looking silly? The man who told me just last night that I shouldn't care what other people think?'

She had him, he knew. 'We're barely going to fit. We're both going to look silly.'

She shrugged, her eyes sparkling. 'I don't care, Dan. I'm being *spontaneous*!'

With a sigh, he went and paid the hire fee.

A few minutes later they were settled in the buggy, Sophie nervously fiddling with the hem of her skirt, running her fingers along the swirls of decorative stitching.

Sensing his eyes on her, she stilled her hands. 'Don't crash,' she said, with a pointed look.

'You just told me how safe this is,' he said. It earned him a glare. He winked at her. 'I'll do my best.'

They scooted slowly—because the buggy had a top speed of forty kilometres an hour and *not* because of Sophie's death grip on the handrail—through the criss-cross streets of Georgian and Edwardian cottages.

Slowly the whiteness eased out of her knuckles and Sophie relaxed back into her seat. 'This is nice,' she said as they left the town centre and headed towards the beach, the salty sea breeze caressing their skin.

He agreed. The close confines of the buggy pressed Sophie's thigh against his, leaving only a thin layer of cotton and denim between them. Their shoulders collided with every bump and crack in the road, and their feet fought for space in the narrow footwell.

It should have felt cramped and uncomfortable, but it didn't. Instead he struggled to concentrate on the road rather than the woman beside him. And to control the buggy rather than his body's reaction to her.

It didn't take long to get to the beach, and he pulled off the road at a hill that offered uninterrupted views of the rapidly setting sun where it looked to be hovering mere centimetres above the infinite horizon.

'Just in time,' Sophie said, making no move to climb out of the buggy. Neither did he.

They sat in silence as the sun made its lazy dive into the ocean. Long, long minutes while their bodies touched and they both stared straight ahead, as if in denial of the fizz and hiss of the sparks flying between them.

He wasn't about to lie to himself—of *course* he wanted Sophie to change her mind. But he wasn't crass enough to have planned tonight purely for that purpose—he did, genuinely, just want to spend time with her. Which was odd in itself.

In the past ten years he'd taken women to restaurants, cocktail bars, concerts, shows...hotel rooms. But never on an unplanned, rambling exploration of Fremantle. Or anything even resembling what they were doing.

Except, of course, this *wasn't* a date.

It was difficult to believe that when the urge to turn and kiss her was near-overwhelming.

But he couldn't. Not yet. She had to say the word. As badly as he wanted Sophie, he couldn't kiss her unless she knew exactly what she was signing up for. A fling. Short-term.

It was all he was capable of.

The tension was almost a physical thing—thick and heavy. Sophie could have cut it with a knife if it had been in any way possible to squeeze one between them.

Which it wasn't. She was terribly—and wonderfully—aware of exactly how they were sandwiched together.

There had been a moment when the little, buzzing scooter-buggy had rolled to a stop and she could have stepped out. Created that tension-defusing space they so badly needed.

Ever since she'd agreed to join him tonight the tension had been growing. And growing. She'd told herself it was all just fun and easy and meaningless. *Ha!* A wasted effort.

But acknowledging that she liked him and wanted nothing more than to turn *right this instant* and touch her lips to his achieved nothing. Because she knew she couldn't handle a fling with Dan Halliday.

She just had to accept it—she was a serious relationship kind of girl. Keeping things platonic was the sensible, *right* thing to do. Even if they'd well overstepped 'businesslike', there was no reason they couldn't complete the rest of the project as, well, friends.

But they were never going to achieve that if they continued to sit in silence, doing nothing to shatter the tension cocooning them and escalating with every second.

She cleared her throat, the sound awkward above the distant splash of waves and the squawking chatter of seagulls.

'It's weird how we were so similar as teenagers and are so totally different now,' she said, trying her best to sound calm and relaxed and *not* as if she was pressed thigh to thigh to the most attractive man she'd ever met. 'I still can't get my head around it.'

'You kissed the most popular girl in school, too?' he said, shooting her a teasing grin.

She shoved against him lightly with her shoulder—not that she had to move far. 'You know what I mean. Head in a book, totally focussed on studying. It just doesn't seem to *fit* you, you know?'

He shrugged. 'Maybe it never did.'

They both stared straight ahead, their gazes not wavering from the sliver of a semi-circle that was all that remained of the sun.

'Do you mean you didn't *want* to study so hard? Did your parents put a lot of pressure on you?'

She'd been lucky—in a way. The pressure she'd put on herself had been completely self imposed. She'd hated being put down a year and had been determined to prove that it wasn't because she was stupid—as some heartless kids had teased. It hadn't taken long for success—and the need to achieve it—to become a habit.

'No,' he said, and then after a long pause added, 'Maybe a little. But don't get me wrong—I wasn't one of those unfortunate kids forced to follow their parents' dreams. I wanted to be a lawyer as much as they wanted it. Actually more, I think. I associated law with success and recognition—and a lot of sillier things that are important to a seventeen-year-old like fancy cars and a beautiful wife.'

Wife, he'd said. Not girlfriend.

'Is that what you meant when you said you had experience in obsessing over goals? Was that to do with your career?' Then she added, before she lost her nerve, 'Your marriage?'

His gaze swung back out to sea just as the sun finally sank beneath its blue-black surface.

He swallowed, and the hands that had been resting relaxed on his lap tightened into fists.

'I'm sorry,' she said. 'It's none of my—'

'Yes,' he said.

But that was it. He made no move to elaborate further.

Questions waited impatiently on the tip of her tongue, but she didn't say a word, knowing that pushing Dan was a sure-fire way to end this conversation. And she wanted him to keep on talking. Not just because she couldn't fully comprehend his spectacular metamorphosis from what he'd once been to the languorous, live-in-the-moment player he now was. But because she wanted to understand him.

Finally, after even the last dawdling rays of sunset had seeped out of the sky, he spoke.

'I won't do it again. Get so caught up in where I'm going that I completely lose touch with what's happening in the moment.'

'What *was* happening?'

He shook his head. 'It doesn't matter.'

But obviously it did. It was evident in every rigid line of his body.

She wanted to ask him more, but there was no point. He'd as good as constructed a wall between them—liberally plastered with 'Keep Out' signs.

'Is that what you think *I'm* doing?' she asked instead.

'Missing out on what's happening in the moment?' He turned towards her, his eyes locking with hers and seeing right into her soul. 'Missing out on what could happen *right now*?'

No. They couldn't. *She* couldn't.

It would be easier if she could drag her gaze away from his, but it was an impossible task. His lazy exploration of her face…her lips…it was hypnotising.

She closed her eyes. 'What would be the point?'

'Of doing something not on your project plan?'

She bristled, snapping out of her almost-stupor. 'Don't be ridiculous. Whatever you might think, I don't live every aspect of my life to some pre-packaged schedule.'

He didn't say a word, but his expression was blatantly disbelieving.

No longer were the cramped confines of the buggy a good thing. Despite its open sides, the vehicle was suddenly absurdly suffocating.

Sophie launched herself out of her seat, stumbling on the

bitumen in her haste for distance. She strode away—one stride, two, three...

Where was she going?

She came to a halt, her arms crossed, staring at absolutely nothing.

She wasn't the type of person to flounce away from an argument.

Maybe she would be if she made it a task in her project plan...

No! Dan was *wrong*.

'Sophie?'

She jumped, surprised to hear Dan's voice directly behind her. She didn't move even when his fingers curled gently around her upper arm.

'I get why you have your lists and plans, Soph,' he said, standing close enough that she could feel his body heat. 'But you're not a little girl any more. Maybe it's time to relax a little—let life happen rather than planning it all.'

She shrugged away from his touch, spinning around to face him. 'What's so wrong with having a plan, really, Dan? It's worked out well for me so far—school, career, *everything*.'

'Everything? How about Rick?'

She went totally still, stunned. 'I don't project manage my love life,' she said coolly. 'I didn't exactly require a written selection criteria.'

'Except now?'

'This isn't real.' She sighed heavily in frustration. 'I know this isn't normal. I *told* you it wasn't normal.' She paused, meeting his eyes in what remained of the fading light. 'And what do you suggest I do instead, exactly? Be more like you, perhaps?' She paused. 'And who exactly would *that* be?'

'Not more like me, Sophie. More like *you*.'

The strange words tumbled about in her head for long, long seconds.

'I *am* me.'

'Are you? That life you had in Sydney with Rick—was that what you really *wanted*, or what you'd always *planned*?'

These words she couldn't process. Not right now. She'd been happy in Sydney with Rick. It had been what she'd always wanted. Hadn't it?

'Why do you care, Dan?'

'Because, like I said, I know what can happen.'

'So, what? You feel the urge to share your cautionary tale with every person you meet?'

'No,' he said. 'Just you.'

It derailed her momentarily.

'Why me?' He looked a little off-balance, as if unsure of the reason himself. 'Why do you want to fix *me*?'

'I don't want to fix you.'

'You just think I'm living my life all wrong.' She gave a short little humourless laugh. 'That's all.' And it hurt. A lot. It was just what she needed—someone else who didn't think she was good enough.

'No, I don't. I like you, Sophie.'

He said it as if that explained everything.

'Why are you so upset?' he continued, as the streetlights flickered on behind them, providing enough light to outline the sharp line of his jaw. 'Why care what I think if I have it so wrong?'

She shook her head. 'You *are* wrong. I'm not the automaton you think I am.' She stepped towards him, driven by a bottomless ache inside her. 'I think and react...' She pressed one palm to his chest, and pushed once—hard. But he didn't move. Not even a centimetre. 'And *feel*...'

All the fight faded from her against the immovable wall

of Dan. She dipped her head, the hand on his chest curling as it relaxed and just lay there defeated for a moment.

But before it could fall away, and before she could succumb to the prickle of unwanted tears, his hand covered hers, holding it where it lay.

His other hand tipped her chin up.

'I know you feel, Soph.'

When you let yourself.

Maybe he wasn't thinking those words, but Sophie was. She as good as heard them—crystal clear and unforgiving.

And *right*.

Who was she kidding? It had taken her *six months* to let out all the pain that Rick had inflicted—and even that had been to a total stranger in a bar. Six months of distracting herself, keeping her mind busy—planning her holiday and planning her new life.

She'd been staring determinedly at a tiny freckle on Dan's cheek, but now she let her gaze wander to his eyes.

How did she feel about Dan? Attracted to him, definitely. And she liked him, too. Enough to know that what she was about to do was a very stupid idea.

But that was exactly why she was going to do it.

One kiss—how could it hurt, really? Could it hurt to succumb to the tingles that rocketed through her body whenever he touched her? To the urge to make his heart, beating so strongly beneath her palm, thump even faster—for her?

She left her right hand where it lay, let her left hand creep up and behind his neck, her fingers brushing against his short-cropped hair. She stood on her tiptoes, her attention flickering between his eyes and his mouth.

Ah, there it goes, she thought, as the pitter-patter of his heart accelerated nicely.

'Are you sure, Soph? I thought you didn't want this?'

She raised an eyebrow, her lips a whisper from his.

'Really, Dan. I'm trying to be spontaneous and you're going to analyse it? I'm living in the moment—just like you said.'

She'd meant to kiss him then—to lean that little bit closer and cover his mouth with hers.

But he beat her to it. *He* kissed *her*.

His mouth was firm. Warm. Nice.

No, nice was completely the wrong word. *Amazing. Perfect. Right.*

His arm wrapped around her, pulling her close. His heart raced, and so did hers. Her body shivered at the sweep of his hand across her back—hot through the thin cotton of her dress.

His tongue brushed against her bottom lip and she instantly deepened the kiss, exploring the shape of lips, his teeth, his tongue.

The hand on his heart slid upwards, a casualty of her almost desperate need to feel his heat. Her hand threaded into his hair and would have pulled him closer if doing so had been physically possible.

The kiss went on and on, their mouths breaking apart only to reunite at different angles. Her hands roamed over his shoulders, his over her back, her waist.

Sophie's head and body spun with sensation and the electricity of her body's reaction. She could feel *his* body's reaction against her belly. A warning that she really needed to take a step backwards. And soon—before this went too far.

Just not yet.

In the end it was Dan who broke the kiss, dragging his lips away from hers and breathing in the salty air in big, slow gulps.

'My place. Let's go.'

His rough voice was enough to break the spell and she stepped away, rubbing her arms against the sudden cold.

'That might take a while in the buggy,' she said, nodding in its direction.

'Oh,' he said, the single word laden with what would have been comical disappointment if she hadn't felt exactly the same way. 'Well, okay. My place—after we return the *Scoot Car.*'

She shook her head. 'No. It was just the one kiss.'

'What?'

She walked past him, making herself put one foot in front of the other and climb into the buggy rather than stopping and wrapping herself around him again.

She heard the crunch of gravel as he walked around the vehicle. He slid in beside her, his hand resting on the ignition but not turning it.

'What was that, Sophie?'

She couldn't look at him. 'Just a kiss,' she said quickly. 'A moment—like you said. Nothing more.'

'And you think you can stop at just one kiss?' His voice was deep and dangerous in the almost darkness.

'Of course,' she said immediately, firmly and clearly. She had to.

'The offer still stands, Soph. Just say the word.'

'I won't,' she said.

She sensed his smile even though she couldn't see it. 'I wouldn't be so sure.'

CHAPTER EIGHT

Monday 14th November, 9:00 a.m.

From: Sophie Morgan
To: Dan Halliday
Subject: Meeting cancellation
Dan,
The planning meeting on Wednesday is cancelled.
Please refer to the attached notes and map prior to
Sunday's barbecue.
I will see you at the bar on Saturday.
Kind regards,
Sophie

Monday 14th November, 9:45 a.m.

Text message from Dan:
Soph, there's no need to be embarrassed. You don't
kiss half bad.

Monday 14th November, 9:47 a.m.

Text message from Sophie:
Please confirm that you received my cancellation
email.

Monday 14th November, 9:50 a.m.

Text message from Dan:
Received. But I don't remember a planning meeting. Is
our date still on?

Monday 14th November, 9:52 a.m.

Text message from Sophie:
No. There was never a date. It was never real.

FOR the first time in her life Sophie was almost late to work.
Not because she was disorganised, or because of bad traffic or anything like that. Simply because it was far easier to
drive aimlessly through the streets of Subiaco than to gather
up the courage to drive into the wine bar's car park.

Eventually it was the certain knowledge that Dan would
never let her forget it if she *was* actually late that finally
made her slow down, flick the indicator and turn the steering wheel in the bar's direction. It was only as she dumped
her bag in the small staff room that she remembered *never*
only had a lifespan of just three more weeks. After that it
wouldn't matter. Once the wedding was over she wouldn't
see him again.

That should have made her feel better, but it didn't.

And that was bad.

It just wasn't sinking in—no matter how many times she
told herself that those long minutes of madness on the beach
were simply that: moments. Discrete moments in time that

she could now box away and shove to the dustiest recesses of her mind—never to be thought of again.

That wasn't going so well for her.

Instead, her memories of those moments would leap out at her, in full Technicolor, at the most inopportune times. Like at her job interview the other day. Or while trying to think calming *Yes, you can work with him and keep your distance* thoughts on her way to work. Hence her driving about in circles.

It had occurred to her briefly, while twisting herself into knots as she tossed and turned in bed following that incredible kiss, that she could just cancel their agreement.

No risk of any more kisses then!

But it seemed pretty gutless to go down that path. She believed Dan when he said he needed her at the bar, and she wasn't about to let him down. Also, it would totally stuff up her project, and she definitely didn't have time to rustle up a new fake boyfriend in time for the wedding.

And, more importantly, it did seem pretty pathetic that she had so little faith in her self control. If she ended their agreement it would be because she felt she was in real danger of capitulating and becoming the latest in Dan's long line of casual and easily discarded girlfriends.

No, thank you.

So she'd emailed him and cancelled their meeting. *Not* because of the kiss—so she kept telling herself—but because there was no need. If she counted Saturday night as their second date...*no* fake date/planning meeting, well, the project was right on schedule.

She'd also decided to have another crack at the whole 'professional relationship' thing. She'd figured it would make life easier—make sure Dan didn't get the wrong idea or anything—although it had been difficult to maintain when she'd received Dan's text messages. She'd smiled as she'd read them, but had made herself text super-serious messages back—not the flirty, teasing words her fingers had itched to type.

Noticing the wall clock's minute hand tick ever closer to 5:00 p.m., Sophie quickly tied her short black apron around her waist. Taking a deep breath, she straightened her shoulders, eyeing the door with steely determination.

She could do this—walk through that door, act professional.

But before she had the opportunity the door swung open and Dan strode into the room. His height and width made the tiny room even smaller, and she took an involuntary backward step.

'Sophie,' he said by way of greeting, punctuating the word with a curt nod.

'Uh, hi!' Far from her target of 'casual' she could only manage 'oddly high-pitched'.

He walked past her, picking up his jacket from the back of a chair. 'There's an issue at the other bar I need to sort out, so I'll see you tomorrow afternoon?'

She nodded, and seconds later he was gone—back out through the door and into the night.

And that was good, right? That she didn't have to work with him tonight, and that he was finally—after resisting right from the very start—maintaining a professional distance?

It was as if the kiss had never happened—which was exactly what she wanted.

Right?

The argument between two of his more flamboyant chefs took less time to untangle than expected, leaving Dan at an unexpected loose end.

He considered returning to the Subiaco bar, but knew if he did it would be purely to see Sophie—his new bartender didn't need supervision any more. And somehow he didn't think he'd get a hell of a lot of paperwork done with Sophie mere metres away.

Besides, after her formal email and text messages he'd already decided on his plan of attack—so to speak. Sophie had made it clear that she'd reverted back to her default defensive position: ultra-professional. So he'd go along with that.

For as long as it lasted. Which he really didn't think would be very long at all.

Did Sophie really think they could both stop after just that one kiss?

He didn't. No way.

But Sophie needed to figure that out for herself, and his instincts told him the best way for that to happen was to keep his distance for a while.

With that in mind he made a quick phone call, and promptly invited himself over to his parents' place for dinner. He drove the short distance to their leafy riverside suburb, winding his way through streets liberally populated with opulent mansions—only the occasional modest 1950s home peeking out amongst the triple garages, glass-edged balconies and angular architectural 'features'.

Unlike Sophie, he hadn't grown up in the house where his parents now lived. That elegant but much smaller house had been a few suburbs away. Over the years, as his parents' legal practice had grown, so had the size of their home. Likewise its location had become even more fashionable with every move. Now, in retirement, they lived in crazily expensive and crazily picturesque Peppermint Grove, in an oversized home complete with river glimpses.

It was a great place—no question—but a tiny part of Dan kind of liked how Sophie still got to sleep in her old room. It was a nice idea—growing up in just the one house, maybe one day bringing your own kids over for sleepovers with their grandmother...

What?

He parked his car on the furthest edge of the curved driveway and took great pains to erase *that* unwanted little daydream. It had been years—*years*—since he'd painted such fanciful pictures in his mind.

Surely by now he should have got it through his thick skull that daydreams like that were as fragile and insubstantial as the head on a pint of beer?

He shoved the car door open and climbed out just as his mother opened the front door.

'Dan! Hi!'

He leapt up the sandstone steps to the doorway two at a time, grinning when he saw his mother's Saturday evening attire.

'Looking lovely in your aqua velour tracksuit tonight, Mum,' he said, earning himself a dazzling smile.

She propped a hand on her slightly plump hip and struck a runway model pose. 'Oh, this old thing?'

He laughed, and she stood on her tiptoes to kiss his cheek.

Dan followed her inside, through the high-ceilinged hallway and past the professionally decorated front rooms. In the open plan kitchen/dining room his dad sat at their curved glass table—'It's a statement piece, darling,' his mother had explained once—surrounded by small mountains of manila folders and lakes of scattered white paper.

'Enjoying retirement there, Dad?' he asked, taking the seat across from him.

His dad looked up, brushing his shaggy grey-streaked hair out of his eyes. 'It's an interesting case,' his dad offered by way of explanation—as he always did.

He asked his dad questions about the case as his mum prepared dinner, and later helped relocate the landscape of paperwork to the study. This elicited much muttering from his mother about the most appropriate original location for said paperwork, and his dad swiftly countered by saying that he much preferred to be near her when he worked. This earned his dad the biggest beef-and-rice-stuffed capsicum and an extra dollop of creamy mashed potato, all swimming in homemade tomato sauce. It was Dan's favourite of the traditional Croatian dishes his mum regularly made.

'Do you ever miss it?' his mother asked as they all mopped up the remains of their dinner with crusty bread.

Knowing exactly what she meant, he got straight to the point. 'I'm not and will never be a lawyer again, Mum.'

'But you were interested in your dad's case.'

He nodded, familiar with this conversation and frustrated that they were having it yet again. 'I was. But that doesn't mean I want to change careers.'

Right on cue, his dad chimed in. 'Such a shame—top of your class and everything.' He even shook his head in bemusement.

'Do we need to discuss this again?' He couldn't even get annoyed with them, as he knew they came from a position of genuine confusion rather than outright disapproval. They were proud of the wine bar's success, in their own way, but not in the same way they'd been when he'd got into law, or when he'd graduated, or got his first job.

They were also convinced—although maybe just slightly wavering after all these years—that he was just 'in a phase'. Still recovering from the horrendous mess that had been the end of his short marriage. But he was far from that empty shell he'd been when Amalie had left him.

He had countless regrets from that period of his life, but as far as he was concerned buying the bars was one of the few things he'd got right. It had been the best thing he'd ever done for himself, with the only ongoing fly in the ointment being his parents' disappointment. They missed the obsessively focussed uni student who had talked so excitedly about one day following in their footsteps and running their practice himself.

He didn't.

His dad stacked their plates and carried them to the kitchen while his mum studied him across the table. He had her to thank for his olive skin and almost black hair, but she watched him with hazel eyes, so different from the pale blue of his father's and his own.

'Nina's pregnant again,' she said. 'She'll be due in May—isn't that great?'

He smiled, genuinely thrilled for his young cousin. 'That's great news. I'll give her a call this week.'

His mum nodded slowly, and the atmosphere—which hadn't really recovered from the awkwardness of the law conversation—went all off-kilter again. He braced himself for the inevitable question.

'So…are you seeing anyone at the moment?'

He had to laugh at her transparent attempt at casualness.

'I think next time I come to dinner I'll just confirm my commitment to my current career and my single status the moment I walk in the door.'

His dad laughed from behind him as he stacked the dishwasher. 'Please do. It would save your mother some angst.'

His mum shot a glare in the direction of the kitchen. 'I do not angst.' She sniffed. 'I just care.'

And she still harboured hope of the future appearance of miniature Dan Hallidays. He was eternally gratefully that he'd restrained himself from blurting out the fact of Amalie's pregnancy all those years ago. It would have killed his mum to know just how close she'd been to becoming a grandmother.

And he absolutely mustn't tell her about that silly little daydream he'd had about Sophie.

No, not *Sophie*. About a hypothetical woman whose mother hypothetically still lived in the family home.

Definitely *not* Sophie.

His mother was looking at him in a funny way, her head

tilted at an angle. 'Hang on. Dan—you *are* seeing someone, aren't you?'

He met her curious gaze with steady, emotionless eyes. 'No, I'm not.'

'Oh, he *is*!' his mum said, and all but clapped her hands in delight. 'Tell me—who is she?'

Dan's jaw clenched.

His dad returned to the table, slapping him on the shoulder as he passed by. 'Good job, son. Tell us all about the lucky lady.'

'There isn't one to talk about.'

His parents shared a long look, and then turned back to him with matching knowing grins.

He couldn't even be bothered arguing any more. They'd made up their minds—why and how, he had no idea.

'I'm so pleased for you, darling,' his mum said, reaching out and grabbing his hand.

'There's no need to start planning the wedding, Mum. It's nothing serious.'

He wasn't sure why he'd confirmed Sophie's existence. Possibly a misguided hope that doing so might defuse the situation—making it clear that it was a purely short-term arrangement.

He'd been wrong. His words had simply ratcheted up that enthusiasm. He shouldn't have said anything. It was cruel to get his parents' hopes up. Their marriage—and marriage itself—was so important to them.

As it had once been equally important to him.

He must have been the only guy in Perth under twenty-five who'd dated women with the end goal of marriage. But then it had all been part of his plan—that pretty painting he'd had in his mind. Degree, job, house, marriage, babies...

He'd seen it, so crystal clear, his picture-book definition of success.

His huge mistake had been tackling each task with the

same close-minded focus that had elicited his high marks and his brilliant straight-out-of-university career. The ideal attitude for work—the worst for marriage.

And he hadn't even been close to realising that until it was far too late.

His mum was still watching him with a beaming smile, wedding confetti practically shining in her eyes.

But his dad, also silently observing him, wore a totally different expression. He watched Dan with concern and contemplation, the gears ticking over in his mind plain to see. He finally spoke. 'You know, Dan, one day you'll need to forgive yourself. It's never just one person's fault when a marriage ends.'

His mum blinked, surprised by the statement, but then nodded and smiled at him with encouragement. As if he was supposed to suddenly burst out with, *Yes, you're absolutely right! It wasn't my fault that my marriage collapsed and I didn't notice until the moment my wife walked out the door. Thank you. I'm cured! I'll go get married and have your grandchildren tomorrow.*

He was being unfair, he knew.

Because, of course, his parents didn't know the full story.

CHAPTER NINE

The Sophie Project 2.1 (Project Manager: S. Morgan)
Task Four: ~~The Second Date~~ (cancelled)
Task Five: Emma's Barbecue

EVEN though they were right on time for the Sunday evening barbecue, the number of cars crowding the lawn and street meant they needed to park some distance away. Dan effortlessly lifted the Esky out of the back of her mum's hatchback—the same Esky Sophie had dragged and hauled into the car with much difficulty before picking him up. If nothing else, a fake boyfriend was super-convenient when it came to the lifting and shifting of heavy objects.

They began to walk down the hill towards Emma's house, shaded by the vast jacarandas that dotted the footpath with blue and purple flowers. They walked in the same silence they'd maintained during the drive after their polite, stilted conversation had completely dried up. Sophie kept her gaze straight ahead, terribly aware of the man beside her and the jumble of delicious sensations his closeness triggered: a shiver whenever they accidentally touched, liquid warmth in her belly whenever she looked at his lips.

'Sophie, slow down.'

His hand on her arm stilled her instantly, and she made herself shrug away from his touch.

'Why?'

He pushed his sunglasses onto his head, meeting her eyes with his clear blue gaze. 'Have you forgotten why I'm here? About the project?'

She shook her head. 'Of course not.'

He raised an eyebrow. 'You sure? Because last time I checked a woman in love doesn't stalk ahead of her boyfriend as if he doesn't exist.'

She tugged at the strapless neckline of her blue-and-grey maxi-dress. He did have a point. 'Maybe we just had a fight?'

He grinned. 'Sure—if that's the image you were going for. I thought it was more "blissfully happy", but we can go with "utterly miserable" if that's what you'd prefer.'

She bit the inside of her lip to stop herself returning his smile.

'Fine. I'll stop stalking.'

'Good news,' he said, and they continued on their way. Sauntering, not stalking.

Three houses before their destination Dan caught her hand, lacing his fingers with hers deliberately.

She stiffened, but with other couples approaching the house from the opposite direction made no move to extract her hand.

'Is this *really* necessary?' she whispered.

He leant close, his breath hot against her ear. 'What do you think?'

No, it's not.

But for some reason, rather than saying the words, she let

the tension ease from her arm and shoulder and just kept on holding his hand.

Because it would help the 'blissfully happy' image, of course.

She darted a glance up at Dan, expecting a raised eyebrow or a smug expression. She saw neither—just his kissable lips kicked up in the sexiest of smiles. And there were all sorts of promises swirling about in his knowing gaze.

She just had to say the word.

Sophie looked away.

Their hands fell apart as they negotiated the narrow steps to the front door, but not before Emma—standing at the threshold to welcome the steady stream of guests—had seen them. Emma's eyebrows were raised in completely unsubtle interest during their short introductions, disappearing further into her choppy blond fringe when Sophie managed to utter the all-important words: 'This is my boyfriend, Dan.'

Dan went ahead of them into the house, and Emma grabbed Sophie's arm before she could follow him.

'Where on earth did you find *him*?' she asked, her eyes following Dan's jean-clad butt down the hallway. 'You've been back in Perth for, what? Five minutes? And you've managed to unearth *that*?'

'Speed dating,' she said simply. 'I recommend it.'

As Dan disappeared around the corner Emma dragged her attention back to Sophie. 'I'll have to give it a try some time.'

Sophie laughed. 'Emma, you're married.'

She shrugged, her eyes sparkling. 'Surely it's okay if I only go for the view?' She paused, shaking her head. 'Far out, Soph. That guy is one hell of a way to forget about Rick.'

For once Rick's name didn't trigger some visceral reaction. No bottomless ache, no stabbing pain. Nothing.

So she smiled broadly, unable to resist her old friend's enthusiasm. 'Yeah,' she said, 'I know.'

It had been a long time since Dan had taken a woman to a barbecue. Or, more accurately, had a woman take *him* to a barbecue. The women he dated figured out pretty quickly that he wasn't going to invite them to dinner with his friends or get-togethers with his mates, and certainly not to any family events. For some women this didn't matter. For the ones to whom it did—who decided that they wanted more than something fun and mutually satisfying—well, it was at that realisation that they generally walked. And that worked fine for him.

So it was strange to be at this barbecue with Sophie—to be 'the boyfriend' again. He'd expected the strangeness, of course. But not absolutely hating it was the real surprise. Even though it was all fake, he'd still expected it to feel unequivocally *wrong*—in the same way the very idea of being in a relationship felt wrong to him.

He wouldn't go so far as to say it felt *right*, though. Having Sophie introduce him to friends as her boyfriend, and the subsequent small talk he engaged in about how they'd met and so on—well, that was all a bit weird, of course. But it was working. He'd lost count of the number of people who told him how *thrilled* they were that Sophie had moved on from her broken engagement.

And, if he was really honest with himself, he could think of a lot worse ways to spend his Sunday evening than sitting in a lovely back garden on a plastic folding chair next to Sophie, sausages and potluck salads piled onto the paper plates on their laps.

Earlier, as he'd held her hand on the footpath, she'd relaxed—just a little—and the awkward tightness of her body had softened before him. But more than a flicker of wariness still danced in her eyes—on the few occasions she'd met his gaze, at least.

Holding her hand had been a diversion from his game plan, no matter which way he looked at it. Part of the fake boyfriend show? Maybe—if he completely ignored the fact that he was hardly the type of guy to consider public hand-holding essential boyfriend behaviour. He knew what it had been—a not exactly subtle excuse to touch her.

So, yeah, not really consistent with the 'keeping his distance' plan. But hardly worthy of regret—and besides, it hadn't escaped his notice that when he touched Sophie she was several orders of magnitude less sensible. Instead she was more natural, more…uninhibited.

Possibly a state of mind he should be pursuing more vigorously…

She leant over and whispered in his ear, 'Thank you for tonight. You're playing this perfectly.'

'I don't know,' he said, the cogs in his brain turning over efficiently as inspiration struck. 'Do you think we've put on enough of a show?'

She considered his question seriously, her forehead crinkling. 'What do you think?'

He shook his head solemnly. 'We could do better.'

She chewed on her bottom lip. 'What should we do?'

He leant just a little bit closer—close enough to smell the vanilla of her perfume. 'I think what we're doing right now is a good start. Is anyone watching?'

Her gaze flickered away from him. 'Yes. A few people. Karen is. You remember—the bride-to-be?'

'That's perfect, right?'

'Yeah. So what do we do?'

'I could kiss you—'

'*No.*'

Far more than just a flicker of wariness in *that* look. More like a *Don't even think about it, buddy!* glare.

Well, it had been worth a try. 'Are we back to the kissing rules?'

She inclined her head slightly. 'Yes, definitely.'

'So I guess putting my hand on your knee is off limits, too?'

She glowered at him. But he didn't miss the merest hint of a grin shaping the corners of her lips.

'There you go—whispering and sharing a private joke. How much more in love could we get?'

Her gaze dropped downwards for a moment, before slowly creeping up again. Ah, he recognised this expression— Sophie in perfectionist project manager mode. 'Maybe you *should* kiss me,' she said, as matter-of-fact as if she was talking about the weather. Then, with a pointed, no-nonsense look, 'On the cheek, of course.'

'Of course,' he said. If she wanted to pretend this was just about her project, that was one hundred percent fine with him.

Despite her businesslike words there was barely a gap between them. They'd both crept ever nearer as they'd talked, drawn together like magnets.

All he had to do was shift his weight forward, dip his head slightly to the side, and his lips would brush her skin. But he took his time.

He inhaled her subtle scent. He silently acknowledged the moment her project manager mask slipped and a blush warmed her delicate skin. And he smiled as she shivered at the touch of his breath on her cheek.

Then, finally, he kissed her.

It wasn't enough. And it was a million times worse than when he'd last kissed her cheek, as this time he knew exactly what he was missing out on.

He straightened. Cleared his throat.

'How was that?' he asked, picking up his plastic fork and stabbing at a piece of potato salad.

'Very convincing,' she said, her voice brisk but just the tiniest bit uneven. 'I don't think anyone would ever think it was fake.'

He nodded.

This whole charade would be a hell of a lot easier if it didn't feel so real.

'Sorry to interrupt you two lovebirds!'

It was Emma, her bubbly enthusiasm snapping Sophie out of whatever off-balance, dreamy place Dan's chaste kiss had sent her to. She'd been diligently slicing up her sausage, and it was only at Emma's voice that she realised she'd reduced it to dozens of tiny inedible pieces.

She put her plate under her seat, hidden by the skirt of her full-length dress.

'Do you need some help, Emma?' she asked, adding hopefully, 'In the kitchen?'

Some distance from Dan was just what she needed. *Twice* now she'd let down her guard—when she'd held his hand and now with their kiss. No matter which way she spun it—both were utterly unnecessary. Dressing it up as part of the project was just lying to herself.

'Don't be silly. You're a guest. I just wanted to let you know that it's time to start warming up those vocal cords!'

Oh, no.

'Sophie sings?' Dan asked with obvious interest.

'I don't,' Sophie answered quickly, just as Emma said, 'Oh, yes, she does!'

'I don't believe it,' Dan said.

'You'll see,' Emma said happily. 'Brad bought me a karaoke machine for my birthday!'

Sophie all but shuddered in horror as Emma sashayed away.

'I'm going to need a drink,' she muttered, getting to her feet.

Minutes and a few liberal mouthfuls of Verdelho later, she didn't feel any better. She returned to her seat in the corner of Emma's large paved patio. Dan watched with laughing eyes as she approached.

'*This* I have got to see,' he said. 'I never would have picked you as the karaoke type.'

'You were right. I'm not. Emma is referring to a short period in my *un*wild and *un*crazy youth when I may have made some dubious decisions with the assistance of copious amounts of alcohol.'

'Decisions involving singing in public?'

'Sadly, yes. Although—in my defence—I was always a backup singer. Karen and Emma would share the lead.'

Her two old friends were excitedly setting up the karaoke machine beneath a porch light that acted conveniently like a spotlight. A spotlight she had absolutely *no* intention of standing in.

Unfortunately she had very little say in the matter, and soon found herself exercising her dreadful singing voice as Emma's—very quiet—backup singer.

'So singing lessons were never on one of your to-do lists, then?' Dan asked as she returned to her seat.

'Very funny,' she said. 'I did warn you.'

He just grinned at her.

As the night wore on and nearly every other guest was dragged into the spotlight—all with various degrees of success—Sophie's mortification faded. Guests soon made the patio a dance floor, spinning and bouncing around to everything from heavy metal to nineties boy band to power ballads.

She and Dan didn't dance—not because she didn't want to, but because she wasn't silly enough to put herself in a position where there were even more legitimate opportunities to touch each other. Dan's occasionally boyfriendish arm around her shoulder or waist as they chatted with other guests was already doing her in—she couldn't handle it if they were on the dance floor and something slow suddenly came on.

If she found herself pressed against Dan again, arms wrapped around each other just like they were at the beach—well, she had a terrible feeling that any self-control or sensible note to self would be hurled out of the metaphorical window.

So when a slow dance *did* come on they were standing together, the couple they'd been talking to having added themselves to the sea of swaying bodies the instant the first familiar bars were played.

Karen's fiancé Ben was at the microphone, but before he'd even sung the first word of the song Sophie's feet had begun to shuffle even as her heart plummeted.

She moved without volition—the helpless Pavlovian result of months and months of practice.

Practising in the Surrey Hills dance studio near her house. Practising in her lounge room with the coffee table shoved up against the sofa.

Feet moving, hands guiding, bodies swaying—Rick and her laughing.

It was their wedding song.

She closed her eyes, taking deep, deep breaths, battling against the waves of unexpected and unwanted emotion that flooded over her.

Tears of frustration stung her eyes. She'd thought she'd finally started to move on—that Rick no longer had the power to hurt her.

'Sophie, are you okay?' She could barely hear Dan. The song's verses seemed many times magnified as they echoed through her skull, her bones and her heart.

She didn't respond, just busied her rogue feet with the act of walking into the house and out onto Emma's front yard. She shouldn't still be able to hear the song, but it followed her, repeating itself over and over in her head.

What she was feeling wasn't about Rick at all, she realised. No, instead the song was like a soundtrack to a time in her life when everything had been perfect. When a man had loved her for exactly who she was and hadn't given a damn that she wasn't some package deal. A time when she'd believed that her infertility really didn't matter. Not at all. That she was enough.

And it had all been a lie.

She *hadn't* been enough for Rick.

And this song—this song she'd once loved—wouldn't let her lie to herself any more.

Maybe she'd never be enough for anyone.

Dan caught her hand as she charged down the driveway. 'Sophie. *Stop.*'

She wrenched her hand free, using far more force than necessary. 'I have to go.' And she kept right on walking away—away from that song and, she hoped, the emptiness inside her. She broke into an awkward jog, her flat leather sandals slapping like gunshots on the footpath.

Dan effortlessly overtook her, blocking her escape route with his body. He didn't touch her again, just stood there.

Sophie realised the song was gone. Now she could hear her uneven breathing—the only sound in the deserted dark street.

'Do you want to tell me what's going on?'

She shook her head. How could she possibly explain?

'No, not good enough, Soph,' he said, his voice firm. 'It was that song, right? As soon as it started you shut down.'

'It was my wedding song,' she said brusquely. 'You know—the first dance as a married couple? It just brought up some bad memories, that's all. I was just being silly.'

Dan didn't buy her *I'm all fine now* tone, she could tell.

'Sophie?' It was a woman's voice, low and concerned, behind her. Emma.

Oh, God, she'd just made a total fool of herself.

She turned and faced a worried-looking Emma. 'I'm sorry, Em. I just needed some fresh air.'

It was a good indicator of their long lasting friendship, even if they had rarely seen each other in the past few years, that Emma didn't point out that there was plenty of fresh air in her backyard.

'Are you okay?' Her gaze flicked to Dan over Sophie's shoulder.

No. 'Yes,' she said. 'But we might head off now, I think. I have a job interview first thing tomorrow.'

Emma nodded reluctantly. 'Let's catch up for a coffee soon, okay?' she said as she retreated back to the house.

'I'll just go grab the Esky and your bag,' Dan said, following Emma inside.

Sophie leant against the trunk of a jacaranda, watching them walk up the stairs and then seeing the fly screen slam behind them.

She hadn't even had her bag—or her car keys. Where exactly had she thought she was going?

Away.

But that, of course, was the problem. The emptiness inside her couldn't be escaped—the inability to start her getaway vehicle notwithstanding.

Even her project plan couldn't fix it. So what if she'd decided to tell every prospective boyfriend that she was infertile? What would that achieve, really?

It would just accelerate the inevitable.

Disappointment.

Meaningless words meant to reassure.

Then rejection. Always rejection.

Even her relationships before Rick—before her boyfriends had hit an age when children were high on their to-do lists—had been temporary. There had always been an unspoken, underlying understanding that she was not a woman men chose to settle down with. She'd known it. And then Rick had made her believe that she'd had it all wrong, and she'd revelled in what she now knew was a lie.

The type of man she wanted—a man who'd propose marriage and a home and a life together—why would *he* want her?

Dan—a man who was the antithesis of the man she wanted—walked back towards her, empty Esky bouncing against his leg. She drank him in as he walked, backlit by the light on Emma's front porch.

Broad shoulders, lean hips, long legs.

And he wanted *her.* Suddenly the fact that he came with an expiry date didn't matter. The pull—the *connection*—between them was so strong that resisting him already felt like a battle she would never win. So why resist? Why not stop all her over-thinking and justifications and sensible decisions and just let go? Give in to this unfamiliar spectacular spark and let herself experience what her body so badly wanted? What *she* so badly wanted? And what now felt like the most natural, most perfect, most necessary thing in the world?

Then in three weeks he'd be gone, and she'd never need to tell him she was broken inside.

She met his eyes, pouring all the pain and frustration and

need she felt into her gaze. He stopped dead, his grip on the Esky's handle failing. It fell onto the grass with a thud. And then, without a word, he walked to where she stood, still propped against the tree. Her bag landed at her feet and his hands pressed flat against the jacaranda's trunk on either side of face.

His eyes hadn't shifted from hers, but she could see the question in his gaze.

She swallowed. 'This isn't about my project plan, or about you trying to make me more spontaneous or something, okay? This isn't me saying "the word", or whatever you called it.'

He nodded.

'This is about *me* wanting *you*.' His eyes glinted in the moonlight. 'And *you* wanting...*me*.'

It took everything she had not to look away or to blush. But she managed it, keeping their gazes locked together as he leant towards her, right up until she felt his breath hot against her lips. A split second before his mouth covered hers her eyes slid shut.

And then he kissed her. No preliminaries this time, just demanding, determined and sure. The touch of his tongue made her shiver and sent her hands from her sides to his waist.

She was deliciously hemmed in, with his palms still flat against the bark, so without the option of threading her hands into his hair, like before, this time she made do with exploring the shape of his back.

It was far from a hardship to run her fingers along his muscular ridges and planes through his shirt, or to drag her nails down his spine, halting only when her fingers hit the leather of his belt.

He kissed her expertly, passionately and voraciously, as if she was something special, and as if he couldn't get enough of her. He tasted crisp and clean, with a hint of cinnamon from the apple crumble they'd both had for dessert.

She sighed when he settled his weight against her, and he groaned into her mouth when she gave in to temptation and snuck her fingers under the hem of his T-shirt. His skin was warm and smooth—and far too covered in clothing. She pushed the fabric upwards, barely aware of what she was doing.

Dan's hands fell to her waist and she tensed in anticipation, wanting to feel his hands on her. All over her.

But then his mouth backed off from hers—and then completely away when she automatically followed him with her lips.

His body was still tight against her, and she dipped her hands into the valley at the small of his back and pressed him even closer against her. His hardness to her heat.

'Hell, Soph,' he said, low and dangerous. 'We can't do this here.'

She knew she should feel embarrassed, but she didn't. It should also have shocked her that her first instinct was to tell him *Don't stop.*

But luckily, somehow—despite the way her body thrummed with anticipation—a small part of her normal sensible self was able to force her hands from Dan's back and coherent, rational words from her mouth.

'Your place. Now.'

CHAPTER TEN

THE necessary frustration of returning her mother's car and leaving a note on the kitchen counter—all the while thanking her lucky stars that her mum was sleeping—was considerably offset during the too long taxi drive to Dan's house. They sat quite respectably, on either side of the back seat—nothing for the driver to see during his frequent glances in the rear vision mirror.

But Dan held her hand, drawing gorgeous little circles and swirls with his fingers on the sensitive skin of her wrist. It was so innocent, but the sensations it set off like fireworks inside her were anything but.

Finally, outside his townhouse, Dan all but dragged her from the footpath to his front door, kissing her even as he turned the key in the lock. They spilled inside, the door slamming shut and then both of their bodies slamming against it. Their mouths came together almost violently in their quest to become ever closer, lips grazing teeth, tongues tangling.

Sophie's hands started right where they'd left off, catching the hem of his T-shirt and shoving it upwards with steady determination. They broke apart while Dan pulled the fabric over his head, but they were back together before it hit the floor.

Her hands skimmed over his back, and then around and over his chest. He was all firm, hard, hot skin, only a few hairs smattering his torso.

Dan's clever hands explored her, too, following the shape of her hips and waist. He took big handfuls of her dress, until the fabric was bunched at her waist and her naked legs were rubbing against his roughness of his jeans.

And then his mouth lifted from hers.

'No...' she whispered, and she felt him smile against her jaw.

Her hands raced to his hair, to tug him back to her lips, but he ignored her, pressing hot, slow kisses beneath her ear, down her neck, along her collarbone. She let her head fall back against the door as he continued his leisurely journey, her body a luscious juxtaposition of ever-increasing tension and languorous, liquid heat.

'You're just perfect,' he said roughly.

The words felt almost as good as his touch.

And then his strong arms caught her beneath the knees and he swung her up into his arms.

Automatically her arms tightened around his neck, and she tried to meet his eyes in the darkness.

'Are you serious?' she said. 'I'm too heavy.'

Although he made her feel light as a feather.

He carried her effortlessly past a flight of stairs and into a bedroom, depositing her gently beside the bed.

'Pay attention, Soph,' he said, the moonlight revealing the heat and intensity in his gaze. 'You're perfect.'

Early-morning light poked through gaps in the wooden blinds, painting Dan's body with slivers and dapples of sun-shine. Sophie ran her finger along the curve of his back, tracing every dot and stripe. Some softly, some harder, and some with the gentle scrape of her nails.

'Good morning to you, too,' he said, sleepy and husky and sexy as hell.

He rolled over, propping himself up on an elbow. Now she could properly see the body she'd had so much fun exploring, and it looked exactly as it felt—powerful, smooth and lean. Not over-inflated muscle on muscle, just hard-angled strength—from his beautifully broad shoulders all the way down to his toes.

Not even a sheet covered them. The bedcovers had been kicked off, or more likely were just a casualty from all the fun they'd been having.

He was studying her, too, his gaze heavy-lidded and as admiring as when he'd first seen her naked skin. No one had ever looked at her like this, with such shiver-inducing intensity. Under his gaze she didn't think to feel modest, or to suck in her stomach, or to catalogue her flaws. In fact, when he was looking at her she forgot she even had them.

She reached for him, her index finger circling a perfect sphere of light on his breastbone. He reached for her, his hand moving in a gentle caress from the curve of her hip to the dip of her waist.

So what happened now? How did one go about having a no-strings-attached, who-cares-about-the-future, living-in-the-moment fling?

Were there rules? A handshake?

Dan's eyes met hers, almost grey in the filtered light. 'I can see you thinking,' he said. The pad of his finger outlined the creases in her forehead. 'And here,' he said, his finger drifting downwards to where she'd sucked her bottom lip subconsciously between her teeth, brushing against her and then away.

She released her lip, running her tongue over the spot where he'd so briefly touched her.

His gaze darkened.

'You're welcome to distract me,' she said.

And he was kissing her almost before the words had left her mouth.

'Dan!'

Sophie's voice was loud and harsh—and far from the beautifully sleep-fuzzed whisper of a few hours earlier. He sat up, shaking his own foggy head, to find Sophie out of bed, still naked, doing a commendable impression of a headless chicken. She picked up his jeans before tossing them aside. Then did the same to his shirt, before scurrying out of the bedroom—to where, he had no idea.

'What are you looking for?' he called out, rubbing his bleary eyes.

'The *time*,' she said, her tone now unquestionably panicky. 'Who doesn't have a bedside clock, anyway?'

He could hear the urgent smack of her bare feet against his hardwood floors as he hauled himself out of bed, tugging his boxer shorts on quickly.

'I use my phone as an alarm,' he said, trying to remember where he'd left it.

He heard a frustrated groan. 'I cannot *believe* you don't even have the time set on your microwave. What is wrong with you?' A pause, then a muttered, '*Where* did I put my handbag?'

He spotted his phone on the floor, where it must have fallen from his pocket, just as he heard a shriek from his living room.

'Oh, my God! It's half past nine!'

He walked out of his bedroom to see Sophie, a look of horror on her face, standing in the long rectangles of sunlight thrown by the frosted glass panels of his front door. The contents of her handbag were scattered at her feet and she held her phone out to him in abject despair, as if by taking it from her hands he could somehow turn back time.

'Your interview,' he said, understanding finally dawning.

'Yes,' she said. 'At ten.'

'In the city?'

She nodded.

'Well, hurry up, then. I'll get you there in time.'

Her jaw actually dropped, and she stared at him for long, confused moments.

'Pardon me?'

'It's ten minutes' drive from here. You'll get there easy.'

'Easy?' she repeated. 'But my suit is at my mum's. Twenty minutes away. I'll never make it back in time.'

He shrugged. 'You'll just have to wear what you wore last night.'

'What I wore last night?'

'Unless you'd prefer to cancel your interview?'

She shook her head. 'No, that would be even worse.'

'So it's decided, then?'

She rubbed her forehead. 'Oh, God—yes, I guess it is.'

'Shower's that way,' he said, pointing down the hallway.

She padded towards the bathroom as he admired her rear view. He supposed it was a little heartless to check her out when she was in the midst of such a momentously shocking occasion: *Sophie Morgan was running late.* But really he had no choice in the matter. Looking at Sophie was a compulsion. It had been long before last night.

'I don't suppose you have any make-up stashed away somewhere?' she said, not sounding even a little bit hopeful.

'Sorry,' he said. 'All out.'

'I don't *believe* this,' she said, just before he heard the hiss of running water.

Ten minutes later they were in Dan's car, Sophie dabbing at a just-discovered tomato sauce mark on her dress with a damp teatowel.

'I don't believe this,' she repeated. 'This is a disaster.'

He didn't comment, deciding that keeping his mouth shut was probably the best way to go, given the tension radiating off Sophie in waves.

'You think this is funny, don't you?' she said.

'No,' he said, figuring the single word was relatively safe.

Apparently not. 'You *do*! You think this is good for me—being late for something.'

'Of course not. Being late to a job interview is not something I'd wish on anyone. Particularly you.'

She fell back into her seat and blew out a long, frustrated sigh. 'Sorry,' she said. 'That was unfair.' And they fell into awkward silence.

Now that he'd had a shower and his brain had finally started to kick into a gear that could think beyond a naked Sophie walking around his house, he was getting a little tense himself.

What was going on here? His standard *modus operandi* the morning after was to get up early—requiring setting his alarm, which he had obviously forgotten—and then take the lady in question to breakfast at his favourite café in Subiaco. It was a good plan on two fronts: 1. He loved a good breakfast, complete with bacon, sausages and other artery-clogging delights, and 2. It circumvented the dangerous illusion of intimacy waking up together in bed inevitably created.

But he had let himself wake up with Sophie and he'd liked it. A lot. And, even worse, after they'd made love it hadn't even occurred to him to get out of bed. No, instead they'd fallen asleep again in each other's arms.

In. Each. Other's. Arms.

Was that really a good idea, given Sophie's predisposition for long-term meaningful relationships? What was she going to think? That it was more than just one night together?

Was it more than one night together?

Yes, probably. He'd suggested a fling—it felt like for ever ago—and that was most likely what she was intending. Or maybe not. *No*, just one night—just as she'd said it was only that one unbelievable kiss on the beach after the sunset.

Did it matter? Did he care?

It shouldn't. He shouldn't.

The effort to not care was making his muscles bunch and his jaw tighten uncomfortably.

Sophie cleared her throat. 'Thank you for driving me in. And for being so calm when I'm being a psychotic hot mess.'

Hot, yes. The rest, well—that was just Sophie. He got it. Running late to an interview must feel like the end of the world to her.

He also didn't feel calm. He felt confused. On edge.

He nodded tightly.

'You should feel pretty proud of yourself, really,' she said. 'For distracting me enough that I forgot about my alarm. About the interview, actually.'

He couldn't help but smile. 'I can't apologise for that,' he said.

'You shouldn't,' she said softly.

They fell into silence again, but it had a different essence this time.

'Ah…' she said finally. 'Um…are there any guidelines or something else I should know about for this?'

'For what?' he said, shooting a quick glance at her before returning his attention to the still heavy morning traffic.

Her head was down as she fiddled with the teatowel in her lap.

'You know—*us*.'

'*Us?*' he said, far more severely than he'd intended. Habit, maybe. An automatic reaction to a woman connecting herself to him in such a way.

She laughed without a hint of humour. '*Wow*. Way to

panic, Dan. I just meant—you know—our fling. Or whatever it is.'

The car slid to a stop at a red light. The high rise venue for her interview was only a minute or two away.

He didn't know what to say. He was still processing his body's unexpected reaction, its sudden release of tension from his jaw through to his toes. He'd all but sagged in relief at the knowledge that Sophie wanted more than a single night together. And his relief bothered him. A lot.

The light went green and he still hadn't spoken. He could see Sophie out of the corner of his eye—fidgeting, bouncing her knees. Maybe about the interview. Maybe about what he was going to say. He pressed his foot to the accelerator and the car continued towards their destination.

He still didn't know what to say.

Should he just end this now? Before it went any further? Before it got even more complicated? He didn't like how he was feeling right now. As if his world had been knocked off-balance.

He nosed the car into a loading bay—the only possible place to drop her off on the sardine-packed CBD street. He couldn't park there, of course, so he kept the motor running, searching for words that stubbornly evaded him.

Sophie opened the door, her action almost violent, then twisted and leapt out of her seat in a stiff, ungraceful movement. She stuck her head back into the car to snatch up her handbag.

'Thanks for the lift,' she said, her voice tight.

'Sophie, I—'

She met his eyes. Raised her eyebrows. The only make-up she wore was a moisturiser she'd unearthed in the bowels of his bathroom cupboard—a misguided gift from his mother, he suspected. Yet she was still beautiful. Dark, dark blue eyes, porcelain skin, rose coloured lips that tasted just as gorgeous as they looked.

She squeezed her eyes shut. Shook her head rapidly once, twice.

When her eyes reopened they were cool.

Then she straightened, slammed the door, and was gone—her gauzy summery dress swallowed up by a footpath awash with starched shirts and pinstriped suits.

All things considered, the interview went remarkably well. And there were a heck of a lot of things *to* consider. Her clothes, for one. So, *so* inappropriate for an interview. And she didn't think she'd ever stop cringing at the memory of the Managing Director's expression when he'd noticed her purpley-black-painted toenails. *Ugh.*

No make-up, for another. Now, she'd never considered herself particularly vain. Not the type to wear a full face of make-up to the supermarket on a Saturday morning, for example. But she'd *never* gone to work without wearing make-up. She wouldn't say it was like armour, or anything dramatic like that, it just made her look good. Professional. Polished. And she liked that.

So, not surprisingly, without make-up she felt like an unprofessional ragamuffin.

But really, once she'd got past a heartfelt apology for her appearance, she could put aside the way she looked, because she couldn't do a single thing to fix it. She was on time, she was otherwise well prepared for the interview, and that was that.

Unfortunately she couldn't put aside the ache inside her. *That* was what made the interview remarkable—the fact that she managed to conduct the entire thing like a rational, intelligent human being.

And not like the very, very stupid person she felt like.

After the interview she visited the company's bathroom and stared at herself for what felt like ages in the unforgiving fluorescent lit mirror.

What had Dan seen when their eyes had met? When she'd been standing on the footpath as stiff as a board and he'd been sprawled, casual as you like, in his luxurious leather seat?

Had he seen the fraud she suspected she was?

Oh, under the jacaranda tree it had all been about the *want*, about the *need*. But in the morning, when he'd looked at her as if she was something exquisite, caressed her as if he would never get enough, she'd bought it. All of it.

Stupid. *So* stupid.

She'd been happy to settle for a fling, knowing deep down that it was all he was capable of.

But he didn't even want that. She'd had the most incredible night of her life, and he was going to discard her as if it was nothing.

Well, not *as if* it was nothing. It must have *been* nothing to him.

Nothing? *Really?* Did she really believe that?

She studied her face: the smattering of freckles she normally hid beneath make-up, the tired smudges beneath her eyes. She didn't look great. It was a fact.

But in the car just before, when their gazes had caught and hung for an age, she'd known—*known*—that he hadn't been comparing her to the bevy of beauties she was sure he was accustomed to. He'd been looking at *her*, connecting with *her*.

Last night hadn't been nothing. She was sure of it.

But the one thing she was even more certain of was that he wasn't going to do a thing about it. She'd seen the moment he'd mentally slammed the door on any chance of more between them. He'd probably seen the stupid stars in her eyes and it had frightened him.

Something—his ex-wife, maybe—*something* had damaged him.

She'd walked away before he'd had the chance to speak.

She hadn't wanted to hear his non committal words. Well practised, she imagined, from dismissing any other women who'd even hinted at getting too close.

But not hearing it hadn't made it hurt any less.

So where did that leave her? A night of hot, sweaty sex to fill the void left by the myth of her previous life and she was left feeling even worse than before.

Brilliant.

Although it probably was for the best. One night and she ached inside. How would she be in a week? Two weeks? Right now she barely knew him and she felt something. Could feel her traitorous romantic self lying in wait to fall for him. Because she didn't think it would take much at all to fall in love with Dan Halliday.

She pulled herself together, shoved her hand in her bag to find the familiar sharp folded edges of *The Sophie Project*. As always, it soothed her. She might have royally stuffed up the boyfriend part of the plan, but it would be okay. The wedding would be awful, but she'd survive—and she'd still have the rest of her plan. The rest of her new life to plot and schedule, and tick off neatly as required.

Who knew? Maybe a miracle would happen and she'd get *this* job. Maybe they wouldn't see massive oversleeping as a flaw in the prospective manager of their multimillion-dollar projects. Maybe.

She walked to the lift, the slap of her sandals an embarrassing echo in a marble tiled hallway more accustomed to stiletto heels. In the lift she hugged herself, watching the glowing floor numbers tick slowly downwards.

As the doors slid open she fished in her handbag for her phone, in readiness to call a taxi. Her head was down as she scrolled through her phone numbers for a taxi service when she heard a deep voice say her name.

She looked up, knowing it was Dan but not quite believing it until she saw him—propped against one of the pillars that dotted the skyscraper's foyer.

Shouldn't he be running for the hills?

He straightened his long body, walking towards her with steely intent.

'I didn't get to answer your question before. About the guidelines.'

She raised an eyebrow. 'I think you did.'

His gaze flicked away for a second, then back. 'No.' A pause. 'I didn't. Can we go somewhere quiet to talk?'

'This is fine,' she said, having no interest in delaying or extending this conversation in any way. She crossed her arms, waiting for him to continue.

'Look, Sophie, I like you...'

The words were as awkward as fingernails on a blackboard. Here it came. Surely there'd been no need for him to hang around? She'd already got it. Loud and clear.

It was fun, but I'm just not looking for a relationship.

Ugh. She couldn't bear it. 'Dan,' she said. 'Really, you don't have to bother. You're freaked out that I want something more from you, but I don't. I knew exactly what I was getting into. Sex. And that's it. I was hoping to keep the fun going a bit longer—you know, until the wedding—but if you'd rather not...'

What was she doing? Why prolong the inevitable? Did she really believe that she could do it—have a fling with Dan and not have it hurt like hell at the end?

He was looking at her with wide eyes that searched her face. 'You just want something short-term? That's it? Nothing more?'

She snorted. 'Geez, Dan, you really *do* have tickets on yourself, don't you? I think you're right—what you said the other week. Maybe a fling is just what I need. I'm not ready for another relationship. Not yet.'

He blinked, but she knew she'd convinced him. She thought she might have half convinced herself.

Three weeks. With Dan. How many nights was that? Twenty-one? Mmm.

And she'd still get her wedding date. *The Boyfriend Plan* would remain on track.

All she had to do was remember why she'd kissed him under the tree outside Emma's. This was *only* about the want, about the electric chemistry between them and—how could she have forgotten this?—about the fact she didn't have to reveal the real emptiness inside her. Not to him, when it was only a fling.

If she'd just remember that, really—what could go wrong?

CHAPTER ELEVEN

THE first night of their fling Dan had taken her to dinner. To—in his words—'the best little Indonesian restaurant' in Northbridge, where the chairs were plastic, the floor faded vinyl and the lighting fluorescent.

It had been great, the food delicious and their casual conversation barely hiding the electricity that snapped between them. Following an impromptu—*ahem*—enthusiastic kiss outside a darkened shopfront before they'd even made it back to the car, the short drive back to Dan's had seemed impossibly long...but so definitely worth it.

The second night they'd had a fancy dinner—at Dan's place. Fully catered for by his chefs. Dan had tried—and failed—to convince her that his culinary skills went beyond his ability to reheat cannelloni in the oven. Although she wasn't going to complain about his creative uses for the strawberries and cream they'd had for dessert...

By the third night, when he picked her up from her mother's once again without giving her any warning about where they were going or what they were doing, Sophie decided he'd proved his point.

'Are you ever going to let me know your plans? Or is this going to be over two weeks of surprises?'

He glanced at her across the centre console before refocussing on the road. 'When it's so much fun watching you trying to figure things out? What do you think?'

She grinned. It was the strangest thing, but she was kind of *enjoying* having absolutely no idea what her plans were each evening. It was unexpectedly liberating to be unable to prepare or over-think what they were doing.

The lack of planning fitted perfectly with the whole fling, really—its very existence, of course, being completely unplanned. And also probably illogical. And not very sensible.

It was the first unwise decision she'd made so consciously—given her decision to waste years of her life with Rick had not seemed so unwise at the time. And so far it was fantastic.

Not that she'd thrown out *The Sophie Project*—not even close!—but Dan was like a drug: her daily dose of disorganisation amongst the regimentation of her charts and checklists.

On night three, Dan really had cooked for her—to prove his point—but by night four it was definitely her turn to be in charge.

By unspoken agreement they never confirmed their plans—or lack thereof—until late afternoon each day. They also never discussed when they would see each other next, which gave each night together a sense of impermanence that somehow heightened the intensity of each meeting.

Or maybe that was just how things were between them?

Sophie wouldn't let herself consider that point in too much detail.

So on night four she had Dan drive them to the same beach where they'd first kissed, stopping for a paper-wrapped package of fish and chips on the way. On the beach, they arranged themselves on colourful towels as they watched the sun set—with the thick cloud of tension that had hung between them at this same beach a few weeks earlier now replaced with humming anticipation.

Sophie studied him as he looked out to the still-glowing horizon, a lone seagull eating the remainder of his salted and vinegared chips beside him. They'd talked all evening—about the bar, about her old job in Sydney, anything, really. But it was nice, this comfortable silence. It felt so easy to just *be* with Dan.

The trill of his mobile phone made her jump and disturbed the bird. It retreated with a squawk and a few angry flaps of its wings.

Dan checked the caller ID and answered with an apologetic nod in her direction.

'Hi, Mum!' he said, and he leisurely rose to his feet, walking a few metres away, his bare feet sinking into the deep sand.

Sophie curled her own toes, hugging her knees to her chest. She hadn't really known what to expect with their fling—but whatever it was it had *not* been this. This was like all the best bits of a new relationship without any of the uncertainty or unnecessary complications. Knowing they had a deadline left her greedy to spend time with Dan without the fear of looking too keen or too desperate or any of the other myriad of angsty things that she usually tended to worry about.

Dan walked back towards her, his phone in his pocket. He reached out for her, pulling her to her feet. 'Ready to go?' he asked.

She'd been so busy watching him that she'd barely noticed how dark it had become.

'Yeah,' she said, pressing a quick kiss to his mouth.

They packed up quickly and headed towards the car.

'I won't be able to see you tomorrow,' Dan said as he unlocked the doors.

Sophie feigned nonchalance, determined not to ask why and to ignore the little kick of disappointment in her belly.

'Family dinner,' he said. 'My mum was just calling to ask what I wanted her to make.'

'That's nice,' she said, more relieved than she should be that he'd told her. Why? Was it really any of her business where he was when they weren't together?

Of course not.

'What are you having?' she asked, to distract herself as they climbed into the car. Hadn't she just decided that this fling was fabulous and completely free of uncertainty? And here she was, over-thinking.

Why couldn't she just let herself enjoy it for what it was?

Dan launched into an enthusiastic summary of the menu for the following evening as they drove back towards his house, describing the traditional Croatian dishes: *Pasticada*—marinated beef with gnocchi—and *blitva*—spinach with loads of potato, garlic and salt.

'That sounds amazing,' she said.

Dan grinned. 'It is. My mum would love to cook for you. I should take you one—'

The casually spoken words came to an abrupt halt and an awkward silence descended.

Sophie's mouth opened and closed a few times—but, really, what could she say? So she spent long minutes focussing on popping the naive little bubbles of hope that had formed, completely unwanted, inside her.

She knew Dan hadn't meant to say that. He didn't mean it.

Eventually they made it back to Dan's, and Sophie slid from her seat with no idea what to do. Should she call a taxi—go home? Dan had as good as built a wall between them, adding to it brick by brick with every passing second.

'Look, Dan, how about I—?'

But then he was beside her, crowding her against the car in the best possible way.

'Sophie,' he said with a hoarse whisper, and when his lips touched her she knew what he was doing. Erasing what he'd said and re-establishing exactly what they had.

Something hot and heavy and amazing...

And temporary. Definitely temporary.

Dan woke up before Sophie, as he had every morning that week, before even the earliest dawn light had forced its way through his window. He wasn't about to repeat the mistakes of that first morning they'd spent together—so he was already up early to swim before spending the rest of the day at one of his bars.

But, as always, he found himself dawdling. Letting his eyes adjust to the darkness so that he could watch Sophie sleep in the moonlight. It had been four of these mornings now, and she'd still never stirred as he watched her, tracing the curves and valleys of her body with his gaze.

If it bothered her, his early-morning disappearing act, she hadn't said a word.

And that surprised him. He hadn't believed her—not really—when she'd told him that all she wanted from him was a no-strings-attached fling. He hadn't forgotten the way she'd looked at him in his car the morning of her job interview, let alone that first time they'd made love. Her vulnerability, her depth of feeling, had been there for all to see—terrifying enough for him to know he had to end it after only one night.

But he hadn't been able to do it. He'd let himself believe what he was so sure was a lie so he could have what he wanted. Sophie.

For three weeks. Well, only two and a bit, now.

It seemed he'd been wrong. Sophie hadn't shown the

slightest hint of wanting any more than he was prepared to give. Instead it was *him* saying stupid, silly things. Where had the almost invitation to meet his parents come from? It had been ten years since he'd last taken a woman to meet his family, and he had no intention—*absolutely none*—of changing that.

And yet the words had still slipped out. For a few seconds he'd imagined Sophie sitting beside him at his mum's funny 'statement piece' table: chatting, eating, laughing with his family.

He needed to make sure that didn't happen again. He *didn't* want that—not with Sophie, not with anyone.

He was lucky Sophie hadn't mentioned it—had seemingly forgotten the words had ever been said. Which was good— excellent, even. She understood exactly what their fling was: a bit of fun with a concrete, immovable end date.

So, with one last, long look at the beautiful woman sprawled beside him, he hauled himself out of bed and far away from her.

When Sophie woke, she knew she'd be alone. But even so, she found herself rolling over, reaching out with her hand, checking just in case...

But *no*. The sheets were empty and had long gone cold.

The first morning he'd left a note, but after that, nothing.

She told herself it didn't bother her, and that she really did need to adjust to this whole no-strings-attached thing, but still it stung. Just a little.

Especially when she compared it to that first morning, and how it had felt to fall asleep in his arms.

There had been no repeat of that, and she wasn't com- plaining—not really. It was her decision just as much as his—for, no matter how intimate, how intense it felt when she and Dan made love, they needed to maintain their boundaries. Otherwise it would be all too easy to read more into their relationship. To think they even *had* a relationship, actually.

She knew that. He knew that.

It was sensible. It made things easier.

But still it stung.

After a quick shower, she headed home. It was still terribly early, but that was unavoidable. Test-driving cars might need to be shuffled a bit higher on her project plan task list. Returning the little red hatchback before her mother started work—or catching public transport if her mum needed the car for the night or if Dan had picked her up—well, it didn't really fit with her perception of what a glamorous fling should be.

When she unlocked her front door and stepped inside to find her mum seated in the middle of the couch, cereal bowl in lap, obviously waiting for her, she immediately decided it was not her new car that needed to be reprioritised. No, it was finding a new place to live.

Awkward conversations the morning after—with your mother—*definitely* did not a glamorous fling make.

'Have a good night?' her mum asked.

'Uh-huh,' she said, and a memory of Dan's body pressed up hard against her as he'd kissed her voraciously against his car popped, desperately unwanted, into her head. She blushed.

Her mum raised an eyebrow. 'Are you sure this is a good idea, Sophie? So soon after Rick?'

She had to give her mother points for waiting days before *The Talk*. Although Sophie hadn't exactly missed her pointed looks of concern.

She shrugged. 'It's nothing serious, Mum, okay? I can handle it.'

'Nothing serious to him, maybe,' her mum replied softly, and Sophie stiffened.

'For either of us,' she said firmly.

'You spend every night with a man you aren't serious about?' her mum asked, scepticism lining her face.

'I'm not seeing him tonight,' she said, choosing to ignore the fact that if she'd had her way she would be seeing him, every night. And not just because of the sex, no matter what she told herself.

'Hmm.' Her mum swallowed a mouthful of cereal, chewing slowly while all the time holding Sophie's gaze.

Her mum didn't believe her for one moment. She was sure Sophie was falling for him, and was sure she was going to get hurt.

And it wasn't news to Sophie that she was probably right. She'd gone into this knowing she was perched on the edge of a precipice—millimetres away from certain disaster.

But whether or not she'd already toppled over— Did it really matter? Walking away from him now would be no easier than watching him walk away from her.

And he would—in two weeks' time.

So she might as well, as she'd said with such bravado, *have fun* until then.

She would deal with the consequences later.

CHAPTER TWELVE

MORE than a week later Dan sat in his office and stared at his computer screen with eyes that refused to focus. He could hear the familiar sounds of a kitchen hand completing the final tidy-up of the kitchen, and he'd already heard the door slam multiple times as his staff headed home for the night.

It was Saturday, so Sophie was out there somewhere. She'd insisted on working, no matter how many times he'd told her that as far as he was concerned their deal was off. He was going to the wedding as her *bona fide* date. Not *bona fide* boyfriend, of course, but close enough that there was no longer any need to barter her waitressing skills.

But she'd insisted. *We had a deal*, she'd said. And then she'd given him the most withering look when he'd suggested he pay her.

He'd barely seen her all night. With the new bartender he wasn't needed behind the bar, so he'd just kept his normal eye on things, but otherwise been stuck to his office. He'd sorted out boring administration stuff while he'd spent far too much time thinking about Sophie.

Surely he should have hit his Sophie quota by now?

It had been thirteen days—twelve nights—since they'd agreed to have their fling, and so far he hadn't come close to having enough of her. They hadn't planned it, but the pattern of those first few days had continued, and they'd spent nearly every night together. One night they'd go out to dinner—and be in bed before dessert. Another they'd intend to go out—but never make it through the door. And for the remainder they just stopped even bothering to try. They'd eat takeaway while sitting cross-legged on his floor and then make love—on the couch, on the bed, against the wall...

The office door swung open. Sophie was a split second behind it. 'Everyone's gone but the cleaner,' she said. 'Are you ready to go?'

He shook his head. 'Come here,' he said gruffly.

She grinned and walked towards him. The room was lit only by the lamp on his desk and the glow of his computer screen. Her dark clothing blended into the darkness when the door clicked shut behind her.

She leant down and pressed a chaste kiss to his lips, but the soft touch wasn't even close to enough. His body had been anticipating this moment for hours—his blood simmering impatiently through his veins. Now he had her, he wasn't about to wait any longer.

He wrapped an arm around her waist, pulling her onto his lap with enough purpose to swivel the big leather office chair violently. She laughed as she fell against him, her breath warm against his neck.

'Very smooth,' she said.

He shrugged. 'Always.'

She snorted. 'Right. Nothing says suave like eating Chinese noodles out of plastic containers.' That had been dinner last night. 'And there I'd been, imagining you romancing women with silver service dining and the ballet.'

'Would you rather we went to the ballet?'

God, he hoped not.

She shook her head. 'What we're doing has been working just fine for me.'

Having her on his lap, legs hooked over the arm of his chair, was working pretty fantastically for him, too.

He kissed her—properly this time—his hand sliding under the fabric of her shirt to roam over the smoothness of her back and waist, holding her close against him.

She kissed him back with passionate enthusiasm, her arms looping around his neck.

By now he should be used to this, but every time they kissed it was just a little bit different. Sometimes fun. Sometimes impossibly intense. Sometimes slow. Sometimes desperate.

Sophie squirmed against him as he trailed kisses down her neck, her pretty sighs rapidly unravelling his control. But this was supposed to be just a prelude. They weren't alone yet.

And then she went still. Laughed.

Not the reaction he'd been aiming for.

'I don't believe it,' she said.

'What?'

She nodded over his shoulder at the computer screen that was now behind him. 'Dan Halliday has a project plan. And...' She laughed again. 'Is that a *spreadsheet*?'

He spun the seat around so he was again facing the desk. Sophie rearranged herself on his lap and leant forward to study the documents on the screen.

'I run a business—of course I have plans. The bars don't run themselves.'

She turned to look at him, raising an eyebrow. 'This is a five-year plan. A very, *very* detailed one.'

'So what?'

'You aren't as wild and spontaneous as you'd like me to think, are you?' she said, her eyes sparkling.

Rather than replying, he stood, lifting and turning her so

she sat on the edge of his solid hardwood desk. She gasped as he stepped between her legs, his hands firms on her hips. The humour in her expression was instantly replaced with heat, and her tongue darted out to moisten her lips.

'That sounds like a challenge to me.'

Sophie remembered hearing vaguely, right at the back of her mind, the cleaner call out a goodbye. She probably should've been embarrassed that she'd completely forgotten about him the moment Dan had kissed her. What if he'd heard them through the thin walls?

But now she lay—on Dan's *desk!*—completely spent, her breathing gradually slowing and returning to normal, and not for one second did she regret what had just happened.

It had never been like this for her before. This constant, continuous need for another person. This urgency, this want. He made her feel like someone else and yet paradoxically completely and totally herself. She barely recognised this woman who could make love with such abandon. But she revelled in how good, how right it felt.

Belatedly she registered that, unlike every other time they'd made love, Dan was not holding her in his arms, or kissing her, or making her smile with cheeky little whispers in her ear. Instead he stood with his back to her, his shoulders rising as he took long shuddering breath after long shuddering breath.

'Dan?' she said, her voice a husky tenor she barely recognised.

He shook his head. 'No condom,' he said, as if he couldn't believe it.

'It's okay,' she said, without thinking.

He turned, his gaze taking her in, propped up on her elbows, her knees bent at the table edge, her feet swinging in an unconscious rhythm. She stilled them.

'What do you mean it's okay? You could be pregnant.'

No, she couldn't.

Finally reality crashed in on her—brutal and uncompromising. She sat up, slid off the desk, searching for her underwear. For the first time she noticed the papers, the pens and other casualties of their passion lying scattered all over the floor.

Dan had located his boxers, and as she watched he dragged on his jeans in a rough, angry movement.

'I've *never* been so careless… How could I—?'

He muttered to himself as he paced the room. It was as if she wasn't even there.

She spotted the scrap of hot pink lace and satin and stepped into her underwear, then tugged down her shirt and refastened her bra. It didn't make her feel any less exposed, or any less guilty.

It's not your fault. We both got carried away…

Maybe. But she was the one who could end Dan's unnecessary torment. She knew he must be beside himself—that this was nightmarish for Mr Anti-Commitment.

She stood in front of him, halting him mid-stride. He rubbed his temples, looked at the floor, looked at her, looked at the door.

It didn't take a psychic to know exactly what he was thinking. He wanted nothing more than to put as much space between them as possible.

'It'll be okay,' she said again.

Now his attention locked on hers. 'You can't know that. Not for sure.'

Yes, she could.

She opened her mouth. No words came out.

He sighed. 'I know—odds are everything's fine. But what if it isn't?' Then his eyes widened hopefully. 'Unless you're on the pill?'

She couldn't lie outright to him. She shook her head. 'No.'

They stared at each other for long, long moments. At any one of those moments she could have chosen to tell him.

Why couldn't she? What was the problem?

Of any man, surely Dan was the most likely to be okay about her infertility? She'd be out of his life in a week's time, so why would he even care?

Weeks ago, on their first date, she'd justified not telling him because he didn't need to know. That excuse had just become invalid.

So it had come down to the other reason—the *real* reason she'd never told him when she'd blurted out and shared so much else with him.

She didn't want him to know. She'd *never* wanted him to know.

She'd told herself that the beauty of this fling was that she wouldn't have to tell him. But she'd lied to herself and pretended it was just generic resistance to revealing something so personal. That it wasn't about Dan, in particular, it was about having a man want her without knowing how flawed she was.

But of *course* it was all about Dan. It had been all about Dan from the beginning.

It wasn't that she couldn't handle yet another man rejecting her for her infertility—she couldn't handle that man being Dan.

At some point she'd closed her eyes.

Dan's finger brushed across her cheek as he tucked a strand of hair behind her ear. Her eyes slid open as he ran his hand across the top of her head, flattening what she only then realised must be the birds' nest of her hair.

'You look like you've been ravished,' he said, but his attempt at lightening the atmosphere fell horribly flat.

So they stood there together, mirror images of each other's misery.

He, because he thought there was a chance she might be carrying his baby.

She, because she knew—one hundred percent, gut-wrenchingly guaranteed—that she was not.

When Amalie had left him, Dan had bought the bar without any real planning or due consideration or anything even vaguely resembling the way he—the old Dan—normally did anything. That had been exactly why he'd bought it, and it had been perfect in its incongruousness.

It had distracted him, and given him a base on which to build his new life. And now the bar—well, *bars* now—was like a symbol. Proof that he'd changed from the person he'd once been to who he was now. The bars soothed him.

So it made sense that he went to his bar on Sunday morning—the morning after his brain explosion—when he'd let his hormones, his lust, suffocate his common sense. He certainly couldn't stay at home, where memories of Sophie were everywhere, even though she'd been careful never to leave behind any of her possessions.

The moment he stepped into the bar he realised his idiocy. The bar was where they'd met, where Sophie worked, and where last night they'd had the most overwhelming, all-consuming sex of his life. Today the bar had absolutely no chance of being his refuge.

He had the disconcerting thought that maybe it never would again.

So he drove to his parents' place. It was somewhere he'd never taken Sophie—a space where he could pull himself together, iron things out in his mind, without having memories of Sophie confusing him.

'This is a nice surprise!' his mother said when she answered the door. Then she must have seen something in his expression, because she did her standard 'worried mother' thing—reaching out to squeeze his hand and saying, 'Honey, is everything okay?'

He hadn't thought it possible, but it was right about then that he started to feel even *more* stupid. What was wrong with him?

Why couldn't he be logical and rational about this? Sophie was probably right. The odds were in favour of her not being pregnant. He had friends who'd tried for months or years before their wives or girlfriends had finally conceived. Given that, what was with all this panic? Why his rush last night to get home—alone—and as far away from Sophie as possible?

Although last night it hadn't been just him doing the running. Sophie had looked every bit as stricken as he'd felt, and had retreated equally fast. He hadn't heard from her this morning—although that in itself was not unusual. Since their fling had started they'd only communicated at night.

He followed his mother inside and sat quietly at the kitchen bench as she fussed about, making him a cup of coffee. She plonked it down in front of him and perched on a stool to his left.

'Do you want to tell me what's wrong?'

'No,' he said. 'Nothing's wrong. I just thought I'd pop by.'

She slanted him a pointed look. 'Dan—do you really think I'm that stupid?'

'Am I really that transparent?'

She looked at him shrewdly. 'Not usually, no.'

Just today. Great.

'Is it to do with work?' she asked, after a few minutes had passed.

That was a relief, at least. He didn't have his problem tattooed across his face.

Which should be unsurprising, though, given he couldn't identify the problem himself.

Was he angry at himself for forgetting about protection?

Yes, definitely.

But if it was just that, then surely this was where his logical self should kick in, telling him there was no point over-reacting? Chances were it would be fine, and he should just wait a few weeks until he knew for sure either way. And, if Sophie was pregnant, deal with it then.

All very sensible.

All things he did not want to discuss with his mother. But there was something else bothering him—something that sat just out of reach and he couldn't grab on to, certainly couldn't define.

'No, it's not work. But I don't want to talk about it. Or think about it.'

Fortunately his mum heard his unspoken plea: *Distract me.*

So she did—or tried to—launching into a monologue about the events of the past week since he'd last spoken to her. Who she'd caught up with for coffee, the name of the book her book club was reading, that sort of thing. His dad joined them later, following some highly unsubtle facial expressions and hand gestures from his mother. Then he heard all about his dad's case, its latest developments, a series of precedent cases he was investigating.

He nodded and smiled at all the right places, but although he was listening barely any of it sank in. His brain was just too packed full of thoughts of Sophie. It seemed no matter where he went memories of her followed him.

How she'd looked—her hair a tangled mess but still beautiful—as she'd slept beside him. She wasn't a neat sleeper—she generally had an arm thrown above her head and her legs arranged all askew. But he liked that—the contrast to the perfectly groomed, perfectly organised Sophie she was by day. And it suited her, that sleepy disarray. It matched her innate passion—something he never would have guessed she possessed until they'd kissed that first time. After that it had seemed crazy that he'd never noticed it before.

Because Sophie's passion was in everything she did. He'd been so wrong to think that her spreadsheets and project plans sucked her dry of all feeling. Instead they channelled her passion, her dogged determination to make the absolute most of her second chance at life. Maybe he didn't always agree with what she was doing, and maybe her actions raised his eyebrows—her memorisation of cocktail recipes and her plan to take him clothes shopping came to mind—but she was always moving forward, always being authentically herself.

He loved that about her.

Loved?

Something of what he was feeling—shock, for example—must have been evident, for his mum reached out and squeezed his hand again.

'I'm sorry, honey. This wasn't the right time to tell you.'

He took a moment for the words to sink in. He couldn't recall a word his mum or dad had said in the previous few minutes. Now they stared at him with obvious concern.

'Tell me what?'

His parents shared a long look.

'That Nina lost her baby a few days ago,' his mum said quietly.

He blinked. 'But I just spoke to her the other day, after you told me she was pregnant. She said everything was fine.'

Her mum nodded. 'Sometimes things go wrong. It's not fair.'

Dan swirled his half-drunk and barely tasted coffee round and round in its mug. He felt sick for his cousin, who'd chatted to him so excitedly on the phone. She'd been so happy, but now her baby was gone.

He knew how that felt.

He stood up and walked outside onto the wide expanse

of jarrah decking. His parents' perfectly manicured oversized garden was glorious in the midday sun, and while he
couldn't see them, he could hear magpies in the branches of
the ancient gumtrees.

No one followed him, leaving him to sit, alone, at the top
of the steps leading down to the lawn.

It had been so long since he'd let himself think about his
loss. About the baby he'd wanted so desperately. He could
still remember how he'd felt when Amalie had announced
her pregnancy: total euphoria. So all-encompassing that he'd
not even noticed his wife's lack of the same. Because somehow he'd made her pregnancy all about *him*—about what
he wanted and when, and about silly things: his excitement
about remodelling the spare room as a nursery, about teaching his son or daughter how to swim, about one day his child
following in his already successful career footsteps.

All about Dan. Him, him, him.

He'd been so caught up in that—in *his* plans and dreams
for the future—that he'd not spent any time in the present.
So he hadn't seen what was happening right in front of his
face.

And then it had been too late—far too late. His baby was
gone. His wife had begun divorce proceedings.

So he'd changed his life. Become the opposite of the man
he'd once been. Shoved aside his old hopes and dreams—at
first because it had hurt too much and later because he'd
decided it wasn't worth the risk of hurting like that again.

Or of hurting someone else like that again.

Was that it? Was that what had caused him to toss and
turn all night? The niggling sensation that maybe his long-
discarded dreams did not lie as dormant as he'd thought?

Because even once his initial knee-jerk, confirmed-bach-
elor, ultra-cautious reaction had finally blown over—and it
had taken hours after Sophie had climbed into her car and

driven away—he'd not let himself consider—*really* consider—what he'd feel if Sophie *was* pregnant.

How would he feel? If Sophie was carrying his child? *Their* child?

Scared. Anxious. That was to be expected.

But that wasn't all. Somewhere deep inside him, amongst the fear and the hurt and the angst of ten years earlier, was a tiny pinprick of hope.

Burning warm and bright.

CHAPTER THIRTEEN

The Sophie Project 2.1 (Project Manager: S. Morgan):
~~*Sub Project: The Boyfriend Plan*~~

SHE had to end it.

Soon. Immediately, really.

Sophie lay fully clothed on her bed—the same narrow bed she'd slept in as a child and as a teenager. She was now blessedly alone, as her mother had left for her Sunday evening rock 'n' roll dance class after a morning full of concerned motherly *Are you okay?*s and *Do you want to talk about it?*s. She was very grateful her mother hadn't rolled out any *I told you so*s. Although she definitely would've deserved them.

Was it really only two weeks since Emma's barbecue? Two weeks since she'd thrown herself into something so hot and so wonderful with Dan—and simultaneously so ill-advised and so stupid?

It seemed impossible.

Last night she'd driven home in floods of pathetic tears, juggling the bone-deep emotions that roller-coastered about inside her. On the surface she'd cried for that old ache, that old emptiness, its familiarity doing nothing to lessen the hurt. But beneath that the real pain lingered, and for once it had nothing at all to do with her infertility.

It was irrational, she knew, to be so devastated by Dan's reaction. They were having a fling—a fling with such a clear end date that of *course* he would panic at the possibility of being tied to her for ever. She knew a pregnancy was impossible, but *he* didn't, and his fear had been etched all over his face.

What had she expected? Some romantic platitude? A promise that they would get through this together?

Ha! Ridiculous.

Right from the start she'd known what they had and all that Dan would ever offer her. She'd thought she'd recovered from her silly little slip-up on the first night, when she'd confused sex with intimacy and had thought she'd been handling her first attempt at a no-strings-attached fling with remarkable aplomb. She'd actually *believed* that!

And then they'd both forgotten about protection, and her first reaction had been sorrow that she would never have Dan's child.

Completely forgetting that Dan certainly didn't want children with her.

So she'd been kidding herself. She hadn't jumped into bed with Dan purely because he made her feel wanted and needed—although of course that had been part of it.

The main reason—the reason she'd been hiding from herself—was that she liked him.

Really, *really* liked him. Daydreaming-of-for-ever liked him.

Her inability to tell him the truth had made that clear. She didn't want him to know, because the last man she'd loved had rejected her for what she was incapable of giving him.

She just couldn't risk that happening again—not so soon.

And that, of course, was the terrible irony of all this. Dan didn't even know about her infertility and he *still* didn't want her. She was tying herself up in knots over telling him something that to him would be completely irrelevant.

She didn't even know if he *wanted* children! Their conversations had certainly never veered towards the future, but based on his general attitude towards relationships and marriage it didn't take much to connect the dots. It seemed as if she had found a guy who genuinely didn't want children... there was just the pesky little problem that he didn't want her, either.

She had got embarrassingly far ahead of herself. She'd actually let herself believe the intimacy they shared was more than physical! She'd totally forgotten—or, if she was honest, deliberately ignored—the fact that Dan was always going to walk away from her.

So delaying the inevitable was doing her no favours.

She needed to end it now.

Belatedly, Sophie realised that *love* had crept into her thoughts.

Did she love Dan?

She couldn't even bear to consider it.

A loud knock on the front door was like a thunderclap in the perfectly silent house. Sophie scurried to the door in her comfiest tracksuit pants and a faded singlet, hugely relieved she hadn't been crying. At least her mother's visitor wouldn't have to suffer *that* unfortunate, blotchy-faced vision.

She opened the door, speaking before it had fully swung open.

'Sorry, my mum isn't home at the—?'

The sentence died an abrupt death at the ghastly reality of who it was framed in the doorway.

'Can I come in?' Dan said.

So he was going to beat her to the chase, then? End it himself?

Unsurprisingly, it didn't make her feel any better.

She didn't say a word—just stepped aside to let him in. As he walked past she could smell the familiar scent of him—crisp aftershave mixed with the ocean-fresh washing powder she'd seen in a box in his laundry.

They both stood awkwardly in the middle of her mother's lounge room, a slight breeze softly rattling the venetian blinds.

Sophie didn't know the appropriate etiquette in this situation. Did you offer a man a drink or a seat when he was visiting for the purpose of dumping you?

She decided *no*, and simply crossed her arms and stood there—waiting.

'Sophie,' he said. 'I'm sorry about last night. I over-reacted.'

She nodded. 'And?'

He looked confused. 'And…I'm *really* sorry.'

She met his gaze. 'Come on. I saw the way you freaked out last night. Isn't this where you say it's been fun, but maybe it's best we end it now?'

'Is that what you want me to say?'

'Yes,' she said. *No.*

His brow crinkled. 'Why?'

She shrugged, feigning nonchalance. 'This was never supposed to be anything serious, Dan. Don't you think last night cut a bit too close to the bone? We've only got a week to go—wouldn't it be easier to end it now?'

'You want to end this? End us?'

She laughed—a short burst of ugly sound. 'I thought you were very clear that there isn't an *us*. That there will never be an us.'

What was she doing? Why bother to explain?

Why couldn't she channel some ultra-sophisticated woman who effortlessly flitted from affair to affair?

He stepped towards her. 'What if I've changed my mind?'

What?

'But you don't do relationships.'

Another step closer.

'Maybe I'd like to make an exception.' He was watching her, his gaze steady and intense, his brilliant blue eyes piercing her soul. 'If that's okay with you?'

He meant it.

It was so unexpected, so startling, that constructing a sentence was suddenly completely beyond her. 'Oh.'

'Oh?' he said with a smile. But she saw the hint of vulnerability behind it.

Was this really happening?

'Why?' she said.

'I don't know,' he said, low and seductive. 'I think we fit pretty well together.'

He was close enough now that his breath fanned her cheek, and her fingers itched to reach out and touch him. All she had to do was give him the slightest signal and she'd be in his arms, his mouth on hers, his hands all over her body.

She took a deep breath, desperately trying to prevent herself from dissolving into a boneless puddle of want. His nearness never failed to accelerate her pulse and heat her skin, and it would be easy—so, so easy—to just...

No. This was too important. She *needed* to understand.

'What else? Surely I'm not the only woman you've been sexually compatible with?'

The stark words were intended to strip all hint of romance from what they'd shared together, and they were effective—to a point. Dan took a step backwards.

'What's going on here, Soph? There's more than something physical happening between us—or am I imagining things?'

Again she was trapped by an inability to lie to him. She shook her head.

'Then why? I thought this was what you wanted?'

'But it's what you *don't* want. So what's changed, Dan?

Why does a confirmed bachelor suddenly want a relationship? And what makes him change his mind overnight?' She took a deep breath, locking her gaze with his. It didn't make any sense, but she needed to be sure. 'The only thing I can see that's changed is now you think I could be pregnant.'

'You could be.'

'I'm *not*,' she said, her voice immovably firm.

He moved closer to her again, this time reaching out for her, rubbing his hand along her upper arm. Her skin goosepimpled at his touch.

'That is what's changed,' he finally conceded, and her whole body tensed in response. 'I've avoided relationships since my divorce because I was so scared of repeating past mistakes. But you—' he smiled as his gaze explored her face '—you've reminded me of what I'm missing out on. That's sometimes it's worth the risk of making a mistake.'

His words should be making her glow with happiness. He thought she was special. Maybe even thought he could fall for her.

But she needed to know the truth.

'What happened? Between you and your wife?'

Now it was his turn to tense. She saw him put the familiar shutters and 'Keep Out' signs in place. She'd seen them often enough.

But then he shook his head, and all the barriers fell away.

'I told you, didn't I, that I once had my own life plan?' She nodded. 'It was a good one. Degree, fiancée, great job, nice house, marriage, pay rises…babies.'

Sophie sucked in a harsh breath.

'I had this image in my head—like a painting of what success was supposed to be. I don't know where I got it from, but I was obsessed with it—and obsessed with achieving it as quickly as possible. I didn't see the point of waiting around. I wanted *everything*, and I wanted it *now*.' He shrugged, but looked anything but casual. 'And as I'd got everything else in my life whenever I wanted it, I had no reason to think I wouldn't.'

'So you became a lawyer, got married...'

'And Amalie got pregnant.'

Oh, God. Oh, God. Oh, God...

She couldn't look at him, so she looked at the floor as her limbs went heavy with dread.

'I was so excited. It was what I'd always wanted, you know?'

Sophie nodded—a stiff jerking action. Was this really happening? *Dan* wanted kids? She looked up as he ran his hands through his hair violently—an angry, furious movement.

'I'd just forgotten to make sure it was what Amalie wanted too. She was younger than me—a couple of years. It never occurred to me that she didn't want a baby as badly as I did. I barely registered her lack of enthusiasm; I was so caught up in my own.'

Dragging her eyes away from him seemed impossible now. Every line on his face was taut with decade-old torment. She reached for him, grabbing his hand.

'But Amalie couldn't handle it. I came home from work one day to find her sitting at the kitchen table. She told me she was leaving me, that she'd made a mistake—she wasn't ready for marriage and kids and happy families.' He paused, took a deep breath. 'She said she wanted her youth back.'

More than anything Sophie wanted to turn back time and rewrite their whole conversation. Why did she have to ask? Why did she have to push? Why was she putting Dan through this agony?

But it was like a hurtling boulder now—impossible to stop.

'Amalie...she...' Another deep breath. This one a little shaky. That weakness was shocking in such a strong man. 'She'd aborted our baby.'

It was as if she could feel his pain, shooting from some-where inside him and flowing from where their hands joined. Her heart shattered for his loss.

'Oh, Dan…' she said, any other words she could think of manifestly inadequate. She wanted to throw her arms around him, somehow absorb his emotions and dilute his hurt. But she could do nothing but stand there, the horrible knowledge of where this conversation was headed freezing her to the spot.

He shook his head. 'I've never told anyone that. No one even knew she was pregnant but us.'

'You blame yourself,' she said. A statement.

'She felt trapped. She said it was the only way out.' His gaze flicked away, over her shoulder to the quiet suburban street through the window. 'I was so focused on work and what I wanted I wasn't paying attention. I wasn't listening.'

'But you were married. I assume you'd discussed having children?' He nodded. 'But she changed her mind?'

'Yes.'

Frustrated anger bubbled inside her for what Dan had had ripped away from him.

'Abortion wasn't her only option. That was her choice and not your fault.'

He shook his head again, dismissing her words. 'I screwed up my marriage.'

'And that's why you avoid relationships?'

'Until now,' he said, his gaze reconnecting with hers. 'I *am* a different person to who I was then, and besides, I know you'll never let me take over your life.' He grinned, but she didn't return his smile. 'When I thought about it, when I got past all my default panicking and over-reacting last night, I imagined how I'd feel if you *were* pregnant. And I realised I didn't feel like I'd expected. I know it wouldn't be what we'd planned, and it'd be far from ideal, but—well, it made me feel kind of good. Like I'd been given a second chance.'

Sophie's gut churned. Her throat tightened inexorably.

'And if you're not pregnant, then… Well—I'd like to just see what happens. Maybe one day…'

The hopeful sparkle in her eyes triggered an icy wave of nausea. How was this possibly fair? How was it fair that she'd met this man who wanted her—wanted a future with her—but also wanted children? How could this have happened again?

'I'm not pregnant, Dan.'

He looked bemused. 'I know it's probably unlikely, and that all this must be a bit of a surprise. I mean, it's a pretty big surprise for me, too—'

'Dan. *Stop.* I need you to listen to me.'

Finally he seemed to register that she wasn't reacting normally.

He squeezed the hand he still held. 'Did I read this wrong? You're *not* interested in anything longer term?'

'You didn't read me wrong.'

His broad smile would have been beautiful if she'd been any other woman.

She held his gaze as she struggled to find the courage to speak again. As the silence lengthened Dan's smile gradually fell away.

'Dan, I *know* I'm not pregnant. It's impossible.' She had to force her lips to move, blinking away the beginnings of fat, ugly tears. 'I can't have children.' A shuddering breath, but she had to make sure he understood. 'I'm infertile.'

Silence.

She was sure time stood still as the all-consuming nothingness enveloped them. She couldn't hear a thing—not even the sound of her own breathing.

Stupidly, she'd hoped she'd somehow got it wrong. That by a second chance he'd meant a future with her—alone. That another child was not intrinsic to his rediscovered hopes and dreams.

His gaze didn't shift from hers, but it changed. She saw it. The moment that sparkle, that hopeful, excited flicker, faded before her eyes.

And finally disappeared.

No, she hadn't got it wrong.

He dropped her hand and it fell, heavy and useless, against her thigh. *Then* the silence lifted—only to be replaced with the roaring in her ears.

She staggered away from him—away from his sudden coldness. From his unvoiced but oh, so obvious rejection.

The backs of her knees hit the couch and she fell awkwardly, her hip smacking its arm before she landed in its enveloping softness. She welcomed the pain, the reminder that she was alive when she felt as if part of her was dying.

Too late, he spoke.

'Sophie, I'm so sorry...'

Dan didn't know what to do. Certainly not what to say.

His words trailed off, useless and without meaning.

Sophie sat exactly as she'd landed on the couch, awkwardly and uncomfortably, her gaze trained on nothing through the wide lounge room window.

He felt pole-axed. Unloading his ten-year secret had lifted a weight he'd had no idea he was carrying. Nothing would erase his loss, or his guilt, but telling Sophie—having her know—it had helped. He hadn't planned it, but it had felt right.

And then...

She'd told him. And he'd been sure he felt something break deep inside.

'Have you figured it out yet?' she asked, her eyes shining with unshed tears but still not looking in his direction.

'Figured what out?'

'The real reason Rick dumped me. Isn't it obvious?'

He went to her, planning to sit beside her, but now she

met his gaze and shook her head. A sharp, clear directive:
Stay away.

'Didn't he know?' He had a thought. 'Did *you* know?'

She choked out a bitter laugh. 'He knew. I've always
known—it was the cancer. For ever ago.'

'But he changed his mind?'

'Yeah. Funny thing, that. Men wanting to get married and
have children. Who would have thought it?'

He let the dig deflect off him as he remembered something she'd told him that first night. Rick's new girlfriend
was already pregnant.

Dan ached for Sophie, and without thinking he reached
for her.

'Don't.'

They fell into another infinite silence.

'You don't have to stay,' she said finally.

'I don't want to go,' he said. And he didn't. He wanted
nothing more than to drag her into his arms and do *something* to obliterate the misery that cloaked her.

'But what would be the point, Dan? Aren't we right back
where we started? Short-term material only?'

'No...' But even as he spoke he was blindsided by the
truth of her words.

Her infertility changed everything. His time with Sophie
had shown him what he wanted—had shown him what he
was missing out on. He was older, wiser, but the core of his
old dream remained.

And he wanted the whole deal—he wanted marriage. He
wanted kids. He *needed* to rewrite his past—to correct his
past mistakes. To heal his ancient pain.

'Who would have thought it?' she said, her tone high
pitched and false. 'Dan Halliday, the ultimate bachelor,
wants to settle down and have kids!'

'That is what I want,' he said, regret weighing down

his words. 'I'm sorry, Sophie.' As if that was even close to enough.

She surged to her feet, a whirlwind of jagged emotions. She slammed into him and his arms embraced her naturally, hers wrapping untidily behind his neck.

And then she kissed him—a kiss that tasted like salty tears and passion and want and need and…love?

He kissed her back, powerless to do anything but caught up in her desperation and realising that it was also his. Burning, swirling, edgy desperation that felt as if it would go on for ever—and then ended far too soon.

They broke apart, panting.

'Is that enough for you?' she asked. 'Can *I* be enough for you? Just me?'

She stood before him, her expression raw and revealing.

With every awful passing second he sensed her slipping away from him. But he was helpless—completely helpless to stop it.

Suddenly she straightened her shoulders and walked with stiff-legged determination to the front door. She wrenched it open, her face perfectly expressionless and unmoving.

'I love you, Dan,' she said, as if it was a curse. 'But it's time for you to go.'

CHAPTER FOURTEEN

The All New Sophie Project (Project Manager: S. Morgan)

SOPHIE hung up her phone with some satisfaction as she walked briskly down the city street. Her new plan was already off to a fantastic start. She'd just been offered a job—from the purple-painted toenails interview, no less. She had high hopes for this plan—primarily because it had absolutely no reference to men, or boyfriends, or wedding dates, or anything even vaguely related to the opposite sex.

And that was A Very Good Thing.

This time her plan was truly just about *her*. Now, finally, she'd be able to get her life on track.

She arrived—early, of course—at the café where she was meeting Emma for lunch, so had a few minutes to fish her ubiquitous project plan out of her handbag and spread it out carefully on the table.

Using a new red felt-tip pen, bought specifically for the purpose, she crossed out *'Get a fabulous job that you will love!'* She'd decided to think positive with this plan. It was tempting to cross out *'Buy totally impractical yet super-sexy car'*, but she did still need to confirm the finance on the lipstick-red hard-top convertible she'd test-driven that morning. With that in mind, she phoned her bank.

Emma arrived just as she ended the call, and she scribbled out the car task with much enthusiasm as Emma slid into her seat.

'Ah, Sophie and her project plans!' Emma said, smiling. 'I remember these from school. You're the only person I know who project-managed her Year 12 group assignments. What's this one for? Buying a house? A holiday?'

'My life,' she said simply.

Emma barely raised her eyebrows. 'Really? How does that work?'

Sophie spent a few minutes running her through the project.

Emma nodded. 'So where does the delicious Dan fit in with all of this?'

She quickly folded up the project plan and shoved it in her handbag. 'He doesn't.'

'No?' Emma said.

'Yes,' she said dryly. 'As of a few days ago.' Sophie was impressed by how nonchalant she sounded—not as if she could rattle off, almost to the minute, how long it had been since Dan had walked out through her front door.

'What happened?'

'We wanted different things,' she said. That was a significant understatement.

Emma nodded, but her old friend wasn't about to let her get off that easy. 'What kind of things?'

'Oh, the usual.' She shrugged. 'He wants children. I can't have them. You know.'

'Oh, Soph,' Emma said, dragging her chair around the table so she could wrap her arm round her.

And so the whole story came out—with a few selected

omissions. The interlude up against Emma's jacaranda for one. More importantly the baby Dan had lost, for another.

But Emma got the gist of it, not even blinking when Sophie admitted to the lies she'd told her, and had planned to tell at Karen's wedding.

'We should have thought about how you'd feel, Sophie. I've never forgotten the indignity of being a single person at a wedding. After what happened with Rick, of *course* you considered it a nightmare.'

'Trust me—it's the least of my worries right now,' she said. 'I'm actually kind of looking forward to it.'

It would a blessed few hours' distraction from the blow-by-blow re-enactment of that last conversation with Dan that spun like a carousel around and around in her mind.

How had she managed to shut Rick out of her thoughts in the aftermath of their break-up? She'd tried her old techniques, her methods to keep her mind busy, but they'd all failed. It felt as if twenty-four hours a day all she could think of was Dan.

Dan. Dan. Dan.

It was awful.

Hadn't she read somewhere that the time it took to get over a break-up was approximately half the length of the actual relationship? With that formula she should have been over Dan in practically a matter of hours. Given she hadn't given Rick a second thought in weeks, and at the moment couldn't fathom forgetting about Dan, she decided that theory had substantial flaws.

'I can't believe he said that,' Emma said with a sad shake of her head. 'That he couldn't love just you. He seemed like such a nice guy.'

'Well,' she conceded, 'he didn't say that, exactly. I said that. He just didn't disagree.'

Emma's eyes lit up. 'So he *doesn't* believe that?'

'Yes, he does,' Sophie said, remembering his expression

with too much clarity. There was no doubt in her mind as to what he thought. Just like Rick, Dan needed her to come as some package deal. He wasn't interested in faulty goods.

'Has he been calling you?' Emma asked, surprising her.

'Yes,' she said. 'But I haven't answered.'

'Uh-huh. So how do you know for sure?'

'I just *know*.'

Emma snorted. 'Why? Because it all went according to your plan?'

Sophie jerked away from Emma's no longer comforting arm. 'What are you talking about? I didn't *plan* the break-up.'

'Maybe not, but had you already decided what was going to happen? Maybe you convinced yourself that his rejection was inevitable?'

Sophie bristled. 'Emma, if there'd been any hint of another outcome I would have grabbed it. I'm in love with him.'

'Oh, Soph,' Emma said, pulling her close again. 'Maybe this is my delusionally romantic, happily married self talking, but I saw something special between you two. Do me a favour—next time he calls, answer. Just so you're sure.'

Reluctantly, and two strong coffees later, Sophie agreed.

But Dan didn't call her again.

Dan had tried calling her for three days. Not crazy, stalker-type phone calls—just a single phone call each day. Asking her how she was. Asking her if she'd talk to him.

But she'd never responded, and eventually he'd decided he was just being pathetic.

It was over. What was the point?

He didn't really even know what he wanted to talk to her about. To apologise for his less than well-handled reaction? Definitely. But what else?

It wasn't as if he could make it all better with a *Whoops!*

Changed my mind. I actually don't want to have children. Because that wouldn't be true.

To be brutally honest, he didn't have a clue what he wanted to say to her. He just knew he wanted to see her again. He wanted to somehow make everything magically right.

But of course he knew that was impossible.

On the day of the wedding he went to his parents' place for lunch. At home, he'd tried his best to pretend it was just a normal Saturday, and that absolutely nothing special or unusual or of any concern was happening that day.

He'd failed, dismally, so had headed for Peppermint Grove, shoving all thoughts of Sophie alone at the wedding she'd so dreaded out of his mind. Or at least trying really, *really* hard to do that.

Much to his frustration, he was no more successful once he arrived, but he did his best to pay attention to the conversation.

His legs jiggled as his parents spoke, his toes tapping on the polished wooden floor. He had absolutely no idea what they were saying. None.

This time he couldn't even nod or smile at the appropriate places. They could easily have been speaking in another language. Or gobbledegook. Or discussing their plans to join a cult in Far North Queensland. He heard absolutely nothing.

Eventually even his long-suffering parents got sick of him.

His father reached out and took his untouched plate away. 'Is there somewhere more important you need to be, Dan?'

That sentence sank in, hitting him like a lightning bolt and shuffling his convoluted thoughts into something clean and simple and straightforward.

Yes, he did need to be somewhere. He needed to go to the wedding.

He might not be able to offer her anything more, but he

could hold up his end of their deal. Help her cross something else off her project plan.

One wedding date.

On his way.

Thanks to the carefully photocopied invitation stored neatly in the back of his own project file—complete with handy map—Dan had absolutely no problem getting himself to the wedding venue. He was even on time—well, close enough.

He turned down the long red bitumen driveway of a winery, cutting between perfectly parallel rows of vines to park outside the timber and iron reception centre, its wide verandahs promising spectacular views of the Swan Valley.

But he paid little attention to the scenery as he followed the hand-painted signs to the ceremony. He crested a hill to find the wedding spread out beneath him: a white narrow carpet leading to a rose-entwined gazebo, guests fanned out in a near perfect semi-circle, the metallic ribbon of the river an undulating, glistening backdrop.

There were a *lot* of guests—so many that it took him several minutes before he found Sophie. But there she was, right in the thick of it beside the aisle, the silver glint of her purse reflecting the glare of the sun.

It was just as he joined the very fringes of the crowd that it occurred to him that maybe this wasn't his best idea.

Around him couples stood, hand in hand or arm in arm, some talking, some looking perfectly content to just be in each other's company. A mother squatted down to her child's eye-level to explain how important it was to stay perfectly quiet during the wedding; her daughter nodded solemnly in reply. An older woman with gleaming white hair twisted awkwardly in one of the few seats, her expression vivid with joyful anticipation of the bride's impending arrival.

Around him everywhere was love.

If he'd been able to accept Sophie's love he'd be right

beside her now. His arm around her, the supple press of her body against him.

He'd deserve to be here then.

Now he was the last person she'd want to see. He was— far too late—absolutely sure of that.

A man in front of him stepped aside, revealing Sophie only metres away.

She stood, her back to him, the straps of her dress display- ing a perfect V of skin—skin that looked even more fragile and pale than usual against the dark silvery-grey fabric. Her hair was up, looped and pinned, and when she turned her head just slightly he could see a hint of her deep pink lips.

He wanted nothing more than to go to her, but knew he had no right. What had he really expected to happen? For Sophie to be *grateful* he'd come? For her to agree the past few days had never happened and go back to how it was before?

There was about as much chance of either of those things happening as of him returning to a career in law.

He realised that coming to the wedding had never been about Sophie. It was all about him. He'd needed to see her one more time.

But now he had to go.

He turned just as every other person in the vicinity did exactly the same thing. The bride had arrived.

With a quick getaway now impossible, he slid behind two tallish guests and hoped to hell Sophie hadn't seen him. He risked a glance at her. He was the only guest not watching the bride make her way towards the aisle.

He needn't have worried. Sophie's attention was one hun- dred percent focused on her old friend, a telltale sheen to her eyes. Happy tears—not the other kind that he was far too familiar with.

He didn't take his eyes off Sophie as the bride continued

her journey, his gaze greedy as he made the most of this last time he would see her.

And then, finally, the bride arrived beside her groom and the ceremony began.

At first Dan barely paid attention, but soon found himself caught up in the undeniable beauty and romance of the moment. The firm, respectful handshake between the father of the bride and the groom; an only slightly stumbling poetry reading from a young girl; the stolen private smiles between the couple who kept getting lost in each other's eyes.

'I, Ben, take you, Karen, to be my friend, my lover, my wife...'

It was a perfect moment. Picture-perfect, really—as the click and whirr of many cameras attested.

It was just like his moment with Amalie, all those years ago. They'd stood together just the same—although in a church rather than under the afternoon sun. He'd thought he'd loved her so much then, and had dreamed of their picture-perfect future: their home together, their future children...

Now Karen was saying her vows. 'I promise to be there when you need me, to comfort you and encourage you, to be your best friend everlasting...'

They were so different from his more traditional vows. These were all about togetherness, support. Friendship.

Had Amalie ever been his best friend?

He knew the answer to that. He'd been so caught up in achieving his goal—striving for some mythical watercolour-painted perfection—that he'd never stopped to just *be*. To be with his wife. To be together as a couple just for who they were and not for what they could achieve together. Not for what life goals she could help him tick off his list.

That mistake had cost him his marriage and his child.

Sophie had made him realise that he *was* ready to try

again. To do it right this time and not repeat his old mistakes.

Something—the sparkle of sunlight against her hair, or maybe just that constant magnetic pull between them— drew his gaze to Sophie as she turned, her darkest blue eyes capturing his with shock. Then joy—for a fleeting second— before transforming to distress in an instant.

Suddenly the truth was obvious. Painfully, embarrassingly, wonderfully so.

He loved Sophie.

And if he didn't do something quickly he *was* going to make the same mistakes. Hell, he'd already made one hugely massive one—walking away from Sophie because she could never have his children.

Was it really children he desperately wanted? Or the chance to rewrite history? And what had driven him to tell Sophie his darkest secret? The possibility that she was carrying his child? Or the reality that he had fallen in love with her?

He could never replace the child he'd lost, just as he could never have a 'do-over'—even if Sophie *could* have children. To think he could only diminished the memory of his child, and reduced what he'd had with Sophie to little more than cardboard characters following a decade-old script.

Sophie deserved more than that. *He* deserved more than that. He was a different person. He'd grown, he'd changed— and so had his dreams. This was his chance to re-start his life after years of punishing himself.

He had been partly right. This *was* his second chance— but just not the way he'd thought. He'd always ache for the baby he'd never got to meet, and he felt a pang of sadness that with Sophie he would never have children—but that pain was incomparable to the agony of losing her.

In a perfect world, yes, he would want children with

Sophie. But that was the key thing: *with Sophie*. Without her, what would be the point?

By pushing Sophie away he was robbing himself of a chance at happiness—and all for some stupid picture in his head.

It was time for a new picture—a picture of just him and Sophie, together. Laughing, living…loving.

And he realised with bone-deep certainty that *nothing* was missing from that picture. With Sophie he'd have everything he needed.

This time the picture was all about love.

If she'd ever forgive him.

The sudden wave of applause jolted Sophie out of the grip of Dan's relentless gaze. She turned to witness the final seconds of Karen and Ben's kiss, trying as hard as she could to focus on them and not on Dan's unexpected appearance.

What was he doing here?

She could feel his eyes still on her, but she kept her body rigidly turned away as the bridal party made their way back down the aisle and away for their photos. She didn't look at him as the guests drifted back up the hill to the champagne and canapés that awaited them.

When they were finally alone, she did turn to face him. She'd known he hadn't left—had felt his presence so assuredly she'd had no doubt he hadn't moved.

She crossed her arms, flicking her gaze up and down his length. He wore a charcoal suit and a pale green tie—the perfect coincidental match to her silver-and-grey outfit. They would've looked great together…

'Why are you here?' she asked, forcing herself back into the present and out of dreams of what could've been. So what if they'd look good together? She should know by now not to judge based on the superficial. Dan was certainly far from what he'd seemed.

'I thought I'd be your wedding date—'

'I'm doing just fine, thank you,' she said, her words brisk and crisp. 'Your services are no longer required.'

He nodded. 'I know. It was obvious the moment I saw you.'

She shifted her gaze, focusing on the knot of his tie. 'Then why are you still here?'

He walked a few paces towards her, but she walked backwards an equal distance, not willing to close the gap between them.

'Watching that ceremony, I realised I made a mistake. Sophie, I—'

She snorted. 'Don't tell me *you* got caught up in the romance? Mr Anti-wedding?' She let her gaze creep upwards, meeting his. 'I don't want to hear some soppy declaration that will wear off before Karen's honeymoon's over. I *heard* what you said on Sunday, Dan. I know what's important to you. I can't give you what you want—simple. A relationship between us is a waste of time.'

There. The pointlessness of them perfectly encapsulated.

If only she could dismiss the still-raw, pulsing emotions inside her so easily.

But he didn't seem to be listening. He strode towards her and too late she realised she'd backed herself up against the gazebo. She was planning to dart around him and away— far away—when she saw the look in his eyes. They were intensely blue. Electric. A shade she'd never seen before.

So, despite her better judgement, she stayed.

'You know what, Sophie? Bad luck. You are *getting* a soppy declaration—like it or not.'

Her stupid bruised heart leapt, refusing to listen to her sensible self. Nothing that Dan would say could possibly fix things.

'I feel like I've been stumbling around in the dark for ten

years,' he said. 'Convinced that by becoming the opposite of myself things would be okay.'

'But now you realise that you aren't really the person you thought you'd become,' she interrupted, her voice heavy. 'That you still want the same things—a wife, children.'

'No,' he said. 'That's where I got it wrong. I mixed up how I felt for you with the old Dan from before. I made the mistake of thinking about where that feeling could take me, not appreciating and experiencing it for what it was. Sophie, you've transformed what was once dark inside me to light. I can't comprehend not having you in my life.'

She wouldn't let the words sink in—wouldn't let herself believe them. 'But you wanted a second chance at a family. I can't give you that.'

'No, Sophie. I *have* a second chance, period. I can't replace my child—no more than I can replace you. Being with you is what's most important to me. Just you.'

The words were beautiful, and so tempting.

'No,' she said firmly, shaking her head. 'You'll change your mind. One day you'll realise that your life isn't complete without children. That you want more than just me.'

Even if he *did* mean it today, she knew it would never, ever last. It would just be a matter of time, and she couldn't put herself through the awfulness of loving Dan while a clock ticked inescapably downwards.

'Is that what Rick told you?' he asked, his eyes so full of care and understanding that she ripped her gaze away. 'That he had to have children?'

'Yes,' she said tightly.

His expression shifted abruptly to the tense lines of anger. 'Did he say you weren't enough for him?'

She nodded, her gaze fixed on the ground. 'He said he *loved* me, but it wasn't enough.' A pause, and then nothing more than a whisper, *'I'm not enough.'*

He reached for her, but she turned away, his touch just a

brief brush against her arm. 'Sophie, you're all I want. All I need.'

'How can I ever trust that?' she said, sorrow mixed with frustration. 'How do I know that you won't just wake up one morning and resent my infertility? Rick said he never wanted children, and look what happened with *him*. And with you—you *do* want children!'

'I thought I did,' he said.

Sophie swallowed, her throat suddenly so dry it was like swallowing shards of glass. 'Right,' she said, disbelief sharpening her tone. 'That's not something you can just turn off and on like a light switch.'

'Do you have some experience in that?' he asked, and now looking at him was an impossibility.

She hugged herself, staring unseeingly out at the river, the sun's reflection off its surface making her squint.

'I never had the chance to want children,' she said. 'Remember?'

'The chance to have them and to want them are different things,' he said softly. 'Do you want children?'

She made herself meet his eyes, hurt and confusion warring inside her. Why would he ask her this? The question she'd always pretended didn't exist?

'No. Yes.' A sigh. 'I don't know. I *hate* that I never got the choice. It hurts too much if I think about it.'

That made it a *yes*, she realised.

'So am I enough for you, Sophie?' Dan asked, his eyes still that blue that seemed to see everything—right through into her heart. 'I can't give you children. And if you wanted to adopt there's no guarantee. It would just be you and me.'

'Don't be stupid. It's *my* fault we can't have kids, no—'

'It is *not* your fault,' he said, the ferocity of his quiet tone shocking her into silence. 'And you know what? If that's the price to pay for having you, then that's fine with me. *You* are more important to me than anything else in the world, Sophie.'

This time when he reached for her she didn't shrug him away. His fingers ran down her arm from shoulder to elbow to wrist, linking his fingers with hers.

Slowly his words were seeping in—right through her—despite her efforts to resist.

'So, Sophie—*am* I enough for you? Is my love enough for you?'

Love?

For a moment she was sure her heart stopped beating.

Could he really love her—her alone? It was what he was telling her, but how many ways did he need to say it before she could let herself believe?

He was asking her to love him with the same limitations that life had imposed upon her. To love just him.

But the thing was the depth of emotion she felt for Dan *didn't* have boundaries. In fact it felt limitless.

Was that how he felt about her?

She looked up at him, searching his face for a hint of *something*. Something that would prove what he was saying wasn't real. Something false, something fragile, something unsure.

But there was nothing. The only way she could describe the way he was looking at her was with *love*. Boundaryless, limitless love.

'Yes,' she said, finally allowing the knowledge of Dan's love to thrum in glorious rhythm through her veins. With every beat of her heart she felt that ache, that hollowness inside her, ebb and flow away.

He tugged at her hand, pulling her close. But the tiniest of spaces still separated their bodies as she lost herself in his gaze.

'You know what?' he said. '*Enough* is the wrong word,

Soph. I love you. I want to spend the rest of my life with you. And at the end of all of those days I'll still be wanting more.'

Convinced that if her heart beat any faster it would burst, she reached for him with her free hand, sliding it along the lapel of his jacket and curving it behind his neck. She stood on tiptoes even as she drew him closer. 'I know what you mean,' she said, her lips a breath away from his. 'I love you, too.'

And then she kissed him, with love and with hope as her body shimmered with happiness.

He pulled her tight against him, cradling her with his strength.

When finally they broke apart—just a little—he murmured against her neck, 'So, is for ever something I can interest you in?'

'Just you and me, for ever?'

He caught her chin with his fingers, holding her perfectly still as their gazes locked and held.

'Just you and just me. Just us.'

She smiled, memorising the angles and planes of his handsome face and, most importantly, the way he was looking at her. As if she was the most precious, most beautiful, most amazing thing he'd ever seen.

She'd never felt this way—never thought she could be loved this way.

But it was happening. It was real.

'Yes,' she said. 'For ever suits me just fine.'

Dan smiled at her with joy and with love.

And for the first time ever, no matter how hard she searched, she couldn't locate that perennial emptiness inside her. She didn't feel broken or damaged or faulty.

She was whole.

* * * * *